CAPTAIN'S
FURY

BOOK FOUR OF THE CODEX ALERA

JIM BUTCHER

ACE BOOKS, NEW YORK

"Jim Butcher is a brilliant world-builder."
—*Midwest Book Review*

Praise for
CAPTAIN'S FURY

"Sharp tactical plotting, hazardous cross-country travel, and a dash of sardonic humor mark Butcher's fourth Codex Alera novel . . . Butcher deftly deploys intrigue, conflicted loyalties, and hairbreadth action to excellent effect. Few writers balance military realism and cinematic swashbuckling with so much skill or wit. Series fans will welcome . . . the strong climaxes resolving most of the immediate conflicts, while newcomers will have no trouble navigating the well-developed landscape." —*Publishers Weekly*

"The fourth Codex Alera novel further develops the world and characters of its predecessors and confirms Butcher's mastery of action-filled fiction." —*Booklist*

"I couldn't put this one down . . . great work." —*SFRevu*

"Readers are transported to a distant world that feels like a cross between ancient Rome and ancient Britain in this complex tale of war and personal growth. Battles are conducted on the field and in the heart, and everywhere in between. Despite this, there is a strong current of love that makes all the fights worth the effort. Once again, Mr. Butcher demonstrates his versatile talent, which never fails to engage his audience." —*Huntress Book Reviews*

"The story is beautifully told. The characters are real, complex, and not always good people. Tavi is someone the reader can identify with and truly root for." —*MyShelf.com*

continued . . .

THE BERKLEY PUBLISHING GROUP
Published by the Penguin Group
Penguin Group (USA) Inc.
375 Hudson Street, New York, New York 10014, USA
Penguin Group (Canada), 90 Eglinton Avenue East, Suite 700, Toronto, Ontario M4P 2Y3, Canada
(a division of Pearson Penguin Canada Inc.)
Penguin Books Ltd., 80 Strand, London WC2R 0RL, England
Penguin Group Ireland, 25 St. Stephen's Green, Dublin 2, Ireland (a division of Penguin Books Ltd.)
Penguin Group (Australia), 250 Camberwell Road, Camberwell, Victoria 3124, Australia
(a division of Pearson Australia Group Pty. Ltd.)
Penguin Books India Pvt. Ltd., 11 Community Centre, Panchsheel Park, New Delhi—110 017, India
Penguin Group (NZ), 67 Apollo Drive, Rosedale, North Shore 0632, New Zealand
(a division of Pearson New Zealand Ltd.)
Penguin Books (South Africa) (Pty.) Ltd., 24 Sturdee Avenue, Rosebank, Johannesburg 2196,
South Africa

Penguin Books Ltd., Registered Offices: 80 Strand, London WC2R 0RL, England

CAPTAIN'S FURY

An Ace Book / published by arrangement with the author

PRINTING HISTORY
Ace hardcover edition / December 2007
Ace mass-market edition / December 2008

Copyright © 2007 by Jim Butcher.
Cover art by Steve Stone.
Cover design by Rita Frangie.
Interior text design by Kristin del Rosario.

ISBN: 978-0-441-01655-6

ACE
Ace Books are published by The Berkley Publishing Group,
a division of Penguin Group (USA) Inc.,
375 Hudson Street, New York, New York 10014.
ACE and the "A" design are trademarks belonging to Penguin Group (USA) Inc.

PRINTED IN THE UNITED STATES OF AMERICA

10 9 8 7 6 5 4 3 2 1

For my angel. For everything.

ACKNOWLEDGMENTS

Many thanks to Jennifer and Anne, for their ongoing perseverance in dealing with me; to the Beta Foo Asylum, though by this point, I don't think any of you people are going to recover; to the fine folk at NERO Central, without whom no one would pound on me with boffer weapons; and to my dog, without whom I would not be reminded daily that I am essentially little more than a ridiculous human being who has somehow swindled somebody into paying me to write down conversations with my imaginary friends.

CAPTAIN'S FURY

⨳ PROLOGUE

Amara soared down in a slow, gradual descent through cold, heavy rain as she neared the camp of the Crown Legion. Cirrus, her wind fury, held her aloft on the shoulders of a miniature gale, and though she wore the leather clothing any flier found necessary, she almost fancied she could feel her skin chafing through it, and she was definitely sick of shivering with the cold.

A trio of armored figures took flight and swept toward her upon their own furies' gales, and Amara slowed, hovering in place to meet them. It was the third and last perimeter around the camp, and one of the knights flashed a challenge in broad hand signals to her while the other two took position above her, ready to dive upon her if necessary.

Amara recognized the men by sight, just as they would recognize her, but in these troubling times, a familiar face was not necessarily any assurance of a friendly party. She gave them the countersign, and only then did the three Knights Aeris take their hands from their weapons and form up around her in a friendly escort as she wearily flew the last mile or so to the camp.

Amara did not land at the standard location, just outside the camp's palisade. She'd covered more than three thousand miles in the past three days, and the very thought of walking through the camp was nearly enough to knock her unconscious. She came down just outside the commander's tent, despite the regulations against it and the debris Cirrus's approach would scatter all over the area. Her legs quivered, all rubbery with fatigue, as she settled her weight on them and ceased maintaining the effort to direct Cirrus.

"Countess," murmured a small, slender man, his few remaining grey hairs shorn close to his scalp, Legion style. He was rather dapper in his fine tunic, but Amara knew that Enos, a former Cursor himself, was one of the deadlier knife hands in Alera. Mild disapproval in his voice did nothing to dampen his smile. "Soaring in here as bold as you please, I see."

"I'm sorry to make extra work for you, Enos," Amara replied, as they stepped underneath a nearby pavilion, out of the rain.

"Nonsense. I'll get one of our Subtribunes Logistica to tidy up. We valets are far too important for such things, you know." He offered her a warm towel, and after she had used it to wipe her face and hands, he pressed a steaming cup into her fingers.

Amara sipped at the thick broth and let out a groan of pleasure. Long flights always left her enormously hungry, and there'd been far more flying than eating over the past few days. "Bless you, Enos."

"Not at all, Countess," he replied. "The least I can do for someone who just beat the previous flight speed record from here to the capital by a full day."

"The First Lord doesn't pay me to lark about," Amara said, and flashed him a smile. "How much did you win?"

"Fourteen silver bulls," Enos said, his tone unrepentantly smug. "Lord Aquitaine's head valet just can't seem to help himself when it comes to gambling."

Amara finished the broth, and Enos immediately filled her hand with another mug of tea. She sipped it. Delicious. Perhaps she'd manage to walk all the way to a warm bunk before she collapsed, after all. "Is he available?"

"The captain is in conference with Lord Aquitaine," Enos said. "But he insisted that I take you to him as soon as you arrived."

"Aquitaine," Amara murmured. "Very well. Thank you, Enos."

Enos bowed his head to her with another smile, and Amara strode over to the commander's tent. Winters here in the south weren't nearly so frigid as in Alera's more northerly reaches, but they were generally cold, rainy, and miserable. The tent was doubled, one slightly larger one outside another, creating a small pocket of warmer air between the interior and the outdoors. Amara opened one flap after another, and strode into Captain Miles's command tent.

It was a fairly spacious arrangement, lit by a trio of bright furylamps hung from the central post. The post itself was part of the large sand table in the center of the tent, one currently molded in the shape of the topography between the Legion's camp, at one end, and the city of Kalare at the other, with small models representing the various forces scattered about it. Other than the sand table, the room contained a writing desk, several camp stools, and a single small trunk and bedroll resting upon a folding cot, Miles's only personal gear.

"And I'm telling you that it's the only way," growled Miles. He was a man of average height but built like a stone rampart, all stocky strength. His armor bore the dents, scratches, and permanent scorch marks of the action it had seen since the beginning of Kalare's rebellion. There was grey threaded through his short, dark hair, and as he paced the length of the sand table, studying it, he moved with a slight but definite limp. "If we don't move in concert, we'll risk defeat in detail."

"Don't be such an alarmist," the second man in the tent said. He was far taller than Miles, long-limbed, and sat on a camp stool with an easy confidence that made him seem to fill more of the tent than Miles. There was something leonine about him, from dark golden hair that hung to his shoulders to his dark, hooded eyes, to the casual strength evident in his shoulders and legs. Aquitainus Attis, the High Lord of Aquitaine, wore a red silk shirt, dark leather trousers, and evidently felt no need to wear armor. "If two years here have shown us anything, it's that Kalare can no more easily maneuver through the fens than we can. The chances that he'd be able to catch your force in time are minimal."

Miles glared at the other man. "I note that if we follow this plan, your own forces will be completely insulated from danger."

"If it works," Aquitaine countered, "we roll up Kalare's mobile forces before summer is fairly under way, and besiege the city within two weeks after."

"And if it doesn't, my men face everything Kalare has left on their own."

"It *is* a war, Captain," Aquitaine said in a mild tone. "There does tend to be the occasional risk."

Miles snarled out something under his breath, and his hand fell to the hilt of his sword.

Aquitaine's teeth flashed in a slow, feline smile. "Captain, don't you think we should hear from the good Countess before we discuss this further?"

Only then did Miles glance over his shoulder and see Amara. There was color high in his cheeks, and his eyes glittered with anger. He glowered at Amara for a moment, then shook his head, composed his expression, gave her a nod, and said, "Countess, welcome."

"Thank you, Captain." She nodded to Aquitaine. "Your Grace."

Aquitaine gave her a speculative stare and a bland smile. Amara refused to allow herself to show the discomfort she felt under the man's gaze. Aquitaine was quite probably unsurpassed in furycraft by anyone in the Realm, save the First Lord himself—and Gaius was no longer a young man. Though she had never seen him using it, she knew Aquitaine was a man of tremendous power. It made her uncomfortable to be such a singular object of his attention.

"What news from the Crown?" Miles asked her.

"There is to be a council assembled for the War Committee to determine the course of this season's campaign," Amara said. "The First Lord requests and requires your attendance, Captain, and yours, Lord Aquitaine."

Miles made a rude noise. "First a committee. And now a council."

"It's a committee *for* the Committee," Aquitaine murmured, his tone suggesting that the subject was one of the few in which he was in wholehearted agreement with Captain Miles. "Ridiculous."

"When?" Miles asked. "Where?"

"Three weeks from yesterday, my lords—at the Elinarch."

"Elinarch, eh?" Miles said. He grunted. "Be nice to get to meet this young virtuoso running the First Aleran. Heard a lot of talk about him."

Aquitaine made a noncommittal sound. "If Kalarus decides

to push our positions in person while we—" By which, Amara thought, he means himself. "—are away, our forces could be hard-pressed."

Miles shrugged. "Intelligence reports suggest that the rumors of his invalidism are true. I understand he sustained rather severe injuries in a fall, courtesy of Count Calderon. They seem to have incapacitated him."

"That may be precisely what he wishes us to think," Aquitaine pointed out, "to say nothing of his heir. Young Brencis lacks in experience, but his crafting talent is considerable."

"The First Lord has given us a command, Your Grace," Miles said.

Aquitaine rolled his eyes and sighed as he rose to his feet. "Yes, of course. The old man plays the music, and the rest of us dance. Captain, under the circumstances, I believe we can continue this discussion later."

"Suits me," Miles said.

Aquitaine nodded to them both and strode out.

Miles watched Aquitaine depart, took up a soldier's tin mug that sat on the sand table, and threw back a long draught of what smelled like ale. "Arrogant jackass," he muttered. He glanced up at Amara. "He's doing it again."

"Doing what?" Amara asked.

Miles gestured at the sand table. "Inflicting casualties on Gaius's loyal troops."

Amara blinked. *"How?"*

"Nothing I could prove in a court. Aquitaine's Legions fight beside us, but they're always just a little bit too slow, or too fast. When the fighting starts, the Crown Legion ends up taking the worst of it." He slammed the mug back down onto the sand table. Granules of sand flew up from the impact. "My men are dying, and there's not a crowbegotten thing I can do about it."

"He's very good at this sort of thing," Amara said.

"And I'm not," Miles replied. "He wants to use us up on Kalare, leave us too weak to oppose *his* Legions once all the fighting is over."

"Hence your argument over strategy?" Amara guessed.

Miles grunted and nodded. "Bad enough fighting a war against the enemy in front of you, without having one marching next to you, too." He rubbed a hand over his bristling hair. "And the Committee has too much influence on our strategies. Committees don't win wars, Countess."

"I know," Amara said quietly. "But you know the First Lord's position. He needs the Senate's support."

"He needs their *funding*," Miles said in a sour tone. "As if he shouldn't have the right to expect their loyalty in a crisis simply because of who he is." He turned and slapped the empty mug off of the sand table. "Two years. Two years of slogging through these crowbegotten fens, fighting Kalare's madmen. We should have driven straight through to Kalare the same season he attacked. Now the best we can hope for is a hard fight through the bloody swamps and a siege of the city that might last years. I've had three men die of sickness for every one slain outright by the bloody enemy. I've seen bad campaigns before, Countess, but this is enough to turn my stomach."

Amara sipped at her tea and nodded. "Then should I assume you wish the Crown to know that you want to be relieved of your command?"

Miles gave her a flat stare of shock. Then he said, "Of course not."

"Very well."

"Who would you trust with it, if not me?" Miles demanded.

"I only thought—"

"What? That I couldn't handle it?" Miles snorted. "No. I'll think of something." He turned back to stare at the sand table. "But there's a major problem we've got to address."

Amara listened, stepping to the table beside him.

"Kalare and his forces aren't hard to contain. If he moves too far from his stronghold, we'll crush them or else move in and take the city behind them. We have the numbers for it." He nodded toward the table's "north" end. "But the Canim are another story. Since they were thrown back from the Elinarch, they haven't pitched in on Kalare's side, but they haven't been fighting against him, either, and their presence secures his northern flank."

"While *his* presence secures the Canim's southern flank in turn."

"Exactly," Miles said. "That's bad enough. But if they re-deploy to actually *support* Kalare, it's going to change the balance of power here dramatically."

"That's one of the reasons I'm here," Amara told him. "Gaius sent me to find out what you need to finish off Kalare."

"One of two things. Either we commit more—dependable—forces here in the southern theater and drive to a decisive victory, or we neutralize the Canim in the northern theater so that we can hit Kalare from two sides at once."

Amara grimaced and nodded. "I suspect that will more or less be the subject of the council at the Elinarch."

Miles nodded grimly, and scowled at the miniature forces deployed on the sand table. "Bloody rebels. Bloody, crowbegotten Canim. If that new captain, Rufus Scipio, was all the rumors say he is, you'd think he'd have driven the dogs back into the bloody sea by now. He probably just got lucky."

"Possibly," Amara said, keeping her face carefully neutral. She'd been anticipating Miles's reaction to the identity of the new captain for some time, and didn't want to tip him off now. "I suppose time will tell."

"Lucky," Miles growled.

"You are a lucky man, Aleran," Kitai said, her tone brisk and decidedly cool. "A lesser woman than I would have broken your neck by now and had done with you. Why not leave well enough alone?"

Tavi looked up from where he sat on the ground, panting with effort. "It isn't well enough yet," Tavi replied. "I'm still not where I want to be. And I haven't been able to work any manifestation at all."

Kitai rolled her eyes and dropped lightly from the tree branch upon which she sat to the springy grass of the little dale. The Marat girl wore a cavalryman's leather breeches along with one of Tavi's spare tunics—not that anyone with eyes would mistake her for a man. She'd taken to shaving her silken white hair after the fashion of the Horse Clan of her people—completely away, except for a long stripe running over the center of her head, which was allowed to grow long, the effect something like a horse's mane. Her hair and pale skin contrasted sharply with her brilliant green eyes—eyes the precise color of Tavi's own—and gave her striking features an edge of barbaric ferocity. Tavi never tired of looking at her.

"Aleran," she said, frowning. "You can already do more than you ever thought you would be able to. Why continue to push?"

"Because willing a manifestation of a fury is the first step to all of the most advanced crafting techniques," he replied. "Internalized crafting is all well and good, but the impressive things all rely upon manifestation. Bursts of fire. Healing. Manipulating the weather. *Flying*, Kitai. *Think* of it."

"Why fly when you can ride a horse?" she asked, as if it was one of those questions only an idiot could have inspired her to utter aloud. Then she frowned and hunkered down on her heels, facing Tavi, and met his eyes.

Tavi felt his eyebrows go up. It was a piece of body language she only used when she was in earnest. He turned to face her, listening.

"You are pushing yourself too hard, *chala*," Kitai said. She touched his cheek with one slender hand. "The Legion's war. Your work for Gaius. These practice sessions. You miss too many meals. You miss too many hours of sleep."

Tavi leaned into the warmth of her touch for a moment, and his eyes closed. His body ached, and his eyes burned most of the time, lately. Savagely painful headaches often followed hard on the heels of his practice sessions, and they made it difficult to eat or sleep for a time afterward. Not that he had much choice but to sacrifice time he might otherwise use to eat or sleep. Command of the First Aleran was responsibility enough to consume the full attention of anyone, and his duties as a Cursor required him to gather information from every available source and report it back to his superiors in addition to his duties as the Legion's captain. Only the inexplicable resilience that he suspected came as a result of his bond to Kitai had left him with enough time and energy to teach himself all that he could of what meager furycraft he'd been able to grasp. Even so, the pace was wearing on him, he knew.

Kitai was probably right.

"Maybe," Tavi admitted. "But there's not a lot of choice

right now. It takes years of practice to develop crafting skills, and I'm about fifteen years late getting started."

"I still think you should tell someone. It might go faster if you had a teacher."

Tavi shook his head. "No."

Kitai let out an exasperated sound. "Why *not*?"

"Because what I can do now isn't much," Tavi said. "Not in the greater scheme of things. I'd rather what little I *do* have come as a surprise if I'm ever forced to use it."

Kitai shook her head. "It isn't worth the risk that you might harm yourself by trying to learn without some instruction."

"I went to the Academy. I know all the theory," Tavi said. Every dreary, humiliating, failure-ridden hour of those classes was burned into his memory along with his other childhood nightmares. "It's been two years, and we're fine."

"So far, perhaps," she said. "I know little of furycraft, Aleran, but I know enough to respect how dangerous it can be. So do others. Would it not deter your would-be enemies if they knew you were a mighty furycrafter?"

"Yes, but . . . but we still don't tell anyone," Tavi said stubbornly.

"Why not?" Kitai demanded.

He broke their gaze and looked away for a long moment. "I'm not sure," he said quietly. "It isn't time yet. I feel it. I know it." He shook his head. "I don't know how to explain it to you any better than that. I need you to trust me."

Kitai frowned at him, then leaned over and placed a gentle kiss on his forehead and rested her temple against his. "You are insane. And I am insane to pay any attention to you. Very well."

Tavi leaned his head gently against hers. "Thank you."

"I reserve the right to change my mind, of course."

"Of course," Tavi said, letting a tired smile shape his mouth. He took a deep breath and steeled himself. "All right. One more try to call out that boulder fury, and we'll call it a day."

"No," Kitai said, her tone perfectly firm. "Enough practice for the day. There are urgent matters that require your attention."

Tavi blinked at her. "What?"

With a single, sinuous arch of her back and motion of her arms, Kitai stripped out of the white tunic, and pressed her naked skin against Tavi's chest. Her arms twined around his neck, and her mouth lifted to his in a scorching kiss.

Tavi made a faint sound of protest, but the scent of her, of crushed wildflowers and clover and faint soap rose up and overwhelmed his senses, and the sheer, passionate fire of the kiss, the heat in her mouth and urgent hands left him unable to do anything but respond in kind. Suddenly, Tavi could think of no very good reason to dissuade the Marat girl, and could only vaguely remember why he might have thought he should try. His hands glided around her waist, stroking over the soft, pale skin of her naked back, tracing the slender strength of the muscles just beneath her fever-warm skin, and he returned the kiss with rising ardor.

Kitai let out a low, hungry sound, and all but ripped Tavi's tunic from him. She pushed him, but he turned with the force of it, spinning to press her down into the thick grass. She let out a wicked, sensual little laugh, and arched up to meet him as he kissed her again. Her hands ran over his shoulders and back, her nails scraping deliciously over his skin, the sensation so intense and intoxicating that he didn't see the cavalry trooper who had approached them until her boots were an arm's length from his nose.

Tavi let out a yelp and felt himself begin to blush from the roots of his hair to his toenails. He fumbled for his tunic and sat up again, fairly certain that he was about to expire of pure mortification.

Kitai lay languidly on the grass for a moment, apparently unconcerned with her nakedness, and let out a regretful little sigh before she began to sit up as well. "Hello, Enna."

"Good day, Kitai," replied the trooper. Enna wore Aleran-style boots and trousers, as Kitai did, but sported a coat of leather armor modeled after the lorica of the Legions. Like Kitai, her hair was trimmed into a long mane allowed to flow down her back, but unlike her, the trooper's hair was dyed a vibrant shade of blue. The Marat woman, a veteran of the Horse Clan, gripped a cavalry spear casually in one hand and stood grinning down at the two of them. "You needn't stop on my account, you know. It's about time I got to look at more of this Aleran you've chosen."

Kitai returned her grin. "See to it that looking is all you do."

Enna tilted her head to one side, studying Tavi with a frankness that accomplished the impossible, by making him feel even more embarrassed than he already did. "Is he always pink like that?" Enna asked. "Or is it merely something he does to amuse you."

"Bloody crows," Tavi muttered, shoving his arms back into his tunic.

Kitai let out a peal of laughter, then said, "He amuses me constantly, cousin."

Enna frowned, and said, "But he's not a horse."

"No one is perfect," Kitai replied smoothly.

Tavi cleared his throat and reminded himself who was captain of this Legion. "Centurion," he said, forcing his voice into the deliberate, calm tones he always used when conducting Legion business. "Do you have something to report?"

Enna's amusement and interest lingered in her eyes, but she came to attention and saluted him, striking one fist to her heart. "Captain. Sir Cyril's compliments, and he thought you would want to know that Ehren has returned."

Tavi gave her a sharp glance and inhaled deeply. His heart leapt in his chest, somehow transfixed by relief and anxiety at the same time. Ehren had returned alive from his dangerous mission into the occupied Aleran territory now held by the inhuman Canim, and Tavi felt mightily relieved that he was back in one piece. Ehren's mission had not called for him to return this soon, though, and that was the cause of Tavi's anxiety. If Ehren had cut the mission short early, it was because he had discovered something that couldn't wait. Tavi had several ugly speculations on what might be important enough to merit such an action on behalf of his friend and fellow Cursor, and the least unpleasant of them was more than a little troubling.

"Kitai," Tavi said quietly, and glanced at her.

The Marat girl was already several paces away, drawing her tunic back down over the supple curve of her back. She untied the horses from where they'd left them.

"Enna," Tavi said, "ride ahead. Tell Tribune Maximus that I want all four of his alae ready to move, and alert Tribune Crassus that his Knights had better be prepared to ride as well."

Enna nodded sharply. "Yes, sir. What shall I tell the First Spear?"

"Tell him I want the Battlecrows mounted up," Tavi said. "Beyond that, nothing. Valiar Marcus knows what needs to be done better than I do."

By that time, Kitai had returned with the horses, and Tavi swung up onto his own mount, a long-legged, deep-chested black he'd dubbed Acteon. The stallion had been a gift from Kitai's aunt Hashat. Well, not a gift, precisely, since the Horse Clan did not see their totem beasts as property. From what Tavi understood, he had been entrusted to the horse's care in matters where speed was necessary, and the horse had been entrusted to his, in matters of everything else. So far, the arrangement had worked out.

Tavi wheeled Acteon as Kitai mounted her own barbarian-bred steed, a dappled grey mare who could run more tirelessly than any Aleran horse Tavi had ever seen. Enna turned and loped swiftly over to her own roan, equipped with the minimal amount of tack the Marat called a saddle, and sent it into an immediate run. There would be little point in attempting to keep pace with her—no riders on the face of Carna could match the pace set by the Horse Clan of the Marat.

He didn't need to say anything to Kitai. The two of them had ridden out so often that by now, it was a matter of routine to send both their horses leaping into a run at the same moment, and together they thundered back toward the First Aleran's fortifications at the Elinarch.

"I *know* there haven't been orders yet," Valiar Marcus thundered, scowling at the stable master. "Even if they never come, it's good practice for my men. So you bloody well *get* those mounts prepared for the Battlecrows, and you do it *now*, or I'll have your lazy ass on a whipping post."

The stable master for Alera's first mounted infantry cohort gave the First Spear a surly salute and hurried away, bawling orders at the grooms who cared for the extra mounts. Marcus scowled at the man's back. You practically had to kick the man all the way to his job to get him to fulfill his responsibilities, and he was getting too old to spend that much energy on fools.

Good help, it seemed, remained hard to find, regardless of the fact that the Realm was fighting for its life against the greatest threat to its integrity in at least four hundred years.

Marcus stalked through the lines of the First Aleran, their tents stretched in ruler-straight rows within the sheltering walls of the town at the Elinarch, the enormous bridge that stretched over the broad Tiber River. He stopped to have a quick word with a number of senior centurions along the way, putting them on alert that something was happening in officer country. As often as not, a stir in officer country meant that the rank and file of the Legion was about to be ordered to hurry up and wait, but it was always good for the centurions to look prepared and unfazed, no matter how sudden or urgent the news.

Marcus strode through the town. It had grown considerably in the two years the First Aleran had been using it as a base of operations. In fact, the southern half of the town had been rebuilt from the paving stones up and made into a fortress that had withstood two ferocious assaults from the Canim's elite warriors and twice as many tides of their howling raiders—before the captain had taken the initiative and begun carrying the battle to the Canim invaders, hard enough to teach them to keep their distance from the Elinarch. The streets were crowded with refugees from the occupied territory to the south, and in the marketplaces the price of food had climbed to outrageous levels—there simply wasn't enough to go around, and the demand had driven prices to unheard-of heights.

Marcus marched through all of it without slowing his pace. No one hampered his progress. Though he wasn't a tall man, and though he did not look particularly more formidable than any other *legionare*, the crowd seemed somehow to sense his purpose and determination. They melted out of his path.

Marcus reached the command quarters just as hooves began to make rhythmic thunder on the paving stone. Half a dozen of the First Aleran's Marat auxiliaries rode down the street, clearing the way for the captain and the Marat Ambassador, returning early from their daily ride, and six more brought up the rear. Ever since those deadly Canim assassins that had come to be known as Hunters had tried their luck against the captain and his woman, the young man had never been left unguarded.

Marcus frowned. The captain's *singulare*, his personal bodyguard, normally a shadow rarely seen more than a few paces away from his back, was still missing from the camp. There was no explanation as to why, or where the man had gone. Marcus, though, had no business querying the captain on the matter. As the First Spear, the senior centurion of the Legion, he had unparalleled access to the command structure, when compared to any other foot soldier of the First Aleran—but even his comparatively broad authority had limits, and he dared not press them.

It would make people begin to ask dangerous questions.

Marcus shook off the unpleasant line of thought and the uneasy quiver that ran through his stomach whenever he allowed it to occupy his attention.

"Marcus," the captain said. The two traded a quick salute. "What have you heard?"

"Just got here, sir," Marcus replied.

The captain nodded. "I've sent orders to have the auxiliaries ready to ride, as well as the Battlecrows."

"Already done, sir," Marcus said.

"Good man!" The captain flashed Marcus a quick grin, startling for its boyishness. The past two years had made even Marcus occasionally forget how *young* the captain really was. His poise, courage, and intelligence had guided the now-veteran Legion through a deadly war of maneuver with an unforgiving foe, and he had stood front and center, facing the danger with his men every step of the way. They loved him for it. The young captain wore the mantle of command as naturally and capably as if he had been born to it.

Which was only natural, because, of course, he had.

Marcus's stomach twisted again.

It was easier to think of him as the captain. Whatever else the young man might be, in time, right now he was the captain—and a captain worthy of Marcus's loyalty. Worthy of his respect.

Worthy of your honesty, whispered a poisonous little voice in his heart.

"Come on," the captain said, his eyes and his thoughts both clearly focused on the command building. "If Ehren's back this soon, it means he's got something that can't wait. Let's find out what."

Valiar Marcus, whose true name was not Valiar Marcus, followed Captain Rufus Scipio, whose true name was not Rufus Scipio, into the fortified stone command building, and struggled with the sudden instinct that the days of pretending he was someone else were only too numbered.

Steadholder Isana of the Calderon Valley grimaced as the wagon hit a rough spot in the road and made her blur a digit in the column of numbers she was tabulating on the little lap desk. She spared a moment to take a breath and calm down, reminding herself firmly that the frustration was a result of long weeks of labor and travel, and not the ineptitude of the wagon's builders, driver, the beasts pulling it, or the engineers who originally constructed the road.

She reached for a fresh piece of paper but found the wooden box empty. "Myra," she called to the cart driver's daughter. "Have you any more paper?"

"Yes, my lady," called a young woman's voice. The wagon creaked as someone moved about the front seat for a few moments, then the curtain to the covered back of the wagon parted, and a scrawny, frizzy-haired darling of a girl appeared, holding out a fresh sheaf.

"Bless you, child," Isana said, taking the paper.

"Of course, my lady," Myra said, beaming. "Did you know that we're in the refugee territory now? The guard showed me and Papa the sight of a scare-mish with the Canim that happened right here by the road."

"Skirmish, dear," Isana corrected her. "And yes, I know that there's been fighting on both sides of the river, on and off."

Myra nodded, her dark eyes intent, her young face serious. "This caravan is very important, isn't it, my lady?"

Isana began the botched page anew. The eagerness she felt in the girl's presence was undermined by a sense of slowly dawning worry, an emotion Isana felt as clearly as she felt her own weary impatience, thanks to the constant, steady presence of her water fury, Rill. "Yes, it is," she said, keeping her tone steady and calm to reassure the girl. "That's why we're so well protected. The food and supplies we're bringing to the refugees will help them survive the coming winter."

"And without it they'd starve," Myra said. "We're helping them."

"Precisely," Isana said.

"And it's here because of you!" the girl said.

That was an oversimplification of staggering degree, but there was little point in trying to explain it to the carter's daughter. "The supplies and money came from a great number of important and generous Citizens," she replied. "The leaders of the Dianic League. I'm only keeping things organized."

Myra frowned. "But Papa said without you, all those old biddies wouldn't have done anything!"

Partly true, though she should hardly like to be the one to call, say, Lady Placida an old biddy. But Isana *had* managed to parlay the exposure she'd been given as Lady Aquitaine's rallying standard for the Dianic League into something far more useful than a trough for her patron's thirst for power. Lady Aquitaine had not been at all amused at what Isana had done with the personal influence she'd gained, but if she'd tried to undermine Isana's relief project, it would have turned a great many minds in the League against her—and Lady Aquitaine knew it. The barely simmering edge of irritation that had tinged Lady Aquitaine's presence every time Isana had spoken to her recently was almost reason enough to have endured the endless hours of effort she'd needed to gather support and put the relief column together. Though if she admitted it to herself, that small victory was nothing compared to the misery and suffering the caravan would alleviate.

Isana was *helping*. She was doing something good, something that she could be proud of—something Septimus would have been proud of.

Isana fought off a smile and a faint shimmer of tears at the same time. "Everyone wanted to do something to help the refugees, child. They only needed someone to give them a way to do it."

Myra chewed on a fingernail and studied her steadily. "Papa says you're important."

Isana smiled at the girl. "Everyone's important."

"Myra," came the carter's voice from the front of the wagon. "Come away now, and let the Steadholder work."

"Coming, Papa," the girl said. She gave Isana a smile and scampered back out of the wagon's rear.

Isana went back to her work on the inventory, and didn't look up from it until the caravan halted for its midday rest. She kept working while the carters and mule skinners took their lunch. *She* hadn't been walking or driving or loading all morning, after all.

A shout of challenge went up outside from one of the caravan's mounted guards, and Isana felt herself tense up. The caravan, while not transporting a great deal of liquid wealth, *did* have a considerable amount of material of use and value. It was too large a target for bandits, but there was always the chance that the Canim might seize the food and supplies in order to feed their own doubtlessly hungry soldiers.

No furor arose, though, and Isana relaxed and kept to her inventories, until the trotting hoofbeats of an approaching horse came up to the wagon and stopped.

Isana looked up, frowning faintly, concentrating on her link with Rill—and suddenly bolted up from where she sat, spilling ink on her most recent page, and not caring in the least. Her heart pounded in a fashion entirely too girlish to suit anyone of her age or her station or responsibilities, and she found herself fidgeting with her hair and straightening her dress. Then she stared in dismay at her ink-stained fingers. Doubtless she had just managed to spread smudges over her entire outfit, and possibly upon her face as well. She felt a blush rise to her cheeks.

Boots hit the ground outside the wagon, and the horse shifted its weight. Someone knocked on the sideboards.

Feeling mildly ridiculous, Isana parted the curtains with one hand and descended from the wagon, emerging into the noonday sunshine of the earliest days of spring in the Amaranth Vale.

A man of average height stood waiting for her, his dark

hair shorn to regulation Legion length, his armor plain and showing signs of use. The features of one side of his face were strongly carved, striking. The other half of his face was marred by horrible burn scars centered around the shape of the Legion brand for cowardice, high on his cheekbone. He wore a simple sword at his side, and the scarlet half cape of a Legion *singulare*.

Isana felt her heart speed up again as she smiled at him. "Araris."

His face turned up into one of his rare, swift smiles, and his eyes all but glowed from within. The sudden warmth of his emotions flooded over Isana, and she felt as if she might float up off the ground. She could feel his happiness and excitement at seeing her, his affection, and a certain, lazily controlled hunger for her that she knew would draw out spots of pink high on her cheeks.

"Isana," he said quietly. She offered her hand. He took it and bent over it, brushing his lips over the backs of her fingers. Isana felt the warmth of his breath as an impact that spread deliciously up her arm to dance along every fiber of her body.

He straightened, eyes sparkling, fingers tightening very gently around hers. "You look . . ." His eyes wrinkled at the corners. "Inky."

Isana tilted her head back and laughed.

"And beautiful," he said. "I've missed you."

"And I you," she replied, covering his hand with her other one. "What are you doing here? We were to arrive at the Elinarch in another two days."

Some of Araris's smile trickled away. "I bring you word. Can we speak here?"

Isana glanced around them. The carters and their crews were sitting down to a simple lunch at the cook's wagon, farther down the line. There was no one nearby. "I believe so."

Araris nodded once. "I am sent to caution you, of course, to remember that while you may be Tavi's blood kin, you have never met Rufus Scipio. You must take every precaution not to reveal his identity."

"Of course." Isana sighed. "I'm not quite senile yet. What else?"

Araris regarded her with a steady gaze for a moment. Then he said, "When he was a child, it was right and proper that you should make decisions for him." He leaned forward, his fingers tightening on hers, giving his words gentle emphasis. "He is no longer a child."

Isana felt her shoulders stiffening. "What do you mean?"

"I mean," he said, in that same gentle tone, "that he has a right to know, Isana. He has a right to know the truth. He has a right to make his own decisions now."

Isana jerked her chin up, the habit of two decades of worry and caution condensing into a flash of outrage and anger. "Oh? And who are you to decide such a thing?"

Araris's face never wavered. "His *singulare*, Isana. His bodyguard and protector. I safeguard his well-being and ward his life and freedom, with my own if necessary. And in my judgment, ignorance may prove dangerous to him. Even deadly."

Isana bit her lip and looked down, unable to meet Araris's calm, unwavering eyes, awash in his continued, steady love, acutely aware of his concern for her, his respect, and his absolute sincerity.

He touched her chin with his fingertips, lifting her eyes to his. "Isana," he said. "He's your son. It is your place to tell him. He should hear it from you." He shook his head. "But if you can't—or won't—I will."

Isana flinched a little at the words, if not his quiet, steady tone. "Has it come to that? Really?"

"Yes."

The simple answer held absolutely no room for doubt. Isana bit her lip. "He'll . . . Will he understand? Why I had to do it? Lie to him . . ." She shook her head. "He's grown so *fast*, Araris."

"He'll understand," he said quietly. "Or he won't. Either way, he deserves to know. He needs to know."

Isana shivered, and without being asked, Araris stepped forward, putting his arms around her. She leaned against him gratefully, closing her eyes. His armor was warm from the gentle sunshine, and he felt steady, immovable, like an obdurate stone in a rushing stream. He was that. He had always been there for her, and for Tavi, had always watched them, helped them, protected them, his presence and his trustworthiness something so elemental that she'd barely thought to question it, any more than she would have tested fire to be sure that it was hot, water to be sure it was wet.

All the same, it was a daunting thought. Telling Tavi the truth, after so many years of hiding it from him. From everyone.

"I don't want to tell him," she said quietly.

Araris nodded, silent and steady.

"But you're right."

He nodded again.

"I'll tell him."

◻◻◻CHAPTER 1

"My ass hurts," said Antillar Maximus, Tribune Auxiliarus of the First Aleran.

"My ass hurts, *sir*," Tavi corrected him.

"Hey. Sacred right."

Tavi grunted where he lay prone and peered steadily through the yellow-and-brown winter grass of the Vale at the valley beneath them. "Just imagine if you'd marched here instead of riding."

"No thank you, sir," Max replied. "I'm too busy imagining I decided to take a few more terms at the Academy so that I could practice my earthcrafting with wealthy and beautiful Citizen girls, sir, instead of riding around the back of beyond looking to pick a fight with big, scary monsters."

The two of them lay low, and Max's voice was pitched barely louder than a whisper, for all that it never stopped running. As long as they didn't stand up and present the enemy force marching through the valley below with a beautiful silhouette, they were far enough above them to avoid being seen. Probably.

"I make that four thousand," Tavi murmured after a moment. "You?"

"Forty-two hundred," Max replied promptly. For all his complaining, the big Antillan was every bit the trained observer Tavi was. In fact, Tavi trusted his friend's estimate over his own.

Tavi frowned, thinking. "Figure one cohort for camp security . . ."

". . . and one more for scouting ahead and behind as they march," Max continued the thought.

"Bloody crows." Tavi sighed. "A full Legion."

Max let out a grim sound of agreement. "Looks that way."

Tavi felt a cold little shiver run along his belly.

In the valley below, an army of Canim marched steadily through the dry grass. The wolf-headed warriors moved with steady purpose, a good three thousand of them spread in a loose, horseshoe-shaped arrangement around a core of solid, heavily armored troops marching in ranks. Three thousand raiders shifting position would not have stirred Tavi to launch any kind of assault. Conscripted Canim, with a minimum of military discipline, the raiders were dangerous only by virtue of their numbers and their tremendous size and strength. The average Cane stood between seven and eight feet tall, and that was in their standard, half-crouched posture. Standing erect, they would have been a foot taller than that, and the sheer speed and power held within those lean frames was terrifying.

Still, the Canim army now occupying much of the territory of the cities of Ceres and Kalare could afford to lose three thousand of their dregs. It was the core of disciplined troops marching at their center, members of the elite Canim warrior caste, that had drawn Tavi from the fortifications.

A thousand of those hardened, disciplined, supremely dangerous troops represented a tithe of the Canim's total number of heavy infantry. In all their clashes with the Canim, the First Aleran had killed a relatively limited number of the warrior caste. Canim losses had been almost universally drawn from among their raiders. Nasaug, the leader of the Canim forces, never used his best troops except in devastatingly well-timed assaults, and the vast majority of Aleran losses had been at the hands of the Canim warrior caste.

Ehren's report of a thousand of them shifting position had represented an opportunity to inflict serious harm upon Nasaug's troops. A thousand were not so many as to be undefeatable, but more than enough to represent a significant loss to the enemy's prize corps of troops. When Tavi had learned which territory they were moving through, he had ordered his most mobile and dangerous units into the field at once.

The Canim warriors were walking through a death trap.

This particular valley had remarkably steep walls, and the lattice of tiny streams that ran through it provided enough water to ensure a growth of luxuriant grass—which had not yet flushed into the lush, verdant sea of green it would become within a few more weeks. For now, it was a ten-mile-long, one-mile-wide box filled with kindling and a thousand of Nasaug's finest.

The First Aleran's Knights Ignus were already in position, with the far more numerous Knights Aeris beside them. At Tavi's signal, the Knights Ignus would set the valley ablaze while the Knights Aeris used their furies to call forth a gale and send a sudden riptide of fire and fury over the foe. The Battlecrows stood at the head of the valley, ready to set a back-fire and blockade the valley's only means of egress, while Max's cavalry stood ready to sweep down from the other end of the valley and crush any Canim who managed to escape immolation.

Which was why the *second* Legion marching beside the Canim company was a problem.

They were Alerans.

Better than four thousand Alerans in full Legion regalia marched beside the most dangerous historic foes of the Realm, under banners that did not correspond to any of the great cities of Alera. Worse, they were moving in good order. Two years ago, Tavi would never have understood how difficult such an apparently simple maneuver actually *was*. It took serious discipline to achieve such uniform movement, and was evidence of a disturbing amount of competence on behalf of whoever was training those troops.

"Give me a lens, please," Tavi said quietly.

The big Antillan rose a little, leaned over Tavi, and held his hands out on either side of Tavi's face, fingers spread. The air between Max's palms blurred, and suddenly the force below them seemed to rush hundreds of yards closer, as Max's furies bent the air, magnifying Tavi's view.

"Those aren't Kalaran banners," Tavi murmured after a moment's study.

Max let out a skeptical grunt. "Maybe Kalare didn't want to be openly associated with them."

"He's already attacked his neighbors without warning, kidnapped several family members of his fellow High Lords, and had dozens and dozens of Citizens murdered by his pet maniacs," Tavi pointed out. "You really think he's worried about covering up his involvement with the Canim at this point?"

"Put that way," Max said. "No."

Tavi let out a little snort of a breath. "Take a look at their gear."

Max moved his hands up to hold before his own face. A moment later, he reported, "It's old. I mean, everything looks to be in pretty good shape, but the armor is of a design that went out of use years ago. There are lots of missing pieces, too. Mismatched greaves, nonstandard-length spears, that kind of thing." Max grunted. "Never seen any banners like that, either. Brown and green? Who uses brown and green for *banners*? They're supposed to be *visible*. That's the *point* of banners."

"Exactly," Tavi said quietly, watching the enemy column's progress.

"They're almost in position," Max said, lowering his hands. "Once their leading elements hit that old streambed, there's no way they're getting out in time."

"I see them," Tavi said.

Max nodded and said nothing for a minute. Tavi watched the disciplined but partially equipped Legion march steadily in step with the far larger Canim.

"Sir," Max said, "they're in position. It's time to signal Crassus, sir."

"It doesn't make *sense*, Max," Tavi said. "This has got to be a Legion of volunteers from within the occupied territory. Why would they be fighting *beside* an army of invaders?"

"Who knows? Maybe Nasaug is forcing them into it. Holding their families prisoner or something."

"No," Tavi said. "Nasaug is too smart for that. You don't take a man's home and family away, demand that he serve and obey you, and then put a weapon in his hand and give him four thousand friends just as angry and well armed as he is."

"Sir," Max said, "at this point, the longer we delay the attack, the more the Canim vanguard is going to be able to pressure the Battlecrows at the head of the valley."

"*Why?*" Tavi demanded to no one in particular. "Why are they *down* there?"

Max's voice gained a tense edge. "Captain, at this point it's academic. Should I order the attack?"

Tavi stared at the valley below. Fighting the Canim was one thing. He'd been doing that for a while. He respected them enough to regret the necessity of killing them though he knew he had little real choice in the matter. It was war. If Alerans didn't kill the Canim, the Canim would promptly kill Alerans, and it was as simple as that.

Except that the cobbled-together Legion below was not made up of Canim. They were Alerans. They were people Tavi had sworn to safeguard and protect.

But they were also the enemy. Two years had taught him that no matter how experienced the army or how skilled the commander, the calculus of war had a single, unalterable constant: death.

More than four thousand Alerans were about to die, and die horribly, and they shouldn't have been there at *all*. Tavi could not afford to let such a tempting target as the vulnerable column of Canim regulars get past—even if the only way to get them was to destroy the strange Legion with them, whoever they were.

His duty was clear.

Four thousand Alerans. He was about to murder more than four *thousand* fellow Alerans.

"Bloody crows," he whispered.

Tavi fought the sudden urge to throw up as he raised his hand and began to flash the signal that would travel down the relay line, ordering his men to begin the attack.

Before he could lift his arm enough to give the signal, Tavi felt an odd, sourceless, faint sensation of shock and surprise. He puzzled over it an instant before he realized that the emotions had not been his own. He had sensed them, if only dimly, coming from another source nearby, and Tavi whipped his head around in a sudden panic.

The enemy scout wore loose clothing of plain homespun that had been intentionally stained with earth and plant juices. He was a blocky little brick of a man, not tall, but with grotesquely overdeveloped shoulders and a neck that was literally thicker than the base of his skull. Despite his ragged clothing, he wore genuine *legionare's* boots, and though his leather sword belt shone with age, it bore a genuine *gladius* at his hip—and there was nothing old or ragged about the short, powerfully curved hunting bow in his hands. He had emerged from the tall grass and scrub on the ridge not ten feet away.

Tavi got his legs underneath him and whipped his knife from his belt, releasing the heavy blade into a throw almost directly from its sheath. There was no time to grip the knife properly, to set himself to throw or to aim. The knife tumbled through the air, and Tavi noted that even if it had hit point on, instead of landing almost flat against the enemy scout's upper arm, it wouldn't have inflicted anything more than a scratch.

But that hadn't been the point of the throw. The scout released the arrow strung to his bow in an instinctive snap shot, but flinched away from the whirling knife, and his arrow flew wide.

Tavi charged after his knife, put his head down, and plowed an armored shoulder into the scout's belly. The shock of impact jarred his shoulder and neck, and the scout let out a sickly sounding croak as he fell. Tavi came down on top of the scout, seized the man's homespun tunic in both hands, and slammed his helmeted forehead against the scout's face. Tavi felt the shock of the blow through the steel, and heard the scout's nose break with a squishy crunch.

The scout reacted by lifting one iron-strong hand and clamping it down on Tavi's throat. Tavi felt the fury-assisted strength of the scout's arm, and knew that if he didn't do something, the earthcrafter would snap his neck.

Tavi brought his armored knee up in a savage blow that struck home between the scout's legs, and, for a single instant, the power in that deadly arm faltered. Tavi slammed his helmet against the scout's face again, then again, and the man sagged limply back to the ground.

The entire fight had taken all of three or four seconds.

Tavi fell back from the man, his throat on fire. It was hard to suck air in through his mouth, and for a second he feared that the enemy scout had managed to crush his windpipe, but after a few seconds more he was able to gulp down great breaths of air.

Max had his sword out and had been on the way, but Tavi's reaction had been the swifter, and the big Antillan's face was pale. "Bloody crows," he hissed. "Captain?"

"I'm all right," Tavi choked out. "Did they see? Did they hear anything?"

Max rose to a low crouch and looked slowly around, then dropped down again. "There'd have been some noise by now." He met Tavi's eyes. "Captain. You have to signal the attack *now*."

Tavi stared at the senseless young man lying limp in the grass. He reached up to touch the front rim of his helmet, and his fingers came away wet with blood.

"I know," Max said, his voice low and hard. "I know you don't like killing. I know that they're our own people. I know this is hard and horrible. But that's what war *is*, Captain. You've *got* to order the attack."

"Signal Crassus," Tavi said quietly.

Max let out a low breath of relief and nodded, beginning to rise.

"Do not engage. Fall back to the rally point and meet us there."

Max stared at Tavi, his eyes widening.

Tavi continued, wiping his hands clean of blood on the dry grass. "Get word to the Battlecrows to abandon their position and fall back."

Max remained still for a moment. "Captain," he said quietly. "We aren't going to get another opportunity like this one."

Tavi narrowed his eyes as he looked up at his friend. "We're leaving, Tribune. You have your orders."

"Yes, sir," Max said at once, and very quietly. Then he paced off through the grass where he would, Tavi knew, begin flashing hand signals down the line of riders.

Max returned a moment later and watched the enemy forces below begin to march out of the ambush area and beyond their reach. "Bloody crows, Calderon. Why?"

"Why not burn four thousand of our own people to death?" Tavi asked. He gestured at the downed scout. "Look at him, Max. What do you see?"

Max stared down at the unconscious man for a moment. Then he frowned, leaned closer, and tugged aside the man's tunic a bit before he rose again. "Muscles are all lopsided, misshapen. He's been chained to a wheel or a plow, for them to develop like that," he said quietly. "He's got lash scars." His right cheek twitched in a tic that Tavi thought Max didn't know he had. "Curling over his shoulders. More on his belly. Collar scars on his neck, too. He's a slave."

"He *was* a slave," Tavi replied quietly. "No collar now." He nodded down at the army below. "We wanted to know what could make an Aleran fight beside a Cane, Max."

Max grimaced, and said, "They're freeing slaves."

Tavi nodded slowly.

"How many?" Max asked. "How many do you think they have?"

"Can't be too many," Tavi said. "They don't have a lot of gear, if this man's equipment is any indication. And if they were raising really large numbers, Ehren's spies would have heard something about them. Which makes sense."

"How?" Max said.

Tavi nodded at the slave Legion below. "Those men know that if they lose, they're dead men, Max. Some slaves have it bad, but a lot of them don't. My guess is that the ones willing to fight are a lot less common than the ones who just want to stay low and quiet until the fighting is over."

"But those are going to fight like the crows are coming for them," Max said, his voice grim.

"Yes," Tavi said quietly.

Max was silent for a minute. Then he said, "All the more reason to order the attack. I know why you didn't do it. Great furies know I agree with your principles. But a lot of men are going to have to die to stop them now. You could have done that without a loss. It's going to cost us."

"It won't cost as much as creating a Legion of martyrs," Tavi said quietly. "If I'm right, then right now, four thousand slaves have taken up arms. If we'd wiped them out, Max, if we'd proven to every slave in the occupied territory that Alera didn't give a crow's feather about their lives, Nasaug wouldn't have four thousand fresh troops ready to fight. He'd have forty thousand terrified, outraged volunteers. Read history, Max. The Canim have." Tavi shook his head. "Men fight hardest for their lives—and for their freedom."

Max drew in a slow breath, his rough, appealing features drawn into a pensive frown. "This was a trap," he said quietly. "We were offered those warriors as bait."

"This could have been a trap," Tavi said, nodding. "But Nasaug doesn't plan operations with only one purpose if he can possibly help it. I think this was something else, too."

"What?" Max said.

"A message." Tavi rose, nodding to the downed scout. "Come on. We'd better clear out before his friends notice that he's missing and come looking for him." Tavi leaned down and rolled the limp man onto his side.

"What are you doing?"

"Making sure he doesn't choke on his own blood," Tavi said. "Let's move."

They moved at a crouch out to where they'd left the horses, hidden in a thick copse of evergreens. "Tavi?" Max asked.

"Yes?"

"Is that really why you didn't order the attack? Did you really think it was a trap?"

Tavi regarded his friend steadily. "You think I felt sympathy for them."

"No," Max said. "I bloody well know you did, Calderon. I know you. But we're at war. I'm not sure you can afford that. I'm not sure the men can afford it."

Tavi paused beside Acteon, one hand on the saddle, one on the reins, and stared at nothing in particular. "I think," he said quietly, "that I have a duty to Alera, Max. All Alerans." He took a deep breath and mounted. Then he said, his voice distant and very calm, "And yes. That's why I didn't kill them all."

Max mounted a moment later and rode up beside Tavi as they moved back toward the rally point. "That works for me." He glanced back at the ridge behind them and let out a low chortle.

"What?" Tavi asked.

"Your *singulare* has been walking around in your shadow

for almost two years now. The first day he's not here, you charge out into the field and get yourself half-choked to death. He's going to be furious. So's Kitai."

Tavi let out a rough-sounding chuckle. It grated painfully in his throat. "Don't worry, Max. I'll deal with them."

Max's smile faded. "Senator Arnos was hoping to put a big new feather in his cap for this conference with the First Lord. He and the War Committee are not going to be happy about you letting those regulars get away."

Tavi felt his eyes narrow as his smile turned into a simple baring of his teeth. "Don't worry, Max," he said. "I'll deal with them, too."

ᚻᚻᚻᚻ Chapter 2

"First Spear!" bellowed a *legionare's* voice.

Valiar Marcus had spent more years in the Legions than many of the volunteers in the First Aleran had been drawing breath. Though he'd had the third watch, and been asleep for less than an hour, his feet swung off his cot and hit the cheap rug that he'd thrown over the bottom of his small, but private, tent. He already had his tunic and boots on by the time the *legionare* reached his tent.

"Centurion," panted Vilius, a young *legionare* in the cohort's third century. "We've got reports of movement on the road to the east. A large force."

"Bloody crows," Marcus swore. "The relief column." He struggled to draw conclusions, but his sleep-fogged mind wasn't cooperating. He shook his head with a growl and forced it to do its duty. "Captain will have the cavalry, the Knights, and the Battlecrows on the road. He'll try to hold the Canim off long enough to get the column into the city's walls." Fidelias turned to his armor and strapped into it, fastening the row of ties down its center front with fingers that flew with the effort-less speed of long practice. "Prime Cohort will form up on the earthworks on the far side of the refugee camp. Tell Tribunes Martinus and Kellus that I recommend that they form up the Seventh and Ninth on First Cohort's flanks. We march in five minutes."

Vilius slammed his fist against the armor over his heart and dashed from the tent.

Once he was gone, Marcus grimaced and rubbed savagely at the clenching cramp that had formed on one side of his neck. He must have pulled a muscle, sitting up that fast out of a dead sleep, but crows take him if he was letting any of those young men see it.

Maybe he was getting too old for this sort of thing.

Five minutes later, the Prime Cohort, double the size of any other cohort at eight centuries strong, moved out of the heavily fortified gates of the town on the northern side of the Tiber. They went out at a run, boots striking hard in unison on the paving stones, then becoming a muffled thunder as the column wheeled out over softer earth. Marcus led the column beneath the wan, cloud-obscured morning sun, running beside the first rank and calling the pace. They passed through the tent-and-shanty-filled warren that stretched for half a mile in every di-rection around the town of Elinarch.

The earthworks at the far side of the refugee camp were not the simple packed-earth walls that the Legions had used for time out of mind. Instead, they had been built from clay taken from the bed and banks of the Tiber, then baked into a substance harder than most stone via the use of firecrafting. Those walls were fifteen feet high and twenty thick, and if they didn't have the sheer, obdurate strength of furycrafted battlement stone, they were far more serviceable than stan-dard earthworks or a wooden palisade.

Marcus led the cohort up onto the walls over the wide-mouthed gate, where the men took up positions with practiced speed. He bellowed at the few who performed with slight im-perfections, and had the entire Prime Cohort in position and standing ready before the *legionares* of the Seventh and Ninth cleared the city walls and came pounding toward them.

Half an hour passed in nervous silence while, behind them, refugees began a slow, confused retreat into the safety of the city's walls. Overhead, several Knights Aeris went flashing by, driven by torrents of wind, flying to and from the east. Marcus felt the familiar singing tension of fear that always came with preparation for a battle. Defending the city from an attack from this particular flank had been a worst-case scenario, and no one had thought it would actually come to that—but if the Canim had crossed the river, then he and the other men here, at the forward defenses, were about to have a very bad morning. Worse, every one of them knew it.

So Marcus spent his time pacing steadily up and down the wall, berating troops for an improperly fastened sword belt here, a small patch of rust on a breastplate there. His growled imprecations were creative, gratuitously foul-mouthed—and familiar. They were all the reassurance he could offer his men. They were all he could offer himself, as well.

Tribune Tactica Kellus, who had himself been a centurion when he first signed on with the First Aleran, paced briskly down the wall from the Ninth's position and nodded to Marcus. "Centurion."

Though as the First Spear, Marcus exercised command of the Prime Cohort, made up of its finest *legionares*, Kellus still outranked him. Marcus saluted, and nodded. "Sir."

"Have you any idea what's going on?"

He shrugged. "Reports of an unknown force east of here."

Kellus grimaced. "I know *that*."

"Then your guess is as good as mine."

"Another drill, you think?"

Marcus pursed his lips. "No. I don't think so, sir. I know the captain's mad for them, but this doesn't feel right."

Kellus grunted. "Can't be the Canim, can it? They've never been able to cross the Tiber in numbers."

"Maybe they worked it out," Marcus said. "Either way—"

"On the wall!" came a call from below.

Marcus turned to find a dapper, aging little man in the livery of a Legion valet standing below. "Good morning, Magnus."

"Permission to come up and speak to you?" called the valet.

"Granted." Marcus beckoned the valet, who hurried up the stairs and arrived on the battlements, laboring to catch his breath.

"Centurion, Tribune," Magnus panted, nodding. "We just got a messenger in from the captain. He wanted me to tell your men to stand down."

Marcus lifted his eyebrows.

"It *was* a drill, then," Kellus said.

Marcus frowned and turned to stare intently at the road to the east. "No," he said quietly. "I don't think it was."

For a moment, there was nothing but the haze of a morning that had not yet become warm enough to burn off all the mist. Then, ranks of marching soldiers appeared in the east. Two long, broad columns of them, in fact, came marching along on either side of the road, leaving room for the relief column's wagons and draft animals in the center. Marcus frowned, and began counting, before he realized what he was actually looking at.

"*Two* Legions?" he murmured.

"Yes," Magnus said quietly.

"And flying the blue and red," Marcus noted. "Like us."

The senior valet squinted out at the approaching troops. "Ah, I thought as much. These are the Senate's new toys. The Senatorial Guard."

Marcus grunted. "Arnos's pet project, right?"

"The Senator is used to getting what he wants," the valet replied. "And with the war stretching on, his arguments have gained much more support in the Committee, the Senate, and among the Citizenry."

"And now the Senate has its own Legions, too."

The old valet nodded. "Ambitious, that Arnos, commanding two-thirds the fighting power of a High Lord. He controls them completely."

Marcus blew out a breath. "So the good news is that the Canim haven't crossed the river." He said the next sentence a bit louder, knowing word would spread rapidly up and down the wall. "No fighting today."

"And the bad news," the valet said in a quiet tone, "is that—"

"The War Committee has come to Elinarch to play," Marcus said, his tone souring.

"Great furies help us. Yes."

"Thank you, Magnus," the First Spear said. "Looks like this has turned into your kind of fight."

The Legion's senior valet sighed. "Yes. Now if you'll excuse me, I'll toddle off and try to figure out where we're going to *put* everyone." He nodded to them and departed again.

Kellus came to stand next to Marcus, scowling at the incoming Legions. "We don't need their help here," he said. "We've held it ourselves for two years."

"We've bled for two years, too," Marcus said quietly. "I won't mind letting someone else do that part for a little while, sir."

Kellus snorted and departed to return to his own men, where Marcus thought he should have bloody well been standing to begin with. The young Tribune was right about one thing, though. Arnos's presence here—and in command of two full Legions, no less—was anything but a good sign.

Marcus knew who truly owned Arnos's allegiance.

An hour later, Valiar Marcus and his men returned to their quarters in the city, and Marcus returned to his own tent, aching for sleep. He drew the tent's heavy flaps closed, tied them there, and then began to unfasten his armor.

"May I help you, my lady?" he asked quietly, as he did.

There was a quiet, pleased sound from the direction of his camp stool, simple canvas on a wooden frame. The air shimmered for a moment, and a woman appeared there, seated primly, dressed in a rather plain russet gown. The gown did not suit her features, any more than an old rope halter suited a finely bred horse. She was lovely in a way that few women could match and none could surpass, dark of hair and fair of skin, seemingly in the flower of her late youth.

Marcus knew better. Invidia Aquitaine was neither young, nor particularly flowery. There was nothing delicate or fragile about her. In fact, he reflected, she was one of the more dangerous people he'd ever known.

"I'm not wearing my perfume," she said in a velvet-smooth

alto. "I was careful to move nothing in the tent. I'm quite sure you didn't see me through my veil, and I made no sound. How did you know I was here?"

Marcus finished unlacing the armor and shrugged out of it. The surge of relief in his shoulders and neck at the sudden absence of its weight was heavenly. Then he glanced at her, and said, "Oh. It's you."

Lady Aquitaine gave him a very direct look for several long seconds before her lips parted and a low chuckle bubbled from them. "I have missed you, Fidelias. Very few people have nerve enough to offer me insouciance, these days."

"Doesn't Arnos?" he asked her. "The way I hear it, he never shuts his crowbegotten mouth."

"Arnos offers me a number of assets," Lady Aquitaine replied. "Sparkling wit and clever conversation are not among them. Though I will grant that he is skilled enough in . . . other social pursuits." Her mouth curled into a merrily wicked little smirk—just a schoolgirl, out to amuse herself, all in good fun.

Fidelias didn't believe it for a moment, of course. "My lady, I don't wish to seem rude—"

"But you had late watch last night, and have not slept, I know," she said, her tone turning businesslike. "I, of course, have other concerns as well." She studied him for a moment, then said, "That face you're wearing. It really doesn't suit you, you know. All the scars. The lumpy nose. It's the face of a mindless thug."

Marcus—Fidelias—sat down on the edge of his cot and began unlacing his boots. "I earned this face, as Marcus."

"So I've been told," she replied. "Valiar Marcus is quite the hero of the Realm." Her eyes remained very steady. "I have wondered, from time to time, if you have forgotten that Fidelias is most decidedly *not*."

Fidelias froze for just a beat, and sudden trepidation made his heartbeat race. He cursed himself for the slip. He'd been soldiering so much, the past two years, that he'd lost some of his edge for intrigue. Lady Aquitaine would have read his reaction as quickly and easily as she might have looked at a playing card. He forced himself to bottle up his emotions as he finished removing his boots. "I know who I am, and what I'm doing," he said quietly.

"I find it odd," she said, "that you have not reported anything to me about this young captain, Rufus Scipio."

Fidelias grunted. "I've reported to you. Young commander, natural talent. He led the Legion through something that should have killed them to a man, and they wouldn't hear of having him replaced with a more experienced commander, after. He's fought a campaign against the Canim that should go into the history books."

Lady Aquitaine lifted an eyebrow. "He's held on to a single city while taking back less than fifty miles of territory from the invaders. That hardly sounds impressive."

"Because you don't know who and what he's done it against," Fidelias said.

"The War Committee does not seem impressed with it."

"The War Committee hasn't stood to battle against an army of fifty thousand Canim with nothing but a half-trained Legion with an understrength corps of Knights to support it."

Lady Aquitaine bared her teeth in a sudden, brilliant smile. "So *military*. That suits you, I think." Her eyes roamed over him. "And the exercise has agreed with you, it would seem."

Fidelias kept himself from reacting at all, either to her words, to the sudden low fires in her eyes, or to the subtle wave of earthcrafting that swept out from her, sending a quiet, insistent tug of desire flickering through his body. "My lady, please. Your point?"

"My point," she said quietly, every word growing sharper, "is that rumor is running rampant that this young Scipio commands Legions as if born to it. Rumor has it that he has shown evidence of subtle and potent furycrafting, to such a degree that he withstood attacks that all but annihilated the officers of an entire Legion. Rumor *has* it that he bears a startling resemblance to Gaius Septimus in his youth."

Fidelias rolled one shoulder as his neck cramped again. "Young men in Legion armor, in Legion haircuts, all look pretty much the same, my lady. He's tall, yes. So are a lot of young men. He's a natural talent at command. But he's got less furycraft than I do. He barely passed his basic crafting requirements for his first term in the Legions. You can look them up, in Riva's records."

Lady Aquitaine folded her hands and frowned at him. "I'll have to take a look at him myself, Fidelias. But frankly, he's too well positioned to ignore. He commands the loyalty of an entire Legion, after all—and a Legion that contains not one, but *two* sons of Antillus Raucus, both of whom possess their father's talents. And he's operated in complete loyalty to Gaius. I'm not prepared to entertain the notion of a bastard of the House of Gaius running loose with that kind of power to support him. Not now." She smiled, and it was a cold, cold thing. "We're almost there. Gaius will fall. I will not have some upstart playing havoc with my plans now."

Fidelias took a slow breath, keeping himself carefully under control. If Lady Aquitaine sensed the sudden turmoil of his emotions now, he was as good as dead. "A reasonable precaution," he said. "What would you have me do?"

"Remain where you are for now," she said, rising. She flicked a hand, idly, and the features of her face melted, changed, and rearranged themselves into a far plainer set of features that looked nothing like her. Her hair changed colors and took on streaks of grey, and her body slumped slightly, as though aging several years within a few seconds. She lifted a bundle of clothing she'd held in her lap, and looked precisely like any of a hundred washerwomen who worked for the Legion—but for the hard shine in her eyes. "And soon," she said, "when the time is right, my dear spy, I'll send you the word."

"To what?" Fidelias asked quietly.

She paused at the tent's flap and looked at him over her shoulder. "Why, to kill him, of course."

Then she was gone, vanishing into the rising bustle of the camp outside his tent.

Fidelias—Marcus—shut the tent flap again and saw that his hands were shaking. He returned to his cot and lay down upon it.

Kill the captain.

If he did not, he wouldn't survive it. Though they eagerly cultivated betrayal in others' retainers, the Aquitaines did not tolerate it among their own. Fidelias knew. He'd killed half a dozen of them himself, at Lady Aquitaine's bidding. He'd turned against Gaius Sextus, his liege. He'd betrayed his fellow Cursors. He'd turned upon his own student, and he knew Amara would never forgive him. He'd done it all at her command, because he had believed that she and her husband were the least destructive choice for Alera's future.

That was before he'd met the captain, before the young man had, somehow, hauled survival and victory out of the ashes of chaos and despair—and personally risked his life to save Marcus's own along the way.

Now, Invidia Aquitaine commanded him once more.

Kill the captain.

Marcus ached to his bones with fatigue, but he lay staring up at the sloping canvas walls of his tent, utterly unable to sleep.

◦◦◦◦◦ CHAPTER 3

"Captain," Valiar Marcus said. "They're ready for you."

Tavi rose and straightened the hem of his rich crimson tunic, beneath the armor, and made sure that his formal half cape draped properly. He'd never actually had occasion to wear his dress uniform before, and after two years of regular use, his battered armor looked rather shabby when framed by the splendid crimson fabric.

"Sword, sir," Marcus said. The old centurion's weathered face was sober, but Tavi thought he saw amusement in his eyes.

Tavi glanced down and sighed. Regulations called for a sword to hang straight along the seam of the trousers, but he'd taken his cue from Marcus and several other veterans, and belted his scabbard on at a slight angle. The change made a small difference in the ease of drawing a blade, and a smart soldier sought every advantage he could. Regulations, however, were regulations, and Tavi took a moment to resecure the weapon properly. Then he nodded to the First Spear and strode into the conference room.

The conference room had been built in the heavy stone command building back when the First Aleran had repulsed the initial Canim onslaught. The room, with its large stone sand table, and its classroom-style slateboards on the walls, had been intended to host the command staff of a pair of Legions—twice what had ever actually put the room to use. Now, though, the place was stuffy and close, and crowded with twoscore of the most powerful men and women in Alera.

Tavi recognized only a few of them by sight, though he could deduce most of the others from their colors and reputations. Gaius, of course, sat at the front of the room, on a small platform raised a few inches over the floor. He was flanked by a pair of Crown Guardsmen, and Sir Cyril, as the nominal host of the proceedings, sat beside him, his metalcrafted replacement leg gleaming in the light of the furylamps.

Around the room were several other notables of the Realm: High Lord and High Lady Placida were front and center in the first row, seated beside the elderly High Lord Cereus. Sir Miles, Captain of the Crown Legion, sat beside him, though Tavi had no idea why Miles's mouth was hanging open like that. After all, surely someone had told Miles about Tavi's role as Rufus Scipio. Toward the back of the room, leaning indolently against the wall, like a bored schoolboy, was a man that could only be High Lord Aquitaine. Several men whose body language declared them cronies of Aquitaine stood nearby him. On the other side of the room from Aquitaine was Countess Amara, standing in precisely the same posture, probably as a subtle mockery of the second-most-powerful man in the Realm—and certainly in a position where she would be able to watch everything the High Lord and his associates were doing. Senator Arnos, head of the War Committee, and a dozen aides and associates occupied the entire second row, and Tavi could feel the man's cold, calculating eyes lock onto him as he entered.

"Ah," Gaius said, his deep, mellow voice filling the room

when he spoke. "Welcome, Captain Scipio. Thank you for coming."

Tavi bowed deeply to the First Lord. "Of course, sire. How may I serve?"

"We've been briefing everyone on the recent developments in the course of the rebellion," Gaius replied. "Sir Cyril assures me that you are the best man to give us a concise recounting of events here." Gaius gestured at the front of the room. "If you please."

Tavi bowed his head again and strode to the front of the room. He bowed to the assembled nobles and Legion captains, took a deep breath, ordered his thoughts, and began. "As you all know, the First Aleran has been holding the Tiber against the Canim incursion since it originally landed on the Night of the Red Stars, two years ago.

"Since that time we have fought a number of sizeable engagements against the Canim, and have seen many smaller actions. It has not been easy—"

"It can't have been *too* difficult," Senator Arnos said. The Senator was a small man, his fashionably long hair slicked back and held in a tail. "After all, a novice commander held off an invasion force that outnumbered his own half-trained Legion ten to one or better—assuming your force estimates are accurate."

Tavi felt a flash of worry and anxiety at the hard, annoyed tone in the Senator's voice—and felt it quickly transform into a surge of anger at what his words were implying. Tavi reminded himself that if anyone intended to discredit him, baiting him into an emotional reaction would be an ideal way to go about it, and he reined in his emotions. "A number of factors played to our favor," Tavi responded, his voice calm and even. "Most important of which was a schism in the Canim leadership, between the leader of the warrior caste, Nasaug, and the leader of the ritualist caste, Sarg. We were able to play them off against one another and foil their initial attack. Their numbers are not in question, Senator. They have been verified from multiple sources in the time since."

"Yes, yes," Arnos said impatiently. "The question I'm sure everyone's eager to have answered, Captain, is why you haven't swept the dogs into the crowbegotten sea by now. Numbers advantage or not, your Knights trump anything the Canim have."

Tavi just looked at the man for a moment. Then he took a deep breath, and said, "Centurion."

Marcus entered, carrying a T-shaped metal contraption the size of a cart horse's yolk. He took up position beside Tavi and held the object up for everyone to see.

"This," Tavi said, "is a Canim weapon. It's an innovation on a standard bow, and we call it a balest. It's capable of throwing a solid steel projectile nearly two-thirds of a mile, if the wind is favorable, and it hits with enough force to punch cleanly through a breastplate, the man beneath, and out the other side."

Arnos rolled his eyes and made a faint sound of derision.

"I've had more Knights killed by this weapon, Senator, than any other in the Canim arsenal," Tavi said. "They're used by highly trained specialists, and almost always at night. If our Knights Aeris try to approach, every crowd of Canim seems to have one of their marksmen hidden in it, and they go out of their way to protect them. This weapon is the only one we've managed to capture over the course of two years—and the Cane who used it managed to escape."

"Captain," drawled High Lord Placidus in his easy, mellow voice, "could you give us an idea of just how effective these marksmen of theirs are?"

"They don't have the precision of a skilled Knight Flora, Your Grace," Tavi replied. "But they're very close. And the raw power of these weapons more than compensates. Given that they apparently have orders to wait for Knights to make their appearance before firing, they have proven to be an effective tactical countermeasure."

"Even assuming this ... toy ... gave a Cane the same combat effectiveness as a Knight Flora," Arnos said, and his tone suggested that he clearly did not believe that it might, "you need only take similar tactical measures to prevent them from employing it effectively."

"Except that Nasaug has a great many Canim he can train to use a balest," Tavi said. "We have a sharply limited number of Knights, and we cannot afford to lose or replace them."

Tavi turned to the rest of the room. "This weapon hasn't determined the course of the conflict on its own, of course. I simply use it to illustrate that the Canim have proven to be a more devious, resourceful, capable, and well-equipped foe than we had previously believed."

Arnos made a disgusted sound. "Are we to believe that in centuries of conflict against these animals, we have simply been too blind to see what was in front of our eyes?"

Tavi shook his head. "The Canim Alera fought previously were never this well organized or this numerous. Furthermore, prior to this incursion, we had never seen the appearance of their warrior caste in numbers."

"I just don't understand this situation at all," High Lord Cereus said. He passed a long-fingered, liver-spotted, but steady hand back over his balding scalp. "The behavior of these creatures just isn't at all what I would have expected. My own nobles and soldiers report to me that these Canim have been allowing Alerans simply to *leave* the occupied territory, unmolested, provided they go peaceably."

"Clearly an indicator of their lack of control of the situation," Senator Arnos said, rising, "as well as a telling point in regards to their strategic ineptitude. No real commander would allow such a potentially valuable resource to be lost at all, much less allow it to be given to the enemy." He turned to the room. "In fact, the ineptitude of command in this entire region has—"

"Excuse me, Senator," Tavi said, keeping his tone polite. "I'm happy to field whatever questions you or the other Citizens may have." He faced Arnos without smiling. "But I believe protocol dictates that I have the floor."

Arnos turned to face Tavi, color flushing his cheeks.

"Quite right, Captain," Gaius murmured from his seat. Though his phrasing remained polite, his voice calm, there were hard inflections on his words that left no doubt as to the First Lord's lack of amusement. "Senator, I ask your patience in this matter. Everyone will have an opportunity to be heard, I assure you. Captain, please continue with your thoughts on the Canim war leader's unexpected generosity in releasing Alerans from the occupied territory."

Tavi bowed his head. "Nothing generous about it, sire. It's genius."

Gaius nodded, his eyes on Arnos. "Explain."

"It gives him nothing but advantage," Tavi replied. "The largest problem facing the entire region of the rebellion has been the supply of food. The fighting has resulted in many fields being destroyed, others damaged, and it has degraded the ability of the entire region to bring in a steady harvest. Add more than a hundred thousand hungry Canim to the equation, and as a result, everyone's forces have been trying to secure all the food they can."

Lady Placidus raised her hand. "Excuse me, Captain. A hundred thousand? I had understood that our estimates placed the number at somewhere near half that."

"A hundred thousand is a conservative estimate, Your Grace," Tavi said, bowing his head politely to the High Lady. "The Canim who came here did not come simply as an invading military. They brought their dependents with them. Females and young. I say one hundred thousand, but I don't know the real number. No one does. They're going to great lengths to protect them."

A low mutter went through the room.

Tavi cleared his throat and raised the volume of his voice slightly. "By releasing Alerans in the occupied territory, Nasaug solves several of his own problems and hands us several new ones. The local Alerans are most familiar with local furies and will have the most ability to take action against his troops. By getting rid of them, he simultaneously robs any resistance within the territory of most of its strength, conserves his food supply by reducing the number of hungry mouths that would consume it, *and* burdens us with the refugees. Now, we are forced to find some way to feed them, as well as to keep our limited number of forces deployed in such a fashion as to shield them from potential enemy aggression, hampering our ability to operate aggressively against them.

"It's a smart move. It's typical of his thinking. And it's working. We haven't had any deaths from starvation, yet—but lack of sufficient food was probably responsible for a number of fatal illnesses last winter. The relief column organized by Steadholder Isana of Calderon might—might—hold us through until harvest, but the refugee camp here is only one of a dozen, spread around the outskirts of Canim-occupied territory."

There was a moment of pensive, even worried, silence.

"Captain," Gaius asked, his rich, calm voice bringing the fearful pause to an end. "I assume you have attempted to apply standard Legion doctrine in your battles against the Canim."

"Yes, sir," Tavi said.

"And how would you characterize its effectiveness?"

"It has been of limited value, sire."

Gaius glanced around the room. "Why?"

"The Canim don't play by the rules, sire," Tavi said.

In the front row, Captain Miles had apparently recovered enough to snort out a rough breath of a laugh.

The creases at the corners of Gaius's mouth deepened slightly. "Explain."

"They don't rely on furycrafting, sire," Tavi clarified. "They can't use it, and have no need for it. As a result, they don't think in the same terms, strategically. For example, they have no particular need for the use of causeways, the way an Aleran Legion does, if it wants to move rapidly. They avoid causeways whenever they can, forcing the Legion to march overland, which gives them a significant advantage in the field. They march faster than we do.

"We've compensated for this to some degree, by introducing training for overland marches, the addition of auxiliary units of cavalry—"

Aquitaine murmured something at the back of the room. Tavi only caught the phrase "naked barbarians," but the men standing with him let out low, growling laughs.

"—as well," Tavi continued steadily, "as the addition of a cohort of mounted infantry."

"Mounted infantry?" asked High Lord Cereus.

"They ride to the fight, then dismount, Your Grace," Tavi clarified. "It lets us field a solid block of *legionares* to support our cavalry and our Knights, and provides us with greater tactical flexibility in the field."

Arnos let out a derisive snort. "This is all beside the point, Gaius, and we all know it. Captain Rufus Scipio's tactics and Sir Cyril's strategies have, I admit, managed to hold on to the region and contain the Canim threat. It's quite possible that, given how badly outnumbered they have been, they were even appropriate to the task at hand. But that situation is now at an end."

The Senator rose and addressed the room at large. "I have two outsized Legions of the Senatorial Guard, fresh and made up purely of veteran *legionares*, now camped outside. Between them and the remnants of the First Aleran, we will sweep the beasts back into the sea and end this humiliating charade." He turned to Lord Aquitaine, specifically. "I anticipate that we will bring the war in this theater to a conclusion by midsummer, at which point we can increase the pressure on Kalare's remaining forces and restore order to the Realm."

Tavi stared at Arnos blankly for a moment. Was the man *insane*? True, the two Legions of the Senatorial Guard contained nearly ten thousand men each—but unless the mathematics instructors at the Academy had done Tavi a grave disservice, it still meant that the Canim's forces outnumbered the Alerans by well more than two to one. Those were not impossible odds by any stretch of the imagination, but they were daunting—and they did not take into account any former-slave forces the Canim might have raised.

"Such an undertaking would be . . . premature, Senator," Tavi said. "Until we have learned more about the additional forces being raised by the Canim."

That drew every eye in the room.

"What?" Sir Miles sputtered.

"The Canim have armed at least one Legion of former slaves," Tavi said. "We presume that they're offering freedom in exchange for—"

"Does this matter?" Arnos demanded, scorn open now in his tone.

"They're our fellow Alerans," Tavi spat. "Many of the people who stayed probably did so because they had nowhere else to—"

"Immaterial," Arnos said, arching an eyebrow. "As you yourself have pointed out, every loyal Aleran has already left the occupied territory."

"That *isn't* what I said—" Tavi began.

Arnos's well-cultured baritone overrode him effortlessly. "Those who remain behind—whether they are taking up arms against the Realm or simply supporting the Canim for their own personal profit—are traitors." His smile was sharp and hard. "They deserve nothing but a traitor's death."

A number of men raised their voices at that point. Tavi began to join them, but there was a sudden presence at his side, and Tavi turned to find the First Lord standing beside him.

"Be silent," Gaius said quietly.

"But, *sire*," Tavi began.

"Be *silent*," the First Lord hissed. His eyes turned to Tavi and gave him a single, hard look, so full of authority that the young Cursor never so much as considered doing or saying anything else.

"Yes, sire."

Gaius nodded once, as the impatiently raised voices grew louder. "I need you exactly where you are—in command of the First Aleran. Don't give him an excuse to remove you."

Tavi blinked and could only stare blankly at Gaius.

"I'm sorry I couldn't do more for you here, lad," the First Lord continued. "My support doesn't mean what it once did, I'm afraid. Today, I'm little more than the chair of a meeting."

"I didn't even get to tell them about what Ehren's contacts have learned or the theories we've drawn from it."

Gaius's lips compressed for a moment. "He doesn't want to hear it. Arnos and his friends have plans for what happens next in the region, and their plans do not necessarily leave room for such minor inconveniences as fact."

Tavi ground his teeth. "He's a fool."

"He's a fool with the backing of the Senate," Gaius corrected him. "And he is the lawful commander of the Guard—and the First Aleran, I might add. He'll be assuming command in the region, with Sir Cyril as his senior advisor."

Tavi took a deep breath. "What would you have me do?"

"Your best," the First Lord said. "Work with Sir Cyril. Mitigate the Senator's idiocy. Save as many lives as you can."

"If Arnos does what he says, Nasaug is going to hurt us, sire. Badly."

"Three months," Gaius said. "Keep things together here for three months."

"What?" Tavi asked quietly, confused. "Why three months?"

"Because by then, the war with Kalarus will be finished, his rebellion over, and we'll have regular Legion commanders to spare. Once the Senate's 'state of emergency' is over, Arnos can go back to pushing soldiers around a sand table where he belongs."

Tavi blinked at him. "How is that going to happen, sire?"

The First Lord arched a greying eyebrow at him. Tavi noted, for the first time, that their eyes were now on a level with one another.

Gaius's eyes glittered with dark humor for an instant. "That would be telling." He cast a glance at the tumult Arnos's comments had created. "The task I'm handing you is unenviable. Can you do it?"

Tavi looked up at the discord swirling around the Senator and narrowed his eyes. He knew all too well the kind of price the *legionares* were forced to pay when their leaders made even relatively small and honest mistakes. What Arnos was proposing was barely this side of insanity, and the suffering that his actions could inflict on noncombatants in the occupied territory was a thing out of the young captain's nightmares.

Something had to be done.

"Yes, sire," Tavi said quietly. "I can."

◌◌◌◌◌Chapter 4

"Well," Amara murmured to the First Lord as they departed the command building. "That could have gone better."

"Actually," Gaius said, "it went as well as could be expected." He strode purposefully toward the area of the square typically used by Knights Aeris for landings and takeoffs. That area of the camp was kept policed of detritus and debris, so that the gales caused by fliers' windstreams sent a minimum number of objects flying around.

Amara had to hurry her own steps to keep up with the much taller First Lord. "I thought the young captain held his own rather well."

"Rather *too* well," Gaius said testily. "Great furies know, Arnos needs someone to bleed his ego to manageable levels, but Scipio isn't the one to do it. I need him right where he is."

Amara shook her head. "I spent some time in the town last night, doing a little listening in the wine houses."

"Amara," Gaius chided her. "You're serving as my liaison now, not as an intelligence agent."

"Habit, sire," Amara said. "His men think new grass sprouts up in his bootprints and flowers bloom where he spits. They'd never stand for his removal."

Gaius made a thoughtful sound. "Really? He's that highly regarded?"

"I watched three brawls last night between *legionares* from the Senatorial Guard and those of the First Aleran. Every one was started by commentary about Scipio."

"How'd his men do?"

"They won three times." Amara shook her head. "They're a tough group, sire."

"After two years out here alone, they'd have to be," Gaius

murmured. "I wanted to send them more help, but the pressures elsewhere were just too great. Especially with the increased pressure on the Shieldwall."

Amara glanced around them, making sure no one was immediately nearby. "And it kept Scipio isolated from the rest of the Realm."

Gaius gave her a sharp look.

Amara shrugged. "There are rumors, sire."

"Rumors," Gaius said.

"About Scipio. About who his father might have been." Amara drew in a deep breath. "The rumors say that he bears a remarkable likeness to Princeps Septimus, sire. And they say that a man named Araris—a man who might be Araris Valerian himself—is his personal *singulare*."

"Rumors, Countess," Gaius said.

"I thought so, too," she said. "Until I saw Captain Miles's face, when T—When Scipio walked in." She looked up at the First Lord. "It was like he'd seen a ghost."

Gaius's voice hardened slightly. "Rumors, Countess."

"Rumors you wanted to strengthen," she said quietly. "That's why you held the meeting here instead of summoning everyone back to the capital. Out here, where he's surrounded by his men, confident, obviously in command—and where none of them would be in a position of authority over him and where you could oversee the situation. You're priming them to accept him as something more."

The First Lord glanced down at her, and the corners of his mouth twitched though his voice remained stern. "I already know you're clever, Countess. You don't have to prove it to me. It's considered good form to let such things go unsaid."

Amara kept herself from smiling and gave him a grave bow of her head. "Of course, sire. I'll keep that in mind."

Gaius glanced back over his shoulder, toward the command building. "They really think that much of him?"

"They love him," she said.

Gaius stepped out onto the swept-clean stones of the flight area. "It was like that with Septimus, you know," he said quietly.

Amara tilted her head to one side, listening in silence.

"He had that quality about him. People loved him. He gave

them . . ." Gaius shook his head. "Something. Something that made them feel that they could do more than they ever had before. That lifted them up. Made them greater. He gave them . . ."

"Hope," Amara suggested.

"Yes," Gaius said quietly, and his voice turned puzzled. "It wasn't any kind of furycraft. It was *him*. I never understood how he did it." The First Lord shrugged. "He must have gotten it from his mother."

"Sire—" Amara began.

Gaius lifted a hand in a weary gesture. "I am not like Septimus. Or Scipio. I still command respect in some. In most, though, all I inspire is fear." His eyes were unfocused, his voice thoughtful. "I am not a good person, Amara. I have had reasonable success as a First Lord, but . . . I don't have their compassion. Only resolve."

Amara only stared at the First Lord, in silence. He rarely spoke of himself in a personal sense. It was at moments like this that Amara felt the real difference in their ages—for though Gaius looked like a man in his midforties, perhaps graced with early silver hair, he was in truth approaching eighty years of age. He had seen a lifetime of intrigue and betrayal, and no small share of personal tragedy of his own. She had grown used to the image he projected—that of a man of fantastic power, inhuman will, and effortless personal and political grace.

It was in moments like these that she was reminded of what he truly was—a weary and almost viciously lonely old man.

Amara had made mistakes enough in her young life to give her a small but steady burden of regrets. Gaius's decisions affected many more people than her own. How many regrets did the old man have piled upon his aching shoulders? How much darker were the dreams that came to haunt him? How many times, over decades in the treacherous world of Aleran politics, had he longed for someone to turn to, to talk to, to lean upon—knowing that there was no one, and never would be. Not after the death of his wife and son, the last of the ancient bloodlines of the House of Gaius. Everyone looked at the First Lord and saw exactly what he wished them to see: the leader of the Realm, the power, and the riches.

Only in the last year of working with him had Amara realized how unutterably alone Gaius truly was.

It took extraordinary courage to lead the life he had lived, to endure in the face of all the problems, the enemies, the demands placed upon him. Even if she had the furycraft to do it, Amara would not be the First Lord for all the riches of Alera.

She drew herself up, faced him squarely, and said, "I serve you, sire."

Gaius regarded her intently for a moment, then briefly put a hand on her shoulder. "Countess," he said, "it is entirely possible that I am not worthy of such loyalty. Summon the coach."

"Yes, sire." Amara raised one arm and flashed a hand signal at a group of Knights Aeris of the Crown Guard waiting on a nearby wall. The men secured harnesses to an aerial coach and lifted into the air, descending to the landing ground with the First Lord's coach, along with an escort of a score of Knights Aeris in the Crown's scarlet and blue. Gaius traded some words with the commander of the Knights, then entered the coach. Amara came in after him.

Wind roared, and the coach rose up and away from the fortified town. Amara took a moment to regard the Elinarch, rising in a graceful arch over the grey-green waters of the slow, deep, steady Tiber. At one point in her life, Amara thought, she would have resisted anything but a direct command to ride in an air coach. After all, why ride when one could be reveling in the power and freedom of flight?

Granted, that was before the First Lord had her flying over the entire width and breadth of the Realm for most of two years straight. After being worn to exhaustion, over and over again, Amara had come to the conclusion that perhaps a little bit of decadent relaxation while someone else did the heavy lifting might not be a bad thing. She had no intention of making a habit of it, but she'd worked hard enough to earn the occasional respite.

Especially given how long it had been since she'd seen Bernard.

Amara sighed. Bernard, her secret husband. Cursors were supposed to devote themselves solely to their duties. Cursors served the First Lord and the Realm, and their devotion was expected to be selfless and undivided—though, like active *legionares*, who were also supposed to remain unwed, Cursors generally took lovers. The only thing truly forbidden was marriage.

Of course, that was precisely what she had done.

Amara should never have allowed herself to fall in love with the formidable Count of Calderon. Regardless of how steady and caring he was, how strong, how handsome, how patient and loving, how passionate and skilled and—

Amara's heart sped up, and she arrested her train of thought before she began to blush.

If love was so easily overruled by banal reason, it would not be love.

"Thinking of the good Count Calderon, Amara?" Gaius asked her. His eyes glittered with amusement.

"You don't know it was him," Amara replied. "Perhaps I've taken a dozen new lovers by now."

The First Lord's mouth quivered. Then he erupted into a rich, genuine bellow of laughter. It didn't last before he subsided, belly shaking, to stare out the window of the coach. "No," he said. "No, not you."

Amara took a moment to compose herself. She often forgot that Gaius was as skilled at watercrafting as he was with fire or earth or metal. Worse, he was a perceptive individual who had been dealing with people two or three times as long as Amara had been drawing breath—all of which meant that it would be all too easy for him to discern awkward, potentially dangerous specifics. Her relationship with Bernard was a dangerous topic of conversation around Gaius.

Especially since it felt like it had been at least ten thousand years since her husband had touched her, or kissed her, or made her cry out in—

Crows take it. She was a grown woman. It was entirely unfair that simply *thinking* of Bernard should reduce her to a starry-eyed schoolgirl like that.

Amara cleared her throat, took her notebook from the cabinet built into the base of the seat, and proceeded to change the subject. "Very well, sire. We should arrive back in the capital sometime early tomorrow morning. The reports from High Lord Antillus should be waiting for you when you arrive, and the final movement orders for the Rhodesian Legions should be in effect by then which—"

The coach swept into heavy cloud cover, and she paused to murmur a furylamp to life.

"Countess," Gaius said gently, before she could. The First Lord reached out and folded the notebook shut, setting it aside. "Come with me, please."

Amara blinked at him.

Without preamble, Gaius turned and opened the door of the coach. Wind howled in a sudden scream, whipping their clothing about, and the coach slewed slightly to one side as the sudden drag made the coach's progress uneven.

The First Lord stepped out into empty air, lifting away from the coach so smoothly that he might have been moving out onto solid ground.

Amara lifted her eyebrows, but followed him, summoning Cirrus to support her as she left the confines of the coach for the cold, clinging, dark grey dampness of the heavy clouds. They kept pace with the coach for a moment, and Gaius exchanged a nod with the leader of the accompanying Knights Aeris. Then he slowed pace, and within seconds the air coach vanished into the clouds, leaving Gaius and Amara hovering alone in featureless grey.

Gaius flicked a hand through the air, and the roar of wind suddenly vanished. For a second, Amara expected her windstream to collapse and send her plummeting toward the ground, but Cirrus's support remained steady. Her hair still whipped around her head, as it always did, especially in a hover—only the sound vanished, dying to nothing more than the sigh of a quiet breeze. Around them, Amara could hear the distant grumble of thunder, as somewhere, miles away, a spring storm gathered in the cloud cover.

"Sire," she said, confused. "The coach."

Gaius shook his head. "I'm sorry I couldn't tell you before, Amara, but secrecy was absolutely imperative. No one can know where we're going, when we left—nothing."

She frowned and folded her arms against the ongoing

winds. She wasn't wearing her flying leathers, and she was surprised at how quickly a chill began settling into her skin.

"I take it we're not returning to the capital," she said quietly.

"No," Gaius said.

She nodded. "Why am I here?"

"I need someone I trust to come with me."

"Where, sire?" Amara asked.

"Kalare," Gaius said quietly.

Amara felt her eyes widen. "Why there?"

His voice stayed quiet and steady. "Because I've been sitting in the capital playing diplomat for too long, Amara, and this chaos"—he gestured with a hand, taking in the entirety of the Realm beneath them—"is the result. Allies and enemies alike have forgotten who I am. What I am. I can't allow that to go on any longer."

Lightning flickered somewhere in the distant clouds, sending a flood of silver light through the swirling mists behind the First Lord.

"I'm going to remind them, Cursor." His eyes hardened. "I'm going to war. And you're going with me."

ᐳᐳᐳᐳᐳ CHAPTER 5

Isana made sure her hood was well up, and was grateful for the unusually sharp chill that lingered in the springtime morning air. It gave her an unquestionable justification to have her hood around her face. She wasn't trying to avoid being seen visiting Captain Rufus Scipio, precisely, since the director of the relief column would quite naturally need to speak to *someone* on the First Aleran's staff. But Tavi felt it was better if she went unrecognized and attracted no notice—or questions—at all, and she heartily supported his caution.

As promised, Araris was waiting at the front doors and escorted her past the two *legionares* on sentry duty there.

"Good morning," she murmured, as he led her into the building. It was an almost ridiculously overfortified structure, all of the same battlecrafted stone that was generally used only for fortified walls. The halls were more narrow than most, the ceilings lower, and Isana noted with surprise that at the first staircase, Araris led her down, not up, to where a leader's quarters were typically located.

"Good morning," he replied. His posture and voice were both politely formal, but she could sense the warmth that lay beneath them, radiating out from him like heat from a banked fire. She was certain that he *knew* she could discern his actual emotions, as well, and the sense of sudden satisfaction in that unspoken trust was a pleasant little thrill, something akin to feeling his fingers intertwine with hers. "We go down two flights to get to his office."

"Did the Senator displace him?" Isana asked.

Araris shook his head. "The Canim's sorcery evidently proved quite dangerous. Some kind of lightning bolt wiped out the First Aleran's original officers. When the Legion's engineers built this building, they made sure to put yards and yards of fortified stone over and around the captain, to avoid any repetition."

Isana shivered. She'd heard about the attack. If Tavi hadn't been sent out to run messages for then-Captain Cyril . . . "I see," she replied.

Araris snorted. "The valets set up Arnos on the top level. I suspect they're privately hoping that the Canim will try another lightning bolt and brighten everyone's day."

Isana repressed a wicked little smile. "Sir Araris," she chided. "That isn't a very kind thing to say."

"Arnie doesn't have kindness coming," Araris replied. Isana felt a gentle surge of contempt flow out with the words.

"You know him," she said.

"We went to the Academy together," Araris replied.

"You didn't get along?"

"Oh, he was at my throat constantly—whenever I wasn't actually in the room," he said. "Arnos never had anything to say to my face." Araris reached up with one hand to rub lightly at the mark branded over one cheek. "He was always small-minded, egotistical. He hasn't changed."

"He's dangerous," Isana said. "Isn't he?"

"Here? Now? Very." He came to a stop before a heavy, closed door, and turned to look at Isana.

She met his eyes, and her mouth suddenly felt dry.

He reached down and took her hand gently in his. He squeezed tightly once. "You can do this."

She bit her lip and nodded. "What if—"

He laid two fingers lightly over her lips and gave her a quiet smile. "Don't borrow trouble. Just talk to him. He loves you. It will be all right."

She closed her eyes tight for a second and brushed the faintest ghost of a kiss against his fingers. Then Isana took a steadying breath, nodded, and said, "Very well."

Araris turned and opened the door for her. "Captain," he announced quietly. "Steadholder Isana to see you."

A resonant, deep-chested voice answered in a tone of distracted confidence. "Thank you, Araris. Send her in, please."

Araris gave Isana another small smile, then stood aside, and Isana walked into Tavi's office. Araris shut the door behind her.

The office was supremely utilitarian, even stark. There was an old wooden desk, scarred from use, several chairs, and several shelves filled with books and papers and writing materials. The cold stone floor was covered by a few simple rugs, and a box beside the lit fireplace was filled with a neat stack of cordwood. A door led off into another room, and a plain, medium-sized mirror hung upon the same wall.

He sat at the desk, a quill in hand, scrawling something hurriedly across the bottom of a page. There were several stacks of them spread across the desk, evidence of what appeared to be several hours' work. He finished writing, set the quill aside, and rose with a broad smile.

Isana stopped in her tracks. The man who stood up was enormous, even taller than her brother Bernard, though he had a more wiry build and the slenderness of youth. His dark hair was cropped short, and he wore a suit of battered Legion armor and a sword on one hip. His features were angular, strong, attractive, though a fine white line across one cheek spoke of a wound too severe to heal without leaving a scar.

Tavi's eyes, though, had not changed. They were green and bright, lit from within by the intelligence of the mind behind them.

How like his father he looks, Isana thought.

"Aunt Isana," Tavi said, and wrapped his arms around her.

She was about to caution him to be careful, but he was gentle, making sure not to crush any armored steel ridges against her. She made up for it by hugging him back as hard as she could. He was real, and safe. She hadn't seen him face-to-face in years, but there was no mistaking that he was her son, no hiding the genuine burst of warmth and love and delight that radiated from him as she hugged him.

They stood like that for a time, before Isana broke the embrace. She lifted her hands to cup his face, her eyes swimming with tears, her cheeks already aching from smiling. "Hello, Tavi."

He kissed her on top of the head. "Hello, Auntie. It's been a long time."

She leaned back to arm's length, looking him up and down. "Longer for some than others," she teased. "Goodness, you've grown even more. What do they put in the water here?"

He grinned. "Yeah. It sort of snuck up on me. But I think I've stopped growing, finally. These trousers have fit me for almost a year."

"Thank goodness. If you got much taller, they'd have to raise all the ceilings in here."

Tavi shook his head gravely. "Nonsense. This is the Legion. The ceiling is at regulation height. It is the responsibility of every *legionare* to be sure that he is regulation height as well."

Isana laughed. "I'm glad to see you haven't lost your sense of humor."

"Never that," Tavi said. "My mind has been gone for a while now, but that's no reason not to laugh at things. How's Uncle His Excellency?"

"Bernard is well, as are the folk at home. Which reminds me." She untied the pouch from her belt and opened it, rustling through several papers, before she drew out a folded, sealed letter. "Frederic asked me to give this to you."

Tavi smiled and took the letter. He cracked the seal and his eyes flicked rapidly over it. "That girl he rescued, eh? Beritte must be miffed. How's that working out for them?"

"About the way most marriages do. They have a lot to learn about how to treat one another."

"I'm glad for him," Tavi said. "If I get time, I'll write something to send with you when you go back. But in case I don't, would you give him my congratulations?"

"Of course."

Tavi smiled at her and gestured to the fireplace, where a kettle hung from a hook close enough to the flames to keep the liquid inside warm. "Tea?"

"Please."

Tavi drew out a couple of the room's chairs, putting them close together, and held one of them for her. Then he took a pair of tin cups down from a shelf and poured steaming tea from the kettle into each. He added a spoonful of honey to Isana's, the way she liked it, then splashed three of them into his own, before returning to her.

They shared a cup of tea, chatting quietly about people and places back home in the Calderon Valley. They talked for a time of Tavi's duties at the Elinarch, and of Isana's journey in assembling the relief column, until Tavi rose to get them both fresh cups of tea.

When he settled down again, Isana said, "Tavi, I hope you know how proud we are of you. Your uncle and I. You've grown into a remarkable young man."

He blinked at her a couple of times, then carefully studied the surface of his tea. Isana's sense of his emotions revealed pleasure in the compliment, and pride, along with large helpings of embarrassment. His cheeks colored slightly. "Well," he said. "I couldn't have done any of it without you and uncle. Teaching me. Preparing me."

Isana felt a little stab of guilt. Preparing him was probably the single greatest thing she *hadn't* done.

She sipped a little more tea, and then frowned down at its surface. "Tavi," she said. "Is it safe to talk here?"

He cocked his head slightly to one side, and she felt the spike of curiosity that flashed through his thoughts. "Yes," he said, with total confidence. "No one can overhear us in here. Why, Aunt Isana?"

Isana took a deep breath. "There's something we need to talk about," she said.

Tavi's face turned red again. "Look, a lot of that is just rumor. I mean, the men get to talking over drinks and every little story grows in the retelling."

Isana blinked at him.

"I mean, it's not like I'm hosting revels or anything. Everyone likes a good story like that, though, and the truth of it isn't as much fun."

"Tavi," Isana said in a firm tone. "What in the wide world are you talking about?"

Tavi froze with his mouth open for a second. Acute chagrin flooded out from him in a wave Isana could practically *see*. Then he swallowed, and said, "Um. Nothing?"

Isana arched an eyebrow at him.

Tavi sighed, blushing again. "I was talking about Kitai. She and I . . ."

"Ah," Isana said. "You're together."

"Um. Yes."

"In more than one sense of the word, I take it?"

"Well. Yes," he said miserably. "But it isn't like we're . . . I mean, *some* of the Marat are, um, sort of indiscriminate when it comes to that kind of thing, and a lot of their riders are around me every time I move around, so it's inevitable that some idiots are going to start spouting rumors about it, but it isn't really like that." Tavi paused to take a breath. "Kitai and I are just . . . together."

Isana sighed. "Stop. Neither one of us wants you to elaborate, Tavi." She turned her teacup idly in her hands. "Well. This could become . . . very complicated. I should have had this talk with you sooner."

"Um," Tavi said. He might have become a fully grown man now, but Isana was familiar with his uncomfortable squirming.

He'd always done that when he'd been caught red-handed as a child. "You don't have to have *that* talk. I had that much figured out by the time I was about ten. I mean, caring for the sheep and all . . ."

Isana shook her head and surprised herself with a quiet laugh. "No, no, not *that* talk," Isana said. "You don't understand—"

She was interrupted by the sound of the door opening. She turned to find Araris standing in the door. "Captain," he said quietly, frowning. "We just got word from one of the men. Senator Arnos's *singulares* are on the way to see you."

Tavi's chin jerked up sharply. "Why?"

Araris shrugged. "No details yet. They're up at the front door now."

"This seems like a good time to speak to Maximus and Crassus about this week's training schedule. Send a runner to them."

Araris thumped his fist to his heart and departed. Tavi bit his lip, glancing around the little office. He opened the second door behind the desk, and said, "Auntie, could I convince you to wait in my chambers? I'd just as soon not explain to the Senator's flunkies what you're doing here."

"Of course," Isana said, rising. She paced quickly through the door. It was difficult to see much without any lamps, but the modest-sized chamber looked as functional and stark as his office, except for the rumpled, double-sized bed. If nothing else, she supposed, the Legions had done that much for him. Anyone who could convince Tavi to keep his room clean couldn't be entirely bad.

Tavi shut the door most of the way, put a finger against his lips in an entirely unnecessary gesture of caution, and then returned to the office. Isana heard him putting the chairs back into position, and heard a tinny clink as he presumably placed one of the tea cups back onto its shelf. His shadow moved across the narrow opening of the cracked door, and he settled down at his desk. Paper rustled. A few seconds later, the door opened again, and several sets of heavy footsteps entered the room.

"Just leave my breakfast tray on the shelf," Tavi said in an absentminded tone. "And none of your nagging. I'll get to it when I get to it."

There was a short, hard silence, broken only by the sound of Tavi's quill scratching on paper.

"Excuse me?" said a woman's voice. It was a quiet voice, one used to speaking in soft tones and whispers, but to Isana's ears, it carried such malice and barely contained rage that she actually flinched away from it.

"Oh," Tavi said. "I beg your pardon. You aren't the valet."

"No," said the woman's voice. "I am—"

"Did the valet send my breakfast with you by any chance?" Tavi asked, his tone innocent and friendly. "I'm starving."

"He did not," said the cold voice.

"I'm sure he meant to," Tavi said. "Do you think you could yell up the stairs and see if it's on the w—"

There was a loud, sharp sound of impact—a hand being slammed down onto the surface of Tavi's desk, Isana judged. There was a rustling, sliding sound of a neat stack of pages slithering off the edge of the desk and onto the floor.

"You are not funny," said the cold voice. "And I will cut your throat before I tolerate any more of it. Do you understand me?"

Isana shifted position slightly. She couldn't see the woman Tavi was talking to, but she could see his face in profile. He sat in his chair, hands on his desk, and regarded the speaker with a calm, remote expression. There was no mockery to it. There wasn't *anything* to it, despite the fact that his life had just been threatened, and it chilled Isana a little to see that expression on his face. He appeared to be relaxed and confident, and she couldn't catch even a hint of his true emotions.

"I understand," Tavi said quietly, "that if you continue to show disrespect unbecoming a soldier, ignoring even basic military courtesy—such as knocking on a commanding officer's door before entering—and speaking to me in that tone, I'll have you bound to a flogging post until the ants can crawl up your hair to get at your eyes."

There was another pause. Then the woman's voice said, "You don't know who I am, do you?"

"Or care, particularly," Tavi said.

"My name," she said, "is Navaris."

Tavi's expression never flickered, but this time Isana sensed a pulse of surprised recognition, and then a low current of tightly controlled fear.

Tavi leaned forward, and said in a congenial murmur, "It's possible that playing *singulare* for the Senator has not brought you the fame you had hoped it would. Never heard of you." His eyes stayed steady for another strained, silent moment. "Well, Navaris. When you first walked in, I assumed you were here for the décor and the charming company. Now, though, I'm thinking that you might have had something else in mind."

"Yes," came the answer.

"How exciting. Maybe you even had a specific reason to visit."

"Yes," Navaris growled.

He glanced past Navaris, eyes scanning the room. "And these four. I take it they're here to help."

"Yes."

Tavi sighed and sat back in his chair. "Navaris, this will go a lot faster if I don't have to play guessing games." His voice went flat. "Tell me what you want."

There was another long silence, and Isana realized with a sudden flash of panic that as Tavi had sat back in his chair, his hand had slipped around behind it, and his fingers were on the hilt of a dagger that had been secured to the chair's back.

There was something thick, even drunken, about Navaris's voice when she finally answered. "Senator Arnos sent me to gather up your intelligence reports on recent activity in the occupied territory. You are to turn over to me every record, every copy, and every list of information sources for the Senator's personal review."

Tavi shrugged his shoulders. "I'm afraid I can't help you."

"These are *orders*," Navaris replied. "If you refuse to obey them, it's treason."

"Which is punishable by death," Tavi said. "I vaguely recall reading as much, somewhere."

"Give us the papers," she said. "Or you are under arrest."

Isana's heart pounded hard in her chest.

"I don't think so," Tavi said. "You see, Navaris, I'm afraid you don't have a leg to stand on, legally speaking. You're a *singulare*. You aren't an officer. You sure as the crows aren't *my* commanding officer. In fact, you aren't in my chain of command at all."

Navaris's voice came out as if through clenched teeth. "These are the Senator's orders."

"Oh," Tavi said, nodding as though at a sudden revelation. "Then they're in writing. Let me see them, and the papers are all yours." He lifted both eyebrows. "You *do* have legal orders, do you not?"

After a brief pause, Navaris said, "You saw him. He resisted arrest."

There were several harsh, masculine mutters.

"Get your fingers off that sword, *singulare*," Tavi said, his voice an abrupt whip crack of authority. "Draw that weapon against me, and I'll gut you with it."

There was the sound of several blades slithering from their sheaths, and Isana leapt to her feet in sudden terror.

A new voice broke into the conversation. "If I were you," Araris said in a level tone, "I would do as he says."

"Or not," said a bluff, cheerful voice that was laced with a desire for violence—Antillar Maximus. "If you all want to dance, I'm game."

"None of them got to draw steel before we did," said a third voice, that of a young man Isana didn't recognize. "If things start up now, they won't even get their weapons clear of their sheaths. That doesn't seem fair."

"Right you are, Crassus," Max said. "Right you are."

Isana felt a surge of murderous fury from the room— Navaris, she felt certain. It was a white-hot anger, something that seethed with malice and hate so intense that it almost seemed a separate entity. It was an irrational, bloodthirsty thing, a kind of madness that Isana had only encountered twice in her entire life.

For a moment, Isana felt sure that Navaris would attack in any case. But then that raging fire suddenly died into stillness, snuffed out as quickly as a candle dropped into a pond.

"You think you've accomplished something here," Navaris said quietly. "You haven't. You'll see that in time."

Tavi looked at her as if she hadn't spoken at all. "Please convey my apologies to the Senator that I could not act without confirming his orders. Regulations can be inconvenient at times, but they are, after all, what holds a Legion together. Thank you for your visit."

"Fool," Navaris said.

"*Captain* Fool," Tavi responded. "Good day, *singulare*. Araris, Crassus, please escort the good *singulare* and her helpers to the door."

For a second, nothing happened. Then there was a shuffling of feet, and then the shutting of a door, then silence.

Isana leaned against a wall and closed her eyes, her heart racing, slightly dizzy at the sudden relief, both of her own fears and of the intense emotions that had crowded the little office.

"Crows," Maximus breathed. "Was that who I think it was?"

"Phrygiar Navaris," Tavi said, nodding.

"What was she doing here?" Max asked.

"Getting humiliated, mostly. Especially there at the end."

Max barked out a short, coughing laugh. "You don't do things by halves, do you Calderon?"

"It saves me the time of going back to finish later." Tavi rose from the chair and came to the door. "And speaking of Calderon."

Isana opened it, aware that her hands were trembling in reaction to the tension of the past several moments. The room was now empty, but for Tavi and Maximus.

Max lifted his eyebrows at Isana, and his surprise was palpable. "Oh. Good morning, Steadholder."

"Good morning, Maximus," she replied. At least her voice was steady, she thought. She looked at Tavi. "That woman is dangerous?"

Tavi nodded. "One of the top ten or twelve swords in Alera."

"More like one of the top six or seven," Maximus said, his

tone serious. "And she's done more actual killing than any two blades on the list."

Isana shook her head. "What were you thinking, insulting her like that?"

"I was thinking that I needed to buy time for Max and his brother to get here," Tavi said. He gave her a boyish grin. "Relax, Auntie. I had it under control."

Max snorted.

"Is she acting on the Senator's behalf?" Isana asked.

"Probably," Tavi said.

"Then why didn't you give her the papers?"

Tavi sighed and began gathering up the fallen pages. "The papers are going to tell Arnos something he doesn't want to hear. I think he was planning on making them vanish." He straightened them and turned to Maximus. "Get these to Ehren. I want copies for Sir Cyril, the Senator, and the Tribunes Strategica of all three Legions, as well as to the militia command in town."

Max grunted. "The staff meeting?"

"Yes. Once the information is out, Arnos won't be able to lock it up again."

Isana blinked at him. "What could be so important about them?"

Tavi raked his fingers through his short-cut hair. "From what we've been able to put together, I think I have a good idea of what the Canim are doing. I think if we handle it right, we might be able to call a halt to this war."

"How?"

"Tavi," Maximus said in a tight, warning voice.

Tavi blinked at him. "What?"

Maximus stared at him, then shook his head and gave Isana an apologetic glance. "This is pretty important information. I know she's family . . . but she's also a client of Lady Aquitaine's. It's probably better not to discuss it in front of her." He glanced at Isana again, and said, "It's mostly the principle of the thing, ma'am."

"Crows," Tavi snorted. "Max, she's my family. If you can't trust your family, who *can* you trust?"

A lance of pure guilt hit Isana in her midsection. The comment was so typically Tavi. He'd grown up close to her, to Bernard, and in the rough frontier country they lived in, toil and hazard built up trust in one another to a much greater degree than in the more settled regions of Alera. As far as Tavi was concerned, in the Calderon Valley, family always supported, always defended, always helped . . . and always told the truth. He believed it.

Oh, it was going to hurt when Isana shattered that belief. It was going to hurt both of them unbearably.

"That's all right," she said quickly. "It was an inappropriate question in any case. Of course, it's better to be careful."

Tavi gave her a searching look, but shrugged and nodded. "Get a move on, Max. We don't have much time."

Maximus banged his fist against his chest, nodded to Isana with another apologetic glance, and hurried out.

Tavi rose, frowning in thought. "I'm sorry to cut this short, Auntie, but . . ."

"I understand," she said quietly. "I have duties I should be attending to as well."

Tavi smiled at her gratefully. "Dinner tonight?"

"That would be lovely."

Tavi suddenly blinked. "Oh," he said. "I can make a couple of minutes right now, if you like. What was it you wanted to talk about?"

She couldn't do it. She couldn't bring herself to hurt him like that.

If you can't trust your family, who can you trust?

"Nothing important," she lied quietly. "It can wait."

CHAPTER 6

"All right, Captain," Sir Cyril said. He grimaced a little and shifted slightly on his seat, finding a more comfortable angle at which to rest the metal leg that had replaced his own from the knee down. "If you're ready, why don't you lay out what you've learned."

Tavi nodded and stepped up onto the raised platform at the head of the conference room. Though the visiting dignitaries had departed, the room was still crowded, this time with the officers of both Legions of the Senatorial Guard and the First Aleran. Except for Max, Crassus, and one or two of the other Tribunes in the First Aleran, Tavi was by far the youngest man in the room.

"Thank you, Sir Cyril," Tavi said. "The First Aleran has been engaged in active operations against the Canim forces to the south for almost two years, ever since the Night of the Red Stars. We repulsed their initial and secondary efforts to take the bridge. Once additional pressure was brought against their eastern flank by the forces of High Lord Placidus, they were forced to divert much of their infantry to the east, and we drove their garrison out of their position at Founderport. The Founderport militia holds the city, and we stand ready to reinforce it should they need it. It's our only stronghold south of the Tiber, but the Canim don't dare assault it for fear of being pinned between the First Aleran and the city walls."

"We're aware of this, Captain," came Arnos's voice. The Senator, resplendent in formal Senatorial robes of blue-and-red silk, sat in the first row. The two Senatorial Guard captains sat at his left hand, and Navaris and one of her fellow *singulares* sat at his right. "You needn't continue reminding us of your accomplishments. Everyone here acknowledges that you've had some success in your efforts here."

Tavi felt like grinding his teeth together but kept himself from actually doing it. Crows take him if he'd let this silk-robed dandy rattle him so easily. Besides, his instincts warned him that it would be a mistake to let Navaris see his self-control slide.

Navaris. The woman was a legend among the Cursors, the single most successful and highly paid cutter in Alera. She'd killed seventy-three opponents in legal duels, another sixty or seventy in fights that were allegedly cases of self-defense, and rumor had it that another hundred mysterious murders could be laid at her feet with reasonable accuracy—and if she was anywhere near as good at covering up her crimes as she was at dodging the legal consequences of her swordplay, Tavi figured that she might have killed who knew how many more, successfully disposing of the corpses afterward.

Navaris didn't look as dangerous as she was. She was an inch or two under six feet tall and made of whipcord and rawhide. She had colorless grey eyes and wore her salt-and-pepper hair in a short Legion cut that did nearly as much to massacre any sense of femininity about her as her lean, hard build. She wore black riding leathers and a long, dueling sword at her hip. Her eyes were flat, and they looked at the world as if everyone in it was simply one more practice target set up in a swordmaster's training hall. If she'd drawn on Tavi in the office, he doubted he could have lasted more than a second or two against her.

She was also, if Tavi judged rightly, quite insane.

He dragged his eyes from Navaris back to the Senator. "Pardon me, Senator. I was only laying out a common point to start from."

Arnos gave him a sour look and waved an impatient hand. "Get on with it."

Sir Cyril, seated at the very end of the first row, lifted his chin, and said, "Begin with Vaucusgard."

Tavi nodded. He turned to the slateboard behind him, and in a few quick strokes drew out a rough map of the region, marking the Elinarch, the Tiber, and Founderport. "Vaucusgard is a timber-cutting steadholt that's grown into a small town," he told the room. He marked its position, about thirty miles south of the Elinarch. "When we were pushing the Canim from their positions in Founderport, they fought like mad to hold Vaucusgard."

One of the captains beside Arnos, a man named Nalus, grunted. "Walls?"

"No," Tavi said. "No serious fortifications at all in fact. Not much in the way of defensible geography, either. But we brought them to battle there for two days before they finally ran."

"Why'd it take them that long to break?" Nalus asked.

"They didn't break," Tavi said. "They retreated in good order, and after two days of fighting, we weren't in any shape to argue with them about it.

"Since then, most of our clashes have been more like heavy skirmishes than a pitched battle, while the Canim consolidated their positions. During that time, several of the Crown's Cursors who had been sent to assist the First Aleran infiltrated the occupied territory and began gathering intelligence."

"What did they learn?" Arnos asked.

"First, sir, that the Canim aren't letting everyone leave peaceably as we first thought. They've been holding back members of two professions, refusing to let them leave: carpenters and shipwrights."

Arnos frowned heavily. "Then . . . their defense of the timber-cutting steadholt had a definite purpose."

Tavi nodded. "They were taking materials. Wood that had been seasoning in storage, mostly."

"Seasoned wood?" Tribune Tactica Kellus was standing against a side wall, not far from Tavi. "Why seasoned wood, sir?"

"Because, Tribune," Arnos said in a tight voice, "you can't build ships out of green wood."

Tavi nodded, a little impressed despite himself. Arnos's mind worked swiftly—when he chose to use it. "Exactly, sir." He turned and marked a point on the rough map, at the very bottom of the slateboard, a distance of perhaps a hundred miles. "And we think they're building them here, at a town called Mastings. It has a long inlet from the sea, and already had the facilities in place to support the building of a dozen ships at a time. We think that its capacity has been expanded."

"You *think*?" Arnos said.

"It's conjecture, sir, but it stands up pretty well. The Canim have set up defensive positions at the mouth of the inlet, and they're turning away or appropriating any ships that try to sail to Mastings. Their patrols in the area are three times as thick as they are elsewhere, and the main body of their troops is located somewhere in the area. It's difficult to be sure, because they are refusing to let any Alerans into the city, unless they're one of the shipwrights or carpenters being pressed into service."

"Then how do you know their main body of troops is there?" Arnos demanded.

"The agents in question tracked food shipments, sir," Tavi said. "Either Mastings is playing host to an extremely large number of Canim, or its people have decided to abandon life as a seaport and take up the cattle trade."

"Ships," grunted Captain Nalus again. "What do they want with bloody ships?"

Tavi answered. "The Cane who led the initial incursion, Sarl, ordered their ships burned behind them when they landed. You could see the fires lighting up Founderport from five miles away."

Arnos scratched at his chin, studying the rough map. "Ships will give them a number of options they don't have now," he said. "They'll be able to move swiftly up and down the coastline—the dogs can sail, I'll give them that. If they build enough of them, they'll be able to move their entire force to support Kalare in the south, or to keep us running in circles up here."

"Or, sir," Tavi said. "They might . . . go home."

Arnos turned a look of pure disbelief upon Tavi.

"It's possible, sir. The majority of the Canim now in Alera did *not* want to be stuck here. That's why Sarl had to burn the ships. And they have their dependents to think about, too. They want what any of us would want in a similar situation." He shrugged. "They want to go home."

Arnos simply stared at Tavi, saying nothing.

Tavi ground his teeth. The good Senator was offering him

plenty of rope to hang himself with, and he knew it—but he also knew that he had to at least try. So he took a deep breath, and pressed on. "Given how static the conflict has been over the past several months, we might have an opportunity here."

The room was very quiet, until Arnos asked, in a polite voice, "What opportunity?"

No use stopping now. "To negotiate," Tavi said.

"Negotiate," Arnos said. "With the Canim."

"Senator, we want the Canim gone. The possibility exists that they want to *be* gone. I think it's worth exploring."

"Negotiate," the Senator repeated. "With the Canim."

"They *do* have an ambassador, sir," Tavi pointed out. "Alera has parleyed with them before."

"An ambassador who infiltrated a band of Canim warriors and trained beasts into the capital itself and attempted to *murder* the First Lord, yes," Arnos agreed. "An ambassador who is currently imprisoned and awaiting execution."

"Trial," Sir Cyril said in a very mild voice. "Awaiting trial. His guilt has not been proven."

Arnos gave Cyril a scornful glance. "His troops. His people. Even if he didn't plan it, he *should* have known about it and stopped it. Either way, the fault lies with him."

"Nonetheless, it may be an option worth looking at."

"I see," Arnos said quietly. "After the Canim have invaded, killed thousands of Alerans, displaced hundreds of thousands, burned cities, and conspired with a rebel in a plot to help him ascend to the throne we should . . . what? Give them room and board while we build ships for them? Fill their ships with provisions and gifts? Then send them home, with our blessings?"

"Sir—" Tavi began.

"I can see the advantages," Arnos continued. "They would return home and tell their entire race that Alera was so cowardly and weak that not only could we not defend our own lands against them, we were frightened enough to pay them tribute to get them to leave us."

"That isn't what—"

"And in a year, or two years, or five, they'll come again, and in far greater numbers. They will demand another round of tribute." Arnos shook his head. "No. We stop them here. Now. We scour them from the face of Alera. Every last one of them. We show the Canim that there is a price to be paid for such things as they have done."

Several low growls of approval vibrated through the room. None of them, so far as Tavi could tell, from anyone in the First Aleran.

"We might be able to beat them," Cyril put in. "But it's going to cost us a lot of men. Men we'll need in the south, when we move against Kalare."

"Men are going to die, regardless of what we do," Arnos shot back.

"Granted," Cyril said. "I simply prefer that we avoid killing them unnecessarily. As a matter of professional principle."

Arnos narrowed his eyes at Sir Cyril.

"I might point out, sir," Tavi added, "that even a temporary cessation of hostilities would provide us with more time to gather intelligence and maneuver to better advantage."

"And more time for the enemy to build attack vessels and become a far more mobile threat. More time for the traitor-slaves to train and equip. More time for them to fortify their positions." Arnos turned a gimlet gaze on Tavi, and said, "There will be no negotiation, Captain."

"Sir," Tavi said, "if you would only give me a little time to contact the First Lord and—"

Arnos's face flushed red, and his voice became harsh, hard. "There will be *no* negotiation, Captain!"

"But—"

"One more word out of your mouth," Arnos spat, "and I will suspend you from duty and have you flogged. Do you understand? Captain?"

Tavi clenched his jaw shut on an utterly unwise answer and gave the Senator a single, sharp nod instead.

Arnos glared at him for a few seconds, and nodded. His voice dropped back into a calmer register, and he rose. "Thank you for your report, Captain," he said, as he went to the front of the room. "That will be all."

Tavi stalked over to take his seat at Sir Cyril's right hand. "Crows take it," he muttered under his breath.

"It hardly came as a surprise," Cyril replied.

Tavi growled in his throat.

"Easy," Cyril cautioned him. "You've pushed enough for today. I think we might have gotten through to Nalus, at least."

Tavi glanced aside, to the Guard captain. Nalus was frowning thoughtfully at the rough map, as Senator Arnos made a little speech about defending Alera from the Canim scourge.

A shiver ran down Tavi's spine, and he looked past Nalus to find Navaris staring at him with blank eyes. The cutter held his gaze for a moment, then gave him an unsettling smile.

Tavi looked away and suppressed a shudder of discomfort.

"Gentlemen," Arnos was saying, "we have been on the defensive for too long. We've stood upon walls and bridges for too long. It is high time that we went forth to meet this threat, and show them what it means to cross the Legions."

That won a lot of murmurs of approval from the room— again, from everyone except the officers of the First Aleran.

"And so as of right now," Arnos continued, "our offensive has begun." He turned and drew a bold stroke on the slateboard, from the Elinarch straight down to Mastings. "We bring their main body to battle and wipe them out before they can get these ships built. We march at dawn, two days hence. Prepare your men. Dismissed."

The room broke out into noise as the men stood, already talking, and began shuffling toward the exit. Within a moment or two, Tavi and Cyril sat alone.

Cyril stared at the map on the slateboard for a moment, and then rolled his eyes. "Of course. March directly toward the objective in a straight line." He sighed. "How many strong points does Nasaug have to work with along that route?"

"Three, maybe four," Tavi said. "Plus a lot of opportunity to hit our supply lines as we march. And then the city itself."

"Can we force through them?"

"Depends," Tavi said. "If Nasaug is willing to take heavy losses, he could stop us cold."

Cyril shook his head. "He won't. He'll hit us as hard as he can while keeping his own losses to a minimum."

Tavi nodded. "Bleed us all the way to Mastings. Then bring the hammer down."

"How long will that take?"

Tavi shook his head, calculating. Thanks to Ehren's hard work, he'd had detailed maps to work with in his own planning, and he was familiar with the territory they'd be fighting their way through. "Call it ten weeks, unless we get lucky." Tavi squinted at the map. "And I'm not feeling all that lucky."

"A lot can happen in ten weeks," Cyril replied.

"I should talk to him again," Tavi said. "Privately. He might be more receptive to the notion of negotiating if he isn't surrounded by people."

"He's always surrounded by people," Cyril said. "And it won't do any good, Captain."

"But it's so *stupid*. Nasaug is willing to talk."

"You don't know that," Cyril said. "He's never sent any kind of word suggesting it."

"It isn't their way," Tavi replied. "To a Cane, talk is cheap. Actions are what speak loudest. And Nasaug's actions are clearly stating his intentions. He's willing to work with Alerans, rather than simply slaughter them—and he wants to leave."

"Perhaps," Cyril said. "Perhaps you're right. If I was in charge, I'd give what you're saying some serious thought. You've earned that." He shook his head. "But I'm not, and neither are you. If you bring it up again, he'll have an excuse to replace you. Don't give it to him."

Tavi exhaled through his clenched teeth. "There's got to be a way."

"Then find it," Cyril said, pushing himself up out of his chair. "But do it in your spare time. Keep your focus on the here and now. They might not know it, but a lot of people are depending on you for their lives."

"Yes, sir," Tavi said.

They exchanged a mutual salute, and Cyril limped out, leaning on his cane. A moment later, Maximus leaned his head in the door. "Hey there, Captain. What's the word?"

"We're marching," Tavi replied, rising to walk to the door. "Send Tribune Cymnea to my office, please, so we can start on logistics. Put the men on notice." He looked up and down the hallway, frowning. "Hngh. I would have expected Marcus to be here. Have you seen him?"

"Not today."

"When you do," Tavi said, "send him to my office, too."

"Yes, sir," Max said.

Tavi went to the slateboard and swiped a damp cloth over it until the markings had been erased. It was sloppy of Arnos to leave his marching orders—such as they were—displayed for any idiot to wander by and see. "All right, Tribune." He sighed. "Let's get to work."

◦◦Chapter 7

Marcus looked around the shabby tent-tavern, one of many that had sprung up in the refugee camp. He hadn't been to this particular establishment before, but he'd seen many like it in his day. Admittedly, few of them had been quite this squalid. The canvas of the tent was sloppily patched with tar rather than being properly repaired. The floors, which could at least have been swept smooth and laid with rushes, were simply mud. The legs of the trestle tables had sunk six inches into it, and their surfaces would have been too low if the benches in front of them hadn't sunk down as well.

Marcus stared at the mug in front of him. The beer had chunks of something floating in it—probably grain from the fermenting pots, but one could never be sure. It didn't smell like beer should. It smelled something like dirty water, only not as pleasant. He'd paid for it with a silver bull, and the copper rams he'd gotten back had been shaved so badly that the horns on the inscribed side were almost entirely gone.

It was intriguing, in a way. The refugee camp had done what hardship always did to people. In some of them, it brought out a greatness of spirit that was almost unbelievable. Fidelias had seen men with next to nothing literally give cold children the cloaks off their backs. He'd seen families with barely enough food to survive take in one more homeless child, find a way to stretch a blanket over one more freezing body. He'd seen *legionares* of the First Aleran, sickened by the suffering they'd seen while on drill, take their pay directly to market, spend it all on food, and take it to the camp to be given to those who needed it.

In others, though, it brought out the worst. He'd led squads that buried the corpses of people who'd been killed for their threadbare cloaks and the rags they'd had wrapped around their feet. He'd seen men demanding things of women in lieu of money, seen those who had what others needed demand degradation and humiliation from them before they would share it. He'd seen the bruises and broken bones that had come as the result of fear and frayed tempers. The sickness brought on by exposure and too little food—even here, in the gentlest lands of the Realm. And all of it, all of that sad, pitiable, loathsome humanity began to clot together somehow, to become a near-visible vapor, a stench in the air that smelled like . . .

Well. It smelled like this beer.

Marcus pushed his mildewed wooden mug away a little and did his best to ignore the smell. Then he took the little furylamp from his pouch, murmured it to life, set it out on the rough table, and waited.

The washerwoman entered the nameless tavern and paused in the doorway before looking around. It was dark enough inside that his little lamp served as a beacon for her gaze, and she crossed the rough floor to sit down at the table with him.

"Good day," the disguised Lady Aquitaine said. She glanced around the tavern with a sniff. "I always knew you were a secret romantic."

Marcus nudged the mug toward her. "Thirsty?"

She glanced at the mug, turned a shade paler, and gave him a level look.

"Suit yourself," he said.

"Why here?" she asked him.

"No one will recognize me here."

"*I* almost didn't recognize you."

Marcus shrugged. "No armor. Different cloak. My hood is up. I look like everyone else."

"We could have met anywhere," she countered. "Why here?"

Marcus glanced up and met her eyes. "Maybe I wanted you to see it."

The washerwoman tilted her head slightly to one side. "See what?"

He moved his hand in an all-encompassing gesture. "The consequences."

She lifted both eyebrows sharply.

"A lot of times, people who make big choices never have to see what can happen. All of this . . . and worse than you see here, or what you saw on the way here—it's all the result of choices like that."

She stared at him without expression for a long moment. "This is supposed to horrify me?"

"This? This is *nothing*," Marcus replied. "This is what happens when there's a polite disagreement, which is more or less what we've had with the Canim so far. This is what happens when everyone has to tighten their belts a little, but there's still enough to go around. It's worse, in the south. Rampant disease. Starvation. Brigands, looting, mercenaries. Men taking more liberties. Men seeking vengeance for the same." He nodded at the tavern. Outside the damp, stinking canvas, someone with a wet cough was wheezing for breath between fits of hacking spasms. "This is sunshine and sweetbread compared to what could happen."

Lady Aquitaine narrowed her eyes. "If my husband and I continue in our designs, you mean."

"I'd have to know them all," Marcus replied. "And I'm sure that I don't. So it's for you to say."

"One of the things I have always admired about you is your professionalism. This isn't like you."

Marcus shrugged. "It's a secure enough meeting space. I had something to say to you. I said it. What you do with it is up to you."

Lady Aquitaine frowned. She glanced around the shabby tavern for a few seconds. Then she shook her head briskly, took the mug, and emptied its contents onto the floor. She put the mug firmly back on the table. "Keep your focus on the task at hand."

"I would—if he could be bothered to arrive on time."

She shrugged. "He's used to being the most important person around. Important people are always late to meetings."

"Why tolerate it?" Marcus asked.

"I need him," she said simply.

"What happens when you don't?"

She gave him a little smile. "He'll have the opportunity to learn better working habits."

Just then, the tavern's entrance cloth swung to one side again, and half a dozen people entered, cloaked, all of them obviously together and too well dressed for the neighborhood. Marcus sighed. The worst thing about his departure from the Cursors had been the lack of competent professional associates.

One of the cloaked figures turned to the surly-looking man behind the cheap wooden table that passed for a bar. She lifted her hands to her hood and lowered it, revealing her features. Marcus tensed slightly as he recognized Phrygiar Navaris.

Navaris flung a small leather pouch. It struck the barman in the chest, bounced off, and landed on the grimy bar. She fixed the man with a flat grey stare, and said, "Get out."

Marcus could have made the same threat, the same way— but the man would have counted the money first. Marcus didn't blame the barman for taking the purse and departing without bothering to so much as glance inside.

The shortest of the figures looked around for a moment, then hurried to the table and sat down opposite Lady Aquitaine. He sat on his cloak, pulling the hood tight, and he muttered in irritation, glancing around the tent before he flung it back. "There's discretion," Senator Arnos muttered, "and then there's senseless paranoia. Did we have to meet in this sty?"

"Now, now, be nice, Arnos," Lady Aquitaine said. "It smells just as bad on this side of the table, I assure you."

Marcus watched the Senator's *singulares*. Navaris remained by the entrance, looking at nothing, and displaying all the emotion of frozen granite. The other four fanned out around the room, dividing their attention between the easily opened canvas walls and the people sitting at the table. Marcus noted the weapons belted at one man's hip, and the bow one of the others bore in a slender hand. Then he focused on Arnos again.

The Senator was, in turn, staring hard at Marcus.

"Take your hood off," Arnos snapped.

"I think not," Marcus said.

Arnos smiled. It reminded Marcus of a snarling jackal. "Take it off *now*."

"No."

"Navaris," Arnos said. "If he does not remove his head from the hood, you are to take both from his shoulders."

"Yes, sir," Navaris said. She never moved her feet or looked toward Marcus. But her hand had drifted to the hilt of her sword.

Lady Aquitaine made an impatient sound and flicked a hand. The air suddenly took on the tight, somewhat muffled feeling of a windcrafting meant to prevent any eavesdroppers from listening to a conversation. "Arnos, restrain yourself. His hood stays where it is."

"Why?"

"Because you're a brilliant politician, Senator," Marcus replied. "But you're a novice conspirator. I am currently in a position of extreme value. If you are allowed to know who I am, your incompetence will undoubtedly send the entire plan to the crows."

Arnos's mouth dropped open and hung there for a moment.

Marcus took the opportunity to savor the look on the fool's face.

"Indelicately put," Lady Aquitaine said, giving Marcus an arch glance. "But essentially accurate." She held up a mollifying hand. "You're a politician and strategist, Arnos. Not a spy. If we were all equally skilled at everything, there'd be no need for alliances, would there?"

The Senator's face flushed dark crimson. "And this one? What skills does *he* bring to the table?"

"I know things, Senator."

Arnos lifted his chin. "Such as?"

"That you have a talent for finding capable employees, for one," Marcus said. He nodded at one of the hooded men on guard. "Aresius Flavis. Twice champion of the Wintersend Arms Tournament in Alera Imperia. The man who killed the current High Lord of Rhodes's elder brother in a fair duel on the lawn outside the Grey Tower.

"The young woman watching the door is, I believe, Iris the Hawk. She was quite famous for her archery along the Shield-wall, and happened to slay half a dozen of Lord Kalarus's Immortal assassins while protecting Lady Voria on the Night of the Red Stars. Lady Voria was the only survivor of the attack on her guesthouse."

The cloaked figure by the door turned to stare at Fidelias. Then she nodded briefly. He nodded back to her. "The man at the rear wall is called Tandus. He's a mute. He's served in half a dozen different Legions as both a Knight Ferrous and Knight Terra. He's famous for single-handedly storming the gates of Lord Gardus's stronghold, when Gardus abducted some free-man's daughter. He killed thirty men taking her back."

Lady Aquitaine's gaze never left the Senator's face, but her quiet smile slowly grew.

"And him," Marcus said, nodding to the last man, the one nearest the table. "Rivar Armenius. He's young, a Knight Aeris and Ferrous, and claims to have the fastest sword arm in Alera. He's won eleven duels against established teaching masters, nine of them fatal."

Armenius's cloaked figure turned toward them briefly. Then he drew the hood back from young, handsome features, and said, "Ten. Maestro Piter took a lung fever of his injuries."

Marcus inclined his head slightly. "Ten." He turned his gaze to the last member of the Senator's *singulares*. "And, of course, Phrygiar Navaris. One of the more dangerous professionals alive. Utterly reliable—provided she does not lose her temper."

Navaris's hand continued slowly stroking the hilt of her blade.

Arnos stared venomously at Marcus. He folded his hands on the table, lips pressed into a thin line. "I'm not moving ahead blind, my Lady. Show me this man's face."

"Or what, Arnos?" Lady Aquitaine asked, her voice almost poisonously reasonable. "You'll walk away?"

"Why wouldn't I?"

"Perhaps because I know what happened to the first captain appointed to the First Senatorial. His name was Argavus, I believe. So odd that he vanished the night before you marched." Lady Aquitaine's gaze drifted to Navaris. "It would be a shame if someone mentioned the location of the body to the civic legion. An investigation might turn up all sorts of unpleasant facts."

Arnos shrugged, unfazed. "I've endured investigations before. Tiresome, but I manage."

"Yes. It's easier to pass the time when one has so many appetites to indulge." Her eyes shifted back to Arnos, and despite the worn exterior she had adopted, her smile turned sultry, predatory. "I can't help but wonder how often you've endured the wrath of a jealous husband. You *do* remember the wreckage at the piers four years ago?"

The blood drained from Arnos's face. "You wouldn't."

"It's a card I'll only get to play once. I'd prefer not to use it on you, dear Arnos." Her gaze was unwavering. "You are, of course, welcome to unleash your hounds if you think it might do you any good."

Marcus already had a knife in either hand under his cloak. He'd take the Senator himself, and then Armenius, the cutter standing closest to the table. Whatever Lady Aquitaine did, it would be violent, and best used against the more distant opponents, so he would handle those nearest. He was sure she'd be thinking the same thing.

Granted, he wasn't nearly as quick as he had once been. Arnos wouldn't pose a problem, but the young duelist might well prove more formidable. Marcus was certain that he'd have had little chance against the young cutter in a fair fight. It was the main reason he avoided them wherever possible.

Arnos was silent for a long minute, his forehead beaded with sweat, and the tension in the room grew. Then the Senator looked away, chin lifted haughtily. "It's senseless to bicker at this point, dear Invidia, when there is so much work to be done."

A small smile graced her mouth. "I'm glad we agree."

Marcus tried not to exhale visibly in relief and slipped th
knives away again.

"I've ordered the Legions to march forth against th
Canim. What do you see as our next step?"

"Rufus Scipio," she said. "He's dangerous."

Arnos arched an eyebrow. "You can't be serious. He's littl
more than a boy. A good showman for his men, tremendous
lucky to be in the right place at the right time, nothing more."

"I'm less concerned with what he *is* than what he might be
come. Mistakes happen, Arnos, but it's best if he's gone be
fore the Legions march. Can you see to it this time?"

At the shabby bar, Navaris's fingers began caressing th
hilt of her blade.

"My lady," Marcus said, "if I may."

She glanced at him, eyebrows lifting again. "Speak."

"It's too late for something that direct," Marcus said
"There's already been one approach. It's failed. He's on hi
guard, as are his men. A second attempt now could be turne
back upon us."

Lady Aquitaine grimaced and nodded. "Your suggestion?

Marcus spoke carefully, keeping his tone absolutely leve
neutral. "The Legion's loyalty is what makes him a threat t
your plans. Remove him from the Legion, and you remove hi
ability to disrupt events in any meaningful way."

"I can't simply strip him of command," Arnos replied
"Not without cause."

"Thus far," said Lady Aquitaine, "he's been clever enoug
to resist manipulation."

"It won't be difficult," Marcus said. "It's simply a matter o
knowing where to apply the pressure."

CHAPTER 8

It never occurred to Amara that she might have trouble keeping up with *anyone* when it came to flying. After all, no one she'd ever seen, not even High Lady Aquitaine, had been more swift or nimble than she in the air. Amara had won race after race during her days at the Academy. She'd never been overmatched in aerial battle.

But then, she had never tried her skills against the First Lord of Alera.

Within the first few minutes, Gaius had surged steadily ahead of her, even as a cold north wind began propelling them southward with mounting speed. Gaius had swiftly ascended to above the cloud cover, and it was as well he did. Within an hour, she could barely keep *sight* of the First Lord, even with Cirrus to help her.

Amara poured on all the speed she could, and for a time she closed the distance inch by inch—but only for a time. Then she rapidly made headway on the First Lord, until she was keeping pace only a dozen yards behind him. Amara felt gratified at her ability to keep up with him. It was only then that she realized that Cirrus's strength was being bolstered by that of dozens of smaller wind furies she could just barely sense. By the time the sun had passed its zenith, she had come to the grudging realization that in this particular kind of travel, at least, Gaius's raw power quite simply trumped all of her innate talent for flight and her hard-won skill.

He never flagged, either, but kept the pace with grim determination. Only a few times did Amara get a glimpse of the ground below, and each time she did, it was sliding by much more rapidly than it should have, especially at their altitude.

The wind at their backs only grew swifter, and Amara realized that Gaius had summoned forth one of the great wind furies of the far north to speed their way—with what could only be unpleasant consequences for the northernmost cities and towns of Alera, who must have received a fresh blast of arctic cold just as winter began to loosen its grip.

Amara had no way to judge where they were—especially given that she had no idea precisely where they were going, beyond "south." She rarely got a chance to look for any landmarks that might tell her where they were headed. The First Lord, however, seemed to have no such trouble finding his way, and his flight was smooth and relentless.

By the time the sun set, Amara had no more energy to spare for such thoughts. It was all she could do to maintain the focus she needed to stay aloft. Still, Gaius flew on, never wavering, never slowing, as if he had become some implacable extension of the North Wind itself.

Night fell, and Amara had no idea how she managed to stay in the air. She remembered being terribly cold, hungry beyond words, and weary to the point of pain.

At last, the dark shadow of the First Lord, now only a black shape against the stars, began to descend. Somehow, Amara managed to keep up with him as they plunged into more cloud cover and came out the bottom of it into a fine, cold, misty rain. They slowed as he banked around some rolling feature of terrain, and then she saw a dim light beneath them, among thick trees hung with long, long streamers of some kind of green-yellow moss.

Amara remembered setting down among those trees, near a fire that had burned down to a bed of red-orange coals and tiny flickers of flame, giving off the absolute minimum amount of light. She remembered her legs almost buckling from beneath her as she touched down.

Gaius turned to find her standing behind him, if barely, and a look of concern crossed his face. Then he took her arm and guided her to the fire. There was a bedroll there, placed not far from the fire, with a large stone propped up behind the blankets to catch the heat and reflect it back, and Amara nearly whimpered in relief at the sudden warmth.

Then someone pressed a tin mug of hot soup into her hand, and she gulped it down as quickly as she could without burning herself. After that, she remembered thinking how heavenly the bedroll felt beneath her, and merciful dark closed on her.

She woke sometime later. It was morning. Golden sunlight flickered down through a white haze overhead, only occasionally letting a shaft of glowing morning sweep over the ground. There was green all around, so much green, in so many shades, that she wondered why on earth anyone thought a simple word like "green" could adequately describe them all.

It took her a moment to focus her eyes and sort out her surroundings. Forest. Thick, thick forest. Some of the trees were ancient giants whose trunks were broader than she was tall. Many were smaller, clawing for space and sunlight in the shadows of their larger neighbors. Thick brush grew up everywhere, largely soft-looking fronds and ferns. Hanging moss draped off of everything more than a few feet above the forest floor. She had never seen anyplace quite like it, and yet she had the sense that there was something very familiar about it.

Birds sang, but few of them sounded like those she knew. She lay quietly for a moment, taking in the details. A few insects buzzed here and there. She saw a motion in a nearby tree, and saw a shadowy, nebulous form—a wild wood fury, doubtless—vanish among the branches.

She pushed herself up to find Gaius sitting on a stone beside the fire. He had discarded his usual silks of scarlet and blue for a woodsman's tunic and breeches, and he looked surprisingly comfortable in them. He sat with a mug in his hands, his eyes closed, his head tilted up.

"Good morning, Countess," he murmured.

"Sire," she said. "I apologize for last night. I should not have collapsed on you like that."

"On the contrary," Gaius said. "That's the first time anyone's kept any kind of pace with me since I took Septimus to—" He broke off suddenly, eyes blinking open, and stared up at the sky. "I had expected to carry you the last few hours."

"You did have to help me," Amara said.

He shrugged a shoulder. "I was helping myself, Countess. You simply stayed close enough on your own merits to take advantage of it. We made better time than I dared to hope."

She rose and stretched. "Where are we?"

"The western reaches of the Weeping Hills."

Amara frowned. "That's . . . that's in Kalare's territory, isn't it?"

"At its fringes, yes," Gaius said. "Though very few folk live in this area, and the land between where we stand and the sea is all wilderness. In fact, I doubt that there are any living souls, excepting ourselves, within forty or fifty miles, if that. We are some three hundred miles southwest of the city of Kalare itself. Tea?"

"Please." Amara accepted the mug he poured for her from a tin pot hung beside the fire. It felt good beneath her chilled fingers, and she sipped at it very slowly. "Three hundred miles?"

"Yes. And, I'm afraid, we walk from here."

Amara felt her eyebrows go up. "Sire?"

"It's the only way." Gaius gestured at the fire beside him. "Sit, sit. I'll explain."

Amara settled down by the fire and took stock of the camp. There was evidence of a small but complete amount of field gear—bedrolls, cooking utensils, a small set of tools, and what looked like an emergency tent. Gaius must have had it waiting here for them.

"We're going to Kalare," Gaius said.

"Sire?" Amara frowned down at her tea. "I don't understand. The Legions in the field are going there, too."

Gaius shook his head. "They're fighting a campaign to get there. This isn't the same thing at all. I don't need to fight for the territory. I simply need to be there."

"Why not just fly in?"

Gaius shook his head. "Kalarus has been clever. He must have been planning for this since he first succeeded to the title. His network of watch furies is extensive to the point of insanity."

Amara frowned. "Watch furies . . . I don't understand."

"Furies tasked to react to a particular presence—in this case, my own. If I come within three hundred miles of Kalare in the air, he'll know it."

"Can't you just remove them?"

"Of course," Gaius said. "But their sudden silence would warn him of my presence very nearly as effectively as if they started screaming about me. I can only imagine that maintaining such a network is a constant irritant. Likely it's a reflection of his personality. Paranoid, damnably paranoid. Obsessive. Formidable."

Amara nodded. "I don't understand then, what we're doing here."

"There's a flaw in Kalarus's planning," Gaius said. "He'll see any approach from the air—but on the ground, all of his furies are geared to keep watch for me by means of being on the lookout for *my* furies. My power." Gaius glanced up at her. "So I'm borrowing a page from our young captain. I'm walking in. No crafting. Kalarus will not expect that. He would never do such a thing, not in a thousand years, and he is blind to anything that isn't himself."

Amara began to speak, then frowned and sipped at her tea instead, thinking over her words. "Sire," she said after a moment. "That's a long walk. A *very* long walk. Particularly for . . . for . . ."

"A man my age?" the First Lord said, his rich voice amused. "Yes. I'm aware." He glanced back at the low fire, and his smile faded. "But it must be done."

Amara shook her head. "But *why*, sire? What do you hope to accomplish?"

"I'm going to break Kalarus's power, Countess. I'm going to end his ability to continue his rebellion."

"How?"

He shook his head. "That is something I'm keeping to myself for now. Suffice to say that there are greater and subtler matters of furycraft than those such as Kalarus and I prefer not to make widely known. This touches upon such a matter."

"But—"

"Countess," Gaius said quietly. "Are you with me? Or not?"

She grimaced, and glared at the fire. "Of course I am."

"Good. Your only concern is to help me get to Kalare. I won't be able to use any of my own furycraft without alerting Kalarus to my presence—which is to be avoided. I'm going to be relying upon you, Amara, to handle any problems that arise."

Amara felt both her eyebrows go up. "Sire, I'm not incompetent in the field, but it is hardly my forte. I'm not at all sure that I'm the best person for this kind of job."

"I trust you," the First Lord said simply.

She felt a flush of pride and pleasure at the words, but she shook her head. "Then you should trust my advice, sire. I'm not the one you should have with you."

"I should attempt it alone?"

"No," she said, at once, somewhat alarmed. "No, sire. I don't see why you should be trying to do this at *all*, but if you must do it, there are those better qualified to help you."

"The larger our party is, the more attention it is going to attract."

There was no arguing with that. "But sire . . ."

"Enough," Gaius said. "Countess, there are very few people in this world who are worthy of trust. Of those who are, not nearly enough of them are on my side. You're one of those few. I trust your loyalty. I trust your skill. I trust your judgment. In my eyes, that makes you one of the only people even remotely qualified for such a task."

"But there's only *me*, sire," she said. "And I'm not sure I'll be nearly enough. I can only be in one place at one time, have my eyes on one problem at a time. And my crafting skills are not the most advantageous when it comes to this kind of travel."

Gaius set his mug aside and rose. "Ah, now there is a point upon which there can be no argument. But I'm afraid I had very little selection in the matter. There was you—and perhaps one other." The First Lord gave her a brief, sunbeam flicker of a smile, and said, "I'll stretch my legs a bit. We have a little time."

Amara stared after him for a moment, before she suddenly recognized what had felt so familiar about this place. She rose and paced over to the bedroll where she had slept and bent down, lifting the blankets to her nose and inhaling.

The brush rustled gently behind her, and Amara's heart started beating very quickly.

"Good morning," a deep voice rumbled from behind her. "Nice day for a walk."

Amara turned.

A tall, broad-shouldered man came out of the thick forest bearing a pair of freshly caught fish. He was dressed in a forester's brown-green cloak, stone grey tunic, and brown leather breeches. He carried a hunting bow in his left hand, and Amara could see the handle of an axe hanging from a strap over one shoulder. He smiled, teeth flashing, and tossed the bow to one side.

"Bernard," she said, and went to him. She wrapped her arms around his neck, pulled him down to her, and kissed him soundly on the mouth. He slid an arm around her waist and pulled her hard against him, returning the kiss with single-minded intensity.

The kiss was so sweetly delicious that it seemed to blind Amara, as her fingers slid through his dark hair, and as her body suddenly caught fire at the touch of his hands, his mouth.

"Thought you'd appreciate a big breakfast after a long flight," he murmured against her mouth. "I'll cook these for you, if you're hungry."

Amara drew slowly back from him, and met his eyes. "I'm starving," she said quietly. "You can cook the crowbegotten fish after."

Sudden hot fire danced in the back of his eyes, but he affected a puzzled tone. "After what?"

She snarled at him, though she knew her own smile would give it the lie, knocked the string with the fish out of his hand with one of hers, then twined her fists in his tunic. She stepped into him as she put a leg behind his own, pushing.

He was too quick for her, turning her motion against her, and she let herself fall, his body coming down to pin hers against the earth. His mouth found hers again, and she felt herself arch up against him, hips rolling, her body demanding more.

He broke the kiss, his breath broken into rough gasps. "Oh," he growled quietly. "After *that*."

Amara let out a wicked little laugh that broke off as her husband kissed her again, and she returned it with breathless ardor.

┅┅┅┅┅ CHAPTER 9

Tavi focused on the stone in the dale outside the town of Elinarch, blocking out absolutely everything else around him. Nothing existed but himself and the stone, a wind-and-rain-rounded lump of granite the size of a handcart. He breathed deeply, concentrating, then spoke in a clear and commanding voice. "Come forth."

Nothing in particular happened.

Frustration welled up inside him, a red bubble expanding in his chest. He fought it off, concentrating on his breathing, on his focus, and addressed the stone again, reaching out for the fury he knew was inside. "Come forth."

The stone's stillness and silence were nothing short of insulting.

"Crows take it!" Tavi snarled. He clenched his teeth, tried to keep his tone of voice level and confident, and only mangled the words slightly as he gave it one last try. "Come f—"

He wasn't sure exactly what tipped him off. There might have been the faintest hint of sound behind him. There might have been a breath of excitement and feline amusement that ran over the back of his neck. It could have been the subtle, singing tension that he now felt surrounding every blade. Likely, it was a combination of all of those subtle factors. They coalesced into a single thought that flashed into the front of his mind: danger.

Tavi flung himself to one side, drawing his blade as he went.

He whirled on the way, spinning back toward the attacker, his back to the ground, and his blade intercepted a sword descending in a sharp overhand arch. The two blades met, and there was a small explosion of golden-green sparks. Tavi's momentum carried him forward, and his bare shoulder blades hit the grass first. He drew upon the wind blowing through the little vale to give speed enough to fold his body into a ball, bounce a bit off the grass, and then roll back onto his feet.

He wobbled but caught his balance as a rock the size of his head came zipping at his face. Off-balance, he had no time to move, and instead thrust the heel of his hand forward, drawing strength from the earth, and struck the oncoming stone with a single, sharp blow.

The rock exploded into shards and dust. Flying pieces lashed open half a dozen small wounds on his naked upper body and put two new rips in his trousers. His wrist and hand hurt like the crows, but he still had his balance, and as his attacker darted forward with windcrafted speed, he met a blindingly swift stroke of his attackers' sword with his own. He traded three or four strokes running on pure reflex, the blows too swift to allow for any thought, minicascades of sparks scattering around him with each blow.

He never "saw" the opening in his opponent's defense, so much as he felt it, sensed the change coming in the humming sensation of the two swords' furies clashing and blending. He twisted his blade forward in a serpentine thrust, forcing his opponent's blade to engage his, the tip too far to one side to stop him from stepping in close, locking his aching left hand on his opponent's weapon wrist, and applying the pressure of a fury-assisted grip.

"Ah!" Kitai cried out, the sound both pained and amused. "Enough, enough!"

Tavi released her wrist, and the Marat girl lifted her blade in a quick salute, then sheathed it one-handed in a single motion, never bothering to look down at the scabbard.

"That was cheating," Tavi said. "I was trying to concentrate."

Kitai thrust out her lower lip in a pouting expression. "Poor Aleran, needing all his rules to keep him safe."

Tavi swiped a hand at her. Kitai laughed and ducked it.

"Crows, Kitai. You know how hard I've been working. Until I can bid a fury to manifest—"

She threw her hands up in the air. "Two years ago, he has no furies at all, and he is content. Today he has more than he ever hoped to have, and it is not enough."

Tavi growled and shoved his own sword away, also without looking. He couldn't have explained how he did it. He could feel when the tip of his blade was aligned with the metal fittings at the end of the scabbard, a sensation that was comparable to feeling his fingers all in the proper position to tug on a glove. "I'm not going to get opportunities to practice once we march. You know that. This was my last chance to try it for a while."

"And you tried it," Kitai said. She put a hand on her hip and faced him, her green eyes hard. "It didn't work, and you started to lose your temper, at which point it wasn't *going* to work." Her expression softened slightly. "You were only torturing yourself, *chala*."

She was right, Tavi thought, which was annoying, but he could feel her genuine concern for him, sense it almost as if it were an emotion of his own. His watercrafter's perceptions were still inconsistent and often quite vague, but where Kitai was involved, they were clear and unmistakable. Or perhaps the bond they shared was more responsible for the empathy that had grown between them. He wasn't sure.

Kitai studied him, bright green eyes on his, and shook her head. "You think too much, Aleran. Always planning. Always questioning. Always calculating. It's a wonder your head doesn't catch fire from the inside." She glanced up at the sun, then down at the cuts on his chest. "Come. Let me clean that up. He'll be here in a moment."

Tavi blinked and looked down at himself. He had almost forgotten the injuries. He had shut away the pain almost before it had registered on him, and had been holding it away without really thinking about it. Once he did, of course, the crafting faltered, and the cuts burned and stung unpleasantly.

Kitai brought a cloth and a flask of water and cleaned the

cuts and scrapes. Tavi managed to hold still through it all, though it was hardly pleasant. He had to close his eyes and exhale slowly as Kitai cleansed one cut. The Marat girl winced a little and leaned down, placing a gentle kiss nearby the hurt. Then she bound over the two wounds that still oozed a little blood, her motions practiced. They should be, Tavi thought. Great furies knew that they'd had enough practice on one another over the past two years.

Tavi had just pulled his shirt back on when Enna's horse came walking slowly through the entrance to the dale. The horse trooper had one hand clamped resolutely over her eyes. "Captain?" she called. "Kitai told me not to look at you when you were unclothed. How am I supposed to *know* whether or not you are unclothed without *looking*?"

Tavi gave Kitai a level look. "Oh for pity's sake."

She laughed at him. She did that quite often, Tavi thought. The smile that went with the laugh was devastating, and he found himself smiling with her, despite another day's effort, another day's failure.

"It's all right, Enna," Tavi called. "You can look."

"Thank goodness," Enna said, dropping her hand, and beaming at Tavi. Then she gave him a disappointed little frown and sighed. "I miss all the best parts."

"Centurion," Tavi prompted.

She gave him a quick salute. "The man who none of us saw and who none of us are going to remember is here to see you, sir."

"He knows me," said a young man's voice, and Ehren walked around from behind Enna's horse, touching the animal's flanks gently with one hand as he brushed past. He was small, quite a bit under five and a half feet tall, but the reed-thin young man Tavi had met when he first came to the Academy had hardened. Ehren, sandy-haired and unassuming, was still slender—but slender like hunting cats, or dueling swords, rather than like writing quills. He was dressed in rough garb of castaway clothing, most of it ill fitting, and looked like any of ten thousand refugees in the camps.

At a nod from Kitai, Enna withdrew. Tavi went to the young

man and traded grips with him, then considered his clothing with a frown. "Ehren. I never said I was sending you out again."

"Please," Ehren said. "I'm a professional spy, Tavi. I wouldn't be doing you any good standing around here." He turned to Kitai with a smile and bowed gallantly over her hand. "Not that it isn't nice sleeping with both eyes closed, but I'm starting to get soft."

"You've only been back for three days," Kitai said.

"That's just about enough," Ehren said. He lowered his voice conspiratorially and jerked his head covertly at Tavi. "I can't stand working where my superiors can look over my shoulder anyway."

Tavi smiled, but he didn't really feel it. Ehren had worked his way into position in Canim-occupied territory over an entire perilous year. Some of the Canim commanders had spent a great deal of energy hunting for spies and rooting them out. Many such informants had been caught, and had not been seen again. Ehren had, Tavi gathered, very nearly been caught as he left occupied territory—and there was a fresh scar on his brow that he had not explained.

"Is there any word from the First Lord?" Tavi asked quietly.

Ehren shook his head. "You haven't given me enough time to try all the channels."

"I don't *have* the time," Tavi said. "We march tomorrow."

"I know," Ehren said. "But word is that Gaius is with the Legions in the south somewhere. As far as anyone I could reach knows, all of his messages are being routed to someone on the staff—even Cursor traffic. So, either he's come down with a bad case of bureaucratic thinking . . ."

"Or he's up to something," Tavi said. "Crows. Why *now*?"

"Even if he wasn't," Ehren said, "from what you told me, he's given you your marching orders. Maybe you shouldn't be trying to go over Arnos's head like this."

"That was before we knew about Mastings," Tavi said. "Or Arnos's so-called battle plan. Or what he had in mind for the noncombatants. We have to find another option, Ehren."

Ehren lifted both hands. "Which is why I'm dressed for the road," he said. "You want me to see how close I can get to Mastings?"

Tavi drew in a deep breath. "Sort of."

Ehren frowned and tilted his head.

"I want you to get to Nasaug," Tavi said.

Ehren burst out in a laugh. It died young, as he watched Tavi's expression. "Oh," he said. "You were serious."

"Yes."

Ehren shook his head. "Your confidence is flattering, but even if I *could* get close to him, which I don't think I could, I'm not at all sure I could take him. I *saw* him fight at the Elinarch."

"No, no, crows," Tavi said. "If I wanted him assassinated, I'd do it myself." He paused to consider. "Or possibly send Max and Crassus."

"For you," Ehren said, "that was an uncommonly sensible afterthought."

Tavi grinned at him for a second. "This isn't that kind of mission," Tavi said. He flicked open the leather case on his sword belt and drew out a folded envelope. He offered it to Ehren.

The young man stared at the envelope for a moment and exhaled slowly. "Oh. The other part of the Cursor business." He searched Tavi's face for a moment, and said, quietly, "We're messengers for the First Lord, Tavi. This isn't one of his messages."

"If he didn't want us using our initiative, he shouldn't be so hard to contact," Tavi replied.

Ehren chuckled. "Can't argue there. What is it?"

"A request for a meeting," Tavi said. "Between me and Nasaug."

Ehren exhaled. "That's all?"

"Yes."

"We, uh. We don't really know how they're going to react to an official courier. No one's sent any."

"Don't worry about it," Tavi said. "You wouldn't be official."

"Oh," Ehren said. "Crows."

"You don't have to," Tavi said quietly. "I can find something else for you to—"

"Oh shut up," Ehren said, his voice annoyed, as he took the envelope from Tavi's hand. "You think Nasaug will be willing to talk?"

"If he is," Tavi said, "I think we can expect him to behave in a civilized fashion."

"They haven't exactly been a monolithic culture," Ehren replied. "What if some of the other Canim don't hold with Nasaug's way of thinking?"

"I'd advise you to avoid them," Tavi said.

"You don't ask much, do you?" Ehren flashed Tavi an easy grin and slipped the envelope out of sight beneath his over-large tunic. "Time limit?"

"Sooner is better, but take what you need to make the approach." Tavi paused, then offered his hand again. Ehren took it, and Tavi said softly, "Be careful, Ehren."

"Can't have you moaning over how guilty you feel for sending me off to my death," Ehren said, and winked at Kitai. "The Ambassador would never forgive me."

"No," Kitai said. She stepped forward and kissed Ehren on the cheek. "I wouldn't. Walk softly."

"I suspect I'll have less to worry about than you. Take care of each other." He nodded to them, turned, and vanished into the trees without ceremony.

Tavi watched him go and bit his lip.

"He knows what he is doing, *chala*," Kitai said.

"I know."

"He knows the risks."

"I know."

"If this works," she said, "what will you say to Nasaug? What do you hope to accomplish?"

"I don't know," Tavi said quietly. "Yet. But I have to do something."

She stood beside him for a moment, then said, "We should get back."

Tavi took a deep breath and blew it out again. "Right," he said. "Lots to do. And we march at dawn."

CHAPTER 10

Just as Tavi rose to leave his office for the field, Araris shut the door, and said in a very quiet voice, "I have to talk to you."

There were a hundred details still to take care of, and they formed a precise, clear list in the young commander's mind. Tavi buckled on his sword belt as he mentally ordered the list, and reached for his cloak. "Fine. We can talk on the road."

"No," the *singulare* said quietly.

Tavi threw the cloak around his shoulders. "The Senator isn't going to appreciate it if we hold him up. Let's move."

Araris looked steadily at Tavi for a second. Then he locked the door, folded his arms, and leaned back against it. "The Senator," he said, "can wait."

Tavi drew up short and stared at the older man until he had managed to shake the list out of the forefront of his thoughts. He studied Araris for a minute, taking in his wary posture, his obvious tension. Tavi concentrated for a moment and was able to feel a vague sense of unease tinting an iron shell of resolve.

"Oh," Tavi said quietly. "This talk."

Araris nodded. "It's time."

Boots thudded dully on the floors overhead, probably the Subtribunes Logistica moving the Legion's treasury chest along with two full spears of guards.

"Why now?"

Araris nodded up at the world above. "Because you're leaving on campaign. There's always the possibility that you might not come back from it. And because you're a grown man, Tavi. Because rumors are spreading, and you've got to be ready. You need to know. You deserve to know."

Tavi felt a flash of old, hot frustration flare through him, but he pushed it back. "I'm listening."

Araris nodded. "There's a lot. Tell me what you've alread
worked out."

Tavi took a deep breath. "I know," he said, "that you were
singulare to the Princeps Gaius Septimus. I know that he die
at the First Battle of Calderon twenty-two years ago. His *sin
gulares* were thought to have died with him. They were burie
with him at the Princeps Memorium back in Calderon.

"I know," Tavi continued, "that you pledged your loyalty t
me. That Gaius didn't seem to care for that, but that he ke[
you close to me for years."

Araris nodded. "All true."

"I know that Aunt Isana doesn't talk about my mothe
much. Neither does Uncle Bernard." Tavi glanced down. "Th
only thing they've ever said about my father is that he was
soldier." He tried not to let it happen, but his voice turned bit
ter. "Which means I'm just a *legionare's* bastard. There ar
plenty of those around."

Araris looked up sharply. "Bastard? No. No, your parent
were wed, Tavi."

Tavi felt his heart begin to speed up. He'd spent a lifetim
knowing almost nothing about his mother and father. No on
had ever been willing to speak of them in anything but th
vaguest terms. Tavi barely trusted himself to speak. "You . .
you knew them?"

Araris's eyes grew distant for a moment. "Oh, yes," he sai
quietly. "Very well."

"How—" Tavi began, but his throat clenched shu
"Who . . . What did . . ."

Araris held up a hand. "First," he said, "I must tell you thi
I did not want to be the one to speak. That duty by rights be
longed to Isana. But she . . ." He shook his head. "Whe
someone goes through as much grief and loss as she did, i
such a short amount of time, it can leave wounds as surely a
any sword. You can recover from some wounds. But some
times they're lasting. Crippling. And the best you can hope fo
is to survive them."

"I don't understand," Tavi said.

"Isana . . . doesn't think very clearly where you are cor
cerned. Not about this. She loves you desperately, Tavi."

Tavi chewed on his lip and nodded. "I know."

"She's terrified of losing you. It clouds her judgment, I think. Her resolve. I believe that she wanted to tell you the truth long before now. But she'd kept it locked up so tightly, for so long, I'm not sure she knew how to let it out again."

Tavi shook his head. "Wait. Araris—what truth?"

"The truth about your father," Araris said quietly. "The truth about Gaius Septimus."

The bottom fell out of Tavi's stomach upon hearing the words.

He'd known—no, not *known*, but speculated, analyzing what he knew and putting it together in a theory, as the Cursors had trained him to do. It had been an idle exercise, or so he thought, though it might be more accurate to say that he had simply found a new way to daydream about what it would have been like actually to have parents in his life. He'd done that often as a child, spending hours picturing them, imagining what they might have looked like, sounded like, what they might have said.

What life would have been like. How much better it might have been.

Of course, the idea of the Princeps as Tavi's unknown father had a single major stumbling block—the utter lack of furycraft that had haunted Tavi until two years before.

But that wasn't an issue anymore.

In fact, as he thought on it, it should have been more obvious to him. Tavi's crafting was still sharply limited by his lack of ability to control a manifest fury, but had he been in the Academy, he would have earned two or three beads in every single branch of crafting by now. While it was not unheard of for a crafter—especially a scion of the Citizenry—to be gifted in several areas of craft, it was exceedingly rare for anyone but the upper tiers of talent to possess skills that ran the entire spectrum of furycraft.

It should have been more obvious, but he supposed it was possible he hadn't *wanted* it to be true. If Araris was correct, if the Princeps truly was wed to his mother, it meant that he was a legitimate heir of the House of Gaius. It meant . . .

Bloody crows. It meant that the First Lord had an heir.

And it was him. Tavi.

Bloody crows. It meant that the most dangerous and ruthless people on the face of Carna were going to want him dead.

Him. Tavi.

Other pieces fell into place. He could see why Gaius had brought him to the Academy—to give him a sound education. To expose him to the children of the Citizenry. He'd been trained with the Cursors, learning the arts of intrigue and deception. He'd been assigned to a room with Max—another outcast to Aleran high society, just as Tavi himself was. That a friendship of mutual alliance would grow between them had been all but inevitable, and Tavi abruptly felt certain that Gaius had planned deliberately to secure Tavi at least one ally with the crafting power of a High Lord.

And the First Lord's designs hadn't stopped there. Tavi had been sent out into a Legion to learn the arts of strategy, tactics, logistics, and leadership. Granted, Gaius hadn't expected Tavi to wind up in *command* of the bloody thing, but the First Lord—his *grandfather*—couldn't have been terribly displeased with the results.

Gaius.

His grandfather.

He had a *grandfather*.

Tavi knew he was breathing too quickly, and it was making him dizzy, but too many thoughts were spinning through his mind to pay any attention. He wasn't sure if he wanted to scream, or hit something, or run, or laugh, or burst out weeping. His mind was an enormous blur of ideas and memories and possible futures, and only one thing was certain.

Everything had changed.

Everything.

"I've . . . I've . . ." Tavi swallowed and forced himself to stop stammering. "I've known that there were things Aunt Isana wasn't telling me about my parents, but . . ."

Araris closed his eyes and sighed. Then he opened them and faced Tavi. "No, Tavi. There's a lot your mother hasn't told you about your father."

Tavi frowned and opened his mouth to ask another

question—then stopped suddenly as he heard the very gentle emphasis Araris put on the word *mother*.

A lot his *mother* hadn't told him.

Not Aunt Isana.

His *mother*.

Isana. Isana *was* his mother.

Tavi's heart suddenly throbbed and clenched, and the searing flame of shock and pain seared through his vitals. It was as if every tiny wound his heart had received over the years, every little momentary pain of a lonely child, every jab of self-loathing he felt when other children had asked who his parents were, every moment of longing for *anything* to fill that emptiness where his parents should have been—*all* of it came back to him at the same instant, in the same place, the concentrated heartache of a lifetime.

Tavi turned his head and clutched a hand at his chest, fingers sliding over the plates of his armor. The pain wasn't physical, of course—but that made it no less real, and no less terrible.

"Her sister was killed in the Marat attack at First Calderon," Araris said. "Almost everyone was. You were born that same night, in fact." His face clouded with an old sadness. "Isana believed that Septimus was betrayed by another Aleran and that if his enemies learned that he might *possibly* have sired an heir, you would surely be killed. So she hid you. She lied about who your mother was. She watercrafted you during your baths, to slow down your growth. She wanted anyone who looked at you to think that you were too young to be Septimus's child, born too long after his death."

Araris stepped forward and put a hand on Tavi's shoulder. "I helped her," he said quietly. He gestured at his scarred, branded face. "I did this to myself, Tavi. Araris Valerian was thought to be dead, and if anyone recognized me, they would have been awfully curious to note that I was watching over a boy. So I became Fade. A simple slave. The scar was part of the disguise. No one ever looked past it."

Tavi could only stare at the older man. Then he heard himself say, "That's what she wanted to talk about the other day."

Araris grimaced and nodded. "She was trying. She was afraid of what it might mean if she told you."

Tavi's vision blurred over, and the tears seemed to magnify the pain bursting through his chest. "All those years and . . . and she was *lying* to me. She was *lying*." He jerked his head upright as another thought flashed through his mind like a thunderbolt. "That's why I was never able to . . . she crafted me. She slowed my growth. She stunted my talents—and I never *knew* . . ."

"Tavi," Araris said, his voice carefully calm. "Wait. You've got to understand that she did what she did because she loves you. She had very few resources to draw upon, and she did everything in her power to protect you."

"No," Tavi spat. She'd done it to him. The years of humiliation, the bewildered pain as he bore the stigma of a freak, unable to furycraft, scorned and held in contempt by people wherever he went. He hadn't been born a freak, born unlucky, a victim of terrible mischance as he always thought.

Someone had *done* it to him.

His *mother* had done it to him.

Part of Tavi was listening to Araris's words, and part of him knew that the *singulare* was probably right—but it was a very small, very distant part. The pain, the outrage, and the humiliation left very little room for anything else.

"Tavi," Araris said, "you've got to calm down. She did the best she could."

"*No!*" Tavi spat, the anger giving his voice a vicious edge. "She *lied* to me. She *took* my crafting." His voice gained volume, independently of his control. "Do you *know* how many nights I couldn't sleep, how many times I suffered because I was the furyless freak? Do you have any *idea*, all the humiliation I had to go through? How *alone* I was?"

"Tavi," Araris said, voice quiet, as one speaking to a spooked horse, "you've got to control yourself. *Think*, man. She's out there, right now, and she's ripped apart inside. You don't know what is going to happen when you leave on campaign. You don't *know* if you're ever going to see her again. You need to see her. You need to make this right while you still can."

Tavi only stared at him incredulously. "Right? Make this

right? She's been lying to me since before I could stand up, and I'm supposed to make that *right*?" He mopped a hand over his face and felt it shaking as it smeared tears. "You bring this to me today. When we're about to march, and I've got five thousand men to consider. You throw this in my face *today*."

"Tavi," Araris said. "She's your mother. She needs this."

No. Tavi found himself shaking his head. The list came pouring back through his thoughts. This was too much. It was all far, far too much. He had barely slept in the past two days. He was already faced with an enormous and most likely insoluble dilemma in his assignment from the First—from his grandfather. Thousands of lives were dependent upon him. If he truly was the Princeps's son and heir, it meant that *millions* of lives were or would become his responsibility. Not only *that*, but he had just gained a veritable pantheon of foes who were more like demigods than human beings.

And his aunt—his *mother*—had been lying to him for his entire life.

The voice of reason, of understanding, lost the battle to govern Tavi's decisions.

"She had twenty years to talk to me if she needed it so badly," Tavi said, his voice rough. "She had a lifetime. And I have a Legion to move."

"Tavi—" Araris began, his voice a gentle protest.

"*Captain Scipio,*" Tavi snarled. "I have a job to do. Either come with me or get out of the way. Or was the loyalty you pledged me another lie?"

Araris stiffened at that. His eyes flashed with sudden anger. Without a word, he unlocked the door, stepped back, and opened it for Tavi, coming to rigid attention.

Tavi started to stride angrily out the door, but hesitated. He didn't—couldn't—look at Araris, but he could see the man regarding him on the periphery of his vision. Tavi went quiet, listening to the silence. There were no more footsteps above, no sound of voices or doors opening and closing. The command center felt eerily empty.

"It was right there in front of me," Tavi said. "All the pieces. Even inside my name."

Araris said nothing.

"I can't," Tavi said quietly. "Not . . . not now. There's too much." The geyser of confusion and hurt threatened to roar out of control again, and Tavi struggled to slow his breathing, to control it. He glanced aside at Araris.

The *singulare's* face remained impassive as a stone.

"I'll talk to her when I get back."

Araris said nothing.

"I have duties that must come first," he said quietly. "So do you."

Araris was silent for an endless moment. Then, quite deliberately, he lifted his fist to his heart, knuckles thumping gently against his armor. When he spoke, his voice was barely more than a whisper, and his words sent a shiver running down Tavi's spine.

"Hail," he said quietly. "Hail, Gaius Octavian, Princeps of Alera."

ᗕᗕᗕᗕᗕ CHAPTER 11

"Cohort!" Marcus bellowed in a voice that every single *legionare* in the Prime Cohort could hear. "Halt!"

The men's steady steps thudded twice more, then fell silent, as the ranks of the First Aleran reached the crest of the low ridge overlooking the Canim's first defensive position. The Prime occupied the center, of course, as it always did. The Fourth, holding his cohort's right flank, took a moment to dress its ranks. The Seventh, whose Tribune spent more time in drill, had no need to straighten out its lines.

"Three days to get here," muttered one veteran to another, as Marcus passed. "We'd have done it in one. Senatorial Guard. Bunch of tenderfoot pansies, can't march without a causeway."

Marcus snapped his baton back against the veteran's

shield, and growled, "Quiet in the ranks." He gave the man a glare, and said, "You might hurt the pansies' feelings."

No one actually laughed (and great furies help any man who had), but several muffled snorts puffed out of the men of the Prime, and Marcus could sense them settling into the tense, familiar silence of prebattle. No joke or song or stirring oration could take the fear away from soldiers. Oh, it made for a fine story, no question, the stirring speech upon the edge of battle. But when facing an enemy as determined to survive as you were, talk was cheap, and the men on the ground knew it.

The joke had helped, though, providing a small release of tension, and helped the men settle down into the mind-set of victorious *legionares*: that they were professionals with a job to do, and that it was time to get to work.

Marcus stalked up and down the front rank, doing his best to look like he had more interest in his men's discipline than he did in the battle raging five hundred yards away. The sound of the fight washed up to their position like distant surf, mercifully indistinct, a distant rumble of drums, a clamor of horns, an ocean of individual cries and shouts. Marcus glanced at the battle as he paced the front rank, his steps steady and unconcerned.

A few moments later, horses thundered up through the gaps between the cohorts, and the captain, his *singulare*, one of the First Aleran's Knights Aeris, and an escort of Marat cavalry troopers rode along the front rank of the Legion. Marcus turned and saluted as the captain drew his horse up. The captain dismounted and returned the salute. "Good morning, Marcus."

"Sir," the First Spear replied.

The captain swept his eyes over the battle below. Marcus took note of where the young man looked and for how long. Excellent. He was paying attention where he should. He'd always possessed the talent to be a skilled battlefield commander, but even so, he'd come a long way since Marcus had seen him in that first frantic defense of the walls at the Elinarch.

After a silent moment, he nodded once, and said, "What do you think, First Spear?"

"It's their first dance, sir. No telling until it's over."

The battle was being waged along a road—a common trail, not a furycrafted causeway. The gentle, rolling terrain of the Vale narrowed, at that point, where a pair of old stone bluffs faced one another across an open gap. A small town called Othos filled that opening but sported only a modest defensive wall. The town was overlooked by a small steadholt high upon the eastern bluff. The omnipresent crows found on any Aleran battlefield whirled overhead in enormous numbers, like a great, dark wheel circling high above the embattled town.

The Canim had gone to work on the defenses, throwing up earthworks outside the walls of Othos itself, and the wolfish creatures now fought tenaciously to hold the outer wall. The First Senatorial had assaulted up the middle, driving hard down the road for the earthworks. Even as Marcus watched, the first assault began to falter, as *legionares* failed to bull past the enormous defenders. A moment later, the trumpets began to sound a retreat, and the First Senatorial pulled back, falling into interspersed columns.

More trumpets sounded, and in the gaps between those columns, the Second Senatorial charged, hurling fresh troops into the defenders without giving them a chance to recover from the first assault. The Second almost immediately began to push forward, breaching the earthen wall in two places before the Canim managed to plug the gap, driving the Second back. Just as they did, the First Senatorial, having reorganized its ranks and given its *legionares* a chance to breathe, charged forward in turn, smashing into the weary defenders like an axe into rotten wood. They crested the defenses in half a dozen places in the first minute, and then it was the deep, braying horns of the Canim that sounded the retreat.

"Not bad," the captain mused aloud. "That kind of retreat isn't easy to coordinate with a countercharge."

Marcus grunted. "They've had a year and a half to train, sir, while we were on the job."

"True." The captain watched as the Canim defenders fell back to the city wall under the cover of a veritable thunderstorm of missiles. The Canim favored spears sized to fit them, and the crow-eaten things were thick and long enough to spit a cow upon. Driven by the unbelievable strength of the wolf-warriors they could pierce a *legionare*, body, armor, and all, and still retain enough power to wound the man behind him.

Worse than the spears, though, was the sudden thunderstorm of hurled stones. A Canim warrior could hurl a stone the size of a man's head without any particular effort, and they lobbed them in high arcs, so that they plummeted almost straight down upon the hapless Guard below. Armor and helmets of Aleran steel were of limited use against the impact of stones so large and heavy. Even when laboring Tribunes began bellowing the orders for their cohorts to shift to a tortoise formation, the rain of stones disrupted the tight ranks necessary for it, leaving men exposed and breaking upraised arms, even through the shields they wielded.

The primitive missiles were less deadly, in a relative sense, than well-aimed arrow fire, but they possessed a far greater capacity to inflict crippling injuries, and the ranks of the Guard nearest the town walls were badly mauled before they were ordered back to the earthworks and out of rock range.

The retreat left the ground before the walls exposed, and the excited crows plunged down toward the corpses; but not before Marcus was able to get a quick estimate of the fallen. The Guard had left the still, armored forms of between seven and eight hundred *legionares* lying dead on the killing field.

"Bloody crows," the captain muttered in a tone that only Marcus was close enough to hear. Disgust tinted the young man's voice. "The battle's not fifteen minutes old, and he's already lost a tithe of one of his Legions."

Marcus grunted his agreement. "Going to be a lonely walk to Mastings at this rate, sir."

"Especially since they outnumbered us to begin with," the captain spat. "We have to pick our moments for attrition tactics."

"Yes, sir," Marcus said.

The captain drummed the fingertips of one hand against the hilt of his sword. "I hate standing around watching."

Marcus glanced aside at the captain's profile. "You've been given your orders, sir. We're a necessary reserve."

Below, the Guard Legions were massing behind the earthworks. Scaling ropes and ladders were being prepared for the assault on the walls, and half a dozen Knights Terra, recognizable by the preposterously outsized mallets they wielded, gathered in the center to smash down the town's gates.

"Crows." The captain's voice sounded distant and tired. "I tried to warn him."

Marcus caught a movement out of the corner of his eye, and glanced up to see twin arrowhead formations of Knights Aeris streaking through the sky toward the town.

The captain had seen them, too. "There they go."

"Textbook," Marcus agreed.

Another trumpet sounded, and with a roar the Guard plunged forward. Spheres of white-hot flame burst into being upon the walls overlooking the gate, as the Guard's Knights Ignus unleashed their furies upon the defenders.

The missile storm began again, but the two formations of Knights Aeris strafed the battlements, sending Canim flying as they were caught in the enormous gale of the Knights' combined windstreams. The *legionares* charged, ladders and ropes rising, even as the Knights Terra rushed the gate.

The captain's head snapped aside, and he pointed up at the western bluff. "There."

Marcus looked up to see dark shapes rising from concealment atop the bluff, and they were soon mirrored by more movement on the eastern side. Marcus could see forms atop both bluffs moving strangely, but it took him a moment to realize what they were doing.

They were spinning in place.

The stones that began to fall upon the conveniently massed ranks of the Guard made the hand-tossed projectiles of moments before seem like pebbles by comparison. Stones half the height of a man came crashing down, lethal to anyone beneath them, crippling to anyone close enough to be struck as the stone rebounded from the earth and tumbled wildly.

Marcus stared in mute surprise. It would take an earthcrafter of considerable talent to throw stones that size, and the Canim *had* no earthcrafters. Not only that, but even if they had been strong enough to throw the boulders, they could not possibly have been thrown at such speed to such distance—and yet they were doing it.

The captain narrowed his eyes, staring at the bluffs, and let out a sudden snarl. "Slingers," he said. "Bloody crows, they're slingers."

Marcus shot a glance at the captain and peered more closely. The young officer was right, by the great furies. The Canim atop the bluffs were whirling the enormous stones at the end of long, heavy chains. Each slinger would rush forward, get the stone moving, then begin to spin, whirling the boulders in great circles, gathering speed, until they released them to sail out and down onto the Guard below.

Horns blared with frantic authority as the deadly rain disrupted formations and sowed panic and confusion in the ranks. The Knights Aeris formations wheeled up and separated, each soaring toward one of the bluffs, to suppress the slingers and sweep them from their position.

Marcus felt nothing but contempt for the arrogance of the commander who had sent those men into the battle unprepared. It was no fault of Arnos's men, but they were going to die for it.

As the Knights bore down upon the bluffs, they began to fall out of formation. Men twisted and jerked in midair, then began plummeting out of the skies to smash upon the ground below.

"Balests," Marcus grunted.

The captain nodded tightly. Without the Knights Aeris to suppress the battlements, the Canim began the terrible rain of smaller stones again, hurling them down upon the *legionares* attempting the walls. They regained their positions around and over the gate, slamming stones down at the Knights Terra attempting to destroy it, forcing them to draw back or risk a crushed skull.

"Crows," Marcus said. "The only thing the Guard is doing is providing the Canim cover from our own firecrafters." He watched as men struggled and died, as the chaos of the battle took hold of the *legionares*. The pressure on the walls faltered, and Marcus had seen battles enough to know that the Guard would soon withdraw, whether or not their officers ordered it.

The captain snarled again. "I'm not waiting any longer." He turned to Sir Callum, the Knight Aeris who had ridden up with him, and said, "Go."

Callum dismounted and dragged a roll of bright scarlet cloth from his saddlebag. He took a pair of quick steps and flung himself into the air, soaring upward. He let the scarlet banner come unrolled as he did, until he was dragging the twenty-yard signal flag behind him.

Almost instantly, fresh trumpets sounded, silvery notes that seemed to float down from overhead. There was a quiet rumble, like distant thunder, and suddenly horsemen flying the banner of the First Aleran were racing along the top of the eastern bluff. They fell upon the slingers holding those heights, putting a sudden halt to the rain of enormous stones.

On the western bluff, the regular cadence of a war chant drifted down through the morning air, audible over the scream of battle thanks to its rhythm. Along that ridge appeared the solid formation of the First Aleran's Thirteenth Cohort, the Battlecrows, marching at the quickstep for the Canim positions overlooking Othos. Once in position, a concerted battle roar went up from them, and the Battlecrows slammed into the Canim like a single, enormous hammer.

A small sphere of blue fire exploded in the air over the bluff, and was echoed by a second sphere over the other bluff.

"There's the signal," Marcus murmured.

"Sharpshooters cleared," the captain growled under his breath. "Take 'em, Crassus."

Twenty armored Knights Aeris, windcrafters of the First Aleran's Knights Pisces, came screaming down out of the sun. They dived upon the battlements, blinding and confusing the defending Canim long enough to allow them to land and clear out a short section of wall.

The Guard's officers saw them come in and seized the opportunity. Scaling ladders went up in the area the Knights Pisces had secured, and *legionares* began flooding onto the battlements to support them.

Canim horns began to bray again, and the defense crumbled. The Guard surged raggedly forward, still too disordered to press home a charge that might have destroyed a sizeable portion of the Canim defenders. The Guard banners, red and blue fields behind the Senate's silver laurel leaf, were lifted upon the walls. The Guard poured into the town, securing it.

Several minutes later, Marcus let out a slow breath and shook his head. "They let us take it."

The captain nodded. "Could have been worse."

A messenger wearing the livery of the First Senatorial rode up the First Aleran's battle lines, toward the captain and Marcus. The young man dismounted, gave the captain a salute, and said, "His Honor the Senator requests and requires that you meet with him in one hour, sir."

The captain nodded. "My compliments to His Honor, and I will be there."

The messenger saluted again and departed.

Marcus frowned. "Senator isn't going to be happy with you, sir. He ordered you to sit tight."

The captain smiled bleakly. "That's why I waited for things to get as bad as they did before I sent them in. He might scream and rant, but he can't get away with laying charges against me for turning a rout into a victory—and he knows it."

Marcus grunted. "Probably true."

The captain stared down at the dead beneath their dark, shifting blanket of hungry crows. Here and there, among the gleaming forms of fallen *legionares*, Marcus could see the darker, larger form of a Cane. No few of them had fallen, but the Legions had paid a ruinous price to drive the enemy from a position he had never intended to keep.

"Marcus," the captain said.

"Sir."

"Send up Foss and his men. The Guard took a mauling today, and this is the first time their Tribunes Medica have real casualties to treat. They'll need the help."

"Yes, sir."

The captain was quiet for a moment. Then he said, "I wish I could have acted sooner, Marcus. But if I had, Arnos would have had cause to strip me of command."

"Yes, sir," Marcus said, very quietly. "He would have."

The captain rubbed his hands against the sides of his trousers, as if trying to wipe something off them. "All right," he said quietly. "Let's get moving, centurion. It's a long way to Mastings."

CHAPTER 12

Tavi rode into Othos with Araris at his side.

The town's gates had been thrown wide open, though not without effort. Tons of earth had been piled up behind them when they were closed, and the Knights Terra who had been part of the assault were only now finishing crafting it clear.

"Look at that," Tavi murmured to Araris. "Even if they had broken the gates, the Guard couldn't have pushed through all of that. They just wanted to make us stand still while they dropped rocks on our heads."

Araris nodded grimly and called out to the squad who held the gate. "Centurion! Could you direct us to the Senator's command, please."

A blocky man with a centurion's baton and blood on his helmet and breastplate looked down from the walls. He stared at Araris and his branded face for a second, and his lip lifted in a snarl of contempt—until his eyes moved past him to Tavi.

Tavi said nothing. Captains and other important people weren't expected to do the talking. That's what their retainers were for.

The centurion nodded toward the young captain, and thumped a fist to his chest in salute. "Town square, big white house. Used to be the local Count's residence."

"My thanks," Araris said, the faintest trace of irony in his voice, and they continued on their way.

The leggy Marat horses moved at a kind of dancing trot down the central street of Othos, their hooves clopping distinctly on the cobblestones. The air carried a strong scent of Canim, an odor that was pungent, musty, and somehow a little metallic. The streets were very quiet as they kept going. With the exception of several passing squads of *legionares*, they saw no one else. In fact . . .

Tavi's mouth suddenly filled with bitterness, and he swallowed, fighting his stomach back down. "The people. Where are the townspeople?"

Araris's expression became colder, but he remained silent. They passed from midmorning sunlight into one of the vast, cold shadows cast by the bluffs rising on either side of the town. Tavi shivered.

They came to the town square, situated flush against the town's southern wall—and found out where the people of Othos had gone. There were perhaps eight or nine hundred townsfolk seated on the stones of the square, and they were surrounded by lines of grim-faced *legionares*. More of the Guard had taken positions on the southern wall, most of them archers. About half of them were facing the square, rather than to the south, where the Canim forces were, Tavi fervently hoped, still retreating.

The square was completely silent, the men and women and children sitting very still, not speaking. Here and there a dog barked, or an infant cried, and the spring wind occasionally slammed shut a door left hanging open. They were fifty yards away, but even Tavi's limited watercrafting senses could detect their quiet, acidic fear. It was a hideous sensation because unlike his own personal fear, this emotion seemed unable to remain inside him. It was as if each part of him, his limbs, his hair, his very skin, could each feel independent terror of its own, and the sensation rolled over him in a sickening wave.

He looked away from them, closed his eyes, and rested his hand on the hilt of his sword. Tavi drew upon the silent, cold strength in the weapon, let it roll up over him and armor him against the townsfolks' terror. The sensation faded at once, enough to let him get control of himself again, and continue riding.

They rode up to a large white house. *Legionares* were stationed outside its front garden, and Tavi spotted one of the Senator's *singulares*, a small, dark-haired woman with a bow, on watch at the house's front door.

As they dismounted, one of the valets from the First

Senatorial emerged from the house and hurried to take the reins of their horses. "Good day, Captain Scipio."

"Good day . . ." Tavi quickly searched his memory "Tharis, isn't it?"

The valet gave him a quick smile and bowed his head. "Indeed, sir. The Senator is waiting for you. Go inside the front door, and you'll find him in the office on the left."

"Thank you, Tharis," Tavi said.

He glanced at Araris, who nodded. Tavi straightened his cloak and started inside, striding briskly. Araris kept pace walking slightly behind him and to the left, his eyes narrow and wary.

The entry hall of the house held several more *legionares* on guard, and the remainder of Arnos's *singulares*—a nasty-looking bunch, all in all, though none quite so unsettling as Phrygiar Navaris. Upon seeing them, she rose, slender and deadly in her all-black clothing, and approached.

"Good day, Captain," she said politely. No, thought Tavi not politely. Something about her tone seemed subtly inconsistent, as if she was speaking a language she had learned sound by sound, without knowing the meaning behind it. It was an imitation of politeness and nothing more. "If your *singulare* would be so kind as to wait here, the Senator is expecting you."

"Sir," Araris said quietly. It was as close to making a protest as he ever came.

"I'm sure the Senator won't mind if you take position outside the office door," Tavi told him.

Navaris gave them a narrow glance, and said, "Not that it would matter where he was standing, if it came to that."

Araris paused at that and turned very deliberately to stare at the cutter. She returned the stare in kind.

"You're probably right," Tavi said. "After all, there are five of you and only one of him. That's a serious mismatch." He took off his cloak and tossed it at Navaris's chest, as if she was a mere attendant. "So why don't you run along and get another five or six. That should make things even."

The woman caught the cloak on pure reflex, and her flat somehow reptilian eyes flickered with a sudden, incompre hensible light. Tavi ignored her and strode past her to the indicated doorway. Araris followed him, glanced around inside the room after Tavi stepped into it, and took up a position immediately outside the office.

Arnos sat at a desk, reading from the top of a stack of papers. "Captain, come in."

Tavi strode to the front of Arnos's desk and saluted. "Reporting as ordered, sir."

Arnos said nothing. He read to the bottom of his current page, flipped it to the bottom of the stack, and only then looked up at Tavi. He just stared for a moment, and rather pointedly did not invite him to sit. After a long silence, Arnos said, "I ordered you to hold back, Captain. You were our reserve force."

"Yes, sir," Tavi said. "There was no time to consult with you while the Guard was engaged. I saw that the leading elements of the Guard needed support and provided it as best I could."

Arnos gave him a wintry little smile. "Really. To reach the tops of those bluffs, one must ride nearly three miles to the east, and a mile and a half to the west before usable ascents can be found. Which means your units had to cover twice that distance to reach the Canim positions on the bluffs. Which means that you had to have dispatched them almost the moment fighting began."

Obviously, thought Tavi. But that wasn't the sort of remark one could make to a superior officer without making him look like the ass he was. Tavi remained silent.

Arnos snorted a moment later. "Granted, I'm glad they were there when we needed them. But I was counting on your support to be available at need. If the enemy had approached with a more extensive force, for example, I might have needed the First Aleran to reinforce the assault, or redeploy to hold off the second force."

"And the First Aleran would have been there, sir," Tavi replied. "Minus two alae of our auxiliaries and a single infantry cohort."

Arnos tilted his head to one side. "Your howling barbarians, you mean?"

Tavi reminded himself not to be goaded by such an obvious attempt before he replied. "The Marat cavalry, yes, sir."

Arnos made a tent of his fingers and frowned at Tavi. "I was given to understand that they went to battle almost entirely naked. Men and women alike."

"Marat can tolerate greater extremes of temperature than the average Aleran, sir. In their homelands, they generally wear a breechcloth and find it sufficient."

"Mmm," Arnos said, imbuing the sound with skepticism. "How did you convince them to wear uniforms?"

"The Marat have very formal cultural conventions with regards to the giving of gifts, sir. If one is given a gift and does not put it to use, it is considered a kind of insult to the gift-giver. So I went around to each of the Marat who had come to support the First Aleran and personally gave them their uniform and armor." He shrugged. "They have to wear it now, or they'll be insulting me. They're too polite to do that."

Arnos shook his head again. "One might question your judgment, Captain, in sending a crowd of savages on such a critical mission."

"One might question my judgment in sending anyone at all, sir, given my orders. I was confident they would do their job. And they did."

The Senator gave him a flat look for several seconds, then waved a hand, as if brushing away a tendril of smoke or an annoying insect. "The infantry cohort you sent to the opposite bluff. How did they arrive so quickly?"

"That was our mounted infantry cohort, sir," Tavi said. "The one I mentioned at the meeting."

"Ah," Arnos said. "I suppose that today, the concept appears to have been proven somewhat useful."

"That's why we put them together, sir," Tavi replied. "Increased tactical options."

Arnos grimaced. "I disapprove of such . . . unconventional stratagems, Captain. Alera's Legions have kept her safe and growing for more than a thousand years. Their methods have stood the test of time and proven themselves over and over again. I'm not opposed to intelligent innovation, mind you, but it's an incredible arrogance to declare the proven methods of a thousand years insufficient, then to employ untested theories of combat when any weakness in those theories will cost men their lives."

Tavi had to force himself not to retort that his "untested" theories had helped them survive for more than two years, and that his own forces had taken but seven casualties today, none of them fatal, while the Guard's Legions had lost nearly seven percent of their total numbers. "Yes, sir," he said.

"In addition, this violation of your orders is a serious matter. The chain of command must be preserved at all costs. If officers begin to lose their discipline, begin picking and choosing which orders they will obey, it is only a matter of time until such behavior spreads to the ranks—and then we have no Legion. Only a mob of brigands. Do you understand?"

"I understand, sir," Tavi said.

"That said . . ." Arnos shook his head and sighed. "Your display of initiative saved men's lives today, Captain. So I'm going to overlook your disobedience." His eyes hardened. "Once."

Tavi nodded. "Yes, sir."

Arnos picked up another piece of paper from the desk, folded it in thirds, and held it out. Tavi took it.

"Your orders," the Senator said.

"Yes, sir."

"Dismissed."

Tavi saluted and turned on a heel to march out. Just as he reached the door, Arnos said, "Captain."

Tavi turned. "Sir."

Arnos said, "Captain Nalus asked me to thank you for sending your Tribune Medica and the First Aleran's healers up to assist with the wounded. They saved a good many lives that might otherwise have been lost."

"No thanks are necessary, sir." He paused for a beat and added, "After all, we're all on the same side here."

Arnos flipped over the next page on his stack with rather more force than necessary. "That will be all, Captain."

"Yes, sir," Tavi said, and left the office. Araris fell into step behind him as Tavi stalked from the home and back out toward the horses.

"What's that?" Araris asked quietly, as they mounted.

"Our orders," Tavi said. He fought down the sick feeling in his stomach as he unfolded the piece of paper and scanned over it. His horse danced restlessly in place as he did. "Oh," he said. "Oh. Great furies."

Araris frowned and tilted his head slightly.

"He's putting us in charge of the civilians," Tavi said quietly. "The First Aleran is to march them to a field just east of here. And . . ."

His voice broke, and he couldn't recover it. He shook his head and passed the paper over to the *singulare*. He didn't watch Araris read it. He couldn't take his eyes from the families huddling together on the stones of the square, pale, silent, and terrified.

Araris's voice emerged soft with shock and disbelief as he read the last few words of the orders aloud. "There," he said, "to be executed."

ᴄᴏᴏᴏᴏ⊶CHAPTER 13

"Are you quite sure they must come off?" asked the First Lord. "It really seems that it would be more comfortable to leave them on."

They had stopped beside an old and seldom-used trail to take a drink from a convenient spring—and Amara had noted that Gaius had been concealing a limp while the small party's steps had quickened over the last few yards. Now, the First Lord sat on a camp stool Bernard had assembled, and the big woodsman knelt before the most powerful man in Alera, unlacing the man's boots.

"I'm certain, sire," Bernard rumbled. "Sore feet are nothing to take lightly—especially not with so much ground still to cover."

"This is somewhat embarrassing, I confess," Gaius said. "I

have even increased the amount of walking I have done over the past several months, to prepare for this."

"Walking up stairs and over paving stones is a far cry from a cross-country march, sire," Bernard rumbled. His nostrils flared, and he shook his head. "I'm going to slide the boot off now. I can smell some blood, so the stocking might stick. Point your toe, sire, and I'll have it off as quick as I can."

The First Lord grimaced and nodded. "Aye, let's have it done."

Without being asked, Amara moved to stand behind Gaius and brace her hands on his shoulders, steadying him. It was a somewhat startling feeling. Though the First Lord was as hale a man for his years as could be found in Alera, and though he looked like a man in his forties gone to early silver, the flesh of his shoulders felt thin and somehow frail. Amara felt her touch grow cautious. The last thing the Realm needed was for her to accidentally dislocate Gaius's shoulders while Bernard attempted to put his feet right.

The boot stuck, and it was only after a few moments of effort, some careful twisting, and a hiss of pain from Gaius that Bernard was able to get the boot off his foot. As he had predicted, the pale stocking beneath was dark with blood.

Bernard took a deep breath and frowned thoughtfully. Then he looked up at Amara, and said, "Get the cooking pot and fill it with water, if you would, Countess."

There was something tense about the way he held his head, Amara could tell. She paused for a moment and frowned at him, her own expression questioning.

"The water, Countess," Bernard repeated, his voice steady. "I'll need to wet the stockings before I can take them off and see how bad it is."

She gave him a frown, but fetched the pot and headed for the stream as he had bid her. It took him another quarter of an hour to have both of Gaius's feet bare and wiped clean with a cloth, and to inspect the damage. He sat back a moment later, frowning.

"How bad?" Gaius asked.

Bernard looked steadily at him for a moment, before he

said, "I've seen worse. But they're blistered badly. How long have they been paining you, sire?"

"At my age, you hardly notice one pain amidst all the rest," Gaius replied. "The first day wasn't too bad. They weren't comfortable last night, but they didn't get bad until this morning."

Bernard nodded. "The real concern is infection. If we're early enough to stop that, we should be able to handle the rest easily enough."

"Quite embarrassing," Gaius muttered, staring down at his swollen ankles. "Sore feet. This is hardly dignified."

"Travel sores are no respecters of persons, sire," Bernard said. "First thing, let's get you on the ground with your feet up. It will help reduce the swelling and some of the discomfort."

"That would be most appreciated, Count Bernard." Gaius sighed. With the woodsman's help, the First Lord settled himself on the ground, his feet propped up on the stool, where he frowned at them in disapproval while gnawing an apple.

Bernard dumped out the water and went to the spring to refill it, and Amara went with him.

"How bad?" she asked quietly.

He shook his head. "I've seen worse—once. On a Legion runner who had enough metalcrafting to ignore the pain and not enough sense to know he shouldn't. He took infection so badly even my sister couldn't help him. He lost the foot, and the fever burned out most of his wits."

Amara bit her lip and brushed her hair back from her forehead. "That bad?"

Bernard grimaced. "We got to the First Lord more quickly—though great furies know what might have happened if you hadn't spotted him limping."

"Quickly enough?"

"Amara . . ." He sighed. "I don't know."

Amara took a deep breath and nodded. "What can we do?"

"We can have him craft the wounds closed," Bernard said.

Amara shook her head. "No. He can't. Any of his crafting at all will give our position away and make the mission a failure."

Bernard gave her a direct look. "So will his maiming or death, love."

Amara glared at him for a moment, but looked away and shook her head. "Is he in any immediate danger?"

Bernard stood up with the pot full. "He's not going to pitch over dead any moment now, no. If he does take fever, it will take some time to kill him. Days, probably, maybe longer."

"Then we have some time," Amara said.

"We might," Bernard said, "but then again, we might not. An infection could be taking hold while we stand here talking." Bernard folded his arms. "This is a humble little wound. But it doesn't care who he is. It's capable of killing him if he doesn't receive proper medical attention."

Amara folded her arms close to her belly and frowned down at the stream.

"Let me put it this way," Bernard said slowly. He turned to face Amara full on, planting his feet at shoulder's width. "It is beyond foolishness to risk the First Lord's life on something this trivial. I won't allow it."

Amara stared at her husband's face for a moment. "Excuse me?"

"I won't allow it," he repeated, his tone gentle and immovable. "I'll give away our presence myself if I must."

Amara forced herself to keep a hot answer from flying from her lips. "Bernard," she said quietly, "that's treason."

"Not the way I see it," he said. "I'm sworn to protect the Crown. The oath never said anything about protecting the Crown from anyone except himself. You swore a similar oath, I believe."

"You can't make a decision like this," Amara sputtered.

"I already have," he replied. "It's been a long time since Gaius was on campaign, and you've never been on one. You've never seen men die of infection." He looked down and away. "It robs them of everything, Amara. All dignity. All strength. They waste away, so fast you can almost see it happening." He shuddered. "The Realm is barely holding together as it is. Should anything happen to Gaius, should he die like that . . ."

She bit her lip and touched his shoulder. "He knows that there are risks, love. He has chosen to face them."

"He is responsible for more lives than his own," Bernard responded. "What is so important that it warrants risking his *life*?"

"I don't know," Amara replied quietly. "He didn't tell me."

Bernard shot her an incredulous look. "You don't even know why we're doing this?"

She shook her head.

"Then bloody crows, Amara, why are you opposing me?"

"Because I trust his judgment," Amara said quietly. "Because I swore an oath." She paused briefly, and added, "Just as you did."

Bernard grunted, as if to acknowledge the touch.

Amara leaned in close against him, and he slid an arm quietly around her. She laid her cheek against his chest. "If he didn't tell you, either, why are you here?"

Bernard's voice rumbled in his chest, a pleasant buzzing sensation in her ear. "He said he needed a skilled woodsman and scout, someone he could trust." He breathed out a little through his nose, a wisp of a laugh. "And he said you'd be there. I suppose he knew it would be reason enough for me."

Amara lifted her head suddenly to stare intently into her husband's face. "Just as he knew that once we were back together, I would be too distracted by you to ask too many questions." She felt a wry smile twist her mouth. "Until it was too late to change our minds, I suppose."

Bernard frowned, and squinted back toward where Gaius sat, and said, "We're not going a step farther until I know exactly what we're walking into."

Amara frowned in thought for a moment, and spoke slowly. "I suppose my duty would be to oppose you putting an end to this mission. Strictly speaking."

"You did that once before," Bernard replied, his eyes brightening with brief amusement. "You'll recall how it worked out." His expression grew more serious. "You couldn't stop me from compromising us, Amara. And without using furycraft, I doubt he could do it, either. Even if he could walk right now."

Amara nodded slowly, "Just as well, perhaps."

"Oh?"

"It gives us a lever to use on him." She glanced back at the First Lord. "He keeps secrets purely as a reflex action, these days. I can't serve or protect him if I'm kept blind and wandering in the dark. But . . ."

Bernard found her hand with his, and squeezed gently. "But what?"

She felt her lips tighten. "It just doesn't feel right. So many have turned against him. Fidelias . . ."

Tears filled her eyes in approximate tempo with a surge of heated anger, as she thought of her treacherous mentor, and it became impossible to speak.

"It isn't the same, love," he told her quietly. "You're trying to protect him and using your best judgment. It isn't the same thing at all."

"I hope you're right," she said quietly. She shook her head, blinking the tears away before they could fall. Then she nodded once, composed herself, and strode back over to Gaius, Bernard in step beside her.

The First Lord looked back and forth between their expressions, then said, "Ah."

Amara came to a stop before him, and knelt down to put her eyes more or less on level with his own. "Sire, Count Calderon . . ."

He lifted a hand with a little, impatient wave, and glanced at Bernard. "We're not walking another mile until you know what we're getting into? Something like that?"

Bernard snorted through his nose. "Not another step, actually, sire."

Gaius winced, shifting one of his legs. "Is it that bad?"

Bernard approached as well, kneeling down and brushing away a layer of forest detritus with one hand, revealing a number of small white-and-pink crystals. He dropped them into the pan and began swirling the water as he spoke. "Without proper watercrafting? It has the potential to be very bad, sire, yes."

Gaius made a disgusted noise. "I suppose I'd be a fool to bring along an expert woodsman only to ignore his advice."

Bernard's mouth quirked up at one corner. "I'd never say that, sire."

Gaius's teeth flashed white for a moment. "Not in so many words, anyway, eh?" He studied his own raw and bloodied feet. "Your recommendation involves my crafting the injuries away, I take it."

"Or flying to someone who can," Bernard said.

"What are my chances if I don't?"

"If we're in time to prevent any infection, I can probably take care of it on my own. If we're too late . . ." He shrugged. "You'll sicken, take a fever, and eventually die. Our best hope is that you will retain the ability to rectify the problem on your own before the fever takes you too far to sustain such a crafting."

"Which would compromise our mission," Gaius said quietly. "Rendering it an unacceptable option."

"Sire," Amara said. "Your untimely death would be no more acceptable."

The First Lord glanced at her. "Untimely? Yes. But that seems rather unavoidable at this point." He wiggled the toes of one foot and winced. "No infection has set in as yet. I believe our best option is to maintain a positive frame of mind and proceed."

"It's a very real risk, sire," Bernard said, and there was nothing subservient in his voice. "What could possibly be so important that it warrants such a risk to yourself and to the Realm?"

Gaius frowned at Bernard. Then he tilted his head, brow furrowed. "Well, this is an interesting iteration of the *ludus* board. A Steadholder with more power than a paired Cursor and First Lord. I can't stop you from acting without revealing myself, and I am not at all certain that Amara could do it, either."

Bernard nodded. "I've got you by the balls, sire."

Gaius, now leaning up on his elbows, let his head fall back with a brief, tense laugh. "So it would seem. Very well. We will speak of my purpose—after which, we will proceed at our best pace."

Bernard frowned. "I can't promise that."

"We will," Gaius said, and there was a cold flicker at the back of his eyes. "This is necessary, Count. It *will* be done." His voice went quiet. "And as formidable as you are in your current position—yet do I advise you not to test me."

Bernard's hands froze for a moment, as he crumbled some kind of herb into the salted water in the pot. It was the only sign of his discomfort. "I can only promise that I will act on my conscience."

"Well enough," Gaius replied. With Bernard's help, he returned to his seat upon the camp stool and slipped his battered feet into the pot. He let out a hiss of pain and shuddered a few times, but then his breathing steadied. A moment later, he opened his eyes, and Amara pressed a cup of bitter willow tea into his hands. He nodded his thanks to her. "This touches upon your last visit to Kalare, actually."

Amara lifted an eyebrow. "In what way? Not for familiarity, I am sure. We only covered the last few miles on the ground."

"Similar motivation," the First Lord said. "You remember the necessity for bringing Lady Placida back whole and unharmed?"

Amara nodded. "There are several dangerous furies back in her lands that are held in check by her will. Had she died, they would have been loosed on her people."

"Precisely," Gaius said. "And Kalarus, whom I will never fault for lack of ambition, has done something almost as brilliant as it is insane—he's intentionally stirred up furies of terrible power of his own and bound them to *his* will in the same way."

Amara took in a deep breath. "He hopes to preserve his life?"

"Not at all," Gaius said in a sober tone. "He's too proud to suffer through imprisonment, and he knows that we could assume control of those furies once he was taken away and we had time to work. His goal is much simpler, Countess. He hopes to drag as many lives as possible into the underworld with him—preferably including my own."

Bernard scratched at his beard, frowning. "Sire . . . what kind of furies are you talking about here?"

Gaius took a slow breath, and said, "One of the Great Furies, Count."

Amara frowned. "Great furies . . . what . . . I mean, there are actually . . . ?"

Gaius's mouth gained an edge of grim amusement. "You

think we swear by them simply for show? No. They exist, the Great Furies. A dozen or so that I'm aware of. Creatures so old and vast that our entire existence upon this world, a thousand years of growth and strife, is less than the span of an eyeblink to them."

Bernard's frown deepened as he took a clean cloth and began washing the First Lord's feet as gently as he could. "And Kalarus can control this thing?"

"Not even remotely," Gaius said. "But he can annoy it, arousing its wrath—and he can delay its response for a time. When he ceases to do so, Kalus will spend his wrath upon anyone it meets."

"Kalus?" Amara asked. "Like Mount Kalus?"

"For which Kalare itself is named," Gaius said, nodding. "Though it is not only a mountain, but an ancient fire-mountain. It has not spoken in Aleran memory, but Kalarus has stirred it up. When he dies, Kalus will burst free of the mountain and bathe the land in fire." He leaned forward, meeting Bernard's eyes, then Amara's, in turn. "If I let the Legions besiege Kalare, it will mean more deaths fighting on the approach. It will mean that all of Kalarus's forces will have fallen back to the city. It means that an entire campaign's worth of refugees will have fallen back with them."

"Bloody crows," Bernard breathed. "He means to make a bier of allies, enemies, and subjects alike. Of the city itself."

"I can intercede," Gaius said, "but only if I can physically approach to within a few miles and clear sight of Mount Kalus." He took a deep breath. "If I don't intervene, it will mean more lives senselessly lost to Kalarus's spite." His eyes glittered, cold and hard. "I won't have it. Not in my Realm."

"So," Amara said quietly. "The plan is to get you in close enough to deprive Kalarus of his funeral pyre?"

The First Lord nodded. "I never truly understood how horrible life was in Kalare, how he had transformed his lands into a nightmare of slaves and fear. I failed his people. Now he threatens to burn them all alive. I will not allow them to die at the will of that madman."

Bernard looked up at the First Lord, his eyes steady.

"Count Calderon," Gaius said calmly. "Please believe me

when I say that I *will* proceed. Either with you—or through you."

Bernard regarded him without blinking. Then he said, "Your feet are swollen, and those boots aren't going to fit. We'll need to let you rest for a day or so, and I'll try to make your footwear a little more comfortable before we move again." He turned to Amara. "Can you find us a spot to camp, out of sight of the trail? There's no sense loitering here until someone stumbles into us."

Amara rose and went to Bernard's side. She touched his shoulder briefly, and said, "Thank you."

Gaius exhaled slowly, and bowed his head gently to the Count of Calderon. "Aye, Bernard. Thank you."

Bernard glanced from Gaius to Amara, frowning. But he said nothing.

CHAPTER 14

"This is outrageous!" Maximus sputtered, his words oddly flat-sounding within the windcrafting that kept their conversation private. His horse danced nervously at the fury in his voice. "We should hand the son of a bitch his *head* for *suggesting* such a thing!"

"Unfortunately it isn't a suggestion," Crassus murmured. Max's slender brother rode on Tavi's other side and was a good deal less ruffled. "It's an order."

Max's hand flew to the hilt of his sword. "I've got the proper response to that order, right here."

Crassus cast his brother a resigned look, and said, "You aren't helping."

"Crassus is right, Max," Tavi said quietly. "This isn't a problem we can hack to pieces."

"Just you watch me," Max growled. His horse half reared

in response, one hoof striking out as if to crush some unseen foe. Acteon snorted at these antics, but his pace never wavered, and Tavi was grateful that his mount did not seem inclined to the same spontaneous displays of physical prowess of most warhorses. Max calmed his horse with an expert's casual skill, and said, "I'm not letting anyone kill those townies."

Tavi glanced over his shoulder, where the prisoners were being walked out of Othos as ordered, surrounded by Valiar Marcus's Prime Cohort. Tavi had deliberately ordered a slow pace, but some of the elderly among the prisoners were having trouble even so. He caught Marcus's eye and flicked a signal at the First Spear. Marcus slowed the pace even more.

Just as well, Tavi thought. It would give him a little more time to figure a way out of this mess.

"We aren't going through with it," Max growled. "Right?"

Tavi shook his head slowly, more a gesture of irritation than anything else. "The children are clear, at least."

Crassus frowned in thought, then glanced at Tavi. "Age of accountability?"

"Exactly," Tavi said.

Hoofbeats approached. Araris came trotting down the line of horses and offered a thick book to Tavi.

"What's that?" Max asked.

Tavi held up the book, titled, simply, *Military Law*. Then he flipped it open and started searching for the proper reference.

Crassus smiled. "You came prepared, eh?"

"Gift from Cyril," Tavi replied.

"Age of what?" Max said.

"Accountability, you illiterate thug," Crassus said. He flashed a small smile at Max. "Legally speaking, a child under the age of twelve dwelling in an adult's household cannot be held accountable for most crimes. Their parent or guardian is responsible for their behavior."

"So that gets the kids out of trouble," Max said.

"It isn't enough," Tavi said. "It just means we'd have to execute their parents twice." He held up the book. "Arnos has to adhere to the letter of the law. As a Legion commander in a war zone, he's got full authority to pass summary judgment on enemy troops and support personnel."

"With no trial?" Max asked.

"Not if they aren't Citizens," Tavi said. "And Arnos is interpreting the definition of support personnel to include any Aleran who has cooperated with the Canim in any fashion. He says the fact that they let those Canim into their town makes them traitors."

"Against Nasaug's army? They had no choice," Max spat. "Look at them."

Crassus shook his head. "Legally speaking, they had a choice. They could have fought the Canim and died."

"That's suicide."

"But legal." Crassus frowned at Tavi. "Captain, do you think the Senator's sentence will stand up before a tribunal of review?"

"He isn't ordering the execution of any Citizens," Tavi said, scanning pages in the book. He found the proper section and it confirmed his fears. "Crows. Technically, he's acting within the bounds of the law. So it will come down to politics."

Max growled. "If he's successful against the Canim, his judgment will probably be supported."

"And if the campaign goes badly," Crassus said, "his enemies will use it to eviscerate his career."

Tavi ground his teeth. "Not that it will matter to the people of Othos by then."

"There's got to be something we can do, Captain," Max protested.

Tavi grimaced. "If Arnos had put half as much planning into the assault on Othos as he had into this, he'd have taken the town without a man lost." He snapped the book shut rather harder than was necessary and looked at Max. "Legally speaking, my only options are to carry out the order or resign."

"Which is what Arnos wants," Crassus said quietly.

Tavi glanced aside at Crassus, surprised that he would bring up the point. The young Knight Commander had rather pointedly remained entirely silent during any conversation touching upon politics more than indirectly. It was hardly surprising, considering that Crassus's mother had betrayed them all at the Elinarch and his uncle was leading a rebellion that had ground on for most of two years. His father, High Lord Antillus, commanded fully half the forces of the Shieldwall, the vast edifice that walled away the threat of the Icemen in the savage north, and was one of the most respected men in Alera.

All in all, that made Antillus Crassus into a potential wildfire, politically speaking. Tavi had sent the First Lord strongly favorable reports regarding the young lord's skill, capability, and loyalty. If he hadn't, Gaius might well have made sure that a young man with such volatile potential was transferred to a less inflammable post.

All of that meant that Crassus had tactfully remained aloof from the intrigue that touched upon the First Aleran, except where it directly affected his ability to perform his duties. It had not meant, however, that he had closed his eyes to what was happening, and Tavi's respect for Max's younger half brother went up another notch.

"Which is probably what he wants," Tavi agreed quietly. "Either way, he's arguably within his rights, and I've got no legal recourse to refuse the order."

Max let out a chuckle with a hard edge on it. "Like you've ever let little things like laws get in the way."

Tavi frowned. It was true enough, he supposed, but that was before he'd been made aware of the fact that he might be the one expected to uphold and defend those laws one day. Law was what separated civilization from barbarism. Law was what enabled a society to protect the weak from the strong who would abuse or destroy them.

He looked over his shoulder at the poor people of Othos.

The law had been made to defend them. Not to murder them.

"We might have to get creative," he said quietly. He squinted up at the sky. "What I wouldn't give for a storm right now."

Max gave Crassus a speculative look, but the young lord shook his head. "Arnos lost some of his Knights Aeris, but the rest of them would sense it if we tampered with the weather."

Tavi nodded. "We need to stretch this out until dark."

Max grunted. "Why?"

"The Canim like to operate at night. Once night has fallen, who knows? We might be attacked by a force of raiders, and in the confusion the prisoners might escape."

Max pursed his lips, then broke into a smile. "Those crow-begotten Canim ruin everything, Captain."

Crassus frowned. "We'll be ordered to pursue them. There's no way that group could escape any competent pursuit."

"I know," Tavi replied. "We do it anyway."

Crassus rode in silence for a few pensive seconds. "I'm with you, sir. But all you'll do is delay things by a day or so. At most. Then you'll be right back where you are now."

"A lot can change in a day or so," Tavi said, quietly. "Either of you have a better idea?"

Neither spoke, and Tavi closed his eyes for a moment, ordering his thoughts. "The first thing we need is time. We're going to double-check all of the prisoners' identities."

"Sir?" Crassus said.

"Arnos can't possibly fault me being careful to make sure we aren't subjecting a Citizen to an injustice."

Crassus narrowed his eyes and began nodding. "And he'll figure you're doing it to protect yourself from legal consequences. Because that's why he'd do it."

Tavi nodded. "Crassus, confirm their identities and be thorough. Make it take until sundown. Go."

"Yes, sir," Crassus said. The young commander banged a fist to his chest and turned his horse, nudging it into a rather listless trot toward the prisoners.

"Max," Tavi said. "Get Schultz, and tell him to pick two spears of men who can keep their mouths shut. You'll take them and stage a raid tonight, once it's full dark. Something noisy but not too spectacular, and leave a couple of the Canim weapons we've recovered lying around. Arnos will have sent some men to keep an eye on things by then. Handle them, but don't kill anyone if you can possibly avoid it."

"Understood," Max said. He lowered his voice, and said, "Crassus is right, you know. The Senator will only send you after them and relieve you for incompetence when you don't bring them back and carry out the order."

"Let me worry about that, Max. Get moving. I'm going to send word to Cyril to find out if—"

"Captain," Araris interrupted.

Tavi glanced back at the *singulare*, who nodded down the line. Tavi turned to see Kitai thundering up the column toward him, with Enna and a dozen Marat trailing her. As they slowed, Max released the windcrafting that surrounded them, saluted Tavi, and turned his horse to head back down the column.

The Marat came to a halt in a blowing, disorderly clump all around them as Kitai drew her horse up beside Tavi's, her lovely face expressionless. The Marat called to one another, trading what were apparently gibes and boasts in their own tongue. Several of the younger riders, as restless and energetic as their mounts, continued dancing in circles around the larger group, their horses shaking their heads and rearing from time to time.

Tavi turned intent eyes to Kitai right away. It might have looked sloppy and exuberant, but the Marat had long since worked out their own method to veil conversations from any windcrafters who might be attempting to listen from afar.

Kitai's leg bumped against Tavi's as their horses walked, and he could sense the tension in her. They stretched out their hands to one another at the same time and briefly entwined their fingers. *"Chala,"* Kitai said. "I worried for you during the battle."

"You worried for *me*?" Tavi asked. He couldn't help but smile a little. "You were the one leading an attack on an enemy position."

Kitai sniffed. "That was nothing. I didn't get close enough to lift a blade." She cast a general glower around them at the Marat of the Horse Clan. "They got there first."

"Still. It was well-done."

She arched a pale eyebrow at him. "Yes. Of course it was." Her haughty expression faltered, though, and she glanced around them, making sure that no one was close enough to overhear them through the cacophony of the Horse Clan. "There is something you must see."

Tavi nodded at once, flashed a hand signal to the First Spear, and turned his horse out of the slow column of marching men. Kitai's horse wheeled perfectly in time with his, and he supposed that an outsider looking on would have thought that he was leading her and not the other way around. The Marat escort joined them as they cantered to the east and away from the column.

They rode for most of two miles, by Tavi's estimate, the sharp rise of the bluff on their right, until they reached a small copse that had grown up where a burbling spring spilled water down from the higher ground. Two Marat horses were grazing on fresh spring grass outside the trees.

The little company rode up to the copse and dismounted. Tavi passed Acteon's reins over to Enna, and followed Kitai into the trees.

"We took a prisoner, *chala*," she said without preamble, her pace never slowing. "An Aleran. A messenger."

Tavi hissed in sudden excitement. "Yes? What did he say?"

"That he would speak only to you."

They brushed through a few yards of undersized evergreens that hid whatever was beyond them from view. When they emerged, Tavi found himself in a small clearing, where a pair of Marat warriors stood with bows in hand and arrows on strings, calmly regarding a man seated on the ground between them.

Tavi blinked and lifted his eyebrows, recognizing the man—the rebel scout he'd subdued back at his aborted ambush of the Canim column. The man was wearing the same clothes, minus all his gear, which had been placed in a neat pile several feet away from him.

The scout glanced up at him and blinked twice before his own eyes widened in recognition. "You," he said. "Bloody crows."

Tavi felt one corner of his mouth lift in a smile. "Good afternoon," he said. "We've got to stop meeting like this."

The scout looked uncertain for a moment, then barked out a short laugh. "Aye, m'lord."

"I'm no lord," Tavi replied. "Rufus Scipio, Captain of the First Aleran."

The man bowed his head slightly. "Captain. My name is Durias. I'm a centurion of the First Freehold Legion auxiliaries."

"Freehold, centurion?" Tavi asked.

"The capital city of Free Alera, Captain." He lifted his chin with a slight but undeniable glitter of defiance in his eyes. "Our capital. The freemen's capital."

Tavi nodded. "I see. I'm told you bear a message."

The man nodded and slipped a hand inside his tunic.

Both Marat drew their bows, and the deadly steel tips gleamed as they oriented on Durias. In the same instant, Kitai's sword hissed from its sheath.

Durias froze, his eyes very wide. He licked his lips, glancing back and forth between the weapons and Tavi.

"Slowly, centurion," Tavi said, keeping his voice calm. "You'll have to excuse my friends. We've had problems with more than one assassin, and they tend to err on the side of caution."

Durias swallowed and—very slowly—withdrew a small bundle of cloth from beneath his tunic. He bowed his head and offered it out to Tavi on both of his upturned palms. "Nasaug bade me give you this," he said quietly.

Kitai stalked forward and took the cloth, then returned with it to Tavi's side. Tavi frowned down at the cloth. It looked vaguely familiar. Then he realized what he was holding. A plain, worn tunic—specifically, Ehren's tunic, the one he'd been wearing when Tavi had last seen him.

Tavi's fingers trembled a little in their hurry to unfold the cloth, revealing the tunic's contents. Two *ludus* pieces resided within. One was a white *legionare*, the missing piece from his own set. The second was a Knight of black stone, from a much larger, less finely carved set.

Tavi chewed on his lower lip and nodded absently to the Marat guards. They eased back on their bowstrings, relaxing once more, their expressions never changing.

"I recognize it," Tavi said quietly. "Did he send anything else with you?"

Durias nodded. "Nasaug said to tell you that in most games, this would be a poor trade, but that it is one he is willing to offer, provided you—and only you—come to speak to him."

Tavi frowned at the messenger. "Where? When?"

"Immediately, Captain," Durias said. "He is nearby. I am to lead you to him."

"And if I refuse?"

Durias smiled a little and spread his hands. "Then Nasaug will have exchanged a *legionare* for a Knight, and profited thereby."

Tavi considered the pieces on Ehren's tunic for a moment. "Nasaug plays *ludus* well," he said. "Surely he would think me a fool to sacrifice a First Lord for the sake of a Knight."

"He offers you safe conduct, Captain."

Tavi folded the tunic back over the pieces. "And what does he offer as a guarantee?"

Durias regarded Tavi steadily. "His word."

Tavi drew in a deep breath. This could very well be a trap. The Canim were cunning and ruthless when it came to warfare. It was, in fact, a point of pride to them. In war, there was no such thing as cheating, no rules, no mercy. Tavi had no doubt that Nasaug would not hesitate to deny his enemy a valuable resource like Ehren—unless there was a greater gain to be had in keeping him alive.

Simultaneously, though, the Canim of the warrior caste seemed to adhere to a rigid standard of honor. They respected strength, courage, and skill, and Tavi had somehow managed to demonstrate all three during the first desperate days of battle at the Elinarch.

Tavi clenched a fist in frustration. This wasn't merely an offer to parley. It was a test of his commitment to the concept. Nasaug would not make a second offer. To say nothing of the fact that Ehren's life hung in the balance.

Tavi could not afford to let this opportunity pass by, and Nasaug knew it.

Which made it a perfect trap.

Which, in turn, made it a perfect test.

Which made it an opportunity he could not afford to . . .

Tavi shook his head before the circular logic made him dizzy.

He had to try.

"*Chala,*" Kitai whispered, brushing her fingers against his arm. "Are you sure?"

He turned to look her in the eye. "No."

"But you'll go anyway."

"They have Ehren," he said.

She scowled at him, clearly unhappy with his response. "This is foolish."

"Maybe," he agreed.

"Stubborn. Proud. Stupid." She sighed and leaned forward to kiss him lightly on the mouth, her lips warm and sweet. She settled back again, and said, "I would hit you on the head with a rock and drag you away from this. But it would only shatter the rock."

Tavi gave her a quick, warm smile, and turned to the captive scout. "Very well, centurion, get your gear. Whatever happens, this ought to be an interesting conversation."

·◻◻◻◻◻· CHAPTER 15

Durias set off at a quick pace, and the former slave's stocky body moved with surprising grace and speed over the open ground. If Tavi had not been mounted, he would barely have been able to keep the pace, despite having kept himself in training for overland marches beside his own men. As it was, Acteon followed Durias at a lazy canter, and the miles passed by. The bluff beside them gradually dwindled to a steep hillside, then blended into the gently rolling terrain of the Vale.

After about an hour, Durias swerved to the right, leading Tavi into a young wood. They passed through it and descended into a narrow ravine that Tavi could not even see until Durias stepped into it. The ravine wound along an ancient streambed, and the roots of trees dangled out of the rough earth-and-stone walls on either side of him. The path at the bottom of the ravine divided several times, and finally ascended into an old-growth wood, completely enclosed by a canopy of fresh spring leaves. The earth was covered with low grasses, and those sparse enough. Shafts of sunlight peeked through the trees, here and there, and the sound of the wind in the leaves was a constant, murmuring susurrus.

Nasaug was waiting for them.

Tavi recognized the enormous, black-furred Cane at once. Most of nine feet tall, even in his hunched, casual posture, the Cane wore armor of bloodred steel, and bore an enormous, slightly curved sword in a scabbard at his side. His ears flicked forward, orienting on Tavi and Durias, and Tavi saw Nasaug's nostrils flare as he quested for their scents.

Tavi took a moment to scan his surroundings. If he needed to flee suddenly, he wanted to know which direction offered him the best chance of evading pursuit. More to the point, he was sure that Nasaug was not the only Cane present. Tavi couldn't see them, but the wolflike beings rarely operated in anything but groups.

Tavi nudged Acteon forward, and the horse snorted and tossed his head at the feral predator smell of the Cane. He sidestepped for a nervous second, but Tavi guided him forward with a light touch on the reins, and the battle-trained mount continued, until they stopped perhaps ten feet from Nasaug.

"Captain," Nasaug growled. His voice was a deep, resonant thing, though his Aleran was chewed and mangled by his fangs and jaws as he spoke it. He tilted his head slightly to the right.

"Nasaug," Tavi replied, mirroring the gesture. "Where's my man?"

The Cane's ears twitched in what Tavi recognized as a gesture of approval. Nasaug growled something under his breath, and another Cane, smaller, his fur grizzled and thick with scars, appeared from around the trunk of the tree, leading Ehren with him.

The Cursor's wrists were bound with leather straps, his shirt was smeared with grime, and there were dark circles under his eyes, but other than that he seemed whole.

Tavi reached into a pocket and withdrew the black ludus piece Nasaug had sent. He tossed it to the Canim leader, who caught it with a casual flick of one pawlike hand.

Nasaug nodded to Tavi and growled something else. The older Cane drew a knife from his belt, and Tavi felt himself tense up. His concerns were groundless. The knife parted Ehren's bonds, and then the old Cane returned it to its sheath.

"Go to your captain," Nasaug growled.

Ehren eyed him warily but walked quickly over to stand beside Tavi.

"You all right?" Tavi asked.

"Mostly embarrassed," Ehren said. "They caught me before I could approach them openly."

Tavi nodded, drew his knife from his belt, and offered the hilt to Ehren. The Cursor took it with a nod of thanks, and promptly turned to watch their backs.

"You returned a scout to me," Nasaug growled. "I return one to you. The scales between us are balanced."

"Agreed," Tavi said. "Your troops fought well today."

"We do what we must," Nasaug replied. "Why do you wish to speak with me?"

"To discuss a solution to our problems."

"Problems," Nasaug said. A bubbling snarl that was the Canim equivalent of a chuckle vibrated through the word. "Of which problem do you speak?"

"I have come to believe that our peoples are dying needlessly," Tavi replied. "This war profits neither your Realm nor mine."

"We fight for our lives, Captain," Nasaug growled. "Another day is profit enough for me."

"And we fight to defend against an invader," Tavi replied. "We both have motivation in plenty to wage a war. But it is my hope that there is mutual advantage to be gained by peace."

Nasaug's gleaming black eyes narrowed, and his ears remained perfectly still, focused on Tavi. "Explain."

"I want you to leave Alera," Tavi said. "But it makes no difference to me how you go, so long as you are gone." He gave Nasaug a small smile, showing a few teeth. "We both know that you can't hold out forever. Even if you defeat these Legions, others will be raised and sent against you. And still others will be should they fall. You're too badly outnumbered, and you know it. Sooner or later, Alera will grind you into dust."

Nasaug's chest rumbled with a warning growl—but he said nothing to contradict Tavi's statement. "I will not surrender to your kind."

"I would never ask it of you," Tavi replied.

"What, then?"

"Tell me how long it will take you to finish your ships."

Nasaug's lips peeled back from his teeth in surprise. He growled something in Canish that Tavi didn't catch, before saying, "Longer than I would prefer."

"My new commander believes you intend to employ them against Alera."

"Ships carry troops," Nasaug said. "I don't need them to take my troops to Alera. They are already here."

"You want to go home," Tavi said quietly.

Nasaug was silent for most of a minute before he answered Tavi, his rumbling voice barely audible. "Yes."

"In other words," Tavi said, "I want you gone—and you want to leave. It seems to me that we are each in a position to solve the other's problem."

"In a rational world, perhaps," Nasaug said, "but we are in Alera."

Tavi nodded. "We are. Because Sarl led your people here."

"Sarl." Nasaug's voice rumbled with harsh rage, and one of his feet flicked backward, scattering dirt and old leaves. "He was a coward and a fool."

"You never truly supported him," Tavi said. "That's why he burned your ships behind you."

Nasaug said nothing.

"Why?" Tavi asked him. "Why did you follow him here?"

"He had the proper authority. I had orders. It was my duty to follow them, no matter how insane they might seem."

"I understand," Tavi said, unable to stop a wry note from entering his voice.

"And he had . . ." Nasaug let out a growl of frustration. "There is no Aleran word. He had charge of many warrior-caste families."

"Hostages?"

Nasaug made a small slashing motion with one paw-hand. "Not the same."

Tavi frowned. "But Sarl does not command you now."

"No," Nasaug said.

"Given the chance, would you depart peacefully?"

The Cane tilted his head to one side, eyes narrowing. "Your forces have begun a war season against us. They do not seek a peace."

"What if that changed?" Tavi asked. "What if the First Lord ordered them to go no further? Would you be willing to withdraw your support from High Lord Kalarus and enter a truce until your departure?"

Again the Cane entered a pensive silence.

Tavi pressed him. "There has to be a reason Sarl did what he did, Nasaug. He loaded every boat he could find with every Cane he could find and sailed them across the full breadth of the sea to land here. He was a coward, and we both know it. He was running from something, wasn't he?"

Nasaug remained still.

"If he was running from what I think he was," Tavi said quietly, "then you and your men are badly needed at home. The Legions are coming for Mastings, Nasaug. If they take it, they will burn your ships and any hope you have of returning home. Even if they don't take it, this time, they will bleed your ranks, attack your supply lines, and hinder your shipwrights in every way they can imagine." He leaned forward, meeting the Cane's eyes. "The fastest way for you to get home with the strongest possible force is to agree to this truce."

Tavi settled slowly back in his saddle and watched Nasaug, waiting.

"Captain," he said, after a time. "You are *gadara*. But not all Alerans are."

"*Gadara*," Tavi said, frowning. "Enemy?"

Nasaug made another slashing negative gesture. "Not the same. You have my respect. But you do not lead them. You do not speak in the voice of Gaius Sextus. And your people have proven to us, many times, that they are not worthy of trust."

Tavi frowned. "How so?"

"Because you are monsters," Nasaug replied, his tone implying that he was stating the perfectly obvious. "You are worse
than starving beasts. You slaughter one another by the thousands over matters of leadership. Your people crush those without power and take whatsoever they wish from them for the
simple reason that they can." The Cane's muzzle lifted in a gesture of contempt. "You betray, enslave, and brutalize your own
kind, Aleran. Your *own*. If you treat your own folk this way,
what fool could possibly believe you would act any differently
toward mine?"

Tavi felt himself rock back a little at the vehemence in
Nasaug's voice. He had never really considered things from
that point of view. Slavery, of course, had been a problem for
years. It would likely continue to be one for years more. The
furycrafting-based system of Citizenship, title, and privilege
was utterly inflexible, and how well he had known the futility
of laboring beneath it.

Nasaug continued. "We came upon those you had enslaved
and set them free. And because we had done it, when they
sought arms to defend that freedom, we supported them. But I
know, and you know, that your Legions will not rest until they
have been destroyed—for seizing what by rights should belong to all."

"That is the way of some Alerans," Tavi replied. "It is not
my way—nor the way of my lord, Gaius Sextus."

"Perhaps not, *gadara*," Nasaug said. "But words are nothing but air."

"Unless they are followed by action," Tavi countered. "I
am here only because you gave me your word."

"I have shown you my word is good," Nasaug said.

"Then let me show you the same of mine," Tavi said.

"How?"

"What would you consider sufficient action?"

Nasaug let out a thoughtful, rumbling growl. "One whose
word I trust over my own was once a guest of honor in your
land. I am told that he is held prisoner in some stinking house
of stone in Alera Imperia."

"You mean Varg," Tavi said. "Yes. He is held prisoner."

"Varg did not behave dishonorably."

"How do you know that?" Tavi asked.

Nasaug flexed one paw-hand, extending his claws. "He is Varg."

Tavi was silent for a moment, then nodded. "He did not behave with dishonor. Quite the opposite. He warned us of the coming of a foe called the Vord."

"And he rots in a prison because of it," Nasaug snarled, baring his fangs. "Your word may be good, Captain. Perhaps we can make an arrangement whereby I can leave your haunted land peacefully. But it will not happen without Varg."

Tavi glanced down at Ehren, who shot a nervous glance up at him.

"If I bring you Varg," Tavi said quietly, "will you be willing to withdraw your strength from Kalarus? To draw back to Mastings, build your ships, and depart this land?"

Nasaug glanced aside, at the grizzled old Cane beside him. Neither of them said anything or moved, but Tavi felt sure they had communicated with one another nonetheless. Nasaug turned back to Tavi and nodded, once. "Yes. But this agreement will have no bearing on how I wage war against you. Until I see Varg and speak to him, face-to-face, your Legions will pay in blood for every step of ground they wish to take."

"I understand," Tavi said quietly. "If it can be done, it will take some time."

Nasaug nodded. "Then until that time, *gadara*, we will seek one another's throats." His fangs shone again. "Go from this place." He raised his voice, and called, in Canish, *"Do not touch him."*

"Ehren," Tavi said quietly. "Mount up behind me."

He leaned down and gave the Cursor an arm up, and Ehren scrambled up onto the saddle behind Tavi. Tavi exchanged an Aleran-style nod with Nasaug, and then turned Acteon and rode calmly and quietly from the clearing. He passed Durias, who also nodded up at him, and then they moved steadily away.

Half an hour later, as they came out onto ground Tavi recognized, he let out a slow breath and pressed Acteon into a swifter pace over open plain.

"You came here alone?" Ehren demanded. "Are you insane?"

Tavi flashed a grin back at his friend. "You're welcome."

Ehren shook his head. "I really feel I should point out that there's no way you're going to get them to release Varg."

"But Gaius can," Tavi replied. "He'll see the sense of it at once."

"If you can reach him, maybe," Ehren replied. "What if you can't?"

Tavi opened his mouth to give Ehren a sharp-edged retort—and was cut off by a sudden blast of furious wind.

Acteon reared and skittered wildly to one side as a sudden gale threw up dirt and dust, blinding them all and deafening them with its roar. Acteon lunged and bucked, panicking, and Tavi lost his seat, crashing to the ground beside Ehren.

Tavi had to squeeze his eyes almost entirely shut, but he could just barely see the gleaming forms of Knights Aeris descending around them, along with an eight-harness air coach.

The coach landed, its bearers settling it to the ground, and one of them hurried to open the door.

Phrygiar Navaris emerged from the coach, slender in black, her face set in an odd little smile. Behind her, the rest of the Senator's *singulares* also appeared, to be followed, finally, by the Senator himself.

Arnos, still in his silk robes, walked calmly over to them, flanked by his bodyguards. He stood over Tavi for a moment, a chilly little smile of satisfaction on his face.

"And now we know how your supposedly gallant Legion managed to survive for so long against so many Canim," he said quietly. "You've been conspiring with them the whole while, Scipio."

"That isn't true," Tavi snarled. "And you know it."

Arnos swept his hand around at the circle of Knights Aeris. "I know no such thing. You were seen meeting with one of the Canim officers, and I have better than a dozen witnesses who will attest to it. Furthermore, you were engaging in parley with the enemy against my express orders to avoid giving any impression of weakness or lack of resolve on our part."

Arnos lifted his chin, staring down at Tavi. "It gives me no pleasure to do this, Rufus Scipio. But I place you under arrest for refusing to follow a direct order of your superior officer in time of war. You will be taken to the nearest stockade and held there until such time as a military tribunal can be assembled for your trial."

Tavi just stared at Arnos, shocked by what he was hearing, cursing himself for being careless. He'd warned Max that Arnos would have had watchers in place by that evening. He should have been smart enough to realize that Arnos already had *him* under surveillance—probably by several of his Knights Aeris, hidden behind crafted veils.

He'd taken a chance and gotten burned.

He'd failed.

"Navaris," Arnos said. "Take the prisoner into custody." An unmistakable glitter of malice danced across his eyes. "Find someplace to lock him away until we can find time to try him for treason."

◁◻◻◻◻▷ CHAPTER 16

Valiar Marcus glared at the young mother who had approached them from the group of prisoners. She had spotted his distinctive centurion's helmet with its scarlet crest, or the baton he carried in his hand as a symbol of his rank, and she walked over to him, trailing a young *legionare*. The plainly dressed woman had evidently overwhelmed the young man via sheer force of personality, and he gave Marcus a half-shamed, half-pleading look as he hurried to keep up with her.

"Centurion," she said. She made part of a curtsey, likely the best she could do while carrying her young daughter on one hip. The child was silent, her blue eyes very wide. "No one will speak to us. No one will tell us when we may return to our homes."

Marcus kept the glare going for a few moments, but it was forlorn hope. The young mother was not going to be dis-uaded. "Ma'am," Marcus said, "I'm going to have to ask you return to your place with the other prisoners."

"I'm not going anywhere until I get some answers," she aid quietly.

"Yes, ma'am, you are," Marcus said. "It's safest for you ere."

The woman clenched her jaw in frustration. "I don't under-and what else you need from us, centurion. None of us are rmed or bore arms against the Legions. None of us know nything that you didn't find out hours ago. There's no *reason* or us to be sitting here, even if that nice young man is being o painstaking in asking about our Citizenship . . ."

Her voice trailed off, and her face set in a pensive frown—en in a sudden, sick mask of fear.

Marcus felt his knuckles tightening on the baton in frustra-on, and only a whisper of cracking wood let him realize that e had inadvertently summoned fury-born strength to his mbs. He'd seen that look on other women, in other places, nd he hated it. "Ma'am," Marcus said quietly. He pointed at e prisoners with his baton. "Go sit down. Now."

She stared blankly at him for a moment. Then she took a wift breath, and said, "My name is Estellis." Her arms tight-ned on her child. "This is my daughter, Estara."

Marcus turned his face away sharply at the words. Crows ke it. He didn't want to know the woman, or her name—or, reat furies help him, the name of her child. Their death war-nt had already been signed. And it was his fault it had been. heir blood was going to be on his hands—perhaps literally. e did not want to know their names.

Some part of him could feel nothing but contempt for his wn dismay. It had been his suggestion, after all, that the Sen-tor order the captain to kill another Aleran. He had assumed at Arnos would seize upon the opportunity to do so as soon s prisoners were taken from the Legion of rebel slaves. He ad assumed that the order would descend upon, at most, one-r twoscore of enemy soldiers. It would have been a point of principle that he did not think the captain would have bee willing to compromise.

Marcus forced himself to turn his face back to Estellis an her daughter Estara, and to look past them at the hundreds freemen of Othos. Dozens of families. Women. Children. El erly. How could Arnos have *considered* such a monstro course?

Because you told him to do it, fool.

The young woman . . . Estellis stared at him, her face pal She did not allow herself to weep—doubtless for the sake her daughter, who clung sleepily to her side—but her ey shone with the effort. "S-sir . . ." she said quietly. "The ch dren are hungry."

Crows take Arnos, Marcus thought viciously. *Crows ta him and eat him whole.*

There was still some hope. Antillus Crassus was taking h time about verifying each prisoner's lack of Citizenship. Ma cus might not have noticed it if he hadn't been working wi the young man for the past two years, but it smelled like t young Tribune was stalling.

Crassus wouldn't be doing that on his own initiative. I was dutiful nearly to the point of insanity, and always work with quiet, industrious efficiency. So, unless he had sudden decided to start dragging his feet, he was still attending to h duty.

So. The captain was up to something.

Marcus did not know what he intended. Legally speakin he had only two options—but the young man had a talent f discovering previously unnoticed avenues of action. Perha he could do it again.

Please let him do it again.

Marcus was already steeped in blood. Much more, and would drown.

He kept his expression colder and harder than stone. If t prisoners went into a panic, great furies only knew what mig happen. "Ma'am," he said. He began to repeat his order, b instead he found himself meeting the gaze of little Estara. I breath left him in a long, slow exhalation. "Estellis," he sa quietly. "I assure you that my captain is doing everything he can to get you back to your homes as soon as possible. But until that time, you are on the front lines of a war, around men who have seen hard battle today. For your own safety, you need to return to the others." He considered the little girl again, and said, "I'll see what can be done about food."

The young woman stared at him, straining, Marcus knew, to discern if he was telling her the truth, or simply lying to her and sending her back to await slaughter, like some foolishly wayward cow. She needn't have bothered. Even if she'd had an enormous amount of talent and practice at the watercrafter's art of truthfinding, he could have told her that the sky was green with perfect conviction.

"I . . . very well, centurion." She dipped into another awkward curtsey. "Thank you."

"*Legionare,*" Marcus growled.

The young *legionare* came to attention. "Sir."

"Please escort Mistress Estellis and her daughter back to the others." He nodded to her. "Ma'am."

The woman gave Marcus one last, uncertain glance as she turned, then walked with the young *legionare* back to where the prisoners sat.

A veteran *legionare*—though to be fair, any of the fish who'd come this far with the First Aleran deserved to be called veterans—named Bortus leaned slightly toward Marcus. "Centurion? What *are* we going to do with these people?"

"Keep your teeth together, Bortus. When I know, you'll know." Marcus watched Estellis and Estara sit down again and grimaced.

Whatever he was going to do, the captain had best hurry.

Tavi sat silently in Arnos's wind coach, cursing his own stupidity. He should have known better than to proceed upon such a potentially incriminating rendezvous when he might have been under aerial surveillance.

Of course, there had been little enough he could have done under the circumstances. His own Knights Aeris, weary from the exertions of the morning's battle, had not been at hand, and they were really the only way he might have reasonably known about being observed from high above. Even if they had been at hand, of course, he had moved away from any potential support to meet with Nasaug. He began to berate himself instead for his inexcusably bad judgment in doing so—but the potential to reach some other outcome than outright war with the Canim had demanded that he take the risk.

Perhaps it was neither stupidity nor poor judgment, but simply an unfavorable conjunction of opportunity, chance and human will that allowed for no particularly desirable outcome—from his point of view, at least. It had certainly been a fortunate enough morning for Arnos.

It could have been worse. Ehren had not been recognized as anyone other than a local freeman—had Arnos known he was a Cursor of the Crown and accorded the rank and privileges of a Knight as a result, Tavi suspected that he would not have been allowed to live to bear testimony about what had happened. Instead, he had been bound, tossed on the luggage rack atop the coach, and was to be dropped with the condemned prisoners back at Othos.

Assuming Ehren came out of the situation alive, he should prove to be a major lever in any tribunal examining Arnos's charge of treason. All Tavi needed to do was claim he was engaged in a prisoner exchange for a critically placed agent of the Crown—which had the considerable merit of being entirely true.

It would be pleasant to be able to throw that into Arnos's teeth, but Tavi refrained, lest Ehren accidentally tumble from the coach during flight. So he regarded the Senator's detached expression of feline smugness with a blank face, and said nothing. Instead, he sat, missing the presence of his sword far more acutely than he ever had before he'd begun feeling his way through metalcrafting. It currently resided across the lap of Phrygiar Navaris, who sat beside Arnos and stared at Tavi, her serpentine eyes never seeming to blink. The archer sat on Arnos's other side, and the largest of the two men in his retinue of *singulares* sat on either side of him.

"This is probably for the best, Scipio," Arnos said. "It was going to happen, one way or another. This way has the advantage of being relatively civilized."

Tavi didn't bother to answer. The galling thing was that to a certain extent, Arnos was probably correct. Tavi wondered if Gaius had known just how ruthless the man was going to be when it came to removing any possible challenge to his authority. Arnos had been willing to see hundreds of innocent people die to remove Tavi. He certainly wouldn't have hesitated to strike out at anyone who supported Tavi against him.

Tavi narrowed his eyes in thought.

There might be one who he would be slow to oppose.

In fact, this entire situation did not *have* to be a disaster. What was it old Killian had told the Cursors-in-training so often?

Every problem was an opportunity, from the proper point of view.

Arnos tilted his head and studied Tavi through narrowed eyes. "What was that thought that just went by your eyes, Scipio? I don't think I liked the look of it."

Tavi smiled at him. Then he said, "Senator. Men like you need never seek out their enemies. You create them left and right by virtue of drawing breath."

Arnos made a clucking sound in his throat. "You can't

possibly think I am intimidated by your contacts. We all have powerful friends here."

"I don't think you can see far enough to realize what you should fear," Tavi replied. "Crowbegotten shame, really. You have gifts. You could do a lot of people a lot of good, if you so chose."

The Senator's eyes went flat. "If I so chose, *Scipio*," he said quietly, "I could have Navaris spill out your entrails here and now."

Tavi shook his head and nodded at the coach's window. "If you'll look beneath you, Senator, I'm fairly sure that you'll see a picket line of riders below us—close enough to be within sight of one another, and relay signals back to the camp. I ordered them not to accompany me to my meeting, which means that they followed me just far enough back to stay out of sight. They saw your men take me, I'm quite sure. Individually, they aren't faster than a wind coach, but working together, in good light, on a clear day like this one, they can send word even faster. Odds are excellent that the camp already knows you've arrested me."

The Senator narrowed his eyes. Then he turned aside and muttered something to the archer. She, in turn, opened a window on the roar of the windstream outside. She flagged down one of the accompanying Knights Aeris. They had a brief exchange of hand signals. The Knight vanished from the window and appeared again a moment later, flickering an affirmative signal at the archer.

Arnos pressed his lips together and waited for the archer to shut the window again.

"Kill me if you like, Senator," Tavi said, before Arnos could speak. "But you might find yourself faced with quite a few awkward questions." He leaned forward. "And I am *not* some freeman whose death might be easily ignored."

Navaris's hand dropped to the hilt of Tavi's *gladius*, and her lips split in a snarl.

Arnos seized Navaris's sword wrist in one hand, his eyes locked on Tavi's. "Now, now, good lady. Let us not lose our tempers. It has been a trying day for all of us." He smiled a little. "Granted, only one of us is to be tried for treason."

"We'll see," Tavi said.

"We will most certainly see you tried and hung, Scipio," Arnos said. This time, there was no posturing in his voice, no overt grandstanding in his manner—almost no inflection on his words. "Even if events conspire to clear you, in the long run, your role in history is ended. Your Legion will be led by another. You will play no role in this campaign. You will gain no power, no renown during the most vital series of battles for five hundred years while others rise to power instead. Your reputation will be tainted regardless of the outcome of the tribunal: After the shadow of treason has fallen upon you, you won't be trusted to command a squad in a civic legion, and we both know it."

Tavi sat quietly. It was worse, this calm delivery of fact, than any of Arnos's previous sneers and glowers. He bowed his head before it, the way a man might when faced with the inevitable cold of winter's first wind.

"You are already dead," Arnos said. "Dead enough to be of no more use to your patron. Dead enough to be no more threat to me." He glanced away from Tavi as if he was suddenly no longer significant enough to notice. "You're dead, Scipio. It is over."

The wind coach tilted as it began to descend, back to the Guard-occupied walls of Othos.

"From here," Arnos said, "we can proceed in an agreeable, civilized manner—or we can do it the hard way. May I take it that you will cooperate? It will make things much easier upon your men."

Tavi didn't look up. He simply said, "Very well."

"You see, Navaris?" Arnos murmured. "He can be reasoned with."

Tavi sat quietly and left his head bowed.

It made it easier to conceal the smile.

The coach landed in the Othos town square, now standing empty of anyone but *legionares* of the Guard. As Tavi watched, a full century of *legionares* rushed out to form up in ranks facing the coach—a personal retinue, like his own perennially proximate gang of Marat riders, if somewhat more numerous.

The *legionares* snapped to attention as a valet hurried out to open the door of the wind coach.

Tavi and the two large *singulares* exited first. The two men stood on either side of him. At one point in his life, he mused, the presence of such large men so obviously skilled in the arts of violence would have intimidated him quite effectively. Given, however, that the taller of the pair still came half a hand short of Tavi's height, and given both his training and his more recent but mounting knowledge of furycraft, the most that they managed to do was elevate themselves in his thinking to the first targets he would need to deal with, should the situation devolve.

When Arnos emerged from the coach, flanked by his other *singulares*, Tavi fell into pace beside him. His escorts were taken off guard by the confident motion, and wound up trailing him by a step, more like attendants than anything else.

"Senator," Tavi murmured, nodding with a polite smile to the centurion of Arnos's personal guard. "It occurs to me that a certain amount of reciprocity might be called for."

Arnos glared up at him for a moment, and Tavi imagined the man torn between continuing the amicable facade and ordering his *singulares* to beat him senseless. "You're in no position to demand anything."

"Nor do I make any demands," Tavi replied. "I simply wish to point out that you are quite correct. I'm beaten and politically dead."

Arnos stared at him as they mounted the stairs to the house he'd claimed, and his eyes narrowed in suspicion. "You have some point?"

"The people of Othos," Tavi replied, arching a brow at Arnos. "You have what you want. There's no need to carry through with the executions now."

"Oh, I don't know," Arnos said, his tone conversational. "Setting an early example might well smooth things down the road. I should think the fate of Othos would do a great deal to inspire the folk of other villages to be more active in their resistance of the enemy."

"Or inspire them to turn their hands against you."

Arnos shrugged. "Freemen out here have little in the way

of capability to do our forces any harm. They are virtually without furycraft." Arnos gave Tavi a chill little smile. "Imagine what that would be like. Scipio."

Tavi regarded the man steadily for a long moment. Tavi's assignment to the First Aleran as a Cursor and spy for the Crown had never been intended to go on for so long. A lot of people had seen his face in the capital, and sooner or later someone must have twigged to the identical facial features of Rufus Scipio and Tavi of Calderon.

Arnos was Lady Aquitaine's creature. Offhand, he couldn't think of anyone else with both enough intelligence resources to obtain the information, and motivation to share that fact with Arnos. It was an educated guess, but Tavi felt fairly confident of it.

For the immediate future, though, it hardly mattered where Arnos had gotten the information—it only mattered that he *did* have it, and therefore knew that he could strike at Tavi's patron by visiting harm on Tavi. "You've gotten what you wanted. Those people have done you no harm, Senator."

"Nor given any help. I owe them nothing."

"And that's reason enough for you to murder them?"

Arnos shook his head once. "This is a war. The innocent die. They are killed by battles, caught in fires, they starve, they grow sick. It is unavoidable. No commander worth the rank lets his mind be distracted by such things."

"Ah," Tavi murmured. "Quite distracting, humanity."

Arnos let out a bark of laughter. "Please. Your heart bleeds no more than mine does. How many tears did you shed for the officers over you who died when you took command, hmm? How many men did you order to their deaths? How many bodies of the innocent have you seen during your stay here— and how long has it been since the sight of them made your gorge rise?"

Sudden, red rage flashed through Tavi at Arnos's words, but he suppressed it savagely. It was a near thing. Two years in the field had killed hundreds of the men he commanded and exposed him to depths of suffering he could never have imagined only a few years before.

"You are the same sort of creature I am, Scipio, or Tavi of

Calderon, or whoever you imagine yourself to be. You simply serve a different master."

Tavi frowned at the man steadily. Arnos was unruffled and, unless Tavi was mistaken, he was entirely sincere.

How could any sane person be so callous? The lives Arnos directly destroyed would not be the only blood on his hands. The repercussions would be shattering. Disease would run rampant. Children would be orphaned. Steadholts would be decimated, their harvests stifled for lack of labor. The shortage of food would drive men into brigandage and murder. Other men would kill for vengeance, while the women and children, as in all wars, suffered the most. The furies in the area, thrown out of balance by all the deaths of those wielding them, would devolve and go feral, causing even more problems and endangering anyone who crossed their paths.

Tavi had seen it on a much smaller scale around towns and villages engulfed by the war. It was a nightmare. If Arnos continued this way, the first snows of winter would fall upon a land of death and decay presided over by fat, croaking crows.

How could the man even *conceive* such a thing?

Tavi blinked. The answer was simple.

He didn't know.

Arnos simply didn't know.

Though he was one of the most respected men in the Collegia Tactica, Arnos had never actually served on a campaign. He had watched the morning's assault from his air coach high above, looking down upon the tiny figures running about far below him—the same viewpoint he would have enjoyed at a *ludus* board, or on a sand table.

He had been too far away to see the blood or hear the screams, or to smell the stench of death. Bloody crows, the man was directing Legions on a campaign against an implacable foe, yet he didn't even wear armor. Tavi was well aware how quickly the tides of battle could shift—his own dented armor bore testimony enough for it.

It wasn't real to Arnos, Tavi thought. Or rather, what was real and what was going on in the Senator's mind were two different things entirely. He was used to talking about war in abstract, comfortably distanced terms. He hadn't been there on

he ground, and while he might have had an intellectual appre-
ciation of the loss of human life that would ensue, he didn't
know. He hadn't experienced it himself.

Tavi shook his head. "I take it back," he said quietly. "You
aren't going to do anyone any good."

Arnos crooked a finger at Navaris. "I'm sure this house has
a cellar or basement or storage closet of some kind. Lock him
in it."

"Arnos, please," Tavi said. "Rescind the order. Those people don't deserve to die, and you know it."

Arnos ignored him. "After that, take the servant and throw
him in with the prisoners. He's obviously in collusion with the
local rebels."

Tavi ground his teeth in sheer frustration, his hands balling
into fists.

Navaris's snake eyes flicked to him, and her sword slid
three inches out of its sheath.

Tavi heard it then, before anyone else seemed to. In the
years since forming the strange bond with Kitai, his senses
had grown steadily more aware. Not acute, precisely, so much
as they seemed to be losing distinction in their respective acu-
ity. Scents had grown steadily more available, familiar, and
recognizable, until they distinguished places and objects in
his memory almost as readily as familiar faces distinguished
different people. Sounds, too, had changed. They hadn't become any louder, really, so much as they had become increasingly more distinct, until he could frequently sort out who
was moving around him, and which steed they were mounted
on, based on little more than the unique sounds of their
breathing.

This was a very low sound, one that most people would not
notice until it grew more prominent.

Horses.

Hundreds of them, gathering speed.

Crows. This was not what Tavi needed right now.

Navaris roughly seized his arm with her left hand, and only
then did she notice the sound. She froze, turning her head toward the northern gates of the city. There was an enormous,
thundering crash, and then the low growl of hoofbeats turned

into a staccato roar, as a tide of hundreds of hooves struck upon the cobblestones of Othos.

Bloody crows. This was definitely something *none* of them needed right now.

Unless . . .

A column of cavalry from the First Aleran surged into the square from the far side, with Antillar Maximus leading them. The column immediately began splitting apart, falling into ranks with parade-ground precision. He'd brought all four alae of cavalry, and they broke into two units—the original Aleran alae and the second unit of Marat riders. As Tavi watched, he saw the Battlecrows bringing up the rear. They dismounted and formed up in a battle square between the cavalry units.

The First Aleran's veterans had moved with tremendous speed, and they were in position and ready before the Guard could react to their appearance. Trumpets blared in dozens of conflicting calls, drums rolled, and the Guard began assembling into ranks, facing the First Aleran. They were disorganized and confused, but what they lacked in coordination they made up in numbers.

Antillar Maximus, armor and helmet shining in the afternoon sun, turned his horse toward the house the Senator had appropriated and trotted toward him, somehow imparting an arrogant swagger to his mount's gait. He stopped ten feet in front of the first rank of opposing *legionares* and gave Tavi a casual nod. "Captain." He spoke loudly enough to let the entire square hear, smiling amiably.

"Good afternoon, Tribune," Tavi said, also loudly. "What do you think you're doing here?"

"There's a situation back at our camp that requires your attention, sir," Max said. "I took the liberty of bringing a spare horse for you." He turned the amiable smile to Arnos. "I'll have my captain back, Senator."

Arnos glared at Max and drew himself up, lifting his chin. Given his silk robes, and the fact that the Senator was shorter than most women, it looked somewhat ridiculous. The increasing numbers of Guard *legionares* arriving moment by moment, however, did not.

"Tribune," Arnos barked. "You and these men will disperse, return to camp, and await my orders."

"You heard the man, Captain," Max drawled. "Get on the horse, and we'll get back to camp."

"Disperse, Tribune!" Arnos snarled. "Now!"

From the north side of the town, drums rumbled. The sound of the *legionares* of the First Aleran singing a quickstep marching song drifted through the air.

Arnos turned to Tavi. "Order them to stand down."

"I'd like to, Senator," Tavi said, "but I've been relieved of command."

"I'll kill them," Arnos said. "One and all."

"That's up to you, of course," Tavi agreed. "But you might give a thought to the consequences to your campaign. You can kill them, but it won't be easy. You'll take heavy losses. And when the dust settles, you'll have less than a third of our current numbers."

Arnos narrowed his eyes.

"We're already outnumbered at least three or four to one, sir." Tavi felt his voice harden. "Do the math. And then tell me if you think you can carry this campaign to completion."

Arnos looked from Tavi to Max, to the *legionares* in the square. The marching song of the First Aleran grew louder.

Finally, he hissed through his teeth, and growled, "If I must, I will fall back and gather reinforcements for next year. You aren't getting your command back."

"I don't need it," Tavi said. "Furthermore, I can guarantee that not only will the First Aleran stand down, but that it will willingly march beside you in the rest of the campaign. We both know you're going to need them."

Arnos frowned, suspicious eyes flickering over Tavi's face. "What do you want?"

"Two things," Tavi said. "First, the people of Othos. Rescind the order."

Arnos snorted. "And?"

"Turn me over to Captain Nalus and remand me to the stockade at the Elinarch until my trial," Tavi replied.

"Why?" Arnos demanded.

Tavi glanced at Navaris. "I'd rather not wake up one day

and find that I've somehow sliced open my wrists in my sleep."

Arnos looked back out at the square, which by that time had become a veritable sea of gleaming armor, banners, weapons, and helmets. On the square opposite the First Aleran forces, the banner of Captain Nalus appeared, and began marching through the ranks toward Arnos's command.

"Done," Arnos said.

Tavi nodded once, and turned to Max. "Tribune?"

"Sir."

"Stand down and return to camp."

Max blinked and stared at Tavi. "Sir?"

"That is an order, Tribune," Tavi said.

Max's horse danced nervously in place, and the big Antillan shook his head. "No, sir. I'm not leaving here without you, sir."

"The Senator has found cause to bring treason charges against me. I am confident that I will have an opportunity"—he placed a very slight emphasis on the word—"to clear up the matter in a trial. For the time being the regulations must be observed."

Max arched an eyebrow, took a deep breath, and then reluctantly saluted. "Yes, sir."

"Thank you, Tribune," Tavi said.

Max turned and rode back over to the First Aleran, casting a glance over his shoulder as he went. A moment later, the formations began to break up, turning to depart the city the way they'd come. A collective sigh of relief from seemingly every man in the square sounded like a wind blowing through tall, thick grass.

Tavi felt his own legs sag with relief. A disastrous clash with the Guard had been averted, and the people of Othos were spared—one problem neatly solving another.

The easy part was over.

From here on out things were going to be a lot more difficult.

⌐⌐CHAPTER 18

Marcus approached the command tent and nodded to the guard outside. "My name is Marcus. Captain Nalus sent for me."

The guard, a young *legionare*, came to immediate attention and snapped a precise salute. "Valiar Marcus, sir, he's expecting you. He said to go in, and he'll be along in a moment, sir."

"Don't call me sir, sonny," Marcus said. "We're all infantry here."

The young *legionare* grinned and banged out a more natural salute, then swung open the tent's flap.

Marcus returned the salute, if more casually than was strictly proper, and stepped inside the tent. It was a bit larger than necessary and was set up around a central table, rather than having tables line the walls, leaving the center open. That was typical of Nalus. He liked his men facing one another as they worked—talking, communicating. He was a great one for talking, Nalus.

Marcus tended to prefer the other arrangement. It meant that you always knew the man who was working behind your back.

The cot at one side of the room was double-sized, and a stool and a large harp rested at its foot. Marcus walked over to the harp and ran a calloused hand along its wooden frame.

The tent flap opened, and Captain Nalus walked in. Marcus turned to him and gave him a sharp salute. "Captain."

Nalus nodded back. "Centurion." He closed the tent flap behind him.

Marcus offered the man a grin and his hand. "Been a while."

Nalus took his hand and smiled in return. "Marcus. Thank you for coming."

"Well, you're a high-and-mighty captain now. How could a mere centurion refuse?"

Nalus snorted. "It's not much like when we were serving High Lord Antillus," he said, his tone wry. "Is it?"

"Not much," Marcus replied.

"Great furies know," Nalus said quietly, "there would never have been any of that business about executing civilians." He was quiet for a moment. "Made me sick, Marcus."

"On the Shieldwall," Marcus said quietly, "you always knew who the enemy was."

Nalus frowned at him for a moment, then grimaced and shook his head. "You've got me all wrong. Crows take the politicians, Marcus, and the politics with them. That isn't what I signed up for. I'm just a soldier."

Marcus grunted. "You joined the wrong outfit if you wanted to avoid getting involved."

Nalus shook his head, crossed to a cabinet in the corner of the tent, and took out a dark bottle. He took a long pull from it, and then offered it to Marcus. "This isn't about choosing sides, Marcus."

Marcus looked at the bottle for a moment. He made no move toward it. "Then what is it about?"

Nalus took another drink. "A lot of years ago, you taught a young subtribune a lot about being a soldier. And a spoiled brat a lot about growing up."

Marcus snorted. "They didn't come much greener than you. That's for sure."

"You were my teacher. You gave me good advice then. I'm asking for your advice now."

Marcus stared at Nalus for a moment. Then he shook his head and reached out for the bottle. He took a swig, and the almost-flavorless hard root-liquor favored in the frozen north of the Realm burned down his throat. "Faugh," he muttered. "You can get any kind of liquor here, and you stick with this?"

"Grew on me," Nalus said.

Marcus grunted, and said, "Absent friends."

"Absent friends," Nalus replied.

Marcus took another pull and passed the bottle back to

Nalus. He waited until the other man drank, then said, "What do you want to ask me?"

"You know I've been given custody of Captain Scipio."

"Aye."

Nalus shook his head. "He's made some requests. He wants to talk to some of his officers before I send him back to Sir Cyril for safekeeping."

Marcus grunted. "And?"

Nalus stared at Marcus for a second. "And? Does he really expect me to allow it? The last thing any of us needs is for him to give some order to his men to the effect of 'the good Senator can go to the crows.' Or maybe, 'kill that fool Nalus and get me out of here.'"

Marcus nodded. Then he said, "Ask him not to."

Nalus arched an eyebrow. "Excuse me?"

"Ask him not to do that."

Nalus let out an exasperated little laugh. "Just like that? And take his *word* for it? Oh, the Senator would *love* that."

Marcus took the bottle and swigged again. "You asked."

Nalus stared hard at Marcus for a full, silent minute. Then he swallowed more of the northern liquor, and said, "Really?"

"He gives you his word," Marcus said, "he's good for it."

Nalus exhaled. Then he said, "And you're good for yours."

Marcus took another pull and grimaced. "Mostly."

Nalus finished the bottle and idly tossed it under his cot. He frowned, brow furrowing.

Marcus let him think it over for a moment. Then he said, "Still playing that old thing, eh?"

Nalus glanced at the harp and lifted one shoulder in a shrug. "I . . . sometimes it helps me sleep."

Marcus nodded at the double-sized cot. "Thought that's what the women were for."

Nalus flashed a short-lived grin at Marcus. Then he shook his head, and replied, "Not going to be much of that on the campaign."

"No."

"If Scipio talks to his officers," Nalus said, "and tells them to resist Arnos, we won't be able to trust the First Aleran,

Marcus. I may be a fool, but I'm not a crowbegotten fool. We're going to need them by the time we get to Mastings. *I can't* make a bad call on this one."

Marcus clapped Nalus on the shoulder, and said, quietly, "Do what you think is best." Then he turned to leave.

"Marcus?" Nalus asked.

Marcus paused.

Nalus took a deep breath. "I want you to be there."

Marcus turned, nodded, and gave the younger man a salute.

Nalus returned it.

The sandy-haired young Cursor, Sir Ehren, was waiting for Marcus as he walked briskly out of the Second Senatorial's camp, and back toward the First Aleran's. He fell into pace beside Marcus, though his body language remained that of someone moving separately from the centurion. His lips barely moved when he spoke. "Well?"

"The captain asked, just like you said he would. And Nalus will allow it."

Ehren's face lit in a brief, fierce grin. "Good."

Marcus glanced aside at him. "What are you going to do?"

Ehren began to speak, but frowned. "Better for both of us if you don't know," he said quietly.

Thank the great furies *someone* had sense, Marcus thought. The Cursors had taken a lot of losses over the past few years, and he'd come to fear for the quality of the agents that would emerge from the situation. At least this one appeared to have sound judgment.

Ehren gave the slightest twitch of a nod to Marcus and vanished down a side street. Marcus continued on his way, at the same businesslike, unwavering pace, and returned to his tent.

This time, Lady Aquitaine had not bothered with a veil. She sat on his stool in her washerwoman disguise, her face lined with impatience. She rose as he entered, and he felt the air tighten with an interdicting windcrafting.

Marcus nodded to her. "My lady."

"Fidelias," she replied, her tone curt. "What did Nalus say?"

"Scipio has requested a conference with his senior officers," Marcus reported.

Lady Aquitaine narrowed her eyes. "According to Arnos, Scipio stated that he would instruct his officers to support him. But he's a fighter. Surely Nalus isn't going to allow the meeting."

Marcus kept his focus upon the details of his tent—mundane, familiar things that were not at all out of the ordinary and with which he interacted on a daily, regular basis. "I advised him against it," he replied.

Lady Aquitaine frowned at him for a moment.

Marcus straightened the lay of the blanket on his cot and wondered if he was about to die.

She sighed and shook her head. "Will he take your advice?"

"We can hope so," Marcus said. "Nalus takes some time to make his decisions, but he does his own thinking along the way. He told me that if he did have the conference, he wanted me there. At least I'll be able to report on what happens."

"Never underestimate the ongoing value in a talented protégé," Lady Aquitaine murmured, smiling. "Or how many times they go to their former mentors for advice on their most critical decisions. Keep me informed."

"Of course, lady."

"What of the villagers?" Lady Aquitaine asked.

"Released and returned to their homes—although Arnos hasn't issued an official countermand to their death warrants."

She shook her head. "With Scipio out of the picture, there's no longer any reason to threaten them, and there is the potential for serious long-range repercussions. I must admit, my spy, that your suggestion sounded like quite a gamble at first. But it's proven an elegant solution to our problems."

Marcus's stomach twisted. If the captain hadn't played the situation as well as he had . . . Aloud, he only said, "Thank you, lady."

"In your opinion, will the First Aleran support Arnos in the campaign?"

"If Scipio orders it?" He pursed his lips. "I think so, yes. They've fought the Canim for two years now. They want to finish the job."

Lady Aquitaine sighed. "Then it all hinges on Scipio. He has a rather irritating talent for impersonating a fulcrum."

"If he reneges," Marcus pointed out, "there is still the death warrant."

Her face twisted into a moue of distaste. "True. But will it be enough to compel him to keep his word?"

"Partly," Marcus said. "But bear in mind that he plans surprisingly well for the long term for someone of his age. Throwing his Legion's support behind the campaign is, at this point, arguably the best way to keep his men and his officers alive, united, and ready to support him again in the future."

Lady Aquitaine arched an eyebrow at that and waved her hand in a gesture that admitted the possibility. Then she rose and gathered up the laundry, a small smile on her mouth. "I'm not worried about his long-range plans. We're nearly there. You have served me very well, my Fidelias. I shall not forget it."

He bowed his head to Lady Aquitaine, and she departed.

He sank down to sit on his cot and closed his eyes. The panic and fear he'd kept hidden inside him when he lied to Lady Aquitaine's face rushed back through him. His forehead beaded with a cold sweat, and his hands started shaking.

Should Lady Aquitaine come to power, she would need the appearance, at least, of integrity, and Marcus knew far too many damning facts about both her and her husband. True, she had a certain amount of integrity—but also true, she allowed no one and nothing to hamper her aims. It had taken him years to see the absolute, voracious nature of her ambition.

He followed the chain of logic to its most probable conclusion.

Once she and her husband had the crown, Marcus would be a liability, suited only for removal.

Optionally, if she ever realized that he had turned against her, she would wipe him from the earth.

And should the captain ever learn his true identity, Marcus judged that he would react with less dramatic but equally effective prejudice.

Marcus sat on the cot with his hands shaking.

He'd kept the captain alive, at least. That was something. As long as he was alive, the young man would be in action—and Marcus was sure that the captain had no intention of sitting quietly in a cell while the Aquitaines' puppet Senator ran up a string of victories and the prestige and influence that would come with them. As long as the captain was alive and able to act, there was hope for Alera's future.

Just not for his own.

To the crows with it. He'd never planned on dying of old age in any case.

CHAPTER 19

Bernard suddenly froze, then lifted his hand and flattened it out again at his side, the signal to take cover. Amara hurried two steps forward to support Gaius as he went awkwardly to one knee, clutching the walking staff Bernard had cut for him after they'd set out on the trail again. She helped the First Lord to lie down flat on the cool, damp earth, and then followed suit.

Gaius let out a hiss of pain and clutched at his leg before going still and silent again. His expression was twisted into a pained grimace.

Amara laid a hand on the old man's arm by way of encouragement, and frowned at Bernard—or more accurately, at where she presumed Bernard was still standing. The shadows of the very trees and brush of the forest itself had fallen over him like a cloak, and the woodcrafting hid him entirely from view.

She heard a soft step on the ground in front of her, and then the light changed subtly as Bernard's woodcrafting slipped over her and the First Lord. Bernard became visible to her as it happened, though his features were softened and dimmed, as if by a deep shadow. He had his bow in hand as he stood over them, an arrow on the string, and his eyes were focused intently ahead of them.

Then Amara heard it—the click-click, click-click of a walking horse's hooves striking a firm trail. They were joined by the sounds of several more, and within half a minute, she saw the riders appear. There were six of them, all dressed in woodsman's leathers, though each wore a device upon the front of his jacket set with the green-and-grey colors of Kalare. Outriders, then, for a Legion—or more likely bandits who had accepted Kalarus's coin and authority to continue doing what they always did, plus the occasional odd job. They were heavily armed, each bearing a huntsman's bow, a broad-headed spear, and additional blades and axes strapped to their saddles.

They passed by in silence, but for the steps of their mounts. This was the second such patrol they had come across in two days, though the other had been more than twice as far away. These men were close enough for Amara to see the stains on their tunics and the scuff marks on their boots. She found herself holding her breath, straining to remain silent.

The patrol passed by, and Amara slowly began to relax again—until the last rider looked around, then reined in his horse and dropped to the forest floor. He tossed the ends of his reins over a low-hanging branch, and began walking toward them.

Bernard moved very slowly, very calmly. He lifted his bow and drew it in careful, deliberate silence.

The outlaw swerved away from them when he was less than twenty feet off, sighed, and began relieving himself against the trunk of a tree.

Though Amara could not even string her husband's bow, Bernard held the powerful weapon at full draw without a quiver. He remained still, his breathing measured, his eyes half-closed and lazy-looking. Amara felt herself quivering with tension, and she realized that her knuckles had gone white where she had ahold of the First Lord's forearm. She itched to move her hand down to her sword, but refrained. The motion might stir a leaf, or break a twig, and warn the enemy of their presence. More to the point, her sword wouldn't do her any good at the moment, even were it already in her hand. Bernard's bow would be their best defense.

The bandit finished up, muttered something under his breath, and turned to go.

Gaius's weight shifted. Amara glanced sideways at him in alarm. His face had gone pale with pain, and his right leg, the one still recovering from his injuries, was quivering against the ground. It didn't make much noise—but it was enough.

The outlaw suddenly turned, his hand flying to his sword, his eyes narrow as they scanned the forest around them. Amara was lying utterly unprotected on the forest floor, within range of a good, long lunge, and the man was facing her. He simply stared, eyes moving slowly from left to right. He stood there for a full minute, just looking and listening.

Amara's nerves began screaming in anxiety. If the First Lord's leg twitched again, there was no chance, none at all, that the man would miss it. If he had the capacity to craft through Bernard's woodcrafting, he would be within a heartbeat of striking out at Gaius, unless Bernard's first shot was instantly lethal. If the man managed to survive the first shot, even if only briefly, Gaius might not be able to defend himself. If that happened, Amara would have to put herself between the outlaw and the First Lord, and she drew upon Cirrus to give her limbs the speed she would need to interpose herself in time.

All the while, Bernard stood directly in front of the man, bow drawn, never moving.

"What the crows are you doing?" blared a sudden voice.

Amara jerked in surprise, and half panicked as the movement stirred the earth and brush beneath her.

The outlaw didn't hear it. He reacted the same way, whirling in place and drawing his sword.

"Crows take you, Tonnar," the outlaw growled. "Scared me out of ten years of life."

Another outlaw appeared, his horse nudging slowly through the brush toward the first man. "Life you lead, I did you a favor."

"Bastard."

"You don't go off alone, fool," Tonnar said amiably. "Do it again, and Julius will have your balls."

"Julius," the outlaw said, his voice sullen. "He has us riding around in crowbegotten nowhere when there's a war on. You know what kind of loot we could be getting if we were at the real fight?"

"Stomach plague mostly, the way I hear it. We're getting paid steady for this. Don't knock it."

"There's no spy running around out here," the outlaw complained. "We're wasting our time."

"Knights Aeris don't fly this far behind enemy lines for no reason. They either dropped someone off—"

"Or picked someone up, in which case we're out here wearing our asses to nothing for no reason."

"You're riding. You're getting paid. Maybe we find someone, maybe we don't. Either we get the five-hundred-bull bounty, or we go back without anybody trying to gut us. There's no loser here."

"Except me, Tonnar. I have to listen to you run your mouth."

"You don't get that nag back in line, you won't have to listen to anything ever again," Tonnar replied. Then he turned his horse away and continued on in the direction he had been.

The outlaw scowled after him, savagely kicked a stone on the ground.

The stone bounded across the earth and bounced off of Bernard's leg.

Amara tensed.

But the outlaw hadn't seen it. He had already turned to his horse. He mounted, kicked the animal with unnecessary vigor, and sent it cantering after the rest of his party.

Bernard didn't lower his bow until a full minute after the man was out of sight, then he released the tension on the weapon and his breath with the same slow, careful exhalation. He lowered the bow and rolled his right shoulder, as if working out stiffness. Then he turned back to Amara.

"I'm going to shadow them for a bit," he murmured. "Make sure that they're not doubling back. Stay here, stay low. I'll be back shortly."

"Be careful," she told him.

He winked at her, and then turned away. The woodcrafting slid away from Amara, and the dappled sunlight brightened again, bright enough to make her squint against it.

She turned to Gaius, and whispered, "Sire? Are you all right?"

"Leg cramped," Gaius growled softly. "Started twitching." He rubbed one hand hard on his right leg. "Crows, that's uncomfortable. Pardon my language, Countess."

"Yes, sire," Amara said, giving him a small smile. She glanced after Bernard, and said, "We can change the bandages while we're here."

Gaius grimaced but nodded to her. He hauled himself about roughly, sitting up and extending his right leg toward her.

"Well," she said, as she went to work, "what did you think of that?"

"I think our young friend there isn't going to survive this patrol," Gaius replied. His voice tightened as she peeled the bandages from his right foot, revealing the discolored sores that had refused to completely heal. "And I think it's lucky they rode by in front of us. If we'd passed through a few minutes sooner, they'd have walked right across our trail and followed it straight to us."

Amara got out the canteen of salted water and poured it over Gaius's foot. He looked away, his expression distant and cool, but his leg jerked as the cleansing wash entered the sores. Amara set about washing and drying his foot, then putting a fresh bandage over it, before replacing his stocking and the heavy leather slipper Bernard had fashioned for Gaius.

"Quite cool in a crisis, your man." Gaius sighed, once she was finished.

"You noticed. I thought I was going to have to scream, at the end there."

"As was I—though for different reasons. I didn't dare use any metalcrafting to keep the pain down." He smiled and dug into his pack, extracting a flask of water. He swallowed most of it down, and then settled back onto the forest floor again, closing his eyes. "I can't ever remember going for so long without performing any crafting. It's like . . . walking around with my

feet and hands asleep all the time. I hadn't realized how difficult it would be." He shook his head once, then closed his eyes
and dropped into what looked like a light slumber.

Amara didn't disturb him. Though Gaius had insisted upon
moving ahead, each hour cost him considerable effort. Though
he never complained, the pain of his foot clearly wore greatly
on him, and he leaned more heavily on the staff as each day
went on.

She sat down with her back to a tree, drew her sword, and
quietly stood watch over the sleeping First Lord, until Bernard
suddenly appeared from beneath his woodcrafting, half an
hour later.

Amara twitched in surprise and frowned at him.

"Sorry," he murmured. Then he knelt down and hugged
her.

Amara sighed, shook her head, and returned the embrace.
He felt large and strong and warm, and she suddenly felt a great
deal less worried. She knew that it was really a somewhat
ridiculous thing to feel. Bernard, after all, was as vulnerable to
harm as anyone. But somehow, when he was holding her, that
didn't matter. She felt better for no rational reason at all—and
she loved that feeling.

"How is he?" Bernard rumbled quietly.

"The same. Or if he's any better, I can't see it. Bernard,
shouldn't those sores have closed by now?"

"Mmmm," he said. "Older folks can be slow to heal without a watercrafter to help them. He hasn't any fever, and
there's no sign of blood poisoning. I'd prefer it if he rested for
a couple of days, but . . ."

"But he won't," Amara sighed.

"It could be worse," Bernard said. "So long as they close
up before we hit the swamps, we should be all right."

"What if they don't?" Amara asked him.

He leaned back from her and traced a fingertip over her
cheekbone. She closed her eyes and leaned into his touch.

"We'll worry about that if it happens," he said quietly.

Gaius stirred and sat up, blinking his eyes once or twice.
He nodded to Bernard. "Count. Our friends have moved on?"

Bernard nodded. "Yes, sire. It won't hurt us to take a bit of rest here, if you like."

The First Lord shook his head, planted his staff, and clambered to his feet. "No, out of the question. We've no time to spare."

"Aye, sire," Bernard said.

He offered Amara a hand up, and she squeezed his fingers once after she was on her feet. Bernard set off in the lead of the little group again, and Gaius grunted with discomfort on his first few steps, then determinedly lengthened his stride, using his staff to help him.

Amara stared at the limping First Lord for a moment, biting her lip. Then she followed him, glancing frequently around them and over her shoulder, and they continued on their way to Kalare.

⊃⊂ CHAPTER 20

Isana followed the young valet to Sir Cyril's office, on the ground floor of the Legion's command building. Only a single *legionare* was on duty at the door, this time—indeed, since the First Aleran and the Guard Legions had departed, the entire town of Elinarch seemed almost deserted, and any little sound rang out with an eerie clarity in the quiet streets.

The valet led her through a little antechamber and nodded at the door. "There you are, Steadholder."

"Thank you," Isana said quietly. "Should I knock?"

The valet shook his head. "He's expecting you, ma'am."

Isana nodded at the young man and turned to the office door. She opened it and stepped into a rather large office. It was crowded with tables and bookshelves, all of them neatly, precisely stacked with books, papers, and scrolls. One wall was covered entirely by at least a dozen maps on broad sheets of parchment.

Sir Cyril sat behind a much-used wooden desk, and he rose with a polite smile.

Isana felt it when a flash of pain went through the remains of his leg, a savage stroke of agony that bored into the joint of his thigh and hip. Her own leg twitched in sympathy at the ghostly sensation. She felt him assert control over the pain an instant later, smothering the fire of it in a blanket of pure determination.

"No, please, sir," Isana said. "Don't get up."

"Nonsense," Sir Cyril said. He swept into a restrained bow. "It's not often I entertain a celebrity."

She shook her head wryly and replied with a simple curtsey. "Hardly that."

"I disagree," Cyril said, sitting again. He let out an almost-inaudible sigh of relief as he took the weight off of his leg. "I've gotten several letters mentioning that you'd favorably impressed many of the Realm's Citizenry, during your abolition campaign."

"As of yet, no laws have been passed," she said, her voice dry. "It's been two years. I can hardly call that impressive."

"Big change takes time," Cyril replied, his tone a polite disagreement. "And the war has certainly been"—he glanced at his leg and flashed a quick, wry grin at Isana—"a distraction."

"Certainly that," she agreed.

"Even leaving such matters aside, this relief column you organized is a rare thing," he continued. "It's already saving lives."

She shook her head. "Any number of people could have done what I have."

"But they didn't," Cyril said. "You did."

"Someone had to."

He tilted his head and studied her for a moment, then shrugged, and said, "Someone *should* have. It isn't the same thing."

Isana waved a hand. "Sir Cyril, I hope you don't think I'm rude for saying this. But I can't imagine why you sent for me."

He gave her a steady look, and his speculative gaze was in

tense enough that she could almost feel it on her skin. "Can't you?" he asked.

Isana sighed. "Honestly, I can't. I was packing to leave, in fact. So, Sir Cyril, I ask you again. Why am I here?"

Cyril's eyebrows went up. "This is somewhat disappointing." He offered her a whimsical smile. "I was hoping you would tell me." He raised his voice, and called, "Galen! Send him in, please!"

The door opened a moment later, and a tall man in a fine Legion-issue dress tunic entered the—

Tavi entered the room, she corrected herself. His green eyes fell on her, and his step slowed in hesitation for just a moment. She felt a surge of emotion from him, so mixed and confused that she hardly knew what to make of it, other than to sense a good deal of anger mixed through it all, unless it was humiliation or—

Great furies.

Araris had told him.

Isana stared at Tavi for a second, meeting his gaze. He nodded to her, and said, "Excuse me." As he did, the fountain of emotion began to dwindle, until there was nothing more coming from him. He had been able to hide his feelings from her since he'd been eleven years old. It had always made her a little proud of him—as well as exasperated. He'd been entirely too . . . creatively energetic, at that age. She'd needed every advantage she could get to stay a step ahead of his mischief and—

And they were not alone, she reminded herself. She glanced aside at Cyril, then rose, politely, offering another curtsey to Tavi, precisely as she had to Cyril. "Good morning, Captain."

Tavi smiled at her and inclined his head. "Steadholder. Thank you for coming. And thank you for seeing me, Sir Cyril."

Isana tilted her head. "Why aren't you with your Legion, Captain?"

"Mmmm," Cyril said. "I was wondering the same thing myself. Nalus's letter was painfully vague."

"I've been arrested and charged with treason, Steadholder," Tavi replied cheerfully. "They sent me back here in irons, though Sir Cyril was kind enough to accept my parole and have them stricken." He held up his wrists, each of them ringed with bruises and small cuts.

Isana blinked for a moment and fought to keep herself from gasping, or letting out a cry of distress. Not in front of Sir Cyril.

"Treason," Cyril said, sighing. "What happened out there?"

"Long story," Tavi said. He put a hand on the chair Isana had been sitting in, holding it for her. "Steadholder. Shall we sit?"

Isana frowned gently at him, trying to understand what was behind his expression—but he was closed to her.

Yes. She'd known him that well, at least. He'd reacted just as she feared he would.

Crows take Araris, she thought quietly, sadly. *But not until after they've taken me. And the slives who made it necessary to take every measure in reach to protect him—including lying to him.*

Araris had been right, of course. Tavi had deserved to know. But she had wanted to put it off for just one more day, and now . . .

Sometimes it felt like everything she turned her hand to withered and died. It was ridiculous, of course. Not everything had. Her steadholt was prospering, after all. The relief column had been a success. Perhaps it was only when her heart was involved that she had such ruinous bad fortune.

Or, she thought, *ruinously bad judgment. Credit where credit is due.*

They all sat down. Cyril settled in to listen to Tavi, one elbow on the desk, his fist supporting his chin. "This should be interesting."

Tavi leaned back in his chair and somehow managed to look lazily confident even while in a relaxed slouch, his legs stretched out in front of him and crossed at the ankles. Then he started talking.

It didn't take Isana long to realize that Tavi was saying more than he probably should have about the motivations and twisted loyalties behind the events of the past several days—which is to say that he was being completely open and honest.

"Let me get this straight," Cyril said, when Tavi paused for breath. "After Arnos lost many of his own Knights Aeris, precisely as we warned him he would, you then bailed his men out of the trouble he'd bought them."

"You should have heard what was going around the Guard camps before I left," Tavi said, with another grin. Isana had never seen the expression on Tavi's face, but it had been common enough on his father's. Septimus had grinned at frustration and pain, too. "According to the Guard, I waited overly long to help, so that I could play the hero and rub their noses in their inexperience."

Cyril snorted. "Arnos has always known how to play a crowd. After you did that, he ordered you to execute the prisoners. You refused the order, and he had you arrested."

"Not exactly," Tavi said. "I was still stalling carrying the order out. I, ah, had the opportunity for a rendezvous with a representative from the Canim. Arnos caught me after and leveled the treason charges. He refused to rescind the execution order, by the way."

"Executing civilians? Families?" Isana heard herself say. "What kind of madness is that?"

"An increasingly common one, unfortunately," Cyril said soberly. "All this ambition being brewed with self-interest under increasing amounts of pressure." He shook his head and turned back to Tavi. "I assume he was holding them against your good behavior."

Tavi's smile turned sharper. "Yes. Though I found a way to make sure he'd leave them alone."

Cyril tilted his head. "How?"

"I left Crassus in command of the Legion," Tavi said, smirking.

Cyril arched both eyebrows, then leaned his head back to laugh, a short, genuine sound. "That would do it."

"Excuse me," Isana said quietly. "Do what?"

"Crassus's father is High Lord Antillus Raucus," Tavi said, still grinning. "His mother is High Lord Kalarus's youngest sister. Once the fighting is done, Crassus may well be declared Kalarus's heir. He already *is* Antillus's heir. If Arnos ordered him to execute the prisoners, and he refused—"

"Which he would," Cyril said.

Tavi nodded. "—Arnos would have little choice but to press charges against Crassus, if he wanted to maintain the integrity of his charges against me."

"Ah," Isana said, nodding. "And given Crassus's family connections and what will probably be a very influential future, it would be stupid for Arnos to make an enemy of him now."

"Oh, he's stupid enough to do it," Tavi said, "but there's also the fact that if Arnos played that game on the son and heir of Antillus Raucus, the patronage of the Aquitaines wouldn't stop Lord Antillus for a second. He would call Arnos out to the *juris macto* and scatter the leftover pieces all over Alera."

"Only if the old man beat Maximus to it," Cyril noted.

Tavi grinned. "Crows, yes. Max would love an excuse to call Arnos out. Defending the honor of his family and father would be undeniable."

"I'm surprised Arnos let you talk to your officers," Cyril said. "It's not the kind of mistake I'd expect of him."

"He didn't," Tavi said. "Max and about seven hundred veterans were in a position to dispute the legitimacy of my arrest."

"What?" Cyril just stared at Tavi for a second, his face going white. Isana sensed the horror boiling up out of him like some kind of greasy black vapor. Then he shook his head slowly. "Seven hundred . . ." He blew out a slow breath. "That was exactly the kind of situation the Crown wished us to avoid."

Tavi grimaced. "I know. I talked Arnos into letting Nalus handle my arrest in exchange for ordering them to stand down."

Cyril mopped a hand over his face. "Nalus," he said, distantly. "No wonder his letter was so awkward. Decent man. Not terribly intelligent, but I've always thought well of him."

"He asked me to give him my word that I wasn't going to order my men to get me out or refuse to support the campaign. I gave it, and he let me meet with them."

Cyril frowned hard at Tavi, and Isana could feel the anger in it, mixed with a certain admiration. "And your orders to them?"

Tavi blinked, lifting his eyebrows in faint surprise. "To

support the campaign, of course. To do everything they could to preserve the lives of Alerans and secure the Realm against the invaders."

Cyril let out a slow breath, sagging a little at the table, and his relief flooded through the room. "Thank the great furies. There's that much, at least."

Tavi grimaced. "Arnos is planning a campaign of numbers. He's tallied every life to be sacrificed."

Cyril grimaced. "Yes. I suspected as much. Can he win?"

Tavi shrugged. "I think Nasaug does his math a bit differently. Othos was a bloody mess, and at a bargain for the Canim." Tavi's voice lowered, and his smile vanished. "I've got to stop him, Cyril."

Cyril looked from Tavi to Isana, frowning. The room was quiet for several seconds.

"Someone needs to," Cyril agreed. "But there are two problems. First, you aren't going to stop him from doing much of anything from inside the stockade. Second, I don't see any feasible way of doing so, even if you weren't."

Tavi took a deep breath. "I think I might know a way," he said.

Cyril nodded. "This meeting you had with a representative, I expect. What does Nasaug want?"

"Can't tell you," Tavi said. "Safer for both of us."

Cyril leaned back in his chair and put both hands flat on his desk. "You want me to release you."

"Yes."

"I can't do that."

"Yes, you can," Tavi said. "Cyril, if this works, it has the potential to end the fighting entirely. I think those three Legions would do a lot more good flanking Kalarus than running around in circles in the Vale."

"It's a treason charge," Cyril said quietly. "If I release you before you've faced a tribunal, it's a death sentence for me as well: to say nothing of the fact that any irregularity would practically guarantee your conviction."

Tavi made a clicking sound with his teeth. "There's always—"

Cyril cut him off with a wave of his hand and exhaled

through his nose. "All right," he said quietly. "This has gone badly, but it could have been worse. The next thing to focus on is making sure the Legions' supply lines are kept secure. Then we'll turn some attention to your trial defense."

Tavi shook his head. "We don't have time. There's too much at stake."

"Yes," Cyril responded, rather sharply. "But you've been outmaneuvered. You're of no use to the Crown, now."

"I could be," Tavi said quietly. "Let me arrange something. None of the blame will come to you."

Cyril began shaking his head. "Scipio—I am a soldier, and a servant of the Crown. I always have been. And at this moment, the Crown's law says that you are to remain in custody until a tribunal can be assembled. We've worked well together, the past two years. We know one another. We've each earned a certain amount of the other's trust." He gave Isana a quite pointed glance and looked back at Tavi. "But by now you ought to know where I draw the line."

Tavi grimaced. Disappointment and a nauseating sense of dread began to spill through even his formidable discipline. "I do," he said quietly.

"Then you ought to know that I'm not going to play along with some kind of escape fiction." He grimaced. "I can't fight anymore, but I'm tired of everyone making light of the laws of the Realm. Abusing them, like Arnos did. I can't make them stop, but it doesn't mean I'm going to participate in it. I'll be glad to help you—by every legal means at my disposal."

"If you had an order from the Crown," Tavi said quietly, "you could do it."

"But I don't," Cyril said.

Isana's heart suddenly pounded very hard in her chest.

Tavi met Cyril's eyes, and said, quietly, "You do now."

Stars flared across Isana's vision, and she gripped the arms of her chair as hard as she could.

Cyril frowned at Tavi, and said, "What?"

Tavi gave Cyril half of a smile. "Come now, Cyril. You've known since the day you met me that my name wasn't Rufus Scipio."

Cyril's frown deepened. "Yes. I surmised that you were

one of the Crown's Cursors, given the way the Battle of Elinarch turned out. And what you've done since."

"And I am," Tavi said quietly. "But there's more. You've heard rumors about me by now. You've heard rumors about my *singulare*. Araris." Tavi paused for a moment. "*The* Araris. Araris Valerian."

Cyril stared at Tavi. His lips parted slightly.

"That's why I asked her to be here today," Tavi said, gesturing toward Isana. "Why I've spoken so openly in front of her."

Tavi turned to her, and Isana could feel his fear and frustration and anger and something else, something deep and powerful and terrifying for which there was no word. It was a kind of wonder, she thought dazedly, a kind of elation—and at the same time, it was a horror and dread.

Isana had felt it before, long ago. Tears blinded her as more memories came back to sudden, vivid life. *Oh, Septimus. I miss you so much. And in this moment, you would be so proud.*

She turned her face to Sir Cyril, blinking until the tears fell. The older man simply gaped at Tavi, his mouth still open, his eyes wide. Disbelief blended wildly with comprehension, well-aged anxiety with sudden hope. His hands closed into fists, and his voice shook as he spoke. "What," he whispered, "is your name?"

Tavi rose, slowly, lifting his chin. "My name," he said quietly, "is Gaius Octavian." He stepped forward and dropped to one knee, meeting Cyril eye to eye. "Sir Cyril, I trust you. That's why I've just put my life"—he nodded to Isana—"and my mother's into your hands."

Cyril stared at Tavi, his face bloodless. His mouth worked a couple of times, then he turned to Isana. "Your . . . your mother?"

Isana swallowed. Now she understood why Tavi had asked her here—to support him. She was, after all, very nearly the only one alive who could.

A panicked voice within told her to deny it. Without her corroboration, Tavi's story would sound like a wild, desperate, and implausible lie. She had to hide him. She *had* to protect him. She had to—

Isana pressed against that panicked voice, against her own terror.

It was time to stop lying. To stop hiding.

Without a word, she reached for the slender chain she'd worn around her neck ever since she had left the Calderon Valley for Alera Imperia, years before. She unfastened the clasp, and drew it from where it lay hidden beneath her gown. The elegant silver ring, complete with its gem of scarlet and azure, seamlessly joined down its center, caught the light and glittered brightly, throwing flickers of colored fire upon the top of Cyril's desk.

Isana set it there gently, and folded her hands in her lap. "Given me by my husband, Princeps Gaius Septimus," Isana said quietly, "upon our wedding, some ten months before his death." She rose to stand behind Tavi, facing Cyril, and lifted her own chin. "This is our son, Octavian. He was born the night of the First Battle of Calderon. The same night his father died."

Cyril stared at her. Then at the ring. He reached out to pick it up, his hands shaking visibly.

"The mark of his signet dagger is carved on the inside, beneath the stones," Isana said quietly. "He left me the dagger as well. It's in a trunk in my room."

The ring tumbled from Sir Cyril's fingertips, back to the top of the desk.

Cyril shook his head, stammering. "H-how can this be?"

Tavi, still on his knee, turned back to look up at Isana. For a second, she saw him again, the boy she had watched over, fed, cared for, loved. And lied to. Great furies help her, had there been more she could have done to hide him, she would have.

Araris had been right. He deserved the truth.

She met her son's eyes. "What very few know," Isana said, careful to keep her voice steady, her words clear, "is that Septimus had twice been attacked by assassins, in the two years prior to his death. His efforts to discover their employer were unsuccessful. When he took the Crown Legion to put down the rebellion at the Battle of Seven Hills, another assassin wounded him so badly, the night after the battle, that even with his own skills at healing, Septimus barely survived. That was why the First Lord sent the Crown Legion off to the farthest reaches of the Realm—to the Calderon Valley. Officially, it was to rest and recover from the losses sustained at Seven Hills. Only his *singulares* and Sextus knew it was to give Septimus a chance to recover in relative privacy." She grimaced. "Septimus wanted to return to Alera Imperia and dare them to come after him again—to catch whoever was behind it. But Sextus ordered him to Calderon.

"Septimus obeyed, but he wasn't content simply to rest and recover. He began sending out men he trusted to search for answers of his own. And . . ."

And how could she possibly speak of a thousand memories, of the words between them, of how Septimus had become her entire world? How could she convey what it had meant to touch his hand, to listen to his voice, to feel his heart beating against her as he slept? How could she make them know what it had felt like for an awkward holder girl to fall in love with a man so strong and gentle and kind?

"We met there," she said in a whisper. "We fell in love. We married."

Tavi stared up at her, and his expression was no longer a careful mask. He looked up at her the way any hungry child had ever looked up to his mother. He had been starving. For his whole life, he had been starving for the truth, and only now was he about to be sated.

"Septimus learned of a plot against him," she continued. "Several of the other young men of his generation—he wasn't sure who—had formed a cabal, swearing to remove him and displace the House of Gaius from the throne." She swallowed. "I think he suspected that the Marat invasion was engineered by this group of men. And it is my belief that they struck at him there, during the battle." Isana's tears blurred the room once more. "They killed him."

She swallowed and forced herself to continue. "Septimus had sent me from the camp, accompanied by my young sister, Alia, with Araris as my *singulare*, just before the Marat arrived. But I was heavy with child, and I began delivery before we could go more than a few miles. We hid in a cave. It was a difficult birthing. Alia helped me, but died of an arrow wound she'd gotten. That's where Octavian was born. In a cave. While his father fought invaders and traitors, and died so that others would have a chance to live."

Tavi's eyes suddenly shone. His expression didn't change, though the tears began to fall freely.

"I was alone," Isana said quietly. "But for Araris. And he could not protect Octavian from those who had murdered his father. Neither could Sextus. He hadn't protected his own son, and I would not chance mine upon his remorse." She felt her back straighten. "So I hid Octavian away. Araris marked his own face with the coward's brand, knowing no one would ever look for Araris Valerian beneath it, and sold himself into slavery. I purchased him, and he helped me watch over Tavi in my brother's steadholt." She reached out and touched his hair with one hand. "We told no one. Not even Octavian. There was no other way to keep him safe."

She met her son's eyes, and felt his bitterness, his lifelong ache and his newly born fear. She felt his rage. And, beneath all of it, threaded and braided with every emotion, was his love. Simple, strong—tarnished, perhaps, but not broken.

Her son still loved her.

He was angry, and afraid of the future, and broken with sadness about the loss of a father he'd never known, even if he did not himself realize it yet. Though his heart was wounded, the wounds could heal. They would pass, in time.

His love would not.

Isana crouched, bowed her head, and laid her forehead gently against Tavi's. He leaned into her, and his hands suddenly found hers, squeezing tight. They shared tears for a moment—tears of loss and regret and repentance.

Isana whispered, too quietly for Cyril to hear, "I'm so sorry. Your father would have been so proud of you, my Tavi."

Her son's shoulders twitched, and his breath caught in his throat for a second, before he bowed his head and leaned more against her. She put her arms around him in a sudden, fiercely tight embrace. He wept silently, his body jerking several times. Isana held him and closed her eyes.

She opened them again when she felt Cyril's pain. He stood from the desk, wincing as the weight went onto his maimed leg, and limped steadily around it. Wordlessly, he offered the ring and its chain back to Isana.

"Thank you," she whispered.

"You should hide it, my lady," he murmured back. "Until the time is right." Then he shifted position and dropped painfully to one knee.

Isana touched Tavi's shoulder.

He looked up to meet Sir Cyril's gaze.

Cyril bowed his head, deeply. "Your Highness," he murmured. "How may I serve the Crown?"

⋊⋉ CHAPTER 21

Tavi thought it somewhat ironic that the bunk in his cell was considerably more comfortable than his own. Granted, it had hardly been used during the two years since it had been built. The occasional drunken or brawling *legionare* had cooled his heels within, but that had been an infrequent event. In general, Tavi had followed Cyril's example of trusting his centurions to maintain discipline rather than meddling in it himself, and as a result the only *legionares* to see the inside of the cell had been those luckless or stupid enough to screw up in front of their captain's eyes.

Of course, he wasn't their captain anymore. He probably never would be again.

That bothered him more than he thought it would—especially since it was a position that had been thrust upon him by necessity in the first place. He'd only been here, at the Elinarch, for two years, but in that time it had become someplace familiar to him. It hadn't been a happy time. Too many

people had been hurt or killed for that. It had, however, been
an *important* time. There had been joy to balance the sorrow,
laughter to counter the tears. He had worked hard and won
respect as well as shed blood. He had made friends, too, of
those who had fought beside him.

It had become his home.

That was over now.

He lay in his bunk, staring up at the stone ceiling. He
missed his room in the command building. He missed the bustle of the Legion's routine. There were times when he missed
Bernardholt—Isanaholt, he corrected himself. Only it probably wouldn't be that for very much longer, either.

Declaring himself to Sir Cyril had changed all of that.
Learning the truth had changed it.

He tried to sort through his thoughts and feelings on the
matter, but it was a hopeless tangle. Isana was his mother. His
father had been murdered—and his enemies, presumably, were
still at liberty. Should he feel rage at whoever had taken his father from him? It seemed to him that he should, but he hadn't
felt it yet. In stories, a young man in his position should be
making oaths of vengeance and setting out with grim determination to punish his father's killers.

Instead, he just felt numb. Too much had happened too
quickly. Isana's emotions, as she told him about his father . . .
had been exquisitely painful. He'd drunk them down like a man
dying of thirst despite that, but there was no denying that the experience had shaken him severely. Perhaps this oddly peaceful
lack of emotions was simply the result of overexposure, like the
ringing in his ears during the silence after the roar of battle.

He'd felt his mother's grief and regret and anxiety as distinctly as if they had been his own. He had never felt another's
emotions so clearly before—not even Kitai's. He wondered
why his senses had seemed so much more adept when it came
to Isana. Before, he had only imagined her good intentions, her
fears, her motivations in lying to him and everyone else for all
those years.

Now, he *knew*. He knew that she had acted as she had out
of love and desperation, taking the only measures she could to
protect him. He knew how deeply she had loved Septimus and

how viciously his death had wounded her. He knew how much she loved him. When she finally talked to him about it, she had told him the truth, complete and open, not only with her words but with the heart and mind beneath them. He *knew* it. There was absolutely no room for doubt.

She would never apologize for what she had done. Her words had been an apology for the pain he'd undergone, over those years, regret for the necessities she had been forced to; but she would never apologize for doing them. Tavi knew that now. She had done what she thought was right and necessary. He could either respect that or hold it against her for the rest of his life.

He rubbed at his aching head. He was tired. Holding grudges took far too much energy—energy he would need for more immediate endeavors. The past had lain quietly for more than twenty years. It could keep a little longer. The future was all one vast, terrible vagary. It could wait. It always did.

Lives were at stake here and now.

Tavi ground his teeth in frustration and glared at the door of iron bars. It wasn't really an obstacle. He could probably summon up enough strength to rip the door out of the wall, hinges and all. The idea had a certain primal appeal, but it seemed a little excessive. It wouldn't take more than a moment or two to pick the lock, which would make for a better, quieter escape in any case.

The problem was that the door wasn't his obstacle. The law was. Tavi could have ordered Cyril to release him, but it would have required him to violate a number of laws, and that could have repercussions for him in the long run. It was by no means guaranteed that simply *being* Gaius Sextus's blood heir would be sufficient actually to give him the power of a Princeps with which to protect Cyril from such actions. There was no guarantee that Gaius would accept him—and even if he did, there was no guarantee that the House of Gaius would continue holding the Crown.

He hadn't dared to ask Cyril for much, for his own sake. He hadn't told Cyril anything of his plans. He hadn't asked for any cooperation of any kind, in fact. If things went bad, and Cyril was questioned by a truthfinder, later, he would honestly be able to say that he hadn't helped Tavi escape and had no idea where he was going or what he was doing.

Where the crows was Ehren?

Waiting for dark, of course. From inside the cell, Tavi had no way of guessing where the sun was. He stretched, sighed, and settled in to try to sleep. Many soldiers learned how to take immediate sleep during any free moment—but officers rarely had any such time to spare, and Tavi hadn't been able to pick up the trick of it. He lay with his thoughts for two hours, waiting for the sun to go down, until he finally managed to begin to drift off to sleep.

Naturally, that was when Ehren came. Footsteps approached the cell door, and Tavi sat up and swung his feet off the bunk. By the time they'd hit the stone floor, the cell door rattled and opened, and the sandy-haired little Cursor stood in the doorway, dressed in simple and well-made traveling clothes, a bundle of clothing under one arm. He tossed it to Tavi.

Tavi lost no time shedding his uniform and donning the unremarkable civilian's clothing. "Any problems?"

"Not yet," Ehren said. He shook a rather large, rather heavy-looking purse at his side. It jingled. "I wouldn't have thought Cyril had this kind of money."

"Merchant family. They have a lot of connections in the Senate." Tavi finished dressing, paused for a moment to consider, and then laid his uniform clothes out on the bunk, positioned as they would be if he had been sleeping in them. "There."

Ehren snorted. "That ought to make for an interesting rumor or two."

Tavi grinned. "Can't hurt. What about the guard?"

Ehren tapped the purse again. "Two of the girls who used to work for Mistress Cymnea have him pretty thoroughly distracted. We could smash our way through the wall with mining picks, and he wouldn't notice."

Tavi let out a small sigh of relief. "Good. I didn't want anyone to get hurt over this."

"The night is young," Ehren said.

Once Tavi was dressed, Ehren tossed him a long, dark

cloak with a deep hood, similar to his own. They pulled the hoods up and left the cell. Ehren locked it behind them. They left the command building by the back door and hurried away through the darkened streets.

"How long before the wind coach arrives?" Tavi asked.

Ehren grimaced. "There's a problem."

Tavi arched an eyebrow.

"Windcrafters were expensive and hard to find even before the war," Ehren said. "Legions all over Alera have been offering incentives to recruit more of them. All the fliers who haven't gone into the Legions are overworked already, even with their prices raised through the roof."

"I don't care what it costs. We need a coach."

"We aren't getting one," Ehren said. "We're in the middle of nowhere. None of the coaches are willing to fly all the way out to a war zone with empty seats."

"Crows," Tavi spat. "Where are we headed?"

"The docks," Ehren replied. "The others are waiting there."

Tavi stopped and blinked at Ehren. "A ship? We'll have to sail halfway around the coast to get to the Gaul."

Ehren shrugged. "Beggars and choosers. It will take even longer to walk it."

Tavi sighed. They walked down one of the many wooden staircases that led down the riverbank to the extensive docks that lined both sides of the river. Taverns and warehouses lined the waterside, and if the Legions had departed, the traders and rivermen hadn't. The docks were as busy as any other night, and Tavi and Ehren had no trouble blending in.

Ehren led them to one of the larger docks, and out along it to its lone occupant, a lean and ill-favored ship conspicuous for its lack of furylamps—and passersby. No one but themselves seemed willing to pace down its wooden length, and Tavi was just as glad. In the darkness, Tavi could just barely make out the letters on the ship's prow proclaiming it the *Slive*.

Several cloaked figures waited at the bottom of the gangplank, and one of them broke away from the others to walk toward Tavi.

"*Chala,*" Kitai said quietly, and embraced him. "I missed you. You are well?"

Tavi kissed her hair. "I'm fine."

His mother was close behind Kitai. She gave him a smile and an uncertain nod. Tavi released the Marat woman and went to Isana, hugging her.

Tavi felt a sudden sense of relief surge through her. She hugged him back, hard.

"We'll have some time. We'll talk," he said quietly.

She nodded, not speaking, and they broke the embrace.

Araris stepped forward from the shadows and nodded to Tavi. He offered Tavi his sword belt, and Tavi accepted it gratefully, glad to feel the familiar weight of the weapon once more at his side. Araris, his eyes in constant motion, moved silently to stand behind Tavi, watching the length of the dock between them and the shore.

"Captain," Ehren called quietly. "We're ready."

A man appeared at the head of the gangplank and walked quietly down it. He was a little taller than average and lean, and wore a long blade at his hip. He stepped onto the dock and stopped when he was standing just out of reach of Tavi's *gladius*—but within the range of his own weapon. He had a flat, cool mask of a face and the guarded, calculating eyes of a professional swordsman.

"This is Captain Demos," Ehren said. "He was the man who got me back to Alera in time to warn you of the Canim fleet."

Demos nodded to Tavi. "Who are you?"

"Rufus Scipio," Tavi replied.

Demos blinked once and shrugged. "All right. Ehren here tells me you have a job."

"I need passage to the capital and back. I need to move some goods discreetly. Can you do it?"

Demos shrugged. "Probably. If the price is right."

"Let's talk price, then," Tavi said.

"I don't haggle," Demos replied. "You pay it. Or you find someone else."

Tavi studied the man quietly for a moment. Then he shrugged. "How much?"

"Five hundred eagles," Demos replied. "That's just the transport fee. The bribes are an extra expense. So is the food. You pay me half up front, half on completion."

Tavi glanced aside at Ehren, who nodded once.

"Done," Tavi said.

Demos looked between the two of them, then at the others. "Get this straight. You might be hiring me, but I'm the captain on my ship. I don't take orders. I give them. If I give you an order, I expect you to obey it, or you'll swim the rest of the way."

"I understand," Tavi said.

"Still want to do business?"

Tavi held out his hand to Ehren. The Cursor slapped the heavy purse into it. Tavi tossed the purse to Demos, who plucked it out of the air with a lazy movement of his arm.

Demos bounced the purse on his palm once and nodded. His face twitched with an expression that, if it had not been murdered in its birth, might have grown into a smile. "Very well, sir. Welcome aboard the *Slive*. We'll cast off in half an hour." He turned and went back up onto his ship and started calling out commands. Men began moving around the deck, readying ropes and sails.

Tavi grimaced at the ship. "Ehren."

The young Cursor nodded and raised his hand, while a frown of concentration came over his face. The air pressed suddenly against Tavi's ears, more uncomfortable than painful.

"All right," Ehren said. "That's as much as I can do."

Tavi nodded. "How long will it take us to get there by ship?"

"Three weeks, give or take," Ehren said quietly.

"Too long," Tavi said.

"I don't think you thought this through very well," Ehren said. "Let's say we had a coach right now. What did you plan on doing? Telling them to fly up to the Grey Tower, wait until you got back with a nine-foot-tall furry prisoner, then to come back here? Every Knight Aeris who can get off the ground will come after the coach to get him back."

"What?" Kitai demanded.

"What?" Isana said, alarmed.

Araris made a choking noise, but he didn't turn around.

Tavi grimaced. "We couldn't outrun them on horseback either."

"Right," Ehren said. "If only we knew some way to sneak a high-profile Cane out of the capital without being caught."

Tavi gave him a sidelong glance. Ehren's face was creased into a grin. Tavi frowned for a moment, then struck his own forehead lightly with the heel of his hand. "It's already been done. Someone managed to slip Sarl out of the capital and all the way back to the Canim homelands."

"Exactly," Ehren said.

"And you found out how they did it?"

Ehren smirked. "Better. I found out *who*."

Tavi looked up at the ship. "I see."

"Aleran," Kitai said. "Perhaps it would be wise to tell all of us what we are doing."

Tavi chewed on his lip for a moment, then nodded. "We're going to Alera Imperia. We're going to break Ambassador Varg out of the Grey Tower, smuggle him back to Nasaug, and exchange him as a token of good faith for a cessation of hostilities in the Vale."

Araris made another choking sound.

Kitai nodded. "Ah."

Isana folded her arms beneath her cloak. "Is . . . is that all together wise?"

Kitai rolled her eyes. "Why should he start now?"

"The security has been tightened there," Ehren said. "I read a report on it somewhere, three or four years ago."

"I know," Tavi said. "I wrote it. Gaius had it redesigned based on some of my recommendations."

Ehren pursed his lips thoughtfully. "Oh. That does raise some interesting possibilities, then."

Tavi nodded. "But I need each of you there. That's why I've asked you along."

"That," Kitai said, "is the least unwise thing you have said tonight." She peered up at the *Slive*, her eyes tracing the dim shapes of the ropes and the sailors moving nimbly among them. "I have never been on a ship."

"Nor have I," Tavi said. "Ehren, what—"

"Down!" barked Araris, even as his blade cleared its sheath. He swept it in a single, smooth cut, and there was a snapping sound as it cleaved an arrow streaking down the length of the dock.

Tavi crouched as Araris shattered two more arrows with as many sweeps of his blade and looked around them wildly. There were figures out there at the riverbank end of the dock, crouching in thick shadow.

"The ship," Tavi snapped. "Everyone aboard! Move!"

Another arrow hissed, and Kitai let out a breathless cry. Tavi felt a sudden, vague shock of pain run through the left side of his body. The Marat girl staggered.

"Go, go!" shouted Araris.

Tavi seized Kitai, tossed her unceremoniously over a shoulder, and dashed up the gangplank. Isana followed him, but stumbled. Ehren was there at once, supporting her. Tavi made the deck of the ship and hurried to get out of sight of the archer's shooting position. Araris came up the gangplank last, sword still in hand.

Demos took one look, saw what was happening, and began barking orders to cast off. His crew, evidently men who were familiar with the procedures for precipitous departures, leapt into action, and within a minute the ship was being warped away from the dock and out into the slow current of the Tiber.

"Light!" Tavi called, laying Kitai down on the deck. "I need a light here!"

Demos appeared a few moments later, bearing a covered lantern. He handed it to Tavi without a word and went back to calling orders.

Tavi opened the lantern and found a plain candle burning inside. It gave him enough light to see Kitai's injury. The arrow had pierced her left arm, on an angle through the biceps muscle. Her teeth were clenched, though there was more outrage than pain in her face.

"Doesn't look bad," Tavi said.

Isana knelt beside him, and examined the Marat girl's wound. "The head isn't poisoned or barbed, but it's sharp. It's close to the artery. If we try to draw it back through, we could open it ourselves."

Tavi nodded. "Break the arrow?"

"Let me get a proper tub of water first," Isana said. "It's possible that the arrow itself is staunching the wound. I can make sure it isn't a problem."

"Araris?" Tavi asked.

"I'll find a tub," the *singulare* said, sheathing his weapon.

Tavi leaned down and kissed Kitai's hair again. "Give us just a minute," he said quietly. "Then we'll get it out of you."

Kitai set her jaw, nodded once, and closed her eyes.

Ehren leaned down and picked up the lantern. He frowned and moved it. "There. Do you see?"

Tavi looked up to where the candle's light fell upon the fletching of the arrow that had wounded Kitai. The feathers were black, green, brown, with a black band at their base.

He'd seen them before, at close quarters in the Senator's wind coach.

"Iris the Hawk," Tavi said quietly.

"Good thing Demos didn't have any lights up," Ehren murmured. "Even shooting in the dark, she hit one of us."

Tavi made sure the light of the little lantern was blocked from the docks behind them, then rose, staring back at the dock they'd just departed.

A slender figure, sword in hand, stood at the end of the dock, barely visible in the light of the furylamps on the boardwalk: Phrygiar Navaris. Several others came to stand beside her—the rest of Arnos's *singulares.* Tavi fancied he could feel Navaris's serpentine hatred drifting over the water.

"It would seem," Ehren said, "that someone doesn't want you making this trip."

"Then someone," Tavi replied, "is going to be disappointed."

Amara crouched beside Bernard in the wavering light of his woodcrafting as another patrol wound slowly through the forest and away from them. As the last of them went out of sight, she murmured, "Have I mentioned how attractive you've been, the last several da—"

Bernard moved suddenly, and his hand clamped gently over her mouth. He let out a soft breath that nonetheless conveyed a warning, and Amara fell silent. The forest sighed around them, the thickening leaves rustling in a low breeze. She saw nothing, heard nothing. She turned to Bernard, her face set in a question.

He touched a finger to his lips. Then, his eyes unfocused, he raised his bow.

Amara stared at him, hardly daring to move.

Bernard glanced down at the ground beneath him, and she saw his face grow intent. His lips moved.

The earth suddenly rippled out from him in a circle—not a violent upheaval, but a single, rippling pulse, as if someone had struck the ground with a large hammer.

Bits of dust and old leaves leapt up from the ground in a low shower. Not twenty feet in front of them, some of the bracken struck against something solid but unseen.

In the same instant, Bernard's bow bent and thrummed. There was an immediate, ugly sound of impact, and then a man appeared, dressed in leathers and bearing a bow of his own. Bernard's broad-headed, thick-shafted arrow protruded at an angle from the man's back.

Bernard moved, a single bound that took him most of the way to the other man, and Amara could see that he had dropped his bow and drawn his hunting knife from the sheath at his side. The other man straightened, turning, but before he could cry out or bring his own weapon to bear, Bernard was on his back, and bore him to the ground. Amara watched as, with brutal efficiency, Bernard reached around with his knife and cut his throat.

Bernard held the other man down, grinding his face into the dirt until his struggles ceased half a minute later. Then he straightened, slowly, his head up, eyes focused in the direction the rest of the patrol had gone. After another full minute had passed, Bernard turned to Amara and nodded once, beckoning.

Amara turned behind her. "Sire."

Gaius came out of the woods behind them, moving more easily than he had since the first days of their journey, though he still carried the walking staff. The First Lord moved up to stand beside Bernard and looked down at the body. He touched the fallen man's powerful bow with the end of his staff.

"A Knight Flora," the First Lord said quietly. "Like you."

"Never served as a Knight, sire," Bernard said, shaking his head. "Centurion in the auxiliary cohort."

Gaius glanced at him. "Mmmm. But obviously you had the skill for it."

Bernard shrugged. "Knights in my Legion . . . seemed a little full of themselves, sire. Didn't feel like spending all my time with them."

Amara walked up to stand beside her husband, still somewhat shocked at the suddenness of what had happened. She had seen violence before, but she had never seen Bernard engaged in it against another man. She knew he had been a soldier, in his past, but for some reason she had never pictured him killing in such a way. For a moment, his idle chat with the First Lord seemed wildly inappropriate—but only until she saw the faintly sickened expression in his eyes.

She touched his elbow. "Are you all right?" she asked.

He nodded without speaking. Then he looked at his bloodied knife, knelt down, and wiped it clean on the man's clothing. When he rose, his voice was rough. "He'd heard us. Or sensed us somehow. I could tell he had stopped right about there."

Gaius grimaced. "You had little choice, then. Even if he

hadn't seen through your veil, he'd have circled back and picked up our trail."

Bernard nodded. "And the way he was trailing their normal patrol means that he was expecting to catch us moving after they had passed." He looked up and met Amara's gaze for no more than a second. "They know we're out here and that we've got some woodcraft on our side if they spared someone like him to look for us."

"How long before they notice he's missing?" Amara asked.

Bernard took a deep breath and nodded to himself. "As long as possible." He turned to the body, and rapidly went through the man's pockets and a small belt pouch. He discarded everything he found, shook his head, then touched the ground with his fingertips, murmuring under his breath. The earth quivered, and then the body began sinking into it, as if into very soft mud. Within a minute, it was gone from sight altogether, leaving nothing but an oblong, rounded patch of bare earth in its wake.

At Bernard's direction, Amara and Gaius helped him scatter more of the detritus of the forest floor over the bare patch, and he went over it himself, once they were done, until he was satisfied that they had concealed it. "All right," he said afterward. "A man like this, if he'd found our trail, might well take off and follow it alone for a time. Even if the patrol noticed he was gone within the hour, they might not think anything of it if he doesn't show up until the end of the day."

Amara nodded. "It makes sense. What do we do about it?"

"We make a better pace," Bernard said. "As fast as we can, for as long as we can. I can cover our trail pretty well for an hour, maybe two. The farther we get before we start leaving tracks again, the longer it will take them to find our trail using a standard search pattern."

"We've most of the distance still ahead," Amara said. "A couple of hours—even a full day's lead won't be enough. They'll catch up long before we get to Kalare."

"We don't have to beat them to Kalare," Bernard replied. "We just have to beat them to the swamps. No one's going to be able to track us through that." He looked up at Gaius. "We've got to pick up the pace, sire."

Gaius nodded, his expression sober. "I'll manage, Count."

Bernard turned to Amara. "I've got to walk behind us to hide our trail. It's going to take much of my attention. Do you think you've learned enough to hold a straight course?"

Amara swallowed. Over the week they'd been traveling, Bernard had been improving upon her rather rudimentary fieldcraft as they marched and in camp at night. She would never have believed how difficult something as simple as traveling in a straight line could be, once one was surrounded by miles and miles of forest. It all looked the same. The sun was often hidden by the canopy of leaves and branches, assuming it was a sunny day in the first place, and that old chestnut about moss growing on the north side of the trees was entirely unreliable.

As it turned out, there was a great deal more simple know-how than furycrafting involved in navigating overland. That was to be expected, she supposed. The vast majority of Alerans lived in steadholts in the countryside, and few of them possessed anywhere near the talent Bernard did in even one form of furycrafting, much less two. Amara had formed a habit of learning new skills, thanks to her Cursor training, but the lessons had served mostly to make her acutely aware of how much she didn't know.

She had little choice, though. There were only three of them, and even if Gaius had the necessary skill—which she doubted— he would have difficulty enough simply holding the pace.

"I've had a good teacher," she said quietly, nodding.

Bernard gave her a small smile. "All right. Find your points of reference, and let's turn a bit more to the east."

Amara took a deep breath and returned his smile with one she hoped did not look as nervous as she felt. Then she lined up a tree behind her with one in front of her in the direction they wanted to move, and led the way.

They were able to maintain a surprisingly good pace over the next hour. Amara broke into a relaxed lope whenever the ground was smooth enough to warrant it. Though Gaius's face grew lined with discomfort, and though he still favored his leg, he was able to keep up. Bernard followed along several yards behind them, frowning down at the ground and only occasionally looking around him.

After that, though, their pace began to suffer, and more because of Bernard than the First Lord. The woodsman's jaw had locked into a stubborn clench, and he shambled along with heavy feet, like a man bearing an increasingly heavy burden. Gaius noticed Bernard's discomfort and frowned at Amara.

She grimaced, just as worried as the First Lord, but she knew what Bernard would say if she suggested they rest. Amara shook her head in a negative, and kept going at the best pace she thought they could sustain.

By the time the light began to slant steeply through the forest and darken into shafts of sunset amber, Bernard was barely managing to keep himself moving forward. Amara began looking for someplace out of sight where they could rest, and found it in a broad ditch where a stream had evidently shifted its bed. Gaius slipped down into it with a grunt of discomfort, but Bernard was shaking with fatigue when he tried to climb down and nearly toppled headfirst into the ditch.

Amara managed to steady him, and he promptly sat down on the ground, leaned his back against the side of the ditch, and dropped his head forward in exhausted sleep.

"How far did we come, do you think?" Gaius asked quietly. The First Lord was vigorously rubbing his bad leg.

Amara saw it jerking and twitching in a cramp, and winced in sympathy. "Since he began covering our trail? Perhaps eight or nine miles. It's excellent time, considering."

Gaius grimaced. "Nothing like a nice walk to make one appreciate flying, eh?"

"True enough, sire." She moved to him and withdrew her flask from her pack. She offered it to the First Lord, and Gaius accepted it with a nod of thanks and drank thirstily.

"Not precisely my question, though," Gaius said. "How far have we come, in total? I've been a tad distracted myself."

Amara settled down on the ground beside him, the better to keep their murmured words as quiet as possible. "Let me think. It has been nine days since we set forth, of which we have been on the move for a little more than seven." She mused over the terrain they had passed, adding the figures in her head. "Somewhere between one hundred thirty and one hundred forty miles, sire, or so I should judge."

Gaius blew out a breath. "I confess, I thought we would make much better time."

"We're past some of the more difficult terrain," she said. "From here, the hills should become considerably gentler until we reach the swamps." She scratched her nose, and waved away a buzzing midge. "Call it another six or seven days to the swamps. Then our pace will slow dramatically."

Gaius nodded. "The last thirty or forty miles will be the hardest."

Amara glanced down at his foot. "Yes." Gaius caught the direction of her gaze, and arched an eyebrow. Amara felt her face flush. "Meaning no criticism, sire."

"I doubt you could give me more than I've already given myself," Gaius said, his tone light. His eyes, though, darkened a few shades, and his hands tightened into fists. "Hiding from a few squads of searchers. Running until the Count has half killed himself with effort. If we were close enough to Kalare, by the great furies, I'd . . ." He cut himself off, and shook his head sharply. "But that's not yet, is it?"

"No, sire," Amara said quietly. "Not yet. But we'll get you through."

Gaius was silent for a long moment. When he spoke, his voice was weary. "Yes. I expect you will."

Amara frowned at him. "Sire?"

He shook his head. "It isn't that time yet, either."

Something in his tone alarmed her, and she felt her frown deepen. "I don't understand."

"That's as it must be for the present," he said, and leaned his head back against the wall of the ravine. "Rest for a bit. We should try to rouse Count Calderon before long. Cover more ground before nightfall."

"Are you sure you're ready for that, sire?"

"I'd better be, Countess," murmured the First Lord, and closed his eyes. "I'd better be."

CHAPTER 23

Tavi spent an eternity in misery, longing for death to bring sweet release from the unrelenting torment. The others gathered at the side of his bunk on the ship, keeping a deathwatch over him.

"I don't see what all the drama is about," Demos said, his quiet voice filled with habitual disinterest. "He's seasick. It will pass."

Tavi groaned, rolled onto his side, and convulsed. There was little but tepid water in his belly, but he tried to get most of it into the bucket anyway. Kitai held him steady until the heaves passed, and regarded Demos, Tavi, and the bucket with more or less equal distaste.

Demos frowned at the bucket and Tavi. "Though I worry about the water stores, the way he's going through them." He leaned down to address Tavi directly. "I don't suppose it would be possible for you to get this back down again. It would conserve our—"

Tavi threw up again.

Demos sighed, shook his head, and said, "It will pass. Eventually."

"What if it doesn't?" Tavi heard his mother demand.

"I wouldn't worry," Demos said. "It's hardly ever fatal." The captain nodded politely to them and departed the low-beamed cabin.

"Lady Isana?" Kitai asked. Tavi thought that her own voice sounded strained. "Is there nothing your watercraft can do?"

"Not without interfering with the *Slive*'s witchmen," Araris said quietly.

"I do not understand," Kitai said.

"They're watercrafters, Kitai," Ehren said, from the bunk

above Tavi's. Tavi heard paper rustle as the young Cursor flipped a page in his book. "They're necessary to any deep-water ship, to prevent a leviathan from sensing us."

"Leviathan," Kitai said. "Like the thing that came to feed on offal and Canim at the Elinarch?"

"That one was only forty or fifty feet long," Ehren said. "A baby, as they go. An adult leviathan, even a fairly small one, would smash this ship to driftwood."

"Why would it do such a thing?" Kitai asked.

"They're territorial," the Cursor replied. "They'll attack any vessel that sails into the waters they claim."

"And these witchmen prevent that?"

"They prevent the leviathans from noticing the ship," Ehren said. "Of course, if a good storm kicks up, sometimes the leviathans find the ship anyway." After a meditative pause, he added, "Sailing is sort of dangerous."

Kitai growled. "Then could we not put in to shore, where the water is too shallow to permit these beasts to approach, and allow the lady to attempt a healing?"

"No," Tavi managed to growl. "No time . . . to waste on . . . pampering my stoma—" He broke off before he could finish the word and heaved again.

Kitai supported him until he was finished, then pressed a flask of water to his lips. Tavi drank, though it seemed pointless. The water would barely have time to get into his belly before he'd be losing it again. His stomach muscles burned with constant fatigue and throbbed with pain.

Tavi looked up to find his mother looking down on him, her expression gentle and concerned. "Perhaps you shouldn't talk of such things here," she said.

"As long as we keep our voices down, it shouldn't be an issue, Steadholder," Ehren said. "We're at sea. The salt spray makes it all but impossible to work with air furies. Anyone who wants to eavesdrop will have to do it physically."

"He's right," Araris said in a quiet voice. "And don't pay any attention to Demos's sense of humor, Isana. As long as we can keep getting a little water into the captain here, he'll be fine. He'll adjust to the sea eventually."

Kitai made a sound of disapproval that was not quite offensively rude. She had considerably refined her manners during her time in Alera, Tavi thought, but even so the lingering fatigue of having her arm crafted whole again, plus her concern for him, was wearing on her more and more heavily.

"When?" Isana asked quietly. "We've been at sea for four days. How long will it take?"

"As long as it takes," Araris said, his voice patient. Tavi heard the *singulare* rise and move toward the cabin's door. He paused to put a reassuring hand on Kitai's shoulder. When Tavi opened his eyes to look up at him, Araris gave him one of his brief, rare smiles. "For what it's worth, I knew another man who was a bad sailor once."

Tavi felt his mouth twitch, but that was as close as he could get to smiling back.

"I'm going to get some sleep now," Araris said. "I'll sit with him tonight."

Kitai glowered up at the *singulare* as if she would object, but she did not. Tavi supposed that after four sleepless days at his side, the bags beneath her eyes had finally begun to outweigh her pride.

Tavi spent the rest of the day fighting his rolling stomach and giving considerable thought to blissfully brief suicide. He drifted into a sleep broken by disorienting dreams and waves of particularly acute nausea. By the time the daylight had begun to fade, Kitai lay curled up on the lower half of his bunk, sound asleep.

With Araris's help, Tavi staggered out onto the deck once night had fallen. Most of the crew sought their bunks and hammocks after the sun set, and only a few remained on deck. Tavi stretched out at the base of the mainmast, where he hoped the rocking of the ship would be least felt. He watched as the stars began to appear on a fine, clear night, and dropped into a true sleep for the first time in days.

When he awoke, the first thing he noticed was a small but steadily growing pang of hunger in his belly. The night had grown pleasantly chill, though no less clear, and when he sat up he was nearly dizzied by a startling lack of disorientation. His nausea had faded to a faint echo of itself. He stood up slowly and stretched.

"Try to focus on the stars, or else the horizon," said a soft voice at the side of the ship. "It can help, sometimes."

Tavi padded over the deck and stood at the rail with Araris. The *singulare* stared out at the water, his eyes focused into the distance, and Tavi was content to stand beside him in silence for a long while. The sea rushed against the ship, a constant murmur, and their passage left trails of luminescence in their wake. Tavi turned his face into the breeze, tried to ignore the sore muscles of his stomach, and savored the absence of illness.

Araris broke the silence. "Have you talked to her yet?"

"Not really," Tavi replied. "Hasn't been time."

"She loves you. Very much."

"I know," Tavi said quietly. "But . . ."

"That doesn't make it any easier," Araris supplied.

Tavi nodded.

"Do you understand why we did what we did?"

He nodded again. "That doesn't make it much easier, either."

Araris stared out at the waters. Then he pushed away from the railing and padded away. He returned and offered Tavi a flat, rectangular piece of what looked something like very dry bread.

"Ship's crackers," he supplied. "Good for a sour stomach."

Tavi nodded his thanks and gnawed at a corner of the bread. He'd broken stones softer than the stuff, but with enough work he managed to get a few gravelly bits to break off, and they softened in his mouth as he chewed. They tasted a little stale, but his stomach began to feel steadier after only a few mouthfuls.

Between bites, Tavi asked, "What was he like?"

Araris's head turned toward him in the darkness. Tavi could see nothing of his expression—only a glitter from his eyes. Araris stared at him for a time, then turned his face back to the sea. "Arrogant," he said, finally. "Impatient. Short-tempered." His teeth gleamed. "And compassionate. Intelligent. Generous. Fearless." Araris sighed. "Too much so."

Tavi said nothing, waiting.

"Septimus was never satisfied with things the way they were. Everywhere he went, in everything he did, he tried to leave a place better than when he found it. When he saw injustice, he worked to set it right. When he found victims, he offered them succor—then he avenged them. If he sank his teeth into an argument, he'd hold on until he'd won it or it died. I never saw him speak an unkind word to a child, strike a dog, or take spurs to his horse.

"When he fought, it was like a thunderstorm going to war, and I never saw his better with a blade. We would have taken a spear in the heart for him—we, his *singulares*. We all thought he would become a great First Lord. As great as the original Gaius Primus. He was one of the first Citizens to speak out publicly against slavery, you know."

Tavi shook his head. "I didn't."

"He had a habit of making allies of his enemies," Araris said. "You should have seen the brawls he had with Antillus Raucus at the Academy—but they ended as friends. He had . . . a kind of grace, about him. He could face a man down without taking his pride. If he'd lived, he would have . . ." Araris's voice closed off for a moment. He cleared his throat, and said, "Everything would be different."

"If," Tavi said. The word carried far more weight than it should have—bitterness, longing, sadness.

Araris squinted out at the ocean. "And he loved your mother more than air and light. He defied his father's direct command when he wed her. Gaius had other ideas about who would make him a suitable wife."

"Do . . ." Tavi cleared his throat. "Do you think he would have been . . . a good father?"

"He would have loved you," Araris said at once. He frowned. "But . . ."

"He would have been busy making things better?"

Araris was silent for a long time. "Perhaps," he said, the word coming out reluctantly. "Great furies know there was distance enough between him and his own father. But perhaps not. Children can change a man like few other things can."

Araris offered Tavi a flask, and Tavi accepted it. More tepid water, but at least he felt like it would stay down this time.

"Have you given any thought to what we're doing?" Araris asked.

Tavi frowned. "Of course."

Araris shook his head. "I know you've been planning it. You've thought about what we're doing, and how. You've thought about what was to be gained or lost. But I wonder if you've given much consideration to the why of it."

Tavi felt a flash of uncertainty, followed hard by anger. He swallowed both with the next mouthful of water, and said, "Because it's going to save lives."

"It might," Araris said, nodding. "But . . . I wonder if you have the right to make this choice."

"I'd approach Gaius," Tavi said, "but for whatever reason, he's out of reach. I already tried to contact him via my coin. Ehren, too."

"From what you told me, you already did ask him about seeking a diplomatic solution," Araris said. "And he flatly denied you."

"That was before he knew all the details."

"Which gives you the right to decide policy that's going to have a great many repercussions? Leaving aside the legality of what you're doing, what you're attempting is going to be viewed very badly from a great many directions, even if you're totally successful."

Tavi sighed. "You think I'm overstepping my authority as a Cursor."

"I know you're doing that," Araris replied. "I question whether or not you're overstepping your . . . new authority."

"What difference does it make?"

"Your claim to that authority is based upon authority derived from the law and from principles of justice," Araris said, his voice quiet and intent. "If you begin your new role by spitting on that law, those principles, you're undermining your own position. Eroding the ethical foundations from which your authority should derive."

Tavi heard himself chuckle quietly. "Believe it or not, I've thought of that."

Araris tilted his head slightly to one side, listening.

"What I learned from Nasaug, and the opportunity that it

created, is clearly information of critical importance. It would probably influence Gaius's reasoning very strongly—certainly enough to force him to reconsider his earlier decision. Agreed?"

Araris nodded once.

Tavi turned to face him. "But he's gone. I don't know where he is, or what he's doing, but for the purposes of this crisis, he's been incapacitated. Normally, if that happened, we'd consult with whoever was next in the chain of command—and then that person would make the decision."

Araris made a small, skeptical sound. "That's . . . quite a shaky foundation."

Tavi half grinned. "I know," he said quietly. "But . . . if I'm to be what I was meant to be, it means that I have a responsibility to this Realm and its people. And if I don't act, it's going to be a real nightmare." He put a hand on Araris's shoulder. "You ask me how I can possibly justify doing this. But the real question is this: How can I possibly justify doing *nothing*?"

Araris stared at him for a moment, then shook his head and snorted.

They turned back to stare at the ocean again, and Tavi asked, "I need you. Be honest with me. Are you against this?"

"I was against you rushing in without being sure of your own motives," he replied. "Your father was a good man. But he had a tendency to trust his instincts too much. To act without thinking. He leaned on his power to get him out of any problems that arose."

"Not really an issue with me," Tavi murmured.

Araris laughed quietly. "No. You're stronger than he was." He mused for a moment. "And probably more dangerous."

Tavi hardly knew how to respond to that. He lapsed into silence for another several minutes. Then he asked, "Your opinion. Can we do it?"

Araris replied without hesitation. "I don't see how it's possible."

Tavi grunted and chewed on his lip.

Araris sighed and spoke with reluctance. "But that's never really stopped you before, has it?"

Tavi barked out a short laugh, and he saw Araris smile beside him.

"You should get some sleep," Araris said. "You'll need it. Practice tomorrow."

"Practice?" Tavi asked.

Araris Valerian nodded. "You've got your basics with a sword. You're ready for some serious training."

Tavi blinked. He had thought himself . . . well. Quite skilled with a blade. "Do you really think that's necessary?"

Araris laughed. "Your father used to ask me the same thing."

"What did you tell him?"

"As you wish, milord," Araris responded. His smile faded. "And someone killed him. So you're practicing tomorrow, and every day after. And you'll keep it up until I'm satisfied."

"When will that be?"

"When you can beat me," Araris said. He bowed his head to Tavi and nodded toward the cabin. "Get some rest, milord."

◁◁◁◁◁ CHAPTER 24

Isana watched as Tavi's bare back slammed into the bulkhead of the *Slive*'s cabin for the ninth time in thirty minutes. The young man bounced back wheezing, but his sword kept moving, catching and turning two slashes and sliding aside a long thrust from his opponent. He wasn't quite fast enough, though, and a string of scarlet beads appeared along one of his ribs.

Isana winced, more at the flash of frustration and chagrin that came from Tavi than from sympathy for his pain. The wound was a minor one, and Isana could close it without trouble, after practice. It wouldn't even scar. Araris would never inflict anything more serious upon any student, much less upon this one.

Tavi'd had the wind knocked out of him, and it showed when he let out a weak yell and pressed a furious attack against

Araris. The *singulare* blocked every single attack, seemingly by the barest of margins, then made a peculiar, circular motion of his wrist. Tavi's sword rolled abruptly from his grasp and fell to the deck.

Tavi didn't wait a second, pressing in close and getting a grip on Araris's sword arm. He slammed his forehead against Araris's cheekbone, and drove a hard blow into his ribs with another yell. Isana tensed suddenly, half-rising, as she sensed the wave of pure anger now rolling from her son.

Araris absorbed the blows like an anvil—they simply impacted him, to no apparent effect. He seized the wrist of Tavi's gripping arm with his own free hand, then turned, weight shifting in a little up-and-down bobbing motion. Tavi, suddenly drawn off-balance, flipped entirely over, and Araris guided his back down onto the wooden deck. He hit hard enough to make Isana wince again—but not, she was certain, as hard he could have.

Tavi lay there on the deck, blinking up at the sails and the sky, stunned. The sailors, most of whom had been watching the practice, let out a chorus of cheers, jeers, and advice, accompanied by more than a little laughter.

"Temper," Araris said, his voice steady. He wasn't so much as breathing hard. "You're a naturally aggressive fighter, but anger is not your ally in a match like this. You've got to keep yourself centered and thinking. Use the anger. Don't let it use you."

He sheathed his sword and offered Tavi a hand up. The younger man glowered at the older for a moment, then shook his head and took his hand. "What was that wristlock?" he wheezed. "I've never seen that one before."

"It's fairly simple," Araris replied. "You've had enough for one day, though. I'll show you tomorrow, if you like."

"I'm all right," Tavi said. "Show me now."

Araris tilted his head, his lips pursed in thought, then suddenly grinned. "As you wish. Get some water, and we'll go another round. If you can keep your head, I'll show you the lock and the counter."

Tavi recovered his sword from the deck, saluted Araris, and sheathed it. Then he walked over to the water barrel beside where Isana sat on a small folding stool. He smiled at her, dunked a wooden cup into the water, and drank it all down, followed by a second. In the two days since he'd begun recovering from his seasickness, his color had returned, and he'd been shoveling down enough food for two at mealtimes—despite the rather questionable provender to be had from the *Slive*'s cook.

Tavi and Araris were sparring shirtless, apparently to keep Tavi from having all of his shirts cut to ribbons and stained with blood. Isana had been studiously avoiding staring at Araris. She would not have thought that a man his age would look so athletic, without the use of watercraft—but he was very nearly as lean as Tavi, his body hard with flat, ropy muscle. Of course, he'd spent all those years in the forge back at the steadholt, and she'd once seen him practicing there by the light of dying embers, late one night, using an iron bar in place of an actual weapon.

Araris had grown confident and strong again, no longer the broken man he'd become after Septimus's death, and seeing him like that was both immensely gratifying to Isana and more than a little distracting. Her fingertips almost itched with the raw desire to trace those muscles. Instead, she turned back to her sewing, mending one of Kitai's pairs of trousers, where both her eyes and her fingers would have less trouble behaving in an appropriate manner.

"Would you like me to close that for you?" she asked Tavi quietly. "I won't need a tub for something that small."

Tavi glanced at her, and a complex little cloud of emotions drifted around him for a second. Then he shook his head and closed down on them, until Isana could no longer sense anything except for a vague dissatisfaction. "No, thank you. It's not leaking anymore." The words came out with a small, harsh edge. He gave her a guilty little glance, and then a half-forced smile appeared on his face. "Though at the rate I'm going, I might need you to patch up my pride."

Ehren appeared from within the cabin in time to say, waving vaguely at the sea, "I don't think there's enough water available."

Tavi arched an eyebrow. "Why don't you come practice with us and say that again, little man?"

Ehren raised a modest hand. "Thank you, no. I get confused about which end of the sword I should hold. I wouldn't dream of slowing down the advanced class." He turned the gesture into a mocking little fencer's salute and strode off toward the back of the ship, presumably to speak with their captain again.

"Some annoying little person is going to get thrown into the drink someday," Tavi called after him. Then he shook his head, grinning, and turned back to Araris. Isana watched, between stitches. She knew barely enough about swordplay to be able to watch it, but it seemed to her that Tavi was moving more slowly, but also more certainly. She caught a flicker of satisfaction from Araris, as the young man defended against half a dozen swift strokes.

Kitai's voice suddenly rang out from the rigging above. "Sails!" she called. "Dead ahead!"

Men paused in their work. A thrill of apprehension flashed through the air, brushing against Isana like a frozen cobweb. Immediately, Demos's voice began calling out brusque orders, and he swarmed up the ropes into the rigging himself, moving as nimbly as a squirrel through the lines. Isana watched as he gained the crow's nest, where Kitai pointed out something to him. Demos held up his hands in a gesture Isana had often seen used by windcrafters to magnify their view of different objects.

He stared for a moment. Then he came swinging back down through the rigging and dropped the last ten feet to the deck. He shouted more orders, and the ship suddenly pitched sharply to its right. Men scrambled to readjust the sails, while Demos strode back and forth, shouting terms and commands so obscure and confusing to Isana that he might as well have been speaking another language.

Isana rose and walked calmly to Demos's side, once the initial stream of orders trickled off. "Captain," she said. "What's happening?"

Isana took note that Tavi and Ehren had stepped over closer to her, as Demos answered.

"That's the *Mactis* out there," he said, his tone calm. "Red Gallus's ship." He stared out over the waves at a gleam of white sailcloth in the far distance. "I ordered a change of course. Now we'll see what he does."

"Skipper!" called a man from the ship's wheel. "He's changing course to intercept."

"Bloody crows." Demos sighed. "Lady, I recommend that you and yours get into your cabin and stay there."

"Why?" Isana said. "What's happening?"

"The captain of the *Mactis* thinks he's a pirate," Demos replied. "The fool means to board us."

Isana felt her eyes grow very wide. "Oh."

"Can he catch us, Captain?" Tavi asked.

Demos nodded once. "Likely. He picked his position pretty well. The wind is taking us into him, he's got a good current, and Gallus knows this part of the business. Give us a few more leagues, and he might turn back."

"Why would he do that?" Ehren asked.

"Because I'm sailing for the Run."

Ehren froze in his tracks and blinked at Demos. "What?"

Tavi frowned, and asked in a completely different tone, "What?"

"The Leviathans' Run," Ehren told Tavi. He licked his lips nervously. "It's a stretch of ocean where, uh . . ."

"Leviathans," Tavi said. "I get it."

"Not exactly," Demos said. He sounded almost bored. "It's where young males who haven't staked out their own territory tend to congregate."

"Oh," Tavi said. "What do they do there?"

"What every group of young males does," Demos replied. "Fight each other for no good reason. Charge around blindly at full speed just for the crows of it."

"And smash ships to tiny pieces," Ehren added in a very small voice.

Demos grunted agreement and turned to the rail again. "My witchmen are better than his. Let's see if he wants to roll the dice today."

"Captain," Tavi said. "No offense, but have you given thought to . . . well. Taking him on?"

"No," Demos said. "The *Slive* is half the size of the *Mactis*. And Gallus carries extra swordsmen to boot. Three to one odds aren't the kind I like."

"We've got some fairly capable hands ourselves," Tavi said.

Demos looked at him and barked out a short, harsh laugh. "Kid, you're pretty good. But there's a long way between training sessions with a family swordmaster and spilling blood on a rolling deck."

"He's right," Araris said quietly, stepping up to stand behind Tavi. "This fight is better avoided."

Demos looked past Tavi to the older man. "You've fought at sea before?"

"Yes." Araris didn't elaborate.

Demos nodded once. "Listen to your teacher, kid. And get comfortable. It's going to be a couple of hours before we get this sorted out, either way. Excuse me. I need to make sure my witchmen aren't drunk again."

Demos strode off to the stairway down to the hold and descended smoothly.

"That was a joke, right?" Ehren said. "About the watercrafters?"

Isana frowned. She could feel a rising anxiety pouring from the young Cursor. His arms were folded, and one of Ehren's feet drummed nervously on the wooden deck.

Tavi noted Ehren's worry as well. "What's got you so twitchy?" he asked.

"If you'd ever actually seen . . ." Ehren licked his lips. "I'm going to go rifle the bosun's trunk. Bound to be something to drink in there. You want any?"

Tavi frowned. "No. I'm fine."

Ehren jerked his head in a quick nod and glanced at Araris and Isana. "Sir? Lady?"

They declined, and Ehren scurried away, his face quite pale.

Tavi watched him go, frowning, and then went to the ship's railing. He stood staring out at the ocean for a time and occasionally stepped away to pace up and down the rail. After perhaps half an hour, he stalked over to Isana's side and frowned down at her.

"How can you just sit there, sewing?" he asked.

Isana didn't look up from her work. "Is there something else I should be doing?"

Tavi folded his arms, frowning. "The captain said you should get into the cabin."

"He said we all should," Isana responded. "But I don't see you going there."

Tavi frowned at her. "Well. I should be on deck."

"So that someone can trip over you?" Isana asked. She tried not to smile, she honestly did, but felt it on her mouth despite her efforts. "Or perhaps you think your sword is going to be of use in trimming sails. Or warding leviathans away."

He let out an exasperated breath. "At least as useful as your sewing."

Isana set the sewing down and regarded her son steadily. "It's going to be hours before anything happens, and it's a lovely day. From the level of anxiety I'm sensing from the crew and Ehren, they expect that we might well be crushed by a leviathan and dragged into the depths of the sea. Failing that, we can look forward to a desperate struggle against a band of pirates who outnumber us three to one." She turned back to her task. "In either circumstance, the light would be less than ideal for sewing. So I think I'll sit here on the deck and enjoy the sunshine while I may, if that's quite all right with you."

Tavi stared at her, and she could feel his complete shock quite clearly.

She spared him a small smile. "I know you're worried about me. And I know how much you've always hated it that so many things were entirely out of your control. This is another such thing. Denying that won't make it less true."

He looked down at her for a moment, frowning, his mood turning from restive impatience to pensive introspection. Isana had always found her son's ability to focus upon whatever he set his mind on to be somewhat intimidating. He could pour tremendous energy of thought and will into any given task. It must be uncomfortable for him, to say the least, to turn that same focus inward.

He sighed and settled down on the deck beside her stool, resting his shoulders against the bulkhead behind them. He lowered his voice. "If I had . . ."

"The furycraft, yes," she said quietly. "It hasn't solved the First Lord's problems. Even if you had it, you'd merely be faced with a host of different uncontrollable situations."

Tavi was quiet for a moment. Then he said, "But I could protect you."

"Perhaps," she said quietly. "Perhaps not. Life is not notable for its overabundance of certainty."

Tavi grimaced and nodded. "I just thought I'd feel better if you were inside."

She tied off the thread, willed Rill into a fingernail to sharpen it, and cut it neatly. She slipped the needle through thread still wound on the spool and shook her hand gently as the nail returned to normal, stretching her aching fingers. "If you truly think that's best, perhaps you should try leading us there."

He blinked and tilted his head, looking at her.

She laughed. She couldn't help it. She leaned down and kissed his hair. For all that he was grown so tall, and for all that he had learned and become, she could still see the infant, the toddler, the mischievous child, all rolled into the man he was becoming.

"Consider," she said. "Were Gaius in your position—"

"As if he'd ever be without furycraft," Tavi snorted.

"But if he were," Isana pressed, meeting his eyes. "Consider it. How would his retinue react to him, hmmm? If he stood brooding at the rail and paced about like a hungry thanadent, snarling and giving orders that made little sense."

Tavi scowled at her. He began to speak, stopped, then shrugged. "If I was there with him? I'd be worried."

"Quite," Isana said. "Such a display might soothe his own anxiety—but he would be doing so at a cost to others. Is that the kind of person you want to be?"

Tavi tilted his head again, frowning. He said nothing.

"Now consider: If staying locked in the passenger cabin truly was the wisest course of action, would you rush into it if it seemed that Gaius was determined to stay on deck, despite the futility of the gesture?"

"Probably not."

Isana nodded. "That's because Gaius, for all that he is a

manipulative old serpent, is also a leader. He acts. Others follow." She glanced around, and said, "They follow you, too."

Tavi's brow furrowed. "What do you mean?"

"Those with us," she said. "Even many of the sailors. They recognize intelligence, competence, confidence. They regard you—and your evaluation of our situation—with more respect than they would another."

Tavi chewed on his lower lip, and murmured, "I'm frightening them."

Isana saw no need to confirm what Tavi had finally realized. "If Gaius thought his people were all safest in the cabin, what do you think he would do?"

Tavi nodded slowly. "He'd go there. Give them a chance to protest. Save their pride. Help their morale. If he thought that was best."

Isana reached into the garment bag on the deck beside her and drew out one of Ehren's sets of trousers—all of which bore tears and ham-handed repairs that were arguably worse than the rips they'd replaced. "Well, then. It might be wise for you to practice. What do *you* think is the best thing to do?"

Her son shook his head. "That question has been on my mind a lot, lately."

Here it came. She steeled herself against another reflex-flutter of panic. That wasn't what Tavi needed right now. "Oh?"

"It's a lot," he said.

"Yes."

"It's big."

Isana nodded. "Oh, yes."

He whispered. "I'm scared."

Isana closed her eyes. The man's voice spoke with the child's aching fear, and it hurt to hear it, to feel it.

"The thing is," he said quietly, "that I'm not making this choice just for me. If I'm not killed today, or when we get to the capital, or in the fighting after that, or in the trial after the fighting, then . . . what I do will affect a lot of people."

"That isn't precisely uncommon, over the past few years," she pointed out.

"But this is different. This is more."

"Is it?"

Tavi looked up at her, searching her eyes with his. They looked brilliantly green against the dark brown wood stain of the ship's timbers. "What if I can't handle it?" he said quietly. "What if I'm not capable of it?"

"Tavi, you've never needed—"

"This isn't about furycraft," he said quietly, firmly. "It's about me." He leaned closer, whispering. "Do you think I could do this? Take . . . take his place?"

Isana's heart pounded. She set the trousers aside. The fear screamed at her to tell her son no. That he could not possibly enter the insanity that passed for government in Alera and survive. That he would bungle whatever he set his hand to, cause pain and grief to untold thousands.

Instead, she took his hand and held it in both of hers.

"I've had nightmares about this since you were an infant," Isana said quietly. "Every time you did something that . . . attracted the attention of the Crown, every time you threw yourself into harm's way for another, it felt like someone stabbing me with a knife. I was sure that if you kept it up, your father's enemies would see you. Recognize you. Kill you. That's all I could see."

She looked up at his eyes. "But I didn't see what was right in front of me." She clenched his hand hard, and her voice turned fierce. "You have proven, again and again, that you are his *son. His* son. Never let anyone tell you differently."

He stared at her with wide eyes. Then he nodded once, and his jawline suddenly firmed. "Thank you."

"Great furies, don't thank me for this," she said quietly. "I hate it. I hate everything about it."

"Will you stand with me?" he asked.

She leaned down and clasped him, hugging him as tightly as she could, and whispered, "Hail, Gaius Octavian."

CHAPTER 25

Tavi stood in the very bow of the ship, where he would be out of the way of any of the sailors laboring to coax every bit of speed from the *Slive*. The ship leapt forward through the waves, and salt spray occasionally misted over him. He felt Kitai's presence a breath before he heard her bare feet tread quietly on the deck behind him. She stepped up beside him, casually pressing her side against his, and followed his gaze off to the ship's port side.

There, visible even from the level of the deck now, was the recognizable shape of another ship, its sails gleaming white in the afternoon sun, its course steadily converging on theirs.

"They're going to catch up," Kitai said quietly.

"So it would seem," Tavi said. "The crew's getting anxious. They'll start sharpening their knives before much longer."

Kitai nodded. "I feel it, too." She was silent for a time more, and said, "Do these pirates always attack so far out at sea? It seems to me to be a troublesome way to seek a quarrel. We could have fought on the docks and settled it there. Then we could have enjoyed the voyage in peace."

"That would have been far more reasonable," Tavi agreed. "But I'm afraid they aren't reasonable people."

"No. They're Alerans." She shook her head, and Tavi suddenly noticed the absence of the usual good-humored twinkle in her eye when she made such observations. "*Chala*, there is something you should see."

Tavi nodded, and followed her the length of the deck, to a narrow staircase that led down into the dimly lit hold of the ship. Within, the ship looked like any rough wooden building, except for the odd contours of the outer wall and the low ceiling. They went through what looked like a larder, full of boxes and barrels of foodstuffs, and a small workshop where various woodworking tools were stored, along with spare lumber, evidently for repairs. Beyond that, the workshop doors opened into the cargo hold.

It was damp and musty, lit with only a single pair of tiny furylamps. The wooden beams of the ship creaked and groaned around them. Kitai slipped forward, through the mostly empty hold, until they reached the foremost part, just under where Tavi had been standing a few moments before.

There, the flat planks forming the floor of the hold had been left out, exposing the curve of the ship's hull—a space the size of a couple of large bathtubs that was full of what was apparently seawater. A pair of men knelt in the water. Both of them were bare-chested, and both had long hair worn in an odd style of dozens and dozens of tiny braids. Their skin was marked with dark ink formed into abstract swirls and curling patterns. Both men had their eyes closed, their hands spread with fingers wide in the seawater, and they both kept up a constant murmuring under their breath. Their skin had a shriveled look, and they shuddered with the cold.

"The witchmen," Tavi murmured.

"No," Kitai said. "Not them."

Tavi arched an eyebrow at her.

"I asked Demos to show me these witchmen," she said. She walked over to the thick shadows at one side of the hold. "That was when I noticed these."

Tavi followed her, squinting. It was difficult to make out anything in the thick shadows, but his night vision had improved markedly since the bond had formed between him and Kitai. She waited in patient silence for a moment, until his eyes adjusted, and he saw what she had brought him to see.

Chains.

Four heavy rings had been set into the side of the ship, spaced about a foot apart, four feet up from the floor. From each set of rings dangled two sets of manacles, heavy things that could never be broken without fury-assisted strength—and anyone locked into them would perforce be surrounded by the wooden hull of the ship and cut off from contact with the earth.

The hull of the ship, and the floor there beneath the rings was stained, and Tavi was glad that he couldn't see much of it. A faint scent lingered in the air, beneath the mustiness of the ship itself, the foulness of human waste—and blood. That was easily enough seen, dark blotches on the manacles.

"Demos is a slaver," Kitai said quietly.

Tavi took a step back before he took a deep breath. "It isn't uncommon in this part of the world. Most captains have transported slaves at one time or another."

Kitai reached out and touched a chain, running her fingers down the links. "And you see nothing wrong with that?"

"I don't like it," Tavi said, "but men like Demos choose what jobs they will or will not take."

Kitai gave Tavi a rather hard look. "Not that, Aleran. Do you see nothing wrong with the fact that this"—she flicked the chain hard against the ship's hull—"is not uncommon?"

Tavi blinked and stared at her for a moment. "Kitai . . ."

She turned back to Tavi, her eyes narrowed. "You told me that Nasaug called your kind monsters. So would my people if they knew you treated your own like this."

"Not everyone does," Tavi said.

"But everyone allows it," she said, her voice hard. She stepped forward until he could see her features in the dimness. They were green agates. "Is this what you are as well, Aleran?"

He met her eyes for a moment and felt her outrage like the heat of a fire on his face. He began to speak, but stopped. Instinct warned him that nothing he said would answer her question.

Instead, he closed his eyes for a moment and dropped his hand to the hilt of his sword. He reached out to it, sensing the strength of the steel, feeling its latent energy, partially beaten into shape at a Legion forge. Tavi pressed his senses into the sword, taking steady breaths, drawing his thoughts into focus and drawing the power of the sword with them, shaping it, aligning its matter, strengthening its edge.

Then he opened his eyes, stepped, drew, and swept the weapon in a single sweep and backstroke.

Sparks flew up, metal screeched, and the chains clattered to the flooring, the ends of the severed links aglow with heat.

Tavi sheathed the weapon in a smooth, practiced motion, and turned to Kitai.

The Marat girl lifted her chin, her eyes aglow. She nodded once, the motion deep enough to be almost a bow.

Tavi responded the same way, never looking away from her eyes.

"That," she said, "is my Aleran."

Tavi looked up to find that both witchmen had turned and were staring at him.

"If Captain Demos asks," Tavi told them quietly, "tell him to take it up with me."

The witchmen glanced at one another, and then nodded to Tavi in unison.

Suddenly, there was a surge of emotion from above, a sudden wave of sharply increased panic, fear, and anger. It crashed against Tavi, and his balance wavered beneath the force of it. His hand went of its own accord toward Kitai, landing on her shoulder, steadying himself, even as she shuddered and reached out to brace herself against his chest.

The witchmen both let out quiet moans of misery and crouched even lower in the water. They resumed their murmuring, though it was louder now, faster, almost frantic.

Above, on the deck, there was an agonized scream.

Tavi turned and sprinted for the stairs again, Kitai on his heels. He didn't draw his blade—a fine mess he would make of himself if he lost his balance in the ship's roll and gutted himself on his own sword. He came onto the deck to find it in frantic activity, men hurrying back and forth as the ship's officers shouted commands. All of them were crouching, darting from place to place, and casting frantic glances to port.

"Careful!" Araris called. He had his shoulders pressed up against the mainmast on the starboard side. "The pirates have a Knight Flora with them. Crowbegotten good one, too."

Tavi nodded and ducked to one side, putting the solid wood of the cabin between himself and the oncoming *Mactis*. He swept a quick glance around the deck and asked Araris, "Where is she?"

There was another scream, this time up in the rigging, and
a man plummeted from above to land on the deck ten feet
away. An arrow had transfixed his throat, bloodied point emerging from one side of his neck. His hips and one arm were bent
at an unnatural angle, and the sailor made a few frantic gur-
gling sounds, feebly thrashing, as his blood pooled on the
deck.

Araris drew his sword, his jaw tight with anger. "Not in the
cabin. She must be forward."

The door to the cabin opened, and Ehren poked his sandy-
haired head out of it, looking blearily around. "What? What's
going on?"

There was a hiss, a cracking sound, and another arrow
smashed through the cabin's door, just above its latch and so
close to Ehren's hand that its haft touched the bare skin of his
wrist.

Ehren peered owlishly at the arrow. "Ah," he said, and shut
the door once more.

Tavi glanced at the arrow and recognized the distinctive
fletching again.

"Crows take it," he snarled. "Iris the Hawk. Navaris and
the rest of Arnos's thugs are out there."

There was another scream from the rigging, though at least
no one fell to the deck this time.

Kitai leaned around Tavi and peered to port for a moment.
"Four hundred yards at least. This archer is quite skilled."

Tavi called out to Araris, and told him what he had seen.
The *singulâre* let out a sulfurous curse. "How did they catch
up to us?"

"They must have used Arnos's Knights Aeris," Tavi replied.
"They could have learned the ship's identity, and it wouldn't be
too hard to figure out where we're headed. They got in front of
us, flew down the coast until they found a captain willing to intercept us."

"This is going to get complicated," Araris said. "Stay there.
I'll go find Isana."

"We go together," Tavi said. He didn't give Araris a chance
to argue—he just darted forward, moving quickly down the
deck. He shot one swift glance off to port, to see the *Mactis* un-

der sail. At this distance, he could make out the moving shapes of the crew, but he couldn't make out any details. That was good news, at least. It meant Arnos's woodcrafter couldn't pick out specific targets. She was shooting at motions and outlines, not at particular men.

Tavi went forward, crouched as low as he could get, hurrying as much as he could, and had no doubt that the motion looked more ridiculous than was probably appropriate for a Princeps of Alera on the edge of battle. An arrow flashed by, several feet away. One of the feathers must have been loose and dragged the shot wide, because it made an odd buzzing sound as it flew past him.

Tavi crouched even lower and moved even more quickly. To the crows with dignity. He felt more than willing to live with such humiliations, especially when he might *not* without them. The *Mactis* was steadily closing.

They reached the bow and found Isana there, crouched behind the wooden planking of the prow. Tavi rushed forward and threw himself down beside her. Araris and Kitai were hard on his heels.

Isana flinched as Tavi landed, but when she looked back at him, he felt a surge of relief flash through her, only to be replaced with renewed anxiety an instant later. "Are you hurt?"

"I'm fine," Tavi said. "We've got a problem."

Isana lifted a dark eyebrow, her voice dry. "Oh, dear."

"Arnos's Knights are on that ship," Araris said, his mouth set in a tight line.

Isana's back stiffened. "I see. Can we escape them?"

Araris crouched and lifted his head up for a moment, peering over the ship's rail, and ducked down again. "I'm not much of a sailor, but I doubt it."

"Their captain isn't going to turn back because we're sailing into the Leviathan's Run," Tavi said grimly. "Navaris wouldn't let him."

"We have to fight, then," Isana said. "Can we beat them?"

Tavi glanced at Araris.

The man shook his head. "Not if we're outnumbered as badly as Demos believes. Navaris is extremely skilled. I'll have to focus on her completely."

"If we can't run, and we can't fight, what *can* we do?" Isana asked.

"We find some way to change the rules," Tavi said. He rose for a quick peek at the other ship, then glanced quickly at the sea ahead of them. He started to drop down again, when he froze, staring.

Ahead of the ship, the relatively calm seas were washing against slate grey rocks that rose seven or eight feet up out of the waters. There were perhaps two dozen of them, any one of them large enough to smash open the *Slive*'s hull like the lid of an ale keg should the ship collide with them.

"Captain!" Tavi bellowed. "Rocks ahead! Captain Demos, rocks ahead!"

Some of the crew took up the call, relaying it back along the length of the ship. Seconds later, Demos hurried down the deck, crouching low the way Tavi had done it, though the ship's captain moved far more swiftly and confidently than Tavi had.

"Demos!" Tavi called. "Rocks!"

The captain frowned and moved forward, rising to look.

"Scipio?" shouted Ehren's voice from somewhere at the ship's stern. "Where are you?"

"The bow!" Tavi called. "Get up here and . . ." Tavi broke off as Demos's calloused hand clamped suddenly over his mouth.

"Quiet," said the captain, his voice and face unreadable. He let out a pair of sharp, single whistles, and the sounds of sailors talking and calling out to one another abruptly stopped.

Tavi pushed Demos's hand away, staring at him, and lowered his voice. "Why?"

"Because those aren't rocks," Demos said calmly. "They're leviathans."

⋊⊐⊏ CHAPTER 26

"Oh dear," Isana breathed. Demos, like Tavi, was capable of concealing his emotions—or perhaps he simply didn't feel them with any particular intensity. Either way, Isana had been able to discern very little about the man's state of mind at any point during their voyage.

Right now, Demos was radiating a cold, carefully restrained fear.

He stared ahead for a few seconds more, then waved his arm in some kind of signal. The timbers of the *Slive* creaked, and the ship changed course slightly.

"Will we get by them?" Isana heard Tavi ask.

"We might, if we're quiet. This time of the day, they come up to the warm waters at the surface to bask. Provided people don't start shouting"—he gave Tavi a deliberate look—"and that we don't actually bump into one of them and wake him up, the witchmen should let us tiptoe past."

Tavi narrowed his eyes, his brow furrowing. "What if we didn't have the witchmen?"

Demos shrugged. "We'd wish we did. Briefly."

Tavi nodded, his eyes flicking around. Isana watched as a sudden, wolfish grin appeared on his face, accompanied by a surge of excitement.

Kitai, who had been facing away from Tavi, peeking at the enemy vessel and the leviathans in turn, suddenly turned around, and Isana was startled by her expression—a grin that matched Tavi's as perfectly as the green of her eyes. "I like that, Aleran," Kitai said. "Do it."

Tavi nodded and turned to Isana. "I'm going to need your help."

Isana frowned at Tavi, and then nodded once. "To do what?"

Her son glanced aside at the *Mactis*, his eyes narrowed. "Change the rules."

Demos finished securing the straps of a heavy canvas harness around Isana's waist. "Too tight?" he asked.

"I have no idea," Isana replied.

Demos grunted. "As long as you can breathe, it should be fine." He held up a line knotted to a metal clip. He showed it to her, then slapped the clip against a metal ring on the harness and gave it a firm tug. "In these waters, you can only see about ten feet. Remember that the *Mactis* is moving forward, so you aren't just moving toward her. You've got to aim ahead of her on an angle."

Isana nodded. "I'll be able to find the ship. I'm not worried about that." She leaned out around the corner of the cabin and peeked at the enemy ship, now less than two hundred yards away.

He attached a second line to another ring. "Make sure you're at least ten feet down when you do," Demos warned her. "If that archer sees you coming, you'll get to experience bow-fishing from the soggy end. Go beneath the ship to the far side before you come up. Believe me, they'll have all their attention focused on us."

"Why does it seem like you've been involved in this sort of thing before, Captain?"

"While it has never actually happened, of course, I have made a number of plans in the event that I should ever work with a customer who wished his cargo to be loaded or off-loaded without troubling a customs inspector or harbormaster." He tested the knots on the lines. "It is in that spirit of prepared-ness that I had these made for my witchmen. Though I admit, they usually tow crates, not people."

The cabin door opened, and Tavi, Kitai, Araris, and Ehren came hurrying around the corner. Araris's sword was in his hand, and as he came, it flashed in the lowering sun and shat-tered yet another arrow. The enemy archer had not slackened her pace, and her shafts only became more accurate as the distance closed. A dozen sailors now lay wounded or dead.

"Can't someone else do this?" Ehren asked.

"We need a woodcrafter, Ehren," Tavi said. "You're it."

"This will be just like the time you helped us escape that warehouse," Kitai said.

"Except for the *leviathans*!" Ehren sputtered.

"Quiet!" hissed several people.

"Actually, your real worry is the sharks," Demos murmured, his tone practical. "There are always dozens of sharks around leviathans, and we're about to start passing through them."

Ehren's face turned white.

"Come on, Ehren," Kitai said. She stripped out of her tunic and kicked off her shoes without a trace of self-consciousness. "Be a man."

Ehren blinked, and spots of color appeared on his cheeks as he turned his head away and coughed. "Oh, bloody crows." He glowered at Tavi, and demanded, "Why do I keep on following you into this kind of thing?"

"You must enjoy it," Tavi said.

"I must be an idiot," Ehren responded. But he, along with Tavi and Araris, also began stripping down. "Let me get this straight. We hold on to the ropes. The Steadholder drags us over there underwater. I open up a hole in the hull, and we eliminate their witchmen. Then we run back here and sail away while the leviathans eat them."

"Yes," Tavi said.

"How long are we going to be under?" Araris asked quietly.

"I've never done this before," Isana said. "If I was alone, it might take me half a minute to move the distance. Perhaps a little more."

"Double it," Demos said, glancing away from Kitai. "At least." He lowered a rope carefully over the side. "Are you not going to strip down, lady? That dress is going to drag quite a bit in the water."

Isana arched an eyebrow at him. "I assure you, Captain, it won't slow me."

"Ah," he said, nodding. "Try not to splash when you go in."

Isana went to the rail and looked down at the sea beneath them. She had never actually gone swimming in it, much less engaged in watercrafting using salt water as a medium. She had heard that there were almost no practical differences in working with freshwater or salt water. *Almost* hardly seemed a comforting word, given that her watercraft was the only thing standing between them and a number of extremely violent, unpleasant forms of death.

For a moment, Isana felt her hands start shaking. What in the world was she thinking? She was no Knight, nor soldier, nor mercenary, to go hurling herself into the deadly sea for the express purpose of murdering two men whom she had never met, nor who had ever done her harm. She was a Steadholder, used to running a farm—and half the time she'd had that position, she had been traveling around the Realm for one reason or another. What could possibly make her think that she was capable of doing something like this?

Isana caught herself before all the anxiety and rising apprehension around her overwhelmed her thoughts. She took a deep breath, called to Rill, and lowered herself into the sea, parting the water beneath her so that she entered with hardly a ripple, much less a splash.

She stayed under for a moment, using the bond with her fury to reach out around her in the water. The sea was warmer than she expected, and there was a greater sense of buoyancy than in the cold streams and lakes of her home. She closed her eyes for a moment, focusing on the water around her, and immediately felt the presence of the furies laboring for the *Slive*'s witchmen. It was crafting of considerable complexity and effort—allowing the ship to cut smoothly through the waters while simultaneously smoothing those waters only a few feet from the hulls. Isana had no idea if she herself could have managed it, and certainly she couldn't have done it for any length of time. The witchmen kept it up on a continual basis. It was a specialist's form of crafting, then, something that took time to practice and master.

It was probably why the witchmen remained so isolated from the rest of the ship—down in the depths of the hold, as close to the water and as far from the distracting emotions of their crewmates as possible.

She took a slow breath and felt Rill filtering the water. The air tasted slightly of minerals, like the hot springs in the Calderon Valley, but she had no particular difficulty. She willed herself forward and rushed through the water, banked in a half circle, and returned to the side of the *Slive*. It was somewhat daunting, how much water was around her. Isana had never been swimming in so much water that she could not feel either shoreline and the floor of the lake or river she was in. Here, in the sea, the water stretched out in every direction, for as far as her senses could reach, endless rolling blue all around her and endless, grave-cold blackness beneath her.

The water was disturbed behind and beneath her, and Isana darted to one side just as a smooth, sleek form more than ten feet long glided through the water she'd recently occupied. She saw a dark, glassy eye, and a mouth of jagged teeth. And then the shark was past her, and it vanished into the murky ocean in utterly silent grace.

Isana took a moment to deliberately extend her senses, so that she would have at least a little more warning should another shark attempt such a thing, and tried to slow down her wildly beating heart. Then she rose to the surface beside the ship.

Araris was halfway down the rope, leaning down, his expression drawn with worry. She met his eyes and tried to smile at him.

"Are you all right?" he murmured.

She lifted a finger to her lips as she nodded, and beckoned him. Araris turned and lowered himself hand over hand down the rest of the rope, the sinews in his back and shoulders rippling. He kept going once his feet hit the water and slid in slowly and quietly.

The rest of them came down the same way—except for Ehren, whose grip slipped halfway down the line. Isana was ready for it, and Rill was ready to receive him, a vaguely human shape rising from the waves to catch Ehren and lower him soundlessly into the water.

"All right," Tavi murmured. He treaded water beside Isana

and seized one of the ropes on her harness. "Everyone grab hold. We need to hurry."

Isana turned toward the enemy ship as the *Slive* sailed on, and the others maneuvered through the water to catch hold of the trailing lines. It took them longer than she would have thought, and she felt the faint fluttering sensation of at least two more sharks circling fifty or sixty feet away.

"All right, let's go," Tavi murmured. She felt his hand touch her shoulder and squeeze once. His fear came pouring through his touch, but so did a sense of almost-eager elation. Great furies save her, the boy was *enjoying* himself.

"Deep breaths everyone," Isana said. She waited a beat, then she oriented on the receding form of the *Mactis*, reached out to Rill, and dived.

She noticed immediately how much more effort it took to move. A glance over her shoulder showed her that everyone was holding on with both hands, and stripped down to trousers, their bodies moved through the water as smoothly as they could. Even so, the additional weight and resistance to movement was considerable.

Isana ground her teeth. At this rate, it would take even longer than Demos's estimate to reach the *Mactis*, and the others didn't have her ability to breathe while underwater. Surfacing too near the enemy ship would be suicide, and if they stopped to discuss it, the *Mactis* might have sailed beyond her ability to catch up.

There was no help for it. She closed her eyes and redoubled her efforts, spreading more of her fury's attention into the water around her charges so that they cut through it more efficiently. Slowly, they began to pick up speed. The sensation of her bond with Rill became something tangible, a pressure on her temples, and she bent all her attention to her task.

She almost didn't notice it, but Rill's sudden warning made her bank sharply to avoid ramming something large and dark. She followed the contours of the object, pressing ahead. Its surface was odd, pebbly, and laced with barnacles and straggling, hair-fine bits of dark green seaweed. They passed along it for several seconds before it dawned on Isana that they were within arm's reach of a leviathan.

Her heart leapt into her throat, crashed back down into her belly, and began beating very quickly. The creature was huge. It literally stretched out of sight in every direction she looked. They were passing along what might have been a tail, she supposed, a long column of flesh and hide, ridged with bony, protruding plates down its center. Ahead of her, she saw a protuberance of some kind, then they passed over what might have been a flipper, broader than the *Slive*, its end impossible to see in the murky water.

Next she passed several rows of what looked like trenches, or perhaps extrabroad furrows in a field. Ribs. They were the creature's ribs. There was a dull, heavy throb in the water, pressing rhythmically against her, and Isana realized that she could actually *feel* the beating of the leviathan's gargantuan heart.

They continued on, passing another flipper, and then another column of flesh that must have been the leviathan's neck. The whole of the beast, then, must look something like an elongated turtle with no shell.

Its head came into sight. Its skull was very nearly as large as the enormous stone barn back on her steadholt, a structure that could house two hundred various animals, the farm's equipment, and stored food besides. It, too, was almost turtlelike, complete with a jagged-edged beak. Each eye was the size of a small cottage, great glassy black orbs that were almost entirely closed.

From its mouth hung bits of what Isana could only assume was some kind of pale flesh. Whale blubber, perhaps? Even as Isana watched, a chunk the size of an oxcart fell with deliberate grace from the leviathan's maw, and was promptly set upon by a veritable cloud of smaller fish, only to scatter from the path of a dozen sharks. Rill warned Isana of several more sharks nearby but out of sight in the murk, all of them arrowing toward the free meal. Isana's heart beat even faster, and she tried to increase their pace again, desperate to avoid tempting the hungry sharks with the others, literally dangling like bait on a line.

She glanced back behind her as one of the sharks began to edge a bit too near, and found Tavi staring at the leviathan in undisguised curiosity and glee. He saw her look back and glanced up at her. He pointed at the massive leviathan, and his grin widened still further, his smile so sharp and bright that she found herself mirroring it.

By contrast, Ehren, holding on behind Tavi, had his forehead pressed against the line with his eyes tightly shut. Isana could not help but feel that the young Cursor had a perfectly serviceable amount of common sense.

Tavi, after all, had a point. Certainly, the business was dangerous—but they would have been in danger regardless of what they did. And how many people in Alera could claim to have seen something so utterly awe-inspiring as this? Septimus would have had exactly the same look on his face . . .

Which, Isana realized, was important. It said something about him, as a man. His father had always counseled him to caution, to calculation, to committing all of his attention and focus to the task of ruling the Realm. In one of the letters to his son that Isana had read, Gaius had called rule a practical matter of survival. Survival, to the First Lord, was all but indistinguishable from duty.

Septimus had quietly, gently disputed the point with his father, but until now, Isana had never truly understood the simple truth of what he meant.

Survival was not the same thing as living.

Septimus had gone into battle beside his men, despite the inexcusable risk to his person. He had traveled the Realm in disguise, experiencing life outside of Alera Imperia. It was, in fact, upon one of those incognito jaunts that Isana had met him, when a furious cook had turned upon her little sister after she'd broken a plate, and Isana had smacked the woman hard on the cheek and pushed her away from Alia. Isana stood facing the angry cook until the woman muttered something and stormed away. Then, Isana had helped Alia to her feet, and the two of them had walked away with at least a little dignity.

A man she had never seen before came to her with a simple offer of work, and Isana had gladly taken it. Anywhere would have been an improvement over that scullery.

She'd had no idea, at the time, that she and Alia had just

become the maids to the senior officers of the Legion, Septimus's *singulares*, and to the Princeps himself.

It was after that that they had begun to talk to one another. To fall in love—and to wed for love, and not for political gain.

Survival was not enough. One had to live.

Septimus had never articulated it: He had simply *lived* it.

Septimus had been fiercely determined to live. So much so that he had died for it.

Living was a dangerous past-time, and often quite painful— but there was also such joy in living, such beauty, things that one would otherwise never see, never experience, never know. The risk of pain and loss was a part of living. It made everything else mean more; beauty was more pure, more bright, pleasure more full and complete, laughter deeper, more satisfying—and contentment more perfect, more peaceful.

She had, in a sense, betrayed Septimus in how she had treated Tavi after his father's death. She had been focused completely on protecting the boy—on forcing mere survival upon him. How much more would Tavi have seen, and done, and learned, if she had chosen differently? How much different would her own life have been? In reducing Tavi's existence to a matter of survival, she had sheltered him from some pains, but exposed him to others, and robbed him of what he might have had—and in doing so, had robbed herself as well.

The past was gone. Nothing could change what had already been. Looking back at it, letting its wounds fester, indulging in regret was just a different, slower way to die. The living moved forward.

Living.

Isana felt the wild beating of her heart and realized that it did not race entirely and purely with fear. There was also a sense of elation there, of joy. She felt more alive, there in that danger-filled murk, than she had felt in all the years since Septimus had died.

She would have to be a fool actually to *enjoy* this.

She would have to be a liar to say that it didn't have its appeal, as well.

The pressure on her temples increased sharply, and then suddenly faded. Isana was never sure precisely what happened, but they were suddenly streaking through the sea, more swiftly than any shark, and Rill's presence swelled. Isana's senses expanded, exploded, becoming so intense that for a moment she thought that the whole of the ocean had suddenly turned as crystal-clear as a Calderon spring.

She felt the heavy, drowsy presence of the leviathans (twenty-three of them, to be precise) and the endless, mindless swirling of the sharks (three hundred, give or take a dozen). She guided them past another leviathan's tail, noting the brightly colored crustaceans crawling among the barnacles and scales, found the *Mactis* beyond them, and shot forward, beneath the enemy vessel. They rose on the far side, and Isana made sure that they surfaced in total silence.

The others labored to keep their breaths quiet, but they nonetheless gasped for air after the long trip underwater. Isana kept pace with the *Mactis*, just outside of the watercrafting that concealed the presence of the ship from the sleeping leviathans. The witchmen of the *Mactis*, Isana noted, maintained a far more slender watercrafting than the witchmen of the *Slive*. Their work was no less complex, but there was much less of an allowance for the turbulence of the sea—probably because their ship was so much larger than the *Slive*, displacing much more water, and they had a considerably more difficult task in hiding it.

"Ehren," Tavi whispered hoarsely. "Make us a hole."

Ehren swallowed, and kicked over to the ship. He released Isana's line and immediately sank one of his knives into the hull. He hung on, dragged through the water by the ship, put his free hand on the hull, and closed his eyes.

Isana extended her senses toward the ship, and again felt surprised at the sheer clarity of what her crafting revealed. It was almost like when she performed a healing, sensing the pains and damage of a patient's body. She could feel the water all around the ship, in contact with the hull—including a number of places where the patient, gentle force of water had found flaws in the hull, and begun to slowly, steadily seep inward.

She waited for a moment, but when Ehren shook his head in frustration and slid his hand to the next board, she angled her course in closer. "Lower, and about a foot toward the bow," she said quietly. "There's a leak there. They've patched it with tar and sailcloth, but the planks have begun to weaken."

Ehren gave her a quick, surprised look. Then he moved his hand to the spot she'd suggested, and his eyes widened. He closed them and his fingers stiffened, forming something like a claw. He shoved down, forcefully, and his fingers sank half an inch into the wood. He made a satisfied, growling sound and repeated the motion several more times, until his hand had sunk to the base of his fingers into the ship's hull. Then he took a deep breath, made a twisting motion of his arm, and pulled.

There was a soggy-sounding crack, and the plank peeled away from its companions in the hull and snapped. Ehren tossed a two-foot length of board away, grasped the plank just below the new opening, and after another moment of concentration, snapped a second length of board away.

Isana felt intense attention directed at her, and she turned to find Tavi watching her, his green eyes narrowed. He leaned closer to her, and murmured, "What happened?"

She stared back at him for a moment, then shook her head. "I'm not sure."

"Are you all right?"

"I'm . . ." She shook her head. "It's all one fury. All of it. The whole sea. If you can commune with any of it, you can speak to all of it. There's so *much* of it there, and I can't—" She broke off suddenly as Tavi's hand covered her mouth.

"Shhhh," he said quietly. "You were raising your voice. Are you sure you're all right?"

Isana closed her mouth and nodded firmly. "But hurry. We need to hurry. The sun is going down. I can feel them beginning to stir. We don't want to be in the water when they wake."

There was another crack, and Ehren pulled himself up to the hole he'd created and thrust his head in. He leaned back a moment later, his nose wrinkling, and reported, "Bilge. Give me a moment to get through the other side." Then the little Cursor vanished into the hole. He reappeared shortly, and nodded at Tavi, then held out his hand.

Isana felt the elation in her son at the intense experience of

the adventure suddenly fade, and she felt it replaced with regret and steely determination. He kicked through the water,
seized the knife Ehren had left in the hull as a handhold, and
with the Cursor's help clambered inside. He had to go through
the hole one arm at a time, his shoulders had grown so broad,
and Isana was again struck by how very *large* the boy had
grown.

Kitai went next, though the Marat girl hardly seemed to
need Ehren's outstretched hand to help her in. From Kitai,
Isana could sense only what she almost always felt in her—a
kind of detached, feline amusement at the world around her,
and an intense involvement in her senses and environment. Finally, Araris went, though he paused to glance back at Isana.
She felt his worry for her very clearly.

"Oh for goodness' sake," Isana whispered, flipping a hand
at him. "Go. I'll be safer than you'll be."

Araris frowned at her, hesitating.

Isana felt the direction of his thoughts, the sudden, irrational heat of them, and she felt her face heat up. "I like the
way you look all wet as well," she told him. "But now is not
the time."

His eyes widened, and Araris gave her a sudden, very boyish grin and a wink. Then he, too, swarmed up the side of the
ship and through the hole in the hull.

Isana bit her lower lip and waited, pacing the ship. Her
sharpened senses continued to flood her with their newfound
clarity and depth, and it made what would otherwise have been
a very simple process—remaining steady beside the ship—
difficult to focus upon. The motion of the waves, the mindless
and purposeful movement of the sharks, the swirling of the
smaller fish feasting on what fell from the mouths of the sleeping leviathans, all blended together into something beautiful,
almost hypnotic, like a vast dance being performed for no one
but her. The sea around her stretched out, boundless and powerful, merciless and bountiful, and she could feel it all, to such
a degree that for a few seconds, she lost the feeling in her own
limbs, their nerves and muscles vanishing among all the endless motion of the living sea.

Fear and sudden agony hit her like a slap on the cheek. She

had drifted ahead of the *Mactis*, and she hurried to return to her place. There was another stab of confusion and pain from somewhere in the ship—great furies, she couldn't have felt that from *here*, not with such perfect clarity. She couldn't even *see* whoever had been hurt.

Panic native to her own heart clutched at her. Had something happened to one of her own? The bond between loved ones and, especially family, had long been well established as a factor that enhanced a watercrafter's already-acute empathic senses, and if Tavi or Araris had been injured it might account for—

The ship suddenly shuddered in the water. It wasn't a large motion—just a gentle bob, out of rhythm with the waves around it, as the watercrafting around the *Mactis*'s hull abruptly failed.

The next wave crashed against the bow of the ship with a roar like a miniature thunderstorm, and a great cloud of salt spray flew up from the impact.

Isana felt a sudden surge of emotion from the *Mactis*. Disbelief gave way to panic and terror, and every single facet of emotion was blindingly intense. They slashed at her like razors, and she could hardly keep herself moving through the water. On the ship, men began shouting. Boots hammered on wooden decks. The nearest of the shouts weren't twenty feet away, up on the ship's deck above her.

Isana fought to contain her agonized senses, to draw away from them, and as she did, she felt her pace suddenly slow, her progress through the water becoming noticeably more difficult. She gritted her teeth and left herself open to the painful flares of emotion and held pace beside the ship, though her teeth had begun to chatter in sheer, nervous reaction to the fear.

Another minute went by, and no one appeared at the hole in the ship's hull. There were more, harsh shouts from inside the ship, and the ring of steel on steel. Then there was a hissing sound and a low howl of tortured wood, toward the bow, where the witchmen were usually stationed. It repeated itself twice, and then Araris's bare foot kicked a triangular section of wooden hull away from the ship, its edges as clean-cut and smooth as if done with the finest saw. The severed planks fell into the sea. The *singulare* looked out from the hole, spotted Isana, and waved a hand at her.

Isana surged forward through the waves, just as Tavi appeared in the newly cut opening and tumbled into the sea gracelessly, as if he'd been pushed through. Isana darted through the water and pressed one of the lines into his hand, then caught up to the ship again, just as Ehren leapt out and hit the ocean heels first. Kitai came next, diving through the hole, her arms extended, to enter the sea in a graceful dive.

Isana rounded them up, made sure each of them had a solid hold on the line. It was getting increasingly difficult to concentrate, and Isana suddenly realized why.

The leviathans had woken.

The very water of the sea itself had all but begun to boil with a slow and monstrous anger.

They had little time.

Isana pressed as close to the newly cut hole as she dared. There was little point in stealth anymore, and she called out, "Araris! Araris, hurry!"

Steel rang on steel inside the ship. A man let out a cry of agony.

"Araris!" Isana called.

"Crows take it," Tavi snarled. "I was supposed to be the last off."

A dim shape appeared in the opening, and steel clashed again. Isana saw an explosion of violet sparks raining against azure as the blades of two master metalcrafters clashed, and then a sword's blade, scarlet with blood, plunged through the planks of the hull beside the opening.

Araris appeared, weaponless, and stumbled sprawling from the hole in the hull to fall into the sea. The water around him immediately became stained with streamers of crimson.

Isana stared at him, suddenly unable to focus, to think of the proper course of action. Panic upon the ship and rage within the sea pressed against her from both sides, a paralyzing weight.

Tavi reached out and got one strong arm under one of Araris's. Moving as if in a choreographed performance, Kitai seized Araris's other arm, so that he was suspended between them, his face just out of the water.

"Go!" Tavi shouted. "Go, go, go!"

Just then, a sound surged up from the depths. Isana had never heard anything like it. So deep that it rattled her very bones, rising to a louder whistle or shriek that pressed against her eardrums like a handful of dull needles. The surface of the sea itself shook with it, sending up a fine cloud of spray that only rose a few inches above the waters. The sound hit her, and with it came a timeless, inhuman, unthinking rage, and the sheer volume, the emotional mass of it, left her arms and legs shaking with impotent terror.

And then it happened again, from behind them. And again from ahead. And again, and again, and again, as the leviathans sensed the presence of intruders in their sea.

"Uh," Ehren panted, clearly terrified. "Uh, uh, uh. That can't be good."

Isana felt the leviathans begin to move as they came alert, motions so vast that they made the ship seem like a child's toy bobbing on the surface of a millpond. The other creatures of the sea swirled in frantic response, the smaller fish scattering, while the sharks became more restive and eager, moving in swifter and more erratic patterns.

Isana felt it with terrifying clarity when several of them picked up the scent of Araris's blood in the sea and began slicing toward them.

Men on the doomed ship began to scream.

It was too much. Too painful. Isana knew she should have been doing something, acting, but the agony of all that motion, of all that emotion, had become a precise and inescapable torment that no amount of writhing could lessen. She clutched at her head and heard herself screaming through clenched teeth.

Then a strong hand gripped her own, closing with power that barely avoided crushing bones, and Isana grasped at that pain as an anchor in the overwhelming, fluid world that had overwhelmed her senses.

"Isana!" Tavi called. "Mother!"

That word, from those lips, came as a sudden shock,

brighter and warmer and more terrible than all the others, and her eyes snapped open.

"Back to the *Slive*!" Tavi shouted. "Take us back to the ship! Hurry!"

"Aleran!" Kitai cried. There was the sound of water being thrashed to foam, and then a shark arrowed by them, streaming a cloud of dark fluid behind it. Isana turned to see the Marat girl lift a bloodied dagger to her teeth, and seize the unmoving Araris.

"The ship!" Tavi thundered, his voice ringing with command. "Crows take it, you are the First Lady of Alera, and you *will* return us to the ship!"

Her son's voice carried pure steel in it, iron control, and Isana grasped at that strength through the contact of their hands. Somehow, it strengthened her, and she was able to push the overwhelming power being unleashed all around her from her thoughts. Reason returned in a cold, focused rush, just as another shark, the largest yet, made a run at the wounded Araris.

Isana called to Rill, sudden rage at the beast giving her strength, and the shark was flung from the water with violent force, arching into the air to land thrashing violently on the deck of the *Mactis* overhead.

"Hold tight," Isana growled. She could feel the leviathans rushing toward them, the pressure wave of water that surged out ahead of them. The nearest had dived, sinking a mere five hundred feet or so beneath them, and it was rising swiftly toward the ship, rising with nightmarish rage and power, and Isana could all but see what would happen to the ship when the ridge of scaled plates on its back struck the vessel's keel.

She called to Rill again, and they surged forward with such speed that the canvas harness bit into her skin, even through the fabric of her clothing. They shot forward, skimming the surface of the water, and she could hear Ehren's breathless shout of fear blending with Kitai's sudden whoop of excitement. They sailed forward, and Isana banked back toward the *Slive*. Their passage kicked up a curtain of water ten feet high as they turned, barely avoiding the bulk of another leviathan cruising toward the *Mactis*.

Isana called out to Rill, to the sea, and as they flashed toward the *Slive*, the water rose beneath them, building up into a wave that lifted them from the surface of the already-roiling ocean, so that as they reached the ship, and the wave broke upon the watercrafting around it, they simply washed up onto its deck.

Demos was standing there as the furycrafted wave washed over his feet and rocked the *Slive* hard to its starboard side, and his eyes were wide with shock. The ship righted itself in the water, and Demos stirred, turning back to his men, and bellowing orders that could barely be heard over the bellows of angry leviathans.

Isana turned to Araris at once, crouching over him and laying her hands on his abdomen. There was a gaping wound in his side, just below his lowest ribs. She grasped at the split flesh with her hands, pushing it back together, pressing her attention down through her fingers. The wound was massive and uncomplicated, but if the bleeding wasn't stopped, and soon, he would not live.

"I did not go through that torture at Ceres to let you die now," she heard herself snarl. Then she willed Rill down into the wound, found its edges with the fury's help, and began to bind them together, to contain the blood trying to rush from his body. It was difficult, and Isana felt her strength swiftly fading, but it had to be done. She did not relent in her efforts until she felt the artery mend, felt the pressures of his body begin to stabilize.

After that, she finally relented, slumping, gasping for breath, and weary in every fiber of her being.

She looked up to find Tavi staring at her.

She looked around. Kitai was watching her as well, her canted eyes brilliant in the lowering light. Ehren's face was awed. Demos, too, stood watching her, as did a dozen sailors.

"Bloody crows," one of the men said. "She didn't even use a tub."

Isana blinked and stared down at her bloodied hands, at the unconscious man beneath them.

She hadn't?

She hadn't.

Bloody crows, indeed. That was impossible. Only the most powerful watercrafters in the Realm could . . .

There was another vast, sea-shaking bellow.

Isana looked up, as did everyone else on the *Slive*, to see the first leviathan attack the *Mactis*. It rose from the sea, a mountain of armored flesh and frenzied rage. It lifted the *Mactis* from the waves, and the crack of timbers snapping as its keel shattered cut through the twilight. Men screamed, falling from the ruined ship, rendered into toys by the distance and by the sheer magnitude of scale. Some of them splashed into the ocean. Some fell upon the bulk of the leviathan, its hide no more forgiving than the rocks of a hostile shore. Half of the ship stayed afloat for a moment—but only until a second leviathan rammed the first, crushing it between them. Men thrashed desperately for life, insects among the angry titans of the sea. Some of them had managed to get a few of the small boats into the sea, but they could not long remain afloat in that maelstrom, and the growing darkness, the surge of furious leviathans slamming into one another in their rage, and the tortured sea swallowed them as the *Slive* sailed on.

Isana felt the horror in those around them—and the sympathy. She realized that these men, though pirates and scoundrels, though struggling to say alive against a foe who would surely have killed them, had just witnessed one of their own nightmares. None of them desired to see another sailor die the way the men of the *Mactis* had.

Isana shook her head, struggling to separate her senses from those around her. It was too much, and her head had begun to pound again.

"All right," growled a voice whose tone brooked no dissent. Her son, she thought dully. "Show's over. Ehren, get the cabin door. Kitai."

Isana looked up dully as Kitai, still shirtless, calmly picked her up as she might carry a child. The Marat girl gave Isana a small, encouraging smile, while Tavi picked up Araris.

"It was well-done," Kitai murmured to Isana quietly. "We're back safe. Time to rest now."

Isana began to protest. She'd closed the worst of the wound, but Araris would need more attention—and she didn't even know if any of the others had been injured. She began to tell Kitai to put her down and fetch a healing tub.

But somewhere between drawing a breath and using it to speak, she lost the will to keep going and embraced the promise of silence and peace in her exhaustion.

ᴏᴏᴏCHAPTER 27

"Bloody crows," snarled Antillar Maximus. "Right now, the captain's taking it easy, sleeping in his bunk in a nice, comfortable cell back at the fort at the Elinarch, while *we're* getting soaked to the skin."

Valiar Marcus stepped down from the block that let him peer over the First Aleran's palisade and view the enemy position at the ford of the river Aepon. The Canim had employed the talents of the Free Aleran Legions. Their earthcrafters weren't the equals of a Legion engineering corps, and the positions they'd erected weren't made of the multilayered stone of a battlecrafted siege wall, but the heavy earthworks they had raised on the far side of the shallow ford were massive enough to provide a formidable defensive position.

"Bet he's eating hot breakfast cakes right now," Maximus continued. The young Tribune glowered up at the steady rain. "Maybe a morning cup of tea. Probably borrowed one of Cyril's books. Cyril's the sort to have a lot of books."

Antillus Crassus stepped down from his own block and glowered at Max. "I'm certain you never complained this much to Captain Scipio."

"Yes he did," Marcus murmured. "Just never in front of anyone. Except me."

Crassus gave Maximus a very direct look. "Tribune, I hereby order you to stop whining."

"That never worked for Scipio," Marcus noted.

"It's a sacred right," Max said. He chinned himself up on the palisade briefly, then dropped back to the ground again. "Looks like they're getting ready to change the guard."

"Signal the engineers," Crassus said.

Marcus turned and flashed a hand signal at the nearest Marat horseman—in this case, horsewoman, he supposed. She nodded, turned, and galloped to the top of the low hill behind them, and repeated the gesture in broader strokes.

"It isn't going to buy us much time, hitting them during their shift change," Max said.

"It doesn't need to," Marcus replied. "They're expecting a shooting match. A few seconds will make the difference." He turned and nodded to the file leaders of the Prime Cohort. They saluted, and murmured orders went down the ranks. The veterans drew their swords in slithering whispers of steel.

Crassus turned and beckoned a runner. The young man hurried over. "Please inform the Honorable Senator that our initial assault is about to begin."

The runner saluted and pelted away.

Marcus stepped up onto the block again and watched the river.

At first, he couldn't see it happening. The change was too slight. His ears, though, picked up on a change in the constant, almost-silent murmur of the water sliding between the banks. The pitch rose, and Marcus leaned forward, watching intently.

The ford was about three feet deep under normal circumstances—slightly deeper, given the steady rain they'd had during the past week. It was not too deep for infantry to ford, but it was more than deep and swift enough to take a man from his feet if he wasn't careful. Trying to cross the ford in the face of the enemy's defenses would be a slow and bloody business, where the balests and bows of the combined Canim and ex-slave forces would be able to take a terrible toll. It would be possible to grind resistance down, eventually, but a conventional assault would require a hefty price in blood.

Which was, Marcus reflected, probably why Arnos had given the First Aleran the dubious distinction of leading the attack.

Marcus wasn't sure if the captain would have run the battle the same way, but he was certain that he would have approved of Crassus's immediate response to such a bloody scenario—to change the scenario.

"Sir," Marcus growled.

Crassus drew his blade and nodded to Maximus. The big Antillan gave his half brother a grin, and, with a murmur to the Knights Pisces, drew his sword. They immediately readied their own weapons.

Marcus kept his eyes on the river, struggling to see through the almost-lightless evening and the steady rain. The reeds the scouts had placed earlier that day had been stripped to pure, white wood that would be more easily seen in the dark, but even so, Marcus began to wonder whether or not it would do him any good.

Then he saw a gleam of fresh white on the river. And a second. A moment later, a third.

"That's it," he hissed. "Three rods. The river is running less than a foot deep."

"Now," Crassus snapped.

Marcus jerked hard on the rope beside him, stepped down from the block, drew back his leg, and kicked at the palisade. Though it seemed a standard Legion defensive wall from the other side, the engineers had altered a two-hundred-foot section of the fence, and when Marcus kicked down the section immediately in front of him, the others fell as well in a sudden wave, crashing to the earth on the far side.

Cries went up in the other camp, but they were immediately drowned out as Crassus lifted his sword, let out a howling battle cry, and the knights and veterans around him responded in kind. Crassus dropped his blade forward, and the Prime Cohort and Knights Pisces surged forward, with Marcus, Crassus, and Maximus in the first rank.

The First Aleran hit the now-shallow water of the ford and surged toward the opposite bank. Arrows began to fly from the earthworks. In the dark and confusion and splashing water, Marcus knew that only a very skilled or very lucky shot from any Aleran bow would have a chance of downing one of the heavily armored *legionares*. Most arrows skimmed off of the steel helmets, or slammed harmlessly into the steel-lined wooden shields of the Legion.

Some didn't.

Marcus heard a scream on his right, and felt, more than saw, the sudden drag in the integrity of the cohort's formation as someone else went down and slowed the advance of those behind him. An arrow struck sparks from Maximus's helmet, and another flickered past Marcus's ear with an eerie, fluttering hiss.

They were halfway across before the Canim sharpshooters went to work.

The flat, metallic twang of the odd bows was not loud, but they were near enough now to hear it. Each twang was followed almost instantly by the heavy sound of impact—a thud accompanied by the shriek of torn steel. Marcus saw from the corner of his eye as another file leader went down—as did the two men in tight formation behind him. Men screamed, and the advance grew more sluggish.

"Now, Max," Crassus shouted. The acting captain of the Legion lifted his blade, and it was suddenly wreathed in brilliant flame, a beacon and a signal to every man in the Legion—not to mention to everyone in the enemy lines as well.

At the same time, Maximus stretched out a hand toward the waters remaining between the First Aleran and the shore. He cried out, and a sudden swirl of wind went rushing down the river, spinning and twisting into a miniature waterspout that threw up great, shimmering sheets of water, obscuring the flaming sword and its wielder from easy observation.

"Forward!" Crassus cried. The fire on the blade pulsed and shimmered. "Forward! For Alera!"

As he finished his cry, Crassus unleashed the firecrafting he'd been preparing.

Rage poured through Marcus, more sudden, hotter, and more violent than any he had felt in years. Every other thought was scorched away by the fire of his anger, and he found himself letting out another cry of eagerness to meet the enemy in battle.

The hesitation of the advancing force vanished entirely, as nearly eight hundred throats erupted in a simultaneous bellow of raw hostility. The First Aleran picked up speed, building to a furious charge as they crossed Maximus's windcrafted water screen. Driven by that anger, they thrust themselves into the teeth of the enemy, utterly ignoring the missiles that continued streaking toward them, claiming lives.

The First Aleran took its hits as it emerged from the river, and accepted them as a necessary price to come to grips with their foe. They surged up the earthworks, spearheaded by the First Aleran's Knights Terra. They struck the mixed earth-and-stone defenses with their great hammers, triggering a minor landslide—one that could be climbed, up and over the defensive walls. Marcus, Maximus, and Crassus were the first to set foot on the improvised ramp, advancing up to the makeshift battlements.

There, they met the enemy.

Marcus had been ready to face the Canim again, but the former slaves were another matter entirely. As he gained the wall, a boy of no more than fifteen summers raised a bow, fumbling at an arrow. Marcus had no time to think. His arm lashed out, and the young soldier fell back, blood rushing from his opened throat.

Marcus stared at the boy for a shocked second, a single thundering heartbeat that suddenly stretched, elongated, drawing the rest of the world into a deceptively dreamy languor. The rage still burned in him, but for that instant, it existed outside of himself, a part of the background that was neither more nor less important than the sounds of battle.

The boy's neck was marred by collar scars. Old ones. If he truly had been fifteen years of age, then he must have gained his scars when he was scarcely old enough to walk—and Marcus had few illusions about what sorts of uses a slaver would find for a helpless child.

Arnos had named the "Free Alerans" traitors—but crows, Marcus wasn't sure that he would not have done precisely the same thing had he been in their place. The lot of a slave in the southern portions of the Realm was a dismal one, and the tolerance of every man, Citizen or not, had its limits.

Then there was a furious, lupine roar, and the frozen instant ended. Marcus ducked the swing of a curved Canim sword and found himself facing eight feet and several hundred pounds of furious, steel-armored warrior-caste Cane.

Marcus was a competent swordsman, and he knew that his own earthcrafter's strength gave him significant advantages against most opponents. Against one of the Canim of the warrior caste, though, he had no advantage of strength, and he might well be the Cane's inferior at bladework. He had not become an old soldier, though, by fighting for pride, and as the Cane advanced and swung again, Marcus shed the blow at an oblique angle along his lifted shield, shoved forward, inside his opponent's guard, and drove his *gladius* into the Cane's knee.

The Cane howled and lurched. Maximus had seen Marcus press in for the ugly little disabling attack, and before the Cane could recover and hew into Marcus, the young Tribune's sword licked out and back in a single motion, and gore erupted from the Cane's throat.

Marcus got his balance again and menaced a foe that was pressing an attack on Maximus's flank, and they drove forward into a half-panicked group of Free Alerans. Marcus was glad that they didn't put up too much of a fight. He slammed one man to the ground with his shield, dealt out a couple of nonlethal cuts with his blade, then the foe was running. Marcus pressed close behind them, down off the fortifications and onto the ground on the far side, and the men of the Prime Cohort pressed in with him.

There, they met a hastily assembled counterattack from the Canim. The wolf-warriors had gathered thirty or forty of their number—shocking, really, given how little time they'd had to prepare, and indicative of considerable military discipline—and they charged the Aleran forces with blood-maddened howls.

Marcus bellowed, "Shield high, blade low!"

"Shield high, blade low!" the cohort roared back, quoting the doctrine that they'd devised as one of the only viable tactics against the immense foe. The Canim hit the line, but their descending weapons were met by a raised curtain of Legion shields, and the soldiers in the front row concentrated on nothing but dishing out disabling blows to the feet, knees, legs, and groins of their attackers. The Canim had comparatively little experience in fighting a foe so much smaller than their selves.

and the low-line attacks had repeatedly proved to be difficult for them to defend against.

Canim smashed at the Legion's shieldwall. One *legionare's* shield took a blow squarely, rather than at a proper angle for a deflection. Lined with steel or not, the shield splintered under the terrible force of the warrior Cane's blade, and the sword that had done it removed the *legionare's* arm at the shoulder. The man went down, screaming.

Beside Marcus, Crassus caught the blow of an immense cudgel on his shield, and even with his fury-strengthened equipment and fury-assisted strength, he grunted with pain and faltered, his shield arm dropping limply to his side.

Marcus cut across the young officer's front, deflecting the Cane's next blow, rather than attempting to match strength with strength, and thrust up at an angle into the Cane's lower abdomen. The Cane fell back with a howl of pain, and Marcus bellowed two of his veterans into position to shield Crassus.

The press of combat abruptly loosened, relaxing, and Marcus realized that the Prime Cohort, followed closely by the rest of the First Aleran, had cleared the earthworks. Braying Canim horns began to blow, and the enemy moved into a general retreat, falling back from their positions and vanishing into the rain and the dark.

Crassus unstrapped his shield from his left arm, his face pale. Marcus turned and glanced at the young officer's arm. "Shoulder's out of its socket," he said. "Need to get you to a healer, sir."

"Let them have the men who are bleeding, first. I'm not feeling it right now, anyway." He wiped his blade clean on the mantle of a fallen Cane, sheathed it, and looked around soberly. "Have the engineers put the river back on its course and recall them. Deploy the Sixth, Ninth, and Tenth Cohorts to a perimeter. Second through Fifth to erect a palisade. The rest in formation as a reserve."

Marcus saluted. "Sir."

"Wait," Maximus said. He stepped closer to Crassus and lowered his voice. "They're off-balance, Crassus. We need to press the attack, now, while we have the advantage."

"The objective was to take the ford," Crassus said. "We've done it."

"This is an opportunity," Max said. "We've got to press it. We might not get another chance like this to hit them when they aren't ready."

"I know," Crassus said. "It's almost too good to be true."

Marcus glanced up sharply at Crassus, and frowned.

Max scowled at Crassus. "You're giving the Canim too much credit, this time."

"Stop and think about this, Max," Crassus said. "It might hurt, but try to pretend you're a Canim for a minute. When else are you going to get a chance to launch an attack against an Aleran Legion isolated from the other two with it, on open ground, and in the dark, no less?"

Max glanced at Marcus. "First Spear? What do you think?"

Marcus grunted. "This is a textbook target of opportunity, sir. If you don't order the pursuit after a rout like this, the Senator isn't going to like it."

"But do you think this is a trap?" Maximus pressed.

"It would take a bloody brilliant soldier to manage it," Marcus replied.

"And Nasaug is," Crassus said. He glanced at Maximus, then out at the dark, his brow furrowing in thought for a moment. "You don't plan for what you think the enemy is going to do," he said, finally. "You plan for what he is capable of doing. I'm not sending the Legion out there blind."

Maximus shook his head. "I'm not eager to wrestle Canim in the dark, but if you don't order an advance, Arnos is going to have your balls."

Crassus shrugged. "Let him try to collect them, then. We secure the ford, first. Get the men moving, First Spear."

Marcus saluted Crassus and turned to the nearest runner, doling out a list of instructions.

"Meantime, send the Marat on ahead," Crassus said. "They can see in the dark and can outrun the Canim. If they don't find the enemy in force out there, we'll send out the cavalry and keep the Canim on the run."

"I hope you know what you're doing," Max said.

"If we stay put, and I'm right, we save ourselves a lot of

blood. If we stay put, and I'm wrong, we've still taken this position, and there are only two more between here and Mastings."

"Scipio would have advanced," Max said. "I'm sure of it."

Crassus rubbed at his injured shoulder, his expression undisturbed. "I'm not Scipio," he said. "And you have your orders."

Maximus glowered at Crassus for a moment, then slammed his fist to his chest and went to his horse. He mounted, then let out an explosive sneeze. The tall Antillan scowled up at the falling rain and nudged his horse into motion, passing near Marcus.

"Lying in bed with a book," he growled to Marcus. "And with the Ambassador, too, I'll wager."

Maximus nudged his horse into a trot, and a moment later, half an ala of Marat cavalry thundered through the captured earthworks and into the country beyond.

Marcus oversaw the positioning of the remainder of the Legion, with some of the men in advance positions, others erecting the mobile palisade wall behind them, and the rest standing in ranks in the center of their position, ready to march or fight should the need arise.

Once that was done, Marcus returned to find Crassus speaking to one of the senior officers of the First Senatorial Guard. The man was evidently angry, because he gestured extensively as he spoke. Crassus stared at the man with no expression on his face and spoke a single word in reply.

The Guard officer spat something in a harsh tone and strode away.

Marcus approached Crassus calmly. "Trouble, sir?"

Crassus shook his head. "The Senator's man. You were right."

The First Spear nodded. "Let's get you to the healers, sir."

"It can wait," Crassus said. "Apparently we've captured some more balests, and I want to make sure they are properly secured before—"

"With respect," Marcus said, "no, sir, it can't wait. Just because you can't feel the pain doesn't mean you aren't doing more damage to your shoulder. We're going to the healers, sir. Now."

Crassus arched an eyebrow in a gesture nearly identical to

the captain's. Marcus supposed that he had learned it from Scipio. Then Crassus glanced down at his shoulder and gave Marcus a rueful smile. "If I was anyone else, I'd be ordering me to go to the healers, wouldn't I?"

"Yes, sir," Marcus said.

Crassus sighed, nodded, and the two of them turned to walk toward where Foss had set up his tents and healing tubs.

"Marcus," Crassus said quietly. "I haven't thanked you."

"For what, sir?"

"Your support. Your advice. I couldn't have taken over the Legion without your help."

"Comes with the job, sir," Marcus said.

Crassus shook his head. "It doesn't. You're always the one willing to go one step farther. You're the first one up in the morning and the last one to sleep at night. You push us all to do better. You keep discipline among the men without resorting to intimidation or humiliation. If you hadn't already won an honor name in the House of the Valiant, your service over the last few years would merit a place in the House of the Faithful."

Marcus fell silent and glanced away from the young man. They had reached the healers' tents. Several wounded men lay on stretchers on the ground, bandaged while they waited their turns in the healing tubs. Several other men lay senseless on bedrolls nearby, fresh pink skin showing where their wounds had been watercrafted closed, exhausting them in the process.

Lady Aquitaine, in her washerwoman guise, was there, serving as an attendant to the wounded, carrying them water and monitoring their injuries. She glanced up at Marcus, smiled very slightly, and returned to her tasks.

"Fidelar Marcus just doesn't roll off the tongue as well though, does it?" Crassus continued. "All the same, I thought you should know that I am aware of all the extra work you do. Thank you."

Marcus tried not to spit out the bitter taste in his mouth. "You're welcome, sir."

CHAPTER 28

The rain, Amara decided, was a mixed blessing. While the moderate, steady downpour helped to hide their trail and cut down on visibility, reducing their chances of being seen, after three days it had begun to gall. Here at the southernmost reaches of the Realm, rainfall such as this was not unusual this time of year, but Amara had never had to contend with such a relentless downpour.

The nights were uncomfortable, especially because there was no dry wood to be had for a fire. Bernard told Amara that he could have used his crafting to shape the trees into a more effective shelter, or to open a dry hole in a rock shelf, but that he didn't dare risk it, for fear enemy woodsmen might recognize it.

Despite that, Amara's husband was as resourceful as ever about practical matters. He always managed to find some means by which to keep at least some of the water away from them, but none of them were resting very well. If the rain didn't let up soon and allow them something other than a cold meal of traveling biscuits, they were going to run out of them and be forced to eat only whatever Bernard could forage or hunt as they traveled. Amara was not looking forward to raw rabbit.

She glowered up at the sky and wished that she had more practice with crafting the weather instead of flying.

"I know precisely how you feel," Gaius murmured, limping steadily along. "I can't stop thinking about how nice a warm fire and a hot cup of tea would be."

Amara smiled. "Is it that obvious?"

"We're all thinking the same thing," Gaius replied. He squinted up at the clouds. "This is mostly my fault, you know."

Amara glanced aside at him. "Why do you say that?"

"Because it was my mistake. The wind that brought us here was from the far north, cold and dry. I bade it fly south with us, and it met the warm, humid skies over the sea. Rain is the result."

Amara shook her head. "Not a terrible mistake. The rain has probably helped us a great deal."

Gaius smiled, teeth gleaming. "Just between the two of us? I've had all the help I can stand."

Amara laughed, and her eye alighted upon the nearest tree trunk. Perhaps seven feet up, the bark had been roughly gouged and scored to the inner skin with thick, crude furrows.

"Bernard?" Amara called quietly.

"I saw them," he said.

"What are they?"

"Territorial markings," Bernard replied.

"Territorial markings . . . ? Of what?"

"A predator," Bernard said. "Maybe some kind of hunting cat. Maybe one of those big lizards." He stopped and held up a hand, his head tilted slightly to one side.

"They're called garim," Gaius supplied quietly. "They make marvelous cloaks when—"

The underbrush ten feet to the First Lord's left erupted in sudden motion, and something massive and leathery and low shot across the forest floor, its head turning sideways, its jaws gaping to snap at Gaius's legs.

It was an enormous lizard—a garim.

The First Lord saw it coming, and he reacted with admirable speed. He managed to turn and thrust his heavy walking staff into the beast's jaws. The garim snapped them shut, neatly clipping off the end of the staff. Then it spat the wood aside and pressed in on Gaius.

Gaius's maneuver, though, had given Amara precious seconds to act. The Cursor called upon Cirrus, borrowing of the wind fury's swiftness, and the world slowed down to a lazy, syrup-thick dance.

Amara's hand dipped to her belt, and her fingers found the hilt of the knife there. She drew, even as she turned toward the menacing garim, shifting her weight with maddening slowness, and flung the knife at what, to her own perceptions, was almost normal speed.

The knife tumbled precisely one and a half times, struck the creature's scaled hide, and sank several inches into the garim's flank, just behind its forward leg.

The garim reacted more slowly than any animal she had ever seen would have, and Amara had taken most of a step before it suddenly wrenched itself to one side, falling into a slow tumble as it snapped its jaws at the knife, tearing it free.

Amara drew her sword and flung herself at the beast, gripping the short weapon in both hands. The extra speed lent her by her fury would allow her to deal out a powerful blow—and she would need it to cut through its hide if the lack of penetration from her knife throw was any indication.

The steps between her and the garim drifted by slowly, and she had time to appreciate another mixed blessing: Though the gift of speed granted by her fury made her swift enough to intervene on the First Lord's behalf, it also left her with entirely too much time to realize the danger in her course of action.

The beast was much larger than she had thought at first. Though it stood very low to the ground, no more than two feet at the highest point of its back, the garim was built broad and flat, with powerful legs that spread out widely from an overly broad body made from gristle and sinew. It probably weighed at least twice what Amara did, and quite possibly more. Its feet were tipped with heavy claws, its head was solid and blocky, distended with the size of the muscles that powered its vicious jaws. It had eyes like beads of black glass, small and vicious and stupid, and its tail, stretching out in length nearly equal to its body, thrashed about with entirely too much power and speed. Its hide was dark grey-green, and rippled with stripes of darker coloration, giving it ideal camouflage in the rain-drenched forest, and the scales looked tough and thick.

If the garim seized her, it would remove her limbs every bit as easily as it had snapped through Gaius's walking staff. She

could evade it easily, of course, if she had been on her own—
but she wasn't. The creature had deliberately rushed Gaius,
and if she did not force it to deal with her, it would only return
to its attack on the First Lord. She had to fight, which meant
that she had to deal out a decisive, crippling stroke on the first
blow or risk being overwhelmed by the beast's power and
speed.

She would have aimed for the throat, had this been a
thanadent, or a grass lion, or one of the Marat's herdbanes.
The garim's neck, though, was covered in great folds of heavily scaled skin, and she doubted her ability to strike through it.

Unlike the garim, which could snap through *her* neck without any particular effort.

Amara was terrified.

The eyes, she decided. A small target, true, but Cirrus's
speed would help with that. A true enough strike had the potential to kill the beast—and even if she only wounded it, that
might disable the garim badly enough to prevent it from pursuing Gaius. Though if it came to that, she supposed, killing
Amara, dragging her body off into the forest, and devouring
her might prevent the garim from pursuing Gaius as well.

Looking at it from that perspective, Amara thought, she
couldn't lose.

The garim's broad, vicious head swiveled toward her, and
its wide mouth opened, revealing what seemed like hundreds
of curved, vicious teeth.

Amara screamed and thrust the blade down, putting all the
speed and power she could muster into the blow. The tip of her
sword struck just above the garim's beady eye, pierced a thin
layer of skin, and scraped along the thick bone of its skull.
Her forward momentum carried her on, over the low-slung
garim, and she realized with a sick sensation of panic that she
was about to fall.

Amara tried to turn the fall into a diving roll, so that she
would be able to come up on her feet and running—but halfway
through, something struck her in the shoulder and sent her into
an uncontrolled tumble. She hit the ground hard, first on one
knee, then slammed into the ground with one shoulder, and
fetched up against a tree with stunning force. She dropped to

the ground, the world rolling back into normal motion again, as she lost concentration on maintaining the link with Cirrus.

The wounded garim lashed its heavily muscled tail, with which it had just struck her, and doubled back on itself with sinuous, liquid speed. It rushed her, fangs bared. Amara fumbled dazedly for her sword, knowing, even as she did, that the weapon would be of little use. She thrust out as the garim closed on her, and the sword skittered off the hide of its chest. She screamed.

And then a length of wood came out of nowhere and landed with crushing force on the creature's muzzle, slamming its jaws closed and into the ground. Its head rebounded from the earth, and the wood landed again, and again, the blows precisely timed and savage.

The First Lord of Alera flung himself onto the garim, slipping his damaged staff across the beast's throat, and with a snarl of effort and a wrench of his entire body, twisted away, taking the garim with him, rolling the lizard belly-up.

"His underside!" Gaius cried. "Countess, where the scales are thin!"

Amara seized her sword, lurched to her knees, and struck down, through the garim's exposed throat, just beneath where Gaius's staff still held back the creature's head. To her surprise, the sword swept cleanly through the finer, smoother scales there, and blood rushed out in a scarlet fountain.

The garim thrashed wildly, but the First Lord had the creature pinned. Though it flung him back and forth, it could not escape Gaius's hold. Amara struck again and again, until the garim's thrashing slowed, and the First Lord rolled clear of the dying animal.

"My lord!" Amara gasped.

"I'm all right," Gaius panted. "The Count."

Amara rose, looked around wildly, and realized that there was something else about the deadly lizards she had not known.

They ran in packs.

One garim hung thrashing fifteen feet above the forest floor in a willow tree, where dozens of the slender branches had seemingly reached down and wrapped around it. Another thrashed and contorted wildly on the forest floor, bounding up as high as five or six feet above the ground. A woodsman's axe protruded from the dying garim's head, where a powerful blow had sunk the weapon to its eye in the lizard's skull.

And the bloodied Count of Calderon himself was locked in combat with a third garim—unarmed. Like the First Lord, he had managed to gain a position on the beast's back, but he had locked his arms around the creature's throat. Amara could see that blood covered one side of his face, his throat, and half of his upper torso, but he was conscious, his face locked into a rictus snarl.

The garim thrashed wildly, rolling over several times, and its tail whipped about with savage energy, hammering Bernard on his legs and lower back. He let out a howl of rage and pain.

Amara cried out and rushed toward her husband, sword in hand.

Bernard's head turned to one side, and he released the garim with one arm, seizing its tail. The beast rolled wildly, twisting free of Bernard's grip, and scrambled at the forest floor with its powerful legs, to rise and sink its teeth into Amara's husband.

Bernard, though, had found his feet first, and hauled at the garim's tail before it could regain its balance. It scrambled toward him as best it could, and Bernard shuffled away from the jaws, still hauling hard on the tail.

At first, Amara thought he was simply trying to buy time— but by the second circle, the garim began to pick up speed. The beast was the largest of any Amara had seen, and must have weighed five hundred pounds if it weighed an ounce, but the Count of Calderon whirled it up off the ground as if it were a child's toy.

Pivoting in a great circle, Bernard roared in rage and triumph, and slammed the garim's skull against the thick trunk of a tree. It broke with a wet, hollow thunk, like the sound of a melon being smashed open, and the lizard fell to the earth, abruptly and totally limp.

The garim trapped in the willow snarled and tore its way

free of the grasping limbs and fell to the ground behind Bernard. Amara cried out in a wordless warning.

He looked up at her, and then his head whipped around. He flung out his hand, and cried, "Brutus!"

The earth beneath the garim suddenly shuddered and erupted into motion. The shape of a hound the size of a small horse rose from the earth, its shoulders and chest made of flint and loam, its eyes of glittering green gems, its jaws of granite. Bernard's earth fury seized the garim in its stony maw, and the lizard hissed and thrashed wildly as Brutus lifted the lizard entirely off the ground. The great hound continued rising from the ground, like a dog emerging from the waters of a lake, and shook the garim as a terrier would a rat. Amara thought she heard the lizard's neck snap, but Brutus was not satisfied until he had slammed the garim against two trees, and repeatedly hammered it into the ground. By the time the earth fury was finished, the garim was a bloody mass of pulped flesh and shattered bone.

Amara slowed and came to a halt a few feet away from her husband. Bernard watched until Brutus was finished, then nodded, and said, "Thank you." The stone hound champed its jaws twice, shook its head, sending pebbles and bits of mud flying, and sank down into the earth again, turning circles like a dog about to lie down as it went.

Bernard sagged and dropped to one knee.

Amara rushed to his side. "Bernard!"

"It's nothing, I'm fine," Bernard slurred, still breathing heavily. "Gaius?"

"He's alive," Amara said. "Let me see your head."

"Looks worse than it is," Bernard said. "Scalp wounds bleed a lot. Flesh wound."

"I know that," Amara said, "but you've got a lump the size of an egg to go with the cut. Concussions are not flesh wounds."

Bernard reached up and caught her hand. He met her eyes, and said in a quiet, firm tone, "See to the First Lord, Countess."

She stiffened with anger. "Bernard."

"I have a duty to my lord. So do you."

"I also have a duty to my husband," she whispered back.

Bernard released her hand, and growled, "See to Gaius." His tone became gentler, and very tired. "You know I'm right."

She put a hand to her face for a moment, took a deep breath, then touched his head gently. Then she turned and went back to the First Lord.

Gaius lay on the ground with his eyes closed. He opened them as Amara approached, and said, "I haven't done that in a while."

"Sire?"

"Hunted garim. Not since I was about seventeen." He exhaled heavily. "It was considerably less strenuous back then."

His voice was tight with pain, the way it had been at the beginning of their journey. "You're hurt."

"It's my leg," he said quietly. "The good one." He nodded at the still-twitching garim. "I'm afraid this fellow managed to trap it between his hide and a stone. I'm fairly sure it's broken."

Amara bent to examine the First Lord's leg. It was swollen, and his foot rested at an utterly inappropriate angle to the rest of the leg. It had been a twisting break, not a clean snap of the bone. Amara knew that they could be very ugly. "I can't see any bone poking out," she said quietly. "You aren't bleeding. How bad is it?"

"It's only pain," Gaius said, but his voice trembled as he did. "I see that Bernard gave rather a good accounting of himself."

Amara would need to set the leg as soon as possible. They would have to splint it as well. "He killed three of them."

"For killing men, metalcrafters stand supreme," Gaius murmured. "But beasts don't fight like men. Primal. Savage. For them, nothing replaces raw strength. And I think one really couldn't fault my choice in companions on this particular journey." He shook his head and blinked his eyes several times. "I'm babbling. Please excuse me. The mind tends to wander a bit when one is my age—or in excruciating pain."

"We'll do what we can, sire," Amara said.

"The pain won't kill me. Bernard is bleeding. See to him. I believe I'll faint now, if it isn't too inconven . . ."

The First Lord fell silent, and Amara bent to him for a panicked instant. He continued breathing steadily, though, and his pulse was strong. She bit her lip in sympathy, and was just as glad that he had lost consciousness. His injury had to be pure torment.

She took off her cloak, damp as it was, rolled it up, and used it to support his broken leg. Then she rose and went back to Bernard. He had taken off his pack and was fumbling through it rather dazedly. Amara took it from his hands and removed the box of bandages, ointments, and healing salves he carried in it. She cleaned his wound as best she could, but it kept bleeding, as such injuries tended to.

"This will need stitches to close properly," she said quietly. "That means we'll need boiling water. A fire."

"Dangerous," Bernard mumbled. "Too easy to spot."

"We've little choice," she replied. "He's unconscious. His leg is broken. We have to warm him up, then set the leg. Can you have Brutus make a shelter for us?"

He looked at her dully for a moment, and then back at Gaius. "Dangerous."

She put her hands on either side of his face. "Bernard, you've been hit in the head. You're having trouble speaking clearly, much less thinking clearly. I need you to trust me. This is necessary."

He exhaled heavily and closed his eyes. Then he nodded. He opened his eyes again and peered blearily around them, through the rain. Then he nodded at a hillock, and muttered under his breath. "Garim had a den there. Brutus is widening it. Shoring it up. Drag wood in first thing. Let it start to dry. Then we'll move Gaius in."

"Very well," Amara said. She covered his wound with a pad of folded cloth and wound a bandage around his head to hold it closed as best it could until she could see to the injury more thoroughly. "Bernard. It's his good leg that's broken."

Bernard frowned for a moment, then said, "Crows. He won't be able to walk."

"No," Amara said.

"That's bad," he said.

"Yes."

"But there is good news," he said.

She frowned at him.

His nostrils flared as he inhaled. "Smell that?"

Amara frowned and sniffed at the air. There was an over-ripe smell to it, a vegetable reek.

"Only one thing smells like that," Bernard said. "Swamps. We made it. Once we get in there, don't have to worry about our back trail."

"No," Amara murmured. "Only disease. Injury. Lack of food. And more of those garim."

Bernard grunted. "Well," he mused, "we never did get that honeymoon."

Amara blinked at him for a moment, then burst out in a laugh that surprised her with its depth and strength.

He gave her a weary grin, and for a moment his eyes shone with warmth. "That's better. Love it when you smile." Then he took a deep breath and pushed himself slowly to his feet. He touched the bandages and hissed in discomfort.

"Don't do that," Amara said absently. She rose, wincing at a flare of pain in her back. She had almost forgotten the blow from the garim's tail and the tumble afterward. Her muscles and bones, however, had not. "He can't walk," she said quietly. "What are we going to do?"

"We'll handle it, Countess. One thing at a time."

She touched her face, and then the bandages. "I love you very much, you know."

He lifted her fingers from his head and kissed them gently, eyes sparkling. "Who could blame you?"

Amara laughed again.

⟫⟫CHAPTER 29

"Again!" Araris snapped, driving a series of high, whirling slashes at Tavi's head. The *singulare* was not restraining the force of his blows, and it took every ounce of Tavi's concentration and skill to survive them. He found the rhythm of the attack, found the tiny half beat of vulnerability between one of Araris's strikes and the next, and countered low, his body dipping to one side and out of the line of the attack, one hand resting flat on the ground to support his suddenly altered balance, his blade darting in a swift thrust for the large artery in the *singulare's* midsection.

Tavi was an instant too slow. Araris slammed his blade across Tavi's, driving it from his fingers. The *singulare* swung a booted kick at Tavi's face. Tavi rolled away from it. Araris drove his heel down at Tavi's nose. Tavi swatted the blow mostly aside—and found the point of Araris's sword resting in the hollow of his throat.

Araris stared at Tavi, his eyes expressionless, even frightening. Then he drew himself upright and lifted the sword away. "It has to be faster," he said quietly. "The fight is always in motion. You can't wait for the right beat. You have to anticipate it."

Tavi scowled up at Araris. "We've done this every day for a week. It's only one counter. Someone my size is going to have real trouble using it. We both know that. What happened to fighting to my strengths?"

"This is one," Araris said. "You just don't know it yet."

Tavi shook his head. "What the crows is that supposed to mean?"

Araris rested a hand on his midsection where he'd been wounded, wincing like a man with a stitch in his side after a long run. "Any swordsman worth the name won't expect that move from someone like you. They would think it too dangerous, too foolhardy."

Tavi touched his throat, where Araris's sword had been, and glanced at the small smear of blood on his finger. "Why would anyone think *that*?" But he got to his feet, recovered his sword, and faced Araris, ready to go again.

Araris rolled his shoulder, his expression pained, and shook his head. "Enough for today."

They lifted their blades in a mutual salute and put them away. "Is your side still hurting? Maybe I should get the Steadholder to—"

"No," Araris said at once. "No. She has enough to contend with. It's sore, that's all."

Tavi arched his eyebrows, realization dawning in his face. "That's how Navaris got you."

Araris frowned and looked away. "She had too many of Arnos's *singulares* with her. I couldn't have fought them all and lived. So I gave Navaris an opening. I had counted on her to take a thrust to my leg and pin her sword in the hull for a moment." He waved a hand at his flank. "But she hit me here instead."

Tavi frowned. "I saw her sword go through the hull. But it was still stuck there when . . ." His voice trailed off as a little surge of nausea went through his stomach. Araris had been pinned to the *Mactis*'s hull with a sword through his guts. The only way he could have freed himself would have been . . .

Bloody crows. The man had simply sliced himself free on Navaris's weapon. He'd let the blade cut through four or five inches of his own midsection. No wonder it looked like Navaris had slashed him open halfway to his spine.

Araris met Tavi's gaze soberly and nodded. "Without Isana . . ." He shrugged. "Navaris shouldn't have been able to do that. I don't know how she managed it. But she did. I'm pushing us both."

He turned without another word and went back to the ship's cabin. Tavi put his sword away, tugged on his loose tunic, and made his way thoughtfully to the ship's prow.

After their raid on the doomed *Mactis*, the rest of the voyage had been comparatively uneventful, and Tavi found himself growing increasingly anxious. Araris was back on his feet after two days of rest, and they returned to relentless practice on the deck for hours at a time. Araris proved to be one of those swordmasters who believed that pain was the best motivator for learning. Tavi acquired any number of small cuts—some of them quite messy and painful—and a collection of dozens of bruises in various colors.

Despite the pain, the practice sessions helped. He wasn't sure exactly how well he was progressing in his swordsmanship, since Araris always seemed to be just a bit faster than Tavi, his technique and positioning a tiny bit more precise than Tavi's own, but Araris assured him that he was getting better. The practices were exhausting, which Tavi thought was their single largest benefit.

It left him with less energy to worry about the future.

After dinner that night, he was standing at the prow of the ship again, watching dolphins sport in the waters ahead of the *Slive*. Kitai was lying back along a line, somewhere above him and behind him, relaxing as casually as if it had been a hammock, rather than a single rope she held with an ankle and one hand. He could feel her lazy contentment at having a full belly, an interesting day, and a lovely sunset to watch over the rolling waves of the sea.

Tavi closed his eyes and tried to partake of Kitai's contentment. The two of them differed fundamentally in regards to their views on the future. For Kitai, the future was a single enormous matter of relative unimportance. What mattered was the here and now. While preparation for what might happen was useful, it was beneficial more in how it shaped one's character and brightened one's day than for any practical gain it might grant when the future became the present. Kitai, he knew, approved of Tavi's weapons training with Araris, but he suspected it had more to do with the fact that she enjoyed seeing him sweating and shirtless than with her concern for whom he might be fighting in the future.

Tavi's sense of Kitai changed slightly, as her interest was briefly piqued. He glanced over his shoulder and saw Ehren approaching.

"Hey," Tavi said quietly.

"Hey," Ehren said. The little Cursor came up to stand beside Tavi, staring out ahead of the ship. "I talked to Demos. We start up the Gaul tomorrow. After that, it will be another week to get up the river to the capital. Maybe more, if he can't find a decent tugboat."

Tavi nodded. "That's good. I figure we'll be there right around the time of the new moon."

"Always nice for sneaking around springing prisoners," Ehren said. There was tension in the former scribe's shoulders. He folded his arms and leaned one hip against the rail. "I knew she was a skilled healer, but I didn't know the Steadholder's other watercraft was that strong. It surprised me."

"I think it surprised her, too," Tavi said. "Maybe it shouldn't have. She flooded a river at home just before Second Calderon. That's more than most watercrafters can do."

Ehren nodded. "How is she?"

"Araris hung up a hammock for her in a storage room in the hold. She says it's quieter down there. She was up on deck for a while, earlier. I'd say she's getting a handle on it now."

"That's good," Ehren said. He frowned out at the sea, and his voice trailed away into an awkward silence.

"Just say it," Tavi said quietly.

"Say what?" Ehren asked.

"Whatever it is that's bothering you."

Ehren quirked one corner of his mouth up and nodded, staring out to sea. "When we went over to the *Mactis*. You said something to the Steadholder."

Tavi grimaced. "I was sort of hoping you wouldn't notice it in all the excitement."

"I debated doing that," Ehren said. "But . . . these days it seems I have to lie to almost everyone. I don't really like it. And I don't want that to include you."

Tavi smiled a little and nodded. "Thank you."

"Sure," Ehren said. "So. When you told Isana that she was the First Lady of Alera, what you meant was . . ."

"Exactly what I said," Tavi said.

Ehren frowned. Then he blinked and stared at Tavi. "You mean . . . she's really Lady *Caria*? In disguise?"

Tavi blinked. "What? No! Oh, bloody crows, no."

Ehren frowned. "Then I don't get it. The First Lady is the wife of the First Lord."

"Most First Lords would have retired years ago," Tavi said. "Passed their authority on to their heir. Remained as an advisor, maybe."

Ehren frowned. Then he lifted both eyebrows and dropped his voice to a whisper. "The Princeps? Gaius Septimus?"

Tavi nodded silently.

"But he never married!"

"He did," Tavi said. "Legally. And he left her the means to prove it."

Ehren whistled. "If he'd lived . . ." He shook his head. "Well. Everything would be different, wouldn't it?" Ehren studied Tavi's face for a moment, frowning. "But that's not all."

Tavi took a deep breath. "He had an heir by her, Ehren. A son."

The Cursor arched a skeptical eyebrow. "An heir to the Crown? Tavi . . ." Then his expression froze in place. "Tavi," he said quietly, his eyes widening.

Tavi forced himself to smile a little. He shrugged his shoulders stiffly. "I'm not terribly comfortable with it, either."

Ehren glanced around covertly. "Um. How many people know about this?"

"You. Cyril. Araris. My mother."

"And me," Kitai drawled from her perch, without opening her eyes.

Tavi frowned up at her. "I never explained it to you."

She yawned. "Aleran, please. It is not as if you are horribly complex. I have ears and a mind. If I waited for you to speak to me about everything important, it would probably drive me insane."

Tavi snorted and shook his head. He turned back to Ehren.

The young man chewed idly at a fingernail, a habit Tavi remembered well from their days at the Academy together. "Gaius doesn't know?"

"He knows something," Tavi said. "I'm not sure how much."

Ehren sighed. "You realize that it's my duty to inform him."

"That," Tavi said, "is the least of my worries."

The Cursor nodded. "If it's true," he said. "Tavi, I don't

mean to insult you, but . . . an heir of the House of Gaius would be a powerful furycrafter. You . . . you aren't."

"There are reasons," Tavi said quietly. "I don't want to go into it right now."

The Cursor nodded and looked away. After a minute he asked, his voice carrying a slight edge, "How long have you known?"

"You're my friend, Ehren. I don't want to have to lie to you, either." Tavi turned to him and put a hand on Ehren's shoulder, meeting his eyes. "I found out just before we marched out from the Elinarch. Until then, I had no idea."

Ehren searched his eyes for a moment, a line appearing between his eyebrows. Then he nodded slowly. "All right." He chewed on another fingernail. "So what do we do?"

"We continue with the mission," Tavi said. "We get Varg and use him to broker an armistice with the Canim. Then we march south and help Sir Miles put Kalarus down for good."

"Simultaneously stealing the thunder from both Aquitainus and his puppet Arnos." Ehren shook his head. "You can't expose yourself to this kind of risk."

"What risk? I'm not anything yet," Tavi said. "And even if I was, it has to be me who takes the risk. Who else could?"

Ehren rolled his eyes and waved his hands in a vague gesture of frustration. "How can you possibly say something that is so backward while still making sense?"

Tavi laughed. "The point is," he said, "we've got to focus on what's here and now. Have you gone over the list?"

Ehren nodded. "I can buy everything but the coldstones. Those aren't easy to find at any time, much less in the spring. Everyone's saving them up for summer. Even if I find some for sale, they're going to cost more than we have."

"They aren't optional equipment," Tavi said, frowning. "We've got to have them, period."

"I thought you'd say something like that," Ehren said. He glanced up at the rigging above and behind them. "As it happens, I seem to remember a rather successful burglar who terrorized the shopkeepers of the capital a few years back."

Kitai opened one eye. Her mouth spread into her lazy, feline grin. "Good," she said. "I was beginning to grow bored."

CHAPTER 30

At Tavi's insistence—backed by more of Cyril's coin—Captain Demos hired a particularly swift tugboat for the journey upriver, once they had reached Parcia. Tavi had never been to the southern city and seaport at the delta of the Gaul, but there was no time to take in the sights. Parcia was a city of shining white stone, rising on several tiered levels almost like stair-steps, up to an impressive fortified citadel. Though not as large as Alera Imperia, the city of Parcia seemed airier, cleaner, more open.

The crew of the tugboat Demos hired reminded Tavi of Countess Amara, with their dark golden skin and their hair that came in several shades of deep gold, amber, and copper. The crew seemed more cheerful than the rivermen Tavi had known in the capital, and after running lines to the *Slive*, the smaller ship proceeded up the river, propelled by a crew of Parcian men with long poles, walking down either side of the tugboat, singing a working song with surprising facility as they did, pushing the vessels upriver.

In the stern of the smaller ship was a pair of middle-aged women. They settled down on seats slung outside the back of the tugboat, down close to the waterline. They sat dragging their feet in the water, chatting with one another, and doing handwork, mostly sewing. When Tavi asked, Demos explained that they were the wives of the tugboat's captain and first mate, and that they were watercrafters whose furies would convince the currents of the river to pretend that the tugboat and the *Slive* were not there.

The Gaul was busy with traffic, and would only become more so until the trading season slowed again at the end of autumn. Now that the sailors weren't needed to manage the sails, they lounged on deck for hours at a stretch, whenever Demos couldn't fill their time with make-work. As a result, Tavi found that he and Araris had an audience for their practice sessions, and to his intense discomfort they began regularly betting on the outcomes of the practices—not whether Tavi would beat Araris, which seemed a forgone conclusion. The wagers all centered on when and how Tavi would lose and how much of his blood would spill in the process.

The tugboat kept up its pace until several hours after dark, lighting its way with furylamps until the boatmen were too weary to continue, and they would start moving again just as the eastern sky began to lighten. The boat moved with surprising grace and speed up the river, often passing trading caravans on the road beside the water, on their way to Alera Imperia—and quietly, efficiently passed the other vessels being drawn upriver by tugs. As a result, it took them only six days to reach the capital.

"That's a great racket they've got going," Demos observed, as the tugboat maneuvered close to the docks and passed up the lines that would let the dockmen haul the *Slive* into position. "They made a quarter of what I did, just for the run up the river. No pirates, no leviathans, no worries about storms, fresh water, or food."

"Maybe you're in the wrong business," Ehren observed.

"You get to be my age, you start thinking about your retirement," Demos replied. "I like to plan ahead. I like my work, but it's going to be a little energetic for me, eventually."

Tavi stepped up next to the pair of them and nodded to Demos. "We're going to be here two days, three at the most, depending on how long it takes us to—"

Demos interrupted him with a scowl and a raised hand. "Don't tell me. The less I know, the harder it will be to incriminate myself."

Tavi frowned at him, but nodded. "Two days, three at most, and we'll be leaving in the middle of the night."

Demos grunted and beckoned the bosun. "Pay the men. Shore leave until noon tomorrow. Tell Sigurd he doesn't go until the stores are refreshed."

The weather-beaten sailor nodded, then scowled at Ehren,

and said something quietly in Demos's ear. Demos listened, nodded, and frowned at Ehren.

Ehren rolled his eyes, opened his purse, and flipped two silver coins at the bosun. The man caught them, bit them both, and nodded before stumping off to his duties.

"Sailors and their swill," Ehren muttered.

The *Slive* bumped against the heavy rolls of burlap cushioning the edge of the dock, and the dock rats made the ship fast. Sailors lowered the gangplank, and sailors spilled off the ship, for all the world looking like students leaving a stuffy lecture hall.

Ehren gave Tavi a nod and slipped off the ship among the sailors, blending into the rowdy bunch without difficulty.

Demos eyed Tavi. "You aren't going, too?"

Tavi glanced up at the lowering sun. "In a bit."

"Ah," Demos said, nodding. "Glad your man paid my bosun back."

"Why wouldn't he?" Tavi asked.

"Some people have funny ideas about property," Demos said. "They think they can take it, or ruin it, and that they have the right to do so. You'll pay me for those chains."

"I did you a favor."

"See what I mean, about funny ideas?" Demos said. "That's my livelihood."

"No it isn't," Tavi said. "If you were primarily a slaver, your ship would smell a lot worse, and you'd have had more chains."

Demos shrugged. "Worked on a slaver before I got the *Slive*. The money's good, but I didn't like the smell. There's the occasional run, though. I carry all kinds of cargo."

"People," Tavi said, "are not cargo."

"The excisemen in all the southern ports seem to disagree with you," Demos said drily.

"Things change," Tavi said. "Slavery is going to be one of them."

Demos narrowed his eyes and stared at Tavi for a long moment. Then he said, "It hasn't changed yet. You'll pay me for those chains."

Tavi squinted at Demos for a moment. "Or what? You'll weigh anchor and leave us here?"

Demos's eyes went flat. "Excuse me?"

"That's what you mean, isn't it?" Tavi continued. "That if I don't pay you, you'll leave us high and dr—"

Tavi never so much as saw Demos draw his blade. It simply appeared at the end of his extended arm. What shocked him was that his own hand came up every bit as quickly, and his dagger met Demos's blade before it could touch Tavi's skin. Then the planks of the deck suddenly shuddered beneath Tavi's feet, flinging him six or eight inches into the air and robbing him of his balance. He came down windmilling his arms, and wound up on his rump. One of the planks of the deck abruptly folded, supple as a willow wand, and came down over Tavi's knife hand, pinning it painfully to the deck's wooden surface.

Demos stepped forward and drove his sword into the deck between Tavi's sprawled legs, not more than two inches from his groin. The captain growled and squatted down to be on eye level with the young man.

"I've taken your money," he said in a tone full of quiet rage. "That means I do the job. Period. Do you understand me?"

Tavi just stared at him for a moment in shock. Then he stammered, "The ship. The whole ship is a wood fury."

"And she's mine," Demos said. "And you *will* repay me for the property you damaged before this trip is over."

Behind the captain, Tavi saw Araris appear silently on bare feet, his sword in hand. He drifted closer, his face intent.

The door to the cabin snapped open with sudden, vicious force, striking Araris in the shoulder and sending him to the deck in a sprawl.

"And tell your swordmaster," Demos continued, eyes never wavering from Tavi's, "that if he draws steel on me again, he'd better be smart enough not to do it aboard this vessel."

Demos rose, drew the tip of his blade from the planks of the deck, and sheathed it. Turning to Araris, he said, "We both know you'd take me in a fair fight."

Araris rose slowly and sheathed his sword. He gave Demos a slight bow of the head. "When's the last time you were in a fair fight?"

Demos made a curt gesture at the deck, and the plank

pinning Tavi's arm flexed and released him, returning to its original position. "I think I was twelve. I never saw the point. Good day, gentlemen."

Tavi watched Demos stroll away and shook his head.

"Are you all right?" Araris asked quietly.

"That," Tavi said, "is a dangerous man."

Araris rubbed at his shoulder and winced in silent agreement.

Tavi glanced at the sun. "Another hour, and it'll be dark enough to go. There's a boardinghouse on Craft Lane. We'll stay there until we can get everything we need." Tavi frowned and lowered his voice. "How is she?"

"Better, since we've gotten away from the ocean," Araris replied.

Tavi shook his head. "The things she did, Araris. That was some major crafting. That thing with the shark . . . And I've never even heard of anyone moving through the water that way. I thought that the spray was going to start cutting my skin, we were moving so quickly."

Araris frowned. "I don't remember much of it."

"She healed you without using a tub."

Araris's eyes widened slightly. "She . . . didn't mention that."

"I saw Lady Placida do that once," Tavi said quietly. "But that's all. I mean, I knew Isana was a skilled healer, even when compared to Citizen healers, but this is the second time I've seen her do something on such a large scale that wasn't healing."

Araris nodded slowly. "When she flooded that little river, just before Second Calderon."

"Exactly. What she did out there wasn't exactly new. But it's certainly more than she's ever done before. More than even she thought she could do, I'm certain."

Araris drummed his fingers idly on the hilt of his sword. "A lot of times, you don't really know where your limits are until they're tested. I've known any number of people who had a tremendous gift in metalcraft, but who, for whatever reason, never used it." He shrugged his shoulders. "How often is one called upon to hurl an attacking shark onto the deck of a pirate ship, Tavi?"

Tavi flashed Araris a wry grin. "You've known her longer than I have," he said quietly. "Have you ever seen anything else like this? Something that would indicate that her crafting might be a more significant gift than anyone knew?"

Araris shook his head. "You mean to ask if your father ever said anything about it."

Tavi glanced away, suddenly uncomfortable. "Well. Yes."

Araris folded his arms and was silent for a long moment. "It was a long time ago. And . . . for a long time, it wasn't anything I cared to dwell on."

"But if there's anything you remember . . ."

Araris held up a hand and closed his eyes for a moment. "Once. When we were talking about what Sextus would say, when he learned about Isana. Your father had just told me of his intention to marry her and . . ." Araris glanced at Tavi, and the young man felt a flash of the *singulare's* discomfort and shame. "And I told him that there would be the crows to pay if he did. Gaius wouldn't have minded a bastard or two running around—the bloodline has never been a particularly fruitful one. But he definitely had plans in mind for Septimus's wife. He'd have chosen someone not only for political gain, but for their skill at furycraft as well, to keep the royal bloodline strong."

Tavi sighed. "I'm not holding advice you gave my father against you, Araris. Bloody crows, man, you know me better than that. Just tell me what he said."

Araris nodded. "He said that Isana was more than he expected. And that she would be more than Gaius had bargained for, either." He sighed. "But he wasn't necessarily talking about her crafting."

"It sounds like he was. What else could he have meant?" Tavi asked.

"There weren't many people willing to stand up to Septimus, but she was one of them. If she thought he was wrong, she'd call him on it. Not argue, exactly, but . . . he could get most people to go along with him through sheer force of personality. He couldn't bull his way through Isana like that. She never raised her voice, never really seemed to be in conflict with him—but she'd never give an inch, either." Araris shrugged. "Tavi, your father never set much store by furycraft when it came to the important things."

"He never had to work without it, either," Tavi said.

"True enough." Araris's frown deepened. "But . . . Tavi, I don't know if you know this. But the House of Gaius has always been gifted with . . . not prophecy, precisely. But a measure of insight, foresight, that went beyond what could be explained away as simple wisdom."

Tavi frowned. "I've never heard about that."

"It isn't something that's casually bandied about," Araris said. "Septimus was particularly . . . intuitive. He would just casually mention things that were going to happen, weeks or months later. Miles used to write them down. Keep track of them. Sometimes, Septimus would hardly remember mentioning it. I don't think it was anything he had control over."

"What's that got to do with Isana?" Tavi asked.

Araris shrugged. "Just that he might have made the remarks based on an intuition." The *singulare* smiled faintly. "You've got to admit, Isana's done quite a bit more than Gaius would expect out of a woman from a steadholt. She was instrumental in the events of Second Calderon. If not for her, in fact, Gaius would have died the night the Vord attacked his meditation chamber. And according to Countess Amara, only her warning saved her and your uncle from being killed by Kalarus's Immortals—and their actions helped tilt the balance of power in Kalarus's initial attack." He shook his head. "Or maybe he was talking about her furycraft. Maybe she had more power at her disposal than she knew. Or . . ." He frowned.

"What?" Tavi asked, intent. "Or what?"

"Or maybe . . . maybe your father placed more furies at her disposal. Before he died."

Tavi frowned. "Could . . . can that be done?"

"Oh, yes," Araris said, nodding. "The way furies can be passed from generation to generation on a steadholt. Remember when Old Frederic passed Thumper to Young Frederic?"

"I thought that only happened, you know. Out in the country, where people name their furies."

"As far as I know, there's no reason that someone couldn't pass more furies along to someone else, whether they were discrete beings or amorphous. It's just rarely done among the Citizenry. A child with a high potential generally attracts many furies to himself all on his own, of course—Septimus certainly did. But his power would have been significantly greater when his father died or stepped aside and willed the majority of his power to pass on."

Tavi frowned. "And . . . what? You think my father might have willed some of his furies to her when he was killed?"

Araris shook his head. "I just don't know, Tavi. But I think it's significant that both times she demonstrated extraordinary strength, your life was in danger." His eyes went distant, and he smiled very faintly. "It would be just like Septimus, to find a way to protect his son, even years after his own death."

Tavi frowned at that. Araris had said more about his father in the past moments than he had in most of the previous two years. It was a lot to think about.

He closed his eyes for a moment as a sharp little ache went through him. Was his father still there, somehow, watching over him? The very thought was incredibly reassuring, almost unbearably sad, sweetly painful. It was the kind of thing he had dreamed about when he was lonely, uncertain, or afraid.

Like now. He was about to set out to break Varg out of the most secure prison in all of Alera. The Grey Tower was home to some of the most dangerous swordsmen to be found—and, partially in thanks to his own recommendations, its furycrafted defenses were some of the most deadly to be had. And even if the rescue was successful, they would have to elude the pursuit that was sure to be sent after them. As if all of that wasn't enough, there was Varg to consider. Tavi was not at all certain what the Canim warrior's reaction would be once he was free. Varg might well decide his best course of action would be to tear Tavi's throat out and make his own way from there.

Tavi smiled faintly at Araris, and said quietly, "I'll take all the help I can get."

Chapter 31

For Isana, visits to the largest cities of Alera had never been pleasant. The constant pressure of the various emotions of so many people packed into such a small area was a constant distraction. It was a low but steady "noise," like being constantly accompanied by half a dozen nightmarishly persistent crickets. It was never horribly loud, but it didn't *stop*, and the intrusive sensations could make it maddeningly difficult to sleep or concentrate.

Isana feared that she might desperately need all of her concentration in the hours to come.

The rooms Tavi had rented for them were plain, but roomy and well kept. They were outrageously expensive by the standards of the steadholts of the Calderon Valley, but her travels had broadened her outlook somewhat even if they hadn't fattened her purse. By the standards of Alera Imperia, the price was more than reasonable—even if each day's rent would also have paid for the food of an entire steadholt for a day.

The boardinghouse, however, was apparently frequented by merchants who were particularly close about their money. Negotiations of one kind or another were in progress in rooms below and above her, as well as in the house's tiny garden, and from the feel of it, they were ferocious affairs. She tried to rest as best she could, once they were there, but the constant, surging flutter of the city made it problematic.

Isana rose quietly from the bed in the room she shared with Kitai, slipped into her shoes, and donned her dress and cloak. Perhaps if she stretched her legs a little, she would tire enough to rest. She drifted to the window and looked out. The lane below, though it was nearly midnight, was well lit with furylamps, and she could see two different pairs of men in the uniform of the civic legion patrolling. The street would be safe enough.

She turned to find Kitai sitting up in her bed, stretching. "Can't you sleep, either?" the girl asked Isana.

"No," Isana answered quietly.

"It's the watercrafting, isn't it?" Kitai said.

"Partly," Isana said, and the word came out with more of an edge than she had intended. She paused, softened her tone, and said, "Mostly."

Kitai tilted her head. Her green eyes were almost luminous in the dim light from the street's furylamps. "Are you leaving the city, then?"

"I thought I'd take a walk," Isana said. "Sometimes a little exercise helps."

Kitai smiled. "I have need to walk as well. Perhaps we should do so together."

"I'd like that," Isana said. She added, diffidently, "Perhaps you should put some clothes on first, dear."

Kitai's mouth turned up in a slow smile. "Why do Alerans always insist on such things?"

Ten minutes later, they were walking together down Craft Lane. The home of the majority of skilled labor in the city, the houses were almost universally dark and quiet. Few people were on the street. Those few were mostly younger men, late apprentices and early journeymen, presumably returning to their beds after time spent in less sober quarters of the city.

"Kitai," Isana said quietly, "there's something I've been meaning to ask you about."

"Yes?" she asked. She wore her cloak with the hood up, hiding both her decidedly conspicuous hair and the canted eyes of her Marat heritage.

"Regarding you and . . . and Tavi."

Kitai nodded, her green eyes shining with amusement. "Yes?"

Isana sighed. "I need to know about your relationship with him."

"Why?" Kitai asked.

"Because . . . because of things I am not free to share with you, your . . . your friendship with him could cause . . . relations could be a factor in . . ." She shook her head in frustration. "What does your relationship with him mean to you, precisely? Where do you see it leading you in the future?"

"Ah," Kitai said in a tone of comprehension. "*Those* kinds of relations. If you wished to know if we were mating, you should have asked."

Isana blinked, then stared at Kitai, mortified. She felt her cheeks burn. "No. No, that isn't what I meant at—"

"Not nearly often enough, of course," Kitai said with an exhalation somewhere between a sigh and a growl. "Not since we left the fortress. We can't on the ship. Never when the Legion was in the field." She kicked a small stone at the buildings on the other side of the street with a scowl. "Alerans have a great many foolish rules."

"Kitai, that isn't what—"

"He was very clumsy at first," Kitai confided. "Except for his mouth." She smirked, and added drily, "But then, he's always been clever with that."

Isana began to feel somewhat desperate.

"It was as if no one had taught him what it was he ought to do. Which I suppose could be another problem you Alerans have. After all, if no one has any idea how to go about it, no wonder you all get so nervous just talking about it."

"Kitai," Isana said weakly.

"They started paying me for doing what I was doing anyway, in the Legion, and I considered purchasing instruction for him. It seemed as useful a purpose for spending money as any. But I was informed by the women working at the Pavilion that it was improper—and that by Aleran standards, practically anything I did was going to make him happy, provided I did it naked." She threw up her hands. "And after all that fuss about *wearing* clothing in the first place!"

At least no one was walking close enough to hear the conversation. Isana began to mumble something she hoped Kitai would not take as encouragement—then caught a swift brush of the girl's emotions. Isana stopped in her tracks and arched an eyebrow at Kitai. "You're teasing me."

The Marat girl's eyes shone, as she glanced over her shoulder. "Would I do such a thing to the First Lady of Alera?"

Isana felt her mouth hang open for a moment. She closed it again, and she hurried to catch up to Kitai. She was silent for several paces before she said, "He told you?"

"He may as well have," Kitai replied. "His feelings changed every time he spoke about you." Her expression sobered. "I remember what it felt like to have a mother. I felt it in him for you."

Isana regarded the girl for a time as they walked. Then she said, quietly, "You aren't what you appear to be at all, are you?"

Kitai arched a pale brow at her.

"You appear to be this . . . barbarian girl, I suppose. Adventurous, bold, careless of manners and proper behavior." Isana smiled faintly. "I asked about your relationship with my son. You've told me a great deal about it."

Kitai shrugged a shoulder. "My father has a saying: Speak only to those who listen. Anything else is a waste of breath. The answers to your questions were there, if you listened for them."

Isana nodded quietly. "What you have with Tavi . . . it's like your people's other totems, yes? The way your father is close to his gargant, Walker."

Kitai's eyebrows shot up. "Doroga was not mating with Walker, when last I knew." She paused a beat, and added, "Walker would never stand for it."

Isana felt herself laugh despite all.

The Marat girl nodded at that, and smiled. "Yes. It is much the same." She touched her heart. "I feel him, here."

"Are there others, like you? With Aleran . . . I don't know the word for it."

"*Chala*," Kitai said. "No. Our peoples have never been close. And whelps are usually kept safeguarded from any outsiders. I am the only one."

"But what clan would you go to?" Isana asked. "If you went back to your people, I mean."

She shrugged. "I am the only one."

Isana absorbed that for a few moments. "That must be difficult," she said quietly. "To be alone."

Kitai bent her head, a small, inward smile on her lips. "I would not know. I am not alone."

Love, deep and abiding, suddenly radiated from the Marat girl like heat from a stove. Isana had felt its like before, though seldom enough, and the power of it impressed her. She had thought the barbarian girl an idle companion before now, someone who stayed near Tavi out of her sense of enjoyment and adventure. She'd misread the young woman by a great deal, assuming that the lack of emotion she generally felt from the girl had meant that there was no depth of conviction in the person behind it.

"You can hide yourself, your feelings. The way he can," Isana said quietly. "You let me feel that, just now. You wanted to reassure me."

The Marat girl faced her, unsmiling, and bowed her head. "You are a good listener, Lady Isana."

Isana bit her lip. "I am hardly a lady, Kitai."

"Nonsense," Kitai said. "I have seen nothing in you to indicate that you would be anything other than one of nobility, refinement, and grace." She pressed something into Isana's hands. "Hold this for me."

Isana blinked as Kitai handed her a sack of heavy burlap. She looked around. The Marat girl had directed their steps while they walked, and Isana had not realized that they had left Craft Lane. She was not certain where they were now. "Why do you want me to hold this?"

"So I have something to put the coldstone in after I have burgled it," Kitai said. "Excuse me." And with that, the girl stepped into a darkened alleyway, flicked a rope up over a chimney, and calmly scaled the outside of a building.

Isana stared for a moment, aghast. Then footsteps sounded down the street, and she looked up to see a pair of civic *legionares* on their patrol. For a moment, Isana nearly panicked and fled. Then she berated herself sharply and composed herself, slipping the bag underneath her cloak.

The *legionares*, both of them young men, dressed in leather tunics rather than the military lorica, nodded to her, and the taller of the pair said, "Good evening, miss. Are you all right?"

"Yes," Isana said. "I am well, thank you."

The shorter of the two drawled, "On a pretty spring evening

like this, why wouldn't you be. Unless you were lonely, of course."

His immediate and . . . somewhat exuberant interest ran over her, and Isana felt her eyebrows go up. She'd spent comparatively little of her adult life in places where she wasn't known, by reputation at least, if not by sight. It hadn't occurred to her that she would be effectively anonymous, here. Given the apparent youth of a powerful watercrafter, with her hood up and the strands of silver in her dark hair concealed, she would look like a young woman no older than these *legionares*. "Not lonely, sir, no," she said. "Though I thank you for asking."

The taller one frowned, and a practical, professional kind of suspicion rippled across her. "It's late for a young woman to be out alone, miss," he said. "May I ask what you're doing here?"

"Meeting a friend," Isana extemporized.

"Little late at night for that kind of thing in this part of town," the shorter *legionare* said.

The taller one sighed. "Look, miss, no offense, but a lot of these young Citizens from the Academy book time, then don't show up for the appointment. They know they're not supposed to be seen down to the Dock Quarter after dark, so they promise the extra coin to get you up here, but—"

"Excuse me?" Isana said sharply. "Exactly what are you accusing me of doing, sir . . ." She snapped her fingers impatiently. "Your name, *legionare*. What is your name?"

The young man seemed somewhat taken aback, and she felt his flash of uncertainty. "Um. Melior. Miss, I don't want to—"

"*Legionare* Melior," Isana said, pressing her aggression with the kind of self-assurance no younger woman could quite have matched. She reached up and lowered her hood, revealing the silver laced through her hair. "Am I to understand that you are accusing me"—she gave the last word very slight emphasis—"of prostitution?"

The shorter of the two frowned and returned with restrained belligerence, "Well why else would you be out here alone this late with—"

The taller one stepped firmly on his foot. Then he said, "I meant no accusations, my lady. But it is my duty to keep things in order here at night."

"I assure you, young sir, that everything is in order," Isana replied firmly. "Thank you for your concern," she said, then added a slight barb to her tone, "and for your courtesy."

The shorter *legionare* glared at his partner, then at Isana, and seemed to come to some sort of realization. "Oh," he said. "Right."

The taller one rolled his eyes by way of apology. "Very well, my lady," he said, and they continued on their way.

Once they were out of sight, Isana let out an enormous breath and leaned against the nearest building, shaking slightly. A fine contribution to their mission she would have made, from the inside of a cell with any other wayward ladies of the night they'd collected. For goodness' sake, there was even the chance that she might have been recognized as something other than an anonymous Citizen. She hadn't exactly been a celebrity during her previous visits to the capital, but there *had* been a number of speeches on behalf of the Dianic League. There was always the chance, however slim it might be, that she might be recognized.

"That was well-done," murmured Kitai's voice. The Marat girl came down the side of the building with the grace of a spider, landed, and dislodged her line with a flick of her wrist. She hissed as she quickly took a pouch whose neck she gripped in her teeth, and held it away from her face. Little wisps of steam trailed from the pouch, and a small patch of frost had begun to form on its surface. "Quick, the bag."

Isana opened the thick burlap sack, and she realized that it was several layers thick and heavily lined, a sack designed specifically to contain the fury-bound coldstones. Kitai opened the pouch and dropped a rounded stone the size of a child's fist into the sack. The evening air was brisk, but a deeper chill followed the coldstone, and Isana hurriedly shut the heavy sack over it.

"What have you done?" Isana asked quietly.

"Acquired something we need," Kitai replied. "Whatever you said to those two was effective. Could you say it again, perhaps?"

"Again?" Isana replied.

"If needed." She nodded at the sack. "I have to get the rest of them."

"And you're going to *steal* them?" Isana asked. "What if you're caught?"

Kitai jerked her head back as if Isana had slapped her, and arched one pale, imperious eyebrow. "No Aleran in this entire senseless, pointless city has ever caught me," she said, with the perfectly steady confidence of someone telling the truth. Isana could feel that in her voice as well. Kitai sighed. "Well," she admitted. "One. But it was a special circumstance. And anyway, he's asleep right now."

Isana shook her head. "I . . . I'm not certain what you think me capable of, Kitai. I believe that you are skilled at this sort of thing—but I am not. I'm not sure you want me to come along."

"Faster, if we can walk openly on the street," Kitai said. "One woman alone will be questioned. Two women, walking quickly, will not be. And I cannot take the heavy bag along with me. I would have to leave it behind each time I climbed. I would feel better if it was being watched than if I had to leave it lying in some alley."

Isana studied the Marat girl for a moment, then sighed, and said, "Very well. With one condition."

Kitai tilted her head. "Yes?"

"I want to talk to you about Tavi as we walk."

Kitai frowned, her features concerned. "Ah. Is that considered to be appropriate, then?"

"Between us?" Isana asked. "Yes. It's something called girl talk."

Kitai nodded as they began walking again. "What does that mean?"

"It means that you can speak openly and plainly to me without fear of being inappropriate—and I won't be outraged or angered by anything you tell me."

Kitai gave the city around them an exasperated glance. "Finally," she said. "Alerans."

Amara was worried.

The swamps stretched out all around them, an endless landscape of trees and water, mist and mud. Life seemed to boil from every patch of ferns, to drip from the branches of every tree. Frogs and singing insects filled the nights with a deafening racket. Birds and small animals who lived within the trees chirped and cried throughout the day. And always, day or night, the air swarmed with insects, like a constant, buzzing veil that continuously had to be pushed aside.

The terrain was a brutal mixture of shallow water over clinging mud, deeper water that could rise above Amara's chest, and the occasional sullen, damp, insect-infested rise of more solid earth. Twice more, they were rushed by garim, though thankfully none were as large as those lurking around the exterior of the swamp—but they ceased their rush forward when confronted with immediate resistance and simply scattered when Bernard and Amara willed their furies into visible manifestation. The lizards, it seemed, had learned the futility of assaulting wild furies and were quick to avoid those the trio had brought with them.

They were making reasonably good time—so long as one considered that any significant progress was reasonable, in the relentlessly wearying terrain. They had avoided any further mishaps, and they had found a number of edible fruits and berries growing within the swamp. They tasted foul, but would sustain life, for a time at least.

The worst thing about the past several days was how the swamp had absolutely permeated her lower body. She and Bernard were both covered in the thick, rich muck of the swamp floor, nearly to the hips, and constantly walking through water had ruined her boots and left her feet perpetually damp and chilled. They had to stop several times a day just to dry their feet out and prevent them from developing sores. There had been no further encounters with the enemy.

All the same, Amara was worried.

About Bernard.

They stayed in the shelter he'd had Brutus dig for them for less than a day, all told. The instant he woke, he wobbled to his feet and insisted that they had to leave at once. Only the fact that it was already the dead of night, and that the First Lord was still unconscious kept him from staggering into the swamps. But the instant there was light enough to see, he began preparing for the remainder of the journey.

To Amara's surprise, the first thing he did was to skin the dead garim. The soft, supple hide of their throats and bellies had already been ripped open by scavengers and gnawed by insects, and they would be useless for making capes. But the heavy, nodule-studded skin of the large lizards' backs and flanks remained sound. Bernard cut the large sections of tough leather away from the corpses, and laid them flat on the ground. At a murmur from him, Brutus rose and dragged the hides down into the earth. A moment later, they reappeared, the skin side of the leather scoured clean of any remaining flesh.

Bernard went to a willow tree beside the swamp, and drew off a dozen larger branches. Under his hands, they simply came away from the trees, like grapes picked from a vine. Using his wood fury and his broad, capable hands, he bound them together into a long frame within a few moments, complete with wooden handles at either end. He then stretched the hides over the frame and secured and sealed them with thick, resinous sap from another tree.

Twenty minutes after he began, Bernard bore what looked something like a runnerless sled over to the First Lord, and loaded Gaius into it. Then, with repeated nervous glances over his shoulder, he got his bearings and led Amara into the swamps, carrying the frame over one shoulder when the ground was mostly solid, and letting Gaius float in his boat-stretcher whenever they had to wade.

Gaius was asleep or unconscious much of the time. Though

Bernard tried to be careful, the First Lord's stretcher could not avoid every jolt and bump, and whenever it happened, his face turned pale and twisted into a pained rictus.

It wasn't until their second day in the swamps that Amara saw that Bernard's course had begun to waver. At first, it wasn't by much, but as the days went by, Amara saw that his sighting of trees ahead and behind had become increasingly sloppy.

"Stop," Amara said, finally. "Bernard, let's stop for a moment. I need to rest."

Bernard, who had been walking over a low hillock with the First Lord's litter over one shoulder, settled the old man down gently and sank to the ground without a protest, his head bowed.

Amara frowned. He hadn't checked the ground beneath him before he sat, something he had repeatedly emphasized as important during their first day in the swamp. Such places, he warned her, harbored a great many venomous serpents and insects with poisonous bites, and it could be worth as much as a man's life to sit down upon or near one of them. Amara checked the ground around Bernard before she settled down, drew out her water bottle, and drank. She offered it to her husband. He drank as well.

"I need to talk to you," she said quietly.

He nodded without answering.

"I've been watching and . . . and I think your course is wavering."

Bernard frowned and looked up at her. Then he muttered under his breath, and asked, "Are you sure?"

Amara bit her lower lip, met her husband's eyes, and nodded.

His expression became faintly confused, and he shook his head. "How much?"

"It's hard for me to judge. We might be five or ten miles south of our original line of march."

He closed his eyes for a moment, then nodded. "I see."

She took his hand between hers. "Love. Tell me what's wrong."

Bernard swallowed. He shook his head once. Flies and

midges buzzed noisily about them. A rare breath of wind stirred the water at the base of the little hillock and set a dozen frogs to croaking.

Amara leaned closer, and kept her voice gentle. "Tell me, love."

"It's m'eyes," he half whispered. "They're not . . . they're not focusing the way they should. Sometimes I have trouble trying to find the right marker to hold our course. But I thought I was getting it most of the time."

Amara felt her heart beat faster with nervous fear. "You did take a blow to the head, love. It can do things to a person's vision until they've had time to recover."

"Yes," Bernard said. He looked up, squinting out at the swamps, then winced and pushed the heel of his hand hard against his head.

"Pain?" Amara asked.

He nodded. "Wasn't much at first, but . . . it's the light. Everything is too bright. It hurts to move my eyes around."

Amara leaned over and placed her wrist lightly over his forehead. "I've heard of some diseases that can do that, but you don't have a fever."

"I feel fine," he growled, leaning a little away from her hand. "Except for my bloody head."

"That is generally considered to be something important," Amara said. "Even for men."

Bernard smiled faintly at the joke but didn't lift his head. "If I'm not able to do this . . ." He shook his head. "If I can't trust my eyes, there's no help for it. You'll have to take the lead until this has passed."

Amara frowned. "Are you sure?" she asked gently. "You told me that navigating through a swamp was no task for a novice."

"I'm sure that we haven't got much choice," he replied. "You did well enough before."

Amara grimaced. "I'm not sure it will be as easy, here."

"No," Bernard said. "It won't. So it's a good thing you've had some practice."

In the stretcher, the First Lord stirred and lifted his head. He peered blearily around them. "Still in the swamps?"

"Yes, sire," Amara said.

"Bloody crows. I thought I remembered someone saying we were finally out of them. Have you seen the mountains yet?"

"No, sire," Bernard rumbled. "But with the trees and the mist, we can't see more than a quarter mile or so, at best."

"Oh," Gaius murmured, subsiding again. "Well. Have we another blanket? I'm frozen."

Amara's head came up suddenly, and Bernard's did the same. She traded a long look with her husband. Then she went to the First Lord, who lay apparently sleeping once more. She laid her hand on his forehead and felt the fever at once.

"He's running a fever," she said quietly.

Bernard growled. "Check his feet, first. If anything got into his blood, he might have to heal it and take our chances on alerting Kalarus."

Amara used more water to clean her hands, and checked the First Lord's dressing. His sore foot still looked tender, the flesh red and raw, but there was no swelling or inflammation. His broken leg, bound hard to its splint, was swollen still, but the deep and heavy bruising all around it had faded to faint blotches of yellow and green. She cleaned them both with salted water, which elicited no response from the sleeping First Lord. Then she covered them again and turned to her husband. "I don't think it's come in through the wounds. Perhaps it's just a springtime fever."

"Maybe," Bernard said. He rubbed at his head again. "We need to push harder," he said quietly. "Get as close as we can to Kalare, as fast as we can possibly manage it."

"If he keeps getting sicker, he might not be able to craft himself out of it," Amara said quietly.

"All the more reason for haste," Bernard replied.

Amara frowned, but could hardly argue with him. Their choices were unenviable. Allow Gaius to continue being weakened to ensure the surprise attack he said they needed, or have him begin furycrafting immediately, when they were farthest from any support, and where even the First Lord himself might eventually be overwhelmed by enemy numbers. "How much farther?" Amara asked.

Bernard made a brushing motion at the earth in front of them, and immediately the ground almost seemed to boil, dark loam rising to cover the grass and weeds in smooth, rich brown. Another gesture, and a large, semicircular area of the dirt shifted its contours, becoming an irregular, bumpy surface, not too unlike the skin of a garim. "This is the swamp," he said quietly. He took a small stone from the ground and placed it almost a third of the way across. "Here's us."

He gestured with his hand again, and the earth at the far side of the symbolic swamp shifted, rising up into smooth cones in a broad, elegant sweep like that of a strung bow. "Here are the Kalare Mountains. They half encircle the area around Kalare. Once we cross the swamps, we'll have to make our way to the base of the mountains. Then we'll have to press through them until we find one close enough to see the city. Then we'll have to climb it."

Amara blew out a breath. She hadn't fully realized the implications of the distances and terrains involved. She had never fully appreciated the full meaning of her ability to fly, completely ignoring such obstacles. When one had to walk over, and around, and through them, travel became a completely different sort of challenge. "How long will it take us?"

"Under ideal circumstances, maybe two weeks to the edge of the swamps and another day of fast travel to the pass through the mountains. Like this . . ." Bernard shook his head. "Three. Maybe even more."

Amara's heart sank. Three weeks or more of *this*? She wriggled her toes in her boots, or at least tried to. They were so damp and chilled, she wasn't sure that they'd moved at all. "Oh," she said quietly.

"You can't think of it like that," Bernard said.

"Like what?"

He gestured at the swamp. "As three more weeks of this."

"Then how should I think of it?" Amara asked wearily.

"One thing at a time," Bernard said. "For instance. Right now, what we need to do is stand up." Her husband suited action to his words, wearily pushing himself to his feet. He offered her his hand.

Amara took it, and rose.

"Good," Bernard said. He pointed out to her the last two trees he'd used. "Now, find your mark."

Amara did, lining up the two trees, and sighting forward to her next waypoint, correcting their course slightly back to the north. "All right."

Bernard grunted and picked up the stretcher again. "Now we go to your next mark." He glanced up at the sky, and though the sun was hidden by clouds and mist, he winced and shielded his eyes with one hand. "We just keep doing that. Walking to the next tree."

Amara took a deep breath, studying her husband, fearing for him. Blows to the head could take days or weeks to kill a man. What if he'd been more badly wounded than he claimed? What if he was already bleeding inside his skull, and it was only a matter of time before the pressure killed him?

Gaius could heal such an injury.

She bit her lip. She was a Cursor of the First Lord. He had given her a task, and it was her duty to see it through. Even if it cost her life.

Even if it cost Bernard's life.

The thought made Amara's knees feel suddenly weak with dread and simultaneously brought up a burst of anger that burned in her chest. Had she not already done enough? Had she not already given more than enough? She had fought the Crown's enemies tooth and bloody nail. She had overcome creatures of nightmare and men of cruel and destructive means as a Cursor, and her body bore more than one scar received in the line of duty. Had she not done enough for the First Lord that he would ask her to sacrifice the man she loved, too?

It would be easy to stop. She had only to tell Gaius that his fever demanded him to take action to save his own life. Or, if that was not enough, it would be laughably simple to ensure that an infection spread to his wound. All she had to do was be careless for a moment, with a single cleaning, a single slip of the bandages. Gaius could heal himself, heal Bernard, and they could all leave this hideous place.

She thought, for a moment, of a lifetime without Bernard. Without ever again knowing his touch, hearing his voice. Without ever again sleeping beside him, waking in the circle of his arms, knowing beyond any doubt that she was desired, treasured. Loved.

Her husband touched her chin with gentle fingers, and she looked up at him. His eyes, though shadowed with pain, were almost invasively aware. She had no doubt at all that he had guessed the direction of her thoughts.

"What do I do?" she whispered.

He was silent for a moment, before he rumbled, "What your heart tells you is right. As always."

She bowed her head, feeling the burn of impotent, shamed tears in her eyes. She refused, absolutely refused, to let them fall.

She looked up at him again, and said, "We'll walk to the next tree."

·◇◇◇◇◇· CHAPTER 33

Tavi looked up at the evening sky and grimaced at the cheerily shining stars. He would have preferred pitch darkness for the raid. Such conditions made it virtually impossible for any kind of organized activity, but considering that Kitai could see in the dark, his own small group would have been at far less of a disadvantage than the forces of the civic legion, the Grey Guard, and any other troops who might be in position in the capital.

Granted, the deceptive shadows and sourceless glow of starlight could be worse than pure darkness when it came to aiming at a target, but Tavi would vastly have preferred a night so stygian as to prevent him from becoming a target in the first place.

"Staring out the window isn't going to make the time pass any more quickly," Ehren observed.

Tavi turned from the window of his room at the boarding-house and gave Ehren a very direct look.

"I'm just saying," Ehren said, spreading his hands.

Tavi sighed and paced over to his bed. It was after mid-night, and the rest of the house had been asleep for hours. Araris was stretched out on one bed, fully dressed, snoozing. Ehren, in his chair by the door, was patiently sewing a new hem on one of the evening's disguises, his needle moving smoothly and steadily.

Tavi sat down on his bed, drew his sword from its scabbard, and got out his whetstone. He spat on it, and began stroking the sword's edge with focused, deliberate movements.

After a little while, Araris turned his head, opened one eye, and said to Tavi, "Give over, man. If it isn't sharp by now, it's never going to be."

"All this criticism had better not be setting a pattern for the evening," Tavi growled.

Araris turned to Ehren, and said, "Don't take any offense, Sir Ehren. He's always been the sort to start running his mouth when he gets worried about something. It usually got him into one kind of trouble or another."

"I know what you mean," Ehren responded. "There was this one time in class during our final examination . . ."

Tavi let out a disgusted sigh and rose. "I'm going to see if the ladies need anything." He strode to the door, ignoring Ehren's grin, and went to the room down the hall. He knocked quietly, and said, "It's me."

Isana opened the door, smiling. "Come in, dear."

Tavi returned her smile and hoped it didn't look as tense as he felt. "Thank you."

Inside the room, Kitai sat cross-legged on the floor, dressed in dark, closely fit clothing. She was carefully coiling a slender rope. She looked up at Tavi and smiled. "*Chala*. Is it time to leave already?"

"Not yet," Tavi admitted.

"Then why are you here?" she asked.

Tavi scowled. "Ehren and Fade didn't like the way I was running my mouth."

Kitai put down her rope, stared at him for a second. Then she turned to Isana. There was another moment of silence, and both of them burst out into . . .

Into *giggles*.

Kitai and Isana—his *mother*—were *giggling*.

He blinked at them for a moment. Then scowled more deeply, and demanded, "What?"

Their giggles became a regular gale of bubbling laughter, and Isana actually had to sit down on the bed.

Tavi felt his scowl deepen. "Tonight is hardly a laughing matter."

They laughed themselves breathless, and as Tavi grew more frustrated, a single glance at him was enough to send them into fresh bursts of merriment. It wasn't until Isana sat with her hands pressed against her stomach and tears in her eyes that it finally began to die down.

"I'm glad someone's enjoying themselves tonight," Tavi said. "Is everything ready?"

"I believe so," Isana said, her voice still quavering slightly.

"All the pieces of your plan are ready to go, Aleran," Kitai said, nodding. "Not that there is much point in all this preparation."

"Oh?" Tavi asked. "Why not?"

"Because it will not work out the way you expect," she said calmly.

Tavi frowned at her. "You've seen the plans, the guards' positions, the defenses. If you thought it wasn't going to work, why didn't you say anything yesterday?"

"The plan is good," Kitai said. "You did not miss anything."

"Then why would you think it's going to go wrong?"

"Because it always does." Kitai smiled at him. "It is the nature of life. Something unexpected happens. Something goes wrong, and the plan must change."

"If that happens," Tavi said, emphasizing the first word very slightly, "then we'll adapt."

"Tell me this," Kitai said. "In your plans, why did you not tell us what Varg was going to do?"

Tavi grimaced at her. "There's no way of knowing," he said. "I think he'll cooperate, but . . ."

Kitai nodded her head in satisfaction, gathered up her coils of rope and put them in a leather case on her belt. "Just so long as you know that tonight will not go to plan."

"Pessimist," Tavi said.

"Tavi," Isana said, "were the coldstones sufficient?"

He still couldn't believe that his mother had helped Kitai burgle a dozen restaurants in the dead of night. "They should be," he said. "I'm more worried about the armor. It's close, but it isn't perfect."

"One can hardly expect to acquire custom-made, counterfeit suits of armor in two days," Kitai replied. "Not even here in the capital."

"I know, but . . ." Tavi sighed. "There's no way we're getting inside once the alarm is raised."

"We have made the best preparations we can, Aleran," she told him. "There is no sense in letting it worry you at this point."

"Probably," he said.

"But you will worry anyway." She sighed.

"Perhaps it isn't entirely his fault," Isana murmured. "I'm afraid it's a habit he learned from me." She faced Tavi, and her expression became much more serious. "But she's right, dear. Worry is fear in disguise. And fear will eat you from the inside out if you let it." She gave him a faint smile. "Believe me. I know."

Tavi took a deep breath and exhaled heavily. If anyone in all of Alera had good reason to worry—and fear—surely he was that person. At the same time, though, he recognized good advice when he heard it. He might not be able to follow it, but it would probably be smart to try, at least in the long term. "I'll try," he said drily. "But not tonight. I've got enough on my mind without adding more pressure."

Isana smiled at him and nodded. "We'll be ready to go when it's time," she told him.

Kitai snorted as she rummaged through a second belt case, laying out several tools in a neat row. "Only if there isn't someone here distracting us with foolish conversation about things he cannot change."

Tavi was about to say something about the two of them not

liking the way he ran his mouth either but thought better of it. Of all the things he expected to face tonight, paralytic fits of laughter at his expense had been rather low on the list. "We'll go as soon as Ehren's done with the cloaks."

He nodded to both of them and paced back down the hall to his room. When he entered, Araris was standing in the middle of the floor, his body shrouded by a long grey cloak. "Are you sure it isn't going to hang too low?" he asked. "Cloaks look very fine, but they're impractical enough to fight in without making them long enough to trip yourself on, too."

"It'll be another four or five inches higher, once you've got the armor on," Ehren assured him. He glanced up at Tavi and tossed him a second grey cloak, rolled into a bundle. "This seems a little familiar. Try it on."

Tavi unfurled the cloak and donned it. Ehren came over to inspect the hem, which hung halfway down his shins. "Not bad. Not quite uniform length, but it should pass in the dark."

"Right," Tavi said.

Outside, the city's bells struck a single note, as they did for each hour between sunset and dawn.

Midnight.

"All right," Tavi said. He seized his pack. "Let's go."

The first part of the plan was, in some ways, the most dangerous.

The Grey Tower was a nondescript sort of building, utterly lacking in the drama its name—and role in history—implied. It did not look particularly menacing. For that matter, it hardly looked like a *tower*. It was an unassuming stone building of several stories. There was an institutional look to the square structure, with its even, identical rows of windows that spoke more of regularity and economy than of style or art. There was a wide, green lawn around the building, devoid of any decoration and easily watched.

For centuries, the Grey Tower had served an important role in Aleran society, as the sole prison in the Realm capable of holding the upper strata of the Citizenry captive against their will. There were furies forged into the very rock of the Tower, fused into each cell by dozens of the most potently gifted furycrafters in the Realm for the sole purpose of neutralizing the crafting of the Tower's prisoners.

In addition to its protective furies, the Tower was also home to the Grey Guard, a half century of Knights Ferrous recruited specifically for the quality of their character and their loyalty to the Realm. Indeed, there was even a Crown Law on the books that required the Crown to pay any Guardsman offered a bribe three times the offered amount when the Guardsman turned in the person responsible for the attempt. In its centuries of duty, not one single Grey Guardsman had ever accepted a bribe.

All of which meant that there would be no relatively easy escape from the Grey Tower, as there had been from the stockade at the Elinarch's fortifications. In point of fact, no prisoner had ever escaped the Grey Tower—until Tavi and Kitai had overcome the inward-focused defenses of the Tower and its personnel and extracted Antillar Maximus from his cell during the Vord attack several years past.

At that time there had been little evidence of traditional prison accoutrements. There had been no bars, no gates, and no walls around the grounds.

Since then, things had changed.

The first obstacle Tavi had to overcome was the fifteen-foot wall around the outside perimeter of the lawn. It was two feet thick and made of the same interwoven layers of stone that comprised the siege walls of Legion fortresses. The wall's top was coated in a layer of razor-sharp stone protrusions and dotted with sculptures of tiny owls the size of a man's hand—gargoyles.

Gargoyles were fairly common guardian furies, often used in the fortresses and residences of the rich and powerful, and though their appearance could vary greatly, they all had one thing in common—they were built to be large, powerful, and intimidating. The cost in effort and furycraft needed to maintain a gargoyle meant that they were expensive to keep, and since the Grey Tower was a state institution, economy was a constant consideration.

It had been Tavi's idea to employ a greater number of weaker furies. For an effort comparable to the work needed to maintain a single gargoyle, the wall (also Tavi's suggestion) could be completely surrounded with furycrafted sentinels. The owls were not intended to be creatures of violence, as most gargoyles were. They were simply there to raise a shrieking alarm should anyone attempt to climb the wall.

All of which meant that the only way to get into the grounds, other than flying in or somehow vaulting the wall, was through its manned and guarded gate—which opened for no one but the Grey Guard and those couriers and legal personnel who carried a special authorization from the Crown itself.

That was why Tavi, Ehren, and Araris headed for the docks. Tavi led them into a darkened alley just off a street lined with taverns and wine clubs.

"Are you sure about this?" Araris murmured.

"I used to go to the Tower every week to play *ludus* with Varg," Tavi murmured as he unbelted his sword. "I got to know most of the Guardsmen. The men they pick for that job don't like to change their routine. Carus and Gert will be along anytime now."

Araris took off his own sword belt and set it aside. "What if the schedule has changed?"

"It hasn't," Ehren said. "I spread a little money around. They have standing weekly reservations at the Scarlet Lantern."

"Carus thinks he's a wine connoisseur," Tavi said. "Well. Whenever he isn't too drunk to pronounce the word. Gert likes the dancers there."

Tavi frowned, faintly. It made him more than a little uncomfortable to contemplate what he was about to do. He'd been on pleasant speaking terms with them. The two men were loyal servants to the Realm, and had always been courteous with Tavi, then a scrawny young page well short of his full growth. What he was about to do seemed a poor way to repay their fidelity and respect.

Ehren peered around the corner of the alleyway. "Tavi."

Tavi eased up and looked out onto the street. Furylamps were less frequent in this part of town than in the rest of the city, but he could see well enough to identify the two Grey Guardsmen, walking with the carefully steady steps of men who had been enjoying a few well-earned cups on their evening of leave.

Tavi beckoned Araris. The *singulare* moved silently to Tavi's side and passed him a small sack weighted with gravel.

"Drunk or not," Araris said, "they're Knights Ferrous. If they get a chance to draw their blades, these blackjacks aren't going to be of much help."

"And if we go after them with swords on our belts, they could feel the metal coming in plenty of time to draw," Tavi countered.

Araris glanced over his shoulder at his sword, leaning against a wall. "I don't like it."

"If it came down to a contest of blades, we'd have to kill them," Tavi said. "I'm not willing to do that."

"They won't feel the same way about us," Araris said. "No guard or civic *legionare* alive is willing to tolerate an attack by footpads."

"Then we'd better get it right the first time." He glanced at the men coming toward them. They would pass the mouth of the alley in another moment. "Shhh," Tavi murmured, and crouched in the thickest portion of shadows.

A moment later, footsteps approached the alley. The two men walked steadily past. One of them, probably Carus, let out a rumbling belch. Then they were past the alley and continuing on down the street.

Tavi rose from his crouch and stole silently after them. He couldn't hear them, but he knew Ehren and Araris were at his back.

Tavi took the taller man, Carus, as Araris stole up behind Gert. Tavi traded a look with the *singulare*, and they closed the last few steps together.

Tavi swung the blackjack with all the strength of his arms and shoulders, and it slammed solidly into the base of Carus's skull and the top of his neck. The man dropped to the ground like a wet blanket.

Araris swung at Gert, but whether it was because of some small sound that betrayed his presence or because of the Grey Guardsman's instincts, Gert flinched at the last second, and only staggered under the blow.

Gert's sword hissed from its scabbard, even as he staggered, off-balance.

Araris pressed in to strike again, but a wobbling thrust of the Guardsman's sword forced Araris to dodge, spoiling the attack. Gert, wobbling but still on his feet, turned and slashed at Tavi, forcing the young man to leap back.

Nearly panicked, Tavi flung the blackjack at Gert's head, hoping to distract the man's attention from Araris, but the Guardsman's blade slashed through the leather sack, spilling its contents onto the cobblestones. Then he whirled and pressed the attack on Araris.

At least, he did so until Ehren all but flew out of the shadows. The little Cursor bounded into the air, body twisting as he did, one foot lashing out in a kick driven by the speed and strength of his whole body. The kick struck Gert just above his right ear and nearly flung the man to the street. He landed in a boneless heap.

Tavi felt a dizzying surge of relief. "Good work, Ehren. Come on." He seized Carus while Araris and Ehren grabbed Gert, and they dragged the two unconscious men into the alley. Ehren uncovered a small furylamp, and they bound and gagged both men.

Once that was done, they paced down the alley, to where they had cached what they would need for the rest of the evening. Tavi had donned his armor so often, now, that he hardly needed to think about it as he put it on. The counterfeit armor of the Grey Guard, though, was subtly different in design than Legion-standard lorica, and it took him a frustrating moment longer to get it fastened on. Once that was done, he buckled on his sword and donned his grey cloak, one almost identical to those of the two men on the alley floor.

Ehren passed him a bottle of wine. Tavi swallowed a gulp or two, splashed more of it onto his armor and cloak, and passed the bottle to Araris, who did the same. They pulled up the hoods and turned to Ehren. "Well?" Tavi asked.

Ehren studied them critically and nodded. "Pretty good."

"Let's go," Tavi said.

They followed the route Carus and Gert would have used to return to the Tower, shadowed by Ehren. The little Cursor dogged their footsteps until they came within sight of the Tower, at which point he disappeared.

"Relax your knees a little," Tavi murmured to Araris. "You don't look drunk enough."

"Not everyone's had Cursor training," Araris replied. But he did as Tavi said, and they approached the gate.

"Who's that?" called the on-duty guard in sleepy challenge.

Tavi recognized the voice of Tiberus, another of the Guardsmen he knew, and he did his best to imitate Carus's voice. "Come on, Tib," he slurred. "You know who it is."

"About time," Tiberus replied, yawning. "Hold on." He appeared behind the gates, holding a ring of keys. He shambled up sleepily and unlocked the gates.

The instant they were unlocked, Tavi slammed the gate open, hard. It struck Tiberus on the forehead, and he staggered back. Tavi closed on him before the expression of shocked surprise faded, and struck him once, then twice across the jaw with his closed fists. Tiberus rocked back and forth under the pair of blows, then seemed simply to deflate. He sank slowly to the ground.

Tavi winced, shaking his right hand, while Araris seized Tiberus and hauled him into the guardhouse and out of sight. Tavi closed the gate and locked it, then took the heavy ring of keys. He turned and started walking toward the entrance of the tower proper, and Araris fell into step beside him.

They crossed the lawn and walked through the front door of the Grey Tower. Most of the Grey Guard would be asleep now, Tavi knew. A handful of men were on duty, stationed at each floor currently occupied by a prisoner, but not on the stairs themselves. Tavi and Araris went swiftly up the staircase. There were candle-sized furylamps alight at each landing, and they moved as quietly as they could through the dim light until they reached the floor with Varg's cell.

A single guard was on duty in the alcove in the hall adjoining the stairs, an earnest-looking young man Tavi didn't recognize. He sat at a table, writing what looked like a letter. "Is it two already?" the man asked absently. "I thought the midnight bell just—"

The young Guardsman looked up. His eyes flicked between Tavi and Araris, and suddenly widened. He pushed his chair back and began to rise, his mouth opening.

Araris closed the distance before the young guard could stand, his blade appearing in his hand. He lashed out with the pommel, and that Guardsman, too, went down in a heap, his armor clattering.

Tavi stepped over to the stairs, listening for any outcry, but the sound evidently had not traveled down the stone stairway. He let out his breath slowly and nodded to Araris.

"All right," he said. "I'll go get him. Then we'll—"

Somewhere in the building, a bell began to ring in a rapid toll of alarm.

Tavi's heart leapt into his throat. "What happened?" he demanded. "What the crows happened? What did we miss?"

Voices cried out somewhere on the staircase below them. A series of rumbling clanks rippled through the building as the newly installed steel portcullises began to slam down all throughout the building, sealing it off from the outside world.

There was a rumble above him, and Tavi barely managed to throw himself forward, into the hallway leading to the prison cells, before several hundred pounds of steel grating plunged down from overhead and slammed to the floor. He turned and stared at the gate now separating him from Araris and the stairway.

"It doesn't matter what we missed," Araris said. He flicked his sword in a little circle, as if loosening his wrist, picked up the sword of the unconscious Guardsman, and stepped out onto the stairway. "Go get the Cane. I'll hold the stairs."

Tavi nodded, turned, and rushed down the hall toward Varg's cell, while the cries of the Grey Guard grew louder, the alarm kept ringing, and the sound of many booted feet striking stone rose up the stairway.

CHAPTER 34

Varg's cell was a spacious chamber that could fairly be called a suite. The ceilings were high enough even for the ten-foot Cane to stand erect, if he wished, and the cell was divided into a living area, a bedroom, and small dining area. As Tavi approached, the rust-and-musk scent of the Cane bombarded his senses, bringing back the memories of his regular visits with Varg, as well as the memories of the Canim Ambassador's actions during the initial assault of the Vord queen.

Tavi approached the darkened cell, but he couldn't see Varg. Shadows hid most of the suite, but even so, it was difficult to believe that the enormous Cane could have hidden himself. The bed, Tavi thought, was unoccupied, but he couldn't be certain.

He certainly had no intention of opening the door until after he'd spoken to Varg. He might have been on fairly good terms with the Cane, for an Aleran, but Tavi had no illusions. Varg was not his friend. If he thought that the situation might present him an opportunity to escape, and that he could do so by killing Tavi, the Cane would do it. He might regret the necessity, in retrospect, but that wouldn't slow the Cane's claws or fangs for an instant.

Tavi stopped at the door, and called, "Varg! It's Tavi of Calderon. I would speak with you."

In the shadows near the suite's hearth, two flickering gleams of scarlet appeared. A breath later, the shadows stirred, and the enormous shape of the Cane stepped forward into what little light came in from the hall.

Varg looked like something out of a nightmare. Huge, even by the standards of the Canim, he stood nearly ten feet tall. He had fur of darkest black, but it was crisscrossed with so many fine streaks of white, where the fur had grown up through the Cane's battle scars, that in the right light his fur looked almost grey. One of his ears was notched, and a glistening red jewel carved into the shape of a human skull dangled from a gold ring in it. His eyes, black irises against fields of blood-red, studied Tavi with an amused intelligence and, despite his size, he moved as nimbly as a cat as he prowled across the suite to face Tavi.

Tavi leaned his head slightly to one side, exposing the side of his throat. It was a bit of Canim body language similar to a human nod, and Varg returned the gesture, though he did not tilt his head so far as Tavi had.

"You have grown," Varg growled. The Cane's voice was a snarling basso, and his words were mangled by his fangs on the way out of his throat, but his Aleran was perfectly intelligible. "This alarm is your doing, I take it."

"Yes," Tavi said. "I want you to come with me."

Varg tilted his head. "Why?"

"There is little time for talk," Tavi said.

Varg's eyes narrowed but his tail flicked in a gesture Tavi had come to understand as an implied agreement. "Do you act for your First Lord in this?"

"I act to protect his interests," Tavi said.

"But you do this at his bidding?" Varg pressed.

"Our people have a phrase, sir: It is easier to secure forgiveness than permission."

Varg's ears flicked in amusement. "Ah. What are your intentions for me?"

"I intend to get you out of this prison," Tavi said. "Then smuggle you out of the city. Then I will take you to the coast and return you to the commander of the Canim army who invaded two years ago. Hopefully, I'll be able to stop our people from tearing one another apart by doing so."

Varg's chest rumbled with a low growl. "Who leads my people in your land?"

"The warrior Nasaug," Tavi said.

Varg's ears suddenly swiveled toward Tavi, so alert that they quivered. "Nasaug is in Alera?"

Tavi nodded. "He offered to discuss a cessation of hostilities if you were returned to your people. I have come to do that."

Varg paced closer to the bars. "Tell me," he growled, "why I should trust you."

"You shouldn't," Tavi said. "I am your enemy, and you are mine. But by sending you back to your people, I help my own. *Gadara* or not, I need you returned to them, alive and healthy."

Varg's chest rumbled suddenly. "*Gadara*. You did not learn that word from me."

"No," Tavi said. "It is what Nasaug called me."

Steel suddenly rang on steel down the hallway, and flashes of colored light splashed onto the walls of the hallway, where the swords of metalcrafters clashed on the stairs.

Tavi gritted his teeth and turned back to Varg. "Do you want out of this hole or not?"

Varg bared his teeth in his imitation of an Aleran smile. "Open the door."

"First," Tavi said, "I will have your word."

Varg tilted his head.

"I'm the one who is getting you out of here, and I can't do it without your cooperation. If I let you out, you become part of my pack. If I tell you to do something, you do it, no questions or arguing—and I will have your word that you will do no harm to my people while you travel with me."

A scream echoed down the hall. There was a brief pause, then the flickering lights and steely chimes of swordplay resumed.

Varg stared at Tavi for what seemed like a week, though it could not have been more than a few seconds. "You lead," he growled. "I follow. Until you are unworthy of it."

Tavi bared his teeth. "That is insufficient."

"It is the oath my pack swears to me," Varg said. "I am Canim. I will stay in this hole and rot before I become something I am not."

Tavi closed his mouth again and nodded once. "But I *will* have your promise to do no harm to my people until you are returned to your own."

"Agreed," Varg said. "I will keep my word so long as you keep yours."

"Done," Tavi said.

This was the tricky part. Varg had never lied to Tavi, as far as the young man knew—but Tavi thought it more than a little possible that Varg might sacrifice his personal honor if he deemed it necessary to serve his people. Varg would never be able to escape Alera without help, and Tavi thought him smart enough to realize that—but Varg had shown him, more than once, that the Canim did not think the way Alerans did. Varg might have different thoughts than Tavi on the subject of his escape.

But there was no sense in backing out now.

Tavi thrust the key into the cell's door and unlocked it, opening it for Varg. He backed away as seven hundred pounds of fang, fur, and muscle squeezed sideways through the cell door.

Once free, Varg crouched, to put his eyes on level with Tavi's. Then, deliberately, he bowed his head to one side, more deeply than he had before. Tavi returned the gesture, instinctively making his own motion shallower, and Varg flicked his ears in satisfaction. "I follow, *gadara*."

Tavi nodded once. "This way," he said, and strode back down the hallway. The hairs on the back of his neck rose as he turned away from the Cane. If Varg intended to betray him, he would do it now.

A low coughing grunt, the Canim equivalent of laughter, came from behind Tavi.

"No, *gadara*," Varg growled. "The time to kill you has not yet come."

Tavi glanced over his shoulder and gave Varg an exasperated scowl. "How very reassuring."

Tavi drew his own sword as they reached the stairway and found Araris fighting to hold the landing. Two men in the armor of the Grey Guard were down, being hauled away by their companions, but the rest were dressed in little more than their breeches, their hair mussed from sleep. Most of the Guardsmen had been sound asleep when the alarm sounded and had simply seized their blades and come running.

Now, three men faced Araris, though they had to stand sideways on the stairs, pressed together in the tight space. They were fighting cautiously, and while they could not manage to break through Araris's defense without exposing their unarmored flesh to his blades, Araris could not get close enough to strike one without being faced with the two blades of his companions.

"We're ready!" Tavi shouted.

"Go, go!" Araris said. "Hurry, get clear!"

Tavi turned to face the steel portcullis and closed his eyes for a second or two, concentrating. He felt his awareness spread into the sword in his hand, and he could sense the air moving around it as if it had been his own hand. He focused on that awareness, reaching out to the blade's timeless spirit, and poured his own effort and will into the steel, strengthening and sharpening it.

He let out a shout and struck at the portcullis, sure that the fury-enhanced blade would be able to cut them free within several strokes.

A virtual hurricane of sparks flew up where the blade contacted the portcullis, scarlet and blue and violet all mixed together, and Tavi felt the shock of impact lance up through the sword's blade and into his arm. It *hurt*, as if he'd slammed his unprotected fist into a brick wall, and he let out a snarl of pain.

The bars of the portcullis had not been severed. One of them evinced a slight gouge, but other than that, Tavi may as well have struck the furycrafted steel with a willow branch.

"They improved it," Tavi hissed, clutching at the wrist of his sword arm with his left hand. "They crafted the portcullis! I can't cut it!"

"I'm a little busy here," Araris snapped. "Do something!"

Tavi nodded once and sheathed his sword. The new gates, once dropped, had been fitted with a crafting that closed the stone behind them, so that there was no way to lift them again. They were simply locked into the stone around them and could not be moved until the building's furies were persuaded to open the stone above the gates once more. They could not be raised again—but that did not necessarily mean that they could not be moved.

Tavi seized the portcullis with both hands, planted his feet, and reached down into the stone beneath him. He drew upon that steady, constant strength, and felt it flooding up into him through his legs, hips, spreading over his chest and into his shoulders and arms. He gathered in as much of that power as he could, then gritted his teeth and heaved at the steel grate, attempting to wrench it free of the stone around it by sheer, brute force.

The gate's steel might have been crafted to resist the impact of fury-enhanced blades, but that didn't mean it could not be bent by power applied in a different way. The steel flexed slightly and quivered as Tavi pulled. It began to warp a little, no more than an inch or so, then Tavi found himself gasping, unable to sustain the effort. His breath exploded out of his lungs in a gasp, and the flexible steel of the grate flexed almost entirely back into its original shape. Its deformation was barely visible.

A huge, furred arm nudged Tavi gently aside, and Varg stepped up to the grate. The Cane narrowed his eyes, spreading his long arms out to grip the grate at one corner at its top, and the opposite corner at its bottom. Then he settled his feet, snarled, and wrenched at the grate.

For a second, nothing happened. Muscles corded and twisted beneath the Cane's thick fur, quivering with effort. Then Varg let out a roar of effort, and his hunched, powerful shoulders jerked.

There was a scream of tortured rock, and then the furycrafted stone wall of the hallway itself shattered. Pieces of stone went flying as the Cane ripped the steel grate clear of its stone frame.

Varg snarled, tilted the grate to get through the doorway to the stairs, and without preamble flung it over Araris's head and down upon the Guardsmen on the stairs.

Varg hadn't thrown it with any particular force, but the grate weighed several hundred pounds if it weighed an ounce, and it fell flat upon the unarmored guardsmen like some enormous flyswatter, pressing the struggling men down and pinning them.

Araris blinked at the grate, then at the Cane, his mouth opening slightly.

"Come on," Tavi snapped. "Before they get loose. We're leaving."

The Grey Tower's enhanced defenses had been designed to prevent anyone from leaving—but the logic behind its layout assumed that an escaping prisoner would run for the only exit—the front door. Now that the windows were covered with heavy bars, the only way out was through the front door, and the building's security plans had been designed to make it impossible for a prisoner to descend the stairway and exit the building. The heavy portcullis gates isolated each level of the prison from the stairway, and more cut the stairway off from the rest of the building, while still more heavy grates sealed the building's only exit, several floors below.

Which was why Tavi flung himself onto the stairs and sprinted *up* them, toward the roof.

He fervently hoped that Kitai and Isana's portion of the plan hadn't gone as badly wrong as theirs had—or this evening was going to come to an early, painful, and spectacularly bloody conclusion.

⚓CHAPTER 35

Kitai's head whipped around as the alarm bells in the Grey Tower began to ring. She paced over to the edge of the rooftop, peered at the tower, and snorted. "I told him so. You were there."

Isana hurried to Kitai's side. The younger woman stared intently at the Grey Tower and shook her head. "We must hurry."

"What's happening?" Isana asked.

Kitai seized her pack, shrugged into it, and jogged toward the other side of the building. "Someone is ringing bells."

Isana bit down on a sharp retort and instead hurried after Kitai. "More specific, please."

"They went inside only moments ago, and the alarm has been raised. The Tower's defenses and guards have been alerted. They can only get out from the roof, and they must escape quickly if they are to escape at all—which means we must hurry." She lifted a hand and pressed it gently against Isana's chest. "Wait here," the Marat woman said. Then she took a pair of steps, her legs blurring with sudden haste, and flung herself off the top of the building. She bounded gracefully through the air, a full twenty feet or more, and landed on the top of the aqueduct that coursed through this part of the city and passed near the Grey Tower.

Kitai turned as if she did such things every day and promptly produced one of the coiled ropes from the case at her belt. She flung one end, lariat style, across the gap between the rooftop and the aqueduct, and Isana caught it. She blinked up at Kitai. "What do I do with it?"

"Slip one foot through the loop, like a horse's stirrup," Kitai said. "Hold tight with both hands. Then step off the building."

Isana blinked. She glanced over the rooftop's edge. It was a seven-story building, and the fall to the street below would be quite sufficient to crush the life from a woman of far more youth and agility than she. "Um," she said. "And then what?"

Kitai put an impatient hand on her hip. "And then I pull you up and we go help my *chala*."

Isana felt her mouth open. Kitai was not a large person. Certainly, she looked athletic and strong, but it was a slender strength one expected in a dancer or runner. The Marat were a physically formidable people, she knew, but all the same Isana was several inches taller than Kitai and outweighed her. Could the girl support such a weight?

The alarm bells continued to ring.

"Isana," Kitai hissed.

"All right," Isana said, flustered. Then she stepped up to the edge of the roof and slipped her foot through the loop. She pulled the rope tight against her foot, clutching hard with both hands at the level of her stomach.

It was a very, very long way to the ground.

She closed her eyes and stepped off the roof.

She felt Kitai pulling the rope tight even as Isana stepped into empty air, so that she did not fall, so much as swing down in a great, broad arch. The speed of it was dizzying, and she felt a small scream pulled from her lungs in pure reaction. She reached the top of the forward arch and fell backward, clinging desperately to the rope, then forward again. She spun wildly a few times, and then Isana realized that the rope was moving upward in short, solid jerks.

She opened her eyes and looked up to see Kitai, a dark shape against the pale stone of the aqueduct, hauling Isana upward, hand over hand, her feet planted firmly on the stone of the aqueduct. She pulled Isana up over the lip of the stone structure, and Isana managed to sprawl onto it, trembling, her foot tightly pinched by the lariat.

"Come," Kitai said quietly. "Hurry."

Isana freed her foot while Kitai recoiled her rope, then set off at a lope down the length of the aqueduct, which proved to be nothing more than an elevated stone trough carrying a steady volume of water as great as the mill stream back on her steadholt. There was a stone lip a foot wide on either side of the trough in the center, and Isana stepped up onto it and followed Kitai as quickly as she could manage. She kept her eyes focused ahead, on the Marat woman's back. If she looked over the edge of the aqueduct and saw how easy it would be to plunge to her death, she might not be able to make her feet keep moving.

Great furies grant that the wind didn't come up.

Or that her feet didn't strike a patch of slippery moss.

Or that her hammering heart didn't make her head go light for a moment, her balance wavery.

Or—

Isana ground her teeth and focused on Kitai's back and on keeping her own feet in motion.

Kitai came to a halt several dozen steps later, spreading her hands as a warning to Isana. Isana stopped as well, and Kitai said, "It's ahead of us."

"Very well," Isana said. She slipped off her shoes, closed her eyes in brief concentration, and reached out for her connection to Rill. Then she rucked up the skirts of her dress to her knees and stepped down into the stream of water in the aqueduct's trough.

The current was a strong, steady pressure along her calves, though not nearly enough to take Isana from her feet, provided she kept them braced strongly. The water had flowed down to the capital from the mountains many miles to the north, and it was bitingly cold. As Rill manifested around her, Isana gained the insight of her fury's senses, and she was surprised at how clean and fresh the water remained, despite its long trip through the aqueduct's channel.

The guardian fury in the water ahead appeared to her as a sudden, ugly sensation of pressure. An invisible presence in the water, she could sense its malice and its desire to do violence to any intruders. The water ahead suddenly thrashed, then a bow spray of freezing droplets rushed toward her in a line, as if she was being rushed by an unseen shark.

"You'd best get behind me just to be safe," Isana murmured, and Kitai hurried to comply.

Isana had no idea where the designers of the Tower's defenses had found such a vicious fury—or worse, what kind of mind it would take to reshape a natural fury into a dangerous beast—but she had dealt with stronger furies in the wilds of the Calderon Valley. She stood calmly before the oncoming monster, and waited until the last possible moment to flick her wrist and send Rill against it.

Isana felt her senses join with her fury's, as Rill, her presence somehow warmer and denser than the cold animosity of the guardian, slammed against her foe. The water five feet in front of Isana erupted in a cascade of spray as the two furies wound around and through one another, currents of living water twining and intertwining like two impossibly elastic serpents.

Behind Isana, Kitai took in a sharp breath, but Isana was too involved in her connection to Rill to look back at the younger woman. Instead, she focused her senses and her will upon Rill, lending her own determination and confidence to the fury, fusing her thoughts and will with Rill's ever-mutable essence. One did not overcome a water fury by simple force of will, the way other furies might be mastered. Water furies could not be beaten down—only changed, redirected, absorbed. Together, Isana and Rill entangled the guardian fury, blended with it, and separated its cohesive essence, bleeding it away into the steady stream of the aqueduct, diluting it, while Rill's presence remained anchored to Isana's mind and will, holding its shape.

The waters thrashed for several seconds more, then they slowly began to subside as the guardian fury was dispersed into the current. Depending on how strong the guardian fury was, it could take anywhere from days to weeks for it to draw itself back into a cohesive being again—if it did so at all—but Isana felt no compunction about disabling such a dangerous being.

For goodness' sake, what if some foolish youths had gone running along the aqueduct purely out of the exuberance of their years, and not for any sinister purpose focused upon the Grey Tower? A fury like that could drown someone without enough power to fight it off, or strike out at an unsuspecting victim and send him tumbling from the aqueduct to the ground far below.

Isana sent Rill out ahead of them, questing around for any other hostile presence, but found nothing more than the faint traces that remained of the guardian. Then she turned to Kitai and nodded. "It's done."

Kitai nodded, her eyes aglow with interest—even, Isana realized as the young woman passed her, with admiration—and took the pack from her back, stepping to the other side of the aqueduct to stare intently down at the Grey Tower, whose roof was very nearly of an even height with the aqueduct, which passed within thirty feet or so. The roof of the Tower resembled a fortified parapet, complete with crenellations, and statues, ugly, lumpy creatures whose features were largely hidden in shadow, faced outward at the midway point along each edge of the roof.

"There," Kitai said. "Can you see the doors?"

Isana stepped up beside her and could indeed see the doors

from the inner stairway to the roof, twin, flat affairs that lay flush against the stone, like the doors to the root cellar at the steadholt. "I see them."

"They must pass from those doors to the edge of the roof without touching the stone," Kitai said. "Any touch upon the stone of the building will rouse the gargoyles."

Isana nodded and bit her lip, judging the distance. "It's farther away than I thought it would be," she said.

Kitai nodded once and flicked open the other case on her belt. She withdrew a small, heavy-looking cloth sack from it, and a small steel hammer. "Can you do it?"

"Let's find out," Isana murmured. Again, she gathered up her skirts and stepped into the water, reaching out for Rill. "Be sure you stay upstream of me until it's time," she cautioned, and then she focused her attention on the water.

Thirty feet was a long way to throw something as heavy as water, and she had to do it in a constant stream if they were to accomplish their goal. The current in the aqueduct could not sustain such an effort if simply redirected. She would need more pressure to move the water that far, and so the first thing she did was throw out her left hand behind her, palm upraised, and willed Rill to block the stream.

The water instantly stopped flowing past her, and instead began to build up in the trough and then started to overflow it, rising up to the level of the stone lip of the aqueduct. Some of the water spilled over the sides to fall to the ground below, but she caught most of it, allowing the water to rise to fill the aqueduct to the brim for twenty, then thirty, then sixty yards behind her. The weight of all that water was immense, and Isana could feel Rill begin to strain. She waited until the pressure of the dammed stream rose to Rill's breaking point, and then she lifted her right arm, palm up, and opened a way for the water to escape—not forward and down the stream, as before, but arching up to one side, toward the roof of the Grey Tower.

The water shot forth in a geyser, rising in a beautiful arch that reflected starlight and the gleam of the many-colored furylamps of Alera Imperia. For a second, a ghost of a breeze pressed against the stream, and it fell short of the roof—but the breeze died again, and a steady spray of cold water splattered down onto the stone roof of the Grey Tower.

Isana felt a fierce smile stretch her lips, and she remained locked in that position, joined with Rill, sending the waters of the aqueduct rushing over the stone of the Tower, rapidly spreading and filling the parapet with a shallow layer of water.

"There!" Isana gasped. "Kitai, do it now!"

Kitai stepped forward, crouching down at Isana's feet, and with one gloved hand she drew from the heavy little sack one of the coldstones they had stolen the night before. She placed it on the floor of the aqueduct, just upstream of the point where the waters arched up to leap to the roof of the Tower, held it there with her gloved hand, and with the other swung the steel hammer sharply down.

There was a deafening crack and a flash of cold blue light, as the fire fury bound within the coldstone greedily sucked the warmth from the world around it.

Coldstones were expensive works of crafting, containing fire furies far more powerful than those found in furylamps or those used to manage the heat of a kitchen's stove and oven. They were specially bound, and though created to draw in all the heat they possibly could, the bindings placed upon them prevented them from pulling more than a tiny trickle into themselves at any one time. The result was a stone that leeched the heat from everything around it over the course of three or four months— the limit of the stone's construction. Placed in an insulated storage box, a coldstone could keep food placed inside it well chilled, even preserve ice over the course of a hot summer.

But in shattering the stone to which the fire fury was bound, Kitai had loosed it to sate its hunger for warmth in a single, unbelievably frigid instant.

The blue fire of the loosed fury's hunger lashed out through the water in a wave of chilly light. Rill and Isana prevented the cold from rushing back up the stream, and instead it followed the course of least resistance, leaping through the arch of water, freezing it to solid in an instant. The wave of frozen blue fire crashed down onto the surface of the Tower and spread out through it in a glittering haze, freezing the water there into a rough-surfaced sheet of ice.

Kitai let out a whoop of excitement and raised a triumphant fist. Isana, shaking with weariness, released the aqueduct's current, which immediately resumed its course in a surge that gradually began to sink back to its original levels. Her foot slipped, and she almost fell, but Rill swirled around her before she could, supporting Isana and helping her regain her balance. For a moment, the fury appeared in the only physical form Isana had seen it take, the shape of a face—a mirror of Isana's own features, when she'd first bonded with Rill as a gawky, thirteen-year-old girl—that appeared on the surface of the stream, smiled, then vanished once more.

Isana stepped wearily out of the water, her skirts soaked from her near fall, and stood beside Kitai. "Now what?" she asked. Her voice sounded rough, even to her own ears.

Kitai gave her a pensive glance, returned her attention to the building, then down to the grounds below, her gaze roaming warily. She reached into her case of coiled lines again and began taking them out. "We wait here. Once they come out on the roof, I'll throw them the lines, and they'll swing over, just as I did with you. Then we meet Ehren."

"What if . . ." Isana shook her head. "What if they're caught?"

Kitai frowned, her hands moving swiftly and steadily, preparing the lines, her eyes everywhere. "They are not caught yet."

"How can you know that?"

She touched one hand briefly to her chest. "I feel him. Excitement. Fear. Determination. Had he been captured, he would immediately begin blaming himself for failure."

Isana blinked at Kitai. "You know him well, don't you?" she murmured. Then Isana gave the younger woman a thoughtful and rather whimsical smile. "This must be what it feels like when I tell others without watercraft what it is like to sense other people's emotions."

"It doesn't feel the same at all," Kitai said absently. "With him, it is more nebulous, but . . . deeper, somehow. The emotions of others are flat, like a painting, perhaps. His are more rounded, like a sculpture."

Isana frowned over her words for a moment, then caught a sudden flash of emotion from Kitai—realization and chagrin. She turned to stare at the Marat woman. "Kitai," she said. "How could you possibly know that?"

Kitai stared at her, frozen for a heartbeat, her green eyes wide. Then she turned back to her tasks, biting her lower lip.

Isana stared at her in dawning comprehension. "How could you know the difference unless you'd felt it yourself," she murmured. "Watercraft. Kitai . . ."

"Quiet," Kitai said, her voice flat with worry, and nodded to the arched column of ice stretching to the Tower. "Someone will see that soon. Don't make it easy for them to find us and shoot us."

Isana would have been choked silent by the implications in any case. No Marat had ever used furycraft. No Marat *could*. And yet if Kitai truly had knowledge of watercrafting, it meant that she, alone of her people, could wield power through Aleran furies.

Kitai was the only Marat ever to form a bond with an Aleran, and that bonding, Isana knew, somehow shared portions of each being in it with the other. Walker, the gargant bonded to Doroga, Kitai's father, was uncommonly intelligent for a simple beast, and seemed to understand Doroga implicitly. Doroga himself was taller and more heavily laden with muscle than the Marat from the other clans, and Isana knew him to be almost unbelievably strong.

If his daughter had bonded with Tavi in a similar way, then her furycraft could only be the result of that bond.

Had Tavi found the strength inherent in his father's blood at last?

Isana's heart leapt, at once terrified and exultant. In her fear, she had attempted to hide his identity, and in so doing she had stunted the development of his furycraft. She had believed the damage permanent.

Had it been healed? Had her son been given a second chance, despite her errors? Might he have gained the strength that could protect him from the forces that would almost certainly attempt to destroy him once his identity was known?

For years she had despaired of Tavi's fate should his identity ever be learned, and her helplessness to protect him in the face of the vast powers of those such as Lady Aquitaine had been a constant, bitter taste in her mouth.

Now something strange and almost forgotten blossomed to life in her heart, flickering and small but bright against the darkness of her fear.

Hope.

"Kitai," Isana hissed. "Has my son come into his furies?"

Kitai turned to stare hard at Isana.

Before she could say anything, ice snapped and cracked with a sharp detonation, and the doors on the roof of the tower slammed open.

Araris came through them first, looking sharply around him, and even in the dimness, Isana could see the sudden gleam of his teeth as he smiled at the ice coating the roof. His gaze tracked the graceful arch of the column of ice back to the aqueduct, and he flashed his hand in a quick wave at them before turning back to the stairs behind him, beckoning.

Tavi emerged from the Tower, and hard on his heels was a monstrous figure straight out of a nightmare. The Cane, Ambassador Varg, she assumed, towered over even Tavi by at least a full yard, and its black-furred form was both lean and powerful-looking. The Cane emerged into the open air and paused for a moment, then threw his head back, lifted his muzzle to the sky, and spread wide his clawed arms. Then he shook himself, looking for all the world like a dog throwing water from his coat, and dropped into a relaxed crouch, following Tavi as the young man moved with wobbling haste over the ice to the edge of the roof.

Without a word, Kitai whirled the first of her lines and sent it zipping across the empty air to Araris. He caught the rope, and as Kitai played out slack, he sheathed his sword and set his foot in the loop of rope, just as Isana had done. Then he swung out into the open air, swung back and forth once, and began to spin gently as Kitai hauled him upward.

Isana glanced sharply at the young woman. Kitai had no

more difficulty hauling up Araris, complete with his armor and weapon, than she had with Isana, and a second later, Isana recognized the slightly absent focus of Kitai's gaze. She had seen her brother's face holding the same expression, often enough, when he labored on the steadholt.

Kitai was using earthcraft to strengthen her.

Once Araris was up, Kitai flung the next line to Tavi. He, too, secured himself and swung out from the roof of the Tower. Araris, Isana noted, anchored the line behind Kitai, his intent face tracking the young man's progress while the anxiety and frustration he felt over being unable to get his charge to safety any faster pressed against Isana like a sheet of scratchy, sweat-soured burlap.

Then Tavi was clambering up onto the aqueduct, his face flushed with excitement. He gained his feet, glanced at Kitai, and said, "I don't want to hear it."

Kitai smirked but said nothing.

Isana turned to stare at Varg, who crouched at the edge of the room, red eyes gleaming in the dim light. "My word," she whispered. "It's . . . rather large."

"He is," Tavi agreed, putting a gentle emphasis on the first word. He glanced at Kitai, who was readying the last line, one braided out of several of her more slender ropes. "Even if we belay it, are you sure it will hold him?"

She paused to give him a brief and very direct look.

Tavi scowled but raised his hands in a gesture of surrender.

Kitai flung one end of the rope, which had been weighted with a heavy knot, out toward the far side of the aqueduct. The rope whiplashed down and around, completing a circuit of the aqueduct, and Tavi reached down to catch its weighted end as it came around, completing the circle. He passed it to Kitai, who knotted it off against the rest of its length, then flung the other end to Varg.

The Cane caught the rope, glanced at it briefly, and stepped forward to put one paw-foot into the loop on its end.

Then he whipped his head around toward the stairs.

Isana saw a half-dressed man rush up the stairway to the roof, bearing a spear in his hand. He looked around wildly for a moment, shocked at what he saw on the roof, but his eyes locked on to Varg, and he lifted the spear and cast it in one smooth, viciously powerful motion.

Varg twisted as though to leap aside, but his paw-feet slipped on the ice, tangled in the rope, and brought him down. Isana heard an ugly sound of impact, and a furious, inhuman snarl ripped through the night air.

"Varg!" Tavi cried.

The Cane regained his balance in an instant, and Isana could hear the claws of one paw-hand bite into the ice as he reached up and jerked the spear from his leg. It looked like a child's toy in the Cane's hands. Varg raised the spear to throw, but then seemed to hesitate for a second, and instead of casting it point first, he flung it in a sidearm throw, its heavy wooden shaft whirling.

The Guardsman tried to dodge, but it was the Aleran's turn to realize that the ice-glazed roof was treacherous. The man wobbled rather than springing aside, and the wooden haft of the spear hit him with enough force to physically throw him back down the stairway.

Varg spun and lurched toward the edge of the parapet, but as he tried to climb it and swing away, his wounded leg seemed to buckle beneath him. He flailed with one arm, trying to recover his balance . . .

. . . and grasped the naked stone of a merlon.

There was thundering detonation, like a miniature thunderclap, and the gargoyles on the roof leapt into instant, eerily graceful life.

The nearest wasn't five feet from Varg, and it leapt at the Cane. Varg fell back beneath it as it pounced, caught the vast weight of the gargoyle on his arms and his good leg, and flexed, still rolling. Such was the power in the Cane's enormous frame that the gargoyle was flung clear of the parapet and went sailing over the edge, thrashing wildly—until one of its misshapen limbs caught on the braided line that still dangled between Varg's foot and the stone of the aqueduct.

The weight of the gargoyle came down on the line, snapping it taut.

Varg snarled, scrambling desperately, but the ice shrieked as his claws were dragged through it, toward the edge.

The other three gargoyles flung themselves at the Cane.

Varg saw them coming and released his grip on the ice.

The rope hauled the Cane roughly over the parapet, just as the gargoyles slammed against the area he'd previously occupied. All of that weight hammered into the crenellation at the parapet's edge, and the stones, the gargoyles, and the Canim Ambassador plunged down.

The heavy rope, unable to hold so much weight, applied so suddenly, hummed in protest for a split second, then snapped, sending strands whipping through the air. There was a flash of fire on Isana's shoulder and she staggered backward and fell into the chilly water of the aqueduct's trough.

She was paralyzed for an instant, stunned by the pain. She looked down and saw that her dress had been sliced open as if with a knife. Blood flowed freely, soaking the arm of her dress. Hands seized her, someone called her name, then Araris was there, binding something around her arm.

Light rose up from below, sullen and red.

"Oh bloody crows," Tavi breathed. He whirled his head to stare at Araris, his eyes wide with panic. "Araris, he landed on the lawn."

Araris suddenly tensed. "What?" He rose, half-carrying Isana toward Tavi, and over the edge of the aqueduct she could see the lawn around the Grey Tower.

Fires burned there. No, not fires, because no true fire was ever so solid, so still.

Furies of fire had come to life. They had taken the form of some kind of enormous hound, almost the size of her brother's earth fury, Brutus. But, Isana noted dizzily, there were differences. Their rear legs seemed too short, their front legs too long, and their shoulders rose to misshapen lumps. Though they looked solid, they were made from raw, red flame, glowing a hostile, angry red. Flickering fires rose up around their shoulders and neck, like some sort of mane, and a pall of black smoke gathered around their paws and trailed behind them.

They moved suddenly and as one. Their heads turned, wolflike muzzles orienting. Isana followed the direction of their gazes, across the lawn to . . .

To the fallen form of Ambassador Varg. Two of the gargoyles lay shattered around him and unmoving, but the others had begun to twist and thrash their limbs, awkwardly attempting to regain their balance and renew their attack.

The firehounds opened their mouths, and the crackle and roar of hungry flames rose through the night air.

The bells continued to ring, and men began to emerge onto the roof of the Grey Tower.

Tavi's expression hardened and he traded a look with Kitai. Without a word, he leaned over and dunked his long grey cloak into the cold water.

Araris spun toward him, crying, "No!"

Tavi seized one end of the broken line that still trailed from the aqueduct and leapt over the side.

Isana took in a sharp breath as her son flung himself into the maelstrom of angry furies and steel below, but was still too dazed to do anything about it.

"Oh," she breathed, wondering briefly if he'd gone mad. "Oh, dear."

┅┅┅CHAPTER 36

Tavi slid down the slender single strand of the snapped braid of rope and wondered briefly if he'd gone mad.

He'd been fortunate, in that the rope had broken fairly near to its end, and he was able to slide down it until his feet were no more than ten or twelve feet off the ground. He slid on off the end into a fall and tried to absorb the shock of his fall with his legs, letting his body fall backward, arms spread to slap the ground.

It worked better when one wasn't wearing all the armor, Tavi thought, but at least the turf of the lawn was soft enough to absorb some of the impact. It knocked some of the wind from him, but he forced himself to his feet, drew his sword, and rushed to Varg's side, just as the gargoyles regained their feet.

He never hesitated or slowed his steps, but once more reached into the steel of his blade, aligning its substance with his will. He let out a howl as he closed on the nearer of the two gargoyles from its flank, and swung his blade low. A shower of scarlet-and-azure sparks flared where the blade contacted the stone surface of the gargoyle, and the steel of the *gladius* sliced through the granite as if it had been moldy cheese. The blow carried so much force as it passed through the gargoyle's leg that it spun Tavi completely around from one step to the next—in time for him to repeat the same movement, upon the second leg, to another shower of angry light and a scream of tortured stone.

The gargoyle toppled onto its side, arms thrashing—but Tavi had severed its original contact with the earth completely, and the gargoyle began to crumble, beginning at the stumps of its severed thighs, as if bleeding gravel.

The gargoyle's companion evidently recognized the danger Tavi represented and switched its attention from Varg to the young man. Before Tavi had recovered from his assault, the second gargoyle bellowed, a sound like a small earthquake, dropped to all fours, and charged.

Tavi knew that if he waited for the fury to charge, it would crush him to pulp through sheer momentum, and in desperation he reached out for his windcrafting, and the world around him slowed to crystalline clarity, his own movements becoming dreamy and dancelike. Off-balance as he was, he saw that he had no chance of avoiding the gargoyle's rush completely, so instead he simply focused on minimizing the impact. He leapt to one side, body stretching out, arms ahead of him as he spun in midair.

The gargoyle struck him across both calves while his body was parallel to the earth. The force of the collision flung Tavi's legs forward and sent him into a spin. The impact hurt tremendously, and the slowed perceptions of his windcrafting gave him plenty of subjective time in which to experience it, fracturing his concentration. The world rushed back into its normal pace, and he hit the ground hard, landing on his belly. His left ankle burned viciously, and he was certain that he'd just sprained it at the very least. He drew on the steel of his blade, and the pain receded from his perceptions—not so much vanishing as becoming irrelevant, its significance forgotten.

The gargoyle turned in a broad arch, its furiously laboring limbs churning up a swath of the lawn, and attacked again. Tavi was on his feet by the time the gargoyle reached him, and, at the last second, he danced a step to one side, his sword striking cleanly through a section of the gargoyle's misshapen shoulder. Once he'd found the opening, he pressed his advantage, and while the gargoyle tried to turn on him again, Tavi pursued it, staying in close to its flank, so that it could never quite reach him.

The only drawback to the tactic was that he had to keep moving, and he never got the chance to plant his feet and deliver the kind of solidly grounded blow he would need to finish the stone fury, but he hacked it about the head and shoulders again and again with his short blade, carving wedge-shaped chunks from the gargoyle's body. Then his injured foot wobbled very oddly and refused to support him. He fell to one knee, and the gargoyle turned on him.

Without room to build up momentum, the gargoyle's pure mass was less of a threat as it slammed into him, but its strength was prodigious. Tavi stepped under a swiping limb and threw his armored shoulder into the gargoyle's chest, screaming, instinctively drawing up power from the ground beneath his legs. The earthcrafted strength surged through him—

—and stopped the gargoyle in its tracks.

Tavi let out a roar of excitement and drove forward against the earth fury, shoving with every ounce of strength he could muster. He drove it back an inch, and then six, and then suddenly the earth fury was reeling back, overborne, to fall upon its back.

Tavi's sword swept up, and he brought it down in a heavy stroke aimed for an indentation in the gargoyle's chest, a point which he somehow *knew* would be vulnerable.

The sword struck in another shower of sparks, and the gargoyle's torso cracked and split, then shattered into a dozen pieces with a sound like a thunderclap. The sheer force of it threw the pieces apart from one another, where they began to crumble away, some of them still twitching with the fury's presence.

"Varg!" Tavi shouted. "Get up!" His knowledge of the Cane's tongue was hardly exhaustive, but he could say that much in it. "Varg! *Narsh raulg,* crows take you!"

He went to the Cane's side, jealous of every second, and looked at the Cane. Varg's leg was bleeding most, where he'd taken that spear, but it didn't look like it had struck an artery. There was dust from the shattered stone covering his black fur, and there was a small army of gashes and incidental cuts on every part of his body Tavi could see. He didn't know Canim physiology well enough to tell for sure, but Varg's rib cage looked misshapen, and one of his arms was certainly broken.

Tavi ground his teeth and realized that the only reason he could see well enough to take stock of Varg's injuries was that the firehounds had come closer.

There were a dozen of them. Tavi had read the reports of the crafters who had prepared them, and he knew something about them. They had been created to behave according to instincts similar to those of wolves in the wild—to pursue those who ran, on the theory that they would be used to surround anyone attempting to leave the building in a wall of searing heat.

Just as they were doing to Tavi and Varg now.

They couldn't run. If they did, the firehounds would pursue them, growing more agitated and burning hotter. They couldn't stay, either. It would not take long for the Grey Guard to arrive, call the Tower's furies to heel, and clap them all in irons. Tavi looked up at the aqueduct overhead. He could escape that way, if it came to that, but with the heavy rope broken, they had nothing that could haul Varg up and out of reach of the firehounds. Besides, his injuries seemed to be too severe to risk anything so strenuous as tying a rope around him and swinging him through the air.

He had to find another way out. How?

The firehounds trotted in a circle around them, only twenty or thirty feet away, and the grass beneath their feet blackened to ash as they passed over it. The air grew hotter. Tavi raised a hand to shield his face from the heat radiating from the nearest firehound, but it did him little good.

Varg jerked his head once, snapped his jaws, then his bloodred eyes opened. He let out a heavy, rough-sounding snarl, then moved, his body tight with pain, pushing himself to a hunched, labored crouch.

One of the nearest firehounds suddenly rushed in closer, toward Varg, perhaps driven by a predatory instinct to assault the weak and injured first.

Tavi ripped off his soaking-wet cloak and stepped into its way. He swung the cloth at the firehound and it slapped hard against it. A cloud of steam boiled forth from the impact, and the fire fury let out a crackling cry of pain, retreating back to the circling members of the pack. Tavi glanced at his cloak and grimaced. Even the brief touch against the fire fury's surface had burned and charred the cloak, despite the water it had absorbed.

Water. The aqueduct.

Tavi looked up, excited. Surely, there was water enough flowing through its trough to extinguish the firehounds, or at least to send them scurrying away. But he glanced at his own left hand and saw red blisters rising from the scorched skin of his knuckles, where the steam from the impact had billowed back over his hand. With his pain restrained by Tavi's metalcrafting, he hadn't felt the burn his hand had received, but when he flexed his fingers he found them somewhat stiff and reluctant to move. A bad burn.

No good. Even if he could somehow bring the water down on the hounds, the resulting fog bank of steam would broil Tavi and Varg alive. If he couldn't use water, somehow, then how could he—

"Kitai!" he shouted, looking desperately up at the aqueduct. "Kitai! Throw me the backup coldstone and your sword!"

Within seconds, Kitai's *gladius* tumbled down, and its point struck deep into the lawn. Tied to its hilt by its drawstring was one of the heavy, insulated leather bags.

"Good!" Tavi shouted. "Go to Ehren! I'll meet you there!"

"Aleran," Varg growled. He coughed, and it sounded wet.

"I am your enemy. If you die to protect me, I will lose respect for you."

"I'm not going to die," Tavi snarled. "And neither are you. "

Cripple and possibly maim himself, certainly, Tavi thought. But that was better than dying—and at least he wouldn't have to feel it happening. He placed Kitai's sword flat on the ground, opened the pouch, and took the coldstone from it. It burned his fingers when it touched them. Tavi gingerly placed the coldstone on the flat of Kitai's sword, at its base, just above the hilt.

Tavi grabbed the handle of Kitai's sword, gritted his teeth, and tightened his grip on his own blade. Then, with a single, swift motion, he lifted his sword and brought its flat down hard on the coldstone, shattering it between the metal blades.

The fire fury trapped within the stone exploded out from it, greedily devouring the warmth of everything around it. The air flashed several degrees cooler—but it was the steel of the blades that could most readily house the hideous, aching cold within the fury-bound stone.

The swords screamed, a piercing shriek of metallic protest as the cold invaded them. Frost formed on the bright steel surfaces in an instant, and almost immediately, the length of each blade was sheathed in a layer of thick white mist. Tavi felt the cold in his hands, a distant surge of fire that vanished an instant later. Frost formed on his fingernails, and the skin on his hand flushed bright red.

Tavi straightened, nodded at Varg, and said, "Come on."

Then he turned toward the nearest wall and charged the firehounds who stood in their way.

The furies' reaction was immediate. They surged toward Tavi and Varg, their fiery auras flaring in excitement.

Tavi lifted his mist-shrouded blades as the first firehound leapt at him. He juked to one side, careful not to depend wholly upon his wounded foot to support his weight, this time. He slashed at the firehound with one of his frozen swords, and the blade struck the fury's canine skull just above its eyes, shearing the top of its head away. A jet of furious fire emerged in a torrent. The fury let out a crackling scream and thrashed wildly as if in tremendous pain, and the flame rushing from the wound set the lawn beneath it ablaze.

Tavi never slowed. The next firehound rushed in low and Tavi dropped to one knee in a low thrust, skewering the fury on one blade and halting its forward momentum. A sharp, sizzling sound filled the air, and the firehound thrashed wildly. It heaved itself off the blade, and when Tavi rose to menace it again, it cringed away from him.

Tavi went on by, and had to leap over a blazing swath of lawn. He glanced back at Varg, but the big Cane did not bother to leap the fire. He simply loped through it, snarling. The scent of singed fur filled the air.

More of the firehounds followed them, and Tavi dropped back behind Varg. One more got close enough for Tavi to strike, driving it back. Tavi couldn't feel the cold of the swords through his numbed hands, but the mist clinging to the blades was not as thick as it had been. To make matters worse, he could see the front doors to the Tower from where he stood, and the Grey Guard was even now attempting to lift the portcullis that had fallen to close the front door.

Tavi kept on backpedaling, calling to Varg, "We've got to get over the wall!"

Suddenly his arms were seized by large and inhumanly powerful hands. Before he could react, he heard Varg grunt with effort, and then he was flying through the air. He had a split second to realize that the top of the fifteen-foot wall was in front of him, and he hooked an arm over the lip before he could fall again. The stony blades atop the wall cut into his arm in a dozen places. As they did, one of the owl-guardians turned its stony head toward him and let out an ear-piercing shriek, which he felt certain would leave him with a lasting headache.

Provided, of course, that *he* lasted.

He dropped the swords in order to get a better hold of the top of the wall—or tried to. He found, to his surprise, that his numb hands would not release their grip on the blades, no matter how hard he tried to do so.

He gritted his teeth, struggling to reach through the stone of the wall to the earth below, to summon up strength enough to haul his body over the top of the wall, but as he did, his concentration on holding his body's pains away began to falter, and flashes of agony shot through him in a dozen places, like jets of water shooting through the cracks of a failing dam.

Tavi stopped trying to call up strength, took the weapon in his right hand, and with a single, focused stroke, drove it six inches into the stone of the wall, blade parallel to the earth. Then he grunted and lifted his right leg, planting his boot on the flat of the sword. Using it as a solid base for leverage, he twisted his shoulders and hauled his right hand from the frozen blade's hilt. Flesh tore. He bled, but freed of the blade, he was able to use his improvised foothold and roll himself over the top of the wall and off the other side, gathering up more cuts and slashes on his legs, though his armor protected his chest and back from further damage.

The fifteen-foot drop was a bad one, and he landed hard, knocking the wind from him and sending a spear of silver pain lancing along his neck and down through his spine.

Varg's shaggy form appeared atop the wall, and snarls bubbled from his throat as he, too, was wounded. He seized the wall's top with one clawed paw-hand and lowered himself in a more controlled fashion, dropping the last few feet without effort.

All the while, the stupid owl never stopped shrieking. Tavi wearily pushed himself upright. His body was not moving correctly, and though he could not tell precisely why, it stood to reason that he had been injured in the fall. After that first flash of pain, the steely resolve of his mind had asserted control over it, and he couldn't feel any pain now—but the lack of free motion did not seem to be a positive sign.

Varg staggered, crouched again, and had to use one arm to hold himself upright. Tavi could see the Cane's blood dripping on the cobblestones of the street.

Tavi heard men's voices crying out now. They had freed themselves of the tower and would be on the street next.

"Now what?" Varg growled, panting.

"This way," Tavi said, turning away from the direction of the Tower's gate. He tried to set out at a brisk jog, but his muscles didn't seem to cooperate. The best he could do was a hasty shamble—which was probably just as well. Varg looked to be in terrible condition himself. They had not gone far when there was a shout behind them.

Tavi turned and saw thirty or forty Guardsmen, most of them in armor now, round the corner and race toward them.

Hoofbeats sounded from the cross street ahead, and a wagon being pulled by a team of four rounded the corner, rising up onto two wheels for a second as it did. Ehren held the horses' reins, and Kitai sat beside him on the driver's bench.

"There!" Tavi said, pointing. "Come on."

He limped hurriedly toward the wagon, and Ehren waited until the last minute to haul the team to a stop. The horses reared and kicked as they caught Varg's scent. Tavi led Varg in a circle around them and found his mother and Araris in the back of the wagon. Isana looked quite pale, and a bloodied cloth was around her upper arm, but her eyes were open, and she seemed alert. She took one look at the blood all over his legs and his arms, and her eyes widened in alarm. "Tavi!"

"In," Tavi shouted to Varg.

The shouts and boot-steps of the Grey Guard grew louder.

"Hurry!" Ehren said.

Varg's strength seemed to ebb suddenly, just as he began to climb into the wagon. Tavi got behind him, screaming sulfurous curses and pushing at the veritable mountain of muscle and fur. Araris seized one of Varg's arms and pulled. Somehow, they managed to get the Cane into the wagon.

Kitai stood up on the driver's bench, holding a thick sack in one hand. "Aleran!"

Tavi struggled for a second, but with Araris's assistance managed to clamber into the back of the wagon. "Go, go, go!"

The street was too narrow to turn the wagon. Tavi saw that immediately. But when Ehren shook the reins and called for the nervous horses to run, Tavi let out a cry of protest. The wagon would never make it through the group of Knights Ferrous. The blades of the Grey Guard would cut the wagon to kindling as they tried to pass through their ranks.

Kitai reached into the large insulated sack that had been left with the wagon and drew out another coldstone. She lifted it and threw it hard at the side of the nearest building, where it shattered, releasing the fire fury within.

There was a flash of blue as the cold spread into the air—and into the public furylamps that hung at the same level, where it devoured their flame, jumping hungrily from one to the next for a hundred feet in either direction. The street plunged into blackness.

"Yahh!" Ehren screamed to the horses. The beasts charged forward, reckless and terrified—which was, Tavi thought, probably a fair description for what the Grey Guard had to be feeling at the moment. He felt exactly the same way. Men cried out around them, and hooves rang on cobblestones, wheels rumbling as the wagon bounced wildly. There were a couple of cries of pain, then they emerged from the darkness and into another furylit area.

Kitai flung another stone, and once again they were in darkness. It would, Tavi had hoped, hinder any pursuit, slowing the reactions of the authorities—and it was working. At least *something* in the plan had gone right tonight.

After five or six minutes of noisy flight, Ehren slowed the wagon and continued on for several more blocks, changing streets several times, while Araris covered Varg with a canvas tarp. Isana, meanwhile, bound up Tavi's right hand and examined the rest of his injuries with worried eyes.

Ehren pulled into an alley and stopped the wagon. "That's it," he said quietly. "We leave it here. The ship's right through there."

"What about the horses?" Kitai asked.

"My contact will pick them up when he comes for the wagon," Ehren said. "I've arranged for the lamps to be out, so we can get the Cane onto the ship."

"How is he?" Tavi asked. The words came out slurred. Weariness had begun to spread throughout his body.

A growl came from beneath the tarp. "I can walk."

"Good," Tavi said. "Let's go."

"He's hurt," Isana said to Araris. "His ankle looks bad. He needs help walking."

"I'm fine," Tavi said. "Get to the ship."

Kitai let out an impatient breath, and said, "I'll do it." She came around to the back of the wagon and dragged one of Tavi's arms over her shoulders. "Come on, *chala*. Lean on me a little. Good."

Tavi closed his eyes and let Kitai guide him. She kept up a pleasant stream of quiet orders and encouragement, which was far preferable to paying attention to his own rising discomfort.

He was losing his hold on the metalcrafting, Tavi thought. The pain was growing.

He remembered getting to the *Slive*, and then Kitai's hands stripping his armor.

"Varg," he mumbled. "Tell her to see to Varg first. He got hurt."

"No more orders, *chala*," Kitai replied, her voice gentle.

He drifted in pain and stillness for a time. Then there came a delicious, bone-deep warmth.

Then nothing.

◇◇◇◇◇◇ CHAPTER 37

Isana looked up as daylight briefly flooded the hold through the open hatch above. Demos and Fade came down the stepladder into the hold and approached at once. Demos's presence was muted to her senses, as usual, but what she could feel of him told her that he was at least mildly anxious.

"What's the problem?" Demos asked. "They've started combing the docks and searching ships. We don't have much time."

"Already?" Isana asked. "That was fast."

"They start with the places someone might use to leave town in a hurry," Demos said.

"We should leave," Araris murmured. "Set sail right now."

"Ships have been ordered to remain at dock," Demos said.

"Then we should have left last night."

"Which would have told them exactly where to look for the prisoner," Demos said. "No. We stay in dock until they clear us, then when we leave, we aren't looking astern the whole trip." He turned to Isana. "Now what's the problem?"

Isana gestured at Varg. The Cane was far too large to fit into any of the healing tubs on the *Slive*, so instead he lay in the shallow pool in the hold where the witchmen usually stood their station. "It's the Cane. He's badly hurt, and he won't let anyone touch him. He nearly took my hand off when I tried to heal him."

"He's got to be moved," Demos said. "We have fifteen minutes, give or take."

"He isn't going to let us move him," Isana said. "And if he starts thrashing around, it could kill him."

"If he isn't moved," Demos said, "it could kill all of us." He touched the hilt of his sword. "One way or the other, he's in the river in fifteen minutes." The captain went back up on deck.

Isana exchanged a long look with Araris. Then she said, "Get him."

"Are you sure?" Araris asked. "He still looks like he's in bad shape."

"He is," Isana said. "He'd want you to do it."

Araris grimaced, then departed. He returned a moment later, half-carrying Tavi. The young man nearly fell coming down the stepladder, and he had to lean on Araris to walk the short distance to the pool. Isana's heart ached to see how pale her son's face remained, his eyes so sunken that they looked bruised. He'd looked worse last night, when she'd had to heal dozens of small wounds, three fractured bones, muscles that had all but torn themselves apart with strain, burns on his mouth, his throat, and in his lungs from breathing fury-heated air, and the hideous damage to the flesh of his hands.

Restoring a body that had suffered so much punishment was hideously draining upon the victim. He shouldn't have been conscious, much less standing more or less on his own, but his green eyes, though sunken and weary, were alert.

"What is it?" Tavi asked quietly. His voice was still raw, rough-sounding. Even with watercrafting, there was only so much one could do for burns.

"Varg," she said. "I've been trying to heal him, but he won't let me touch him. We have to move him in the next few minutes, before they search the ship."

Tavi blinked slowly once, and for a second, she wondered if he'd even heard her. "Ah," he said, finally. "All right. Try again."

Isana frowned. "I've tried, several times, to—"

Tavi shook his head. He splashed wearily down into the pool, and sat down on the floorboards, not far from the Cane's head, his feet in the water, his shoulders slumped. He gestured wearily for Isana to proceed.

Isana stepped down into the water again, reached out for Rill, and stepped closer to Varg. She reached one hand toward his chest warily, watching the enormous, dark-furred body for movement. Her fingers got to within perhaps an inch of the Cane's fur before Varg let out a growl. His half-opened eyes never focused, but his lips peeled back away from white fangs, and his jaws opened slightly.

Tavi moved with sudden and shocking speed, for the Cane's head. Before Isana could react, her son seized one of the Cane's upright ears hard with one hand, squeezing and twisting, and clamped Varg's muzzle shut with the fingers of his other hand, shoving the Cane's head back at an almost brutal angle.

Then, to Isana's utter shock, her son went for the Cane's throat with his teeth.

Varg's entire, enormous body stiffened, and his clawed paw-hands half rose from the water—but before they could reach for Tavi, they froze in place, and a low growl bubbled in Varg's throat.

She heard her son, then. Tavi, his teeth still closed over the Cane's throat, snarled like a beast. The sound rose, deepened again, then repeated. Isana realized with a shock that he was *speaking* to the Cane.

Varg's bloody eyes seemed to focus for a second or two, and then the Cane let out a low growl and lowered his claws back into the water again.

Tavi opened his mouth slowly, and straightened. He released

the hard grip on the Cane's ear, his hand dropping to grip the fur at the nape of Varg's neck. With the other hand, he kept on holding the Cane's muzzle closed.

He turned his head to one side and spat and snorted, apparently to get fur out of his mouth. "Go ahead," he said quietly, then. "He'll be still now."

Isana stared at him for a moment. "How in the world . . . ?"

He gave her a weary smile. "Just have to know how to talk to them."

Isana shook her head, and glanced at Araris. She hadn't noticed when the *singulare* had stepped up close to Tavi, naked sword in hand.

"Ten minutes," Araris said quietly.

Isana nodded once, called upon Rill, and then laid her bare hand on Varg's chest.

His chest shook with one more growl, but the barely conscious Cane did not move.

Isana closed her eyes and sent her focus down into Rill, and into the water surrounding the Cane. She was immediately startled by how *much* water surrounded Varg. She had seen the Cane's size, of course, but if she hadn't occasionally been called upon to heal wounded livestock, she would never have even contemplated healing a creature so large.

Granted, she had never healed a Cane before. At first, she feared that the wolflike creature would be too different to benefit from the kind of healing she knew, but she rapidly saw that the fear had been groundless. Pain was universal.

She sensed the injuries in Varg as she might have in anyone else. She sent Rill coursing into the Cane's body, closing his wounds, aligning broken bones, easing inflammation and pain. None of the injuries were especially complex or difficult to repair: It was a question of volume. The Cane simply bore so *many* various hurts that she was shocked he had survived so long without any help.

Then there was a hand on her shoulder, shaking her gently, and Isana drew her awareness back into her own body. She looked up, blinking, to find Demos standing over her. "Lady," he said quietly. "We're out of time."

"Oh," she mumbled. "Yes, of course."

Demos regarded Tavi and his grip on Varg for a moment. Then the captain said, "We would have restrained him. If we'd had any chains."

Tavi gave Demos a sour look.

Demos nodded to Araris, then at the pool. "In, all of you." He went to the side of the pool and drew a rope from his belt. He secured one end to a ring on the near side of the pool, the other to a similar ring on the far side. "Everyone get hold of that."

Isana told Tavi, "Varg is unconscious now. I had to do a lot. He'll need help."

Tavi nodded once and glanced at Araris. The *singulare* put his sword away. Each of them went to one side of Varg, dragging one of the Cane's huge arms over their shoulders.

"The rope," Demos said quietly, and Isana shook herself into motion, grabbing on to the rope with both hands. Demos nodded his approval, and said, quietly, "Shouldn't be long."

He closed his eyes and made a gesture with one hand. The hull of the ship, beneath her, suddenly shifted, weirdly fluid, and then simply dropped away, lowering them up to their chins into the waters of the river. As Isana watched, the hull of the ship shifted and then closed over them, leaving a bubble of air trapped against the dome-shaped indentation in the ship's hull.

Then, there was little to do but hold on to the rope in near-total darkness. And wait.

"Tavi," Isana said quietly. "How long have you known?"

There was a moment of silence. To Tavi's credit, he didn't attempt any evasions, even one so minor as asking her what she was talking about. "Almost two years now."

"Why didn't you tell me?"

"At first," he said quietly, "because I thought there were things you weren't telling me. It seemed . . . an appealing bit of symmetry."

Isana felt a stab of anger that came along with the hurt, but she could hardly throw stones at him for keeping secrets. Besides, to a certain degree, he was right. In some ways, she'd had such treatment coming.

"What about later?" she asked quietly.

"I suppose I'd gotten used to it," he said. "I didn't even tell Araris."

"Didn't have to," Araris said quietly.

"What?" Tavi asked. "But until last night I never . . ."

"Asked me to turn out the furylamp in your room," Araris said. "Never missed a day out alone, practicing with Kitai." He chuckled. "You didn't think you could actually work out against me, using some of your metalcraft, and I wouldn't notice?"

"Oh," Tavi said quietly.

Isana frowned. "Araris? You knew? And you didn't tell me?"

"It wasn't mine to tell," he said quietly.

"I see," Isana said.

"Quiet," Tavi hissed.

They fell silent. Heavy boots, too heavy to be any sailor's wear, thumped on the hull above them. Hollow voices, strangely muffled, vibrated through the floorboards. There were shouts, calls, the sounds of things being moved. After several minutes of this, the sounds retreated.

Not long after, the wooden hull of the ship twitched, then parted again, and Isana idly noted the subtle, steady water-crafting worked into the hull that prevented water from rushing in, the work of Demos's witchmen, presumably.

The boards of the hull reached down around them and closed beneath them, lifting them up, until they stood in the witchmen's shallow pool again. Demos stood nearby.

"That went fairly well," he said quietly. "You'll all need to stay here in the hold until we get moving again. They might come back, and if they do, you'll have to get wet again."

"Are you sure they didn't find anything?" Tavi asked quietly.

Demos shook his head. "That would have been suspicious. They found two hidden compartments holding several ounces of aphrodin, a crate of wine bottles that hadn't been marked by the excisemen, and a bolt of silk cloth from Kalare that's supposed to be embargoed."

Isana blinked. "And you weren't arrested?"

"I had cash." He turned to go. "I'll have something hot sent down to you. Once the other two members of your party arrive, and we're cleared to depart, we'll get moving again. Probably sometime tomorrow morning."

Tavi nodded. "Thank you, Demos."

"It's the job," he said, and left.

Tavi pulled himself out of the pool and sank down against the nearest bulkhead, his feet pulled up, knees against his chest. He lowered his head and was asleep again.

Isana looked at the battered young man and sighed. Then she said, "Am I wrong to be worried, about his furies?"

"There's something wrong with his crafting," Araris said. "I'm not sure what. But I've never seen him actually manifest a fury. Not even last night."

"If he could have," Isana began.

"He would have," Araris finished, nodding. He wrinkled up his nose and glanced at Varg, before positioning the Cane to lie with his head out of the pool. "Smells like wet dog in here."

She smiled faintly. "I should resume tending to him. There's quite a bit more to do."

Araris nodded and stepped out of the pool. "How's your arm?" he asked.

"It hurts," Isana said. "But I'm not in danger. Once I've seen to these two, I'll mend it."

He didn't look happy about that, but he nodded. "All right." He began to turn away, but paused. "Shouldn't one of us tell him about . . . us?"

She felt her cheeks color again. "I . . . what would we tell him?"

"That we love each other," Araris said in a quiet, firm tone. "That once things are more . . . settled, that we want to be together."

She looked up at him, and swallowed. "Is . . . is that what you want?"

Araris glanced at her and then gave her a gentle grin. "You know just as well as I do, my lady."

She smiled at him, and despite the cool water all around her, she felt very warm.

Araris settled down beside her son to guard the boy's sleep, while Isana turned her attention back to the wounded Cane.

CHAPTER 38

Valiar Marcus stared down at the spear in his guts in total shock.

The Canim javelin had slipped through a tiny opening between Marcus's shield and that of the *legionare* beside him, thrown with such force that its black metallic head slammed cleanly through his armor.

Marcus realized, then, that he was standing in the second rank. He didn't remember taking a step back. The impact of the javelin must have knocked him there. That was probably why only about ten inches of steel was in his guts. Javelins hurled by a warrior Cane typically transfixed their targets entirely.

And this *was* the weapon of a warrior Cane, he knew, which meant that the Prime Cohort was engaging some of the foe's elites. They would have to alter their formation and advance, now, because the Canim typically flung their spears immediately before a charge. Marcus managed to take a deep breath, and bellow, "Close formation! Shields up! Second and third ranks to spears!"

Spear leaders began repeating the orders, shouting together, and the ranks of the Prime Cohort shifted and compressed. The *legionares* in the second and third ranks put away their swords and readied the five-foot spears strapped to the back of their tower shields. Those spearheads rose in a thicket of deadly steel thorns, just as the Canim warrior caste exploded from the rain-shrouded shadows and struck the lines.

Marcus sheathed his sword and pulled hard on the spear, but it was pinned in the steel grip of his punctured armor, and he couldn't get it free. Battling *legionares* on the front rank jostled the spear's shaft, shoving it left and right, and Marcus felt it as a horribly invasive, quivering tremor in his belly, and his breath was suddenly gone.

He dropped to one knee, and got his shield up in time to deflect a hastily aimed blow from a black-armored Cane. The *legionares* around him drove the Cane back with spears and brutally stabbing swords.

Someone stepped on the spear shaft, and pain that redefined his concept of the word burned Marcus to his core.

He fell, onto his back, and rain poured into his face. He reached to wipe water from his eyes, and Foss said, "Easy there, Marcus. Try not to move just yet."

Marcus blinked. He opened his eyes and looked blearily around him.

He was in the healer's tents.

And it was morning.

He'd been moving the cohort to secure that shaky flank near the woods, and then the spear had hit him.

And now he was in the healer's tents. He'd been injured, and injuries could be disorienting. Someone must have dragged him from the fight.

It was such an immense effort to move his head that after the first couple of twitches, he didn't bother.

He lay in a healing tub, naked, and the water was stained dark with blood. Foss sat at the head of the tub, his head bowed, his hands resting on Marcus's shoulders.

Marcus's eyes tracked down to his belly and found a gaping wound there, as long as his hand was broad. The wound gaped at the edges, and he could see . . . whichever parts of his guts were beneath the wound, he supposed.

"Balls," he whispered.

"Try not to talk," Foss growled. "You have to tighten your stomach muscles to do it, and I don't need you bumping my elbow while I work."

"C-cohort," Marcus said. He tried to look around him, but reclined as he was, he could see little more than that the First Aleran's Tribune Medica and his staff had no shortage of work. Battlefield infirmaries were always like this. Men groaned and screamed and wept. Quiet, determined healers fought their own battle with Death himself, to what Marcus was sure would be the usual mixed results.

"Hold still and shut up, or I'll knock you out," Foss said. "That column that hit you out of that ravine was one of three. The other two went right through the Guard and hit us in the flanks. If the Prime Cohort hadn't held, the Canim would have cut us up but good."

Marcus turned his eyes back up to Foss.

The healer glanced at him and frowned. "It isn't pretty in here. Thirty-four of the Prime dead. Twice that many wounded." Foss scowled. "Now shut up and hold still, before you're number thirty-five."

It was too much effort to nod. Marcus closed his eyes. The sobs of the wounded and the murmur of quiet, determined voices continued, until he found himself sitting up in bed, wolfing down a steaming bowl of mashed meal, bland but filling.

He blinked several times at the bowl and looked up and around him. He was back in his tent, and it was morning again—a different morning, he thought. The sun was out. He felt weak as a puppy and twice as hungry.

He moved his blankets and looked at the scar on his abdomen. It hadn't closed neatly—though it would hardly be the first time that had happened to him. The scar marking the injury was as thick as his little finger, raised from his skin—the hallmark of a vicious injury attended to by an overworked and exhausted Legion watercrafter, worn to the point of collapse from saving men's lives as swiftly and as certainly as possible.

The past two days were little but mist in his memory, a few solid points, with many hours of nothingness in between. That happened, sometimes, when a particularly extensive injury required particularly extensive watercrafting to rectify. He'd been close to gone, then.

He turned his attention back to the simple mash and ate until the bowl was empty.

"Good morning," said a voice outside. Crassus. "Are you up?"

"Not dressed yet," Marcus said. "Just a moment, sir."

"Don't," Crassus said, alarmed. The young man came into the tent. "Healer's orders. You're to stay in bed all of today."

That sounded good to Marcus, but he wasn't about to let the young officer know it. "I'm fine, sir. I'll go talk to Foss about it."

"Captain's orders," Crassus said. "Stay in bed."

Marcus grunted. "Sir." He rubbed a hand over his head. "How'd yesterday go?"

"The short version? Nasaug hit us with better than three thousand of his elites spearheading twenty thousand raiders. They tore through both Guard Legions and threw them into confusion. If you and your men hadn't held, they might have routed us completely."

Marcus grunted and gestured at himself. "I didn't do much of that."

Crassus lifted his eyebrows. "I've had a number of men report that you hacked the shaft off that javelin in your belly and kept giving orders for more than an hour. It wasn't until we started pushing them back that you let them take you to the healers."

Marcus blinked. He remembered nothing of that. "Well. That wasn't real bright of me."

"Under the circumstances, I'll forgive it," Crassus said. "You held. We got everyone rallied up on First Aleran's flanks, and started pushing them back—but it was bloody close." He shook his head. "They left quickly once the tide began to turn. We actually took more casualties than the Guard—the Canim let them run once they'd been broken up and came after us. We got hit hard, but we hurt the Canim as badly as they hurt us."

"Then we're losing," Marcus said quietly. "There's more of them."

"Yes there are," Crassus said. "But we're close to Mastings now. Twenty miles from here to the ruins, and we can see Mastings from there."

Marcus grunted. "They aren't going to give us the ruins cheap. It used to be a fortress. They'll have rebuilt portions, fortified it. We should move on it now."

Crassus nodded. "Arnos is holding us here for two days.

Raiding parties have been hitting our supply trains behind us. We're going to run short on food if we don't hold here for the wagons that managed to get through."

Marcus growled. "They can get an awful lot of work done in two days."

"I know," Crassus said. "But I have my orders, and you have yours." He nodded at the bowl. "I'll have some more brought in. You're to eat it and get some more sleep." His voice sobered. "I'm going to need you."

Marcus put his fist to his heart and bowed his head.

Crassus returned the salute and left the tent. "Excuse me," he said to someone outside. "Could you bring him some more, please? And don't let him go wandering around."

"Of course, my lord," answered a woman's voice.

"Captain, is just fine, ma'am," Crassus said. "And thank you."

Lady Aquitaine came into the tent in her washerwoman disguise, bearing a covered tray. She gave Marcus an elaborate curtsey, and he shook his head at her.

"Captain will do, indeed," she said, casting a narrow glance over her shoulder in the direction of the retreating Crassus. She settled the tray on Marcus's lap and removed the lid. The aroma of fresh, hot food threatened to rob him of his sanity.

"Where on earth did you get fresh eggs out here?" he demanded. "And ham?"

"I'm a woman of means," Lady Aquitaine said. "Eat. I'll talk."

Marcus's stomach howled more than growled, and he fell to with a will.

"Our young Crassus is too modest," Lady Aquitaine said. "He's all but totally responsible for rallying the entire First Senatorial. And Captain Nalus is swearing up and down that the Second would never have survived the battle without Crassus's steadiness and that fool Antillar's cavalry."

"The Senator's less than thrilled with that," Marcus said.

Lady Aquitaine waved one hand. "As am I. Crassus has something young Scipio didn't."

"A title," Marcus said. "Legitimacy."

"Precisely. The son of Antillus Raucus." She shook her head. "I've worked hard to set up Arnos to receive the political profit from this campaign—and in a broader sense, my husband hardly needs more rivals."

"You can't really think Crassus could threaten him," Marcus said.

"No. Not now. But ten years from now, with the credit for a successful campaign behind him . . ." She shrugged. "The wise gardener plucks weeds when they are small rather than waiting for them to take root."

Marcus stopped chewing.

"We'll use him to take the ruins," Lady Aquitaine said. "We'll let him help us secure the city. When we march on the city . . ." She shrugged. "Take care of it, my Fidelias."

"Crassus," he said.

"Yes," she replied.

"That could prove difficult. And if his death is traced to me—to any Aleran, for that matter—it will cast a shadow on the Senator. To say nothing of Raucus's response."

"Which is why I have taken the liberty of procuring one of those Canim balests for you, my spy." She poured him a mug of spiced tea from a pitcher. "It's beneath your bunk. He'll die at the hands of the foes he so bravely confronted, a hero of the Realm."

Marcus nodded and forced himself to continue eating.

"I know you've been injured, and you need rest." She calmly picked up the tray, tugged aside the blankets, and studied his wound. "Goodness, someone made a botch of this." She laid her hand over it, and her eyes went a bit distant. "But it's closed solidly enough, I suppose." She restored his blankets and returned the tray. "Do this for me, Fidelias, and you can finally get out of this place. It hardly suits you, you know." Her eyes glittered. "The next year or so will be very exciting. I'll want you at my side."

He nodded back. "I'll take care of it."

"Excellent," she said, her eyes glittering. "Eat. Rest."

She departed the tent.

Marcus sat quietly for a moment.

Kill Crassus.

Or refuse her orders. Kill himself.

Marcus set the question aside and ate everything left on the tray. He drank the tea and settled down to sleep. He would think things through more clearly after food and rest.

He would need his strength.

Regardless of what he did with it.

▫CHAPTER 39

Dreary days and miserable nights blended into one long, slow, ugly ordeal, and Amara grew heartily sick of swamps and everything to do with them.

The days were all the same. They started at first light, with cold breakfast. Then they would slog forward through endless mud and shallow water. They would stop for rests, but increasingly, as the days went on, the stops seemed to do less and less to allow them to recuperate. Bernard sometimes managed to find dry wood that would burn without giving off too much smoke, but there was never much of it, and he was willing to chance only tiny fires.

They would cook whatever meat Bernard managed to shoot—the garim provided most of their foraged fare, though the meat was tasteless and oily. They could never chance a fire at night, as Bernard said they could be seen from miles away, and without a fire, the nights became something utterly miserable.

They would stop on dry ground to rest—but "dry" was a relative term in the swamps. Moisture seeped in through blankets and clothes regardless of what they tried to prevent it, until Bernard collected enough of the smaller garim hides to provide a single sleeping mat. One of them had to remain awake at all times, so they couldn't huddle together for warmth, and as a result what little sleep Amara *did* get was attenuated by her constant shivering.

And, of course, absolutely every part of the day was accompanied by thousands and thousands of insects that crawled insects that flew, insects that swam, and Amara found herself constantly brushing them from her eyes and nose and ears and mouth, like walking through some endless living curtain.

When first light came, they would rise and set forth again.

And so endless days passed.

Though Bernard claimed to feel better, he did not offer to lead them again, and Amara saw him rubbing at his eyes or temples when he thought she wasn't looking. The First Lord for his part, continued to drift in and out of sleep, and if he did not recover from the steady fever, at least he did not further deteriorate, either.

They had stopped for a meal an hour before, and Amara still hadn't gotten the taste of the oily garim meat out of her mouth, when she saw movement in the swamps ahead. She stopped, holding up a hand, and glanced over her shoulder at Bernard.

They were standing in waist-deep water, and Bernard immediately laid his bow and quiver across Gaius's floating stretcher and crouched until only his head was showing. Amara followed his example. He moved soundlessly through the water to stand next to her, squinting ahead.

Amara lifted her hands and called to Cirrus, willing the fury to bend light in the space between her palms. The air there blurred for a moment, and then came into sharper focus, magnifying her view of the area ahead of them.

There were three men moving through the swamps. They were dressed in garim-hide cloaks, trousers, and boots, and the mottled hides of the swamp lizards blended in perfectly with all the green and grey and brown around them. In fact Amara never would have seen them at all except for—

She willed Cirrus to draw her view even closer to the three men, and she focused on the one in the lead. Around his throat was the gleam of a polished, metallic collar. With her fury's help, she was even able to make out the word engraved on the steel: *Immortalis*.

"Immortals," she whispered. "They're Immortals, Bernard."

He said nothing, but she saw his eyes flicker with concern. The enslaved warriors had been driven beyond madness by the furycrafted collars that controlled them. Kalarus's Immortals had been responsible for the deaths of dozens of Citizens on the Night of the Red Stars. They were virtual juggernauts, entirely insensible to pain, completely focused upon serving their master, Kalarus. Amara had seen Immortals simply ignore swords thrust through their throats, limbs severed from their bodies, accepting hideous wounds more than willingly in order to strike down the targets their master had sent them to eliminate.

"Crows," Bernard murmured.

A moment later, Amara saw something else, through the haze of humidity, beyond the patrolling Immortals.

"Bernard," she whispered. "I can see the mountains."

He took a deep breath. She felt his hand move to her and rest for a moment on the small of her back. "How far?"

"Ten miles?" she guessed. "Twelve?"

He nodded. "Close."

"The patrol is passing us," she said. "We can push through today if we hurry."

She had already begun to move forward when Bernard's hand slid around to press against her stomach and hold her back. "Wait," he said quietly.

"For what?" she asked.

"If Kalarus has his Immortals here," he said, "then they're looking for us, specifically. He wouldn't send them out unless he thought it was that important."

"Agreed," Amara said.

"Those three are the sentinels we do see," Bernard said. "But I'm more worried about the ones we don't."

Amara frowned. "What do we do, then?"

"We watch them," he said. "We wait. We'll see how regular their patrols are and look for a way to slip through between them."

"Wait?" Amara said. She looked at the vague, vast forms of the mountains in the distance. "We're so close."

"We can't get sloppy now," Bernard said, his voice solid, certain. "We wait."

"I thought you were worried about someone catching up to us from behind."

"I am," he said, nodding. "But the men coming behind us have to search miles and miles of swamp, sweeping along in one big, slow line. The Immortals have a much smaller area to watch."

"What happens if they catch up to us while we're waiting?"

"Pretty much the same thing that happens if we rush out there and bump into a gang of Immortals standing sentry in a hidden blind," Bernard said.

"That's not terribly encouraging," Amara said.

"I can't take you anywhere." He gestured around them, pausing to brush a swimming serpent, nudging it gently aside. "No matter how nice it is, you always seem to think it could be just a little bit better."

Amara's stomach twitched in tiny jerks, and her quiet breaths of laughter stirred the water beneath her nose and mouth.

"Plenty of trees," Bernard said. "A beautiful view." He slapped at himself as one of the stinging flies that filled the swamp struck at his ear. "Friendly neighbors."

"You know me, Bernard. I'm just one of those women who needs someone to do everything for her."

His eyes wrinkled at the corners, and he started snorting quiet laughter, too. "Crows, yes. That's you."

"I have a suggestion," murmured Gaius. "If you're both quite finished amusing one another."

Bernard gave Amara a sidelong look and his hand moved under the surface of the muddy water.

She clutched at his wrist and tried to glare at him as her cheeks turned scarlet. "Pardon, sire, of course."

Bernard grinned and turned his attention forward once more.

Gaius coughed a few times. "I would suggest that you wait until near sunset, Countess, and then fly an aerial reconnaissance. It's generally easier to spot hidden sentry posts from above."

"What if they have Knights Aeris about?" Bernard asked.

"We've not heard any windstreams of late," Gaius replied. "Besides. Even if there are enemy Knights Aeris, the Countess is more than capable of handling herself. And in the meanwhile, we can observe enemy movements before drawing any closer."

Amara glanced at Bernard, who frowned pensively for a moment, then nodded. "They already know we're about. It might be worth the risk to know more about what's immediately ahead." He grimaced down at the water. "Going to be a little damp while we wait, though."

"We'll take turns on the stretcher," Gaius said. "I won't need both legs to support my weight in the water."

"No," Amara said. "That isn't going to happen, sire."

Gaius blinked. "Ex*cuse* me? Countess, I believe that I am perfect—" He broke off, coughing again, struggling to smother the sound with his hands. The sound became ugly for just a moment, and then he got himself under control again. "You may," he breathed, "have a point."

They settled in to wait.

During the course of the day, patrols swept by every two to three hours, on varying paths. The last patrol passed to within twenty yards of them, but Bernard had raised a woodcrafting around them, and once more, they remained unseen.

Finally, the shadows began to stretch, and Amara murmured, "I'd best draw back a little way. I don't want to chance them hearing my takeoff."

Bernard nodded once and kissed her cheek. "Be careful. Good luck."

Amara paced silently back through the swamps and found a point of higher ground which she could use to become airborne. She grimaced at all the mud on her and did her best to get the heaviest bits off before she called out to Cirrus. It was a bit of an effort, given the way the mud hampered her ability to will her fury to action, but she took off on the quietest windstream she could manage and ascended several thousand feet, to the edge of her ability to see what was below her in detail.

For a single glorious moment she paused to take a deep breath, her face turned up to the sun, and gently urged Cirrus to dry her clothing. She'd been wearing wet things for so long, she'd almost forgotten what anything else felt like. The air smelled fresh and clean, this high up, and more importantly, it was entirely free of the constant stench of rotting vegetable matter. For that matter, she couldn't remember the last time she had gone so long without flying, and it felt glorious to be in the air again.

She let out a guilty little sigh and turned her mind back to business. Bernard and the First Lord were still down in the muck. It hardly seemed fair for her to waste time reveling in being away from it when they were waiting for her to help them get out themselves. She willed Cirrus to magnify her vision and approached the swamp's edge out of the concealment offered by the setting sun.

At first, she worried that the haze might lower visibility too much to make the overflight practical, but she soon proved able to see the swamp below clearly enough. It did not take her long to spot the three outposts in the general vicinity of their approach.

Two were built up into trees at the very edge of the swamp, and a third was dug out of a mound at the base of a dead tree, overlooking the swamp's edges, shrouded by brush and grown over with vines. That last looked large enough to shelter perhaps a dozen men—and all three posts had dogs tethered nearby.

Amara sailed to several other vantage points to double-check what she had learned, though she didn't dare fly directly over the enemy strong points—without the glare of the sun to keep casual glances away from her position, it would be entirely too easy for a sentry to spot her by accident.

With the sun setting in earnest, Amara descended back into the swamps and hurriedly returned to Bernard and Gaius. She couldn't find them, even knowing the general area in which they'd been, until Bernard lowered his woodcrafted veil and beckoned. She waded back to them and quietly reported what she'd seen. "We can't get through without going by at least one of their watch positions," she concluded. "Which, I suppose, is why they put them there."

"Dogs," Bernard said. "That makes it more complicated."

"Why?" Amara asked.

Bernard shrugged. "I could use Brutus to keep them calm as we went by them—but I can't hold up a veil around us at the same time. And dogs track by scent. Veils won't do much to hide us from them."

"And if you don't hold a veil around us," Amara mused, "we won't make it through unseen."

Bernard nodded. "Likely."

"That isn't a problem," Gaius murmured. "Countess, you can veil us from sight, while the good Count Calderon prevents the hounds from raising the alarm—and it would leave him with enough attention to shoot if we need to silence anyone quickly."

Bernard lifted an eyebrow, thinking it through, and nodded. "True. I didn't know you could do a veil, Countess."

"Uh," Amara said. "I . . . I can't." She flushed. "Not a very good one, anyway. I passed the qualifications in my windcrafting courses at the Academy, but not by much. I've never held one large enough for all three of us, and never for more than a few moments."

"Mmmm," Gaius said. "Have we other options?"

Bernard grimaced. "Not unless you'd like to begin taking action here and now, sire."

Gaius turned his gaze to the east for a time. Then he shook his head, and said, "It's still too soon. We'll need to get through the first pass in the mountains." He studied Amara. "You say your classroom veils were barely passing marks, eh?"

"Yes, sire. I was always so much better at flying. Perhaps I didn't put as much effort into the rest as I could have."

The feverish old man smiled and closed his eyes. "Or," he murmured, "perhaps you needed the proper tutor. Attend."

Chapter 40

Tavi lost track of several days. Not completely, but there was a definite blurring in his memory. He had to get the details from Kitai later, but the long and short of it was that they slipped quietly out of Alera Imperia two days after they took Varg from the Grey Tower.

Demos had delayed their departure until he had secured a cargo to freight down the river to Parcia—since it would look more than mildly suspicious for a ship to arrive and depart without loading or unloading anything. Tavi was only intermittently aware of what was going on, thanks to the extensive watercrafting he'd required after the rescue. He had a fairly clear recollection of the conversation with his mother while hiding in the river, and something about grabbing one of Varg's ears as if he'd been a sheep being stubborn about shearing— but he mostly remembered being ravenously hungry, eating as much as he could fit in his stomach, then stumbling back to his bunk to sleep.

By the time hours had begun once again to proceed one after another in an orderly fashion, they had reached Parcia, and in less than half the time it had taken them to make the journey upriver. Demos unloaded his cargo and within hours they were once again in the open sea.

Tavi promptly got sick again.

He was lying on the open deck at night, several nights later, enjoying the cool breeze and gnawing on a ship's biscuit as his nausea finally began to fade. Araris sat with his back against the mast, his sword on his lap, dozing. Tavi had just begun to consider life worth living again, when the door to the hold opened and Varg prowled onto the deck.

Tavi watched in silence as the Cane paced to the bow. The

vast, dark-furred form, darker and more solid than the evening shadows, faced forward for a time, face lifted to the evening air.

Tavi rose. He held out a hand to Araris as he walked past him. The *singulare* passed over the hilt of his sword, and Tavi took it with him, casually carrying the weapon in its scabbard as he went to stand beside Varg.

The Cane glanced aside at Tavi and down to the sword. His chest rumbled with a sound that could have been amusement or approval. "I was wounded," Varg said. "Unto death."

"Not quite," Tavi said quietly.

Varg lifted a paw-hand in an approximation of an Aleran gesture of acceptance. "I was made whole by Aleran sorcery."

"By the Lady Isana," Tavi said.

"Your mother," Varg said.

Tavi blinked and stared at him.

Varg tapped one claw on the end of his nose. "Your scents are similar."

Tavi snorted out a breath.

Varg turned to face the sea again. "Almost as similar as your scent and that of Gaius Sextus."

Tavi frowned.

Varg let out another amused rumble. "I have said nothing of it to any ears but yours."

"Sometimes it feels like everyone knew but me," Tavi growled. "How long have you known?"

"Since the night you held a knife to my throat."

"I didn't have much choice in the matter," Tavi said.

"You could have chosen to neglect your duty. You did not." Varg leaned his huge, clawed paw-hands on the ship's rail and stared out to sea. "Why did you come down for me when I fell, Aleran?"

"Because you agreed to follow me," Tavi said.

"I might already have been dead."

"There was no way to know that until I went down to look."

Varg grunted. "You could have been killed in coming."

Tavi shrugged. "I wasn't."

Varg bared his teeth. "I respect Gaius's power. I respect his intelligence. But I most respect that he understands what it is to lead." He turned toward Tavi and bent his head gently forward, in the Aleran manner. "As I respect you, *gadara*."

Tavi inclined his head in reply. "Have you eaten?"

Varg coughed out a grunt of laughter. "You have learned what it is to lead warriors." He sounded amused. "These sailors do not like to come near me. I have chosen not to take food from them."

Tavi's eyes widened as he considered what Kitai had told him about Varg's extensive wounds and the crafting that had been required to repair them. "You must be starving."

"I have been hungry before."

Tavi turned to Varg and put the rest of his ship's biscuit on the rail beside the Cane's paw-hand. "Eat that," he said. "I'll see about getting you something more solid."

Varg took the biscuit and tossed it into his jaws. The Cane's teeth crunched the tough block of food as if it had been fresh bread. He flicked his ears in distaste as he worked his jaws, getting the crumbs from between his fangs. "Alerans may be hardier than I thought." He tilted his head and considered Tavi. "The Lady Isana," he growled. "If it is not improper, I would have you convey my respects for her skills."

"Why would you think it improper?" Tavi asked.

Varg picked another shard of ship's biscuit from his teeth with one claw. "Your people have strange customs with regards to mates and offspring. A male may be mated, yet pursue other females. A female may be mated, but bear children of other males, yet pretend they are her mate's offspring, while the mate outwardly acknowledges the children as his own. A man and woman may mate and bear children, but if it is recorded improperly, then shame is visited on the child."

"Shame?"

"Illegitimacy, I have heard it called," Varg said. "Bastard. And you, a child of the House of Gaius, were treated as an outcast. A menial. I do not know if your mother has been visited with shame, or if it would be inappropriate to acknowledge her. The values of such things make no sense to me."

"It's . . . complicated," Tavi said. "Even by Aleran standards. But it would not be inappropriate for you to thank her for her assistance."

Varg bared his teeth and growled. "I do not offer thanks. Your people need me alive and healthy. It was not an act of charity."

"True enough," Tavi said. "I chose an imprecise phrase. It would not be inappropriate for you to convey your respect for her skills."

Varg narrowed his eyes in thought for a moment. "Among my people, a pack leader handles such matters."

Tavi turned to face Varg directly, hand on his sword. "Then I will do so."

The Cane's chest rumbled again, and he flicked his ears in agreement, turning back to the sea. "It is well."

Tavi turnèd from his confrontational stance as well. "Is there anything else you need?"

Varg growled and flexed his claws. "Information."

Tavi considered that, and said, "I will give you what I can."

"I have need," he said.

"Were our roles reversed, I the prisoner in your land, would you share information openly with me?"

"Were our roles reversed, Aleran, your blood would have been drained into jars long since." He drummed his claws on the rail. "And no. I would not share openly." He nodded once. "Tell me what you can about my people here."

Tavi described the last two years in very general terms, giving Varg no information about the positions of Aleran troops, their capabilities, their logistics, or their vulnerability.

When it was done, Varg's mouth dropped open, his tongue lolling out for a second or two. "Sarl is dead by your hand?"

Tavi grinned out at the sea. "It might not have happened if Nasaug hadn't maneuvered him into it."

"But you saw it happening," Varg said. "You used it to your advantage."

"Yes."

"And Sarl died by your hand."

"Yes."

"Well did Nasaug name you *gadara*," Varg rumbled.

"I have a theory," Tavi said.

One of Varg's ears swiveled around toward him.

"The invasion fleet arrived under desperate circumstances,"

Tavi said. "Sarl burned their ships behind them. There was a great deal of internal division. A great many ritualists had come with the fleet, and they were clearly dominant." Tavi frowned. "And they had noncombatants with them. I saw a female with young."

Varg's claws dug into the railing.

"It wasn't an invasion force," Tavi said. "It was more like a colony."

"I do not know this word," Varg said.

"It's when you send a group into a new area. They take with them everything they need to begin building their own society and settle down to make a new home."

Varg flicked his ears in acknowledgment.

"After the night of the Vord attack on the First Lord, Sarl vanished. We now know that he was taken from the capital on a ship and went back to his homeland. We hunted for him for weeks, but we never found him." Tavi squinted out ahead of them to the west—toward Varg's home. "We never found the Vord queen, either."

Varg bared his teeth.

"Sarl was already scheming with the Vord. I believe that he took it with him when he ran. I believe he took it back to your homeland and that it got loose. I think that once he realized what was happening, he took hostages to guarantee the cooperation of Nasaug and his warriors, stole everything he could get his hands on, and ran, trusting his scheme with Kalarus to give him a fighting chance."

"That," Varg growled, "was Sarl."

Tavi nodded. "I think," he said quietly, "that your people are in danger. That's why Sarl burned the ships behind him. He knew Nasaug would return to protect your homeland if he didn't. And that's why Nasaug is building a fleet right now."

Varg said nothing. His body language told Tavi nothing. A moment later, he said, "If it is true, Aleran, then your enemies will be laid low. What reason could you have to help Nasaug return and stop this from happening?"

"Are you kidding?" Tavi asked. "Self-interest. If the Vord destroy your people, sooner or later they will come here. If I send you home to fight them, then one of two things will happen. You will overcome them, in which case Alera is faced with a familiar enemy and is no worse off than before. Or they will destroy you, weakening themselves in the process, making them easier for Alera to fight. Either way, we are better off if your people leave."

Varg considered that for a moment. "If you are right, we share an enemy."

"I'm right," Tavi said quietly. "I know I'm right."

The Cane glanced aside at Tavi. "What do you propose?"

"I return you to Nasaug at Mastings. You finish building your ships and leave."

"So simple," he said. "But it is not so simple, Aleran. You are not honored as your blood should be. Can you compel your Legions to cease fighting? To allow my people to leave?"

Tavi clenched his teeth for a moment but forced himself to admit, "I'm not sure."

"Then how will you accomplish it?"

"I'm not sure," Tavi said. He narrowed his eyes. "Not yet. But it *will* happen."

Varg did not reply.

The two of them stood staring out at the shadowed west before them, and for no explicable reason Tavi suddenly felt cold.

⊶CHAPTER 41

"I don't like it, First Spear," Crassus said quietly. "This was too easy."

They stood within the ruins of an old town on a hill, its name long since forgotten. Odds were that the town had simply withered after the successful port city of Mastings had grown up only a few miles away, but whatever it had once been,

centuries had passed since anyone but the occasional traveler
or passing deer had lived there.

"I was sure they would have fortified this place," Marcus
said. "But I'm just as glad they didn't make us fight to take it."

"Exactly," Crassus said. "They could have—they *should*
have. And they didn't."

"The Canim are good soldiers," Marcus responded. "But
that doesn't make them perfect, sir. And there could have been
any number of factors that prevented them from using this position against us. Whether they made a mistake or just couldn't
get things set up in time, we're better off for it."

"That story sounds weak, Marcus," Crassus said. "Even you
think so."

"Weak, sir?" Marcus asked. "Just because the Canim have
let us take a position we can fortify beyond their capabilities
to assault only miles away from the town they have to protect
at all costs, without giving us so much as a nosebleed over
taking it? Especially when they know how tough we are from
a defensive strong point?" He snorted. "What's weak about
that?"

Around them, the First Aleran continued sweeping the
overgrown streets, the half-collapsed buildings, checking
everything within the tumbledown walls that had once surrounded the town. Both Guard Legions had marched to positions beside the town and were now erecting palisades atop
simple earthworks as an outer defensive perimeter around the
base of the hill.

The hoofbeats of a trotting horse approached, and Maximus
rode his stallion through what had once been someone's living
room. He dismounted and flicked the horse's reins around the remains of a chimney, then approached Crassus and saluted.

Crassus returned it. "Well?"

"They had scouts watching the hill," Maximus said. "Canim
and mounted rebels. We pursued them, but not too hard."

Crassus nodded at his brother. "The city?"

Maximus's eyes glittered. "Saw it."

"How bad is it?"

"Three layers of earthworks," Max said. "Then what looks

like a newly crafted outer wall, around the walls of the town it-self. And they're all lined with troops."

Marcus let out a low whistle.

"How many?" Crassus asked.

"Twenty thousand on the walls," Max said. "No idea how many might have been behind them."

Crassus spat. "Wonderful."

"The good news," Marcus said, "is that at least they're do-ing something we anticipated, sir."

"Under the circumstances, it's hardly comforting," Crassus said. "With that much manpower, they should have had plenty of hands to spare to build up the ruins and make us fight for them."

"Maybe they didn't think they needed to," Maximus said. "They've got us outnumbered already. If we want to take them out, we'll have to go to them, and having a defensible position to fall back on isn't going to mean much when it's miles away."

Marcus grunted in a neutral tone. Crassus was a young commander, but his naturally studious, pensive personality tended to negate the usual recklessness of a leader his age. If anything, perhaps too much so. Waging a military campaign truly was one of the more complicated endeavors anyone could embark upon, and the demands of organization, logis-tics, communications, and internal politics could often create unusual, or even outwardly ridiculous-seeming, scenarios.

Marcus was well aware of Nasaug's skills, which had been sufficient to enable him to survive in hostile territory, cut off from any help and vastly outnumbered on the absolute scale. Only extremely competent leadership could account for such a thing—but even the most brilliant general had finite re-sources. It was entirely possible that Nasaug had reached the limits of his.

It was also, he admitted, entirely possible that the reason the ruins had been ceded without a fight was nowhere near so innocuous.

"Plan for what he can do," Marcus said. "Not what you think he's going to do."

Crassus glanced at Marcus and nodded sharply. "Giving us a nice position here lets them know two things for certain— where to find us and from where we'll approach Mastings." He scratched at the tip of his nose, frowning. "We estimate that he'll have forty thousand troops available to defend Mastings, right?"

"Yes, sir."

"Fine," Crassus said. "Let's suppose he's got thirty thousand waiting for us behind the walls. He could easily have ten waiting in the field, hoping to pin us between Mastings's defenses and their field force."

Max nodded. "Which would get ugly, fast."

"But that isn't a large enough force to take us on its own," Marcus said. "Especially not from fortifications."

"Which gives them even more reason not to let us take these without a fight."

Max stared at Crassus for a moment, then accused, "You think too much."

The young commander shrugged. "I don't see Nasaug sitting quietly behind his walls and waiting for us, either," Crassus said. "It could be that he's planning on hitting us here before the engineers can build the ruins up. So I want to picket the cavalry in a screen around us at five or six miles. If anyone sees anything moving out there, I want to know about it."

Max nodded and banged a fist on his chest, then went to his horse.

Before he could leave, more horses approached, and shortly the Senator, the captains of both Guard Legions, and their immediate attendants arrived.

But not, Marcus noted, the Senator's hired *singulares*. There was no sign of Phrygiar Navaris or her contemporaries. Several burly *legionares* from the Guard were staying close to Arnos—but not his gang of hired killers.

Marcus glanced at Crassus, who seemed to have noted the same absence. The young commander frowned and tapped the tip of his thumb restlessly against the hilt of his sword.

"Captain Crassus," Arnos said.

"Senator," Crassus replied, his tone polite as he saluted. "Welcome. I hadn't expected to see you today."

"No sense wasting time," Arnos replied.

That hadn't stopped him from doing it before, Marcus oted, but he said nothing.

"No, sir," Crassus agreed. He went on to give Arnos the rief facts of what they had learned about Mastings. "I was ast about to set pickets, sir, if you would like to—"

"Good," Arnos said, nodding. "Keep them close in. No nore than a mile or two out. Otherwise, we'll lose them to aiding forces and enemy scouts."

Crassus didn't respond for a second. Then he said, "Sir, if I night respectfully suggest it, I think we'd be better served to ush them farther out. It's a greater risk, but if an enemy force omes at us, they'll have more time to warn us before they rrive."

"Thank you for your suggestion, Captain," Arnos said in a evel tone. "But the enemy hasn't seen fit to come at us openly ver since our last encounter with them. That's why they gave s the ruins today: They know they'll be beaten in the open eld and wanted to preserve morale for the defense of Mast-ngs. If there is a force moving around out there, I doubt it's ery large. The Canim are protecting their ships. They won't pare a significant number of troops for side adventures."

"That sounds logical, sir," Crassus replied, nodding. "But it on't hurt us to have our screen out a little farther."

"It's a long walk to Kalare, young Antillus," Arnos said, his yes hard, but with something jovial in his tone. "We'll need ur riders when we face the real threat in the south. Let's not aste them here, hmmm?"

Crassus's expression became totally neutral. He gave the enator a sharp nod and another salute. "Yes, sir." Then he rned to Maximus, and said, "Pickets to be set at two miles. on't make me say it twice."

Maximus saluted once and departed.

Marcus stood nearby while Arnos went over the order of attle with his captains, and while Crassus demonstrated the uits of a lifetime of preparation to succeed his father's title. hough he could have made several suggestions, the young an kept his mouth shut until Nalus inevitably brought up me of the same points. Crassus would immediately caution

Arnos against the sensible course of action, and Arnos would
just as immediately overrule him. By the end of an hour-long
conference, they had a plan for assaulting the city that at least
stood a crow's chance of success.

When they were leaving, Marcus strode over to Nalus's
horse. "Sir, that girth is looking a bit loose." He nudged Nalus
on the leg and the captain drew it back so that Marcus could
reach the fittings of the broad leather band.

"Don't say it," muttered Nalus under his breath. "I know.
This was too easy. Something's wrong."

Marcus nodded, finished adjusting the saddle's girth, and
slapped the horse on the rump as he walked away.

Crassus fell into step beside him, and they walked toward
the southern edge of the ruins, where the engineers were already at work, preparing to fortify the old town wall.

"Two miles isn't far enough," Crassus growled.

"No, sir," Marcus replied. "Guess it's a good thing you told
Maximus to go to four miles."

"I didn't tell him that," Crassus said, smiling faintly. "You
were there."

Marcus snorted. "Yes, sir."

Marcus accompanied Crassus as he inspected the fortifications and conferred with the Tribune of the engineering cohort. After that came a briefing of the First Aleran's Tribunes,
outlining the battle plan for the following day.

Crassus dismissed the officers from the command tent, and
said, "Marcus, stay a moment."

The First Spear waited.

"Did you notice the Senator's *singulares*?"

Marcus frowned. "Yes, sir. Or rather no, I didn't."

"I'm trying to think of the last time I saw them. I think it
was when we were still near Othos."

Marcus nodded. "That was what I figured, too."

"It isn't hard to work out what someone would send Phrygiar Navaris to do," Crassus said quietly. "If anything's happened to the captain, I'm not going to let it pass. And I'll want
your help t—"

Outside, trumpets began blaring the call to arms. Men began shouting, and boots pounded the ground. Crassus an-

Marcus traded a look, then left the tent, to find the First Aleran in the midst of the structured chaos of a surprise call to arms.

Maximus came thundering up on his horse, and the beast was lathered with sweat and breathing hard. He threw Crassus a quick salute, and swung down from the restless beast. "I ordered the call to arms," he said shortly. "We don't have much time."

"For what, Max?" Crassus demanded.

"You were right. It was too easy," Max said. "The Canim are coming—at least two separate elements coming from the northeast and southeast, and they're converging here."

"Crows," Crassus spat. "How many?"

"So far, better than thirty thousand," Max said.

Crassus just stared at him, his face going pale. "How? How could they have that many in the field?"

"Sir," Marcus growled. "It doesn't matter how. They're here."

Crassus clenched his hands into fists and then nodded sharply at the First Spear. "Assemble, and prepare to move down the hill to support the defense of the palisade wall," he said sharply. "Knights to stay at the crown of the hill in reserve. Maximus, how many of your troops are in?"

"Not many," Max said. "Most are still standing picket."

"Then you're taking over as Knight Tribune," Crassus said. "Get moving."

Max saluted and strode off.

"Marcus . . ." Crassus said.

The First Spear banged out a crisp salute. "Let's get to work, sir."

Isana watched as the *Slive* approached the docks at Fellcove, a small port town on Alera's western coast, many miles south of Founderport and the Elinarch. The place had a seedy look to it, the boards of its houses weathered with age and smeared with tar. From the looks of the docks, one could practically step off of one's ship and directly into the town's drinking house, or its brothel—possibly both.

Ehren stood beside her, smiling. "Don't look so alarmed, my lady," he murmured. "We won't be staying long enough for it to make you uncomfortable."

Isana glanced down at Ehren and smiled. "Does it show?"

"From about a league away," Ehren replied. "Truth be told, I don't care much for the place, either."

"Then how did we settle upon it as our landing point?" Isana asked.

"It's close to Mastings," Ehren said. "The Legions are probably there already, and even if they aren't, Nasaug almost certainly is."

"Shouldn't we have sailed directly to Mastings, then?"

Demos's voice cut into the conversation as the captain came striding down the deck. "The Canim have been rather narrow-minded about commandeering every ship that they can get their hands on. I'd rather keep mine."

"Which makes Fellcove our only real option," Ehren said. "The Canim don't keep a presence here. Something about the smell."

Isana arched an eyebrow. "Surely they don't leave it entirely unguarded?"

"No," Ehren said. "They pay a local, ah, businessman

named Ibrus, to commandeer ships and keep them informed about any naval movements."

"What's to stop him from taking the *Slive*?" Isana asked Demos.

"He's greedy," Demos said. "Not suicidal."

"I've done business with him before," Ehren added. "He's as reasonable as any of his ilk can be."

The ship's lines got tossed out to the dock rats, and the men drew the *Slive* up to the dock and made it fast. Isana noted that a broad-bladed axe had been set out beside the base of each mooring line on the ship, presumably so that they could be severed quickly, if necessary.

The ship's hull bumped against the dock, and Demos nodded to Ehren, holding out his hand. "There you go."

Ehren slapped a jingling leather pouch into Demos's palm, and nodded to him. "Pleasure doing business."

"I always enjoy working with Cursors," Demos replied. "They pay on time, and almost never try to kill me afterward."

Tavi emerged from the passenger cabin, wearing a mail shirt and his weaponry. Araris, similarly clad, also appeared. Tavi nodded and smiled at Isana, before walking over to the hold and growling something in the Canish tongue. An answering snarl rose from the depths of the ship, and then Varg came up the stairs through the cargo doors. The enormous Cane wrinkled his nose and growled something, to which Tavi responded with a bark of laughter. Varg disdained the gangplank. He simply put one hand on the ship's railing and vaulted lightly down to the dock beneath. *Lightly* being a relative term, Isana supposed.

The dock rats all paused in their tasks for a moment, staring at Varg. The big Cane stretched, then deliberately yawned, displaying a mouthful of fangs.

The dock rats went hurriedly back to their tasks.

As Tavi passed Isana on the way to the gangplank, she asked him, "What did he say?"

"That he's glad to get off this ship," Tavi said. "He says it smells like wet people here."

Isana blinked. "I . . . I didn't realize." She glanced at the Cane. "Was he making a joke?"

"I'm not really sure," Tavi said. He gave Varg a wry glance. "I don't think I'm supposed to be. Excuse me." He paced down the gangplank to stand near the Cane.

Kitai climbed down from the ship's rigging and dropped the last several feet to the deck. Over the course of the journey, her hair had begun to grow in again and was now a short, fine brush of white offset by her longer mane. She gave a brilliant smile to one of the crewman, a brawny young sailor with a fresh cut running across his chin. The man visibly flinched and seemed to remember urgent duties requiring his attention elsewhere on the ship.

Kitai murmured to Isana, "I take my shirt off once, and it is as if these Alerans think I have invited them all to mate with me."

Isana glanced at the retreating young sailor. "Oh, dear. Why didn't you say anything?"

Kitai shrugged. "There was nothing to it. He made advances. I objected."

Isana arched an eyebrow. "I see. At what point did your objections draw blood?"

"Here," Kitai said, drawing a finger across her chin. "And another you can't see, right about . . ." She started untucking her shirt from her trousers.

Isana sighed and put her hands over Kitai's. "Later, dear. For the time being, let's just get off the ship." She turned to Kitai and offered her one of the traveling cloaks she had folded over her arm.

Kitai took the cloak, evidently well pleased with herself, and threw it about her shoulders, covering her distinctive hair with the hood. "Though I hardly see the point of wearing any kind of disguise," she said. "Not with the Cane with us."

Isana donned her own cloak. "Humor me."

"Easy enough," Kitai said agreeably.

Araris, now cloaked and hooded, came up to Isana, a satchel over his shoulder. He offered it to her, and she took it, her fingers brushing his. His eyes shone for a moment, and he bowed his head to her. "Ready?"

Isana felt a sudden flutter of amusement mixed with realization from Kitai, who murmured tartly, "Why, I expect she *is*."

"Kitai!" Isana whispered fiercely, her face heating.

"All that fuss about the men in a separate room. I should have shared a room with my Aleran and you with yours. We all would have been happier."

"Kitai!"

"Though I suppose we might not have gotten things done quite as quickly," Kitai said. She tilted her head and gave Araris a frank appraisal. "How is he with his mouth?"

Araris looked considerably more shaken than he had when he'd received his hideous belly wound. "Um, ladies," he said. "Excuse me." He hurried down the gangplank to move to Tavi's side.

Kitai laughed, a merry, silvery sound. "Alerans make this easy."

"You're shameless!" Isana protested, but she felt her mouth turning up into a smile.

"Of course," Kitai said. "It's obviously a side effect of being an unlettered savage." She pursed her lips thoughtfully and glanced at Tavi, who was speaking intently to Ehren. "My Aleran does not know."

"Correct," Isana said.

"You would prefer that he did not know."

"Yes."

Kitai smiled faintly. "There were times when Doroga would meet with a woman, after my mother died. I was much younger. I thought he was betraying her memory. It was painful."

Isana shivered a little at the sudden sense of hollow loss and loneliness she felt in Kitai. The loss of her mother must have affected her deeply, still to bring up such intense emotion years and years later.

"I know better, now. My mother was dead. Doroga should not be expected to spend the rest of his life alone. But it was a difficult thought to hold between my ears."

"I'll tell him," Isana said. "When he doesn't already have so much on his mind."

Kitai nodded. "Then I will not bring it up. I will not lie to him should he ask me, but I will not draw his attention to it."

"Thank you, Kitai."

She inclined her head, and said, "But tell him soon. The next time we stay in an inn, matters can be better arranged."

They descended from the ship to join the others, and together walked through Fellcove to see this man Ehren had mentioned, Ibrus.

It had been sundown when they made port, and it was well on toward full darkness now. Fellcove had very few furylamps on its streets—in fact, the town itself seemed to have none at all. The only lamps in evidence were outside of homes and businesses, doubtlessly personal property. The streets were crude mud tracks, utterly lacking the properly furycrafted stone, or even the ruder, more common cobblestones. Fellcove's filth ran through garbage-choked gutters on either side of the street, and the whole place smelled awful.

Indeed, as they proceeded into the town, Varg seemed to shrink a few inches, his shoulders hunching up even higher, his head lower and often turned aside, as if to seek some respite from the stench.

There was only one street, and it wound back and forth from the ocean up the steep side of a hill. Ehren led them to its very last winding, and to an enormous house that may at one time have looked respectable, perhaps as a residence for a magistrate or a minor Count. Now, its white stone had been stained by years of weather and sun, and most of the windows were out. What had once been a small garden in front of the house had become a patch of weeds and brambles so thick that it had strangled itself to death.

Ehren walked up to the front door of the house, drew his knife, and banged the pommel of his dagger several times upon the door. The door was cheap and weatherworn, clearly a relatively recent addition to the house, and it was marked with the shallow, round indentations of what Isana assumed had to be thousands of other people banging on it with a dagger's pommel.

For a long while, nothing happened.

"Should we let ourselves in?" Tavi asked.

"Oh crows no," Ehren said quickly. "Bad idea." He pounded on the door again. "Ibrus!" he shouted. "I need to talk to you, and I've got cash!"

Footsteps thudded on floorboards inside the house and grew louder. Shortly the door was opened by an enormous man in a food-stained shirt. He had a heavy brow, a thick neck, and something had removed an entire section of his upper lip, leaving his teeth bared in a perpetual snarl.

"Siggy," Ehren said, smiling. "Is Ibrus in?"

The big man's voice was slurred by his mangled face, but its tone was surprisingly warm and mellow. "It's late, Appius. He's told you about his hours before."

"I'm prepared to make it worth his time."

"Heard that one before," Siggy said.

Ehren tossed a pair of coins at the big man, and Isana saw the glitter of gold in the light of the single furylamp outside the front door.

"I'm prepared to make it worth his time," Ehren said in exactly the same voice as before.

"Come in," Siggy said. He pocketed the coins and led them into the entry hall, a large room obviously used as a reception area, centered around a large (and largely defunct) fountain with its own pool. The water was dark and stagnant. Siggy paused for a moment as Varg crouched to come through the door, and stared at the Cane. "Wait here. I'll go get him."

"Charming," Tavi murmured to Ehren, after Siggy had gone.

"It helps to speak the language," Ehren said.

"Appius?" Tavi asked.

"Everybody in this part of the Realm has at least two or three aliases. If you don't pick up a couple, you'll never fit in."

"This Ibrus," Tavi asked. "Can we trust him?"

"Absolutely," Ehren replied, "to do whatever benefits Ibrus most."

Tavi nodded, looking around the shadowy hall. "I don't like it. If there was any other way to secure mounts . . ."

"There isn't," Ehren said firmly.

Tavi growled beneath his breath, looking around them. "Still."

More footsteps sounded, and another light approached. Siggy bore a furylamp in one hand and a heavy cudgel in the other. A man walked beside him. He was a little taller than average and well built, his thick red hair and beard shot with grey. He wore a fine robe, much like those sported by Senators and the most pretentious of the Citizenry, though it was rumpled and stained with what Isana hoped was wine.

"Appius," Ibrus said. He yawned. "I was just finishing a rather fine evening's entertainment, and I cannot adequately express how annoying your presence is."

Isana found herself focusing more intently on Ibrus. Though the man looked and sounded both bored and mildly angry, his true emotions were considerably different.

He was tense. Afraid.

"You're a middleman, Ibrus," Ehren replied. "Everyone wants to see you in the middle of the night—or in the middle of a bonfire. There's not much in between."

"Someday your mouth is going to get you into trouble, Appius," Ibrus said darkly.

Ehren lifted a purse and jingled it. "I'd better move it to where it won't disturb you, then. I need horses."

Ibrus scowled, then rolled his eyes. "Siggy."

The big man held out his hand, and Ehren tossed him the purse. Siggy dumped the coins out in his palm, looked at them, and then dumped them back into the purse, which he handed to Ibrus with a nod.

"There's not going to be much to choose from," Ibrus warned him. "The Free Alerans were grabbing anything they could get their hands on."

"What have you got?" Ehren asked. The two men got down to haggling over horses.

As they did, Isana became increasingly aware of the discrepancy between Ibrus's manner and his actual state of mind. That was nothing unusual, really. Most people could dissemble reasonably well, in that sense. After all, it was part of being polite and showing common courtesy to others. But ever since her venture into the leviathan-haunted sea, her watercrafting senses had become increasingly fine, able to distinguish details and nuance with greater and greater clarity. Ibrus's emotions were not simply a repressed reaction he preferred not to display. He was actively worried, impatient, and increasingly frightened.

"You're expecting someone," Isana said sharply.

The conversation stopped, and every pair of eyes in the room turned to her.

She hadn't meant to say it aloud, but the die was cast. She stepped forward, locking her gaze to Ibrus's and spoke clearly. "Who are you expecting, Ibrus? Why does a simple horse trade frighten you so?"

"I have no idea what you're talking about," Ibrus replied.

Tavi's eyes narrowed. He traded a quick glance with Isana, and said, "You're sweating, Ibrus. Even though it's a lovely, cool evening."

Araris, who had become motionless once Isana began speaking, abruptly moved. His sword cleared its sheath as he spun, and the blade struck through what looked like empty air.

A spray of blue sparks and a ribbon of blood spilled forth from nowhere, splattering the floor and Ibrus's fancy robes. There was a cry of pain and a man appeared, tall, slender, dressed in mail, and bearing a sword. Araris's blade had sheared through his armor like a knife through cheese, and a long, gaping wound in the metal links was matched by the far more gruesome wound in the flesh beneath. The man went down, screaming, dropping his sword to clutch at the innards spilling from his belly.

Isana recognized the man. He had been one of Senator Arnos's *singulares*.

Which meant . . .

There was an enormous roar of shattering stone, and the wall nearest the party suddenly fell inward, toward them, shattering along the way. Isana saw Araris leap back—directly into Tavi, pushing him away from the falling stone. Araris went down underneath the fall of white marble and screamed.

Isana found herself falling backward, and realized that Kitai had seized her by the back of her dress and hauled her away from the deadly rain of marble. Ehren flung himself into a neat forward roll, toward Ibrus, and when he came to his feet again, the young Cursor sank one of his knives to the hilt in Ibrus's throat.

Siggy whirled toward him and leapt on Ehren, flattening the smaller man to the floor. He seized Ehren's throat between two huge hands, and Isana saw the young man's face turn purple.

She rolled and came to her knees, then gestured at the fountain of stagnant water and called to Rill.

A jet of water leapt from the pool and flashed across the room. It slammed into Siggy's maimed face and simply clung to his head, filling his eyes, nose, mouth, and ears. The big man released Ehren's throat in a panic, reaching up to claw uselessly at the water covering his face.

Ehren arched his body and threw Siggy off him. Before the big man could fully settle to the floor, Ehren had produced another knife and flicked its razor-sharp blade across Siggy's throat.

The man's terror flooded over Isana, layer after layer of it, like a landslide of some kind of hideous, stinking mud. It weighed her down relentlessly, magnified by her contact with the dying man, but she kept the tendril of water on his face until his movements went frantic, then suddenly slackened, his fear abruptly vanishing.

Isana released the crafting with a sob and began to struggle to her feet, calling for Tavi. Just as she did, someone smashed the furylamp, which rose up into a brief column of fire and vanished, leaving the ruined house in utter darkness.

Sparks leapt up across the room for a moment as blade met blade, showing Isana a flash image—Araris, his lower legs pinned beneath the rubble of the fallen wall, and another large, muscular man, also one of the Senator's bodyguards, standing over him with a great war hammer raised over his head.

Isana cried out. In the renewed darkness, she could not see her target, so she did the only thing she could think of. With Rill's help, she seized the entire contents of the stagnant pool and flung them in a single, coherent mass toward the man about to kill Araris.

There was an enormous slap-splashing sound and a cry of surprise. Another flash of sparks showed her the man lying dazed on the ground several feet away, and a drenched Araris choking and coughing.

Then someone with an iron grip seized her by the hair. They jerked back on her head, snapping it back to a painful angle, and then a line of fine, deadly cold settled across her throat. Isana froze in place.

Her captor and she sat motionless in the dark for a time, until finally a cold, female voice said, "Get the light back on and report."

Someone produced a pair of small furylamps and set them on the floor nearby, and Isana could see what was left.

Araris lay on the floor, still trapped from the knees down. His hands were empty and spread, and a man stood over him with the tip of a long blade resting in the hollow of Araris's throat.

The man with the huge hammer looked up from lighting the furylamps. "Aresius is dead," he said, his tone neutral. "So are both locals. We've taken two prisoners."

The woman holding Isana said, "Scipio? The Cane?"

The man with the war hammer swallowed. "Gone."

Her captor suddenly pulled hard on Isana's hair, flinging her onto her back on the ground. The tip of a sword came to rest upon her cheekbone, and Isana found herself facing Phrygiar Navaris.

Navaris looked the worse for wear. The skin of her face was peeling, badly, and looked as if it had been blistered. Her short hair was burned to a lighter color, similarly, and her hands and arms told the same tale of too much sun and the exquisitely painful consequences.

"Steadholder," Navaris murmured. "Give me one reason why I shouldn't kill both of you. Right here. Right now."

Tavi had been unable to sense anything of Ibrus's emotions as the man spoke with Ehren. That was hardly unusual. His own watercrafting senses were still somewhat clumsy, certainly in comparison to those of a real watercrafter, like his mother. But all the same, something about their situation had made him uneasy, and when his mother had confronted Ibrus, he was more than willing to back her.

Then Araris had moved, his sword screaming from its sheath and drawing blood from a man who had kept a wind-crafted veil wrapped around himself even as he slipped up closer to their group—specifically, toward Tavi.

Tavi drew his sword, but even as he did, he felt a surge of power shiver through the ground beneath him, and then the head of an all-metal war maul smashed through the nearest wall as if it had been made of beeswax. The whole wall came down, all at once under a wave of earthcrafted power, spreading out from the opening created by the blow of the hammer.

Tavi hardly registered what was happening before Araris slammed into his chest, sending him reeling back from the falling stone. The *singulare* cried out as hundreds of pounds of rock fell on him.

Tavi got to his feet just as Ehren sprinted by him. He felt a thrum of tension in the air behind him, and turned just in time to meet a descending blade with his own. Steel rang on steel, and Tavi found himself facing Phrygiar Navaris.

The woman's face was peeling, the skin red, and healing from what must have been blisters—but her eyes were still just as cold, and her sword moved in a shining blur as she instantly recovered from the parried blow and sent another attack snaking toward him.

Tavi had no time to think about defenses or lessons. Pure instinct guided his arm as he blocked a deadly combination, barely sliding out of the last attack, a cut that turned into a thrust that came slithering toward his belly. Seemingly of its own accord, his hand lashed out as Navaris leaned into the thrust, and his fist struck her in the mouth. She whipped her head aside at the last second, and the blow landed with little force—but her eyes burned with a sudden cold fury.

Tavi found himself forced back on his heels as blow after blow rained down on him. What counterattacks he could manage were weak, and Navaris slapped them aside almost contemptuously. Tavi's heart pounded in terror. He barely caught blow after blow, turning them aside by the barest of margins. Twice, Navaris's sword actually struck his mail shirt, severing rings and sending them bouncing to the ground with sharp, tinkling sounds, and if he escaped with his flesh unbroken, it seemed little more than a stroke of inordinate fortune.

Navaris howled, and her blade blurred even faster. Tavi suddenly became aware that he had fallen out of the smooth rhythm that he had instinctively grasped and used to defend himself, that Navaris's sword had begun to move more evasively, that he was losing track of its motion.

At last, he was slow to recover from a particularly strong parry, and Navaris's eyes blazed as she struck his blade aside, leaving him wide open as her sword descended for a killing stroke.

"Aleran!" Kitai cried. He saw her sword tumble by, spinning, thrown with the inordinate strength of an earthcrafter. It missed Navaris by three feet—

—and smashed into the room's sole furylamp.

The room plunged into darkness.

Tavi dropped straight down, and felt Navaris's sword pass through the air where he'd just been standing.

Navaris cursed, and he felt her slow down, trying to locate him, to feel where his sword was. Struggling went on in the darkness. Someone was thrashing around. A man shouted, and he heard the heavy thud of exchanged blows, flesh on flesh. Then Navaris hissed, and Tavi felt her sword coming at him, a disc of cold, deadly steel inscribed on his mind by the course of her blade.

The force behind the blow was terrible, both physically and in the weight of furycraft behind it, infusing the steel with all the strength of her mad will. Tavi would have to meet that strength with his own, or Navaris's sword would shatter Tavi's—and Tavi would find himself shattered shortly after.

He spun, putting his strength and weight behind his blade, swinging in a stroke that would meet Navaris's squarely, furiously focused on his own sword.

The blades met. Steel chimed on steel, a note that was high and pure and piercing. A blinding shower of sparks erupted from the meeting blades, and Tavi saw a frozen image of the room: Navaris, her teeth clenched in hate. Kitai, bleeding from a split lip, struggling with an armored man for possession of a sword. Isana, kneeling, her expression colder and more terrible than he would have believed possible, a hand extended toward a man who thrashed on the ground, his face completely covered by a blob of dirty water.

Then the darkness returned, and Tavi moved a few steps to one side before freezing again. He clenched his teeth in frustration. The others needed his help, but he didn't dare move toward them. The sound would have told Navaris precisely where he stood, and if he didn't have every bit of his attention focused on her, he'd never be able to defeat her attack.

Again, Navaris's sword came at him, and again, he met it with his own. In the flash of contact, he saw the other armored man flying back through the air and Varg standing over Kitai, his arms extended. Ehren lay unmoving on the floor. Araris's body was arched up in effort, or in pain, as he struggled to free his legs from the rubble.

Tavi took two steps back and froze again, mentally cursing, as he desperately sought Navaris's next attack.

He was utterly unprepared when an enormous hand landed on his shoulder, and only the sudden rusty-musty scent of the Cane's fur prevented him from turning and thrusting in sheer panic.

"Aleran," Varg growled. "It is over. Come with me."

"Go," Tavi whispered.

Varg kept his paw-hand on Tavi's shoulder, roughly directing him. Tavi had to put his trust in the Cane's guidance. If he felt his way along with tentative steps, Navaris could close the distance and kill him—but without someone to guide her own feet, she wouldn't dare rush after him blind. So Tavi broke into a run and trusted Varg to guide his steps.

They emerged into the comparative brightness of the outdoors, and Kitai was coming hard behind them, weaponless, carrying Ehren slung over one of her shoulders.

Tavi took the lead, taking them around the corner of the house, where they would be out of sight of the house's entrance.

"Ehren," Tavi breathed.

Kitai put him down carefully, supporting his mostly limp weight. The little Cursor sucked in his breath as if through a tiny reed, a strangled rattle accompanying it. There were bruises on his throat that were already darkening, and it was entirely possible his windpipe had been crushed. His eyes were glazed and unfocused, while his chest labored to bring in enough air.

"What do we do?" Kitai asked.

"He needs a watercrafter," Tavi said.

Varg knelt down in front of Ehren and peered at his throat. Then he growled, "Give me a quill."

"What?" Tavi asked.

Kitai slung her pack off and reached into it. She opened the pack and produced a writing quill.

Varg took it, and with a quick motion of his claws snipped the quill about two inches from its end. He held it up to the light and squinted at it.

Then he reached down with a single claw and ripped open Ehren's throat.

Tavi cried out, reaching for Varg's wrist. The Cane growled, and said, "There is no time for this."

Tavi stared at Varg for a moment, then leaned back on his heels, and nodded once.

Varg leaned down and thrust a claw into the open wound. Then, his motions delicate in one so large, he thrust the quill into the cut.

Ehren shuddered and drew in a sudden, deep breath. It hissed through the hollow quill, and then hissed again as he exhaled. His breathing slowed and steadied. He blinked his eyes several times, focusing slowly.

"It is dirty," Varg rumbled. "But there was no time to clean it before he would have died. Perhaps your sorceries can cleanse the wound, later." He took Ehren's hand and lifted his fingers to the protruding end of the quill. "Hold this in. If it comes out, you die."

Ehren, pain in his expression, stared up at the Cane and nodded.

"We must go back for them," Kitai whispered.

Tavi held up his hand and whispered back. "We've only got one sword among us, and they have hostages. If we go in again, they'll use Araris and Isana against us. Assuming they don't kill them out of hand."

Kitai bared her teeth in a silent snarl of frustration.

Tavi chewed on his lip, thinking furiously. Then he nodded and looked at Varg. "Ibrus said he had horses. They must be close. Take these two and find them."

"You can't go back alone," Kitai hissed.

Tavi met her eyes, and said, "We aren't going to be able to take them back by force. And whatever happens, we'll need the horses—who won't let Varg handle them. Ehren can't do it either. So go. Now."

Kitai scowled furiously at him, but then she rose and offered Ehren a hand up. Varg lifted his head, sniffed the air for a few seconds, and started off at a shambling lope. Kitai, staying close to Ehren, followed the Cane.

Tavi took off his belt, bent over at the waist, and wriggled out of his mail shirt, letting it fall to the ground. Though it would have provided him some protection in the event of a fight, it also would make noise when he moved. For the moment, stealth was at a premium.

He buckled his sword belt on again and stalked through the darkness back to Ibrus's house, creeping forward until he crouched beneath one of the broken windows outside of the entry hall. There were two small furylamps inside, casting a dim red-orange glow.

"Steadholder," Navaris murmured, as Tavi approached.

"Give me one reason why I shouldn't kill both of you. Right here. Right now."

Tavi's stomach got a sick, sinking feeling. He put his hand on his sword. If it came to that, he would attack them before he stood by and let them kill his mother and his friend.

"Did you hear me, Steadholder?" Navaris said. "This isn't a rhetorical question. If there is some reason I should leave you alive, you should tell me."

Tavi drew the blade perhaps two inches from its sheath.

"I suppose that depends," Isana responded. Her voice was steady, confident.

Tavi froze again.

"Upon what?" Navaris asked.

"How loyal you are to the Senator."

Silence.

"I know who he serves," Isana continued. "Invidia Aquitaine is, in fact, my patron, too. I doubt she'll thank Arnos for interfering in my work. I shudder to think of her reaction should he actually eliminate me."

More silence.

"I spent nearly a year campaigning for the abolition of slavery for Lady Aquitaine and the Dianic League," Isana replied. "And the last six months I've been visiting members of the League raising funds and supplies for the refugee camps. The wives of every Count, Lord, and High Lord from here to Riva have met with me, given me money—and know I was coming to the Elinarch. Are you *sure* he's willing to be implicated in my death?"

"You're lying," the cutter said.

"Can you afford to assume that?" Isana's tone turned frank. "Do you want to make that decision for him, Navaris?"

Tavi felt his mouth stretch into a grin.

"And the *singulare*?" Navaris asked. "Why should I spare him?"

"Scipio is his friend," Isana replied. "Dead, he's of no further use to you. Alive, he's a hostage."

"Dead, he's of no further threat to me, either," Navaris murmured.

"I can't argue with that," Isana said. "I'd be afraid of him, too. Particularly if I was you."

Navaris's voice turned very quiet. "Particularly?"

"Yes. It must be difficult for you in some ways. After all, you've won more duels than Araris Valerian ever fought. You've certainly killed many more armed foes than he ever did. Yet I should think that you've lived your whole life in his shadow. He has such a name, after all. No matter how many times you prove it, he'll still be the best in everyone's mind." She let that sink in for a moment before she said, "If you fight him and lose, well. That would prove it for certain."

Tavi edged up enough to be able just barely to see in the window. Isana sat on the floor between two corpses—Ibrus and his enforcer—and in front of Navaris, as composed as if she was having tea in the capital. Araris was still pinned under the rubble, and one of Arnos's *singulares* was standing over him, a sword to his throat.

Isana was focused intently on Navaris, and Tavi suddenly realized that it was because she was reading Navaris's reactions to her words, using her watercraft to judge exactly what to say to the cutter, to discern what would motivate her.

"Of course," Isana added, leaning forward slightly, "if you kill him here, you'll never have the chance to beat him. You'll never be able to prove beyond all doubt that you're the greatest sword in Alera. Whereas if you return him to your master alive, he'll most likely order you to dispose of him in any case."

Navaris stared down at Isana, frozen, her eyes remote.

"You're better than he is, Navaris," Isana said. "You pinned him against the hull of the *Mactis* like an insect, and if he hadn't run, it would be over. You know you'll beat him if you fight him. Why not give yourself a chance to wipe his name away and replace it with yours?" Isana frowned slightly, and Tavi heard a note of sympathy enter her voice, a bit of sadness touch her eyes. "What else do you have?"

Navaris's nostrils flared, and her right hand suddenly trembled, fluttering at the end of her wrist. Tension entered her lean frame, and her breathing sped up for several seconds.

Then she seemed to slump in place. Her eyelids lowered,

half-closing. "Tandus," she murmured. "Armenius. Bind them. We'll bring them with us."

The huge man whose hammer had smashed the wall nodded and bent down over Araris, levering the *singulare's* hands behind his back and binding them with a heavy leather cord.

The other swordsman shook his head. "We're not going after Scipio?"

"His name isn't Scipio," Navaris said quietly. "It's Tavi of Calderon." She moved abruptly, striking Isana on the cheek with the back of one hand with stunning force, knocking Tavi's mother to the floor.

Tavi's fist clenched on his sword, but he controlled the sudden surge of rage and remained still and hidden in the deep shadows cast by the little furylamps.

"And we won't have to go after him," Navaris murmured quietly. "He'll be coming after us."

ⅨᏅᏅᐧCHAPTER 44

The plan was working perfectly, and that made Amara nervous.

An evening and morning practicing under Gaius's tutelage had drastically expanded Amara's ability to craft a veil. It was not so much a matter of learning something new as it was of being presented with techniques she was already familiar with in new ways. Gaius seemed to have an instinctive knack for picking out the strengths and weaknesses of her crafting, and showed her how to apply the stronger aspects of her personal talents in a new way.

By the time the sun was high, Amara was holding a veil nearly ten feet across, with only a little more effort than it took to fly.

"Excellent," Gaius said, smiling. "I believe Maestro Vircani must have been your windcrafting instructor."

"Yes," Amara said, smiling. She had never imagined herself managing a veil so large with such comparative ease. "Yes, he was. He thought very little of my work, too. Except for the flying."

"Small-minded old goat," Gaius murmured, suppressing another cough. "He was of the school of thought that held that any furycrafting concept worth employing was already being employed, and therefore there was no need to teach multiple approaches to any given task since the one that he knew was already good enough."

"I just never thought thinking of light as a windstream," Amara said. "Only bending it, like for a farseeing. I can concentrate on windstreams all day."

"Furycrafting is as much about imagination as concentration," Gaius murmured. "Bear that in mind when you try anything new in your crafting, Countess. Imagination. Different ways of visualizing your goal. It wouldn't startle me in the least to see you manage quite a respectable level of weather-crafting, should you wish it."

Amara blinked at him. "Really?"

"Certainly."

Bernard murmured, "A breeze to blow away some of these bugs might be nice." He squinted through the grass at the patrolled area. "I'm still not sure we shouldn't do this at night."

"Of course we should do it at night," Amara said. "And that's when they'll expect anyone to try to sneak through their pickets. They'll have more men on duty, and they'll be more alert—whereas if we move through during the day, the men will be less cautious and more likely to be distracted."

Bernard frowned and nodded. "But if one of them does notice us, they'll have awfully nice light for shooting."

"And we'll have nice light for running away—unless you prefer to flee through strange country in the dark."

Her husband's mouth twisted sourly. "I suppose there's no good way to do this, is there?"

"Precisely," Gaius murmured wearily.

Bernard nodded. "Then now is as good a time as any."

"All right," Amara breathed.

Bernard took up Gaius's stretcher and nodded at Amara.

Then he half closed his eyes, and the ground beneath her feet quivered for a moment, a pulse of movement that she could barely detect. A moment later, it repeated, at the pace of a sleeping man's heartbeat.

Amara murmured to Cirrus and felt the light around them change subtly as she brought up the veil. Everything outside the veil blurred, colors twisting and overlapping, shapes softening to mere blobs of color. It was one of the things that made a windcrafter's veil different from one crafted with wood furies. The woodcrafted veil hid and concealed, as long as there were shadows and vegetable shapes to manipulate. The air veil needed no such condition—but it did limit the amount of light that could pass through it, making the world outside the veil look like something seen through poor glass, or murky seawater.

"There," Amara said quietly. "Bernard?"

"Ready," he said.

And they started toward the enemy positions, with Amara in the lead. It took them most of the afternoon to reach the edges of the swamp, where the ground began to rise. Amara almost wanted to hold her breath as they approached the first concealed position. They passed by it, close enough to smell the smoke from a campfire—and to smell the aroma of freshly baked bread. Amara's stomach practically leapt from beneath her belt, and even Gaius looked a little wistful.

It wasn't for another several steps that Amara saw the dogs, great rangy beasts, outside the camp. They were sprawled in the sunshine, asleep, and likely to stay that way under the gentle, slow pulse of Bernard's earthcrafting.

And then they were past the outpost, with their foe none the wiser.

The second watch post was much the same. They walked slowly, steadily by the tree supporting the observation blinds, and no one seemed to detect them. They kept up the same slow, careful pace for several hundred more blessedly dry, firm-grounded yards, uphill all the way.

It couldn't be that simple, could it? Amara had imagined dozens of ways for their efforts to go disastrously awry, but none of them had come to pass. Something had to go wrong.

Something always went wrong. Yet nothing had, and it made her nervous.

A fresh breeze hit them, clean air that smelled of pine, and Amara felt like singing.

And then hunting horns began blowing behind them.

She and Bernard whirled to look back at the swamps, and Bernard cursed. "One of their patrols must have swept by and found our trail. They'll be coming."

Amara felt obliquely reassured by the sudden dour turn of events. Certainly, it meant that a great many madmen were shortly to be pelting after them, determined to wipe them out—but at least she was in a familiar element.

"Very well. Our options?"

"Limited," Gaius said, and coughed some more.

"I can't erase our trail and still carry the stretcher," Bernard said. "We should run for the mountains. Dark's coming on. If we're still free by then, it should give us enough time to get Gaius close enough."

Amara nodded. "Then we run."

She turned and began jogging forward, up the hill, disdaining the windcrafted veil. The enemy already knew they were here. The veil would just be a drain of energy that could better be used to keep moving. Bernard kept up with her, even bearing Gaius's stretcher, though he breathed heavily as they ran.

The land rose steadily, the willows and fronds of the swamps dying away, replaced by fir and pine. The hunting horns kept sounding behind them, and Amara thought she could hear them coming steadily closer.

Amara had never particularly loved running, but the weeks of travel had done somewhat to harden her for the pace, and a gentle effort to guide Cirrus ensured that she never ran short of breath. As a result, her muscles didn't begin burning until well into the first hour, and she kept the pace quick and steady. The ankle the garim had injured twinged several times, and she took care to place her foot carefully; but evidently she'd had enough time to recover from the injury, and she was able to keep the pace she had set for them.

Bernard lumbered along behind her, implacably moving

ahead despite his burden, and though his breathing was labored, his steps never faltered.

Amara found a smooth track leading up toward the mountains and followed it, her shadow lengthening on the hillside in front of her as the sun set behind them. She kept running for another half hour, and felt her arms and legs beginning to shake with weariness.

That was when they heard the hunting horns being blown ahead of them as well as behind. Amara slowed up, looking over her shoulder at Bernard.

"Aye," Bernard panted. "Surprised it took them this long." He came to a halt, breathing heavily, and Amara wished she could send Cirrus to ease his breathing as well—but without being able to sense the changing pressures, the way she sensed her own breathing, she could inflict a number of forms of injury on him, ranging from the inconvenient to the excruciating.

Bernard glanced around, frowning in thought, as he settled the stretcher on the ground, staring up the slope toward the mountains, golden in the setting sun. "They're moving fast. Mounted. We've only got a few minutes." He reached into the stretcher, murmured, "Excuse me, sire," and drew out his bow.

"Mounted," Amara murmured. She went to check on Gaius as Bernard strung his bow. The First Lord was pale with pain. He gave Amara a faint smile, and said, "I hardly have the right to say it, but I th-think I've had enough running today."

"Just rest," Amara said. She dragged the stretcher as gently as she could to one side, under the shelter of some pine branches. Then she went to her husband. "I need to know something."

"Yes," Bernard said. "I was serious when I said I'd never done that with any woman but you."

She slapped his shoulder lightly. "Mind on business, Count Calderon. You can calm animals. Can you uncalm them, too?"

He grimaced. "Spook their horses? Hate to do it. Horses are big, strong animals. Get them scared enough, they can hurt themselves pretty bad."

"They're coming to kill us," Amara pointed out.

"The riders are. I doubt the horses have strong feelings one way or the other."

Amara stopped and stared at him for a moment, smiling faintly. "You can strike down enemy Knights, shoot furious High Lords from the sky, make war on creatures out of nightmares, and fight garim the size of ponies three at a time without flinching. But you don't want to frighten horses."

Bernard looked at something of a loss. He spread his hands, and said, "I *like* horses."

She leaned over and kissed him. Then she said, "I need you to do it."

He winced but nodded.

"Can you tell how many are coming?" she asked.

He jerked his head in a nod and rested his fingertips lightly on the ground. "Eight," he reported after a moment. "There's another group several miles behind them. Much larger."

"Then the first eight are the men who were on duty. The others, perhaps, the men who had been sleeping."

"Yes, dear." Bernard sighed, a smile lurking at the corners of his mouth. "You were right."

Amara peered at the falling sun. "I want to hit them and take two of their horses. Mounted, in the dark, we can get farther."

"And the horses will know their way back to their stables," Bernard said. He glanced toward the First Lord's stretcher. "He can't ride. And in the dark, on this terrain, there's no way we can sling the stretcher between our mounts."

"We don't need to," Amara said. "Remember how you pulled me, back at Second Calderon?"

Bernard grinned suddenly. Amara had been too weary for full flight, and the skies had been heavily patrolled by the enemy. To catch a group of men they'd been pursuing, he'd used his intimate knowledge of the valley's furies to travel on a ripple of moving earth, a feat that only someone with such knowledge could manage. Amara could never have kept the pace, and so she had crafted a cushion of air to lift her from the ground and had held on to a tether fastened to Bernard's belt.

"Might work," he said. "But it will be loud."

"Not as much as you'd think. I can suppress some of it."

"How long can you sustain it?" Bernard asked.

"As long as I need to."

Horns sounded again, upslope, and were answered distantly from behind them. This time, Amara actually caught a flash of movement in the trees.

"All right," she said quietly. "This is what I want to do."

The first rider to come plunging down the trail never had a chance. Amara dropped her veil when he was twenty feet away, and by the time he saw Bernard standing with his great bow drawn tight, it was too late for him to avoid the shot. The Count of Calderon's arrow took him in the bridge of his nose and lifted him from the back of his horse as if struck with a lance. A flash of silver collar proclaimed the man one of the Immortals.

The second rider shouted and lifted his spear, but could do no more before Amara settled a veil around *him*, blotting him from sight and half-blinding him. The man hesitated, slowing, and the horse of the rider immediately behind him crashed into him, screaming in sudden fear at the scent of hot blood.

Horses and men went sprawling, and the equine screams abruptly rose in pitch and volume. Animals bucked and thrashed in pure panic, under Bernard's earthcrafting, sending some of the Immortals sprawling to the ground while others clung to their inexplicably hysterical mounts and were carried in every direction.

Bernard wasted no time. A dismounted Immortal rose, weapon in hand, his eyes gleaming with exaltation as he turned toward his prey. Another arrow slammed into his head, felling him instantly. A third Immortal raised a circular steel shield to protect his face as he charged. Bernard shot him through the thigh, breaking the bone that supported it, and the Immortal went down in a sprawl. Before he could recover, Bernard put a second arrow through his neck in a fountain of gore. The man staggered to his feet despite the horrible wounds, took two wobbling steps forward, and then sank to the earth and was still.

Amara did not dare close with the remaining Immortal on

the ground. She was not entirely unskilled at swordplay, but she was no match for one of Kalare's manufactured madmen and doubted she could kill him without being slain or badly injured herself.

So with a flick of her hand, she dropped the veil that was hampering him and sent Cirrus surging around the Immortal's face and head to cut off his air.

The man staggered forward, sword raised, and Amara kept her own weapon in hand—but she circled away from him nimbly, carefully keeping the distance between them open. The Immortal's face turned pink. Then red. His steps began to falter. His face went purple. At the last, his lips were blue, his chest heaving desperately. Amara could feel him, through Cirrus, struggling vainly to draw a breath.

Then he simply dropped, eyes staring sightlessly, and struggled to breathe no more.

Amara stared at him blankly for a moment.

Then she retched onto the ground in front of her.

She remained there, head bowed forward, hands resting on her knees, and tried to get herself under control.

Bernard's hand touched her shoulder.

"I've . . ." she gasped. "I've never . . . I mean, I learned how, but I've never . . . I thought he would black out, and I could let him go, but he just kept *fighting* . . ."

His fingers tightened on her arm, gentle.

"Bloody crows," she whispered. "That's an ugly way to kill a man."

Bernard withdrew his hand and offered her his water flask. "Love," he said quietly. "Time."

The hunting horns behind them sounded again.

Amara squeezed her eyes shut, nodded once, and straightened. She took the flask, washed the horrible taste out of her mouth, and then drank. As she did, Bernard moved slowly forward, toward the two horses he'd excluded from his crafting—the two lead horses, who were presumably the fastest of the group. Bernard spoke gently, and once again Amara felt the slow, steady pulse of a soothing earthcrafting. Within a minute, he had the reins of both animals, and led them to her.

Amara mounted up while Bernard drew Gaius's stretcher

out of its concealment, then tied one end of a line to it, the other to the saddle of Amara's mount.

Amara turned, focusing on the stretcher, murmuring wordlessly as she willed Cirrus to lift it from the ground. Within seconds, a small whirlwind had gathered beneath Gaius's stretcher, lifting it perhaps eighteen inches above the earth.

This time Bernard took the lead, veiling them as they rode through the darkening wood. Amara followed, dragging the stretcher on its miniature cyclone behind them to wipe away whatever trail they left behind. It wouldn't prevent Kalarus's men from tracking them, but it *would* conceal their numbers and the pace they set, denying the enemy information that might help them make intelligent choices in the pursuit. It would also force them to slow down if they wanted to keep the trail, especially after night fell.

Shadows began to fall as Bernard led the horses north, off the trail and into the thickening forest. He turned east, toward the mountains, in a gradual arc, and all the while the horns of the Immortals sounded in the gloom around them.

Evening turned to dusk turned to twilight. Terrain that had been difficult in dim light became treacherous in the dark, and Bernard slowed them down, allowing the horses to pick their way forward. The night began to turn cold. The strain of all the travel, of the run, of her ongoing furycraft to support the stretcher began to tell on Amara, and she found herself shuddering with cold and exhaustion.

She very badly wanted to sleep. She very badly wanted to fall off the horse and lie still. But she clung grimly to the saddle and stayed upright for what felt like a week. Then a month. Then a year.

And then the horses emerged from the pines, and Bernard let out a grunt of satisfaction.

Amara lifted her eyes. In the starlight, she could see very little, despite the hours her eyes had been given to adjust. It was as if half the stars were simply blotted away—or, she realized, overcast with clouds. She wearily hoped that it wasn't about to start raining, too.

Then she realized what she was looking at, and her heart leapt.

The Kalare Mountains. They rose above them in silent, stark majesty, their enormous peaks casting a shadow over half the starry sky.

Bernard murmured in the darkness, "There's not enough flora for me to veil us along that trail. From here on out, if we're seen, we're out of options. You want to do this fast or slow?"

Amara's teeth were chattering, but she managed to say, "Fast. I'm almost done."

Bernard took a deep breath, nodded once, and said, "Here we go."

Then he kicked his weary horse forward into a listless canter, and Amara followed suit. They hurried up the trail in the dark, and Amara began to feel nervous again. It took her several moments, until they were riding over a level patch of trail that must have been the first pass through the mountains, to realize why.

The Immortals' hunting horns had ceased to blow.

Light hit them first, painful in the mountain night. The horses, too tired to truly panic, threw back their heads and danced nervously. Amara raised a hand, trying to block the painful glare—the great furylamps sometimes used in sieges, surely—and felt Cirrus suddenly falter.

The First Lord's stretcher crashed to the ground.

She sagged in her saddle, saw someone approaching on her right side, and kicked weakly with her right leg. She hit something, but a grip like stone seized her ankle and dragged her off the horse and to the ground.

Bernard roared, and she heard his bow hum. She turned her head enough to see an Immortal stricken cleanly through one lung with her husband's arrow. The man never slowed his pace, seizing Bernard's belt and hauling him to the ground. Bernard turned as he fell, and seized the Immortal, reaching for his throat with fury-borne strength.

The Immortal seized Bernard's hands . . .

. . . and slowly, steadily forced them away.

Bloody crows.

Immortal Knights.

Bernard's eyes widened, and he clenched his teeth in desperate effort, but to no avail. The Immortal twisted suddenly and threw Amara's husband face-first to the ground, rapidly secured a lock on one of his arms, and dislocated his shoulder with a single savage motion.

Bernard screamed.

Amara became aware of more men, then, all fully armored, all bearing the shining steel collar of the Immortals. She looked around dully. Indeed, the light had come from enormous fury-lamps which must have been moved up by teams of horses long before. Armored men were everywhere. Not twenty, or thirty, or fifty, but *hundreds*. All of them Immortals—and led by Knights.

Footsteps crunched over the cold, stony ground. Several gauntlets banged to armored chests. A pair of boots appeared before Amara's eyes, and she looked up.

A young man stood over her. He was a little taller than average, very thin, and dirty. There was something ugly in his eyes, lurking behind contempt and rage and a certain amount of petulance. It took Amara's stunned and weary mind a moment to place the young officer—Kalarus Brencis Minoris, the High Lord Kalarus's son and heir.

"I can't believe this," the young man said. "*This* is the elite team of soldiers First Lord Has-Been sent down with the north wind? *This* is what Father's had me slogging all over the bloody swamps for?"

Brencis shook his head with disbelief and, almost idly, struck Amara across the face with his mailed hand. Pain made her world go white. She felt her neck wrench as it twisted sharply to one side under the force of the blow.

"I could have been sleeping in a *bed*," Brencis snarled. "And instead I'm out here frozen to the balls and bored out of my mind, setting up the trap, worried about a whole cohort of Knights sneaking in the back door, and for *what*?"

Amara tasted blood on her tongue. She lifted her head dizzily.

Brencis spat. It struck her cheek.

"I'm here for *this*?" he snarled. He seized Amara by the hair, baring her throat, and drew his dagger in his other hand. "For two pathetic little sneaks? Two of you? *Two!*"

Light hit them first.

It washed over Amara's back and shoulders in a sudden wave of warmth and color, as if someone had convinced the setting sun to reverse its course and rise once again over the mountainside behind them. The light cast knife-sharp black shadows over the entire mountain, its luminance so brilliant that the glare of the enormous furylamps became utterly insignificant.

Immortals, Knights, and infantry alike, cried out in surprise. Brencis turned white, took a step backward, and lifted a hand to shield his eyes, releasing Amara and letting out a low moan of fear.

And then came a voice.

A voice spoke in a gentle tone that resounded from the stone and the sky, a voice that rang with a depth and richness of power the mountains had not known since their fiery conception—a voice that contained a certain amount of biting amusement as it answered the heir of Kalare's question.

Gaius Sextus, First Lord of Alera, murmured, "Three."

·ᑯᑯᑯᑯᑯ·CHAPTER 45

Reverberations of Gaius's deep, mellow voice rolled through the mountains and echoed from the hills. Though he had spoken in a murmur, it emanated from the very stones, and Amara felt sure it could have been heard several miles away in every direction.

In the wake of that voice, the brilliantly lit mountainside went totally still and silent. Hundreds of Immortals remained motionless in their tracks, shielding their eyes and crouching defensively. Brencis stared past Amara, his mouth gaping and working like that of a landed fish.

The Knight holding Bernard had backed away when Brencis did, and the Count of Calderon slowly sat up, his face white with pain, his shoulder resting at an odd angle to the rest of his body. He traded a glance with Amara, but neither of them spoke, not daring to draw the attention of the enemy to themselves.

It was odd, Amara thought, sitting there on the stony mountainside, exhausted, outnumbered hundreds to one by their foes—and yet for a single, endless moment no one moved, and no one spoke.

And then Brencis let out a sound partway between a scream and a moan, and yelled, his voice cracking into a falsetto in midword, "Attack! Attack! Kill them all!"

The moment was broken.

Hundreds of collared Immortals let out a furious cry and steel rasped in a deadly chorus as they drew weapons. They surged forward, the sound of their boots a sudden thunder.

Amara found herself at Bernard's side, unarmed and far too weary to take to the air. She felt his hand fumbling for hers, as the Immortals came for them, and she interlaced her fingers with his, squeezing tight.

They both looked away from the charging Immortals, at one another, and that was how Amara saw the First Lord, in the corner of her vision, raise a hand and murmur another bone-deep word that rose from the very mountain beneath them.

"No."

There was a sudden noise, lower than the cries of charging Immortals, more piercing than the tread of their boots. It was a rippling staccato of a sound, somewhat like a saw going through wood.

Amara turned to stare as every Immortal, *every single* Immortal on the mountainside suddenly convulsed. Their necks twisted sharply, and the snapping bones were the source of the strange sound.

And then they fell dead.

All of them.

One second, a force the size of two or three Legion cohorts was howling for their blood. The next, the Immortals lay on the ground, twitching and dying, the strange metal collars now bent and misshapen, all deformed so sharply and suddenly that they had broken the necks of the men wearing them.

Amara turned to stare.

Gaius Sextus hovered perhaps ten feet above the mountainside, buoyed by a windstream so tightly controlled that it hardly stirred the dirt beneath him. He was wreathed in the orange-gold flame of an autumn sunset that turned his silver-white hair to bronze. The signs of strain and age that had come on as they traveled were gone. In his right hand was a sword of fire, and fire blazed on his brow in a blinding diadem. His eyes were bright and hard, his face hewn from granite, and such was the majesty and power of him that Amara found herself immediately bowing her head, her hand pressed to her hammering heart.

Behind her, Amara heard Brencis sob in terror. And then she heard the unsteady rasp of a sword being drawn into a trembling hand.

"Boy," Gaius said, his tone growing gentler, even compassionate, "you have a choice. You may choose to stand with your father against me. Or you may choose to live."

Brencis let out a few small, breathless sounds. Then he said, "I'm not afraid of you."

"Of course you are," Gaius said, "and should be."

And with those words, a blue-white shaft of lightning roared down from the clear night sky, and gouged a hole the size of a grave in the solid stone not five yards from Brencis's feet.

"I give you one final chance to live," Gaius said, and his voice was no longer gentle. "Choose."

Brencis sobbed, and his sword clattered to the stony ground. He turned and fled, his boots sliding and scuffing over the mountainside, vanishing into the distance.

Amara rose slowly, afterward, and had to help Bernard rise with her.

"Well," Gaius said quietly. "That's a relief." And with that, he dropped without ceremony to the ground. The blazing light around him—and the light of the furylamps on the mountain—vanished in the same moment.

"A relief, sire?" Amara asked.

Gaius's voice, from the darkness, sounded calmly weary. "By all accounts, young Brencis is quite capable at his furycraft—and I have enough to do tonight without putting him down, too."

"Sire?" Amara asked.

"Surely," Bernard said, his voice strained, "after killing so many men, one more . . ."

Gaius murmured something, and one of the furylamps began to give off a much-reduced amount of light, enough to let Amara dimly see the First Lord as a vague, tall shape, standing over one of the fallen Immortals. "These," he murmured. "These were not men. Men have wills, good Count. Men have choice."

His eyes turned toward Amara for a quiet moment, pausing just long enough to give his last words a subtle weight.

"Kalarus raised these creatures from childhood bound to these accursed collars," Gaius continued. "He took their wills, their choices, away from them. The men they could have been died long before tonight. These were animals.

"What he did was terrible, yet I cannot help but wish he'd done it to more of his *legionares*. Today would be much simplified." The First Lord's voice tightened, quickened. "Let us count ourselves fortunate that Kalarus had the collars all made from the same batch."

Amara blinked at him. "You mean . . . the Immortals could have . . . ?"

"Killed me?" Gaius asked. He shrugged a shoulder. "Perhaps. In some ways, I am no more powerful than any other High Lord."

Amara blinked. "But, sire . . . what I saw a moment ago . . ."

"One needn't be omnipotent to overcome every foe, provided one can appear that way in the enemy's mind." He smiled faintly. "True, I have the means to have slain them all—but accidents happen, and the weight of numbers could tell against me just as surely as they did against my s—" His voice broke. He closed his eyes, cleared his throat, and rasped, "My son."

Amara faced Gaius, silent, watching his face. Not even his discipline could hide the pain in his features, and Amara suddenly ached for the old man.

Gaius shook his head briskly and strode toward Amara and Bernard. He put one hand on her shoulder, another on Bernard's.

Bernard let out a hiss of discomfort—then there was a wrenching pop that dragged a muffled curse from his throat.

"There," Gaius murmured. "Try to move it."

Bernard did, rotating his wounded shoulder slowly. "Tender," he said after a moment. "But it will serve, sire."

Gaius nodded and squeezed Amara's shoulder gently. In that simple gesture, relief and energy seemed to flood into her, weariness washed away before it. She shuddered at the pleasant sensation left when her aches and fatigue vanished.

"Look there," Gaius murmured, and nodded to the east.

Amara looked. Dozens, even hundreds of green streamers of light flickered through the sky, rising from the earth in wavering lines, almost like luminous smoke. They were spaced miles apart in a regular grid.

"Kalarus's sentinel craftings," Gaius murmured. "He knows where I am. And I daresay he's deduced my goal. Right now, Kalarus is gathering every Knight under his command and ordering every *legionare* in his forces to intercept us, so we have little time."

Amara jerked her head in a nod. "What would you have us do?"

Gaius looked back and forth between them. "Guard my back. I should hate to make you walk all this way only to take an arrow in the kidneys when we've all but reached the finish line."

Drums rumbled from farther up the pass. A low moan drifted through the rocks, the faint, basso precursor to a Legion marching song that must shortly follow.

"Sire," Bernard cautioned. "I'm not sure what I can do against numbers like that."

"His forces are spread out in the field, and he has far fewer Knights and *legionares* at hand than he might," Gaius said. "Which was rather the point of this stealth business, yes?"

"True enough, sire," Bernard said. "But fifty thousand or five thousand makes little difference to me."

"I see your point. You need only concern yourselves with his Knights. The others will not be an obstacle."

Amara drew in her breath suddenly. "I understand."

Gaius nodded, eyes sparkling briefly. "You would."

The marching song of a Kalaran Legion became discernible across the mountainside.

Gaius turned to face upslope, narrowed his eyes, and raised his right hand above his head. There was a flash, and then a rippling tongue of fire licked up from his fingers. He closed his hand on the hilt of a sword made of stationary flame.

Amara recovered her sword and hurried to his side. Bernard followed suit, setting an arrow to his bow.

In the pass above, a second body of troops appeared—several cohorts of *legionares*, marching together in a swift, cohesive formation. The Kalaran Legion pressed forward at a quick step, moving steadily toward Gaius's blazing blade.

"Stay behind me," Gaius cautioned them. "Directly behind me."

And then, with a cry of challenge, the suicidally outnumbered First Lord and his retainers charged the oncoming Legion.

⚬ CHAPTER 46

In two years of fighting since the Battle of the Elinarch, Marcus and the First Aleran had never seen the Canim resort to the use of their bizarre sorceries. In the absence of other evidence, they had concluded that the enemy's ability to use them had died with Sarl and the majority of his ritualist compatriots.

The conclusion was incorrect.

The first shock of the Canim charge was repelled by the massed ranks of the three Aleran Legions. The palisade wall was a light defensive emplacement, as such things were reckoned, but it was critical that the outer wall hold until the engineers could fortify the partial wall remaining around the ruined town at the crown of the hill.

"Now we know why they didn't fortify the ruin," Crassus murmured.

"Why do our work for us?" Marcus grunted. He raised his voice, and shouted, "Third Cohort, dress those ranks!"

The Canim had withdrawn in good order after their first charge, but a second and larger force of raiders was already in position. In two years, Nasaug had drilled his own conscripts into something that resembled an actual military force, and the mass movements of the raiders, which had originally been slow, confused, almost tidal, had become disciplined and precise.

Their armament had changed as well, Marcus noted. They had taken the handheld scything swords (originally harvesting implements, for goodness' sake) the Canim raiders had used and mounted them on thick wooden shafts, effectively changing what had been a close-fighting implement into a weapon with far greater reach, one more suited to assaulting a defended position.

Marcus watched the assault coming and felt his heart pounding in fear as the oncoming Canim let out howls and bellowed battle cries. The raiders smashed into the palisade like a living tide of muscle and steel. The Canim raiders fought with far more skill and tenacity than they had at the Battle of the Elinarch, and the new hafted weaponry proved deadly.

Over and over, Marcus saw the same brief, hideous tableau repeated: A Cane raider would swing his hafted scythe overhead and straight down in a smashing, two-handed blow. The tip of the scythe would land hard against the top of a *legionare's* helmet, and with the power and weight and leverage of a full-sized Cane behind the blow, the tip of the simple weapon would pierce even Aleran steel, straight down through the top of the helmet and into the skull of the doomed *legionare* beneath.

It was a deadly tactic. The foe could adjust his aim with relative ease, and there was no practical way for a *legionare* fighting in close formation to dodge the diving tip of the Canim scythes.

Marcus brought his own shield up in time to catch the inner edge of a scythe falling toward his skull, and dropped to one knee. The scythe's edge managed to carve straight down through the steel of his shield, despite the strength of the standard Legion battlecraft that strengthened it. Marcus grunted, summoning strength from the earth to twist the shield, trapping the weapon, and with a powerful blow of his *gladius*, he parted the wooden haft from the scythe head, drove a wounding blow into the Cane before him, and fell back, trying to clear the weapon head from his shield while another *legionare* shouldered into his position—and was promptly felled by a falling scythe as the Cane Marcus had wounded was replaced just as swiftly as he had been.

After that, it became a desperate nightmare of a battle. The Legion spears were not long enough to outreach the Canim haft-scythes, and their comparatively slender wooden shafts were easily shattered by the sharpened inner curves of the scythes. The *legionares*, fighting on raised mounds of earth behind the palisades, fought nearly eye to eye with the Canim, and it did them no favors. The second rank could not press up onto the earthworks and employ their shields to shelter their compatriots in the first rank, and the Legion's favored tactic— the steady press forward with murderous swords thrusting and chopping between miniscule openings in the shieldwall—was simply not an option from the defensive position.

It was, Marcus reflected grimly, a tactic that would have made short work of the Canim. A steady press inside the reach of the Canim haft-scythes would leave the weapons all but useless—but fighting from a static position, the foe's new armament was taking a savage toll on the Legion.

The Canim broke the ranks on the earthworks almost at will, but never pressed their advantage. Why should they? More and more *legionares* stepped up to fight, and more and more went down, helms shattered. Even the heavily layered shoulders of their body armor could not wholly turn aside the force of a well-swung Canim haft-scythe, and the toll of dead and wounded steadily mounted.

"Sir!" Marcus shouted at Crassus. The young officer was

near the front ranks of the battle, and as Marcus watched, he
stepped up over a wounded *legionare*, his face a mask of determination as a Cane swung a haft-scythe in a finishing blow.
Crassus's sword lashed out, and the young Citizen's blade shattered the steel of the Canim weapon in one swing and wounded
the Cane holding it in another. Crassus seized the fallen man
and dragged him back, while other *legionares* pressed up to
take his place.

"Sir!" Marcus screamed. "We've got to press them, sir!
We've got to push them back before they cut the men apart!"

"No!" Crassus bellowed. "Hold the line! You hold that wall
until the engineers signal us, First Spear!"

Marcus's instincts and experience screamed that Crassus
was making the wrong choice—that his naturally conservative
tendencies as a commander, which were so ideal in other circumstances, were fatally flawed this day. The First Aleran
could ill afford such a mistake in leadership.

But it could afford a loss of unity even less.

"You heard the man!" Marcus bellowed, urging his men
forward. "Hold the wall! Hold! Hold!"

He had no idea how much time went by. He was briefly
blinded twice—once by the blood of a Cane, and again by
the blood of a veteran *legionare* named Barus. He was once
caught off guard by a haft-scythe, and only the raised crest
of his centurion's helmet kept him from sharing Barus's fate.
The Cane weapon left a deep crease in his shoulder armor,
and the straps and edges beneath cut into his flesh, but he
kept fighting, kept supporting his men, desperately clearing
the wounded from the line and urging fresh *legionares* into
the fight.

After a lifetime, the trumpets began to blare up higher on
the hill. The engineers had finished their work.

"Fall back!" Marcus screamed to his men in the tumult.
"Fall back to the wall!"

The Canim howled and surged forward as the Aleran *legionares* began to withdraw from the palisade. They hacked
into the wooden barrier, chopping away enough material to
create myriad openings, and began to press the retreating *legionares*.

Without the Knights and the reserve waiting on the hill, it could have become a rout. Several cohorts broke altogether, but Marcus somehow kept the Prime from fragmenting, withdrawing step by step up the hill, fighting all the way. Where discipline began to fail, teams of Knights smashed into the Canim lines, and now the haft-scythes, so deadly in one circumstance, became hindrances in another. Knights Terra and Ferrous smashed through the weapons like toys, piling up fallen Canim like cordwood, and the cavalry's initial charges down the hill left windrows of dead behind.

It would be enough, Marcus saw, as Antillar Maximus, a long blade in either hand, plunged through the ragged remains of the decimated Ninth Cohort and shattered the fragile momentum a squad of raiders had gathered to pursue their advantage. The First Aleran was steadily gaining the security of the thicker stone walls of the ruin, fighting in a shrinking half circle as the men at the rear retreated. Without being ordered, he positioned the Prime at the outer edges of the defense. They would be the last cohort to gain the walls.

A flight of Knights Aeris screamed by, low enough to employ their spears, spitting Canim entirely with the speed of their passing. One man weaved aside from an upraised scythe, but the weapon's point caught in his armor or gear, and he was hauled down into a howling mob of furious raiders. As the Knights Aeris completed their pass and arced around for another, men began to drop, wounded or killed by Canim balests, and they were forced to withdraw.

Increasingly, it was the efforts of the close-combat Knights that made the critical difference as the Canim surged forward into the steadily shrinking Aleran lines. Showers of missiles from the newly crafted walls slowed some of the Canim, but there were simply not enough missiles in enough concentration to break them, and the Knights had to expend more and more effort, now fighting in the ranks with the *legionares*.

That was when the Canim unleashed their sorcery once again.

Marcus had little time to gawk, but he did catch a patch of unusual motion at one of the fallen palisades. A number of Canim figures in mantles of pale, pale leather appeared, filing steadily forward, swinging lit braziers in rhythm in front of them. They fell into a line, facing the hill, and then as one reached their clawed hands into gaping pouches slung across their bodies. They withdrew their hands as one single motion, sending out splattering arcs of scarlet liquid, and as one body the ritualists threw their heads back and howled.

Lines of violet flame sleeted suddenly from the skies. They struck the hillside near the distinctively deadly forms of the battling Knights and erupted into spheres of hellish fire and light. Men screamed and died, and if the skyfire wasn't the enormous destructive force that had struck the First Aleran at the Elinarch two years before, the more precise, smaller eruptions of fire certainly struck with telling effect.

The Aleran lines collapsed. Marcus screamed orders, dragged at wounded men, and had no idea how he managed to avoid all the Canim weapons that came screaming at him. He remembered felling one Cane that had leapt upon a badly burned Knight he recognized as Maximus, and then his weapon was struck from his hand. He fell on Antillar's wounded form, covering them both with his shield, and then there was a flash of steel, and Crassus was at his side, long blade in his right hand, and the curved, heavy blade of a Cane dagger in his left.

Crassus dealt two death strokes in as many seconds, driving the Canim back. "Inside!" he screamed, and rushed forward.

It was not a second too soon. Another delicate-looking line of violet skyfire descended upon him and exploded into a blinding sphere of heat and light. A second later it was gone, leaving a circle of blackened earth behind it—and Crassus with it, untouched by the fire, the bloodred gems in the hilt of the Canim dagger glittering in the lowering light.

A fresh round of cheering howls from the Canim raiders died abruptly as Antillus Crassus unleashed the power of the son of a High Lord of Alera upon their ranks.

Fire engulfed his blade and lashed out in a wave, washing over a hundred of the inhuman warriors. Somewhere, a balest hummed, but Crassus's blade intercepted the blurring missile in a shower of sparks, deflecting it. At his cry, a sudden vortex of wind formed, spinning the ashes and gravel and dust of the hillside into a blinding cloud, shielding the remnants of the Prime Cohort from the sight of most of the enemy.

Marcus got to his feet and seized Maximus by the armor. He dragged him backward, bumped into the wall, and was guided by the hands of other *legionares* to the opening. He retreated through it, shaking with fatigue, and fell to the ground in exhaustion.

Seconds later, Crassus bounded through the opening, and half a dozen Legion engineers rushed forward, laying their hands upon the stone of the wall. The opening quivered and began to shrink, and in seconds it was gone altogether, the stone of the wall smooth and unbroken.

Outside the walls of the ruins, the heavy, braying horns of the Canim began to sound.

"They're retreating!" shouted someone on the wall. "They're falling back!"

"Healer!" Marcus rasped. He turned to Maximus, and found the young man lying senseless, burned, and bleeding. "Healer!"

"Easy," said a voice. "Easy, there, First Spear." Crassus eased Marcus back and away from Maximus. "Go ahead, Foss."

Marcus watched them carry Maximus away. Someone guided his steps to one side and sat him down with his back against a wall. He found a mug of water in his hands and gulped it down at once, then a second and a third. Food came next, and though it was only plain, mashed oats, he emptied the bowl and licked it clean.

Only after he had attended to the screaming needs of his body did he manage to look up, gathering his wits again.

Lady Aquitaine, in her washerwoman guise, stared at him expressionlessly. Then she went back to passing out bowls of food, such as they were, and fresh water to the exhausted *legionares*, who were scattered all over the ruins nearby. Other domestics tended to minor injuries and brought replacements for weapons lost or broken in the fight. Battle-weary soldiers wolfed down food, gulped water, or simply lay in senseless heaps on the ground, asleep, as they did after practically any

battle, much less one as strenuous as this one. Marcus felt like
a mound of worn-out boot leather and wanted nothing more
than to join them.

Instead, he pushed himself to his feet and started stumping
around the immediate area, locating his men as the light faded
from the sky. Of eighty spear leaders in the Prime, twenty-nine
were still fit for duty, including himself. A quarter of his *legionares* were wounded and out of action. Another quarter were
dead or missing—and in the savage battleground they'd left behind, "missing" probably meant that they'd been too badly
mangled to be identified as the Legion withdrew. Another quarter of his men were lightly wounded and awaiting their turn
with the healers. In the merciless mathematics of war, lightly
wounded *legionares* were treated first by the Legion's watercrafters and returned to duty. Those more heavily wounded
were generally stabilized, and then suffered until there were
resources enough to get them back on their feet.

As he took count of his men at the healer's station, Marcus
saw a lot of Alerans suffering.

He went around to the Legion's fifteen Tribunes. Three were
dead. Three more were injured and out of action—including
Antillar Maximus, whose injuries relegated him to the category
of those awaiting additional medical resources. The tally of
losses was sobering. The report from the Tribune Logistica was
even more so.

Marcus found Crassus where he probably shouldn't have
been—visiting his half brother, on a cot in the healer's tents,
alongside all the other men too badly hurt to be easily put to
right. The young man sat beside Maximus, his expression remote.

"Captain," Marcus said quietly.

"You were right," Crassus said without preamble. "We
should have sortied."

Marcus ignored his words. "We're at half our normal fighting strength, sir. More than a third of our supply train was cut
off as they tried to make it inside the palisade, most of it our
livestock. And the only well we can reach on this hilltop has
been poisoned. The Tribune Logistica is working on a way of

filtering the water, but it doesn't look promising. We've already gone through most of what we had in barrels from the wells down the hill, so unless we get some rain, or Tribune Cymnea manages a minor miracle, we're going to be fighting dry."

It was a death sentence for a Legion. A Legion might—*might*—manage a day without food, but without water, men would drop by the score every few moments, unable to fight.

"I was so sure we had to hold," Crassus said. "To tough it out for a few moments more. I thought that any minute, the walls would be ready, and we'd stand them off, like before. I thought that we must have drawn the heaviest attack, that the Guard would be able to reinforce us. "He gestured at his fallen brother. Maximus was covered by light sheets, and Marcus knew that the healers had done it to keep dirt and grime out of the burns. "Max was right," Crassus said. "I thought too much, Marcus. And he's suffered for my sins. Again."

Marcus stared at the back of the young man's head for a moment. If Lady Aquitaine saw Crassus like this, she'd be hard-pressed to hide her satisfaction. He could be no threat to her liegeman Arnos's military laurels, like this.

It would probably never occur to her that in their current circumstances, there would *be* no laurels bestowed, no honors conferred—except, of course, the posthumous ones.

He walked around to the young officer's front, saluted, and slapped him sharply across the mouth.

Crassus blinked and stared at the First Spear in perfect shock. It hadn't been a gentle slap. Blood trickled from the young man's lower lip.

"Crows take you, sir," Marcus said quietly. "You are a Legion captain. Not some teenage bride mooning over her husband off to war. Get off of your ass and lead, before more men wind up like your brother."

Crassus just stared at him blankly. It occurred to Marcus that it was entirely possible that no one had spoken so to the young man in his entire life.

"Stand up," Marcus growled. "Stand *up*, sir."

Crassus stood up slowly. Marcus faced him, and banged his fist to his chest in another salute.

Crassus responded in kind. He studied Marcus for a moment, nodded slowly, and said, his voice very quiet, "Half strength, no meat, no water."

"Aye, sir."

"The Guard?"

"I spoke to their First Spears, sir. They're in worse shape than we are. For all practical purposes, we've got the only Knights on the field. The Guard used a different model of helmet than we did, without the crossbars on the crowns, and those hafted scythes went through them like paper. They've got fewer wounded but a lot more dead."

"Orders from the Senator?" Crassus asked.

Marcus shook his head.

"The other captains?"

"No word from them, either, sir."

Crassus drew in a deep breath. "It seems to me we really ought to have some kind of plan."

"If you say so, Captain."

"Send runners to the Senator and the other captains," Crassus said. "Inform them that I've prepared a pavilion for him, his staff, and the other captains, and that it is ready to receive him immediately."

Marcus saluted and turned to go.

"Marcus," Crassus said quietly.

He paused, without turning back.

Crassus dropped his voice, until only the two of them could have heard it. "We aren't getting off this hill, are we?"

Marcus blew out a breath. "Doesn't look like it, sir."

Crassus nodded. "Thank you," he said.

Marcus went on about following his orders, though he was ready to allow the Canim to kill him, if only they promised to let him get a few moments of sleep first.

CHAPTER 47

Troops surged from concealed positions beside the road, a dozen Canim and twice as many men in the worn gear of the Free Aleran Legion. One moment, no one was in sight, and the next a formidable array of weapons was pointed directly at Tavi's chest.

"Well," Tavi said, his tone impatient, as he reined his nag to a halt. "It's about bloody time."

One of the men had begun to speak, but he blinked and simply stared at Tavi, evidently surprised to be so addressed. Tavi studied him for a moment and decided that he was the most advantageous point of attack. If he didn't manage a successful verbal assault with the first pickets around Mastings, it might take him hours or days of waiting to get to Nasaug, and he doubted his mother and Araris would have that long.

"You," Tavi said, pointing at the man, then indicating the wooden baton thrust through his belt. "Centurion, I take it?"

"Yes," said the young man. "Yes, I'm—"

"Don't you people watch the back door as closely as the front? Bloody sloppy."

The man's face turned red. "Now, see here. You are intruders on a Free Aleran causeway, and as such I am placing you under arrest in accordance with general order—"

"I don't have time to listen to you cite phrase and paragraph, centurion," Tavi said, his tone striking a fine balance of impatience and authority, all of it absent of malice. "Lead me to Nasaug at once."

One of the Canim, a warrior Cane decked in the dark red-black steel plate of his caste, narrowed his blood-colored eyes and growled in Canish to one of his companions, a raider.

"Spit him on your spear. We'll see how much talking he does then."

Tavi turned and stared hard at the Cane who had spoken. Their battered group was not calculated to impress, and consisted of one mounted but unarmored man on a horse who had seen better days, and one rickety wagon drawn by a pair of shaggy mules, driven by a Marat girl, and carrying an unclad Cane and a wounded traveler. They could hardly have passed as bandits, much less anyone of importance enough to demand an audience with the Canim's leader, and if Tavi allowed the warrior Cane to treat them as petty vagrants, they would doubtless be tossed into a cell to languish through being passed from one officer to the next, up the chain of command, and the entire enterprise of the last several weeks could come to nothing.

Varg could probably establish his credentials in fairly short order, but Tavi's instincts warned him not to ask the Cane to do so. Varg had agreed to follow and support him until they reached Nasaug—but only so long as Tavi behaved in a fashion appropriate to a leader. Among the Canim warrior caste, leaders did not detail matters of personal precedence to their subordinates. They established such guidelines themselves. It was how one became a leader in the first place.

Tavi had to establish himself, by himself, at once—and when it came to dealing with a Cane, actions undeniably spoke far more than words.

So, without another word, Tavi swung down from his horse and stalked over to the Cane, staring hard at his eyes. Tavi stopped about six feet from the warrior, and said, in the wolf-warrior's own snarling tongue, "Say that again, please. I didn't hear you."

The Free Aleran soldiers stared. Every single Cane in sight turned his head toward Tavi, ears swiveled entirely forward.

The warrior Cane lowered his chin, and a warning growl bubbled in his chest.

Tavi let out a bark of harsh laughter, showing his own teeth in response. "Is that supposed to frighten me?"

The warrior Cane rested one hand on the hilt of his sword. "Do you want your blood to stay where it is *sochar-lar*?"

Tavi lifted both eyebrows at the unfamiliar word, and glanced at Varg.

"Monkey," Varg supplied, in Aleran. "And male-child."

"He called me monkey boy?" Tavi asked.

Varg nodded.

Tavi nodded his thanks and turned back to the warrior Cane. "Take me to Nasaug," Tavi told him. "Now."

The Cane lifted his lips from his teeth. "Drop your sword and pray that I choose to be merciful, monkey boy."

"Will it take long for you to talk me to death?" Tavi asked. "I can't help but wonder why you, a warrior, are out here leading a group of makers and monkeys, guarding a back road. Sadly. Are you too useless for an actual fight?"

The Cane let out a snarl and moved, sword sweeping from its sheath as he leapt at Tavi.

Tavi hadn't expected quite *that* strong a reaction, but he'd been ready to move since the moment he'd dismounted. He borrowed speed from the wind and slowed everything that happened, drawing his sword to meet the Cane's, pulling strength from the earth and twisting the whole of his body, hips and shoulders and legs, to strike against the Cane's weapon with all the force he could summon.

The Aleran *gladius* rang against the bloodsteel of the Cane's sword, and shattered it in a scream of tortured metal. The Cane staggered, thrown off-balance, and Tavi bulled forward, low, sword sweeping in a cut aimed at the back of the Cane's armored leg.

The Cane jerked his leg clear of the blow that could have severed tendons and rendered him immobile, and Tavi rammed his shoulder into the Cane's belly with all the power of his body and furycraft, actually lifting the huge wolf-warrior clear of the ground, before slamming him to the earth on his back. The Cane's breath exploded from his lungs in a croaking snarl, and before he could recover, Tavi had seized one broad ear in an iron grip and set the tip of his sword against the Cane's throat.

"I am Rufus Scipio," Tavi said calmly. "Captain of the First Aleran Legion. Defender of the Elinarch. I have faced the massed ranks of your army alone and unarmed. I killed the

Bloodspeaker Sarl by my own hand. And," he added, "I beat
Nasaug at *ludus*. I have come to speak to Nasaug, and you will
take me to him."

The warrior Cane stared at him for several seconds. Then
his eyes flicked to one side, and he tilted his head slightly, baring his throat. Tavi released his grip on the Cane's ear, and returned the gesture, more shallowly. The Cane's ears twitched
in what Tavi had come to recognize as a motion of surprise.

Tavi lowered the sword and backed away without letting
his guard down. Then he sheathed the weapon and nodded to
the Cane. "Get up. Let's move."

The Cane growled as he pushed himself up but tilted his
head to one side again and gestured to the other Canim there.
He turned to the Aleran centurion, and said, in mangled Aleran,
"I leave the post in your care, centurion."

The centurion looked from the Cane to Tavi, his face full
of questions, but he saluted the Cane, Aleran style, and began
giving orders to the other men there. The Cane growled to his
countrymen, and the Canim fell into a loose formation around
Tavi, who mounted his horse again and pulled it up next to the
wagon.

"How is he?" he asked Varg quietly, looking down on
Ehren's ashen face.

"Sleeping," Varg replied. The Cane held steady the quill
that still protruded from the slit in Ehren's neck, allowing him
to breathe.

"Aleran," Kitai said, a note of reprimand in her voice. "If
must drive the wagon, it would be courteous of you to let me
handle the fighting."

Varg's ears flicked in amusement.

"Next time," Tavi told her. He glanced at Varg and arched
an eyebrow in silent question.

"Your grammar is terrible," Varg said. He glanced up at the
warrior Cane, as he signaled his men, and their group and it
new escort started down the road. "But you make yourself understood, *gadara*. Calling him 'useless' may have been more
than was necessary to goad him."

Tavi grunted. "It is an insult word to your kind?"

Varg snorted again. "Rear-area duties such as this are ofte

assigned to overly aggressive young warriors, to temper them. They often resent it."

Tavi nodded in understanding. "I'm just glad I didn't have to kill anyone to get through."

"Why?" Varg asked.

Tavi glanced back at the Cane. The question had been delivered in a neutral, almost casual tone, but Tavi sensed that there was more to it than that, in Varg's mind.

"Because it would be a waste of a life that could be better spent elsewhere," he said.

Varg looked at him steadily. "And perhaps because your people do not all enjoy killing for its own sake."

Tavi thought of Navaris's flat, reptilian eyes and suppressed a shiver. "Perhaps."

Varg's chest rumbled in a low, pensive growl. "You begin to understand us, I think, *gadara*. And perhaps I begin to understand you."

"That," Kitai said in an acerbic tone, "would be remarkable."

They reached Mastings in the midst of the afternoon.

The Canim, Tavi saw at once, had turned the city into a veritable fortress, with multiple ranks of earthworks and palisades surrounding a solidly crafted curtain wall, leading up to full thirty-foot siege walls around the town itself. The outermost wall was lined with both Free Aleran and Canim troops, and at the gate they were challenged by another warrior Cane. The leader of their escort went forward to speak with the sentry, and Tavi paused, looking around.

The conversation between the two Canim became animated, but no louder. The Cane at the gate beckoned an older Aleran man over, and the three of them met in a quiet conference. The man glanced at Tavi and frowned, and Aleran sentries on the wall began to gather in, overlooking the group at the gate.

"We've attracted attention," Kitai noted under her breath.

"That was the idea," Tavi replied.

Ten minutes later, no one had come to speak to them, but a runner had been dispatched toward the city, and a rider had left the gates, riding hard toward the north.

Another half hour passed before a group of horsemen

emerged from Mastings and made their way through the extra
defensive walls until they finally reached the outermost wall.
As they did, Tavi squinted at the outer wall, then at all the positions on the inner wall, where thousands of uniformed figures stood on guard.

"Kitai," Tavi breathed quietly. "Look at the guards on the
second wall, and farther in, and tell me what you see."

Kitai frowned at them for a silent moment, and then spoke
suddenly. "They aren't moving. At all."

"They're scarecrows," Tavi said quietly. "Imitations. Only
the guards on the outer wall are real."

"Why?" Kitai breathed.

"To put the Legions off their guard," Tavi said quietly. "The
scouts would never have gotten this close to the city, to see
through it. They'd report back that the city was heavily occupied, and the Legions would count on twenty thousand troops
at least being behind the city walls. Under observation. Safely
located. Then Nasaug could bring the actual troops in unex-
pectedly."

"Nasaug is not planning on fighting a siege, as we thought,"
Kitai said.

"No. He met us in the field, probably before we could dig
in." Tavi shook his head. "Crows, he's good."

Varg growled thoughtfully. "You beat him at *ludus*?"

Tavi glanced back over his shoulder at Varg. "During a
truce to allow him to recover the bodies of his warriors. His
game on the skyboard isn't as strong as it could be, and he un-
derestimated me."

"Understandable," Kitai noted. She glanced at Varg. "I was
also unimpressed with the Aleran on our first meeting."

Varg glanced at Kitai, and his jaws parted briefly in amusement, his ears quivering in a motion Tavi had never seen in a
Cane before.

They fell silent as a group of mounted horsemen approached
from the gates of Mastings, riding swiftly. The horses pulled up
to a halt only a few feet away from them, and the officer who
led the group, presumably a Tribune, judging by his more mod-
ern and well-fitting armor, flung himself from his horse, his
face already scarlet with rage.

"What have we here?" he demanded. "Some of the scum at last?" He whirled on a man in a centurion's crested helmet and stabbed an accusing finger at the ground directly before Tavi. "Centurion. I want the gallows constructed right here."

Tavi narrowed his eyes, and he traded a glance with Kitai.

The centurion banged his fist to his chest and began giving orders to the Free Aleran riders. The *legionares* began hurrying about at once, and someone returned with rough lumber within a moment.

Their Cane escort let out a rumbling growl in his throat, watching the angry Tribune with narrowed eyes, but he did not move or speak. Tavi waited a moment before it occurred to him that he was in the same situation with the young warrior Cane as he was with Varg. He'd declared himself the Cane's superior, and any responsibility for acting in a dispute belonged to him.

He nudged his horse forward a few steps, and said, "Excuse me, Tribune. Might I ask what you think you're doing?"

The red-faced Tribune whirled on Tavi in a fury, one hand on his sword. "Centurion!" he bellowed.

"Sir?"

"The next time the condemned speak, you will carry out their executions at once!"

"Sir!"

Tavi met the Tribune's hard eyes for a long moment, but he didn't speak. He glanced aside at Kitai. The Marat girl's expression didn't change, but she shifted position on the driver's bench of the wagon, and reached back to adjust the unconscious Ehren's clothing. Tavi never saw any indication of it, but he was sure she had palmed one of the many knives Ehren habitually secreted about his person.

From the set of his ears, Varg took note of it. He glanced up at the young Cane, whose ears suddenly flattened to his skull.

Tavi suppressed a grimace. If it came to a fight, they'd have no chance, not even if the young warrior and his entire patrol joined in. There were simply too many of the Free Aleran *legionares* about, and in any normal Aleran Legion, the orders of a Tribune would draw immediate support from every *legionare* and centurion in sight.

Another rider came galloping up from the city, kicking his horse the entire way, and when the beast arrived it was in a near frenzy. It screamed and reared, hooves lashing, and the rider dropped off, threw off his helmet, and drew his *gladius* from his belt.

Tavi recognized him immediately, though the last time he had seen Durias, his features hadn't been mottled with rage.

Something was happening here, something more than merely tension during a time of war. There was far too much emotion in the reaction of the Free Alerans, and such things didn't occur for no reason. It didn't bode well for their situation. Men in such an excited state of mind were capable of anything.

Tavi tensed, readying himself to borrow the wind and draw his sword before anyone could stop him—but Durias stalked over to the hard-eyed Tribune, and without a word, fetched him a blow to the face with the back of his empty hand.

The Tribune reeled. Durias lifted his sword and shoved it hard against the Tribune's armored chest, forcing the man to the ground.

"Stand up," Durias snarled, "and I will strike off your useless head, Manus."

The Tribune looked up in a fury. "Centurion. I will have your *head* for thi—"

Durias leaned back and kicked Tribune Manus in the mouth with the heel of one foot. The man's head snapped back in a sudden spray of broken teeth, and he flopped to the ground, unconscious.

Durias glared at him, then at the nearby centurion. "In his cups again?"

The centurion's mouth twisted in distaste, and he nodded.

"Then get him something harder," Durias said. "If he's too drunk to walk, he'll be too drunk to do something this stupid. Now put the crowbegotten lumber back and get those horses back to the stables."

The centurion nodded and immediately began giving orders that were more or less the precise opposite of those he had just uttered. The *legionares* collected the unconscious Tribune and carried him off.

The blocky Durias, who looked even blockier dressed in armor than he had in a scout's field clothes, turned and walked over to Tavi, putting his sword away as he came. He nodded to Tavi as he approached. "Captain."

"Durias," Tavi said. "Nice to see you again, all things considered."

The Free Aleran centurion twitched his mouth into a faint smile. "I wish I could say the same. We need to get you away from here."

"Not until I speak to Nasaug," Tavi said.

Durias narrowed his eyes, glancing from Tavi to the wagon and its passengers and back. "You're kidding."

"This doesn't seem the appropriate place for levity," Tavi said. "I need to see him."

"You need to be elsewhere," Durias insisted. "Fortunately, in this case the two aren't exclusive. Nasaug's in the field."

Tavi grimaced as Durias confirmed his guess regarding Nasaug's plans. "I see. Lead the way, then."

"Aye." Durias went back to his horse and swung up without bothering to use the stirrups, hauling himself up purely by the muscles in his chest and arms. He nodded to their Cane escort, and said, "Thank you, Sarsh. I'll take them from here."

The Cane tilted his head casually to one side, and growled, "Watch the one on the horse. He's quicker than he looks."

Durias nodded, frowning, and said, "This way."

They followed Durias away from Mastings and toward the north. Once they were well away from the city walls, Tavi urged his horse up alongside the Free Aleran's. "That was quite a reception committee," he said quietly. "What brought that on?"

Durias glanced aside at Tavi, his expression unreadable. "Isn't it obvious?"

"Not to me," Tavi said. "I've been away awhile."

Durias exhaled through his teeth. "Of course you'd say that," he murmured, almost to himself. He glanced back at the wagon. "That's Varg?"

"I'll speak to Nasaug about that," Tavi said quietly.

Durias shrugged. "Fair enough. Then I'll let Nasaug answer your questions as well."

Tavi grunted, but nodded. "One thing more. One of my men is hurt. He needs a healer before we go any farther."

"He can't have one," Durias snapped. He took a deep, steadying breath. "That is, there are none at the city in any case. They're all in the field, and we're already heading their way."

"The ruins?" Tavi guessed.

"Just keep up." Durias nudged his horse into a trot for a few steps, drawing ahead of Tavi.

They traveled for three hours that way, Durias leading them, though Tavi became aware that the countryside on either side of the track they followed was far from empty. Once in a while, he managed to catch vague, flickering glimpses out of the corner of his eyes; movement in a stand of tall grass, or a slightly too-solid shadow among the trees. They were being watched, presumably by Durias's scouts, concealing themselves behind woodcraftings of varying skill.

The track began to show much heavier signs of use as they went. When they rounded a final hilltop and came into view of the ruins on their hill, and the battleground Nasaug had chosen to once more pit his forces against the Legions of Alera, Tavi drew up short for a second, unconsciously stopping his horse. He wished like the crows that Max had been nearby to provide a vision crafting for him, so that he might see the besieged hilltop in greater detail, but a few things were obvious, even from there.

The Legions had been hard-pressed, and their outer palisade wall shattered. They'd taken serious losses while doing so. Tavi could see the gleaming armor of fallen *legionares* lying in rough groups and singly, as often as not mixed with the dark-furred forms of fallen Canim. Presumably, they'd died while buying time for the engineering cohort to reinforce the walls of the ruins, which now stood at a conspicuously uniform, formidable height.

A sea of Canim surrounded the hilltop, and even a glance showed Tavi that Nasaug had trained his conscripts into disciplined troops and equipped them with uniform weaponry— even with their own armor, if lighter than that of the warrior Canim or Aleran *legionares*.

Worse, the Canim had brought forth their ritualists again.

Streamers of violet fire fell upon the hilltop in what was almost a regular cadence, slamming onto the walls and blasting great gouges from the stones, or from the earth when they struck the ground—and presumably from any Aleran unfortunate enough to be beneath one. Sharp, crackling reports resounded from the hilltop in a steady, hollow-sounding thunder.

"Bloody crows," Tavi whispered.

Kitai stared at the hilltop, her expression closed, but he could feel the sudden surge of fear and anger in her.

Durias looked over his shoulder, and said, harshly, "Keep moving."

They pressed on, passing through several checkpoints, where the Canim sentries seemed to have been expecting them. They waved Durias through without speech, though Tavi could feel their bloody eyes tracking his movements.

As they approached what Tavi recognized as the command area of the Canim force, they came upon a nightmare made flesh.

At the base of a small hillock, the Canim were piling bodies.

There were so many corpses that at first Tavi thought that they had been stacking bags of grain, or sand. Hundreds of dead Alerans lay in the oncoming sunset. The smell was something hideous, and both Tavi's and Durias's horses began to shy away from the stench, nervous at the smell of death. Tavi had to dismount, and moved to the horse's head, holding the bridle and murmuring quietly to soothe the beast.

Tavi wanted to look away from the bodies, but he couldn't. Most of them were *legionares*. Many of them wore the slightly differently styled armor of the Senatorial Guard, but many others wore the achingly familiar armor of the First Aleran.

And still others were dressed in the clothing of common holders.

Tavi stared. Among the dead were the elderly. Women. Children. Their clothing was stained with blood, their bodies mangled by brutally violent attacks. If he didn't retch his guts out on the ground, it was only because he'd had so much practice holding them in over the past two years.

It took him a moment longer, but he realized that the Canim were . . . putting the bodies through some kind of process. A pair of ritualists in their pale mantles stood at two separate tables— no, they were more like wide, shallow, elevated basins, tilted at a sharp angle. As Tavi watched, two other Canim, older laborers of the maker caste, by their simple clothing and greying fur, gently picked up the body of a holder woman. They carried it to one of the tables and laid it down on the basin, with her head positioned at the basin's lower end.

The ritualist murmured something, a musical-sounding, even meditative growl—and then reached down with a curved knife and cut the dead woman's throat on both sides.

Blood trickled from the corpse. It drained down the shallow basin, where it gathered and flowed down through a hole at the bottom of the basin, out of a small spigot. There, it poured into a wide-mouthed stone jar.

Tavi could only stare at it in mute astonishment, unable to quite believe what he was seeing. The laborers fetched another corpse for the second basin. As Tavi watched, the first ritualist beckoned a nearby Cane, a young male not more than six feet tall, and far more wiry than an adult. The young Cane gathered up the stone jar, replacing it with another one from a row of similar vessels nearby. Then he turned and loped rapidly away, toward the sorcery-blasted hilltop.

A moment later, the ritualist nodded to another set of workers—only these were half a dozen or so Alerans, also wearing the clothing of holders. They gently removed the woman's body, wrapped it in sackcloth, and carried it to an open wagon, typical of those used as an improvised hearse on the battlefield, where they laid it down beside several other similarly wrapped figures.

Tavi looked up to find Durias watching him from where he stood at his own mount's head. The centurion's face was bleak, but Tavi could read nothing from it, nor sense any of the young man's emotions through his own shock, revulsion, and growing anger.

"What is this?" Tavi demanded. His voice came out confident and cold, though he hadn't meant it to be.

The muscles in Durias's jaws flexed a few times. Then he said, "Wait here." He led his horse away.

Tavi watched him go, then averted his eyes from the basins and the stacked corpses. He walked his weary mount back to the wagon to give it the company of the mules drawing it.

"Varg?" Tavi asked quietly.

Varg watched the rituals with a rigidly neutral body posture. "Blood into jars," he rumbled.

"This is where their power comes from," Tavi said softly. "Isn't it?"

Varg flicked his ears in assent, as bodies continued to be drained and runners continued to carry the filled jars toward the battle lines.

"This is how they used power against us at the Elinarch," Tavi snarled. "They killed our people after they landed and used their blood against the Legion."

"Take no particular offense, Aleran," Varg rumbled. "They are not choosy about which blood they take, so long as it is from a reasoning being. The rituals have killed more of my people than the whole of your race. The sorceries they used to assault your shores, block your skies, redden your stars would have required millions upon millions of lives."

"And you allow them to exist?" Tavi spat.

"They serve a purpose," Varg replied. "They have the power to bless bloodlines. Increase fertility in our females. Increase the bounty of crops, and to lessen the ravages of storms, droughts, plagues."

"And you are willing to sacrifice your people's lives for them to do it?"

"My people are willing to make a gift of their blood upon death," Varg growled. "Though there are times when a particularly powerful ritualist forgets that his power should be used to serve his people. Not the other way around."

"There are women there," Tavi said, his mouth tight. "Children. I thought better of Nasaug."

"And I," growled Nasaug, from behind Tavi, "thought better of you."

Tavi turned around, hand on his sword, eyes narrowed.

Nasaug stood ten feet away, in full armor—armor stained with several shining new nicks and dents and spattered with drying blood. The dark-furred Cane's lips were lifted from his teeth in open hostility, and a naked sword was in one of his hands. Durias stood at Nasaug's right hand, his teeth similarly bared.

Some distant part of Tavi's mind shouted that he should be calm and cautious. He could barely hear it over the outrage and horror, and he met Nasaug's eyes squarely. "Tell your men to get their hands off of my people."

"Or what?" Nasaug said, his eyes narrowing to slits.

"Or I'll bloody well *make* them do it," Tavi replied.

"You are about to die, Aleran," Nasaug said.

Tavi drew his sword. "You'll find me harder to kill than defenseless old holders and children, dog."

Nasaug surged forward—not a leap, but a controlled, blindingly swift rush, his sword gripped in two hands. Tavi lifted his sword, shifting his weight, preparing to slide the enormously powerful blow aside, summoning strength from the earth.

Until Varg hit Nasaug in the chest like a hurled spear.

Nasaug, though huge and armored, was still outweighed by the larger and more heavily scarred Varg. Both Canim went down in an explosion of deafening snarls, and a bestial struggle ensued. Varg knocked the sword from Nasaug's grip, but the smaller Cane sank his fangs into Varg's shoulder, drawing blood. Varg roared, driving a blow at Nasaug's nose, slamming his head aside, his teeth ripping great gashes in Varg's flesh.

The two Canim struggled, rolling and twisting, exchanging blows and rakes of their claws and slashes of their fangs. Though Varg was larger and stronger, Nasaug was armored, and ruthlessly made use of the advantage his greater protection afforded him.

Nasaug managed to slam his armored forearm into Varg's throat, then his jaws opened and his fangs flashed as he snapped forward.

Varg was too swift. The larger Cane fell back, claws hooked in Nasaug's armor, then whirled the smaller Cane off the ground and down onto it in a vicious slam that shook dust from the earth for twenty feet in every direction.

Nasaug tried to roll away but, stunned by the impact, was too slow, and Varg was on his back, jaws on the back of his neck, body pinning the smaller Cane down.

Nasaug let out a howl of anguish and fury, then fell silent.

For a moment, Tavi thought that Varg had killed him. Then he realized that Nasaug still breathed. He simply lay there, unmoving, not struggling, and there was a quality of exhausted frustration in the snarls that continued bubbling from his throat.

Tavi looked up and met Durias's gaze. Then he put his sword away and took a step toward the two Canim.

Varg released Nasaug's throat, and Tavi heard the big Cane growl, almost too quietly to be heard, *"Gadara-lar."*

Nasaug shuddered. Then one of his ears twitched in assent. *"Gadara-sar."*

"Honor," Varg said.

"Honor," the smaller Cane echoed.

Varg rose slowly from Nasaug. The Canim commander turned to face Varg, and each of them bared their throats to one another, Nasaug more deeply.

"Lar," Tavi said quietly. "It means boy."

The two Canim turned their heads to face him.

"Sar," Tavi said. "It means sire. He's your son."

"Obviously," Varg growled.

"And *gadara*," Tavi said. "It doesn't mean 'enemy.' "

"The people of the snows," Varg said, "you call them the Icemen. They have twenty-four words to name snow. Alerans have one. In the same way, Canim have eleven words to name enemy."

Tavi nodded slowly. "Can you tell me what *gadara* means? Describe it?"

Varg gave Tavi a very Aleran-looking shrug. "It means that you are a foe that is equal. Honorable. Trusted."

"A trusted enemy?" Tavi asked. "And you name your son as such?"

"Enemies are far more faithful than friends, Aleran, and

more dependable than allies. One can respect an enemy far more easily than a friend. It is considered a mark of respect," Varg said.

Nasaug, meanwhile, had dropped to his haunches in a relaxed crouch, still panting to regain his breath. Struggling in the armor had wearied him far more than it had his unarmored sire. "Aleran," he said. "Why did you turn an honorable war into a slaughter of makers and females?"

"I didn't," Tavi replied. "I've been gone more than six weeks, bringing Varg to you, as we agreed." He frowned. "Your people didn't kill those holders?"

Nasaug spat. "No. Cavalry from your Legions have been striking steadholts for weeks now." He jerked his muzzle at the draining tables. "So I have allowed the bloodspeakers to drain the blood of the dead and so avenge them."

Tavi lifted a hand to his face for a moment. "These riders," he said. "Alerans?"

"Aye."

"Not Marat?"

"The white-hairs. No."

Tavi exhaled slowly. "Then it hasn't been the First Aleran. Arnos must have ordered the Guard's cavalry to do it."

"That matters little to the dead," Durias said quietly. "Or to their families. Manus's wife and children were killed two days ago. That's why he reacted as he did, Captain."

"Why would Arnos do such a thing?" Kitai asked quietly.

Tavi shook his head. "To ensure that there would be no peaceful conclusion to this campaign, maybe. Or . . ." He glanced at Durias. "Has the Free Aleran Legion engaged the Crown forces yet?"

"No," Durias said quietly. "We've been holding off as long as possible."

Tavi spat a bitter taste from his mouth. "That's why, then," he said. "This campaign has been about ambition from the start. Arnos wants to be sure you have reason to fight. Then he gets the credit for defeating an invader and putting down a slave revolt as well."

"If he wished to anger us," Nasaug said, "then he has succeeded. There will be no quiet end to this struggle, Aleran."

Tavi frowned. "I lived up to my end of the agreement."

"I agreed that if you freed Varg, we would talk. I have talked, and you may go in peace, *gadara*. But I will not allow those who murder makers and females to walk away unpunished." He jerked his muzzle at the besieged ruins. "They will not last the night."

Tavi clenched his jaw. Nasaug was no fool, and he could clearly see that the Legions were already in desperate straits. They'd been taken off guard, and the ongoing sorceries seemed more than able to pulverize what little shelter they had, given enough time.

And blood.

Tavi racked his brain desperately. There had to be some way out of this mess, some way to save the First Aleran, some way to . . .

"And what then?" Tavi heard himself ask quietly.

Nasaug tilted his head to one side.

"After you've killed them," he continued, struggling to keep up with a sudden flood of possibilities. "They'll be replaced by more Legions—and you'll be long gone. But the Free Alerans won't. And you can bet that whatever force comes next will have orders to wipe them out. They'll be the ones to pay for what you do to the men on that hill."

Durias lifted his chin defiantly—but there was something in his eyes that was not at all certain.

"For that matter," Tavi said, "how do you expect to get across the sea? When your fleet came, they used a storm the ritualists summoned to travel swiftly, and they came in large numbers to get through the leviathans. You won't be sailing nearly so swiftly on the way back. How many more ships will you lose? How much weaker will your army be when you finally return to your home?"

Nasaug growled in his throat. "We are willing to face those dangers, Aleran."

"What if you didn't have to?" Tavi asked.

Varg's ears flicked in amusement. "Perhaps you noticed," he growled to Nasaug, "that our young *gadara* is clever."

Nasaug snapped his jaws pensively. "What do you propose?"

"I'm going to give you the man responsible for those deaths," Tavi said. "I'm going to punish those who carried out his orders. I'm going to see to it that the Free Alerans are not treated as criminals for what they have done—and after *that*, I'm going to make sure your fleet gets safely over the sea and back to your home."

"And in exchange for all of this?" Nasaug asked, his tone clearly skeptical.

Tavi gestured at the ocean of Canim surrounding the hill. "You surrender."

Nasaug lifted his lips from his teeth. "What?"

"You surrender," Tavi repeated.

"Even if this was possible, I will never surrender to Alerans or their Legions," Nasaug said. "Too many of them are no better than animals."

"You won't be surrendering to Aleran Legions," Tavi replied. "You'll be surrendering to me, personally—a *gadara*."

Nasaug tilted his head, his ears swiveling forward in concentration. He traded a long look with Varg, then tilted his head to one side. He drew a heavy leather sash from his belt and tossed it to the larger Cane.

Durias's mouth fell open, and he stared at the exchange in pure surprise.

Varg donned the sash, belting it on with practiced movements. "Aleran," he said. "Let us assume that I agree to this proposal. What will you need to make it happen?"

Tavi's heart began to pound in excitement, and he felt a grin try to stretch his lips. He was careful to keep his teeth covered, lest he give the Canim the wrong idea.

"First," he said, "I'll need you to take my wounded man to a healer. I'll need his help."

Varg nodded, and said to Durias, "See to it at once."

Durias glanced at Nasaug, but even as he did his fist was banging out a salute on his chest, and he hurried away.

Varg nodded and turned back to Tavi. "And?"

"Any eyewitnesses to any of the attacks," Tavi said. "I'll need to speak to them."

Varg glanced at Nasaug, who nodded. "It can be done, *sar*."

Tavi pointed at the besieged ruins. "The attack needs to top, at least temporarily."

Varg narrowed his eyes but nodded once. "Is midnight time nough for this plan?"

"It should be," Tavi said.

In fact, it should be plenty of time, Tavi thought. By the ime midnight got there, he would almost certainly have ful-illed his word to the Cane.

And if he hadn't, he'd be too dead for his failure to bother im overmuch.

CHAPTER 48

jaius Sextus fell upon the forward ranks of the *legionares* oming toward them, and terror like none they had known rashed over them.

The flaming brand in his fist cast out a blinding radiance, nd Amara could feel the very edges of the fearcrafting that nbued it. Once before she had borne a flame containing a ıry of terror, and she had barely remained conscious during ıe act. Count Gram's fearcrafting had been formidable, rout-ıg thousands of barbarian Marat and their war beasts alike, ending them screaming from the walls of Garrison during econd Calderon.

Beside the horror Alera's First Lord now sent against the .alaran *legionares*, Gram's fearcrafting had been a momen-ıry flutter of insecurity.

The men nearest Gaius, those file leaders of whatever luck-ıss century had the fortune to make up the column's center, ever got to scream. Their eyes rolled back in their heads, and ; a single man, they convulsed and fell to the stony ground.

Then the screams began.

Hundreds of throats opened in terrorized howls, a sudden

and deafening cacophony. Ranks and files melted like butter on a hot skillet, and Legion discipline vanished like dew beneath a desert sunrise. Some men fell, clutching at their shoulders and chests, bleeding from the eyes, or frothing at the lips. Some sobbed and staggered to their knees, weapons tumbling from fear-numbed fingers. Some turned their weapons upon those near them, panicked beyond reason or ability to recognize their sword-brethren. Most simply fled, casting aside their swords and shields.

Among those hundreds of afflicted souls, one man alone stood his ground. Though his face was ashen, somehow this man withstood that horrible fear, bracing his shield and raising his sword in wavering defiance.

The First Lord's blade of fire swept down, and no shield or sword in all of Alera could have withstood that molten furnace of a blow. In a flash of light, the *legionare's* shield shattered into cleaved halves and droplets of molten metal, parted every bit as easily as his armor and the flesh beneath. He fell in a horrible cloud of hissing gasses and the stench of scorched flesh, and Amara could not help but feel pity that the poor man had been so rewarded for his courage, greater than any of the Legion about him.

Even in Gaius's shadow, unable to see the flame, and shielded from the worst of the fearcrafting, it was all that Amara could do to keep moving forward. The terrible light of the First Lord's sword created a nightmare army of shadow that raced in senseless panic over the slopes of the mountainside and flashed back from polished armor and the bright steel of discarded blades. It created a dizzying display of light and blackness, making it difficult to judge distances or to maintain her awareness of their direction or position. She had grown used to tracking their movements, of maintaining her orientation, and she realized in a sudden panic that she was no longer sure of their way.

Not that it would matter, she realized a beat later. The largest threat the poor, howling *legionares* posed to Amara and her companions was that of a broken ankle to be had from stumbling over the fallen forms of those incapacitated by terror.

Such was the screaming chaos around her that Amara nearly

missed precisely the threat she was supposed to be on guard against—a sudden knot of resistance, discipline, and purpose amidst the horror. Several heavily armored men had gathered around another figure, one holding his hand aloft—a Knight Ignus. Blue fire wreathed that single man's fingers, a counter-crafting, Amara judged, not strong enough to stretch far from his body against the will of the First Lord, but of sufficient power to enable the men immediately around him, Knights Terra by their outsized weapons, to maintain their reason.

"Bernard!" Amara screamed, pointing with her sword. Her voice was lost in the din of maddened men around them, but she sensed his change in pace and dropped into a crouch as he lifted his bow and loosed an arrow that passed close enough to her scalp to stir her hair. The arrow leapt through the shifting shadows—

—and missed the Knight Ignus by the width of a finger. It flicked past one of the Knights Terra and drew a streak of crimson across his cheekbone. The enemy Knights' mouths opened in cries Amara could not hear through the tumult, and they charged, the Knight Ignus at the center of their group.

Amara tried to shout a warning to the First Lord—but Gaius had his face turned away from the threat, his eyes instead focused upon three other men coming from the opposite direction, their faces blank with the detachment of Knights Ferrous, their swords gleaming.

In the corner of her eye, she saw her husband swipe a hand over his eyes in a gesture of frustration and fear as he reached to his quiver for another arrow, but the enemy Knights were too close, and there was no way he would have the chance to loose it.

Amara drew upon Cirrus and the battlefield slowed to a crawl as she dashed forward. She was upon the leading Knight, a man armed with an enormous axe, before he could bring his weapon to bear properly upon her. She slipped aside from a hasty and badly aimed swing and whipped her sword across the man's face with one hand, while giving the axe's haft a sharp downward slap with the other.

The sword stroke did no real harm, rebounding from the ridges of his helmet, though it drew a crimson line across the bridge of his nose—but it did serve to make him jerk his head sluggishly back from the blow. Far more dangerous was the suddenly altered path of his enormous axe. It swept down and around, into the thigh of the Knight beside him, and the fury-assisted blow sheared completely through the luckless Knight's armored thigh.

Both men fell, hampering those on either side of them, and it gave Amara a single, flickering instant of opportunity. She drew a dangerous portion of her fury's essence within herself—far more than she ever had before, far too much—until that instant expanded into a nearly motionless lifetime.

She lunged forward, moving with a speed no body in Alera was designed to bear, and she felt muscles and joints scream in protest and tear like wet paper as she did. She had an age to experience the pain, an eon to aim her thrust, an eternity to focus all of her body's weight and strength and speed upon the gleaming, needle-sharp tip of her *gladius*.

The Knight Ignus saw her coming, and his eyes widened as slowly as ice forming on a winter pond. He tried to draw aside from the oncoming blade, but he did not have the time she did. His head moved a fraction of an inch, no more.

Then her sword's point sank into his desperately widened eye, and the length of its blade followed in slow, dreamlike motion—all the way to the weapon's hilt. The man's head snapped languidly back, and droplets of blood spewed forth in a misty cloud.

Amara felt an explosion of fire in her hand, her wrist, her elbow, her shoulder. Her bond with Cirrus faltered, and everything rushed into a single blurring motion.

Though she could not hear it, she felt her throat go raw with screaming.

Pain and terror wiped the world away.

Amara awoke to find herself dizzily content to remain absolutely still. It took her a mildly astonished moment to notice that she was still moving. Her hair hung about her face—crusted with mud and blood and the filth of their swampy journey. It smelled like rotting vegetables.

Beyond her hair, her hands dangled limply. Her right hand, from wrist to fingertips, was swollen up like a collection of sausages knotted together into a rough doll. The skin was deep purple, one solid, livid bruise that covered it all equally—or so she supposed. It was difficult to be certain because of the mud and blood and flecks of something grey and gelatinous still clinging to her skin.

She was fairly sure something like that ought to hurt. It didn't. She attempted to wiggle the purpled fingers and found them entirely unresponsive. She felt sure that was not an encouraging sign, but for the life of her, she couldn't remember why.

Past her fingertips was stony ground, moving steadily by. Something was pressing up hard against her stomach in steady rhythm. Bernard, she thought. His shoulder. She was draped over Bernard's shoulder. Yes, she could see his swamp-ruined boots, down by the ground.

"Hurry," snapped the First Lord. He sounded steady, confident. That was good. It had almost been more than Amara could stand to see Gaius, who had always been so dynamic, so vital, reduced to a fevered wreck on an improvised litter. He must have watercrafted himself better, lying still on the litter, while Brencis had examined her and Bernard.

It occurred to her that she did not know if even the First Lord's skills could have wholly restored himself so swiftly. She felt a vague sense of worry, that the old man had simply shored up his condition as best he could, then opted to block out the pain of it with his metalcrafting, proceeding as if nothing was wrong. If he was, in fact, operating on the borrowed time given him by a crafted insensitivity to pain, then he was in danger—and that bothered Amara enough to make her move her head and stir her weary limbs in a faint effort to attract someone's attention.

"She's waking up," Bernard said, his tone urgent.

"We're almost there," Gaius said. "Once we've crested this rise, I'll be able to see the mountain Kalarus has prepared, and—" The First Lord drew in a sharp breath. "Knights Aeris are coming, Count. Quite a few of them. We have only moments. I should think we would both appreciate it if some of your salt arrows are ready."

Then there was much huffing and puffing and scrabbling of boots over stone. Amara gave up on her efforts to move and drifted through a haze for a while. She wasn't sure how long it took for things to change, but it didn't seem like a very long time until Bernard slowed, then set her carefully on the ground.

He dropped to one knee beside her, breathing hard, his face set in an expression of pain. He drew the arrows from his quiver and began thrusting their tips into the earth. Then he muttered and laid his hand upon the ground among them.

"Bernard," Amara said. It barely came out, but her husband turned to her immediately.

"Love," he said quietly. "You mustn't move. You've been badly hurt."

"I'm tired," she replied. "But it doesn't hurt."

"Sire," Bernard said, his voice hard. "She's awake. Shivering. I think she's going into shock."

Amara looked to one side, where the First Lord stood staring down, and for the first time she noticed that they were high upon the shoulders of the mountain and that they could see clearly into the vast bowl below them.

There, miles away, twinkled the lights of the city of Kalare, a luminous emerald jewel in the darkness. The smaller clusters of other lights showed where several smaller towns lay in the region around the city, and small, single pinpoints of light showed where dozens of individual steadholts lay. The moonlight shone off the shallow-water fields of barleyrice, turning them into mirrors that were acres across.

Amara had been to Kalare. It was an ugly city, run-down, deprived of any apparent virtue, where the only thing in greater abundance than slavery was misery. After two years of war and economic isolation, it was bound to be even worse, dirtier, poorer, crueler, and more disease-ridden. But from up there on the mountain, from far away, when only the characteristic greenish furylamps of the city were visible, Kalare and its flock of child-cities possessed an eerie and fragile beauty.

"Sire!" Bernard barked. He began jerking arrows from the

ground, their heads now encased in translucent crystal. "She needs your help."

Gaius stood facing a mountain on the far side of the valley, and Amara realized that she shouldn't have been able to *see* the mountain from here, or at least not in the dark. But she *could* see it, a vast black cone backlit by dim red light at its crown.

Bernard nocked an arrow and rose to his feet. "Sire!"

"In a moment, Count," Gaius murmured. "There are other matters that—"

"No," Bernard said. "You're going to see to her. Now."

Gaius's head snapped around. "Excuse me?"

"She's hurt," Bernard said. "She might be dying. Fix it."

"You have no idea," Gaius said from between clenched teeth. "No idea what is at stake."

Her husband faced the First Lord without flinching. "Yes, I do." His eyes hardened. "The life of a woman who was willing to sacrifice everything to get you here. You've planned enough pain for her already, Sextus. Or maybe you think it would be easier to let her die."

Wind whispered over the stones for several empty seconds.

Then Gaius was at her side. He leaned down and laid his hand on her forehead. His fingers were long, rough, and fever-hot. He murmured, quietly, "I'm sorry for what is to come, Amara."

Fire engulfed the entire right side of her body. She felt herself contort strangely, saw the shape of her abdomen alter, watched as her arm straightened, unwinding as it went, almost like a twisted cord. The pain was indescribable, but there was a sensation of silvery ecstasy mixed with it that left her unable to move or cry out. She could only weep, and the stars blurred upon her tears, mixing with the lights of the city below.

There was a roar of wind, the thrum of Bernard's bow, and a horrible, wet sound of impact.

Gaius lifted his hand away from her and rose. "Keep them off me, Count."

"Aye, my lord," Bernard growled, taking position standing over Amara, his bow in hand.

Amara could do nothing but watch as the First Lord stared at the distant fire-mountain and raised his hand.

There was another roaring sound, a windstream, and Bernard loosed another arrow, drawing a scream. Armor clattered against the stones as a Knight Aeris in full gear crashed to the mountainside and slid along it in a bone-breaking tumble, sparks leaping up in his wake where steel armor met stone.

She wasn't sure how long it went on, before the pain began to fade somewhat and she found herself able slowly to sit up—but her husband now stood with his last arrow against the string of his bow, staring up at the night sky with dull, exhausted eyes.

The First Lord let out a sudden sigh, closing his eyes. "Crows take you, Brencis. At least your son had wisdom enough to know when he was beaten. Crows take you and rip out your eyes for forcing me to this."

And then Gaius Sextus suddenly closed his reaching hand into a fist and jerked it back, as if snapping a particularly tough cord.

The night went red.

Blinding light flared from the distant mountain.

It took Amara several dull, thudding seconds to realize what she was seeing.

Fire erupted from the mountain, white-hot, lifting in a great geyser that rose miles into the air. That first rush of blinding liquid flame spattered out for what had to be miles and miles in every direction around the mountain and only then did the earth suddenly move, the mountain jumping as if it had been an old wagon hitting a pothole in a bad road. Rocks fell. Somewhere nearby, a cliffside collapsed in a deafening roar.

Amara couldn't take her eyes from what was happening below. The mountain itself began to spew out a great cloud of what looked like grey powder, illuminated from within by scarlet light. The cloud billowed out in slow, graceful beauty—or so it looked from the distance. She watched as it rolled down over the valley of Kalare. It washed over the poinpoint lights of the little steadholts. It devoured the larger clusters of lights marking the little towns and villages around the valley.

And, within moments, it washed over the city of Kalare itself.

Amara could not help herself. She lifted her hands, tiredly willing Cirrus into a sight-crafting. The grey cloud was not simply ash, as she had at first thought. It was . . . as if fire had been made into one vast thunderhead. Whatever was caught in the path of that scarlet-limned grey flood was instantly incinerated by its touch. She saw, just barely, small moving shadows flying before the oncoming inferno, but if the cloud moved with lazy grace, those tiny figures—those Alerans, she realized—moved at a snail's pace. She herself, one of the fastest fliers in Alera, could not have outpaced that incendiary nebula. Those holders had no chance. None at all.

She stared at the valley below them in numb shock, as more jolts and tremors rattled the mountain beneath her. How many thousands—tens of thousands, *hundreds* of thousands of people had just died? How many families, sleeping in their beds, had just been reduced to ashes? How many children had just been burned alive? How many homes, how many stories, how many beloved faces and names had just been incinerated like so much useless garbage?

Amara knelt there beside her husband and witnessed the death of Kalare—of its city, its people, its lands, and its lord.

A vast cloud of steam rose as the watery valley surrendered to the embrace of the fire-mountain, and their view of that steam vanished as dust from the rockslides and tremors rose up around them, creating a thick shroud that blotted away the stars.

There was still light, though. Light from the blazing mountain and from the burning corpse of the city of Kalare painted everything in a surreal, scarlet twilight.

Only after their view of the valley had been obscured did Gaius Sextus turn away. His gaze slid past Bernard and found Amara. He walked over to her with slow, heavy steps, and faced her, his expression a mask, his eyes showing nothing.

"Had I waited for Kalarus to loose it, Countess," he said quietly, "it would have been worse. Refugees fleeing the front lines would have been forced into the city and doubled the numbers there. Our own *legionares* would have been there. Died there." He sought her eyes, and spoke very quietly. "It would have been worse."

Amara stared at the weary First Lord.

She pushed herself slowly to her feet.

She reached up and found the slender chain around her neck. She wore two ornaments upon it. The first was Bernard's Legion ring, worn there in secret testimony to their marriage.

The second was a simple silver bull, the most common coin in the Realm, marked with Gaius's profile on one side. It was the symbol and badge of office of a Cursor of the Realm.

Amara grasped the ring in one hand.

With the other, she tore the coin and chain from her throat, and cast them into Gaius's face.

The First Lord didn't flinch.

His eyes became more sunken.

Amara turned and walked away.

"Go with your wife, Count," Gaius said softly, somewhere behind her. "Take care of her for me."

▭▭▭▭▭ CHAPTER 49

The Senator's thugs, Isana thought, lacked refinement. She had expected to be bound, of course, but they could at least have found a *clean* cloth with which to hood her.

She blinked and considered that thought for a moment. It sounded, to Isana, remarkably like what someone like Lady Aquitaine would have been thinking, in her position. Until the battle of Second Calderon, Isana's largest practical worry had been the organization of the kitchen at her brother's steadholt. Had she really become so jaded to the dangers of Aleran politics since then that she felt herself qualified to criticize the nuances of her own abduction?

She couldn't help it. She found herself shaking with quiet laughter.

Araris stirred, and she felt the motion as they sat, backs together, leaning gently against one another. "What is it?" he murmured.

"I'm just appreciating the irony of human nature," Isana said, voice pitched very low.

She could hear the smile in his voice. "Any part in particular?"

"Our ability to face enormous adversity, yet retain the capacity to complain about the little things."

"Ah," Araris said. "I wondered if they made these hoods out of old horse blankets as well."

Isana laughed again, mostly a shaking of her shoulders that made little sound, and Araris joined her.

"The sounds of fighting have died down," Isana noted a moment later.

"Yes," Araris said.

"Have the Legions won?"

"They haven't lost yet," Araris replied. "Those trumpet calls were a general retreat."

"They were pushed back from whatever they were attacking, then," Isana said.

"Whatever they were holding," Araris corrected. "A failed assault sounds different. And there are too many wounded."

Isana had been trying hard not to think about the moans and screams of wounded men, coming from not far away. "It's different, then?"

"In an assault," Araris said, "you're fighting on the enemy's ground. Pushing forward. When men fall, it's harder to get them to the rear. And once the retreat is on, a lot more men fall. More of them get left behind, taken prisoner or killed. A defense is different. It's your ground. You've got men standing by to carry the wounded back to your healers and fresh men to step into the places of the fallen, covering their retreat. You wind up with a lot more wounded."

Isana shuddered. "That's horrible."

"It's a horrible situation," Araris acknowledged quietly.

"Rather like ours," Isana said.

He was silent.

"That bad?" Isana asked, nudging her back gently against his.

"You said the right thing to Navaris," he said. "Making her question whether or not she should make the decision for Arnos. It bought us a little time. But she brought us into the Legion's camp in a covered wagon, and in hoods. Then they dumped us directly into this tent, which is guarded. And I'm fairly certain that we're among the men of the First Guard. Nalus is Captain of the Second Senatorial, and he'd bloody well want to know all about any hooded prisoners in his own camp."

"No one knows who we are," Isana said quietly. "No one knows we're here."

"Precisely," Araris said.

"Do you think he'll kill us?"

Araris considered that for a moment. Then he said, without malice, "He'd better."

"What?"

"You're a Citizen of the Realm, Isana. His hirelings assaulted and kidnapped you on his orders. Ehren's a bloody Cursor of the Crown. If he survived, he's going to be able to make a terrible stink, legally speaking. Arnos's best chance to survive it—"

"—will be to make sure there are no witnesses to corroborate Ehren's version of things."

"Probably," Araris said. "Besides, if he doesn't kill us, I'll take him."

The matter-of-fact tone to his quiet voice was chilling. Isana found herself leaning slightly harder against him. "What do we do?" she asked. "Escape?"

"Realistically speaking, we've no chance, even if we get loose. We'll just provide them a wonderful excuse to kill us and make apologies later. Heat of battle, confusion, such a tragedy."

"What, then?"

"If you get the chance, keep Arnos talking for as long as you can," Araris said. "And we wait."

"Wait?"

"He isn't going to leave us here," Araris said.

Isana had no doubt to whom the *singulare* referred. "We are secret prisoners in the camp of what might as well be an enemy Legion, which is itself surrounded by an army of Canim. He is alone. He might not even know where we are. I believe he'll try, of course, but . . ."

At that, Araris burst into a low, rich laugh, loud enough to be heard outside the tent. It was, Isana realized, the first time she'd heard him make such a sound, and her own heart reacted with a senselessly juvenile little burst of happiness to hear it.

"Quiet in there!" barked a man's voice, one of the Senator's thugs, or some random *legionare* pressed into duty as a sentry.

Araris swallowed his laughter and leaned his head back. Isana felt his head touch hers and leaned into the contact, closing her eyes.

"I've been with him for two years," Araris whispered. "You know his heart, Isana. You helped shape it. You've seen him while we traveled—but you don't see what he's become, and you don't know where it came from the way I do."

"Septimus," Isana whispered.

"You don't know how many times he got us out of trouble like this." Araris paused for a moment. "Well. Perhaps not quite this much all at once. But then, it was never a matter of scale."

"You believe in him," Isana breathed.

"Great furies help me," Araris said. "It's almost insane. But yes." He was quiet for a moment more. Then he said, "I love you very much, you know."

She nodded, gently, so as not to bump their skulls together. "I do know. I love you, too."

"I've been thinking," he said. He hesitated. "I mean. Well, it isn't like it's an entirely new thought, but . . ."

The awkward little flutter she felt in his confidence was almost painfully endearing. "Yes?"

"If it's possible," Araris said. "I mean . . . if we both live through this. And if . . . if things work out to where . . . I know it probably won't ever be a real possibility, but . . ."

Isana shivered. "Yes?"

"If. One day. If everything . . . Would you . . ." He took a deep breath. "Would you marry me?"

She'd known the direction of his thoughts, from the wildly unsettled sense of his emotions, but she hadn't anticipated her reaction to them.

She laughed. Again. She laughed herself breathless, laboring to keep it quiet.

"Here?" she demanded finally, half-smothered in laughter. "You ask me *here*? *Now?* Like *this*?"

His back had gone completely stiff. "Well," he managed to say after a moment. "Yes. It's . . ." His voice sobered abruptly. "It's all I have."

She fumbled with her bound, half-numb fingers until she found his. They managed to intertwine some of them, more or less at random.

"It's enough," Isana said quietly.

Araris was carefully still for a moment. "Is . . . Then . . . Yes?"

Isana sighed and squeezed his fingers as hard as she could. "Yes."

He suddenly sagged. "Oh," he breathed. "Oh. Oh, good." He shook his head, stroking one of her fingers with one of his. "For a moment there, I was worried."

The absurdity of *that* statement, all things considered, hit them both at the same time.

They were still laughing together when the tent flap rustled, and Phrygiar Navaris ripped off their hoods, a naked sword in her hand.

Chapter 50

"This one," Tavi said quietly, picking up one of the long blades Durias had brought out for his inspection. He snapped it up to a guard position, whirled it about in a loose circling motion of his wrist, and nodded. He could feel it in the steel, the way it settled in his hand, the subtle vibration of the blade as it ceased motion. The weapon was an old one but of excellent manufacture, its blade notched with battle scars in the torchlight, but still strong, flexible, and true. "What about Ehren?"

"I'll take you to him," Durias said. "This way, please, Captain."

Tavi followed the centurion through the darkened Canim camp and was surprised at how much similarity it bore to an Aleran battle camp—though admittedly, the various stations were spread out over a considerably wider area. Perhaps the Canim measured their camp in strides, the way *legionares* did.

The healer's shelters were crowded, but the sounds coming from them were nothing like those of an Aleran healing tent. Instead of the cries and moans of the wounded, there was nothing but a daunting chorus of snarling and growling in every pitch one could imagine, and it made Tavi glad to be unable to see inside.

Most of the wounded Canim who emerged from the tents were walking under their own power. Those who weren't were almost invariably missing limbs. Somewhere in the background, the mourning howls of individual Canim for their fallen brethren rose into the night sky, haunting and savage and beautiful.

"A year ago," Durias said quietly, "I thought I'd get used to that. Still makes the hairs on my neck stand up."

"We're very different peoples," Tavi said quietly.

Durias turned around and stared at Tavi, his expression surprised. "Huh."

"What's that, centurion?"

"Not sure which surprises me more," he said. "To hear a Legion captain call them 'people' instead of 'animals' or to lump himself into a group with a bunch of slaves who have taken up arms."

"You walk, talk, breathe, eat, sleep. Same as me."

Durias snorted. "Since when has that been reason to regard someone else as an equal?"

Tavi showed Durias his teeth, more in the Canim gesture than the Aleran. "You wear armor, carry a sword—and I'm in your camp."

"Hah," Durias snorted. He shook his head once. "But so what if you're a good talker? Talking is easy."

Tavi found himself smiling more naturally as they walked. "I didn't talk you unconscious last spring, centurion."

Durias snorted and rubbed at his jaw. "No. No you didn't."

"You've been with Nasaug for almost two years, I take it."

Durias nodded. "I was . . . He said he got the idea for Free Alera from me."

Tavi lifted his eyebrows. Then he said, "You're the First Spear of your Legion."

"Isn't hard to be First Spear, Captain. You just serve longer than the others. I was the first recruit."

"Bet that's a good story."

Durias shrugged his oversized shoulders.

"But you aren't captain," Tavi noted.

Durias's brief grin showed, and he gestured at his jaw. "Don't have the fist-fighting experience for it, I suppose."

Tavi snorted.

Durias took them past the Canim hospital area and nodded at a patched old Aleran Legion pavilion, converted into a tent with the addition of what looked like reused canvas sails. "Your man's in there."

Tavi stepped forward and noticed Durias standing precisely in the "shadow" of his body, exactly where it would be hardest for Tavi to turn and strike him with the sword he carried. He checked over one shoulder and saw Durias's hand on his *gladius*. He arched an eyebrow at the blocky young man. "What are you doing, centurion?"

"Preventing misunderstandings," Durias said. "Orders, Captain."

Tavi turned fully toward him, then wordlessly offered his sword, hilt first.

Durias shook his head. "That means more here than it does in your Alera, Captain. Keep yours. Just bear in mind that I have one, too."

Tavi studied the young man for a moment, and realized that he was standing with his back straight, feet spread and ready, hand on his sword, but his weight back on his heels. It was an arrogant stance, by Aleran standards, one that almost begged for a fight—but if he'd been a Cane, Tavi would have recognized it immediately as a stance of nonaggression tempered with caution, as one of respect.

"I'll do that," Tavi said. Then he turned and entered the tent, to find Ehren lying in a tub, his throat bloodied—and an enemy knelt beside him with a scarlet blade in her hand.

Tavi's hand went to his sword instantly—but he restrained himself from drawing steel, and an instant later felt the subtle change in the air behind him as Durias's sword crept half an inch from its sheath.

Antillus Dorotea, High Lady Antillus, the sole surviving sibling of the High Lord Kalarus, and the woman who betrayed the First Aleran to the Canim, glanced up at Tavi as he entered the tent.

Tavi felt her emotions at once—first a flare of anger, swift and hot, then a sudden surge of fear that wiped the anger away. She closed her eyes for a moment, lips pressing together, and he felt the woman will both anger and fear away, replacing them with an intent focus and concentration. She turned her attention back to Ehren, who lay naked in a healing tub, his eyes closed and barely conscious.

She set the knife aside, along with the quill she'd been forced to cut free from the swollen flesh around Varg's original incision. Then Lady Antillus gently pressed Ehren lower in the tub, until his throat was covered by the water, and bowed her head.

A sense of . . . not contentment, precisely, or well-being, but something of both, something too rich and deep to be called merely satisfaction, suddenly flowed from her, as the torn flesh knitted closed, the mottled bruising around Ehren's throat lightened, and Tavi's friend drew in a sudden, deep, wheezing breath.

Tavi stared at the High Lady, frowning, taking in details of her appearance. Lady Antillus had been a beautiful woman, in an aggressive, knife-edged way. She looked young, of course, as all the watercrafters tended to do. She'd dressed in silk in the blues of her husband's House, and her dark hair had been long and lovely.

Now she wore a gown of grey homespun cloth, very simple, plain, and sturdily made. Her hair had been cut into a much shorter, more practical length, and was bound back with a leather cord. She wore a healer's apron, smeared with both the scarlet of Aleran blood and the much darker hue of the Canim. She wore no cosmetics—which Tavi had formerly never seen her without—and no jewelry, either.

Except for the gleaming steel of a discipline collar around her throat.

"This will only take me a moment more, First Spear, Captain Scipio," she said, her voice still as quiet and rich as Tavi remembered. "I apologize that it wasn't done sooner, but my services were needed for the most badly wounded."

Tavi stared at her for a moment, at a loss for words. "H-high Lady Antillus. Good evening."

She glanced up with a small smile filled with the awareness of irony. "Oh please, Scipio. High Lady Antillus is a traitor in line for a cell in the Grey Tower, a trial, and an execution. She would most certainly not be aiding you or—unless I miss my guess, from the number of knives he had hidden on him—a Cursor of the Crown."

Tavi frowned at her, tilting his head. "No. I suppose not."

"Call me Dorotea," she said. Tavi could sense gentle regret in her voice, and more of the same sense of deep fulfillment

"I'm a healer. It's what I do now. If you will excuse me." She bent her head back to her healing and closed her eyes.

Tavi shook his head and glanced at Durias.

"Sarl managed to capture her two years ago," Durias said, his voice pitched to a respectful quiet. "He put the discipline collar on her himself, and ordered her to do no harm, to obey those who commanded her and heal those who had need."

Tavi drew in a sudden breath, understanding. "Only Sarl could have taken the collar off."

"And he died," Durias said quietly. There was real and very deep pain and empathy in the young centurion's eyes as he stared at the former High Lady. "She's stuck with it. If it's removed, she dies."

Tavi exhaled slowly, shaking his head.

"You can't have her," Durias said. "I'm to tell you that."

"There's something a tad hypocritical in your people refusing to free a collared slave, Durias. Is this their idea of justice?"

Durias grimaced. "It isn't that, great furies know. I know what she's going through. So do a lot of other folk around here. But she's too valuable to us—and she deserves to be among folk who know what it's like to live under a discipline collar. Who won't abuse her." He shook his head. "Though there was plenty of that, the first several weeks, before order was established."

Tavi felt sickened, just thinking of it. Granted, High Lady Antillus had been no one's idea of a spirit of mercy and goodness, but all the same, no one deserved the kind of retribution that had undoubtedly been visited on her by newly freed, leaderless slaves. "It isn't just what she's done, or the deaths she's responsible for. It's her son."

A sharp spike of pain jumped across the room to Tavi from Dorotea, a yearning, a sadness, a regret, and a fierce, fierce love. She lifted her eyes to his. "Crassus?" she asked. "Is he . . . is he well?"

"The last I knew," Tavi said. "He knows what you did. He won't talk about it to me, but I believe he worries for you. He wonders what has become of you."

Ehren's color had much improved, and his chest was rising

and falling normally, now. Dorotea lifted her fingers to her collar in a fluttering motion, then lowered them again. "I . . ." She closed her eyes. "I think it's best if . . . if Lady Antillus died in the fighting." She opened them again and sought Tavi's eyes. "She did, you know."

"I . . ." Tavi shook his head. "I don't have time for this."

Dorotea flushed and looked down, bowing her head in a gesture of acceptance. "Where is he?"

"I left him in command of the First Aleran."

Her face went pale, and Tavi had to draw upon the steel in the blade beside him to protect himself from the sudden surge of horror as she turned her head toward the besieged ruins.

"As I said, Dorotea," Tavi said quietly. "I have no time. I need Sir Ehren."

"Y-yes," she said. "Of course." She laid her hand on Ehren's head, bowed her own for a moment, and murmured, quietly, "Wake."

Ehren's eyes blinked open without ceremony. "Eh? Hmmm?" They widened. "Ah!" he said. He took a deep breath, and then several more. "Oh, my word, that's more like it. Thank the great furies tha—"

He turned to thank the healer, saw High Lady Antillus, and let out a squeak. His hands flailed about his naked person, presumably looking for a knife, splashing bloodied water everywhere.

"Ehren," Tavi said. "Ehren!"

The young man went still. He tore his eyes from Lady Antillus to Durias, and then to Tavi. They got a bit wider at each stopping point. "Ah. Well. Some things have happened while I was lying down, I see."

"Yes," Tavi said. "And you've got that look on your face again."

"I can't help it," Ehren said. "You're about to walk to breakfast, aren't you, regardless of who is in the way?"

"Yes," Tavi said.

Ehren sighed. "Let's hear it."

Tavi told him the plan.

"That's insane," Ehren said.

"It could work."

"You aren't going to have anyone come along to bail you out this time," Ehren pointed out.

Tavi grinned. "Are you with me?"

"The plan is insane," Ehren said. "*You* are insane." He looked around the inside of the tent. "I'll need some pants."

ᴄᴄᴄ CHAPTER 51

Tavi rode up to the ruins on the best horse the Free Aleran Legion had to offer, and Ehren rode beside him.

Though most of the bodies had been removed, some had been missed in the fighting and the oncoming darkness—and plenty of bits remained where they had fallen. As a result, the darkness was filled with the rustling wings and raucous cries of the omnipresent black crows, feeding upon the fallen.

Ehren, bearing a torch, murmured, "I hope Nasaug knew what he was talking about when he told us which wall the First Aleran was defending. Otherwise, we're likely to get shot by some nervous archer."

"Bloody crows," Tavi replied, as they passed the shattered palisade. "Look at this mess. Did they try to hold the palisade against an ongoing assault?"

"It happens all the time," Ehren said. "Especially when a Legion's taken a beating. Nervous archers on watch. They're tired. Half-asleep. They hear something. Thwang, wham. Then they shout 'who goes there?' while you bleed."

"Look at all the discarded helmets," Tavi said. "The holes punched in the top. Ancient Romanic writings we found at Appia mention a weapon that could do that—they called it a falx."

"Did the ancient Romanics ever get shot in the dark by mistake?" Ehren asked. "Because I'd really hate the file on me in the Cursor Legate's office to end like that."

Tavi's borrowed horse shied away from a mound of jabbering crows. Birds cried out in the night, and Tavi smiled slightly. "You aren't worrying in the right direction."

"No?" Ehren asked.

"I'm more worried about some enterprising young Cane who doesn't see eye to eye with Varg and Nasaug putting a couple of balest bolts through our backs."

Ehren gave Tavi a sour look. "That's very reassuring. I'm glad I'm carrying the light. They'll shoot you first."

"That's the spirit," Tavi said. He drew his horse to a stop about fifty feet from the walls and lifted a hand in greeting. "Hello on the wall!"

"Don't come any closer!" called a *legionare's* voice. "We'll shoot!"

Tavi squinted at the darkened walls. "Schultz? Is that you?"

There was a short, baffled silence. "Captain? Captain Scipio?"

"Aye," Tavi drawled. "With Sir Ehren beside me. It's a little cold out tonight. Any chance you could spare a cup of hot tea?"

"Come forward," Schultz demanded. "Up to the base of the wall. Let me see your face."

Tavi and Ehren did so, and a pale face peered out at them from beneath a Legion-issue helmet. Tavi recognized the young centurion at once.

"Captain!" Schultz cried.

"Crows take it, Schultz," Tavi scolded. "You know better than that. Even if it looks like me, it could be a watercrafted double. Go get Foss, or Tribune Antillar or Antillus, and have them do a truthfinding on me."

Schultz grinned. "Yes, sir. You stay right there, sir." He paused. "You don't want this kept quiet, or you wouldn't be shouting at the whole wall, would you?"

Tavi felt himself grin in answer. "It's chilly out here, centurion. Bring us in under guard, if you would."

"Yes, sir!" Schultz said. "If you'll move about sixty paces to the east, sir, there's an opening. I'll have them meet you there, sir."

"Thank you, centurion, understood." Tavi turned his horse, and Ehren followed him along the wall. They could hear the mutters racing out along the wall ahead of them—excited soldiers whispering that Scipio had returned.

Tavi could feel the emotion that began pouring down from the wall. Excitement, interest, the tight, aching fear that came along with any action—and, that most vital of emotions to a commander: hope. As Tavi rode beneath the positions on the wall, soldiers stood forward, snapping to attention as if they were being reviewed and not keeping an eye on a potential spy.

The "opening" in the wall proved to be a blank section of stone like any other—except that, as Tavi approached, the stone of the wall itself melted like wax and flowed down and away, leaving an opening in the wall just wide enough to let a horse squeeze inside. Tavi rode through, his knees scraping stone on both sides, and recognized all six of the First Aleran's Knights Flora on the wall above the opening, bows in hand, ready to send deadly accurate arrows winging into anyone who might have tried to take advantage of the opening.

Almost before Ehren's horse was through, the engineers of the First Aleran, half a dozen weary-looking men on each side of the opening, sealed the wall again, coaxing the stone back up into position. Two of the Knights Flora above turned to keep an eye on Tavi and Ehren—as they should have, until their identities had been verified.

Tavi was content to stay right where he was for the moment, in the circle of firelight cast by Ehren's sputtering torch, where several hundred *legionares* could see him clearly. The chatter on the walls had risen in volume, almost drowning out the crow calls and bird cries echoing around the ruins.

Schultz appeared out of the darkness. The young centurion of the Battlecrow Cohort had been a raw recruit when at the battle of the Elinarch. Now he had scars and commendations enough to do him proud in any Legion in the Realm. The centurion bore a tin soldier's mug in either hand, and both of them were steaming in the cool night air. He offered the first to Tavi, and the second to Ehren, and Tavi took the mug of strong tea gratefully.

"There you go, Captain," Schultz said with a salute. "Alleged captain," he corrected himself.

Tavi grinned at him. "Bless you, man." He swallowed some of the hot brew, studying Schultz's manner and bearing, contrasting them against the weary fear that was pouring off of him. The man was putting on an act of carelessly brave indifference in front of the men of the Legion, but he was clearly worried—and with good reason. Tavi didn't see half as many men on the wall as the area covered demanded, which implied that the First Aleran had lost a lot of soldiers to injury and exhaustion. And the tea was too crowbegotten thick. No one took it that strong, no matter how tired they were. The Legion was short on water.

They were afraid. Fear could take the life from a Legion more quickly than any blade, and Tavi reacted at once to combat it as he sipped the tea and spoke within hearing of the men. "Mmm. Were you planning on using this stuff as mortar later?"

"Bricks," Schultz replied. "But that pansy Gregus watered it down."

"I don't want to know with what," Tavi shot back.

A chorus of quiet chuckles rippled up and down the wall.

Schultz grinned and glanced around. "Sir . . . if I might ask . . . why are you back, Captain?"

Tavi sipped more tea. He hadn't realized how achingly tired he was, until he felt some of the drink restoring a bit of life to his limbs. "Hmmm? Come on, Schultz. You never get a straight answer from captains. You should know that by now." He swallowed more tea as the men laughed quietly again. "The Crown's found an even worse mess out there for us to be in, and our orders are to get there right away."

Schultz gestured at the ruins and battered men around them. "And leave all this?"

Instant sounds of feigned disappointment and disgust fell from the walls and the ruined structures in the immediate area.

Schultz had understood what Tavi was doing, and abetted him, releasing some of the pressure on the men. It had been good thinking for a man his age, after the day he'd had, and Tavi nodded his approval at him. "As you were, centurion. You'll have your marching orders soon enough."

"Yes, sir," Schultz said, saluting. The sound of marching boots came nearer, and Schultz faded back as a party arrived, which proved to be Antillus Crassus, flanked by several Knights Terra, and followed by the blunt, stocky form of Valiar Marcus.

"Schultz?" Crassus demanded, his voice strained with anger. "Pulling me out of a command meeting? This had better be good. And who the crows authorized that light to be—"

Crassus came to a dead stop as he reached the edge of the torchlight, and his eyes widened as he recognized Tavi and Ehren. His mouth opened, as if for an exclamation, but then he clenched his lips shut with a visible effort of will and gave Tavi a terse nod instead. "Centurion. Has his identity been verified?"

"No, sir," Schultz replied. "Tribune Foss sends his compliments and asks me to tell you that he is too crowbegotten busy to wander around the camp on errands, sir."

"True enough, tonight." Crassus sighed.

Tavi dismounted and shifted his tea to his left hand, waiting quietly.

Crassus made sure that the Knights Flora were covering him, and then approached Tavi, offering his right hand. Tavi traded grips with the younger man.

"Your name?" Crassus asked.

Tavi's world froze for an instant.

Every detail came into crystal clarity—the scent of greasy woodsmoke from Ehren's torch, the clank of a *legionare's* armor against the stone battlements, the dim gleam of torchlight on battered armor. A patch of Crassus's hair had been burned down to stubble, close to his scalp, and the red stones in the hilt of the Cane-sized dagger on his belt twinkled in the scarlet light. The moon and the stars hung, for an instant, entirely suspended, and Tavi was left alone, in all the universe with a single fact for company:

He'd lived most of his life surrounded in a cloak of lies and half-truths.

After this moment, after this breath, everything would change.

"Most of my life," he said quietly, "I have been known as Tavi of Bernardholt, in the Calderon Valley of Riva. Then I became Tavi Patronus Gaius, and Tavi ex Cursori. In the time you have known me, Crassus, my name was Rufus Scipio, Third Subtribune and later Captain of the First Aleran."

The hilltop, the ruin, was perfectly silent, perfectly still.

Tavi's voice flowed into that stillness, confident and steady, and he could hardly believe it was his own. "But my name," he said, raising his voice so that it rang from the battlecrafted walls and fallen stones, "is Gaius Octavian, son of Gaius Septimus, son of Gaius Sextus, First Lord of Alera."

And as that name fell onto the evening air, the sky bloomed into scarlet light.

Tavi wasn't sure what had happened, but the light was directly behind him, to the south, and it illuminated the entire southern sky as if he'd called the sun itself back from its nightly journey into darkness to herald his presence. It washed over the ruins, revealing the exhausted, startled, awestruck faces of *legionares* covered in grime and blood. It threw his shadow out before him, engulfing Valiar Marcus, and Crassus, and the Knights escorting them.

And it revealed, approaching through the ruins, a second and larger group of men, consisting of a number of armored *legionares* of the Senatorial Guard, Captain Nalus and his seniormost officers—and Senator Guntus Arnos, his *singulares*, and his hangers-on.

Crassus, who had been seeking the sound of truth with his watercrafting senses, went absolutely white with shock, his fingers tightening almost painfully on Tavi's. A beat later, the young Tribune dropped to one knee, and after a baffled second his Knights, the First Spear, then the whole of the First Aleran followed suit. The clank and clatter of arms and armor was like a roar of surf on a stony shoreline.

The Senator stood staring in slack-jawed shock. The hem of his Senatorial robes dropped from his numbed fingers, and landed in dirt made muddy with blood.

"I am Princeps Gaius Octavian," Tavi said, his voice loud and cold. "And I am here to bring a treasonous slive to account for his deeds."

As Tavi spoke, there was a rumble in the earth, so low-pitched that it shook his teeth, and the ground began to a tremble. Tavi's heart leapt, and he almost followed suit in fear of plummeting stonework, seeking shelter under a nearby archway that had somehow survived.

If he scrambled for cover, though, it wouldn't make a terribly regal impression upon those watching. Tavi elected to roll with the situation. He had no idea what was happening, but bloody crows, it certainly added something to the delivery.

He pointed a finger at the stunned senator. "Guntus Arnos! For conspiring with enemies of the Crown in plots that resulted in the deaths of hundreds of serving *legionares*, for the assault upon and the subsequent abduction of the rightful First Lady of Alera by subordinates under your direct command, and for ordering the *murder* of Aleran freemen, holders, and their families, I call you a traitor to your lord, your Realm, and your people!"

Arnos's mouth twitched, and incoherent gobbling noises came from it.

"I call you to account, traitor!" Tavi thundered, and a nearby wall gave way beneath the shuddering earth and fell. "I call you to the *juris macto*! And may the crows feast on the unjust!"

CHAPTER 52

"If you kill me now," Araris said quietly to Navaris, "no one will ever know."

The sword-slender woman stared at Araris with dead eyes.

Then she shrugged.

"I'll get over it."

Isana felt the cutter's decision the instant she'd made it, and a blossom of mad, unholy glee flared out from Navaris as she turned to Araris and lifted her sword.

"No!" Isana cried, struggling against the ropes.

Without warning, the earth suddenly shook.

Navaris staggered, reaching out to seize the tent's central pole to keep from falling. The tent sagged to one side, and its flap fell open, revealing a lurid twilight outside. The earth continued to rumble, and Isana could hear stone falling on stone. Somewhere in the background, a strident male voice thundered in furious speech.

Navaris stared around in angry surprise and shuffled to the tent's opening over the still-trembling ground, eyes roaming back and forth.

Isana felt a sense of bafflement from Araris that must have matched the incredulity on her own face, and just then there was a sharply whistled birdcall from outside.

A voice lifted up in what Isana recognized as a Marat war cry, and the tent was suddenly ripped away around them. Isana had to twist her head down against one shoulder to avoid a trailing rope. The tent flew off, and Isana had time to see a pair of leggy Marat coursers, bearing their barbarian riders, gallop off, dragging the tent behind them.

The sky was lit with red light, which seemed to cast shadows that were somehow subtly wrong for a sunset, until Isana realized that was because they *were*. The ruddy light of sunset poured in from the west. *This* light came from almost directly to the south.

Kitai appeared from the shadows behind a dilapidated stone building. The Marat girl was dressed just as she had been when Isana saw her last, though she bore a heavily recurved Marat bow in her hands, complete with an arrow tipped with razor-sharp, glossy black stone.

Navaris saw her, too. The cutter took a smooth step to Isana's side and rested her sword against the Steadholder's throat.

"Kitai," Isana breathed.

"Good evening," Kitai said pleasantly. She peered at the sky to the south, then turned to Navaris. "What do you make of that?"

Navaris jerked her head to one side in a gesture of suspicion and fixed Kitai with a steady stare.

"I didn't think you knew. I don't know what it is, either," Kitai said. She shook her head and then tipped one end of her bow at Isana. "Walk away from them both, Phrygiar Navaris, or you will die."

Navaris's mouth twitched up into a little smirk.

"Yes," Kitai admitted. "You could probably stop my arrow. But can you stop twenty?"

She twisted up her lips and gave another trilling birdcall, and the shadows boiled over with leather-armored Marat warriors rising from concealment. Every single barbarian bore a bow like Kitai's, and every one of them had a stone-tipped arrow nocked to it.

"Stone-headed arrows, Navaris," Kitai said, her voice steady and empty of malice. "From every direction. No way to see them all. No metal for you to sense."

Navaris's expression went blank. Her eyes flicked around, taking stock of her situation.

"Walk away," Kitai repeated.

Twenty Marat warriors drew their bows at the same time. The creak of the weapons' curved staves and straining strings sounded like an old barn in bad weather.

Navaris never flinched. "If you shoot, I will kill her before I die."

"Yes," Kitai said in a patient tone. "Which is why I have not shot you. Yet. Walk away."

"If I step away from her, what is to prevent you from killing me?"

"Your death doesn't belong to me," Kitai said. "We flipped a coin. I lost."

Navaris lifted her eyebrows.

"Go," Kitai said. She raised her voice, presumably addressing the Marat present. "Neither I nor any of mine will harm you or seek to prevent you from leaving."

Navaris considered that for a second. One eyelid twitched several times, and Isana felt dizzy from the variety and disorienting intensity of the emotions flooding from the cutter. Navaris experienced terror, contempt, joy, hunger, lust, and howling satisfaction all at the same instant, all jumbled up inside her thoughts. Isana could sense the barrier of will that generally kept that hurricane of violent emotion in check.

The barrier quivered like the earth beneath their feet, but it did not break. The formless, colorless mass of will suddenly blanketed the strong emotions, and they vanished into the void that was Phrygiar Navaris. The woman lowered her blade, nodded her head once, and walked with quick, quiet steps from the circle of Marat archers as the red light began to fade from the sky.

Kitai moved directly to Isana's side and knelt down beside her. The Marat woman's eyes never wavered from Navaris's departing form. Once she was gone, Kitai drew a knife, and muttered, "Crazy bitch."

She cut Isana and Araris free of their bonds, and rose. "Hurry," she said. "There's no time."

Araris managed to stagger to his feet, but Isana simply couldn't. Her limbs and back knotted themselves tight when she tried it, and to her embarrassment she found herself unable to stand.

"Help her," Kitai snapped, and Isana found herself being lifted by a pair of brawny young barbarian riders, one of them under each arm. Kitai made an impatient sound and started through the ruins. Araris hobbled after her, and Isana's bearers more or less dragged her along with her tingle-numbed toes dragging the ground, passing too close to the nearest hospital area. The pain and fear of the wounded slammed against her like a frost-coated leather lash.

Isana struggled to brace herself against it, focusing on her surroundings until they had passed the hospital. The red light in the sky had faded almost completely, and was now only a dim band of sullen red on the southern horizon.

"Kitai," Isana said. "Where are we? How did you get here?"

"The ruins outside Mastings," Kitai replied shortly. "My mother-sister's kinsmen lowered a rope for me in the dark. I was sent to find you."

"Why?"

"To prevent Arnos from using you as hostages against Octavian, obviously."

"*Kitai!*" Isana breathed.

Kitai shrugged. "They all know by now, Isana. Right now, my Aleran is declaring himself and challenging Arnos to the *juris macto*."

"What?" Araris demanded. Horror pulsed off of him in a nauseating cloud.

"The *juris macto*," Kitai said seriously. "It means 'trial of the fist.' Though it isn't a literal fistfight. I still do not understand why your people insist on naming things by calling them something else. It is insane."

"I *know* what the *juris macto* is."

"Araris," Isana asked, her voice shaking. "What's wrong?"

"He's the challenger," Araris spat. "What is he *thinking*?"

"I don't understand," she said. "Can't you stand for him? Champion him?"

"No!" Araris half shouted. "He's the *challenger*. He can't have a champion. He *has* to engage in it personally, or the law won't recognize its outcome as valid."

"Tavi can't have a champion?" Isana felt the bottom of her stomach fall out. "But Arnos can." She went cold. "Great furies. Navaris will be his champion."

Araris spat to one side. "That's what she does."

"I told him he should have let me handle it," Kitai said. "But after escaping one prison and stealing Varg from another, suddenly Aleran law is important again."

Feeling had begun to return to Isana's legs and feet, and she shrugged her supporters away, walking on her own. "Is he likely to be hurt, Araris?"

"Hurt?" Araris shook his head grimly. "It's to the death."

Isana stopped in her tracks and stared at Araris. "Can he beat her?"

Araris clenched his fists, frustration and worry pouring off him like heat from a bonfire.

"Araris," she pled quietly.

The *singulare* said nothing, and Isana knew why.

She would have known if he lied to her.

Kitai led Isana and Araris to the First Aleran's command tent, which was by tradition the captain's quarters. It looked like it had been set up in great haste, several of its ropes hanging rather loosely. Inside was nothing more than a furylamp, a camp stool, and a bedroll.

"I think I know what you want to tell him," Kitai said quietly. "I think you know he won't listen."

"I will speak to him all the same."

Kitai frowned, but nodded. "I understand." Then she left.

She returned with Tavi a few minutes later, and the tall young man immediately enfolded Isana in an embrace.

"Thank the great furies you're both all right," Tavi said.

Isana hugged her son back. "And you."

The tent opened and Ehren appeared, carrying a scribe's writing case. He plunked himself down, opened the case, and took out a pen, inkpot, and several sheets of paper.

Tavi released Isana with a smile, and asked, "Well?"

"It looked like the testimony of six different truthfinders wasn't going to be enough," Ehren said. "Until I showed Nalus the affidavits from the witnesses to the attacks on the steadholts. He's thrown his support behind the validity of the charges and the challenge."

"Meaning?" Isana asked quietly.

Ehren bared his teeth in a wolf's smile. "Meaning that if Arnos doesn't accept, he can kiss all his efforts good-bye. He'll have to stand down from his command, just like Tavi had to step down, and wait for a trial." He inhaled and let out a satisfied breath. "I love the symmetry."

"What are you writing?" Tavi asked.

"A declaration of identity and intent," Ehren said. "Retroactively giving yourself permission to release yourself on your own recognizance in order to defend the honor of the Realm. It's going to block Arnos's next move, to claim that you are a prisoner under suspicion and that your presence, and therefore your challenge, is illegal."

"I can do that?"

"Unless someone overrules you, and the only one who can do *that* has been out of touch for a while."

"Good."

Ehren nodded. "I'm just glad Arnos forced us to brush up on the pertinent laws when this mess started. Give me about ten minutes. Then we'll need the signet dagger."

A slender, older gentleman in the tunic of an officer's valet entered the tent, lugging a heavy leather sack. "Ah, there you are, sir," he said. He dropped the sack near Tavi's feet with a sigh of relief. "Your reserve lorica, sir."

Tavi dumped out the sack without preamble, revealing a much-newer-looking set of armor than the one he currently wore. "Excellent. The Free Alerans have decent gear, all things considered, but this set has seen better days. Give me a hand here, Magnus?"

"Of course, Captain," the valet said. "Or is it 'Your Highness,' now?"

Tavi arched an eyebrow at the man. "You don't believe me?"

"That isn't the issue," the valet replied. He glanced aside at the others.

"I'm not keeping secrets from anyone here," Tavi said. He glanced at Isana, and she felt a little knife of resentment accompanying the words. He pushed it down at once, but it had still been there.

Isana winced. However well-intentioned she had been, some mistakes took time to correct. She would have to live with that.

Magnus sighed. "Very well. May I have your permission to speak candidly, Your Highness?"

Tavi's frown deepened. "Of course."

Magnus nodded. "This stunt is idiocy on the grandest and most irresponsible scale in the history of mankind."

Tavi's eyebrows shot up.

"Entirely setting aside the fact that this is the worst possible time and place for you to go public, there are other considerations. The Princeps of the Realm is *not* someone who engages in duels. He does *not* put his person at risk. He does *not* take such chances. He is far too valuable to do so."

"The Realm has had a Princeps again for about twenty minutes, Magnus," Tavi said. "The only people who know about it are within these walls. Even if I lose, the Realm won't—or not much, at any rate."

"Tavi," Isana said, stepping forward. "Listen to him, please. Magnus is right."

Tavi glanced aside at her, and a frown with a trace of uncertainty to it formed a small line between his brows. He nodded slowly and gestured for the valet to continue.

"With all due respect to Princeps Septimus," Magnus continued, "your father made this choice as well." His voice hardened. "And he was wrong to do it. He died. And as a result, Alera has known twenty years of plotting and betrayal and conflict. It has all but shattered as High Lords maneuver for power, inflicting hardship and suffering, and triggering disputes and wars that have resulted in the deaths of thousands—to say nothing of those lost when our enemies sensed that we were becoming increasingly divided and acted upon it."

"Tavi," Isana said quietly. "There must be some other solution to this problem."

Tavi chewed on his lower lip, his eyes unreadable.

"Navaris is one of the best I have ever seen," Araris said, speaking for the first time. "In my judgment, if I fought her, even in a controlled duel, it could go either way. You've got talent and training, but you're still learning. Your chances are not good."

"Agreed," Magnus said. "Risking yourself in a battle is one thing. Throwing your life away in a fight only a fool would place money upon is something else altogether."

Tavi looked at each of them, his expression serious. Then he glanced at Kitai.

"I would be displeased should you be killed, *chala*." She shrugged. "You will do as you think best."

Tavi nodded slowly. Then he took a deep breath, and pointed his finger at the wall of the tent. "Out there," he said, "are tens of thousands of frightened, angry Canim. And thousands more frightened, angry, vengeful ex-slaves. They've got all three of our Legions dead to rights, and in a few hours, they're going to kill us.

"Unless," he said, "I can show them a reason to believe that we're more than a bunch of murdering, crowbegotten bastards who deserve to be killed. Unless I can give them the men responsible for those massacres and get these Legions to stand down and stop threatening the Canim's only means of going home."

"But Tavi," Isana said. "There must be some other way to—"

"While Arnos is in command, there isn't," Tavi said, his voice certain. "He can't back down and leave the Canim in peace now. He'll continue the fight and kill every man in the Legions if that's what it takes to get his victory, and I'm not willing to let that happen."

"Then arrest him," Isana said.

"I don't have the grounds to do so yet," Tavi said. "And if I tried to arrest him illegally, his own people would fight to protect him. We'd do the Canim's work for them. And then they'd wipe out whoever was left standing. After that, the war would continue. More will suffer. More will die.

"The *juris macto* gets us around all of that, and it's the only way I can strip him of his legal authority without taking it to a courtroom."

"But—" Magnus began.

Tavi turned to the old valet, scowling. "It's this simple, Magnus: The Canim are coming. Either I give them Arnos, or they kill us all and take him. The duel is my only way to get at Arnos." He looked at each of them singly and separately. "Does anyone here see another way? Anyone?"

No one spoke.

Tavi nodded slowly. "I'm going through with this. Support me or get out of the way."

He swept his gaze around the room again, and Isana stared, fascinated. She had never seen him like this before. She had never seen *anyone* speak with that much authority and strength. Not since Septimus died.

"I can't," said Araris, his voice very quiet. "I can't let you do this. I'm not going to fail again."

Tavi met Araris's gaze steadily and spoke in a very quiet voice. "This is my fight. My responsibility. Or did you plan on pushing me in front of a wagon to stop me."

Araris's face went pale, and he averted his eyes.

Ehren blew gently on the sheet of paper, then fanned the air with it slowly, to help the ink dry. "Ready for your signature and that seal."

Tavi nodded and turned to Isana.

"I don't have the dagger," she told him quietly. "It was in my bag. I haven't seen it since we were captured."

Kitai stepped past Isana quietly, shrugging her pack off of her shoulders. She reached into it and retrieved a dagger, the steel of its blade and its hilt both showing traceries of scarlet and blue. The dagger's pommel was engraved with the signet of the House of Gaius, an eagle in flight. Kitai passed it to Tavi.

Isana took a slow breath. Then she said, "You took it from my pack."

"I thought I might need it," Tavi said quietly.

"You didn't trust me."

Tavi looked down, turning the dagger over in his hand. "You've had a lot of . . . reservations, about this part of my life. I didn't want to see them get the better of you at a bad moment."

"You didn't trust me," Isana repeated. She shook her head. It was not as though she had given him a great deal of reason to do so, but all the same, it stung.

Tavi signed the document and marked it with the pommel of his signet dagger. He folded it and sealed it closed the same way. "Three hours from now," Tavi said. "On the walls. I want everyone to see this."

"Got it," Ehren said. He took the sealed letter and hurried out.

"If you don't mind," Tavi said to the tent, "I'd like a few minutes alone to change."

Everyone murmured their farewells and left—but Isana paused at the entrance to the tent, and turned to face Tavi.

"Can you win?" she whispered.

He smiled crookedly. "I've never lost a duel to the death. Not one."

"Tavi."

The smile faded, but his eyes didn't waver. "I've got to. For all of us." He glanced down again, and said, "I have a favor to ask of you."

Isana nodded. "Of course."

"My friend is hurt," Tavi said. "Max. And a lot of my men. Do you think . . ."

Isana bowed her head to him. "I'll go to the hospital now."

Tavi closed his eyes. "Thank you." He licked his lips, then suddenly his reserve shattered, and his emotions came pouring through to her. They were achingly familiar to Isana—the fear and insecurity that had greeted her whenever Tavi, as a child, had woken from a nightmare in the darkest hours of night.

She went to him at once and hugged him as tightly as she could. She felt him lean some of his weight against her.

"I'm frightened," he whispered.

"I know," she said.

"Don't tell anyone. They mustn't see."

"I know," she said.

"I love you, Mother."

Isana could feel it as he spoke it, and she held him even tighter. "And I love you, my son."

⚹⊶CHAPTER 53

Marcus paused in the shadows outside of Senator Arnos's well-lit command tent, and listened, watching through the half-open flap.

"Well?" Arnos demanded of one of his cadre of flunkies. "You're my legal advisor. Advise me."

"I'm sorry, Senator," the plump little man said, from the midst of a stack of thick books. "All the legal precedents would seem to be on the Princep—"

"*Scipio,*" Arnos snarled. "His name is Scipio."

"—Scipio's," the man corrected seamlessly, "side. He has . . . technically, of course . . . satisfied the legal requirements to establish his identity, and in the case of a threat of treason or dishonor to the Realm, Citizens of the rank of Lord and above have the right to issue a challenge to any Citizen of the Realm."

"I *know* that," Arnos snarled. "What do I *do* about it?"

The man tried to smile, and his voice came out in a squeak. "You could always renounce your Citizenship, sir."

Arnos slapped him. "Idiot. Get out before I have you flogged."

The little man went scrambling from the tent, and Marcus stepped back to let him pass.

"You could take his advice, you know," said a woman's voice. Marcus recognized Lady Aquitaine's disguise at once.

"Bloody crows and furies," snarled Arnos, his throat tight. "How long have you been there?"

"Long enough to see that you are in a spot, Arnos."

The Senator let out a fairly uncivilized growl. "I'm not backing away now. I'd lose everything I've worked years to build. In my professional opinion, it is time for you to intervene."

"And?" she asked.

"And make it go away," he said, his voice coming through clenched teeth.

"I believe I've made a mistake in you, Arnos. I knew you were a pompous egotist with delusions of grandeur, but I *did* believe you were at least competent."

Arnos stared in silence for a few seconds, then accused, "We had a deal."

"We had an understanding," Lady Aquitaine said. "But you've broken faith with me. You told me that you hadn't acquired any of your troops as mercenaries. But your extremely well-supplied and well-armed and well-paid cavalry seem to have taken it upon themselves to loot and pillage every human habitation they come across."

"Their Tribunes are acting independently of my orders," Arnos said.

"You're the commander of these Legions, dear. You're responsible for what they do. That's rather why one is able to attain glory and respect after a victory. Or don't they teach that at the Collegia."

"How *dare* you lecture me on—"

Lady Aquitaine's voice, though still quiet, turned cold.

"Don't make me raise my hand, Arnos. When I slap someone, he doesn't scurry away after."

Arnos jerked up straight, and his face turned red. "You were willing enough to spill Aleran blood six weeks ago."

"I'm willing to make sacrifices in pursuit of a greater goal," Lady Aquitaine said. "That's not the same as condoning the rape and murder of entire steadholts. There was no profit to those actions. No purpose. It's unprofessional. Idiotic. And I have difficulty tolerating idiots."

"Then you should agree that this conversation is unprofitable, given the circumstances. We need to focus on the matter at hand."

"Oh?"

"We're probably worried about nothing. Navaris is going to introduce our young captain to the crows, and that will solve the problems at hand."

"Will it?" she said in a flat voice. "I've made a decision about the problems at hand, Arnos."

The Senator's voice sounded wary. "What's that?"

"They're your problems," Lady Aquitaine said, her tone pitiless. "Solve them by yourself. If you manage to survive them, I may be willing to renegotiate our relationship. But until then, you're on your own."

Arnos's mouth opened and closed several times.

Lady Aquitaine appeared in the tent's doorway and faced Marcus. She gave him a small smile, then it vanished. She turned, and hissed to Arnos, "Someone is coming."

Marcus took that as his cue and briskly strode to the mouth of the tent. "Senator?" He held up a roll of paper. "I've brought the First Aleran's casualty list for you to look over."

Lady Aquitaine's simple gown was spotted with blood, doubtless from the wounded men to whom she had been carrying water. She took the paper with a little curtsey and passed it over to Arnos.

Arnos unrolled it and glanced at it. "Thank you, centurion. Dismissed."

Marcus saluted and withdrew from the tent. He found Lady Aquitaine walking beside him.

"Sloppy," he said quietly. "Speaking that openly. Someone could overhear."

She made a tsking sound. "I extended the windcrafting to include you."

Marcus grunted.

"The duel is to be held on the south wall of the fortifications," Lady Aquitaine said. "This is the time for the balest, I suppose."

Marcus nodded. "Which?"

She shook her head. "There's something to be had on all fronts of this debacle. If Arnos is vindicated, our would-be Princeps has been dealt with. If Octavian wins, he gets rid of a useless retainer who might well return to stab me in the back when I'm not looking."

Marcus understood the cold-blooded logic of it. "Wait until it's over. Shoot the winner."

"Problems solved," Lady Aquitaine said.

"There might be some problems you aren't considering," Marcus said. "About sixty thousand of them."

The mourning howls of the Canim army drifted through the night air.

She frowned, and rubbed her hands on her arms as if cold. "It's unfavorable. I'd rather not lose the Legions, but the odds would seem to be against it."

"You could improve them."

Lady Aquitaine stopped in her tracks and stared. "You can't be serious."

"Consider the advantages should we succeed," Marcus said. "Between this and the Vord attack in the citadel, you'll be establishing yourself as a true hero of the Realm. You'll gain even more allies."

"Assuming I'm not killed in the fighting, of course," she said. "No. That's not a chance I'm willing to take. Should the battle go ill, I'll take us both safely away."

No you won't, Marcus thought. *I know you, Your Grace. Why remove two liabilities when it's as easy to manage three?*

Marcus brooded for a moment, and when the privacy aircrafting Lady Aquitaine had been holding suddenly collapsed, he all but collided with the captain.

"Ah, there you are," the captain said. "I've been looking for you. Where did you get off to, First Spear?"

Tavi's eyes traveled to the disguised Lady Aquitaine, and his eyebrows rose in time with the corners of his mouth. "Ah-hah."

Lady Aquitaine dropped another curtsey, her eyes on the ground, and her cheeks turned pink.

Marcus coughed gruffly as he saluted. "Captain." He turned to Lady Aquitaine. "I must attend to my duties."

She nodded silently, still blushing—or pretending to be—and kissed Marcus on the cheek, curtseyed again to the captain, and hurried away.

"I didn't know you had a woman," Tavi said, grinning. "Ready to work?"

"Yes, sir."

"Good. I—" The captain frowned suddenly, studying Lady Aquitaine as she left.

Marcus watched him frown pensively. "Sir?"

"Mmmm?" The captain shook his head. "Oh, nothing. She just seemed familiar to me for a moment."

"You may have seen her around the camp, sir."

"That's probably it." The young man rolled his shoulders beneath his armor. "The show starts in an hour. I'd like you to make sure the south wall is cleared of debris and ready."

Marcus saluted. "Will do, Captain."

The captain thumped a fist down on one of Marcus's armored shoulders. "What would I do without you, centurion? Carry on."

Marcus strode away to the wall, rounded up two spears' worth of *legionares*, and proceeded to clear it. Then he hurried back toward the wagons to get his gear. He'd already picked a likely spot from which to shoot. There should be just time enough to collect the balest and reach his position.

And after that, who knew.

He might even get to rest.

As challenger to the duel, protocol required Tavi to arrive at the field first, and his knuckles were white as he climbed up the ladder to the southern wall.

It felt like a very long way up.

Tavi pulled himself up to the top of the wall and made room for Araris, who was coming up behind him. The structure was a standard Legion battle wall, at least in appearance. Given how much material they'd had to raise, and how little time they'd had to do it, Tavi was sure that it lacked the interlocking, interwoven layers of stone that would make it practically invincible to all but the most violent furycrafting. The wall itself was a flat shelf about eight feet across, and crenellation rose along its outer edge. The tops of the merlons rose to a few inches higher than Tavi's head, and the embrasures between them rose to the middle of Tavi's stomach.

The wall was a series of straight sections, each one at a slight angle to the next, following the terrain it had been built upon. It would not be difficult to keep track of the inner edge, which would be handy for avoiding a potentially fatal fall to the ground below. At Tavi's order, his men had left a series of furylamps along the length of the wall, providing plenty of light to see by.

He felt cold. Though spring was edging toward summer, the night was chilly, and the steel of his armor drew the heat from his body.

"Walk a bit," Araris suggested. "Stretch out. You don't want to go into it with your muscles cold and tight."

Tavi followed the *singulare's* suggestion. "How many times have you fought in the *juris macto*, Fade?" He caught himself and shook his head. "I mean, Araris."

The older man smiled, his eyes wrinkling at their corners. "I don't mind it from you," he said. "And I've done it four times. I championed someone else in three of them."

"Four?" Tavi asked, still stretching. "That's all?"

"I don't enjoy hurting people."

Tavi shook his head. "That's not what I meant. From your reputation, I thought it would be dozens."

Araris shrugged. "Quality over quantity, I suppose. I fought the High Lord of Parcia's bastard half brother when he challenged the old man for the throne of his city. Antillus Raucus took offense at a young Knight, even younger than you, who had been sleeping with his sister. I had to intervene on the Knight's behalf."

"You beat a High Lord at the blade?" Tavi asked.

"Like I said. Quality over quantity." Araris frowned. "He's got a scar or two to show for it, but I didn't kill him. And I championed Septimus just before the Battle of Seven Hills broke out—"

"That was *you*?" Tavi said.

Araris shrugged again. "Kadius, a Placidan Lord, had decided that he needed to improve his lands by stealing his neighbors', and Septimus and the Crown Legion were sent to restore order. Kadius challenged the Princeps to compel him to withdraw—and when I killed him, his wife went insane with anger and sent every soldier in her army against the Crown Legion. They had a respectable force of Knights. It was a mess."

"And the fourth was Aldrick ex Gladius," Tavi said.

"With more than a hundred duels to his credit. He used to hire out as a champion, before he took up service with your father. That one got a lot of attention. We went for about ten hours, all the way around Garden Lane and Craft Lane both. Must have been fifty or sixty thousand people that came down to see it."

Tavi frowned, lifted a boot to one of the embrasures, and leaned, stretching out his leg. "But he challenged Sir Miles originally, right?"

"Yes."

"Over what?"

"A girl." Araris narrowed his eyes, looking down the wall past Tavi. "They're here."

A hundred feet down the wall, Navaris pulled herself up from the ladder and rose. The slender cutter wore close-fit armor of leather and light mail, rather than the heavy, steel-plated Legion lorica Tavi wore. She faced him from a hundred feet away, and her expression was empty, devoid of humanity. She carried a long blade and a *gladius* on two belts slung over her shoulder, just as Araris carried Tavi's. Neither of them would burden themselves with a scabbard in this duel.

Arnos climbed up the stairs behind her, and the climb up the ladder had evidently convinced him to rid himself of the tailored Senatorial robes. He was dressed in a coat of mail, and was puffing visibly from hauling himself and the armor up the ladder.

Tavi watched Navaris, willing all expression from his face as well. He was glad she'd come up so far away. It gave him time to get control of the sudden trembling in his hands before she could come close enough to see it. He took slow, steady breaths.

"She's human," Araris said quietly. "She's imperfect. She can be beaten."

"Can she?" Tavi asked.

"She's won a lot of duels," Araris said. "But most of them were the same duel, just with a different face. Someone relatively inexperienced, who let fear rule their thoughts and actions. They were over in seconds."

"I'm relatively inexperienced compared to Navaris," Tavi said drily. "For that matter, so are you."

Araris smiled. "Patience. Don't let the fear drive you. Don't initiate. Mind your footwork, keep your blades in tight, and wait for your opening."

"Suppose she doesn't give me an opening."

"Outthink her. Make one."

Tavi laid a hand on the merlon beside him. "Like you did at Second Calderon."

"Exactly. Very few people understand that swords aren't dangerous, Tavi, nor hands nor arms, nor furies. Minds are dangerous. Wills are dangerous. You are heavily armed with both."

Tavi frowned at that, staring at his opponent, mulling the thought in his head.

His hands stopped shaking.

The ladder behind them rattled, and Captain Nalus heaved himself onto the wall. He had a fresh bandage on his cheek, where a sickle had laid open his face all the way down to his skull. Tavi had heard he'd ordered them to stitch it closed with thread rather than "wasting a healer's energies on a minor injury when other men's lives were in jeopardy."

"Your Highness," Nalus said, nodding at Tavi. "You're ready?"

Tavi accepted his weapons from Araris and slung the belts over one shoulder. "I am."

"Follow me," Nalus said.

Tavi followed the captain, who had agreed to officiate under protest, down the length of the wall toward Navaris. At the same time, the cutter began walking toward them, slim and deadly.

In the ruins below, people had gathered—*legionares*, domestics, camp followers. Thousands of them. Several had climbed atop walls and dilapidated rooftops to get a better view of the top of the wall. He could only just see them in the darkness—but atop one of the nearest buildings, he could make out white hair, and Marat manes drifting on the gentle breeze—Kitai and her people. He nodded to them, and fists thumped simultaneously against leather-armored chests in response, the sound loud in the otherwise-silent night.

They reached the middle of the wall in time with Navaris. Tavi stopped far enough away from her to have time to avoid a sudden draw and lunge, while Captain Nalus stopped halfway between them.

"Phrygiar Navaris," he said. "Are you ready?"

Her flat eyes never left Tavi's. "I am."

"Gaius Octavian," Nalus said. "Are you ready?"

"I am."

Nalus glanced back and forth between them. "I remind you that this duel is to the death. I ask you both if you will concede the point of the duel and spare needless bloodshed."

"I will not," Tavi said.

Navaris only smiled a little and said nothing.

Nalus sighed. "Gaius Octavian, draw steel."

Tavi did so, and offered the hilts of the weapons to Nalus. The captain inspected them both for poison, and handed them back to Tavi, then slung the empty weapon belts over one shoulder.

"Phrygiar Navaris, draw steel."

He went through the same process with Navaris, and took her weapon belts as well.

"Very well," he said. "Neither party may move until I have stepped from between you and counted to ten. Once that is done, both participants are free to act. Do you understand?"

Both replied in the affirmative. Nalus stepped out from between them and hurried down the wall to descend to the ground. It took approximately forever, and Tavi held his gaze against Navaris's for the entire while.

"One!" called Nalus.

"Are you nervous, boy?" Navaris asked quietly.

"A little sleepy," Tavi replied. "A bit hungry. I'll get some breakfast in a bit and have a nap."

"You'll rest," Navaris said. "I promise you that. You won't be hungry, either."

"Two!" called Nalus.

"I'm curious," Tavi said. "How did you survive the sinking of the *Mactis*?"

"Araris killed his witchman. You only gutted yours. We got him into a boat and he hid us from the leviathans."

"Three!" called Nalus.

Her lips spread into a soulless smile. "It took him three days to die. Time enough to get us clear of the Run."

Tavi felt a surge of nausea at the description. Three days . . . Crows, that was a bad way to go. Though he supposed there weren't many good ones.

"I've been looking forward to this," Navaris said.

"Four!"

"Why's that?" Tavi asked.

"Because you're the bait, boy." Her eyes left his for a moment, focusing down the length of the wall behind him. "Once you're dead, Valerian there will come for me." She shuddered. "And *that* will be a fight worth watching."

"Five!"

"You have to get there first," Tavi said.

Navaris tilted her head, her eyes returning to his.

"Six!"

"I'm curious," she said. "Are you truly Princeps Octavian?"

Tavi gave her a copy of her little smile. "We'll know shortly."

"Seven!" Nalus called.

Navaris's breathing began to speed up. He watched her eyes dilate, and a series of eager little shivers ran through her body and down the length of both of her blades.

His mouth felt dry, but he focused on what Araris had told him. Patience. Control. He faced the cutter and touched lightly on the steel of his blade with his crafting, drawing his world into sharp, calm focus.

"Eight!"

Navaris's lips parted, and her body undulated strangely, as if it wished to fly straight into battle without consulting her feet.

"Nine!"

Tavi took a deep breath.

Kitai's voice rang out clear and vibrant in the silence between Nalus's counts, ringing from the stones so that every man, woman, and child looking on was sure to hear it. "Take her to the crows, Aleran!"

"Ten!"

The First Aleran spoke in a single, enormous, deafening voice that shook the stones as the Legion roared its encouragement for their commander.

Phrygiar Navaris's eyes glittered with sudden lust and fury, and her mouth opened in a wordless cry of something eerily like pleasure as she lifted her blades and darted at Tavi.

CHAPTER 55

Navaris was fast. She closed the distance in the blink of an eye, both weapons whirling out in front of her, weaving through a rapid series of slashes broken by the occasional lightning thrust. Before the First Aleran's roar had died down, she had sent half a hundred strokes toward Tavi, and he was certain that only steady retreat and his recent, intensive training with Araris enabled him to stop them.

Colored sparks showered out every time the blades met, and the cuts and parries came so swiftly that Tavi could hardly see through them. He felt as if they were fighting in a blizzard of miniature stars.

Her assault was unrelenting, aggressive, and precise. Her cuts and slashes slammed hard into his upraised weapons, so that he felt the shock all the way to his shoulder when they hit. They were, by far, the simplest attacks to defeat. Her thrusts slithered forward like double-bladed serpents, smooth, almost unpredictable, and impossibly fast. He caught each one as it came in, but only responded with the most conservative of counterattacks, more meant to force her to remain wary of a counterstrike than actually to draw blood.

He missed the next thrust and had to spin to the side, arching his back out. Navaris's sword struck a line of sparks along his belly, glancing off the lorica—and leaving a seared black crease on the Legion steel. If she could strike squarely against his armor, her sword would pierce it like cloth.

Twice, Tavi saw an obvious opening, but Araris had taught him better than that. It had been a deliberate act on Navaris's part, and had Tavi launched his own attack in unthinking response, he would have paid with his life.

And then Tavi felt it—a flicker of surprise and concern that flowed from Navaris, coloring the riot of emotions that spilled from her.

She stepped up the pace and power of her attacks, but not enough to allow Tavi his chance to strike. He was forced to backpedal more quickly, and his defense wavered for a moment before solidifying under the storm of steel and light that threatened to engulf him.

"Footwork!" Araris cried.

Tavi didn't dare glance down at his feet. The cutter would skewer him. But he felt his balance shift for a second and realized that Navaris had driven him back to the edge of the wall—his right heel was hanging over empty air.

Navaris surged forward again, and Tavi knew that if he didn't have room to retreat, he'd never hold off her furious assault.

He called upon the wind and turned the whole world into a hazy, languidly fluid portrait. His blades swept up, simultaneously sliding aside one thrust aimed at his throat, the other at his groin.

Even as he felt the contact, he drew power up through the heavy stone of the wall, pivoted, and flung himself into empty air.

The fury-borne strength of his legs sent him sailing across a twenty-foot volume of open space to land on the rooftop of the nearest building. He landed heavily—there was generally no other way to land when one wore heavy armor—and rolled as the overstrained stonework of the roof gave way in his wake, falling straight down into the dilapidated building beneath him. He gained his feet as the watching crowd erupted into cheers.

Navaris stared coldly at Tavi for a moment, and then down at the wall. With a quick, practical motion, she reversed her grip on her *gladius*, knelt, and with a single thrust drove it several inches into the stone of the vertical surface of the wall's interior.

Then she backed away, long blade in her right hand, took two bounding steps forward, and leapt. Her heels came down upon the quillions of the blade embedded in the wall. The *gladius* bent, then flexed back with unnatural strength, flinging the cutter into the air. She turned a complete flip as she sailed toward Tavi, and landed in a roll on the building's roof, exactly as he had.

Except, he realized with a sinking feeling, that the roof hadn't collapsed under the slender, lightly armored woman's weight. His situation had not improved. At least on the wall he had known where the drop *was*. If he spent much time shuffling around up here, he was sure to find a weak spot and fall right through the roof, and almost certainly through the rotted wooden floors of the building's interior.

Navaris drew a dagger from her belt and stalked forward. She smirked, and Tavi felt certain that she had come to the same conclusions he had about the roof.

They engaged again, and storms of blazing motes shattered from every touch of blade on blade. Though Navaris's offensive potential had been reduced by the loss of her *gladius*, Tavi, forced to keep track of his footing, could not take advantage of it. Bits of rubble threatened to turn beneath his feet, and the furylamps on the wall were just far enough away to offer deep shadows that concealed the sections of rooftop that had already fallen.

Tavi's instincts screamed at him to take the offensive and drive the fight off the rooftop, but he knew it would be a deadly mistake. Patience, Araris had said. Wait for the opening.

But Navaris hadn't given him one.

Tavi barely avoided a neatly executed maneuver that would have disarmed him, and whipped his shorter blade at Navaris's dagger arm.

The blade struck.

Navaris's attack stopped at once, and the two stood poised, barely out of one another's reach, weapons raised. The stillness was eerie, broken only by Tavi's steady, heavy breaths and those of his opponent.

A tiny trickle of blood wound its way down Navaris's hand.

"You pinked me," she said, her head tilted, her eyes narrowed with what felt to Tavi like a sudden and somewhat alarming interest. "That hasn't happened in years."

Tavi didn't move, holding his *gladius* at arm's length in his left hand, in a low guard, his long blade in his right, slightly forward, pommel close to his body, tip aimed at Navaris's throat. Any shifting of his weight or stance would give her an opening for a blow he might not be able to repel. But by the same token, she couldn't move without facing a similar risk.

The hit had been the result of luck as much as skill, but it had certainly caught Navaris's attention. She would be more wary now, harder to strike, and there would be no repetition of his riposte's success. Tavi gritted his teeth. He had to push her, somehow, get her to take more chances, come at him even harder. Otherwise, he would wind up one more name on the list of people killed by Phrygiar Navaris.

But how? There was nothing for him to work with. The woman was apparently driven solely by a desire to inflict pain on others, coupled with an obsessive need to prove her skill. If he used his earthcraft to increase his strength, he was likely to leave her an opening while he demonstrated the danger to her. If he windcrafted greater alacrity into his attacks, it was entirely possible that she'd skewer him before he had the chance to frighten her. Speed alone was no guarantor of success.

But how else to force her into a more aggressive attack without getting himself killed in the process?

Outthink her. Create the opening. Blades and furies aren't dangerous. Minds and wills are dangerous.

There was another way to overcome her skill and metalcraft—by overturning the mind and will that sustained the cautious discipline that could prove lethal to Tavi. In the face of that discipline and skill, he would never be able to take her down blade to blade. Not all weapons were made of steel.

His mother had shown him that.

Tavi suppressed a surge of excitement and focused on his watercraft. The emotions of the mad cutter—and he had no doubt at all, now, that she was completely insane—washed over him in a fluttering tangle of sensation. It blended weirdly with his sense of the weapons in her hands.

"Phrygiar Navaris," Tavi said quietly, keeping his eyes on the center of her mass. Arm and hand motions could deceive, but real movement would always show in her center of balance.

She stared at him.

Any number of things could have caused the woman's madness and obsession, but some were still more likely than others: The deepest joys and most terrible wounds were both to be had from family.

The name Phrygiar, like every other metronym in the Realm, was an indicator of illegitimacy. Children who were not recognized by their fathers and admitted into their Houses legally became members of the "city-house" of whichever High Lord held authority over their birthplace.

That was why Max went by Antillar. His father, High Lord Antillus, had never legally recognized him. Never accepted him. It was fair to say that Max had been driven to a few extreme behaviors, largely in reaction to that fundamental insecurity, the old wound in his soul.

Tavi himself knew what it was like to grow up without a father. The absence had left an enormous hole in him, one that never seemed to completely fill again, and when something touched it, it was agony.

Oh, yes.

If he was right, he could hurt Navaris.

He could kill her with a breath.

"You can't win this fight," Tavi said quietly. "If you beat me, these walls will be overrun with Canim. Everyone will die."

"Probably," she replied, her voice entirely too calm. "But I'll take Araris first."

"Even if it kills you?"

"Yes."

"Why? What's the point?"

"To prove that I am the best," Navaris said. "The greatest blade Alera has ever known."

Tavi forced himself not to sound eager as he replied. "Prove to whom?" Tavi asked quietly.

Navaris did not answer. Pain mixed with the other emotions flooding from her.

"I grew up without a father, too," Tavi said.

Navaris stared. The miasma of her diseased spirit and mind thickened on the word *father*.

Tavi had been right.

He knew how much the slightest touch upon that old heartache could send him into a rage if he was not careful to contain it. Navaris bore a similar wound, but unlike Tavi, the cyclone of fury and hate that roared through her was barely under control on the best of days. True, her will was harder than diamonds—but Tavi was about to hit it at precisely the right angle.

The fight was over. She just didn't realize it yet.

"You aren't going to prove anything to your father, you know," Tavi said. "Even if you defeat Araris and me, you'll die here. The story of what happened will die here."

The tip of Navaris's long blade trembled.

"He didn't want you, Navaris. Do you think a mound of corpses will make him seek reconciliation? Do you think he'd run to wrap his loving arms around a bloodthirsty murderess?"

Navaris's eyes widened until Tavi could see the whites all the way around them, and she gnashed her teeth as an even greater wave of agony ran through her. The cutter's voice shook. "Stop it."

"He won't," Tavi said, pitiless and precise. "He never will. You've become a monster, and you'd bring nothing but shame to his House, just as you bring nothing but suffering to the world."

The cutter began to shake her head slowly, and her wide, mad eyes suddenly glistened.

The woman was in pain—old, old pain, the pain of a wounded child who couldn't understand why it was happening or how to recover from it. Tavi knew it. He'd known it all his life, and it suddenly became difficult to tell where Navaris's torment stopped and his own began.

The woman's pain fed upon itself, and Tavi felt his stomach turn with involuntary sympathy—but he forced himself to continue. "It doesn't matter how many you kill or whom you kill. You'll never be welcome."

She started taking heavy, labored breaths, though neither one of them had moved.

"Your entire life has been a lie. *You* are a lie, Navaris." He lowered his voice, and said, gently, "You're nothing to him. You are *nothing*, Navaris. Nothing but a mad, miserable animal who's got to be put down."

She let out a guttural moan through her open mouth, and the childlike grief suddenly fused with the berserk intensity of her hostility and rage, her self-control shattering into chips and shards.

Something strange happened.

Tavi, his crafting senses, both water and metal, focused simultaneously and more intently than ever before, *felt* the next stroke coming before the center of Navaris's body ever moved, as if her physical intentions had somehow been transmitted to him through her emotions.

Tavi could not say what had changed, precisely, but he knew, he absolutely *knew* that she was about to fling the dagger at his face and follow up with her sword in the instant of distraction it afforded her.

Tavi called upon the wind, and watched as Navaris's arm slowly rose and flicked forward. The dagger flickered end over end—but Tavi had already raised his *gladius* and cut the dagger from the air. Navaris's throat erupted in a howl of feral rage as she came forward, a lightning slash aimed for his throat.

It was the opening Tavi had been waiting for.

He'd practiced it so many times that he had no need to think about it, his body moving with automatic precision. As Navaris surged forward, Tavi let his weight drop, falling under her blade, his body angled on a diagonal to Navaris's line of attack. As his left hand hit the ground, he extended his right arm back, along his side, then snapped it forward in a single, deadly thrust.

His sword sank through her armor and body with effortless ease.

Navaris gasped, her tearing eyes widening. Tavi felt the motion of the exhalation travel up the blade to his hand.

She turned her eyes to him and swept her sword at him, but Tavi released the hilt of his long blade, leaving it buried in her body, and rolled away from the attack. He came to his feet at once, shifted the *gladius* to his right hand, and stood ready.

Phrygiar Navaris took one step toward him. Then another. She bared her teeth in a grimace of madness and hate, lifted her sword—

—and sank down like an emptied flagon. She lay on her side for a moment, eyes staring, and her arms and legs made fitful, twitching motions, as though she believed that she was still fighting.

Then she went still. Tavi felt the rage and pain and grief and terror continue to pour from her. In a few seconds, it died down to a trickle.

Then it stopped.

Tavi stared down at the cutter's corpse. Then he knelt and gently closed her empty, staring eyes. He couldn't remember ever feeling so weary—but his work wasn't done.

Tavi heaved himself to his feet and closed his eyes. He lifted his head to the stars and let the breeze blow the perspiration from his skin.

The wind blew, and silence ruled the night.

☆☆☆ CHAPTER 56

Marcus did not find it difficult to reach his shooting position unseen.

There were grass and brush and trees enough to provide him with a frail woodcrafted veil, and shadows enough to cover what his crafting did not. Over the past two weeks, he'd managed to slip out of camp at night to practice with the Canim balest, and found the weapon accurate enough for his purposes.

Once he'd reached his position, he took a pair of clay jars from a belt pouch. He opened each one, careful to keep his nose and mouth well away from them, and took a single heavy steel bolt from the pouch. He dipped the tip of the bolt into each jar, then waved a hand, calling upon his earth fury, and the two jars and their lids sank gently down into the ground.

He set the bolt aside. Then he summoned up strength

enough to haul the balest into its prepared position. It was an enormous strain, even with his fury-born strength, and he had to be cautious, move slowly, so that he wouldn't slip or lose his grip on the weapon, betraying his position as the bow staves snapped straight again.

Once that was done, he slid the poisoned bolt into its groove in the balest and hefted the weapon.

Silence reigned, the air thick with anticipation.

The duel was over.

Marcus lifted the weapon silently, his arms steady, and waited for the winner to appear.

◻◻◻◻◻ CHAPTER 57

Isana told herself that she would not go to the duel, when there were still so many wounded to tend to. She threw herself into the work, sending her senses with Rill through each wounded body. A man named Foss, the officer in charge of the healer's corps, watched her with the first man he brought over, nodded his head, and promptly started barking orders.

Isana shortly found herself tending to men with the most dire and delicate of injuries. One poor soul's eyes had been viciously slashed by some weapon. Another young man had suffered what looked like a spear thrust through the genitals. A third had been treated for a cracked sternum, but hadn't regained consciousness—his first healer hadn't felt the bruising on his heart that made it labor unsteadily and insufficiently. Isana poured herself into her efforts and, at a steady pace, restored each man to health and exhausted sleep.

She didn't know how many men she worked on, but between efforts she dimly realized that she should have pushed herself to exhaustion after only a handful. She felt tired, of course, but the work seemed easier, swifter, as if her "touch" had become a dozen times more sensitive, allowing her to pinpoint precisely where the damage was, then to direct her fury's healing power with more precision and grace. Her talents had not grown, so much as she was taxing herself less to do the same amount of work.

"Last one," grunted an orderly, lowering another battered young body into the healing tub Isana was using. He was a young man, large and well muscled, and his legs, belly, and chest were covered in savage burns.

Isana winced, and was grateful that the poor *legionare* was unconscious. Burns like that would have left any conscious mind blind with agony, and if her ability to help the wounded had grown, their suffering had been that much more difficult to bear.

The *legionare* settled into the tub, and Isana supported his head, making sure he didn't slip under the water, and was startled to realize that she recognized the man.

It was Tavi's friend, Max.

She closed her eyes and went to work with steady, determined patience. Burns were some of the worst wounds to heal—she would have said *the* worst, until she had spent weeks in nearly constant crafting, dealing with an infection brought on by rancid garic oil introduced into a wound.

Though burns were not that festering nightmare, they were bad enough, and the drain upon the wounded Max would be tremendous, even dangerous. She turned her attention to the maimed flesh and, with Rill's help, got things sorted out. She reduced the damage as much as she could, to the point where she believed it would leave no hideous scarring, but felt the young man's strength waning and dared not press for more.

She leaned back from her efforts and nodded wearily to the orderly. She sat back as Max was taken to a bed, and dried her hands on a towel.

"My lady," said a voice behind her. "If you ever want a job, I can offer you the rank of senior subtribune and start you at the maximum pay grade."

Isana turned to find Foss watching them carry Max off and

shaking his head. "Crows," the Legion healer said. "In a rational world, you'd get *my* job."

She smiled wearily at him. "Thank you, Tribune. I'm sure you could have done as much."

Foss snorted. "You gave a man back his *eyes*, my lady. That's fine work, and I've known maybe two or three healers in my *life* who could do that, and one of *them* was a High Lady. You did more work than any three of my healers, and in half the time. You have a remarkable gift." He bowed his head to her. "Thank you."

She blinked at him several times and felt somewhat flustered. "I . . . You're quite welcome."

Foss nodded and offered her his hand. "We'd better get moving. It's almost time."

"Time?" Isana asked.

"The trial, my lady."

Isana frowned and shivered. As she worked, she'd all but forgotten the duel. Perhaps she'd been hoping that it would be over by the time she'd emerged from all the crafting.

If so, she thought, then she had been wrong to think it. Her son was about to fight for his life—for all of their lives—and she should be there.

The duel was the most elated, ecstatic nightmare she had ever experienced.

The crowd's emotion was a violent sea, a seething cauldron. If she hadn't worked herself to near exhaustion, she would have run screaming for the nearest dark hole—which would have looked rather unladylike, all things considered. As it stood, a bodyguard of eight *legionares* waited outside the healer's tent, evidently assigned as her escort. Each of the men was rather young, though they all had the hardened look of men accustomed to war, and the breast of their armor was decorated not with the red-and-blue eagle of the Crown, but with a similarly depicted black crow.

The crowd parted for her as she approached, and she felt them all around her, people buzzing with excitement and hope, with despair and fear—and with interest.

For her, specifically.

Faces turned toward her, and voices were raised in excitement. *Legionares* and trapped camp followers alike pressed closer, trying to see her, and to her intense embarrassment, the crowd actually sent up a cheer.

The solid forms of her guards gently kept the onlookers from getting too close, but a slender figure slid between the two in front, and Ehren smiled at her. "My lady," he said, bowing his head as he went to her side.

"My goodness," Isana said, looking around her uncertainly. "Ehren . . ."

"They know," he said. "Everyone in the camp knows, my lady, since all the truthfinders took testimony. No story that juicy was going to stay secret for long."

"I see," she said.

"Tavi—" Ehren caught himself and shook his head. "Octavian asked me to stand with you."

"I'd be glad of your company," Isana said quietly. She kept walking, as more people gathered around, staring at her in the dim light of both torches and small, household furylamps. "This is a very strange experience."

"I can imagine," Ehren said. "But if things go well, this is nothing compared to what you'll see in the streets of Alera Imperia someday."

"Oh dear," Isana said.

They took her to a small, open area directly before the wall where the duel was to take place. There was quiet talk all around her, but she paid little attention to it. She focused only upon the two men who began climbing a ladder.

The next few moments passed in eerie silence, as the taller of the two men began to limber up, stretching. The tension of the crowd rose steadily, until Isana felt sure that if she suddenly dropped unconscious, it would hold her upright where she stood.

Then her son followed Nalus out onto the wall, and faced the slender woman who had nearly killed them only hours before. There was brief talk. There was counting.

Kitai's voice rang out in sudden scorn and defiance, and

the gathered crowd roared its fear and tension and expectation into the cool night air.

The two combatants came together, and Isana had never seen anything so bright and beautiful and terrifying. Tavi's weapons erupted in scarlet and azure sparks, while flashes of brilliant, bilious green showered from Navaris's blades. The light was blindingly bright, and every flash left a spot of color burned onto Isana's vision.

She had never seen anyone move so swiftly as Phrygiar Navaris, and she could hardly believe that her son could withstand such speed and fury. They fought in constant, graceful motion, dancelike and deadly, four blades spinning and whirling and thrusting, and the ring of steel on steel, with its accompanying flash of light, grew swifter and swifter.

She could only stare, terrified and fascinated, and if the steadily thickening silence from the crowd was any indication, they felt the same way.

Navaris nearly drove Tavi from the wall, and her heart caught in her throat. Then she saw him turn, somehow impossibly slipping aside from Navaris's blade, and bound through the air like a hunting cat, leaping several yards to land on the roof of another building.

Navaris followed him over, and then the pair of them were out of sight of the crowd below. Steel chimed on steel as swiftly as a drumroll, echoing strangely through the ruins. Spectral light flashed through the air, casting stillborn shadows, gone as quickly as they appeared. Stones clattered to the ground, all dull cracking sounds and heavy thumps of impact.

Isana couldn't breathe. She became vaguely aware of a sharp pain in her hands, and idly thought that her nails had begun biting into her own flesh. The crowd's growing tension and excitement felt as though it could have drawn blood as well. She stared at the roof, hoping, *willing* it to be over.

The swords stopped ringing. The lights stopped flashing.

Isana heard herself moan in her throat.

Silence stretched on and on.

Then there was an enraged scream, a sound so raw, so full

of madness and rage that she could hardly believe it had come from a human throat.

Light flashed but once more.

Silence fell.

"Tavi," Isana heard herself whisper. "Oh, my Tavi."

The crowd remained perfectly still, as motionless as the stones of the ruins around them, and even more silent. It was unbearable to Isana, that tension, and she found herself rocking forward and back where she stood, fighting against the tears that blurred her vision.

"Tavi," she whispered.

And then Marat war cries filled the air.

The barbarians sent up a joyous howling upon their rooftop. The wild, fierce cries of their people danced among the stones. Isana stared, stunned, her mind only sluggishly processing the meaning behind the sounds.

Tavi.

They were cheering for Tavi.

Her son appeared at the edge of the rooftop, and the ruined city went wild.

Alerans cried out in a great roar. *Legionares* began slamming their fists to their chests in rhythmic thunder. Somewhere in the ruins, horses screamed out shrill cries of challenge. Dogs kept by the camp followers set up a howling chorus of their own. Legion drummers pounded on their instruments in glee, and Legion trumpeters sounded their horns. The noise was so loud that a section of ruined wall not far from Isana trembled and collapsed.

A burning cyclone of elation enveloped Isana and threatened to rip the consciousness from her mind. She closed her eyes against it, and only Ehren's support kept her from falling to her knees. The fire was too hot. It had to be turned aside, channeled away from her, before she went mad. She opened her eyes and forced herself to stand straight.

"Hail!" she cried. "Hail Gaius Octavian!"

Ehren gave her a glance, then took up the cry as well.

"Hail Gaius Octavian!"

The *legionares* formed up around her were next.

"Hail Gaius Octavian!"

It spread rapidly from there, from ruin to ruin, century to century, street to debris-choked street.

"Hail Gaius Octavian!"

"Hail Gaius Octavian!"

"Hail Gaius Octavian!"

◦◦◦◦◦ CHAPTER 58

The crowbegotten crowd kept on screaming his name, and Tavi wanted to tear his hair out in pure frustration.

Arnos was getting away.

The Senator had vanished from his spot on the wall, and Tavi spotted him heading into the crowd, lifting the hood of his practical brown cape. That explained why he'd worn the simple traveling clothes instead of the expensive robes, then.

Tavi pointed at him and shouted at his men to pursue Arnos, and the roar of the crowd grew louder. No one set off in pursuit, though, and Arnos was headed into the thickest part of the crowd.

Tavi turned to Kitai and screamed her name.

There was no way she could have heard his call, not over the furor of the crowd, but her head snapped around toward him, her features set in concern.

Tavi flashed her hand signs for *enemy* and *fleeing* and *pursue*. Then he pointed at Arnos.

Kitai's eyes widened, and she turned her head, following the line indicated by Tavi's finger. Her eyes narrowed, and she shouted into the ears of the Marat near her. The barbarians rose and began bounding from one roof and ruined wall to the next, lithe and agile as hunting cats.

One of them landed in the circle of space the detachment

of the Battlecrows had cleared for his mother and shouted something to Ehren. Then he rushed into the crowd.

Tavi signaled him with *stay* and *defend*, and trusted him to work out that he was to stay with Isana.

Ehren nodded and signed back *understood*, which happened to be a motion very like a Legion salute, and stepped closer to Isana, who looked distracted and preoccupied. Little wonder. Even up on the roof, the storm of emotion in the crowd below was grating against Tavi's senses. His mother must have been half-unconscious from it.

Tavi turned and looked at the wall, where Araris waited. He'd never actually made a leap of that distance before tonight, and his ability to jump so far had been strictly theoretical until he'd actually done it. He wondered if he'd be able to do it without a murderous maniac at his back to encourage him.

No help for it. He'd never get through the still-roaring crowd on the ground.

So he focused on his intentions, drew strength from the stone beneath him, speed from the night breeze, and hurtled back across the same space to the battlements.

He'd leapt too hard, and he slammed into a massive stone merlon before he could stop himself. His armor soaked up much of the impact, and he pushed away from the stone as Araris came to his side.

"Arnos!" Tavi wheezed.

Araris nodded once, his eyes intent on the crowd below. "I see him."

"Go," Tavi said.

Araris broke into a run, moving down the battlements, and Tavi followed him, peering down at the crowd, until he saw the brown-cloaked hooded figure roughly pushing his way through them, heading for the far side of the ruined city.

Then Arnos stopped in his tracks and began backpedaling. Tavi looked past him, and saw a pair of Marat crouched on a wall ahead of Arnos, their dyed manes blowing in the wind.

"Here!" Tavi said. He turned to another ladder mounted on the wall, took a few rungs normally, then clamped his boots to the outside of the ladder and slid rapidly down it, until he hit the ground. He turned and hadn't gone two steps before Araris hit the ground behind him. The *singulare* sprinted past Tavi, drew his sword, and ran forward, striking at the stones of the ground as he went. Each strike sent out a shower of sparks, a flash of light, and Araris bellowed, "Make way!" as he went.

The crowd parted before him.

Tavi moved forward, taking his cue from the Marat, who had formed a slowly tightening ring around Arnos in a classic hunting technique. None of them, he noted, were actually attempting to apprehend the Senator. The Marat had a strong sense of the appropriate. Arnos was Tavi's enemy, foremost. Barring any practical considerations that might alter the situation, they would leave it to Tavi to deal with him.

Tavi caught up with Arnos as the panting Senator shoved through a group of camp followers, knocking an old peddler over, and seized a woman by the arms. He shook her, snarling something at her Tavi could not make out over the noise.

"Guntus Arnos!" Tavi bellowed.

Arnos's head snapped around. He bared his teeth, his eyes desperate, and hauled the woman around, putting her body between his own and Tavi's, holding her by the hair. He drew a dagger in his other hand and held it to the woman's throat.

"This wasn't the plan!" Arnos shouted.

Araris took a few steps to the left, and Tavi to the right. Tavi had drawn his sword again at some point. He realized, with a little shock of recognition, that the woman was the First Spear's companion. The noise of the *legionares* and civilians around them became confused and began to dwindle.

"It's over, Arnos!" Tavi said. "Put the knife down!"

"I won't," Arnos spat. "I won't. It isn't going to end like this."

"Yes," Tavi replied. "It is. Let the woman go."

"Madness!" Arnos cried, shaking the woman's head through his grip on her hair. "Madness! You can't let this go on! You can—"

Suddenly both Arnos and the woman jerked, and the steel head of a Canim balest bolt erupted from her chest.

The woman's face went white, and her eyes rolled back in her head. Her knees gave way, and she melted slowly to the ground, her arms spread to her sides, her open mouth to the sky.

Arnos stood in place behind her, and the dagger fell from his fingers. He looked down at the blood flooding from the hole in his chest, where the bolt that had spitted them both emerged. He screamed, a sound full of protest and terror. It was a breathless scream, one with no strength, and his hands scrabbled at his chest, as if he thought he could brush the wound away if only he acted quickly enough.

Tavi walked over to him, Araris at his back.

Arnos was letting out desperate little grunting coughs, and blood bubbled from his lips as he did. His hands kept moving, but his fingers seemed to have gone limp, and he was only slapping uselessly at his lifeblood as it spilled from the massive wound the Canim projectile had left in his chest.

Tavi flashed signals to the Marat. *Archer. That way. Find.*

The barbarians loped into the ruins, eyes bright. Their night vision would give the unseen assassin nowhere to hide.

"Healer!" Tavi bellowed. "Now!"

Arnos turned a look of pathetic gratitude on Tavi, reaching out with his useless hands to grasp at the young man.

Tavi slapped Arnos's hands away with one motion and dealt him a contemptuous blow to the face with the back of his hand with the next. Arnos fell to the ground and landed on his side, shaking his head. He tried to speak, but blood strangled whatever he'd been going to say.

"For the woman. Not for you." Tavi squatted next to Arnos, and said, "I'm doing you a kindness you probably don't deserve, Senator. This is a better death than the Canim would give you."

Arnos's head jerked, and his eyes went out of focus. He made a few thrashing movements, his expression twisting, knotting, becoming absolutely agonized. Tavi didn't want to feel the man's terror and pain and confusion, but he still did. Logically, his actions had merited far more than what he had received—but he was still human, still Tavi's countryman, and someone who, in a perfect world, Tavi would have protected from his own ambition.

Arnos died there in a pool of his own blood, frightened and friendless and broken.

Tavi wouldn't lose any time mourning the fool—but he regretted the needless deaths of so many Alerans. Even the Senator's.

Things like that shouldn't happen to anyone.

Tavi pulled Arnos's cloak over his face and head, and asked Araris, "How is she?"

"Not good," Araris said. He'd torn off his cape, folded it into a pad, and had it pressed hard against her back. "Pulse is thready. I think she's got a hole in her lung, and she might be bleeding into it. We don't dare move her, and—" Araris froze for a second, then leaned forward, his nostrils flared.

"What is it?"

"I think . . . I think this bolt was poisoned."

Tavi leaned down and sniffed himself. There was a faintly corrupt odor from the wound in the front of the domestic's body, underlying a sharper, almost lemony scent. "That's heartfire," he said. "Master Killian taught us to recognize it. It speeds up the victim's heart until it bursts. Blinds them, too. I don't know what the other scent is."

"Rancid garic oil," Araris said.

"I've only read about that. Are you sure?"

"Pretty sure."

"Crows," Tavi said. "She's the First Spear's woman."

Araris shook his head. "Bad bloody luck."

"This way!" called Kitai from behind them. A moment later, she arrived leading a score of Marat and a trio of weary-looking healers, including Tribune Foss.

The bearish Tribune immediately examined the wound and listened as Tavi explained about the poison. Then he and the other healers loaded the woman onto a stretcher as gently as they could and carried her away, while the Marat took position around Tavi.

Tavi watched them go and rubbed at his forehead with one hand. "Get me two horses. Tie the late Senator over one of them."

"You can't ride out to the Canim," Araris said. "They aren't dealing in good faith. Look what they just did to Arnos."

Tavi shook his head and rose. He held out one hand, and said, "Arnos was about this tall."

"Yes," Araris said.

"And the woman was bent back, with the top of her head level with his."

"Yes."

"Arnos's wound was in the center of his chest. Hers was in the same spot, but more to the right, because of where she was standing." Tavi extended a finger in a straight line. "The bolt was traveling horizontally and fast enough to pierce them both. Which means it was fired from fairly short range, from inside the walls."

Araris followed the line of reasoning. "You don't think the Canim did this."

Kitai came to stand beside Tavi. "He thinks Alerans are far more capable than the Canim are when it comes to treachery and back-shooting," she said quietly. "He's right."

Tavi found her warm hand with his, and squeezed tight. She returned it, gripping hard.

"Which leaves us with a question for which we have no answer," Tavi said.

Araris nodded. "If not the Canim," he murmured, "then who did it?"

⟩○○⟩CHAPTER 59

Valiar Marcus stood upon the southern battlements with his men, watching as the Princeps rode forth from the ruins. A second horse, trailing on a rope, carried Senator Arnos's corpse draped upon its back. The sun was rising, the lands around them steadily growing brighter.

The balest had gone the same way as the jars of poison. It had been tricky for a few moments, when the Marat had come looking for the hidden archer, but his woodcrafted veil had served him well, and he eluded them.

The whole thing had gone to the crows, as such plans often did. Marcus had been forced to change position when the Senator bolted. He'd been sure the man would run to Lady Aquitaine, given a chance, but he'd fled even before the duel was over, and Marcus had been forced to shadow him.

Fortunately, it had hardly been difficult to remain unobserved in the frenzy around the duel, and he'd been able to use the reactions of the hunting Marat as a guide to the Senator. The doubled opportunity he'd finally found had been a stroke of fortune he had acted upon instinctively and instantly. Such moments could not be predicted and never lasted. The tiniest hesitation, and they were gone.

He had heard that "Davia," career Legion domestic, had died in the healing tub, as the poison on the bolt set her heart to racing, spreading the deadly taint of the garic oil through the whole of her body, until her life had simply failed.

That was a pity, Marcus thought. The woman was undeniably capable. She could have been a tremendous asset to the Realm, handled properly, and the loss of such potential to the Crown was regrettable. On the other hand, she was stubborn. He doubted she would have cooperated quickly or easily. He was certain he would not have survived the fallout, regardless of what she chose to do. Still. The skills of the powerful bloodlines of Alera were vital to the long-term survival of the Realm, and—

He felt himself smile a little. For a moment there, he'd been thinking like a Cursor.

"What do you think, First Spear?" asked Tribune Kellus. The annoying young officer had survived the battle and had naturally wandered away from his command again to come chew the fat with Marcus.

"Sir?" Marcus asked politely.

Kellus nodded at the Canim army outside, surrounding the ruins. "Think the captain can get us out of this?"

"Difficult to say, sir," Marcus replied.

"I hope so," Kellus muttered.

Marcus drew in a breath and silently counted to three. "Yes, sir."

The Princeps stopped as a group of Canim, with what must have been two or three former Aleran slaves, came out of the enemy ranks to meet him. They faced off about ten feet from one another, then two of the slaves, an armored *legionare* and a black-haired woman in a grey dress, came forward to examine the body. The woman looked at his face and nodded, and then the enemy contingent withdrew—except for a single Cane, an enormous, scarred, black-furred brute, who remained facing the Princeps.

The Princeps dismounted, and walked up to face the Cane—who towered over him by a good three feet.

The Cane drew a heavy sword from his belt.

The Princeps mirrored him.

The Cane reversed his grip on the weapon. The Princeps did the same. Then, moving slowly, almost ritually, they exchanged weapons, and stepped away from one another. The Cane slipped the Legion *gladius* through his belt as a man might a dagger. The Princeps had to slide the massive Canim weapon through a loop attached to his horse's saddle.

The Princeps mounted, and the two faced one another for a moment, probably talking. Then the Princeps tilted his head slightly to one side. The Cane casually lifted one fist to its chest in an Aleran salute, and tilted his head more deeply to one side. Then he turned and strode away.

Horns blared, and within a minute the Canim army was on the move.

And they followed the enormous Cane back to Mastings, away from the ruins on the hilltop.

Legionares stared; and then, as the Princeps rode back to the walls, still bearing Arnos's body, the entire hilltop erupted into cheering, the blowing of horns, the beating of drums.

"He did it," Kellus shouted, pounding on Marcus's back. "Bloody crows and great furies, he *did* it!"

Marcus endured the buffeting without complaining or knocking a few teeth from the young officer's mouth—but just barely. "Yes, sir," he agreed. "He seems to have formed a habit."

The jubilation continued as the Princeps rode back up the hill, and Marcus excused himself, leaving his senior centurion in charge of the cohort. He didn't have much time. The Princeps would call for a council immediately.

Marcus made his way to the healers' tents and found most of them asleep, simply stretched out on the ground, too exhausted to walk back to their bedrolls. He looked around until he found Foss and shook the Tribune's shoulder.

"I should kill you," Foss said blearily. He opened his eyes, blinked them a few times, and said, "Oh. Marcus."

"I'd like to see her," Marcus said quietly.

"Her?" Foss mumbled. Then he winced, and said, "Oh, right. I . . . I'm sorry, Marcus. We did everything we could for her, but . . ."

"It happens," he replied wearily. "I just want to . . . say good-bye."

"Sure," Foss said, his usual gruff tone gentle. He jerked his head at some hanging curtains at the rear of the tent. "Back there."

Marcus made his way back to the curtains and parted them. Six bodies lay behind them, covered in bloody shrouds. He began lifting shrouds, revealing dead, pale faces with grey lips. Five were fallen *legionares*. One was an elderly woman.

None of them was Lady Aquitaine.

Marcus's blood ran cold.

He strode back out to Foss, cuffed the man's shoulder to wake him up, and said, "Where?"

"Back *there*," Foss protested, waving at the curtains. "She was the last we worked on. She's right back there."

"No," Marcus snarled. "She isn't."

Foss blinked at him. Then he rose, groaning, and shambled back to look for himself.

"Huh," he said, after looking around. "I don't understand it. She was right there." He nodded at an empty space at the end of the row of bodies. "Seven of them."

"Now there are six," Marcus said.

"Seven minus one, yeah," Foss said testily. "Look, we've been asleep for a while, Marcus. Sometimes family or friends come for domestics or followers who are killed rather than sending them to a mass Legion grave. You know that."

Marcus shook his head. The surge of fear had faded rather

rapidly, as his exhaustion finally caught up with him. He knew he should be stealing a fast horse and running for his life, but he was just too tired.

Besides, he'd do it again in a heartbeat. And he was finished with running.

He exchanged a few more words with Foss, and then marched out of the healers' tent and toward the command tent. In the end, what difference did it make if he died for this choice or one of the many others that could come back to haunt him?

As long as he was still alive, there was a job to do, a Realm to defend—and a captain to serve.

◻◻CHAPTER 60

All in all, Tavi supposed, it could have been worse.

It took him another three hours to gather up the surviving commanders of the three Legions, hash out exactly what resources were left to them, and get them positioned where he wanted them to be. He set up the watch, arranged for water to be carted in from the wells that hadn't been poisoned, and ordered everyone who wasn't engaged in one of those two tasks to get some sleep.

He suspected it was that last order, more than any of the others, that won him the approval of the officers of the Senatorial Guard.

Then they buried the dead, honoring the fallen, and the First Spear called the roll for the entire Legion, marking the names of the dead on his lists, in half a day of quiet tribute. The wake that night was subdued. There was little alcohol to be had, and too many of their brothers were missing to allow sober *legionares* to forget that lack. For the most part, the camp turned in early.

The next two days were a mess, adjusting the formations of the battered Legions, caring for the wounded, and setting up a proper camp. The First Aleran had taken a terrible beating—almost as bad as at the battle of the Elinarch. Even so, they were in better shape than either of the Senatorial Guard Legions, even though they'd both come in marching heavily overstrength.

The captain of the First Senatorial had been killed in the fighting, and the next-most-senior officer was the Tribune Auxiliarus, whose cavalry had been responsible for the attacks on several steadholts. The man hadn't returned from his most recent patrol—or if he had, he'd somehow learned which way the wind was blowing, and elected not to remain. None of the officers below him seemed willing to risk his possible wrath by taking the command that was rightfully his, and thus tacitly support any charges that might be brought against him.

Nalus suggested that Tavi assign him to be the joint commander of both Guard Legions, and Tavi found it an excellent solution. There were just enough survivors of the two Legions to make a single full-strength Legion in any case, and Nalus immediately folded the two Guard Legions together, "until reinforcements made dividing them practical again."

Kitai and her kinsmen, meanwhile, set out to hunt down the guilty Tribune and his murderers. She'd won the coin toss, that time.

The weather had turned strange. The sky was covered with a pall of grey, and flecks of something that looked like snow but wasn't began to fall from the sky. It took Tavi an hour or two to realize what was falling—ash. Ashes from some enormous fire that could only be explained by the presence of a volcano. Since it also explained the great red light on the night of the duel, as well as the shuddering in the earth, he felt confident in his guess. After a day or so, it slackened, then stopped, and the next day the sky was brighter. Still, it was strange, and it worried nearly everyone.

After two days of reorganizing, repairing, and rearming, the First Aleran, beaten down to seventeen combat-capable cohorts, almost looked like proper soldiers again. The ruins had been neatly cleared of debris and many of the trees that had grown up through it, and the engineers had been hard at work on buildings, repairing their walls and roofs where they could, and converting them to open space where they couldn't. Every hale *legionare* helped them, including Tavi himself, at least for part of the day, carrying away rubble and clearing ground. It was best to keep the men busy. It would improve morale and discourage thoughts of any rash adventures toward the town of Mastings, still filled with the foes who had mauled them so badly.

Tavi found himself commanding the Legions out of the building upon whose roof he had won the duel with Phrygiar Navaris. The rotting wooden interior had been cleared, leaving a soaring roof overhead, and he quickly fell into the routine of command—except, of course, for the missing faces who now lay in the earth.

On the fourth day after the duel, the First Lord arrived.

Gaius Sextus stalked into the command building completely unannounced and narrowed his eyes at Tavi.

"Out," he murmured.

Had the building been on fire, it would not have emptied more quickly.

Gaius idly flicked a hand at the door as the last of Tavi's staff left, and a breeze slammed it closed. He eyed Tavi for a long and silent moment.

Tavi lifted his chin—a gesture of attention, more than aggression, schooled his face to a mask of polite neutrality, and waited. The silence grew heavier, but Tavi didn't let it press in on him, and after a time, Gaius grunted.

"And I thought *I* had made a mess," he said, finally.

"Mess, sir?" Tavi asked. He deliberately avoided the honorific given to the First Lord by everyone in the Realm but his immediate family. Tavi was not, however, feeling quite so bold as to call the old man "grandfather." "I'm not sure what you mean."

"Don't be obstreperous, Tavi," Gaius said. To Tavi's surprise, he sounded almost exactly like his Uncle Bernard sometimes had after one of Tavi's fits of ingenuity, back at Bernardholt.

"Magnus got through to you on his coin?" Tavi asked. "I assume he's taken on the role of watchdog on your behalf."

"Once he recovered from the shock," Gaius said. He walked past Tavi, looking around the room. "Who told you? Araris or your mother?"

"Araris," Tavi said quietly.

Gaius sighed. "Mmmm. Unfortunate."

"That I know?"

"The way you learned. That she kept it from everyone. That Araris consented to it." He shook his head. "Though who knows. It may have been for the best. Concealment may have protected you more thoroughly than my power could have. Though that's over now."

"Sir?"

"Surely you must realize, Octavian," Gaius said quietly, "that a great many people will not be happy about the appearance of an heir. They'll remove you."

"They'll try," Tavi said.

Gaius studied him intently for a moment and glanced around them. "You've no attendant furies. But you overcame Navaris. And there's a touch of . . ." He peered closely at Tavi. "Your talents?"

Tavi nodded quietly.

Gaius stepped forward, sudden tension in his shoulders. "I thought it might happen. What have you been able to do?"

"Internalized crafting," Tavi said. "Earth, metal, water, air."

Gaius arched an eyebrow. "But no manifestation? No discrete fury has come to your call?"

Tavi shook his head.

"It's encouraging, I suppose, and your talents may well keep developing, but . . . it isn't going to be enough to let you protect yourself now."

"I've done fairly well so far," Tavi said, stung.

Gaius grimaced. "Don't be a fool. You were an annoyance before, and one difficult to reach, at that. Now you're an objective—and no one is untouchable, Tavi. Your father wasn't." Gaius paused and coughed several times. It had a wheezing sound to it.

Tavi frowned and tilted his head. "Sir? Are you feeling all

right? You look a little . . ." He nearly said "frail," but hurriedly replaced it with, ". . . pale."

"Am I all *right*?" Gaius asked in a mild voice. "Boy, I told you to stay here and manage Arnos. Instead, you get outmaneuvered by the fool, arrested, then proceed to escape, take up with pirates, assault the bloody Grey Tower, and carry off the most important prisoner in Alera."

"Sir," Tavi said. "I know it looks bad—"

Gaius kept going, ignoring him. "*That* campaign of chaos not being enough, you then return here, declare your identity to the entire world, challenge a senior Senator to the crowbegotten *juris macto*, and as if that was not enough, you strike a truce with the largest invading force ever to attack the Realm, and at least a Legion of armed rebels—criminals, boy—to boot!" His voice rose, stentorian, echoing from the stone walls of the enormous chamber. "You've set policy with no regard whatever for the future! You've broken—no, *shattered* Crown Law! Have you any idea what you've *done*?"

The suggestion of the First Lord's displeasure had sent men hurrying from the room—and his open wrath literally sent tremors through the stone floor and made the room's furylamps flare scarlet in reflection of his anger. Tavi knew that Citizens all around the Realm would have immediately bowed to one knee and averted their gazes in the face of Gaius's outrage. Prudence suggested that Tavi might want to follow the same course.

Instead, Tavi found himself squaring his shoulders, setting his jaw and, somewhat alarmingly, stepping forward to brace the First Lord directly, eye to eye.

"I know what I've done," Tavi said quietly. "I have followed your orders to the best of my ability. I protected innocent Alerans whom I would otherwise have been forced to murder. I made use of the best transport I had to retrieve a prisoner from the Tower—a prisoner to whom you and I both owe our lives, I might add, and who has been unjustly imprisoned for four years for the sake of appearances.

"Then I returned here, parlayed Varg into a summit with the Canim command, and used information they provided me to remove a murdering, treasonous slive from power and see something that almost looks like justice done. And after that, I negotiated to gain the Realm the single largest, best-trained, and most destructive allied force Alera has ever known." He paused a beat, then added, "Sir."

Gaius's expression of wrath darkened, then faltered. He opened his mouth for a moment, then closed it, eyes calculating, and asked, "Allied?"

"Yes, sir."

"Explain."

Tavi did, sharing his theory about the reason for Sarl leading the exodus from the Canim homeland, explaining that he, and the Canim themselves, believed that the Vord were destroying their home, and their people were fighting for the very life of their race.

"I'm not sure we shouldn't let them fight," Gaius said after a moment. "The enemy of my enemy, is my friend, eh?"

"If the Vord are truly the threat I believe they are, I think I'd rather keep the enemies we know than trade them in for new ones."

"A point," Gaius murmured. "But Alera as a whole is hardly going to approve of a truce with the Canim."

"It isn't a truce," Tavi said. "They surrendered. They're prisoners."

Gaius's eyebrows lifted. "They had the city surrounded. They outnumber your local troops by more than five to one. And they surrendered. And while still in possession of a heavily fortified city and retaining their arms, they are your prisoners."

"Mine," Tavi said, "personally, in my capacity as the Princeps of Alera. They have given their parole, and I have accepted it." He offered Gaius a faint smile. "The Realm has known more elaborate fictions, sir."

Gaius's mouth twitched. "Mmmm. What did you offer them?" Gaius asked.

"To allow them to leave," Tavi said. "To provide them with watercrafters enough to get past the leviathans. And to give them support troops for the defense of their homeland."

Gaius frowned and began to speak, but then paused. "Support troops. The 'Free Aleran' Legions?"

"I've taken the liberty of drawing up a proclamation of general amnesty to those in this region who have broken laws in acting to protect their lives and those of their families due to the Canim invasion and Kalarus's rebellion," Tavi said, turning to the table where he'd set the documents aside, "contingent upon their service to the Crown. I've also had a proclamation drawn up declaring the general liberation of all slaves in Kalaran lands."

Gaius accepted the two parchments and scanned them. "Well. At least you didn't attempt to sign them and enact them."

"Naturally not," Tavi said wryly. "That would be overstepping the bounds of my authority."

"Overstepping the—" Gaius shook his head. "As if assaulting the Grey Tower wasn't transgression enough to earn you a death sentence." He spread his hands. "Proving your heritage won't be an issue. Septimus saw to that. But your actions have created a problem, Octavian. You are, by all rights, a criminal."

"And if you use your authority to pardon me," Tavi said, "it will erode what support you have left and undermine my own position in the eyes of the Citizenry."

"Precisely," Gaius said. "Your actions have created an untenable position for us."

Tavi nodded. "If only there was some way my actions might be pardoned as part of a mass amnesty—one in which many Alerans great and small were excused for extraordinary actions taken in good faith."

Gaius stared at Tavi for a long and silent second. Then he stared at the paper in his hand.

"I came to the same conclusions you did," Tavi said quietly. "Once word spreads through the Realm that there's a Princeps again, every cutter in Alera will be able to find work—or the same people who killed my father will come together again to remove me."

"One won't," Gaius said quietly.

"Kalarus?"

"I believe so," he said. "There was never any proof, of course. But I knew." He tilted his head, studying Tavi's face.

"So. You depart the Realm, placing yourself beyond the reach of assassins and High Lords alike." Gaius frowned. "To what gain?"

"First," Tavi said, "I get to make sure that the Canim aren't going to use their fleet just as Arnos feared they would—to shift their attack to a weaker part of the Realm."

"I thought you had a high regard for the honor of the Canim leaders," Gaius said.

"I do," Tavi said. "But there's no sense in being stupid, is there?"

The First Lord's mouth quirked up in amusement. "Go on."

"Second," Tavi said, "I'll be able to gather intelligence on the Canim and the Vord, both of which are going to be valuable in the future."

"True enough," Gaius said.

"And, once I've taken the Canim home and gotten them settled back again, I'll be able to return, claim the amnesty you're about to declare, along with all the rest of the Free Aleran Legion and, perhaps, a few of my own men—"

Gaius smiled faintly.

"—at which point I should be able to return to the Realm without anyone feeling the need to put me behind bars."

"And meanwhile," Gaius murmured, "you gain time to develop your furycraft more deeply. And I am given time to build up greater support for the Realm's Princeps. Which should be quite possible, given all you've done, as well as everything your mother has managed to accomplish." He shook his head. "I must point out that should you be killed while on this sojourn, the entire plan rather falls apart."

"If I stay, they'll kill me," Tavi said. "If I go, at least everything that wants me dead won't be taking it personally."

"Question," Gaius said. "What makes you so sure I'm not planning on sending you south to finish Kalarus's forces?"

"You'd have told me already," Tavi said. "I'd have been given marching orders before we had this talk. Given that you didn't, I assume that the rebellion is over."

"Yes," Gaius said.

"Volcano?" Tavi asked.

"Yes."

Tavi shuddered at Gaius's tone—flat, quiet, empty of humanity. "Are you all right?"

He expected the First Lord to brush the question off. Instead, Gaius shook his head, and said quietly, "I don't believe so. But I have neither the time nor right to indulge in self-pity. How long will you be gone?"

"I expect we'll leave before summer is out," Tavi said. "We'll winter in the Canim homeland. I'll return next spring."

"A year, give or take," Gaius mused. "I can work with that." He walked to one of the tables, took up ink and a quill, and dashed his signature across the bottom of both documents he was holding. "The copies?"

Tavi found the small stack of duplicates Ehren had written out. Gaius read each before signing them. Tavi helped sand and blot the fresh signatures, and for a moment, the rather mundane task occupied their attention.

Gaius left a single copy of the documents with Tavi and took the rest himself, rolling them into a leather carrying case. "Well. There is a great deal of work ahead of us both. Good day."

The First Lord turned and strode for the door.

"Grandfather?" Tavi asked quietly.

Gaius stopped. He glanced over his shoulder, his body language cautious.

Tavi shook his head. "Just . . . trying it out. I've never been able to use it before."

Gaius nodded slowly. "Grandson," he said quietly, as if considering the way the word sounded.

For a long minute, neither spoke.

"You look like him, you know," Gaius said. "A great deal." He gave Tavi a faint smile. "I expect he would have been proud of you."

"You and he didn't get along very well, did you?" Tavi asked.

"As a rule? No."

"What would you have done, if he'd brought my mother to you?"

Gaius shrugged a shoulder. "I'd have reacted badly, I suppose."

"She's my mother, sir," Tavi said. "She was your son's wife."

"Yes."

"I don't expect you to shower her with affection," Tavi said. "But she could be a great help to you. And she deserves your respect."

"I will bear that in mind," Gaius said.

"Do," Tavi said, without threat or malice in his voice. "Or you and I won't get along very well, either, sir."

Gaius showed Tavi his teeth. "Be careful, grandson," he said, making two statements at once, and left the building.

Tavi sank down onto a stool and bowed his head. He wondered what it would have been like to grow up with a grandfather.

Then he shook his head and rose. He had no time for nor right to self-pity, either, and there was a great deal of work to do.

Bernard led them safely out of the immediate area. Whatever pursuit had been behind them when they came into Kalare, it evidently disintegrated with the destruction of the city and the resulting blizzard of ash. When the skies finally cleared again, Amara lifted them both into the air. It was far more work than she would have had to do if she had been alone, but she wasn't trying to set any speed records. Even so, only a day of travel carried them into the lands surrounding neighboring Attica, and to a traveler's inn beside one of the causeways.

They were so filthy from the journey through the swamps that they might not have been able to buy a room at the inn if they hadn't been able to show the innkeeper gold coins as well as silver when he asked to see their money. The first thing they bought was a bath. They wore robes provided by the inn while their clothes were being cleaned, and ate their first proper meal in weeks.

After that, Amara had assumed they would collapse into an exhausted sleep.

Bernard had other ideas.

She couldn't say she disapproved of the direction of his thoughts, either.

Afterwards, sleep came. But she awoke in the deeps of the night, and just lay quietly, listening to her husband's heart beating.

"He didn't give you much choice," Bernard rumbled.

Amara hadn't realized that he'd awoken. It took her a moment to gather her thoughts. "You knew what he was going to do?"

"I suspected," Bernard said.

"You didn't say anything," she said.

"I didn't know," he replied. "And I hoped he would do it differently. Tell you."

"I feel like a fool," she said. "He said he would stop Kalarus from using the Great Fury. It never even occurred to me that he'd do it by setting it loose."

"I know," Bernard said. His arm tightened on her gently.

"If I'd known what he intended . . . I don't know if I could have . . . I couldn't have made myself a part of that."

"I know," Bernard said. "So did he."

"What have I done?" Amara whispered. "I betrayed my oath."

"He lied to you, Amara," Bernard said.

"He never—"

"He deceived you," Bernard said, his tone brooking no dissent. "He chose words he knew would give you the wrong idea to get what he wanted out of you. He knew what he was doing. He knew how you would react. He accepted it."

Amara pressed her cheek against his chest. "He knew about us. That I'd broken the law."

"Amara," Bernard chided, his tone softening, "the First Lords worked out years ago that outlawing marriage among certain personnel is probably the worst thing they could do actually to discourage it. We handled it just as it's done in the Legions. We were discreet and still performed our duties. In return, he overlooked it. Good commanders always handle it that way."

True enough. She'd thought through the logic, tracked

down the motivations, the reason, the simple calculation of the entire situation.

And then the rest of it hit her.

She found herself shuddering against Bernard's chest, weeping. His arms slid around her, pulling her more tightly against him, and she sobbed harder. It was too much, too much. The weeks of toil and danger. The horrible destruction at journey's end. She could still see the tiny, helpless figures, hopelessly running from a fiery death.

And without her help, it could not have happened.

How could Gaius have done that to her?

It hurt. Oh, it *hurt*. She had *trusted* him.

Just as she had trusted Fidelias.

She wept against her husband's chest, feeling miserable and foolish for doing it, and found herself unable to stop for several minutes. By the time she did, she felt emptied out, heavy, lassitude beginning to seep into her thoughts.

Bernard kissed her hair gently, simply present.

"What am I going to do?" she whispered. "I've never done anything else."

"I know a place you could go," Bernard replied. "It's a little rough, but there are good people there. There's a man there who has a lot of folk to care for. He could use the help of an intelligent, courageous, and talented woman."

She tightened her arms around him, just soaking up the warmth of him. "Yes?"

"Mmmmm. Countess Calderon. It suits you. And I've wanted to see you in my colors since . . ."

"Since when?"

"Since I bandaged your ankle," he replied.

"I suppose I'd need some clothes," she said sleepily. "Dresses, perhaps. I've never owned more than one."

"I can afford them," he said.

"I'd never thought about doing this," she said. "Being a wife."

"A wife with a great many hostile wind furies about," Bernard said. "Not to mention a full military garrison to help oversee. I'm afraid there won't be much time for knitting."

"I'm terrible at knitting," she replied with a yawn. "Well. Except for a mail coat, once."

"We can hire someone for knitting, then." He kissed her forehead. "I've hoped we could be together. Actually together."

"So have I," Amara whispered. "I just never thought it would happen."

"With the rebellion over," Bernard said, "there's bound to be better times ahead. It will be a good time to settle down. Maybe even start a family. We'll finally have time to try again."

Amara smiled. "Mmmm. A good wife embraces even the most tedious chores."

Bernard murmured, "Oh, really?" He moved his hand.

Amara's breath caught in her throat as her heat sped up. "Aren't you tired?"

Evidently, he wasn't.

Isana watched Gaius depart the improvised command building from her chambers in the small, restored home across the ruined street. He took to the air and vanished, all in the same motion, as if he had simply become the wind. No more than a handful of people even saw him leave.

"He had the document case with him," she reported quietly.

"Tavi guessed correctly," Araris said. He stood in her doorway, watching her.

Isana turned, glancing uneasily down at the gown she wore—dark, muted shades of scarlet and blue, a sedate gown suitable for the widow of one Princeps and mother of another, and it was quite the most expensive dress she had ever owned. A makeshift wardrobe in the room held several other outfits every bit as costly, and much more suitable for the Princeps Matron than her simple grey dress. The outfits had been a gift from "Free Alera," which Isana suspected in this case meant Varg and his young Aleran aide de camp, Durias.

"I almost wish he hadn't been right," she murmured. "Over the sea. Surrounded by Canim. Facing the Vord."

"Perhaps," Araris said. "Perhaps not. Personally, I'm glad. I couldn't protect him here. Not against the kind of people who will want him dead."

"I understand the reasoning behind it." Isana sighed. "And I know he's developed into something far more than the boy I raised, and that he has obligations and duties, Araris, but crows take it, he's still my boy. I hate to see him go so far from home."

"My lady," Araris said, gently mocking sternness, "a woman of your station should not curse."

Isana gave him a level look, and the swordsman smiled in reply. "I'll watch over him."

She couldn't help but return the smile a little. "You always have."

His smile faded. "It's you I'm worried about," he said. "The First Lord is sure to summon you to the capital to help rally support for Octavian. And Lady Aquitaine isn't going to like that."

Isana waved an unconcerned hand. "She'll adjust. She's practical in that way."

"I'm serious, Isana," Araris said. "You're going to be in danger."

"When have I *not* been?" she asked, and she heard the uncharacteristic note of sharpness in her voice. "Honestly, Araris? I've lived my whole life afraid, and I'm sick to death of it."

Araris frowned at her, folding his arms.

"Somewhere out there are men and women who would gladly conspire to murder my son," she continued in the same tone. "They may well be many of the same souls responsible for murdering my husband." The sudden rage inside her almost seemed to force her chin up, and her words came out crisply bitten. "I won't have it."

Araris's eyebrows climbed.

"I've made many friends, Araris. I've learned a great deal about Alera's leading Citizens. I'm going to find those responsible for killing Septimus. I'm going to find those who might wish to do harm to Octavian. And great furies help them when

I do." She felt her voice shaking with the ferocity and weight of her feelings. "Don't waste your time being afraid for me. I don't care who they are. I'm going to find them. And destroy them."

He walked across the room to her and ran the fingertips of one hand over the curve of her cheek. "That," he said quietly, "is what I'm afraid of."

Isana's sudden, hot fury faltered, and she lowered her eyes.

He lowered his head until he caught her eyes. Then he leaned in and kissed her lightly on the mouth, returning to gaze intently at her. "Don't become what you aren't, Isana."

She leaned her cheek against his hand. "I wish that we . . ."

He stepped up and put his arms around her, and she leaned against him gratefully. "Shhh," he said. "The time isn't right yet. If we wed now, it would cause issues, now that Octavian's name is loose. He will need all the support he can secure, at first. If wild rumors about our relationship and how it's tied to Septimus's death start circulating, it will make the work much harder."

"They'd do that, wouldn't they?" She sighed. "I'm sorry."

"It's all right," he murmured. "I can wait. For you, I can wait."

She found herself smiling a little. "What do I do?"

He hugged her tight. "Keep your eyes and ears open. Don't let them drive you to behaving as they do."

She held him in return, and they were silent and together for several moments.

"I'd best go," he said quietly. "I don't want to get too far from him."

Isana nodded. They kissed again, and Araris hurried toward Tavi.

Isana watched him go, and bit her lip as the door to the command building opened and she caught a glimpse of Tavi.

Of Octavian.

She thought of what it would be like to bury him, and shuddered.

That would not happen. She would do whatever she must in order to make sure of it.

The invasion might have been turned back, the rebel High Lord put down, but it seemed obvious to Isana now that those had only been the first eddies of the winds of change—and that the storm was just beginning.

Look for the fifth book
of the Codex Alera . . .

PRINCEPS' FURY
by Jim Butcher

Now available from Ace Books

THE DRESDEN FILES

Wizards are cool.

I mean, come on. When it comes to fantasy, you can't swing a cat without hitting a wizard somewhere, striding through the shadows and wars of epic battles of light and darkness, uncovering lost knowledge, protecting, inspiring, and guiding others toward the future. Merlin, Gandalf, Allannon, Dalben, Belgarath, Raistlin, Goblin, and One-Eye—and their darker counterparts like Morgana, Arawn, Soulcatcher, and Saruman. Wizards wield secrets as warriors do swords, driven by a vision that lets them see and know more than mere mortals, gifted with a power that makes them treasured allies—and terrifying foes. Throughout fantasy fiction, when the need is most dire it is the wizard who stands to face balrogs and dragons, dark spirits and fearsome beasts, natural catastrophes and dark gods.

Harry Blackstone Copperfield Dresden, wizard for hire, is happy if he manages to pay the rent for another month. He's in the Chicago Yellow Pages, under "Wizards." He's the only entry there. Most people think he is some kind of harmless nutball at best, and a charlatan-psychic at worst.

But then, most people haven't seen what Harry's seen. Most people don't know the truth: that the supernatural is perfectly real, existing quietly side by side with most of humanity's perceptions of reality. Trolls lurk under bridges, and faeries swoop down to kidnap children. Vampires prowl the shadows by night, restless ghosts rise up from the darkness of the grave, and demons and monsters to boggle the mind lurk in the shadows, ready to devour, maim, and destroy.

A few people know the truth, of course. Wizards such as Harry know. So do a few of the cops, like Lt. Karrin Murphy, head of Chicago P.D.'s Special Investigations division, who knows the touch of the supernatural when she sees it and who hires Chicago's only professional wizard to come in as a consultant when an investigation begins to look like an episode of *The X-Files*.

And other people learn the truth the hard way, when something out of a bad dream shows up at the front door. For those poor mortals, the supernatural becomes a sudden, impossible, terrifying nightmare come true—a nightmare no one can help them wake up from.

No one but Harry Dresden, that is. Hauntings, disappearances, missing persons, murders, curses, monsters—you name it, and Harry knows something about it. More than that, he shares the convictions of his literary ancestors—a deep and genuine commitment to use his power to protect those who cannot protect themselves, to stand between the darkest beings of the supernatural and his fellow man.

When the need is most dire, when the night is most deadly, when no one else can help you, give Harry Dresden a call.

He's in the book.

Jim Butcher's newest Harry Dresden novel, *Small Favor*, is now available in hardcover from Roc Books.

Now available in hardcover

Princeps' Fury

BOOK FIVE OF THE CODEX ALERA

by

New York Times Bestselling Author

JIM BUTCHER

War-torn Alera struggles to rebuild—while politicians and nobles maneuver for power. But from the south comes news of death and devastation unlike any have ever known—for the Vord have come to Alera.

For a thousand years, Alera and her furies have withstood every enemy and survived every foe.

The thousand years are over...

penguin.com

THE CODEX ALERA SERIES BY
JIM BUTCHER

New York Times Bestselling Author
of the Dresden Files Novels

Book One: *Furies of Calderon*

"Sharp, fast moving, full of deadly
dangers and double-dealing."

—Simon R. Green, *New York Times* bestselling author

Book Two: *Academ's Fury*

"A fresh approach to magic and a cast
of appealing characters."

—*Library Journal*

Book Three: *Cursor's Fury*

"One of the best volumes yet in
this entertaining series."

—*Locus*

Book Four: *Captain's Fury*

"Few writers balance military realism and cinematic
swashbuckling with so much skill or wit."

—*Publishers Weekly*

penguin.com